Terra Tempo

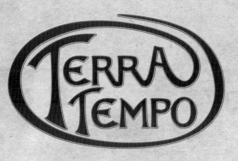

TERRA TEMPO

THE FOUR CORNERS OF TIME

Written by **David Shapiro**

Illustrated by **Christopher Herndon**

Color by **Erica Melville**

 CRAIGMORE CREATIONS

Portland, OR

First edition January 2013.
Printed in the United States of America.

Library of Congress Control Number: 2012944924
ISBN: 978-0-9844422-6-3

Content Director: David Shapiro
Art Director: Erica Melville
Lettering: Erica Melville
Color assistance: Brian David Smith, Wade Liostro, Caroline Knecht
Jacket art: Christopher Herndon

CRAIGMORE CREATIONS

2900 SE Stark Street, Suite 1A
Portland, OR 97214
www.craigmorecreations.com

To my father, Gary Shapiro, for his ongoing
support of Craigmore Creations & to the Hopi
for their inspiration through time.
-DRS

To Gaddy.
-CMH

To DMC.
-ETM

INTRODUCTION

Previously, in *Terra Tempo: Ice Age Cataclysm!*, the
twins Jenna and Caleb discovered that their Uncle Al
was traveling time with the use of an unusual map.
The children found the map and Uncle Al's journal
documenting his time travel adventures and decided to
"borrow" them for an adventure of their own.

Initially skeptical about the validity of Uncle Al's
writings, Jenna, Caleb, and their friend Ari try out the
method of time travel that is detailed in the journal.
A portal opens and they find themselves 15,000 years
in the past, at the end of the Pleistocene period—also
known as the ice age. Not only were there giant beasts to
contend with, but the landscape of the Pacific Northwest
was changing as the largest recorded floods were washing
over the earth. An inland freshwater sea in Montana had
burst its confining ice dam and was raging across Idaho
and central Washington, pooling hundreds of feet deep
in the valleys of western Oregon.

Giant short-faced bears, fierce 600-foot high waves
of water, herds of wooly mammoths and packs of dire
wolves were just a few of the hazards of the time.
Luckily, the children had the supernatural assistance and
friendship of the giant mythic thunderbird, Yakama, to
help them across the landscape. The trio pooled their
skills of survival, orienteering, and paleontology and not
only survived, but had fun exploring the ice age.

The children's adventure led them through multiple portals as they investigated the short time before and after the great ice age flood. On the cusp of a great wall of water they made it back to modern Portland, Oregon where their uncle was waiting for them. He was stern as expected, but happy to see them safe and home. The children returned to their parents as if nothing but a long day of summer had occurred, but not before Uncle Al let slip knowledge of a larger time travel mystery and the secret investigation into the "curious nature of things and the curious things in nature."

Here, in the second book of the *Terra Tempo* series, the adventures of Jenna, Caleb and Ari continue in the American Southwest. Find out what happens as the time travel adventure deepens and the children face more than the elements and beasts of the past!

CHAPTER
ONE

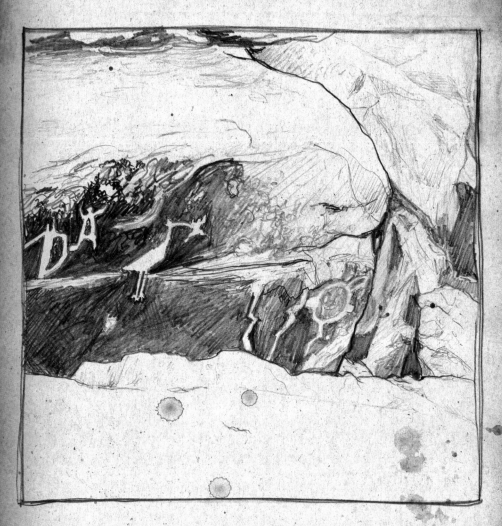

FOUND IN
THE PAINTED DESERT

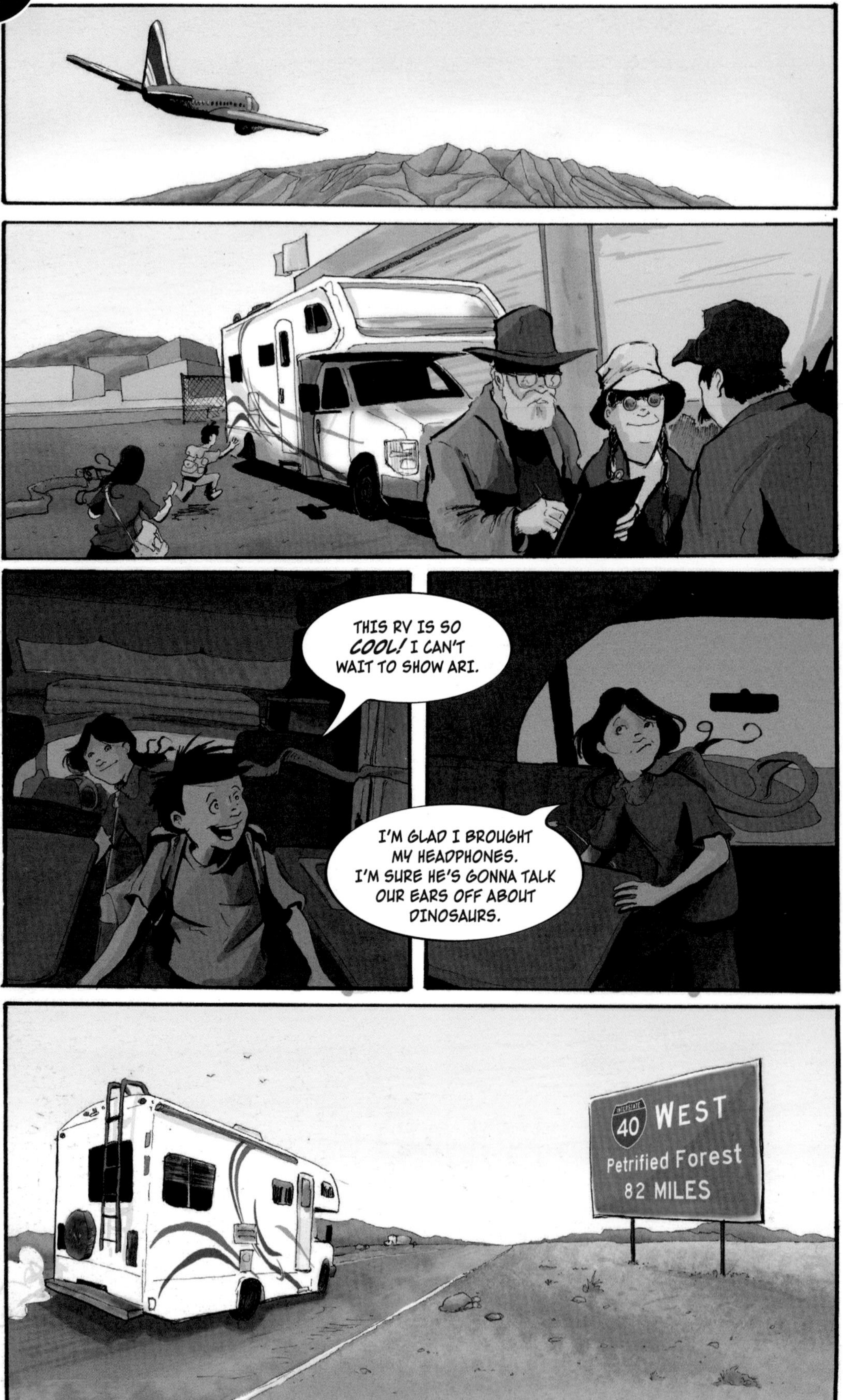
THIS RV IS SO *COOL!* I CAN'T WAIT TO SHOW ARI.
I'M GLAD I BROUGHT MY HEADPHONES. I'M SURE HE'S GONNA TALK OUR EARS OFF ABOUT DINOSAURS.
INTERSTATE 40 WEST
Petrified Forest
82 MILES

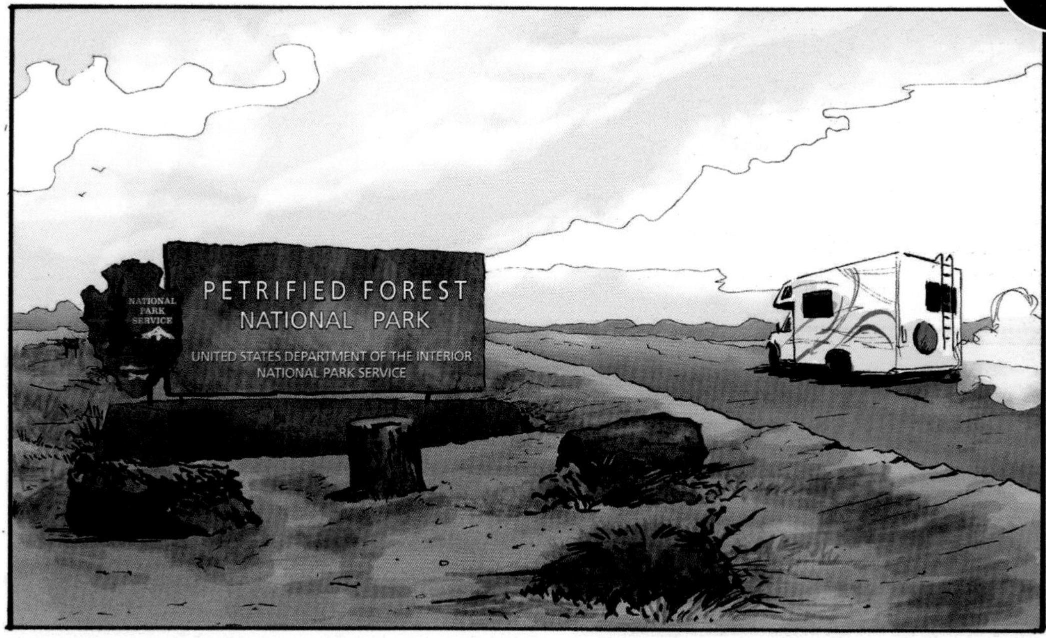
NATIONAL PARK SERVICE
PETRIFIED FOREST
NATIONAL PARK
UNITED STATES DEPARTMENT OF THE INTERIOR
NATIONAL PARK SERVICE

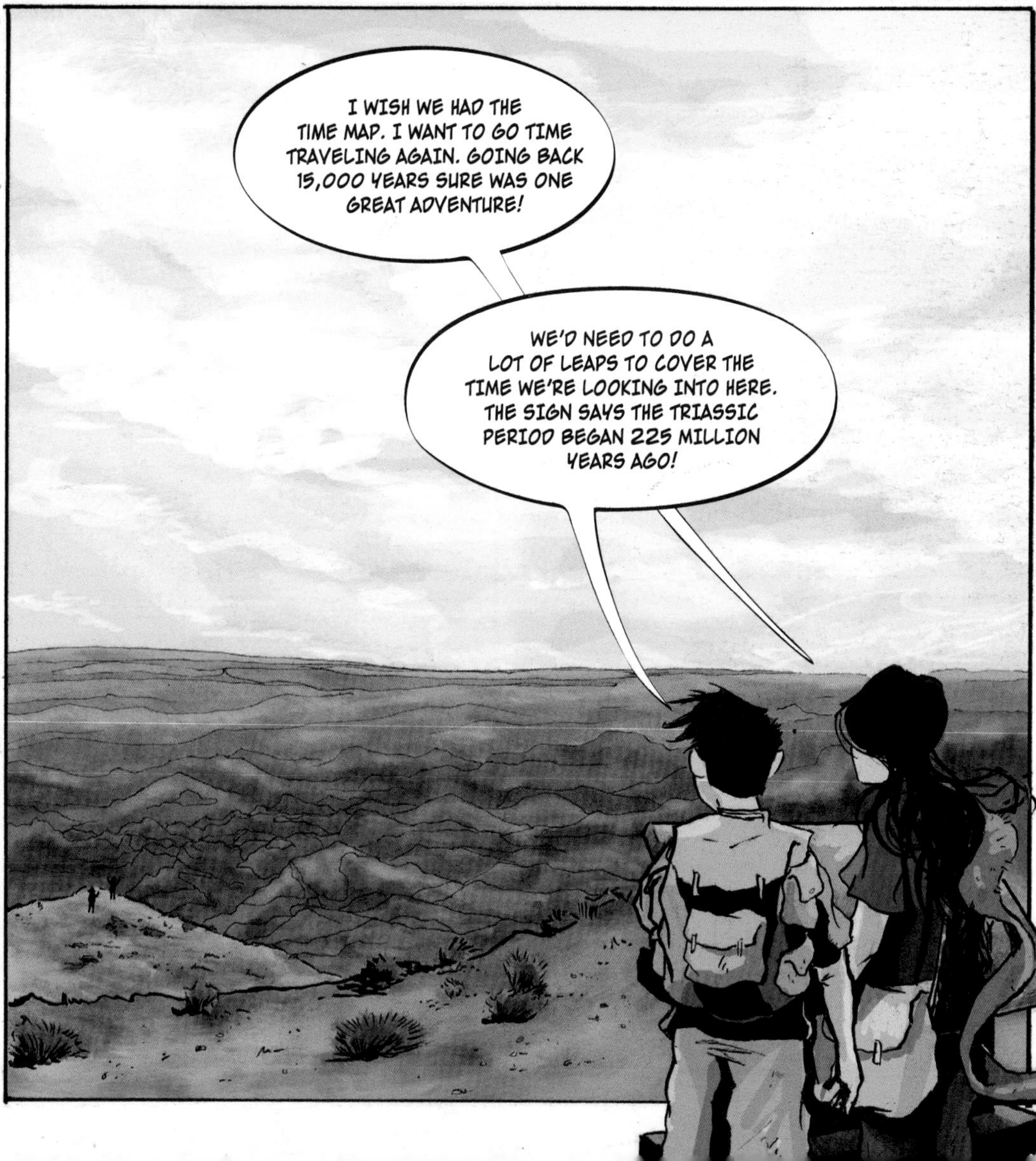
I WISH WE HAD THE TIME MAP. I WANT TO GO TIME TRAVELING AGAIN. GOING BACK 15,000 YEARS SURE WAS ONE GREAT ADVENTURE!
WE'D NEED TO DO A LOT OF LEAPS TO COVER THE TIME WE'RE LOOKING INTO HERE. THE SIGN SAYS THE TRIASSIC PERIOD BEGAN 225 MILLION YEARS AGO!

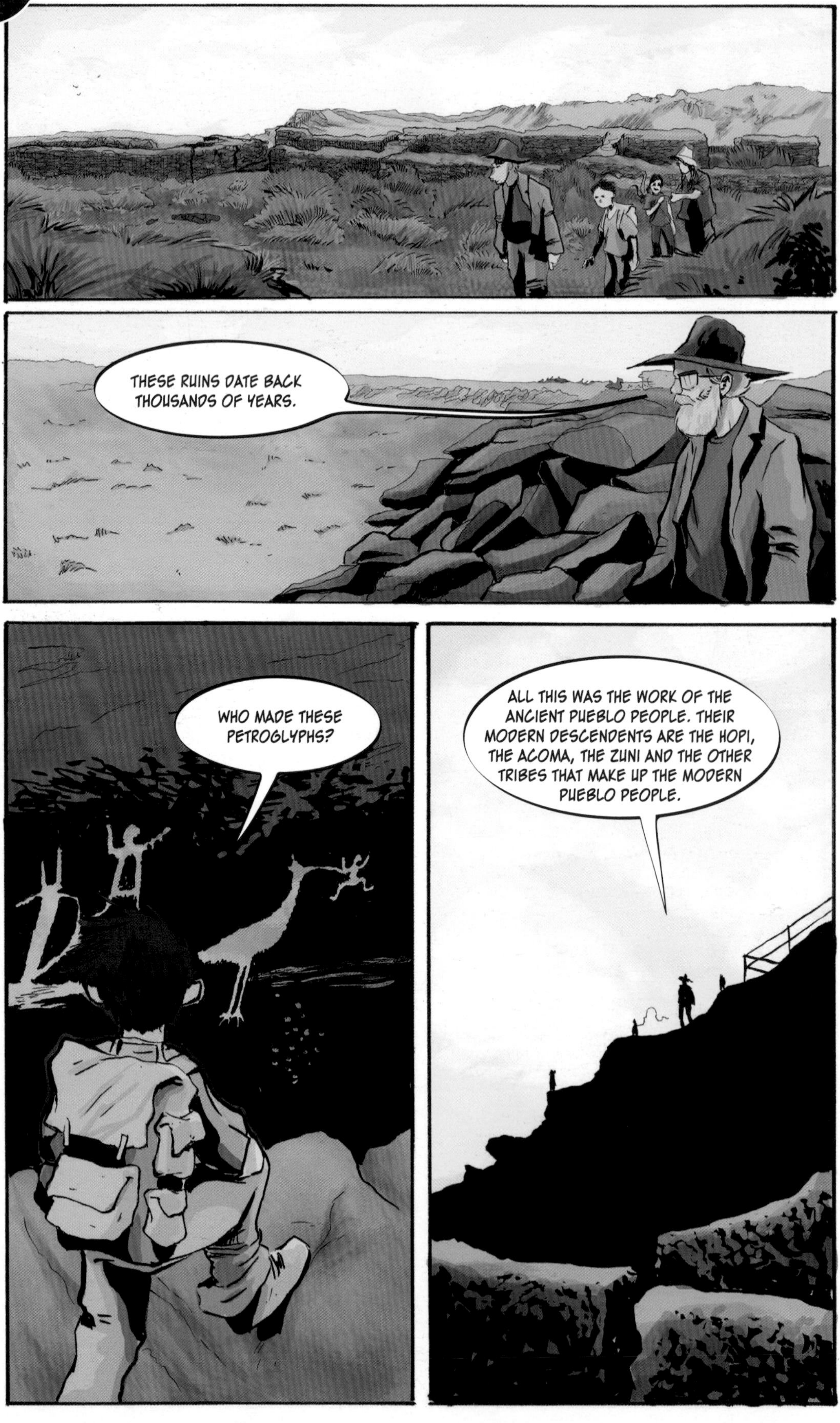
THESE RUINS DATE BACK THOUSANDS OF YEARS.
WHO MADE THESE PETROGLYPHS?
ALL THIS WAS THE WORK OF THE ANCIENT PUEBLO PEOPLE. THEIR MODERN DESCENDENTS ARE THE HOPI, THE ACOMA, THE ZUNI AND THE OTHER TRIBES THAT MAKE UP THE MODERN PUEBLO PEOPLE.

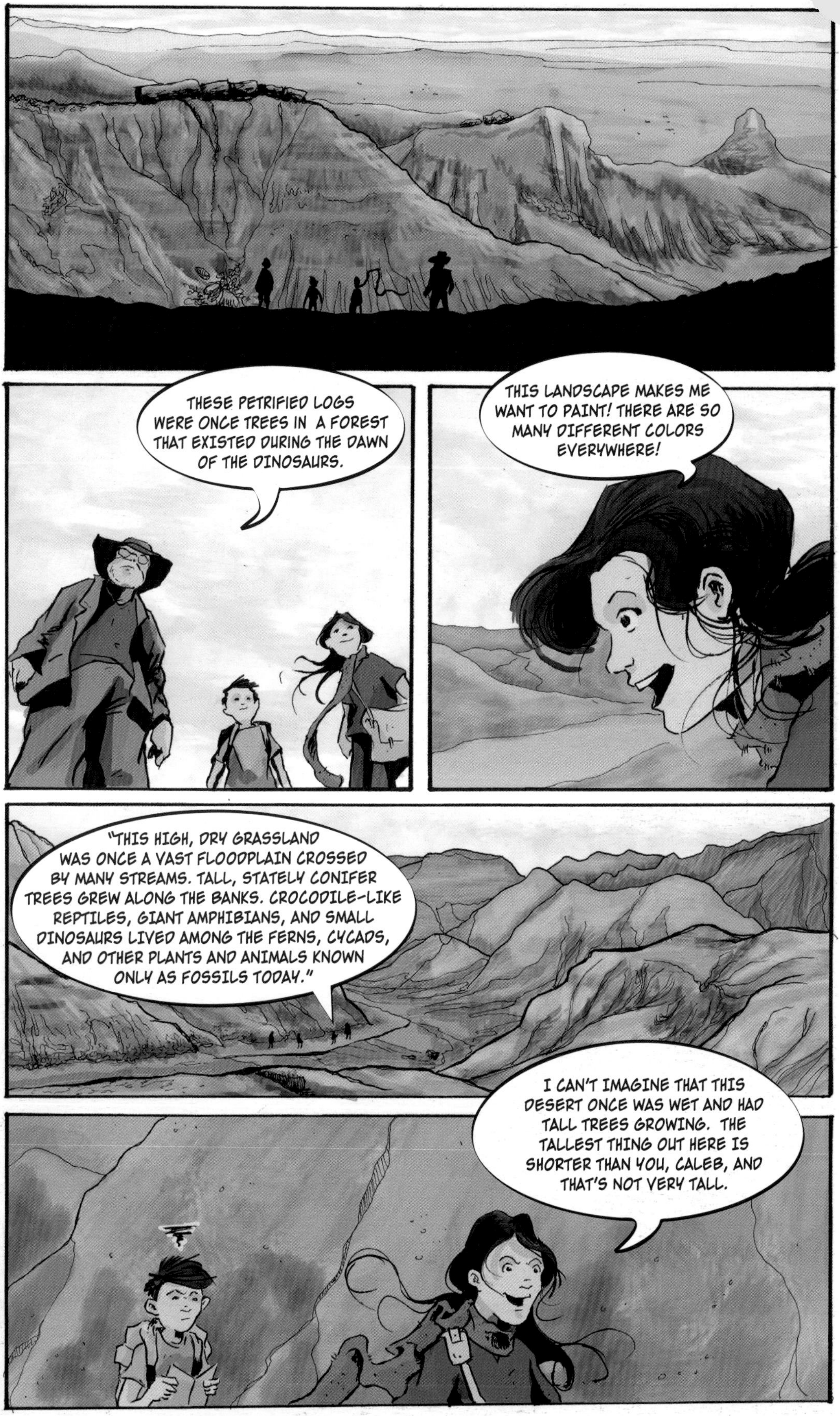
THESE PETRIFIED LOGS WERE ONCE TREES IN A FOREST THAT EXISTED DURING THE DAWN OF THE DINOSAURS.
THIS LANDSCAPE MAKES ME WANT TO PAINT! THERE ARE SO MANY DIFFERENT COLORS EVERYWHERE!
"THIS HIGH, DRY GRASSLAND WAS ONCE A VAST FLOODPLAIN CROSSED BY MANY STREAMS. TALL, STATELY CONIFER TREES GREW ALONG THE BANKS. CROCODILE-LIKE REPTILES, GIANT AMPHIBIANS, AND SMALL DINOSAURS LIVED AMONG THE FERNS, CYCADS, AND OTHER PLANTS AND ANIMALS KNOWN ONLY AS FOSSILS TODAY."
I CAN'T IMAGINE THAT THIS DESERT ONCE WAS WET AND HAD TALL TREES GROWING. THE TALLEST THING OUT HERE IS SHORTER THAN YOU, CALEB, AND THAT'S NOT VERY TALL.

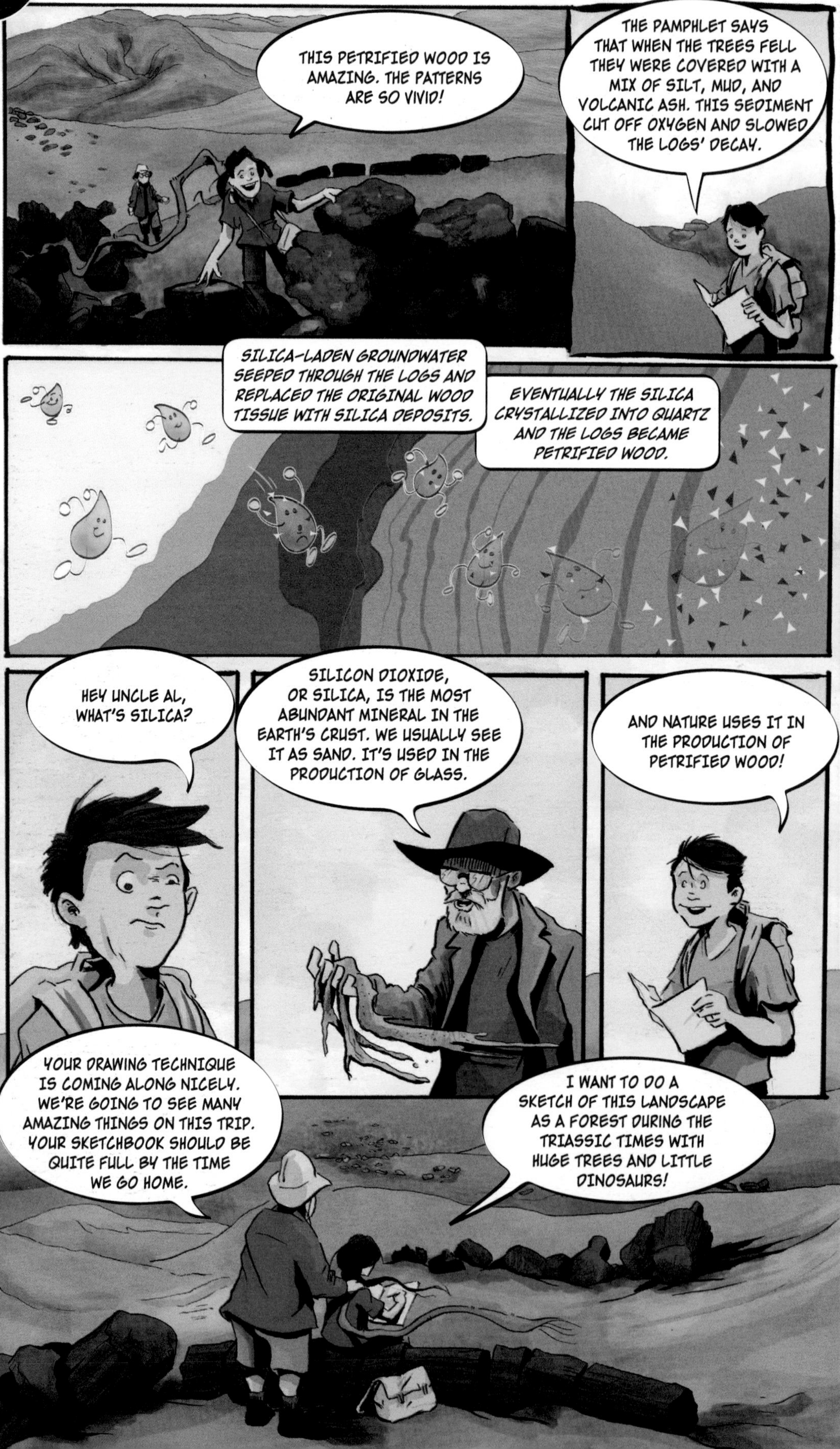
THIS PETRIFIED WOOD IS AMAZING. THE PATTERNS ARE SO VIVID!
THE PAMPHLET SAYS THAT WHEN THE TREES FELL THEY WERE COVERED WITH A MIX OF SILT, MUD, AND VOLCANIC ASH. THIS SEDIMENT CUT OFF OXYGEN AND SLOWED THE LOGS' DECAY.
SILICA-LADEN GROUNDWATER SEEPED THROUGH THE LOGS AND REPLACED THE ORIGINAL WOOD TISSUE WITH SILICA DEPOSITS.
EVENTUALLY THE SILICA CRYSTALLIZED INTO QUARTZ AND THE LOGS BECAME PETRIFIED WOOD.
HEY UNCLE AL, WHAT'S SILICA?
SILICON DIOXIDE, OR SILICA, IS THE MOST ABUNDANT MINERAL IN THE EARTH'S CRUST. WE USUALLY SEE IT AS SAND. IT'S USED IN THE PRODUCTION OF GLASS.
AND NATURE USES IT IN THE PRODUCTION OF PETRIFIED WOOD!
YOUR DRAWING TECHNIQUE IS COMING ALONG NICELY. WE'RE GOING TO SEE MANY AMAZING THINGS ON THIS TRIP. YOUR SKETCHBOOK SHOULD BE QUITE FULL BY THE TIME WE GO HOME.
I WANT TO DO A SKETCH OF THIS LANDSCAPE AS A FOREST DURING THE TRIASSIC TIMES WITH HUGE TREES AND LITTLE DINOSAURS!

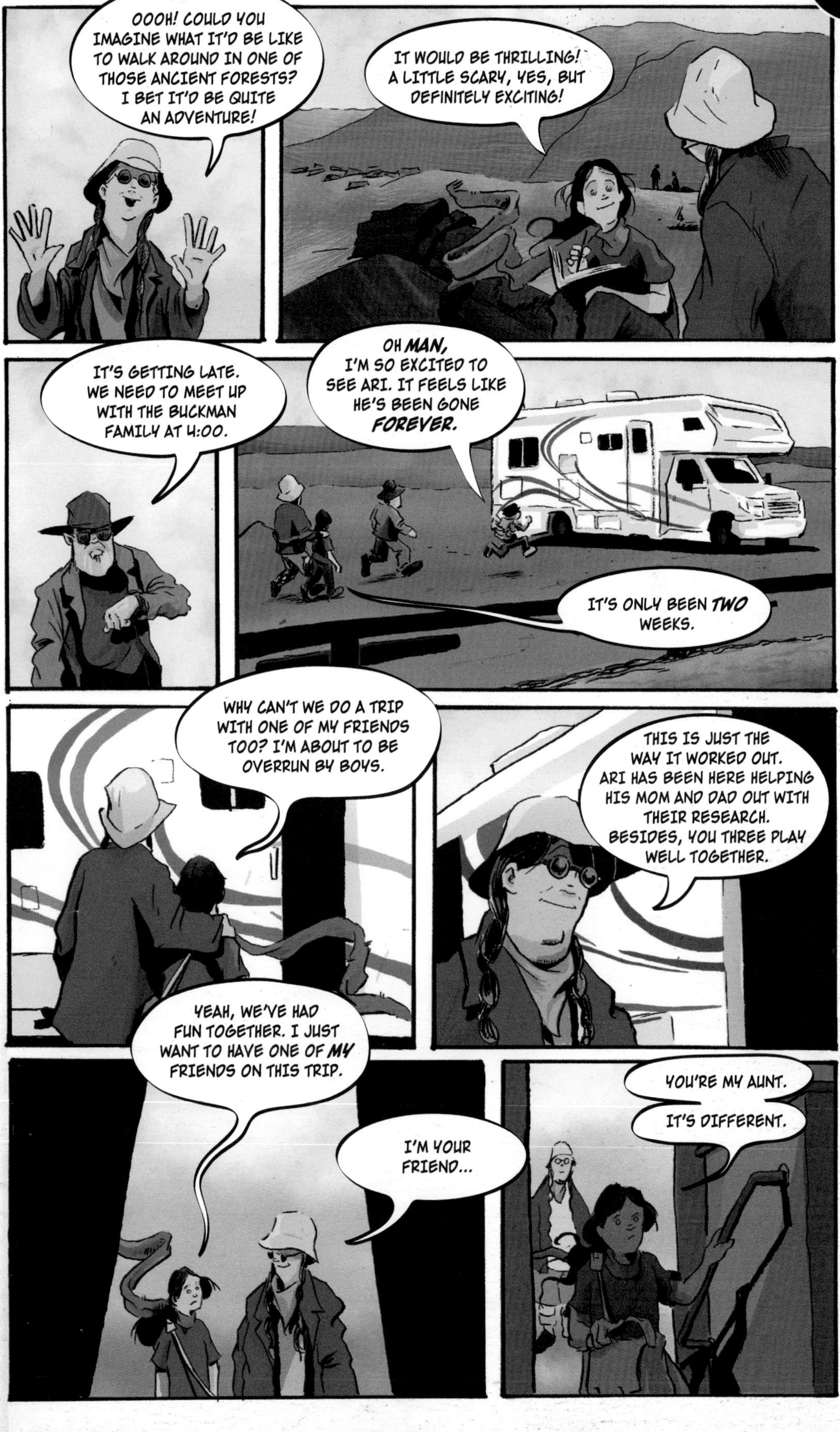
OOOH! COULD YOU IMAGINE WHAT IT'D BE LIKE TO WALK AROUND IN ONE OF THOSE ANCIENT FORESTS? I BET IT'D BE QUITE AN ADVENTURE!
IT WOULD BE THRILLING! A LITTLE SCARY, YES, BUT DEFINITELY EXCITING!
IT'S GETTING LATE. WE NEED TO MEET UP WITH THE BUCKMAN FAMILY AT 4:00.
OH MAN, I'M SO EXCITED TO SEE ARI. IT FEELS LIKE HE'S BEEN GONE FOREVER.
IT'S ONLY BEEN TWO WEEKS.
WHY CAN'T WE DO A TRIP WITH ONE OF MY FRIENDS TOO? I'M ABOUT TO BE OVERRUN BY BOYS.
THIS IS JUST THE WAY IT WORKED OUT. ARI HAS BEEN HERE HELPING HIS MOM AND DAD OUT WITH THEIR RESEARCH. BESIDES, YOU THREE PLAY WELL TOGETHER.
YEAH, WE'VE HAD FUN TOGETHER. I JUST WANT TO HAVE ONE OF MY FRIENDS ON THIS TRIP.
I'M YOUR FRIEND...
YOU'RE MY AUNT.
IT'S DIFFERENT.

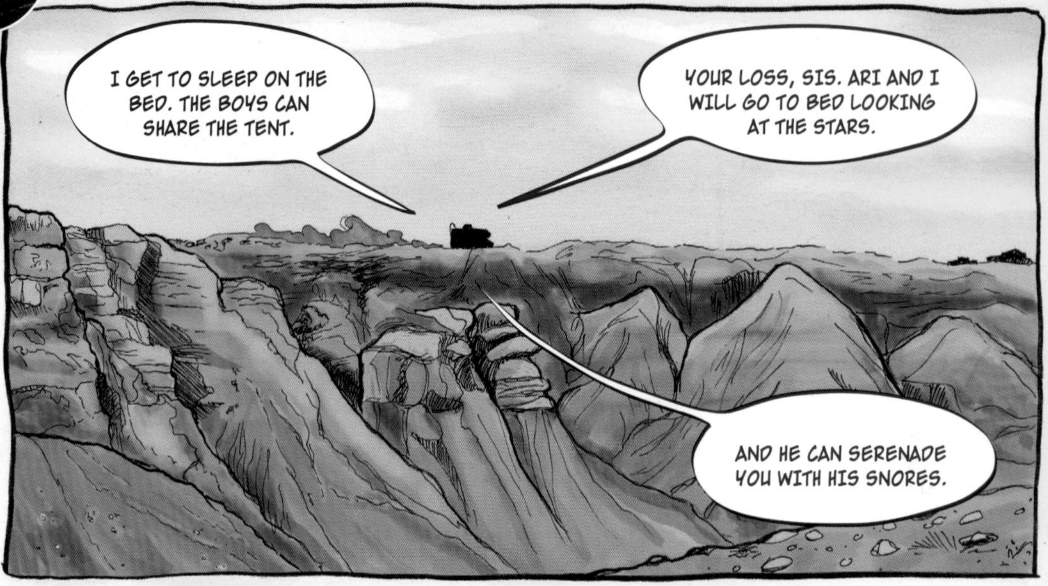
I GET TO SLEEP ON THE BED. THE BOYS CAN SHARE THE TENT.
YOUR LOSS, SIS. ARI AND I WILL GO TO BED LOOKING AT THE STARS.
AND HE CAN SERENADE YOU WITH HIS SNORES.

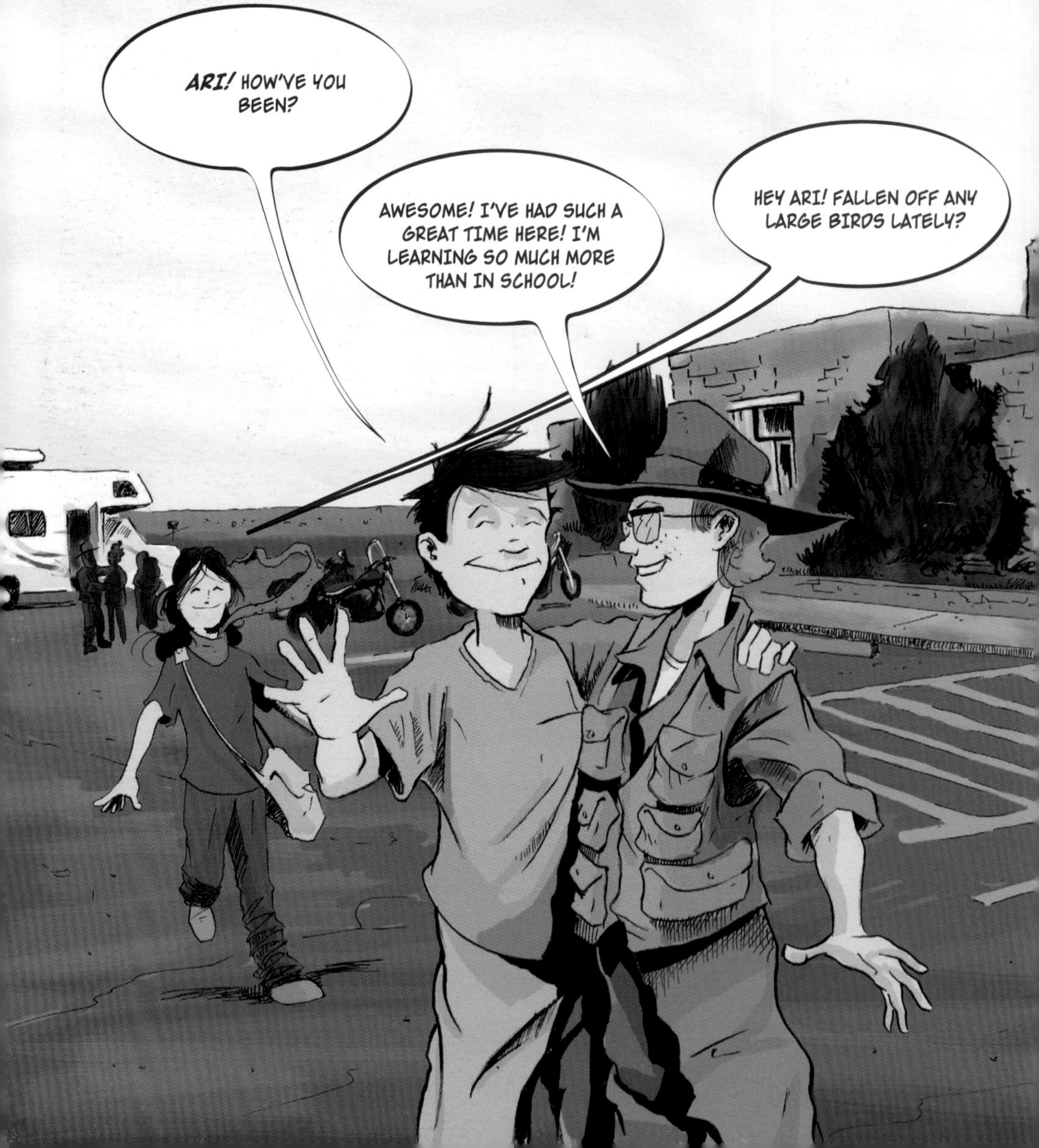
ARI! HOW'VE YOU BEEN?
AWESOME! I'VE HAD SUCH A GREAT TIME HERE! I'M LEARNING SO MUCH MORE THAN IN SCHOOL!
HEY ARI! FALLEN OFF ANY LARGE BIRDS LATELY?

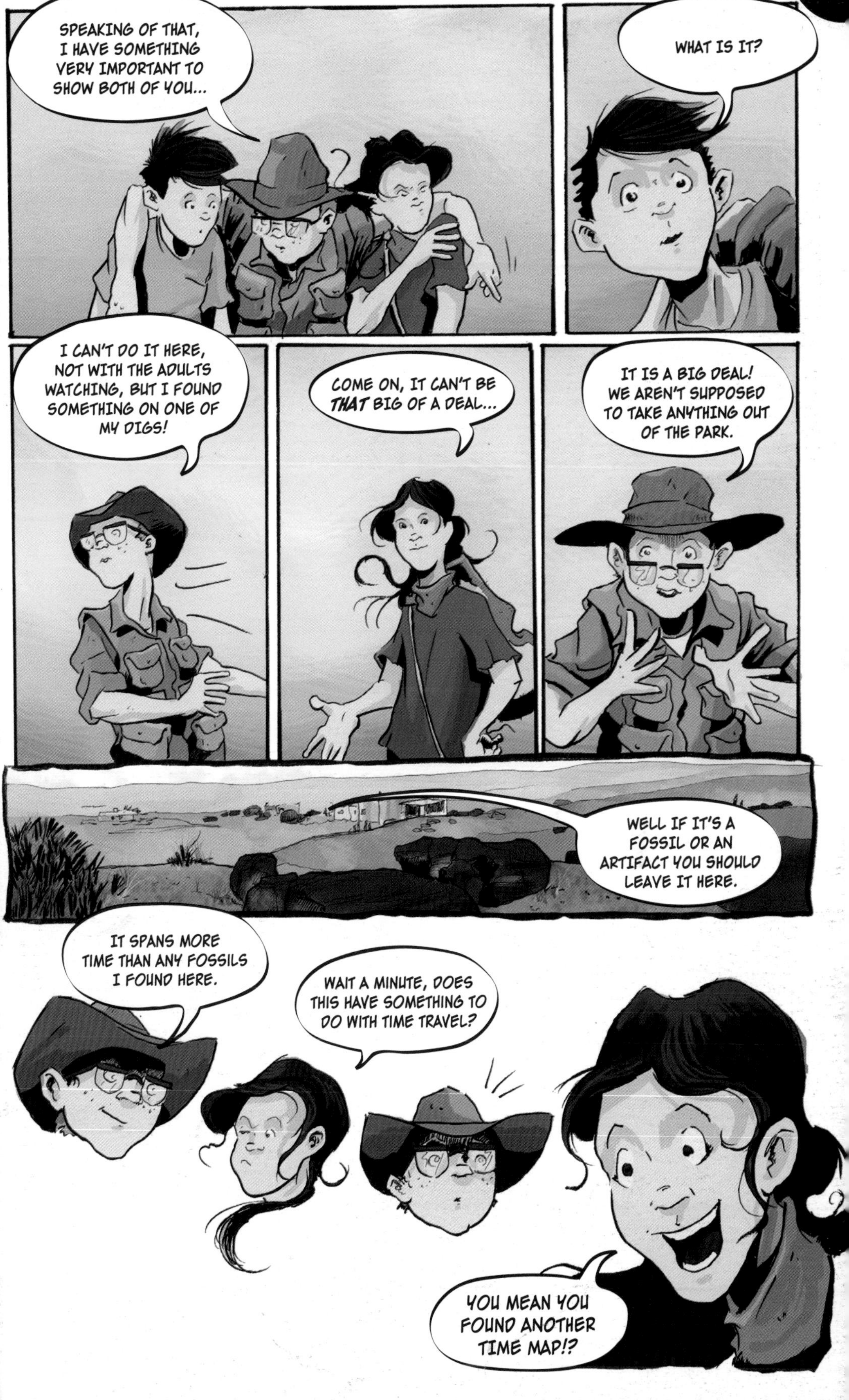
SPEAKING OF THAT, I HAVE SOMETHING VERY IMPORTANT TO SHOW BOTH OF YOU...
WHAT IS IT?
I CAN'T DO IT HERE, NOT WITH THE ADULTS WATCHING, BUT I FOUND SOMETHING ON ONE OF MY DIGS!
COME ON, IT CAN'T BE *THAT* BIG OF A DEAL...
IT IS A BIG DEAL! WE AREN'T SUPPOSED TO TAKE ANYTHING OUT OF THE PARK.
WELL IF IT'S A FOSSIL OR AN ARTIFACT YOU SHOULD LEAVE IT HERE.
IT SPANS MORE TIME THAN ANY FOSSILS I FOUND HERE.
WAIT A MINUTE, DOES THIS HAVE SOMETHING TO DO WITH TIME TRAVEL?
YOU MEAN YOU FOUND ANOTHER TIME MAP!?

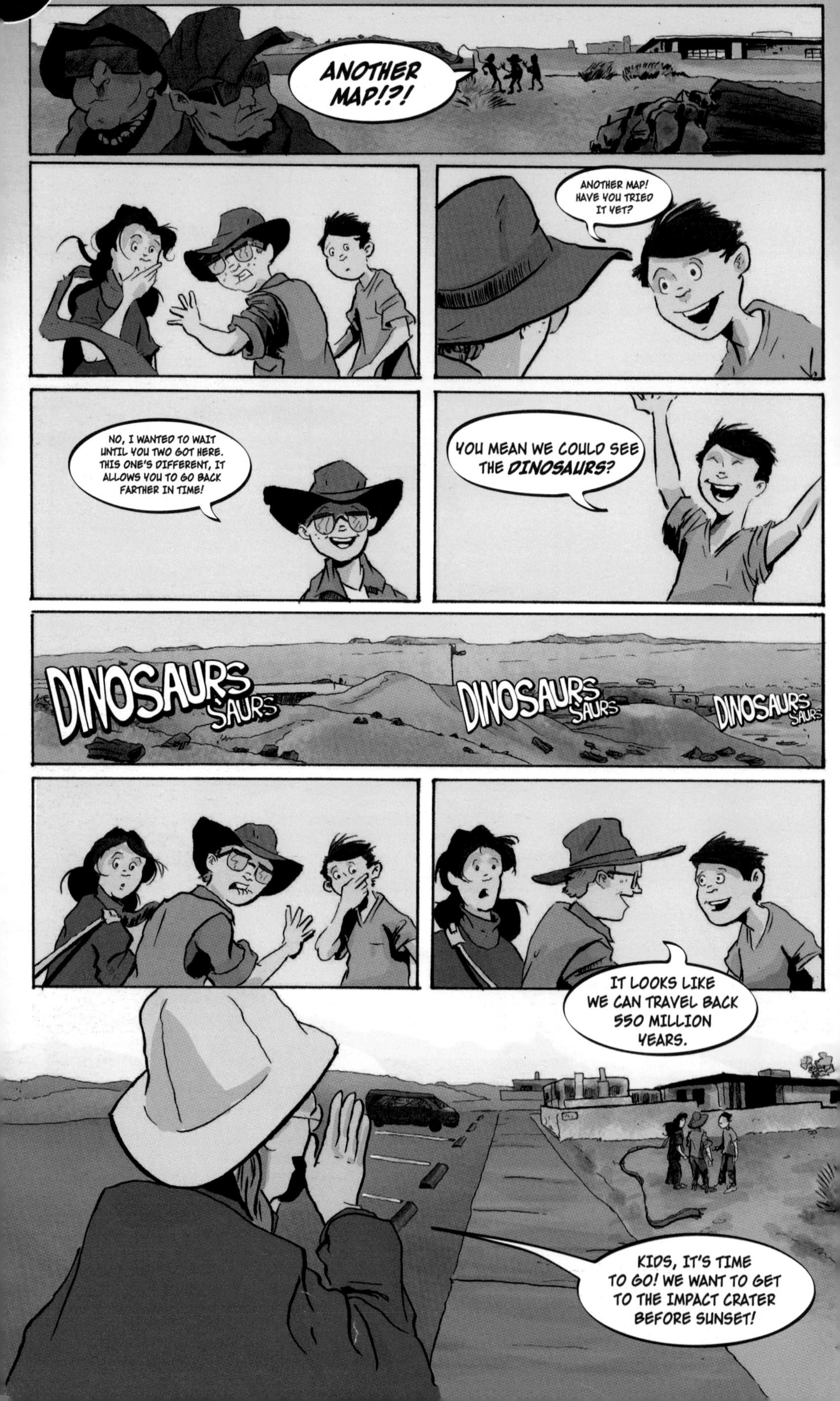
ANOTHER MAP!?!
ANOTHER MAP! HAVE YOU TRIED IT YET?
NO, I WANTED TO WAIT UNTIL YOU TWO GOT HERE. THIS ONE'S DIFFERENT, IT ALLOWS YOU TO GO BACK FARTHER IN TIME!
YOU MEAN WE COULD SEE THE *DINOSAURS?*
DINOSAURS SAURS
DINOSAURS SAURS
DINOSAURS SAURS
IT LOOKS LIKE WE CAN TRAVEL BACK 550 MILLION YEARS.
KIDS, IT'S TIME TO GO! WE WANT TO GET TO THE IMPACT CRATER BEFORE SUNSET!

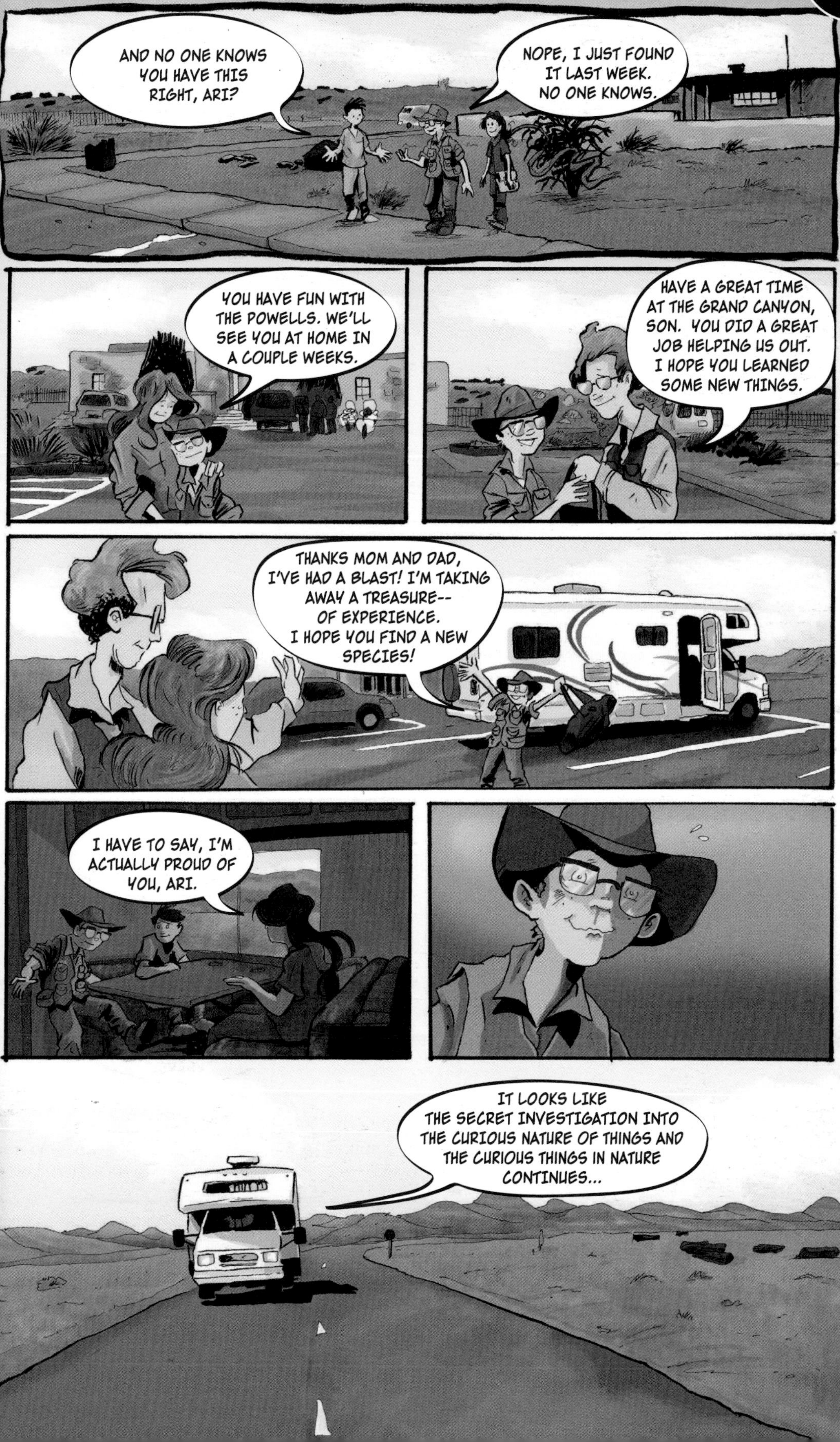
AND NO ONE KNOWS YOU HAVE THIS RIGHT, ARI?
NOPE, I JUST FOUND IT LAST WEEK. NO ONE KNOWS.
YOU HAVE FUN WITH THE POWELLS. WE'LL SEE YOU AT HOME IN A COUPLE WEEKS.
HAVE A GREAT TIME AT THE GRAND CANYON, SON. YOU DID A GREAT JOB HELPING US OUT. I HOPE YOU LEARNED SOME NEW THINGS.
THANKS MOM AND DAD, I'VE HAD A BLAST! I'M TAKING AWAY A TREASURE-- OF EXPERIENCE. I HOPE YOU FIND A NEW SPECIES!
I HAVE TO SAY, I'M ACTUALLY PROUD OF YOU, ARI.
IT LOOKS LIKE THE SECRET INVESTIGATION INTO THE CURIOUS NATURE OF THINGS AND THE CURIOUS THINGS IN NATURE CONTINUES...

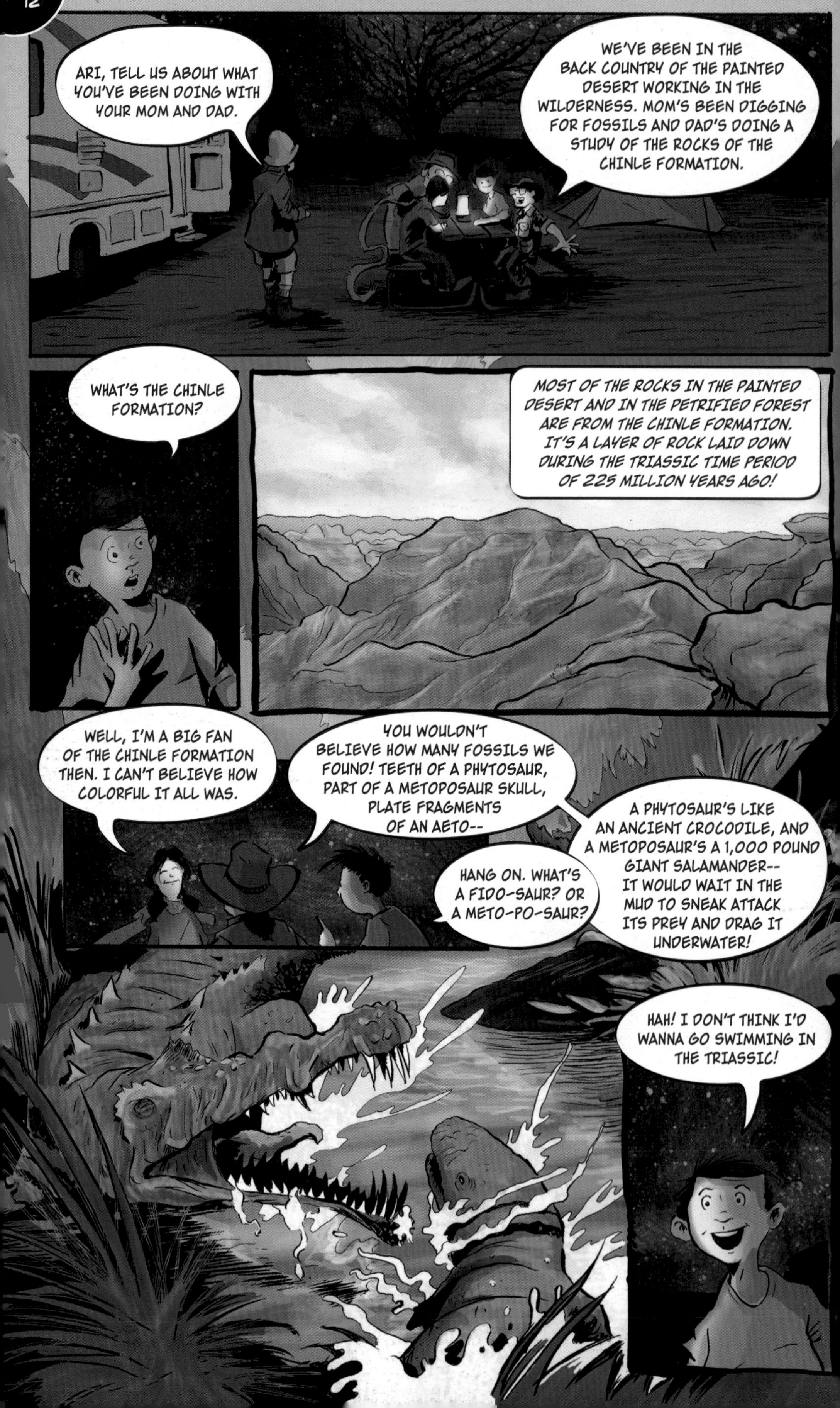
ARI, TELL US ABOUT WHAT YOU'VE BEEN DOING WITH YOUR MOM AND DAD.
WE'VE BEEN IN THE BACK COUNTRY OF THE PAINTED DESERT WORKING IN THE WILDERNESS. MOM'S BEEN DIGGING FOR FOSSILS AND DAD'S DOING A STUDY OF THE ROCKS OF THE CHINLE FORMATION.
WHAT'S THE CHINLE FORMATION?
MOST OF THE ROCKS IN THE PAINTED DESERT AND IN THE PETRIFIED FOREST ARE FROM THE CHINLE FORMATION. IT'S A LAYER OF ROCK LAID DOWN DURING THE TRIASSIC TIME PERIOD OF 225 MILLION YEARS AGO!
WELL, I'M A BIG FAN OF THE CHINLE FORMATION THEN. I CAN'T BELIEVE HOW COLORFUL IT ALL WAS.
YOU WOULDN'T BELIEVE HOW MANY FOSSILS WE FOUND! TEETH OF A PHYTOSAUR, PART OF A METOPOSAUR SKULL, PLATE FRAGMENTS OF AN AETO--
HANG ON. WHAT'S A FIDO-SAUR? OR A METO-PO-SAUR?
A PHYTOSAUR'S LIKE AN ANCIENT CROCODILE, AND A METOPOSAUR'S A 1,000 POUND GIANT SALAMANDER-- IT WOULD WAIT IN THE MUD TO SNEAK ATTACK ITS PREY AND DRAG IT UNDERWATER!
HAH! I DON'T THINK I'D WANNA GO SWIMMING IN THE TRIASSIC!

KIDS, WE'RE GOING TO BED. PLEASE DON'T STAY UP TOO LATE.
WE'RE GOING TO WAKE YOU UP EARLY TO GET A LOOK AT THE IMPACT CRATER BEFORE WE GO TO THE GRAND CANYON!
ALRIGHT, ARI. LET'S SEE THE MAP.
I FOUND IT INSIDE OF THIS CYLINDER DEEP IN THE SOIL.
IT COULD HAVE BEEN THERE FOR OVER 200 MILLION YEARS!

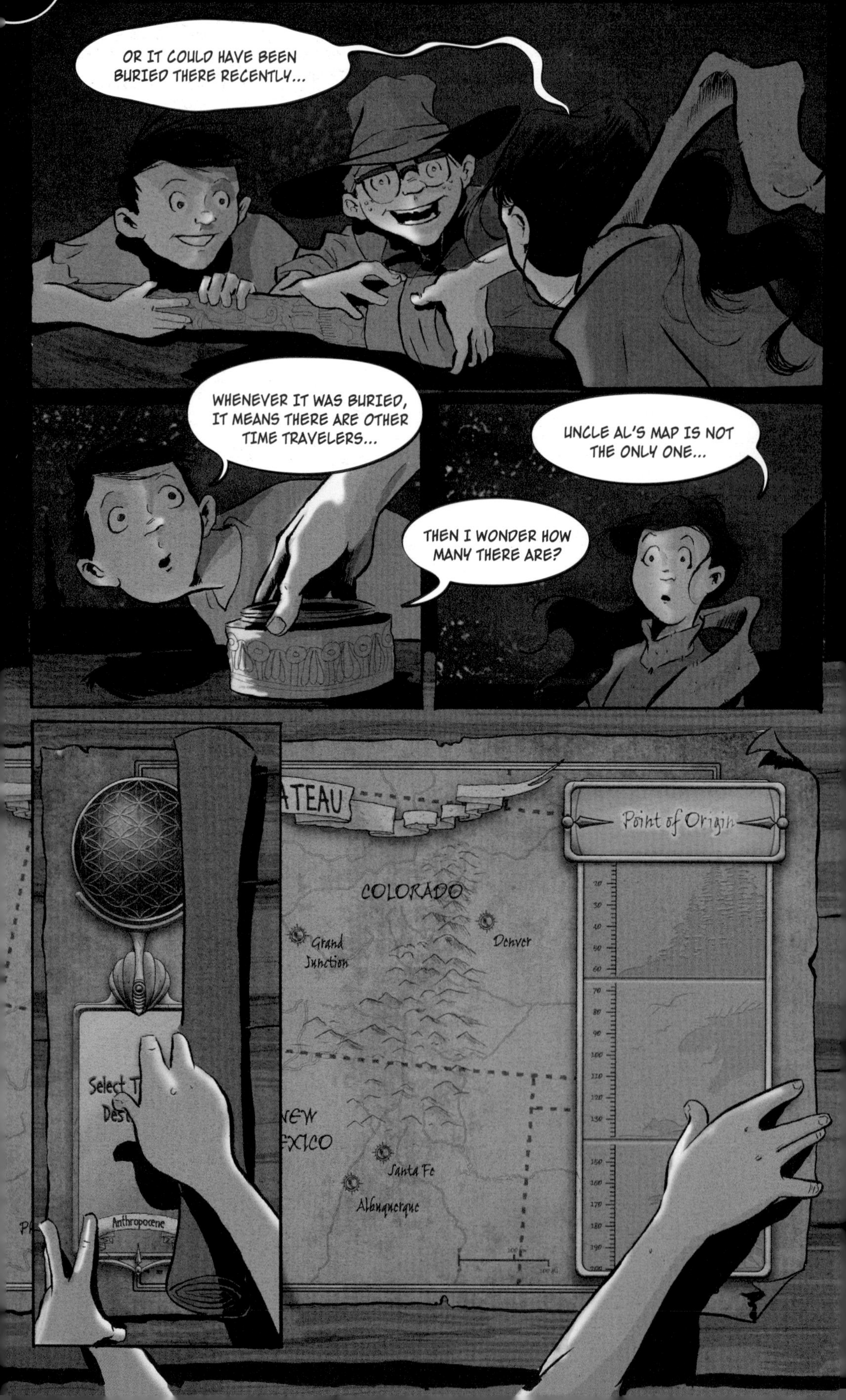
OR IT COULD HAVE BEEN BURIED THERE RECENTLY...
WHENEVER IT WAS BURIED, IT MEANS THERE ARE OTHER TIME TRAVELERS...
UNCLE AL'S MAP IS NOT THE ONLY ONE...
THEN I WONDER HOW MANY THERE ARE?
Point of Origin
COLORADO
Grand Junction
Denver
Santa Fe
Albuquerque
Anthropocene

THIS MAP'S A MORE ADVANCED VERSION OF UNCLE AL'S MAP. THE CHANTS ARE IN SOME OTHER LANGUAGE INSTEAD OF THE CHINOOK JARGON. IT CAN GO WAY FARTHER BACK IN TIME.

AND IT'S NOT OF THE PACIFIC NORTHWEST.

NOPE. IT'S OF THE COLORADO PLATEAU.

BUT WE'RE IN ARIZONA.

COLORADO PLATEAU

UTAH

COLORA

Grand Junction

Blanding

Tub

NEW MEXICO

Santa Fe

Albuquerque

UTAH, ARIZONA, NEW MEXICO, AND COLORADO.

THE COLORADO PLATEAU IS NAMED AFTER THE COLORADO RIVER. THERE IS MORE OF THE PLATEAU IN UTAH THAN THERE IS IN COLORADO. BUT THE PLATEAU IS IN PART OF ALL THE FOUR CORNER STATES.

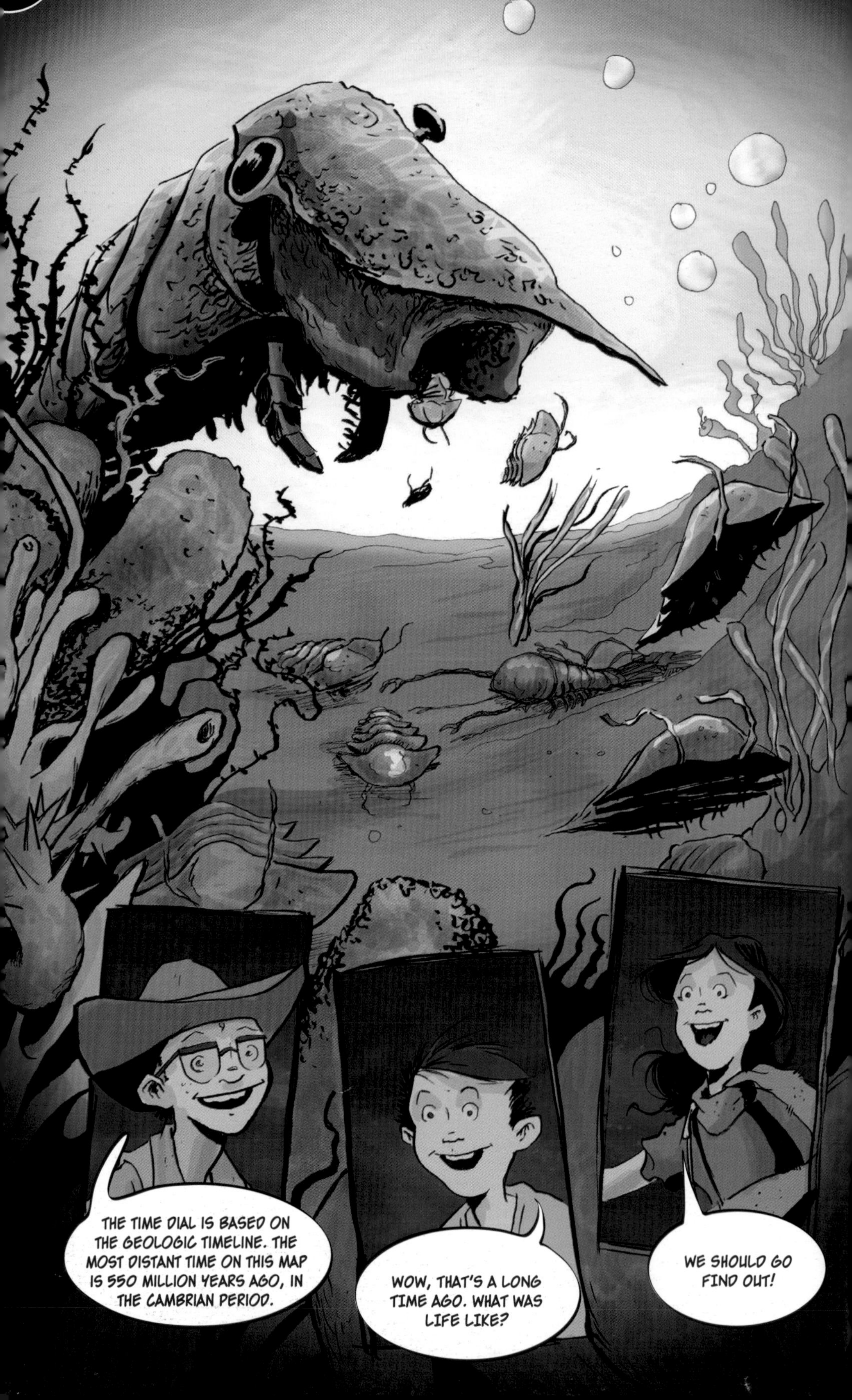
THE TIME DIAL IS BASED ON THE GEOLOGIC TIMELINE. THE MOST DISTANT TIME ON THIS MAP IS 550 MILLION YEARS AGO, IN THE CAMBRIAN PERIOD.
WOW, THAT'S A LONG TIME AGO. WHAT WAS LIFE LIKE?
WE SHOULD GO FIND OUT!

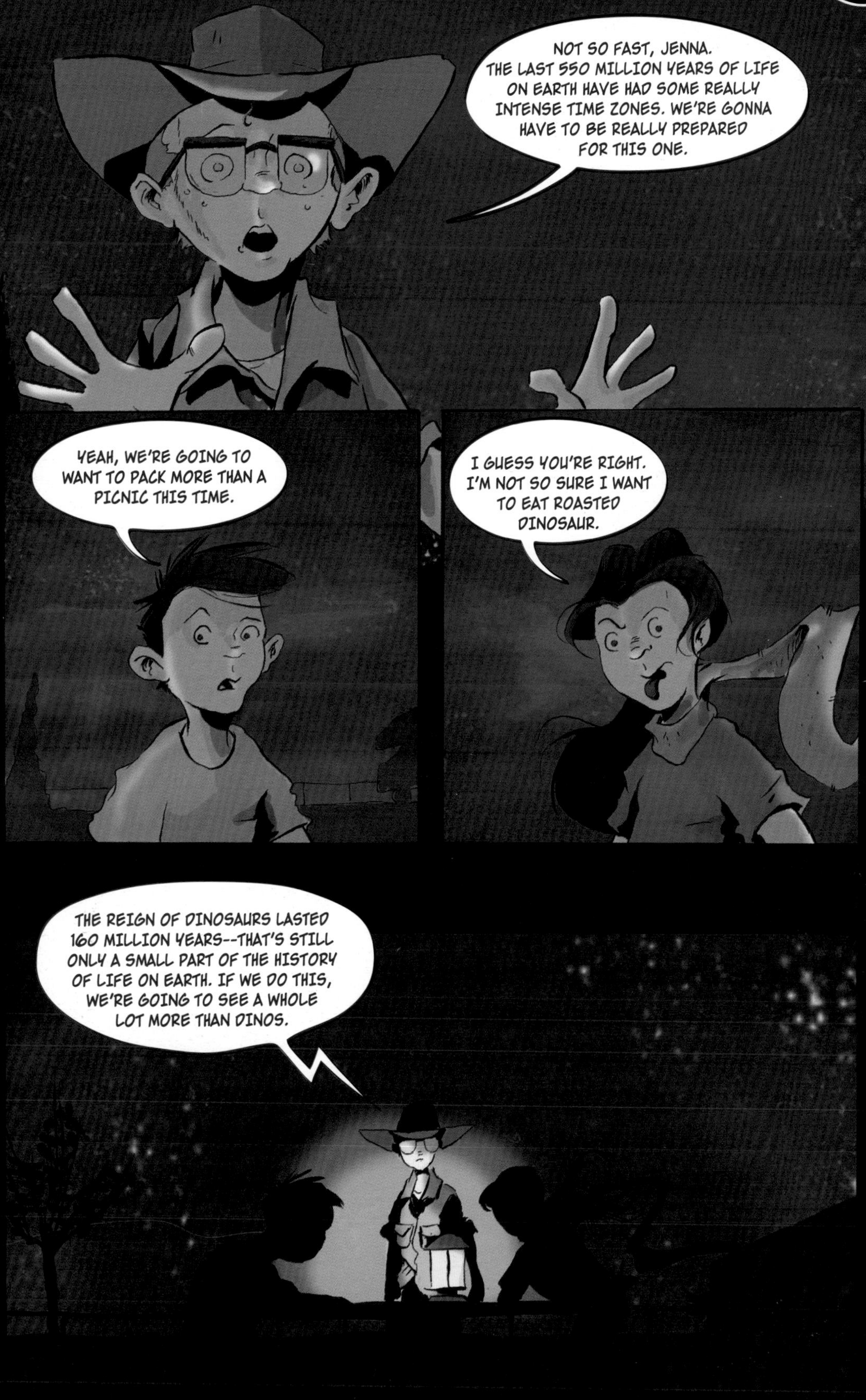
NOT SO FAST, JENNA. THE LAST 550 MILLION YEARS OF LIFE ON EARTH HAVE HAD SOME REALLY INTENSE TIME ZONES. WE'RE GONNA HAVE TO BE REALLY PREPARED FOR THIS ONE.
YEAH, WE'RE GOING TO WANT TO PACK MORE THAN A PICNIC THIS TIME.
I GUESS YOU'RE RIGHT. I'M NOT SO SURE I WANT TO EAT ROASTED DINOSAUR.
THE REIGN OF DINOSAURS LASTED 160 MILLION YEARS--THAT'S STILL ONLY A SMALL PART OF THE HISTORY OF LIFE ON EARTH. IF WE DO THIS, WE'RE GOING TO SEE A WHOLE LOT MORE THAN DINOS.

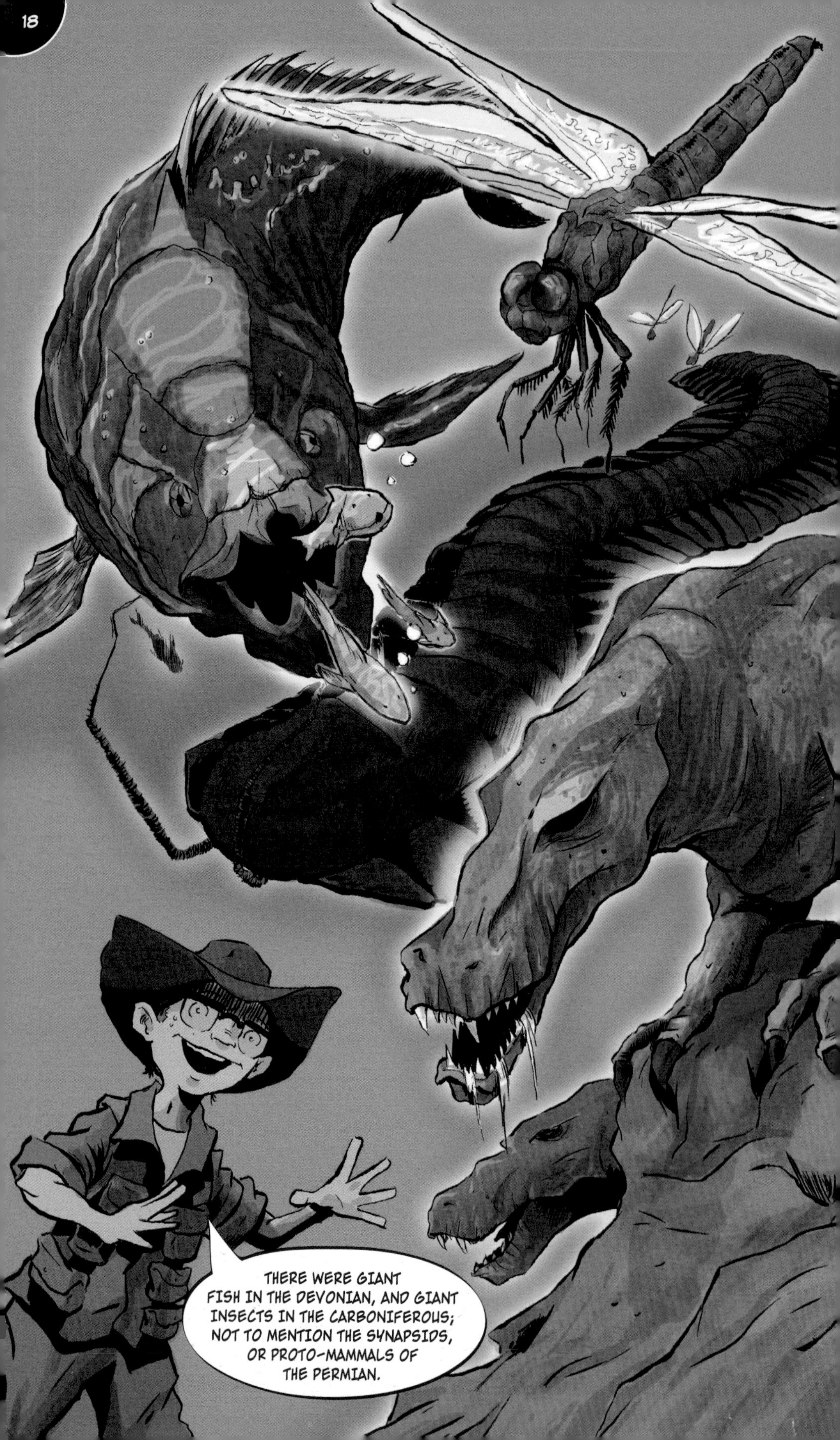
THERE WERE GIANT FISH IN THE DEVONIAN, AND GIANT INSECTS IN THE CARBONIFEROUS; NOT TO MENTION THE SYNAPSIDS, OR PROTO-MAMMALS OF THE PERMIAN.

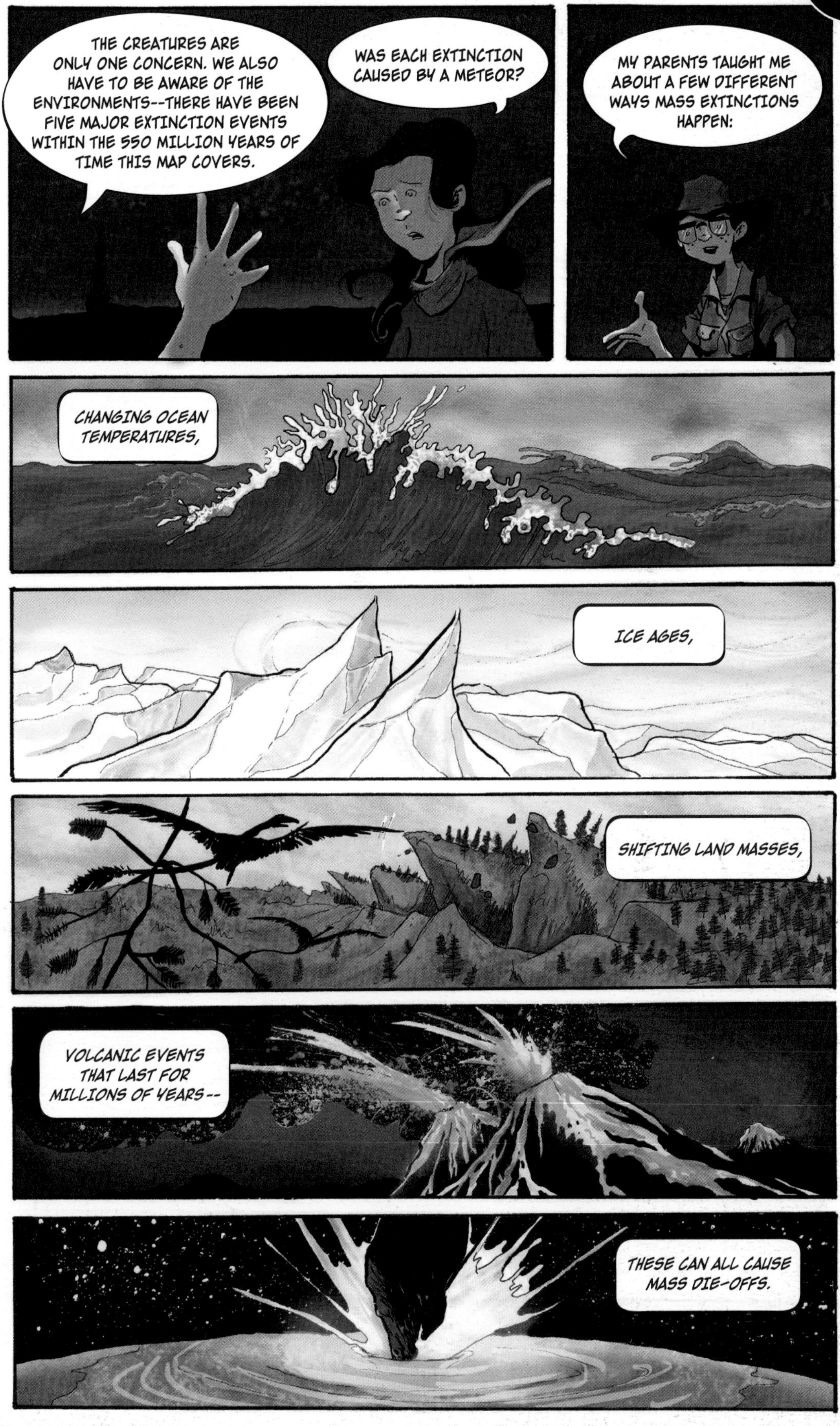
THE CREATURES ARE ONLY ONE CONCERN. WE ALSO HAVE TO BE AWARE OF THE ENVIRONMENTS--THERE HAVE BEEN FIVE MAJOR EXTINCTION EVENTS WITHIN THE 550 MILLION YEARS OF TIME THIS MAP COVERS.
WAS EACH EXTINCTION CAUSED BY A METEOR?
MY PARENTS TAUGHT ME ABOUT A FEW DIFFERENT WAYS MASS EXTINCTIONS HAPPEN:
CHANGING OCEAN TEMPERATURES,
ICE AGES,
SHIFTING LAND MASSES,
VOLCANIC EVENTS THAT LAST FOR MILLIONS OF YEARS--
THESE CAN ALL CAUSE MASS DIE-OFFS.

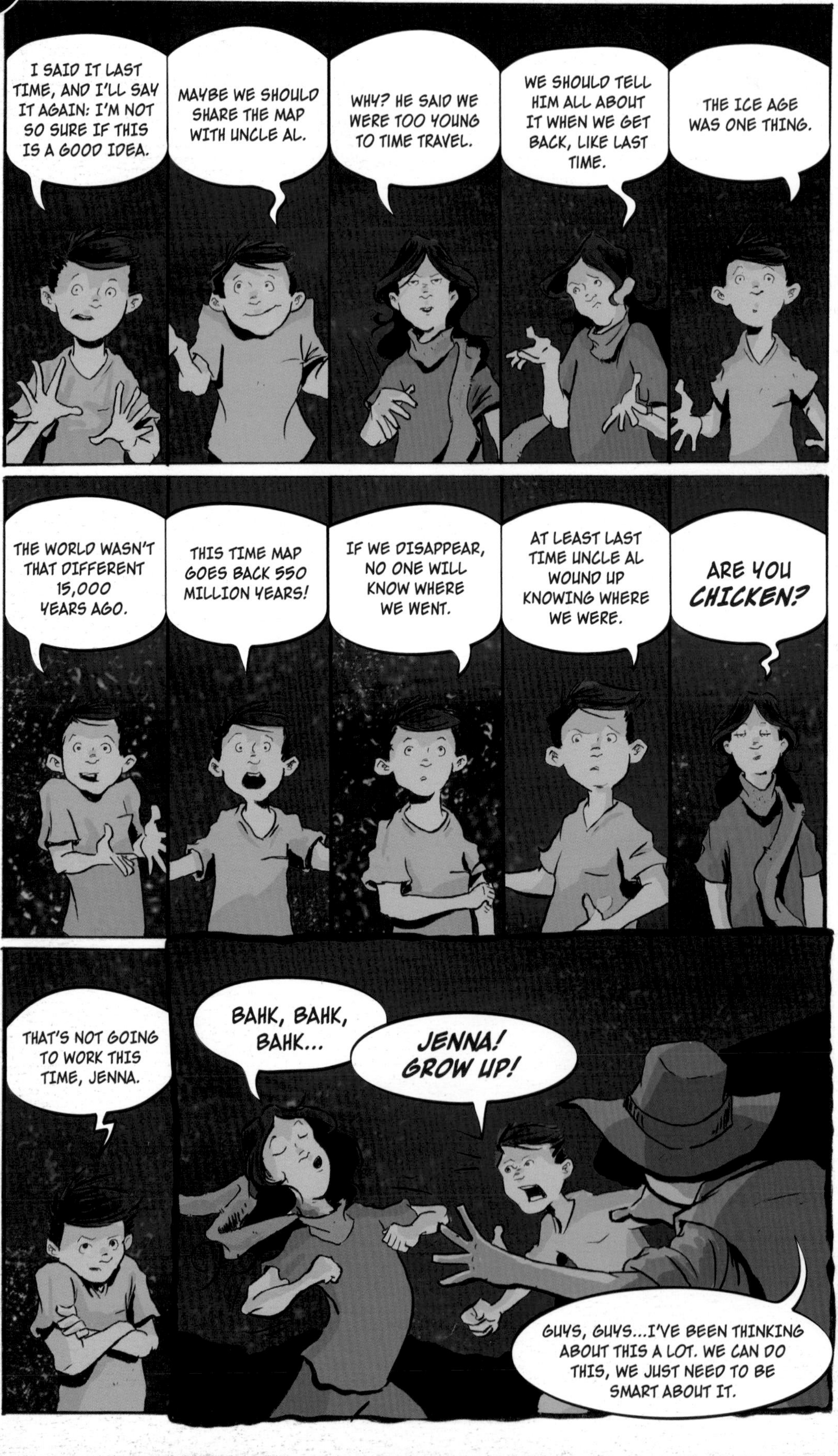
I SAID IT LAST TIME, AND I'LL SAY IT AGAIN: I'M NOT SO SURE IF THIS IS A GOOD IDEA.
MAYBE WE SHOULD SHARE THE MAP WITH UNCLE AL.
WHY? HE SAID WE WERE TOO YOUNG TO TIME TRAVEL.
WE SHOULD TELL HIM ALL ABOUT IT WHEN WE GET BACK, LIKE LAST TIME.
THE ICE AGE WAS ONE THING.
THE WORLD WASN'T THAT DIFFERENT 15,000 YEARS AGO.
THIS TIME MAP GOES BACK 550 MILLION YEARS!
IF WE DISAPPEAR, NO ONE WILL KNOW WHERE WE WENT.
AT LEAST LAST TIME UNCLE AL WOUND UP KNOWING WHERE WE WERE.
ARE YOU CHICKEN?
THAT'S NOT GOING TO WORK THIS TIME, JENNA.
BAHK, BAHK, BAHK...
JENNA! GROW UP!
GUYS, GUYS...I'VE BEEN THINKING ABOUT THIS A LOT. WE CAN DO THIS, WE JUST NEED TO BE SMART ABOUT IT.

LAST TIME WE TIME TRAVELED, WE JUST JUMPED INTO IT. THIS TIME WE CAN PLAN IT OUT BETTER. JENNA, LET'S REALLY STUDY THIS MAP AND KNOW WHAT WERE GETTING INTO. I CAN HELP US FIGURE OUT WHERE--AND WHEN--NOT TO GO. WE'LL AVOID ANY OF THE MASS EXTINCTIONS, WE'LL BRING PLENTY OF FOOD AND WATER.

WE CAN ALSO HAVE A SAFETY SYSTEM AND LEAVE A NOTE FOR YOUR AUNT AND UNCLE TO FIND IF WE DISAPPEAR.

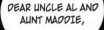

DEAR UNCLE AL AND AUNT MADDIE,

IF YOU'RE READING THIS IT'S BECAUSE WE WENT TIME TRAVELING AND ARE IN TROUBLE SOMEWHERE IN THE DISTANT PAST.

OF COURSE, YOU HAVE NO WAY OF TIME TRAVELING WHERE WE ARE, SO YOU CAN'T REALLY HELP US.

LOVE, JENNA, CALEB, AND ARI.

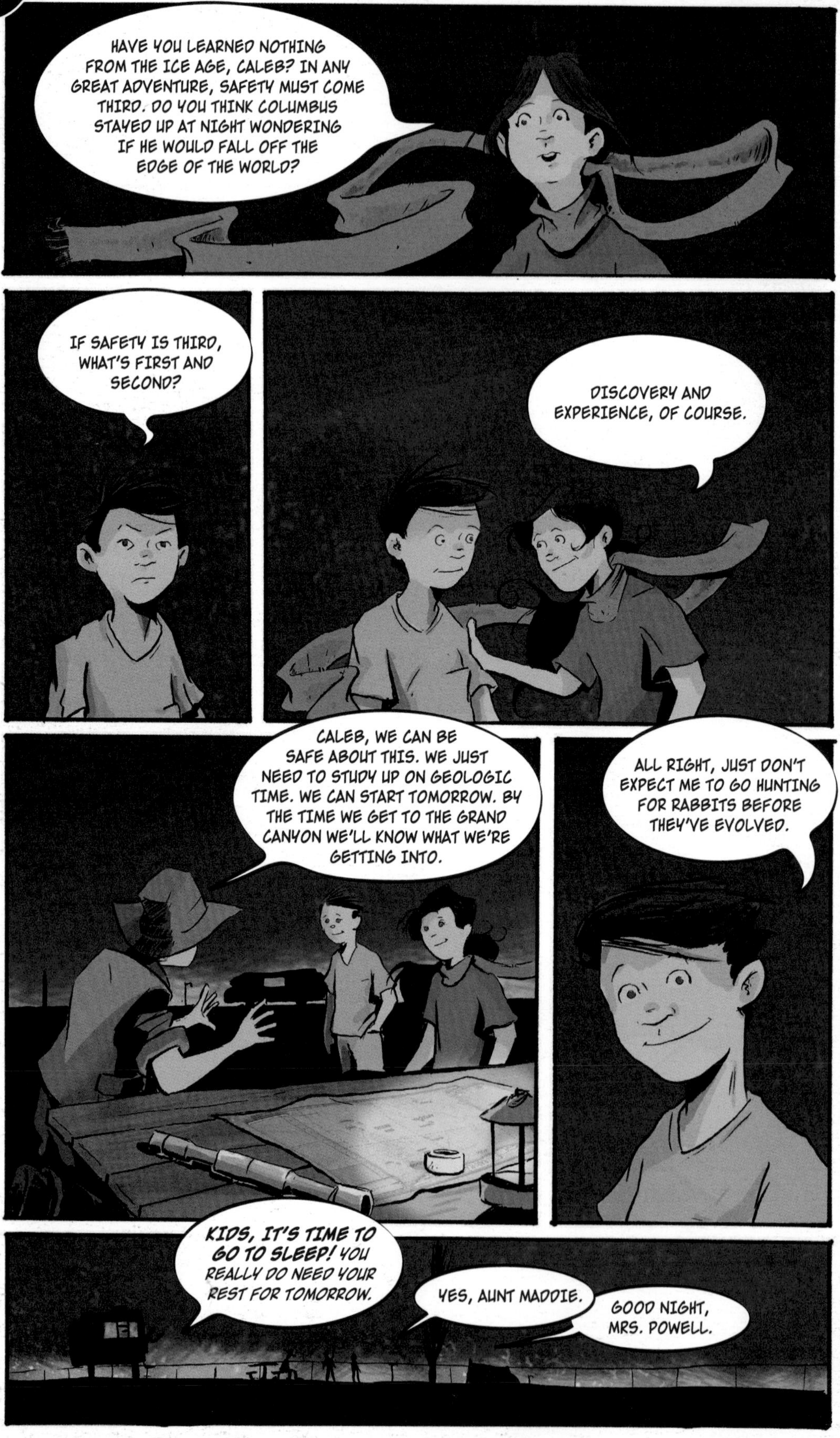
HAVE YOU LEARNED NOTHING FROM THE ICE AGE, CALEB? IN ANY GREAT ADVENTURE, SAFETY MUST COME THIRD. DO YOU THINK COLUMBUS STAYED UP AT NIGHT WONDERING IF HE WOULD FALL OFF THE EDGE OF THE WORLD?
IF SAFETY IS THIRD, WHAT'S FIRST AND SECOND?
DISCOVERY AND EXPERIENCE, OF COURSE.
CALEB, WE CAN BE SAFE ABOUT THIS. WE JUST NEED TO STUDY UP ON GEOLOGIC TIME. WE CAN START TOMORROW. BY THE TIME WE GET TO THE GRAND CANYON WE'LL KNOW WHAT WE'RE GETTING INTO.
ALL RIGHT, JUST DON'T EXPECT ME TO GO HUNTING FOR RABBITS BEFORE THEY'VE EVOLVED.
KIDS, IT'S TIME TO GO TO SLEEP! YOU REALLY DO NEED YOUR REST FOR TOMORROW.
YES, AUNT MADDIE.
GOOD NIGHT, MRS. POWELL.

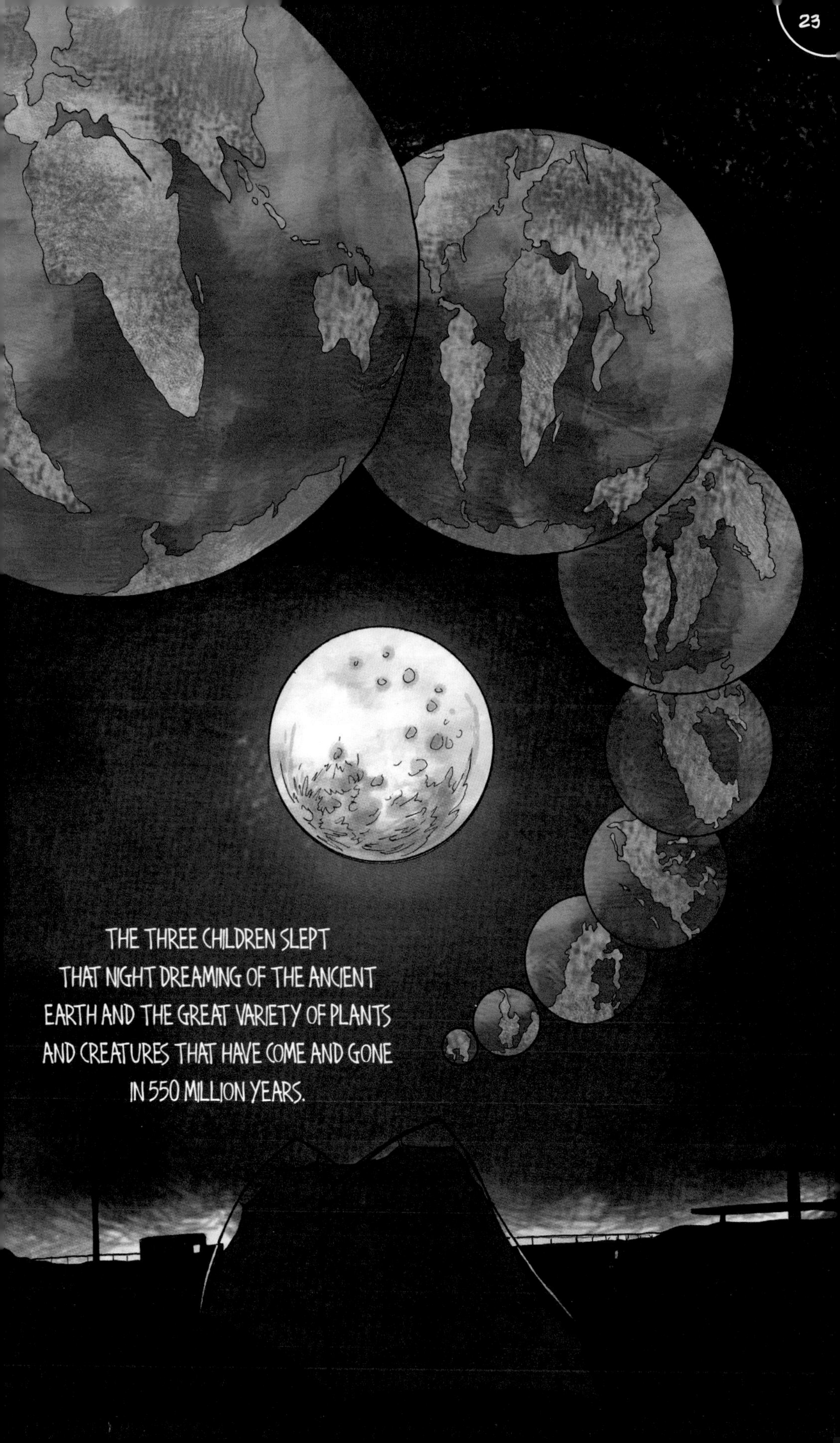
THE THREE CHILDREN SLEPT
THAT NIGHT DREAMING OF THE ANCIENT
EARTH AND THE GREAT VARIETY OF PLANTS
AND CREATURES THAT HAVE COME AND GONE
IN 550 MILLION YEARS.

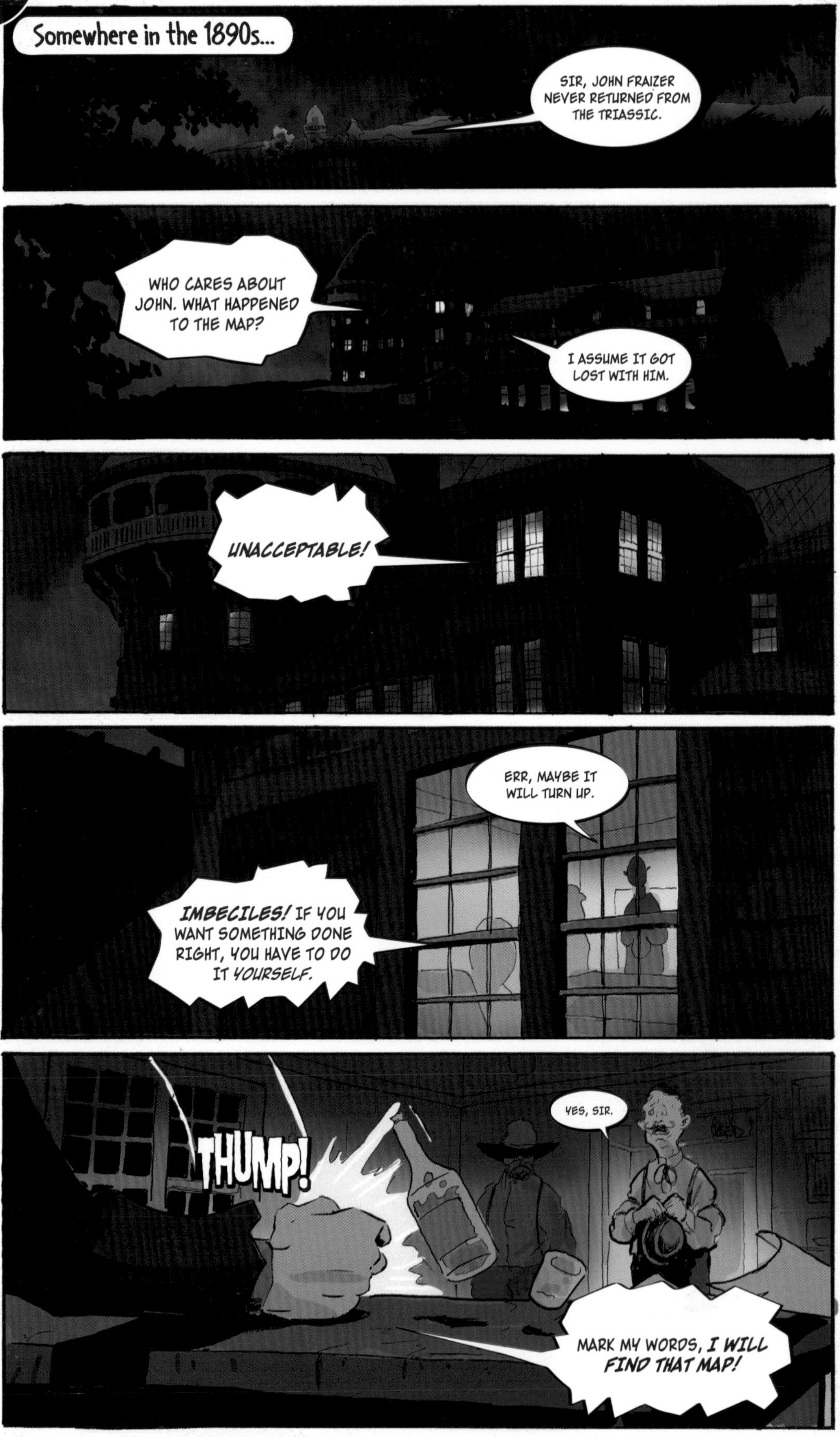
Somewhere in the 1890s...
SIR, JOHN FRAIZER NEVER RETURNED FROM THE TRIASSIC.
WHO CARES ABOUT JOHN. WHAT HAPPENED TO THE MAP?
I ASSUME IT GOT LOST WITH HIM.
UNACCEPTABLE!
ERR, MAYBE IT WILL TURN UP.
IMBECILES! IF YOU WANT SOMETHING DONE RIGHT, YOU HAVE TO DO IT YOURSELF.
THUMP!
YES, SIR.
MARK MY WORDS, I WILL FIND THAT MAP!

CHAPTER
TWO

GRAND IMPACT

WOW, THIS WAS ONE DEEP IMPACT! KIDS, I HAVE ALWAYS WANTED TO SEE THIS PLACE.
KEEP IN MIND, THIS WASN'T THE METEORITE THAT KILLED OFF THE DINOSAURS.
THE PAMPHLET SAYS IT HIT 50,000 YEARS AGO, DURING THE PLEISTOCENE EPOCH.
BOY, DO WE KNOW ABOUT THAT TIME.

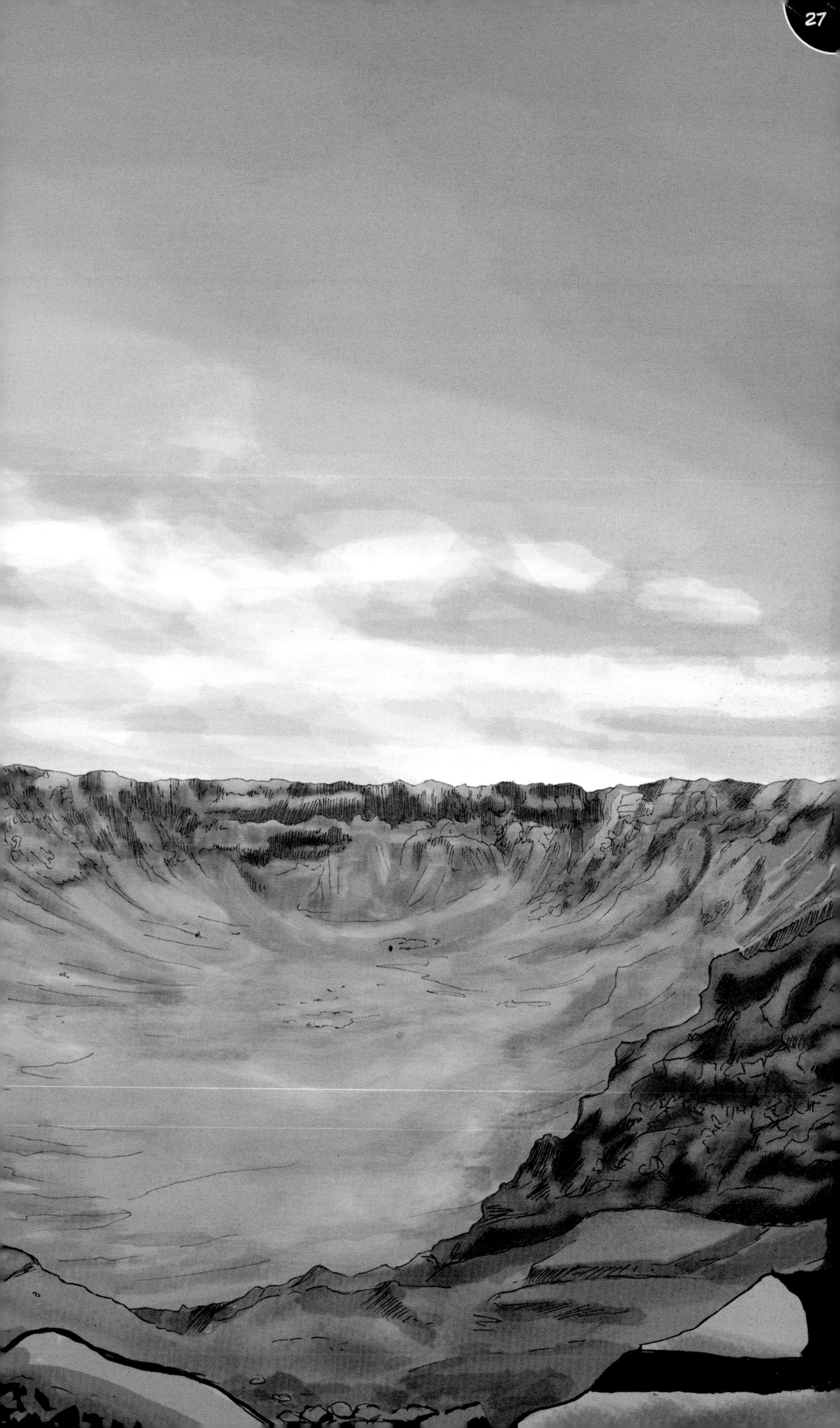

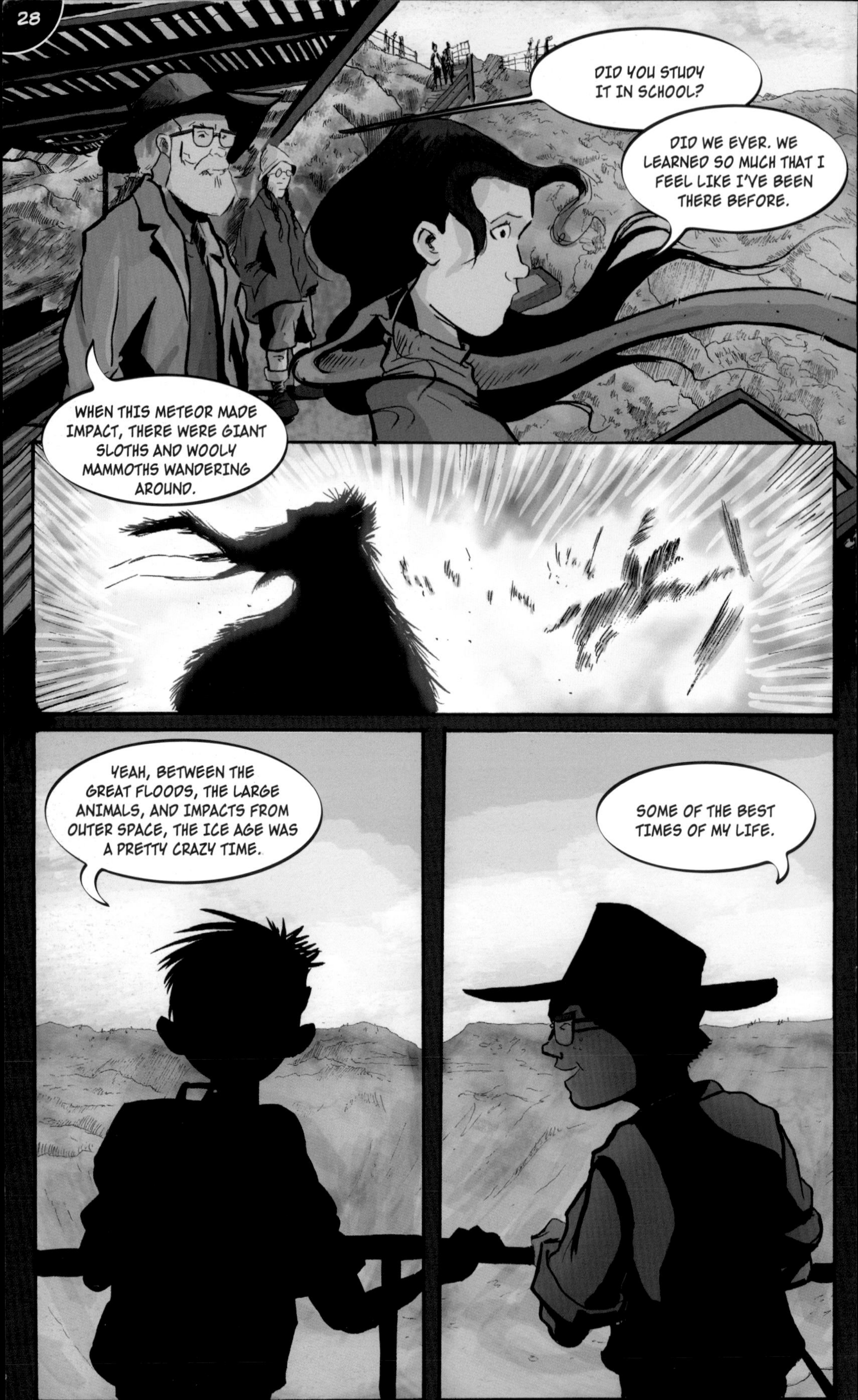
DID YOU STUDY IT IN SCHOOL?
DID WE EVER. WE LEARNED SO MUCH THAT I FEEL LIKE I'VE BEEN THERE BEFORE.
WHEN THIS METEOR MADE IMPACT, THERE WERE GIANT SLOTHS AND WOOLY MAMMOTHS WANDERING AROUND.
YEAH, BETWEEN THE GREAT FLOODS, THE LARGE ANIMALS, AND IMPACTS FROM OUTER SPACE, THE ICE AGE WAS A PRETTY CRAZY TIME.
SOME OF THE BEST TIMES OF MY LIFE.

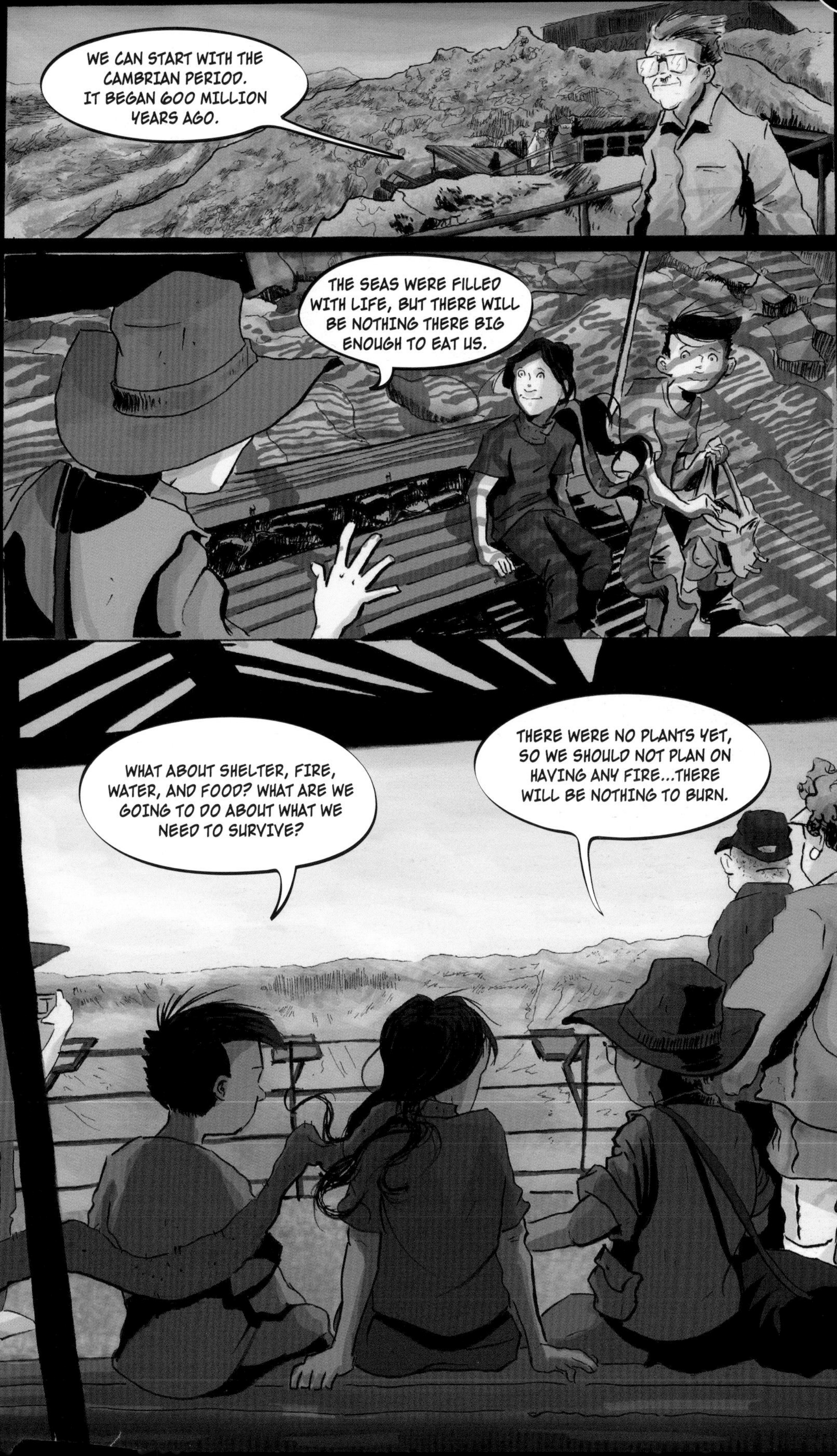
WE CAN START WITH THE CAMBRIAN PERIOD. IT BEGAN 600 MILLION YEARS AGO.
THE SEAS WERE FILLED WITH LIFE, BUT THERE WILL BE NOTHING THERE BIG ENOUGH TO EAT US.
WHAT ABOUT SHELTER, FIRE, WATER, AND FOOD? WHAT ARE WE GOING TO DO ABOUT WHAT WE NEED TO SURVIVE?
THERE WERE NO PLANTS YET, SO WE SHOULD NOT PLAN ON HAVING ANY FIRE...THERE WILL BE NOTHING TO BURN.

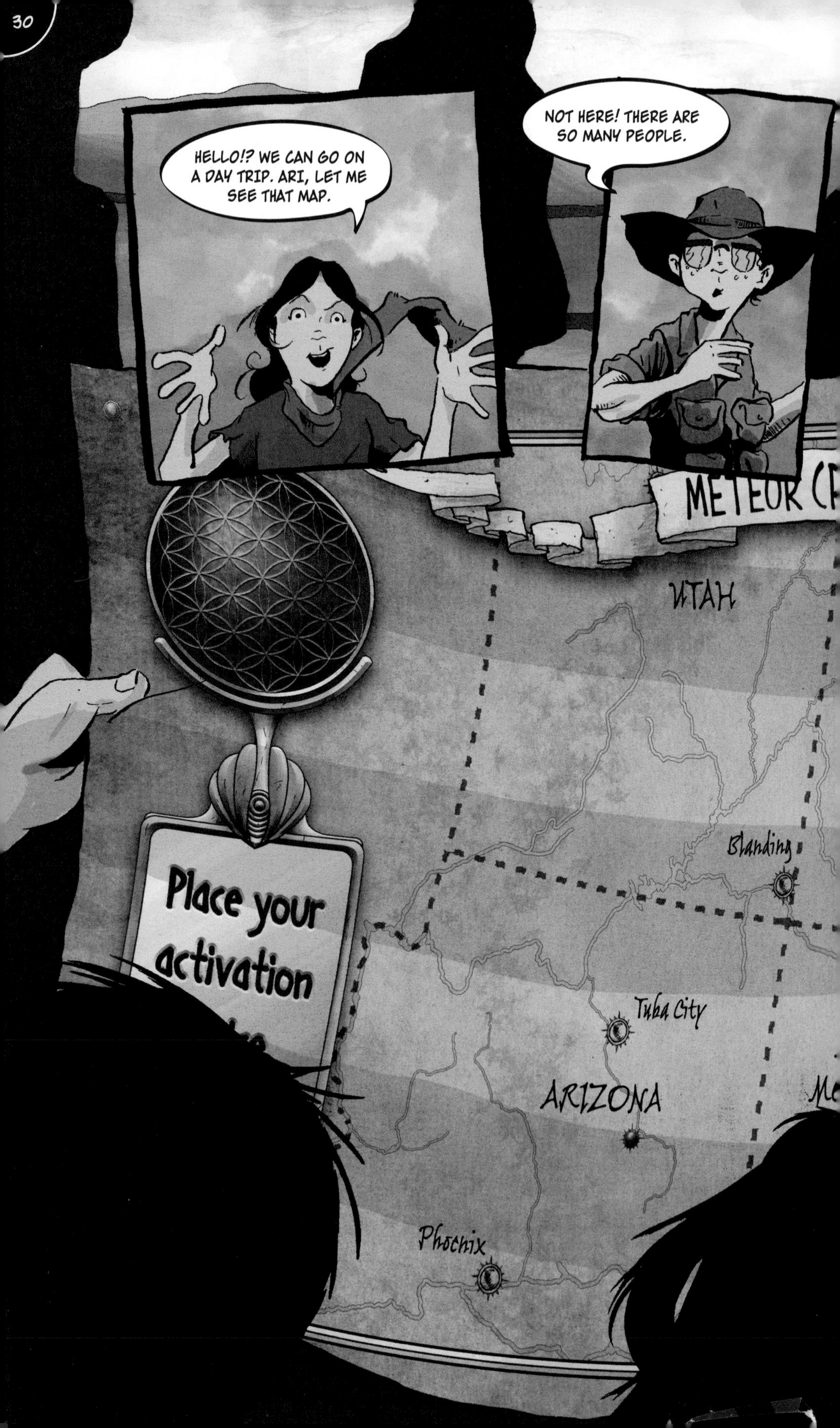
HELLO!? WE CAN GO ON A DAY TRIP. ARI, LET ME SEE THAT MAP.
NOT HERE! THERE ARE SO MANY PEOPLE.
METEOR CR
UTAH
Blanding
Tuba City
ARIZONA
Phoenix
Place your activation

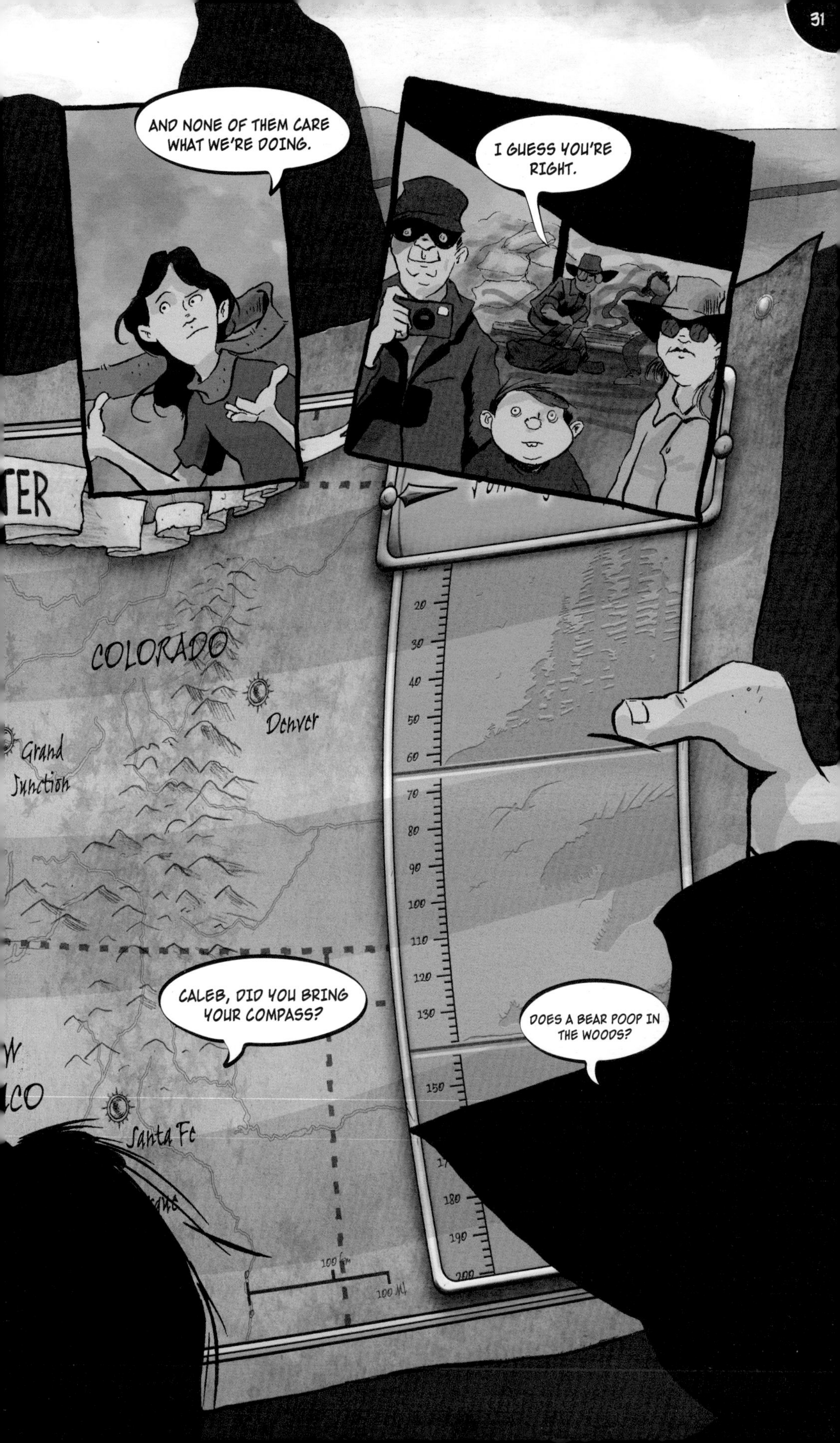
AND NONE OF THEM CARE WHAT WE'RE DOING.
I GUESS YOU'RE RIGHT.
COLORADO
Denver
Grand Junction
Santa Fe
CALEB, DID YOU BRING YOUR COMPASS?
DOES A BEAR POOP IN THE WOODS?

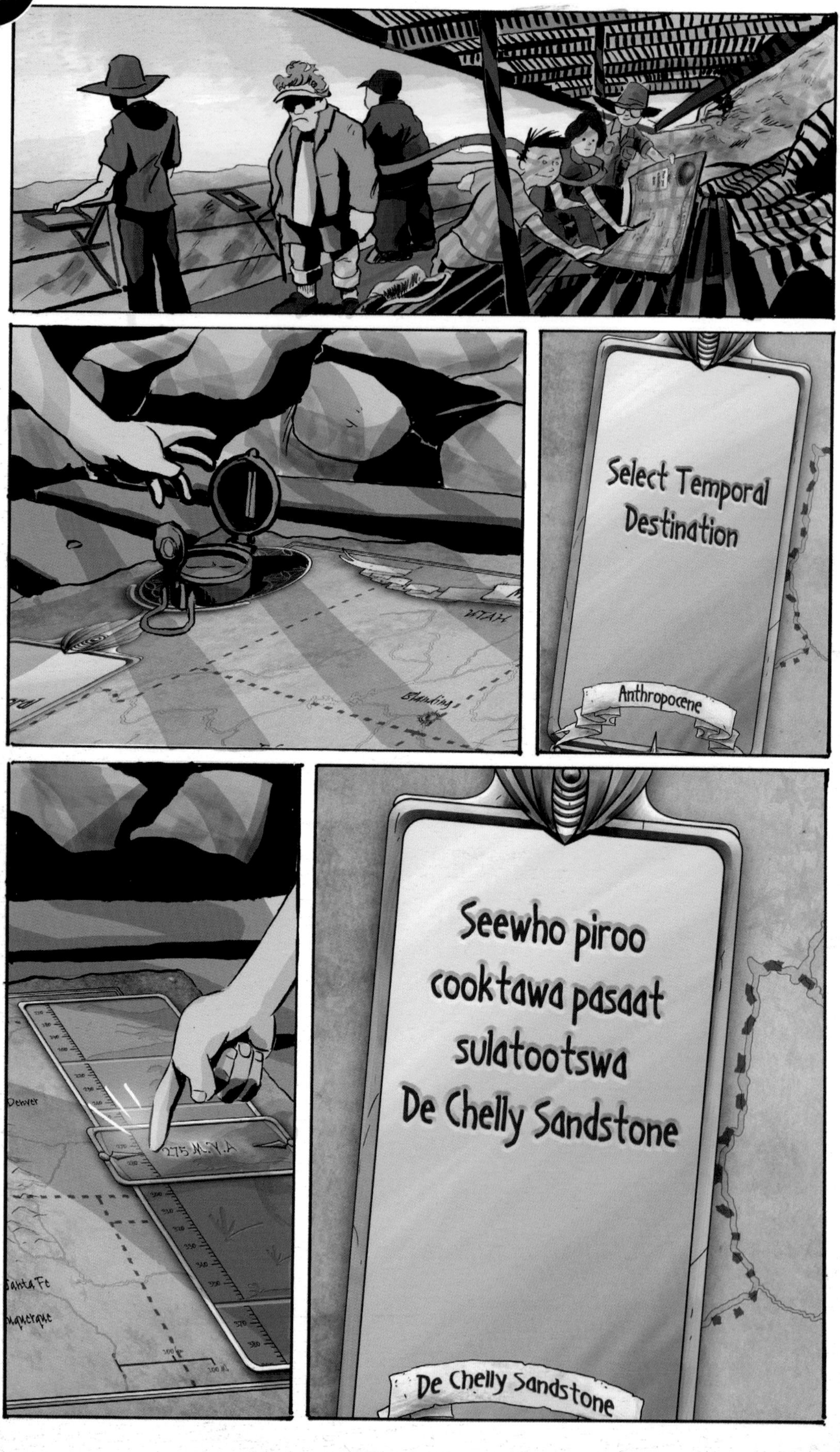
UTAH
Blanding
Select Temporal Destination
Anthropocene
Denver
275 M.Y.A
Santa Fe
Seewho piroo cooktawa pasaat sulatootswa De Chelly Sandstone
De Chelly Sandstone

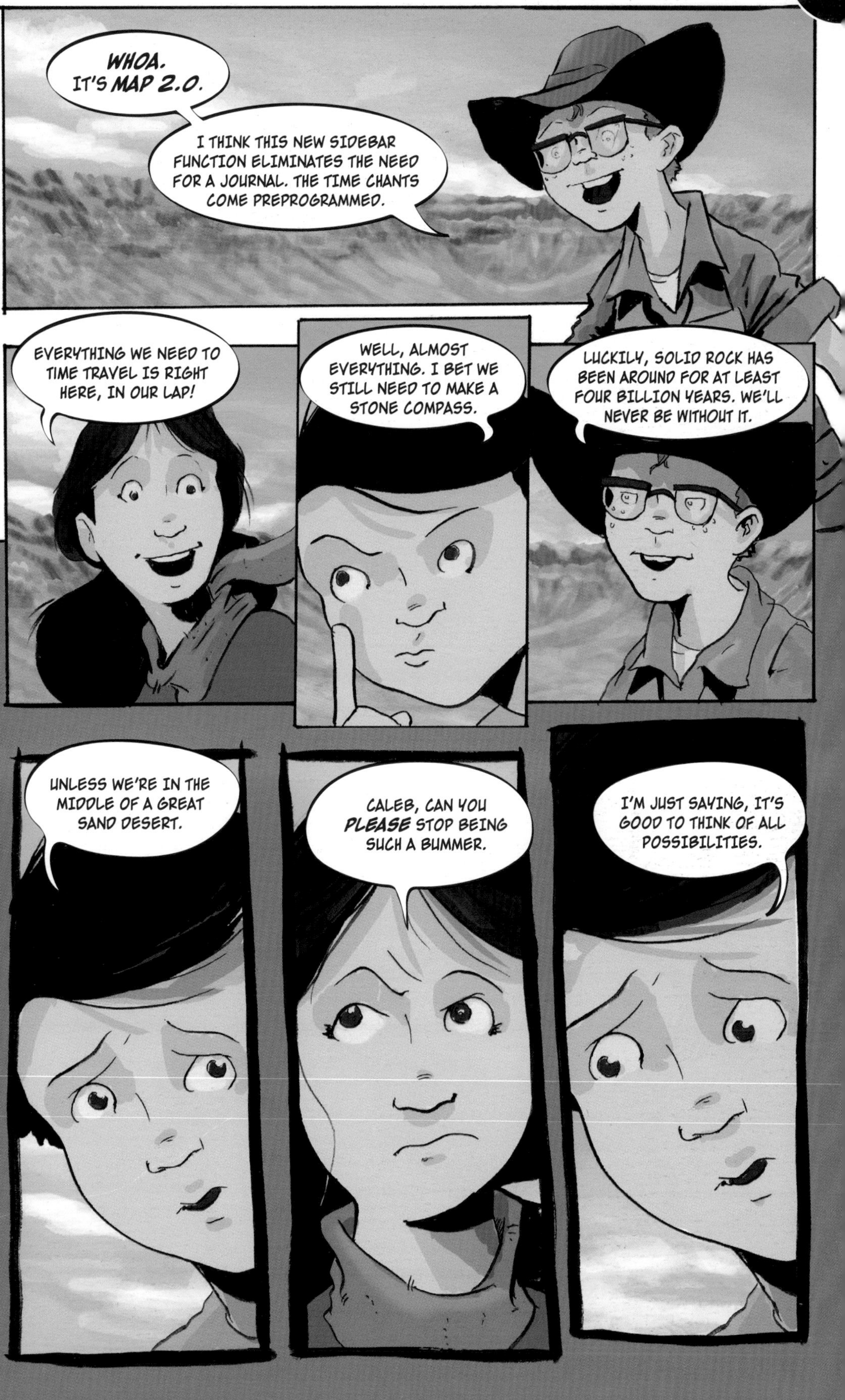
WHOA. IT'S MAP 2.0.
I THINK THIS NEW SIDEBAR FUNCTION ELIMINATES THE NEED FOR A JOURNAL. THE TIME CHANTS COME PREPROGRAMMED.
EVERYTHING WE NEED TO TIME TRAVEL IS RIGHT HERE, IN OUR LAP!
WELL, ALMOST EVERYTHING. I BET WE STILL NEED TO MAKE A STONE COMPASS.
LUCKILY, SOLID ROCK HAS BEEN AROUND FOR AT LEAST FOUR BILLION YEARS. WE'LL NEVER BE WITHOUT IT.
UNLESS WE'RE IN THE MIDDLE OF A GREAT SAND DESERT.
CALEB, CAN YOU PLEASE STOP BEING SUCH A BUMMER.
I'M JUST SAYING, IT'S GOOD TO THINK OF ALL POSSIBILITIES.

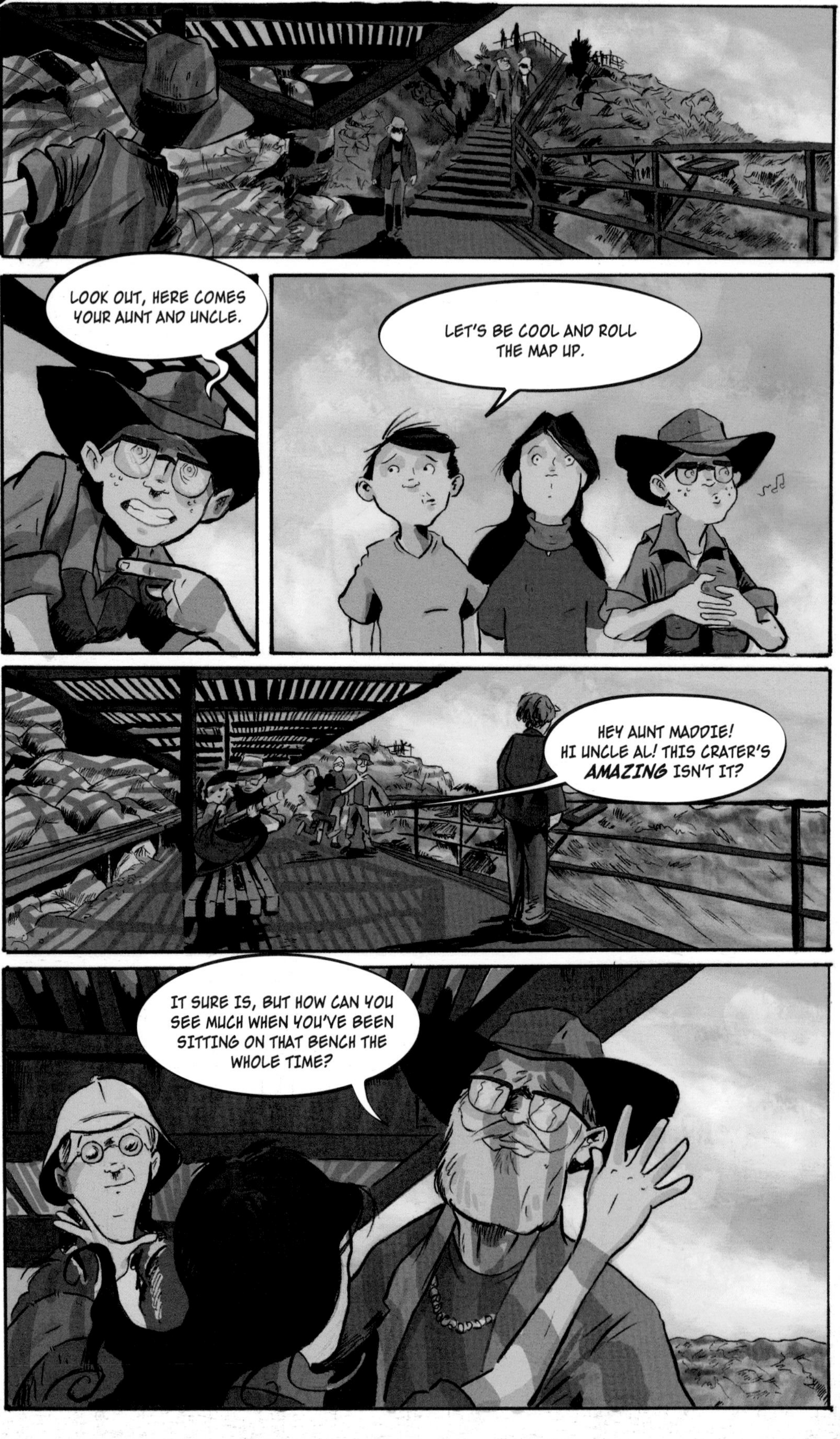
LOOK OUT, HERE COMES YOUR AUNT AND UNCLE.
LET'S BE COOL AND ROLL THE MAP UP.
HEY AUNT MADDIE! HI UNCLE AL! THIS CRATER'S ***AMAZING*** ISN'T IT?
IT SURE IS, BUT HOW CAN YOU SEE MUCH WHEN YOU'VE BEEN SITTING ON THAT BENCH THE WHOLE TIME?

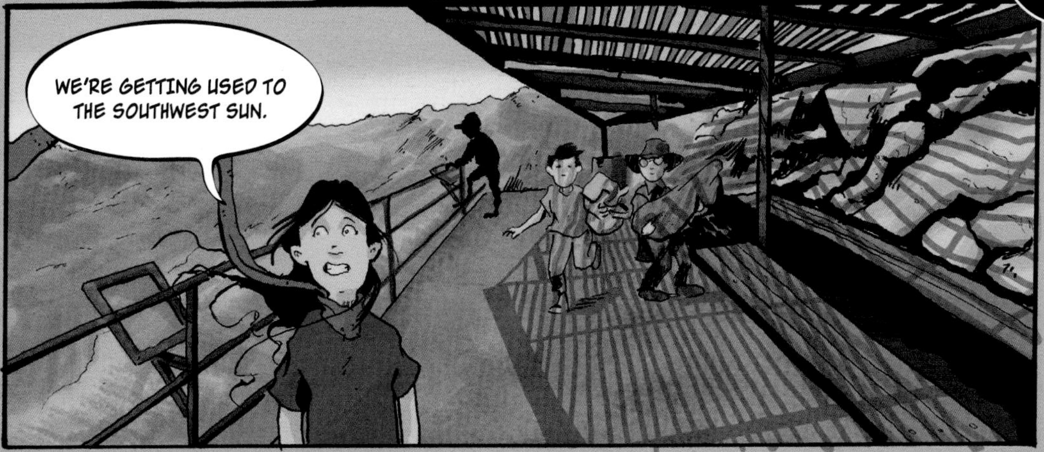
WE'RE GETTING USED TO THE SOUTHWEST SUN.

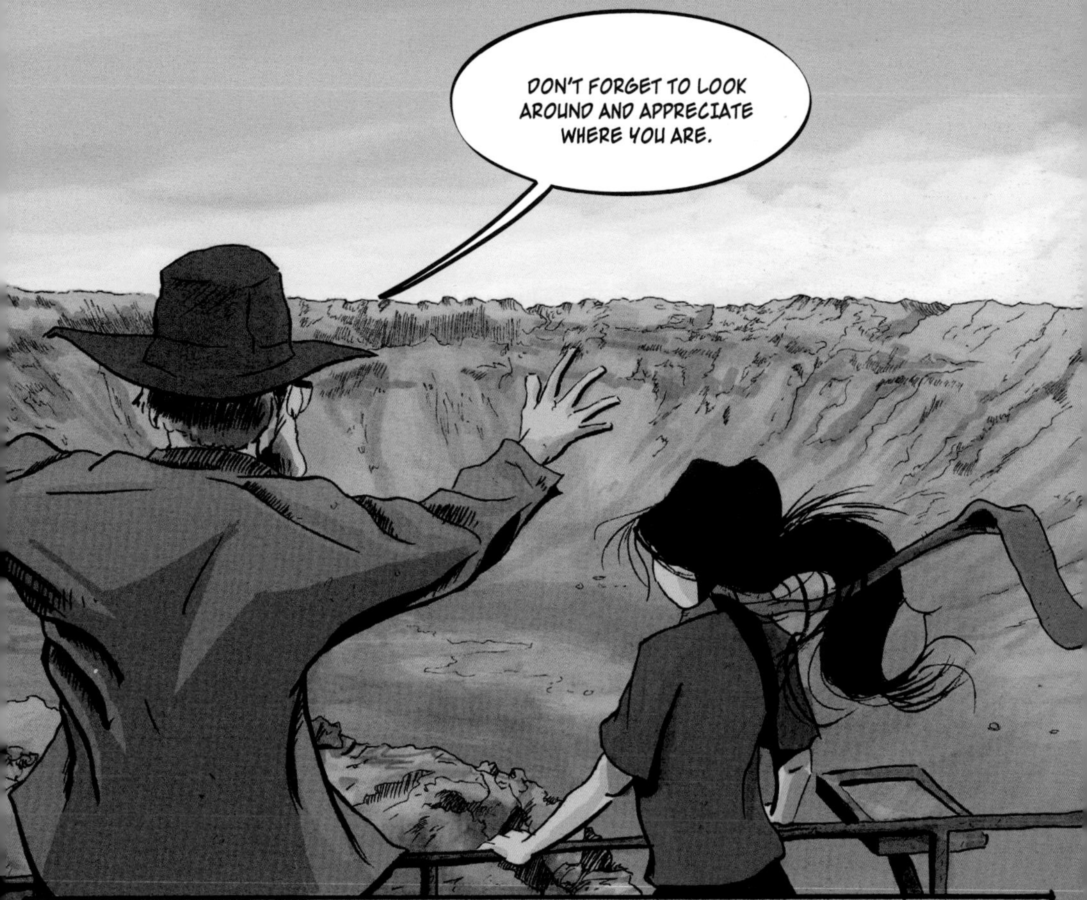
DON'T FORGET TO LOOK AROUND AND APPRECIATE WHERE YOU ARE.

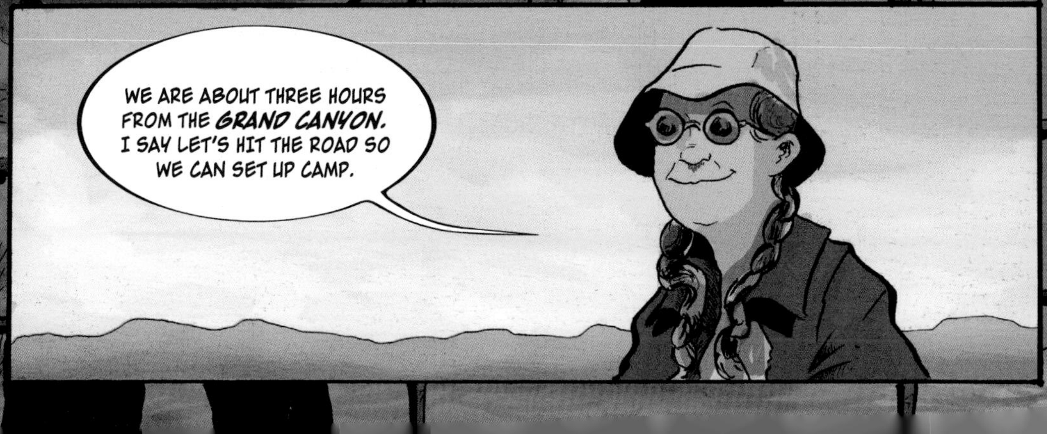
WE ARE ABOUT THREE HOURS FROM THE ***GRAND CANYON.*** I SAY LET'S HIT THE ROAD SO WE CAN SET UP CAMP.

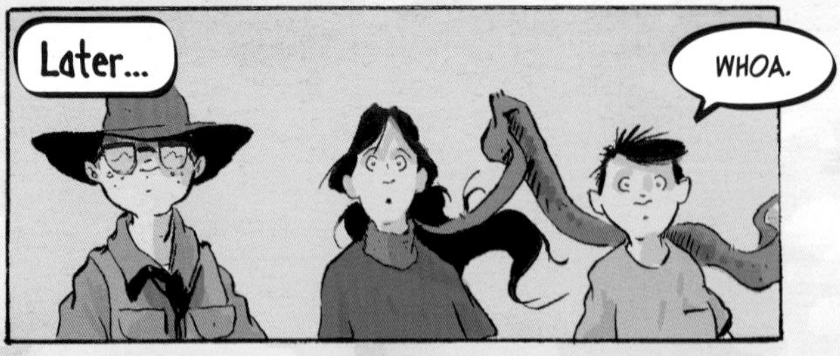
Later...
WHOA.

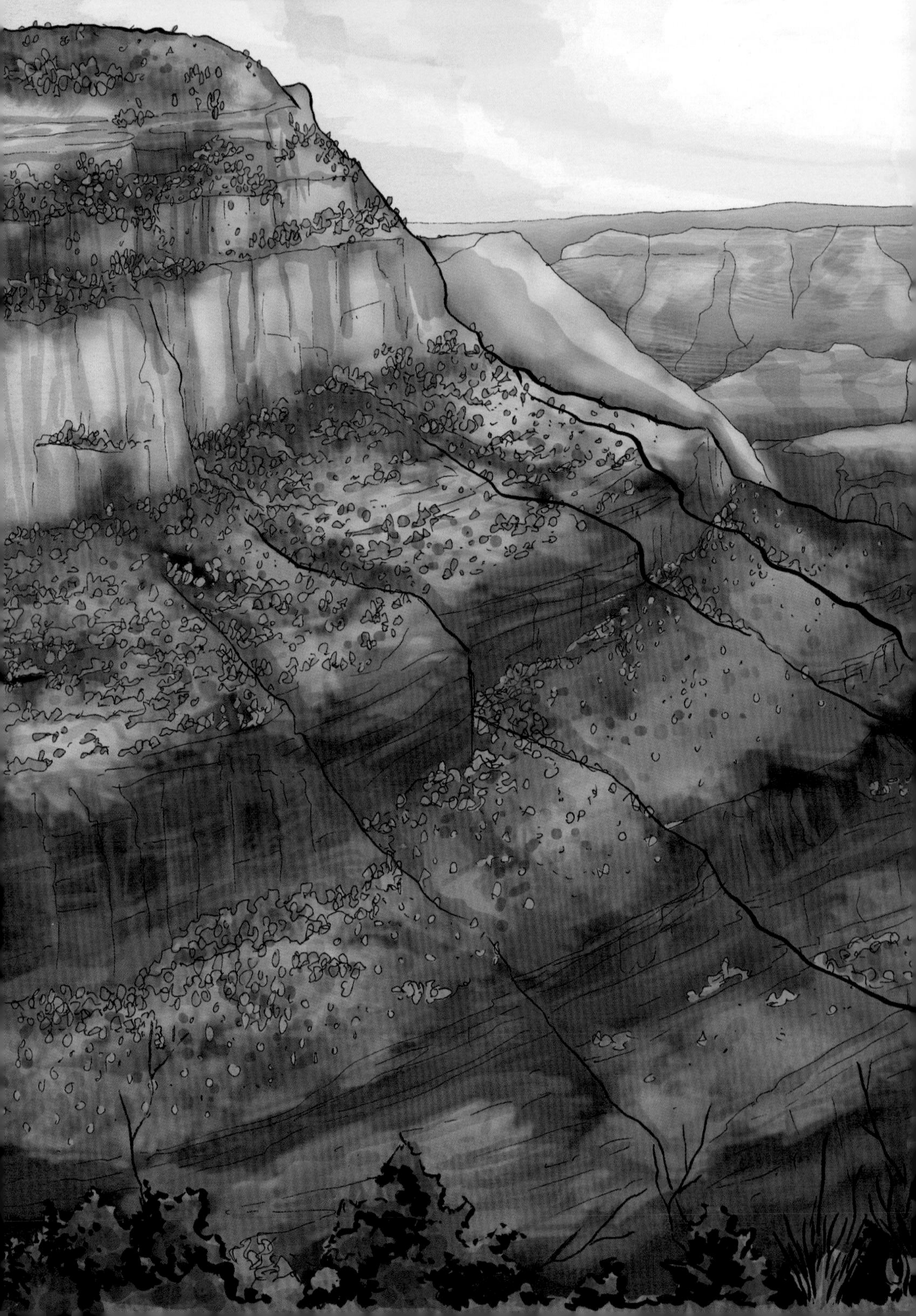

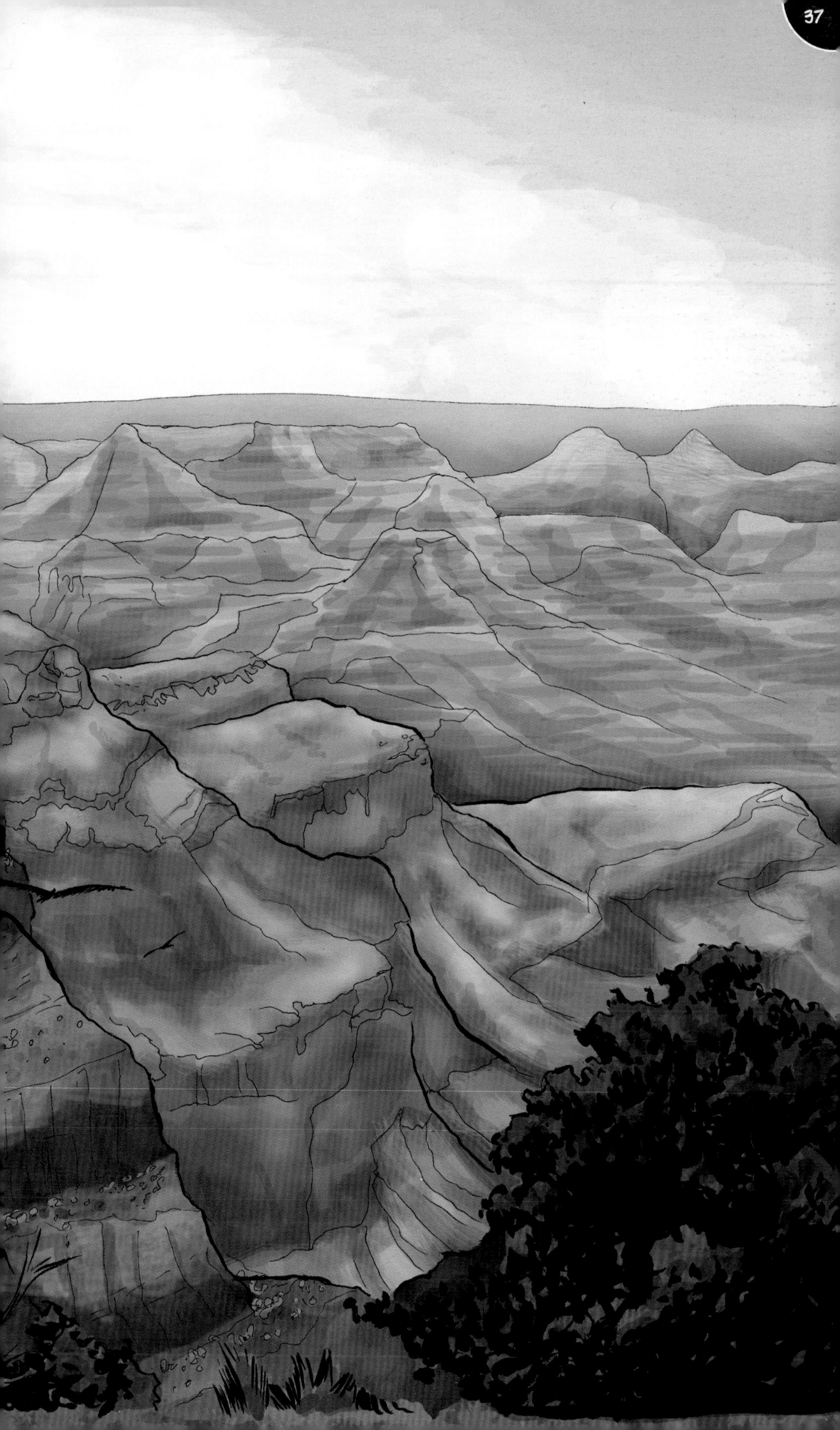

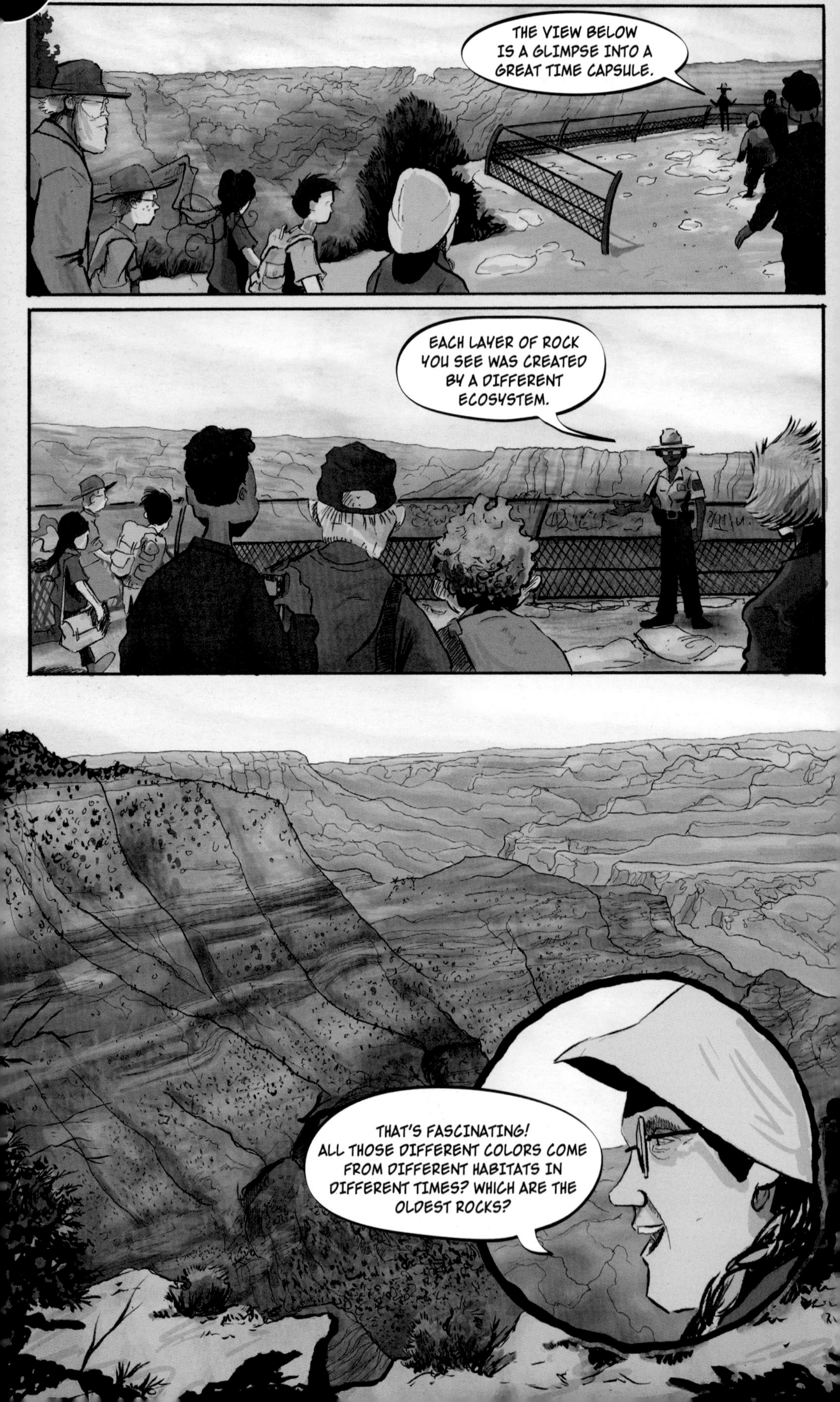
THE VIEW BELOW IS A GLIMPSE INTO A GREAT TIME CAPSULE.
EACH LAYER OF ROCK YOU SEE WAS CREATED BY A DIFFERENT ECOSYSTEM.
THAT'S FASCINATING! ALL THOSE DIFFERENT COLORS COME FROM DIFFERENT HABITATS IN DIFFERENT TIMES? WHICH ARE THE OLDEST ROCKS?

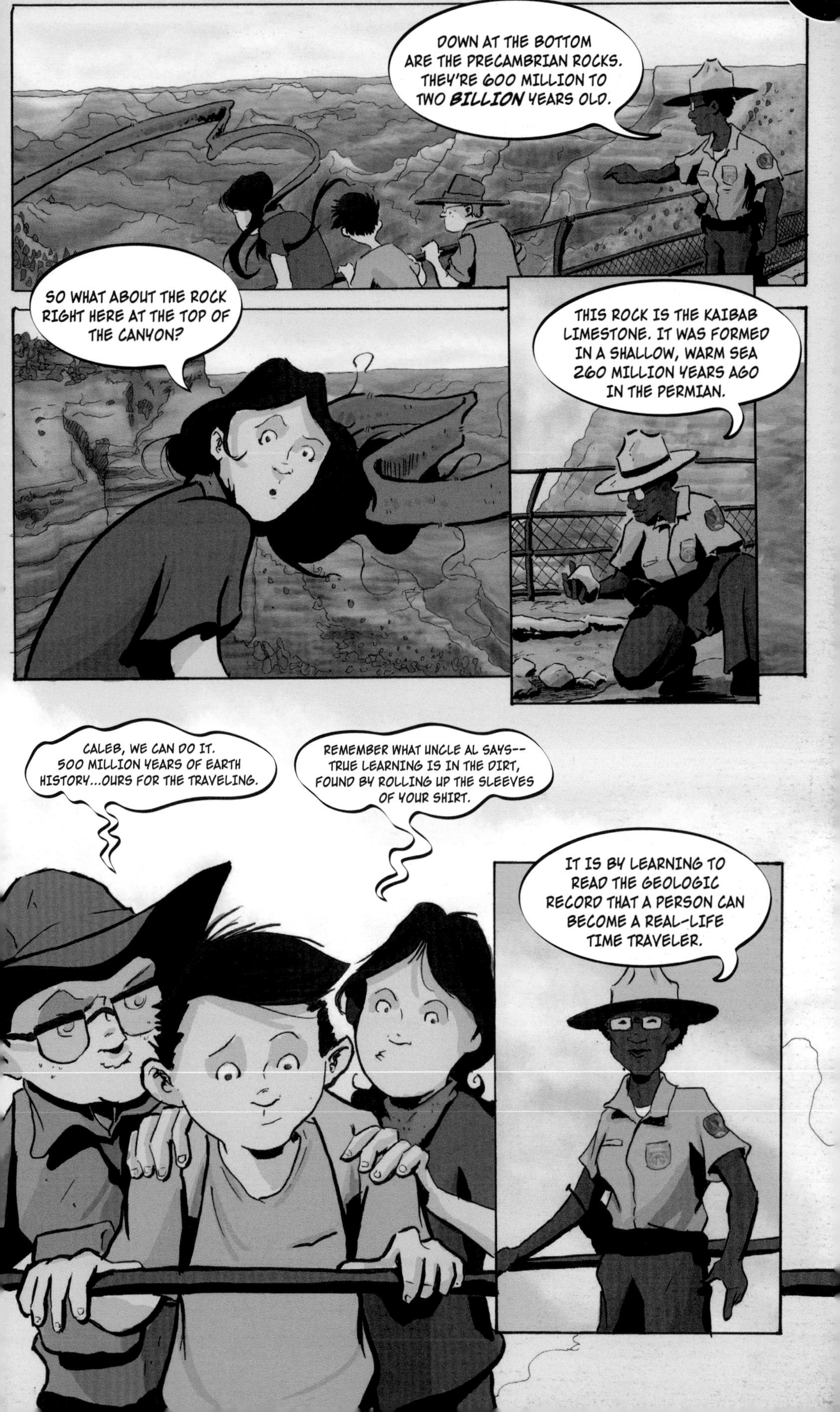
DOWN AT THE BOTTOM ARE THE PRECAMBRIAN ROCKS. THEY'RE 600 MILLION TO TWO BILLION YEARS OLD.
SO WHAT ABOUT THE ROCK RIGHT HERE AT THE TOP OF THE CANYON?
THIS ROCK IS THE KAIBAB LIMESTONE. IT WAS FORMED IN A SHALLOW, WARM SEA 260 MILLION YEARS AGO IN THE PERMIAN.
CALEB, WE CAN DO IT. 500 MILLION YEARS OF EARTH HISTORY...OURS FOR THE TRAVELING.
REMEMBER WHAT UNCLE AL SAYS--TRUE LEARNING IS IN THE DIRT, FOUND BY ROLLING UP THE SLEEVES OF YOUR SHIRT.
IT IS BY LEARNING TO READ THE GEOLOGIC RECORD THAT A PERSON CAN BECOME A REAL-LIFE TIME TRAVELER.

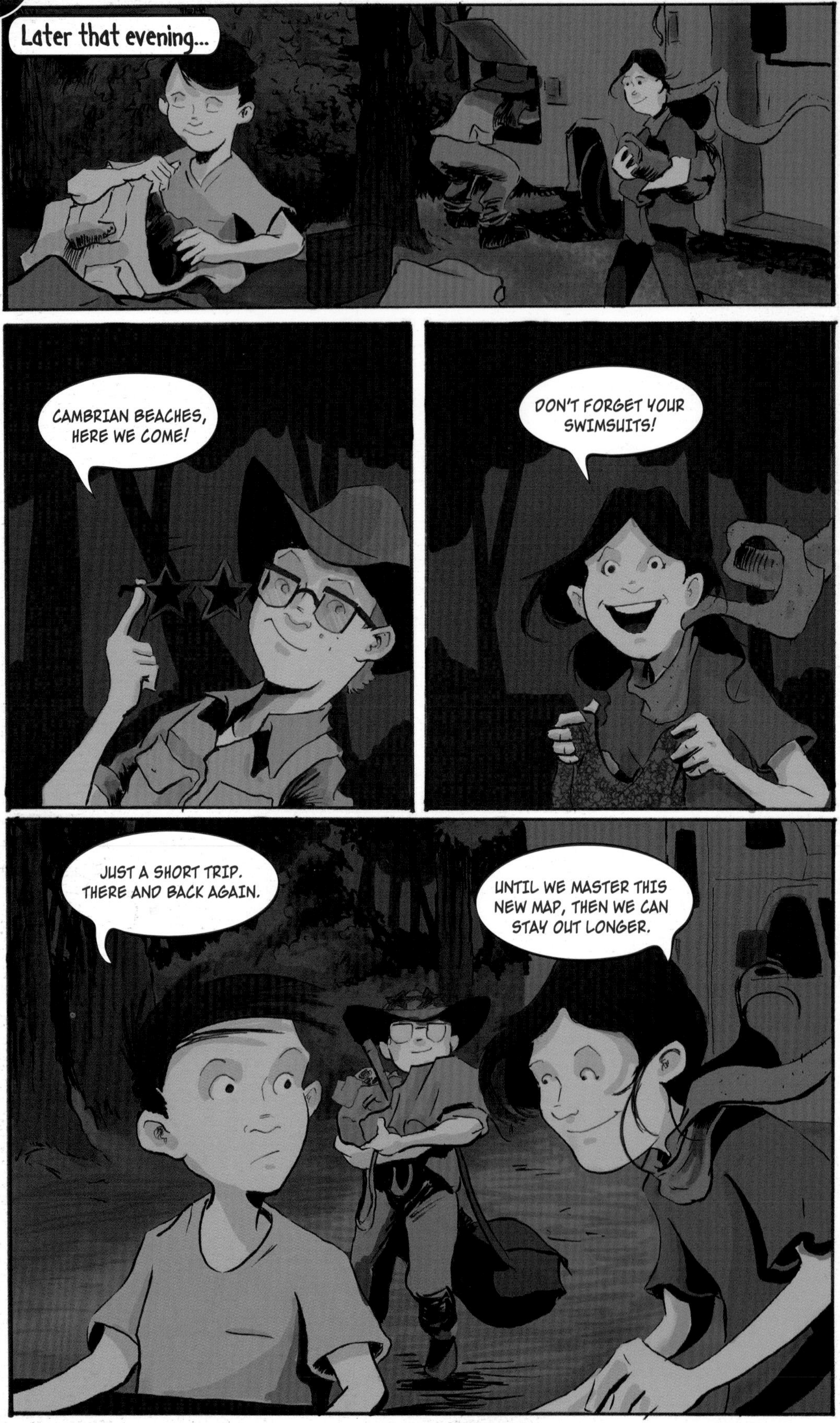
Later that evening...
CAMBRIAN BEACHES, HERE WE COME!
DON'T FORGET YOUR SWIMSUITS!
JUST A SHORT TRIP. THERE AND BACK AGAIN.
UNTIL WE MASTER THIS NEW MAP, THEN WE CAN STAY OUT LONGER.

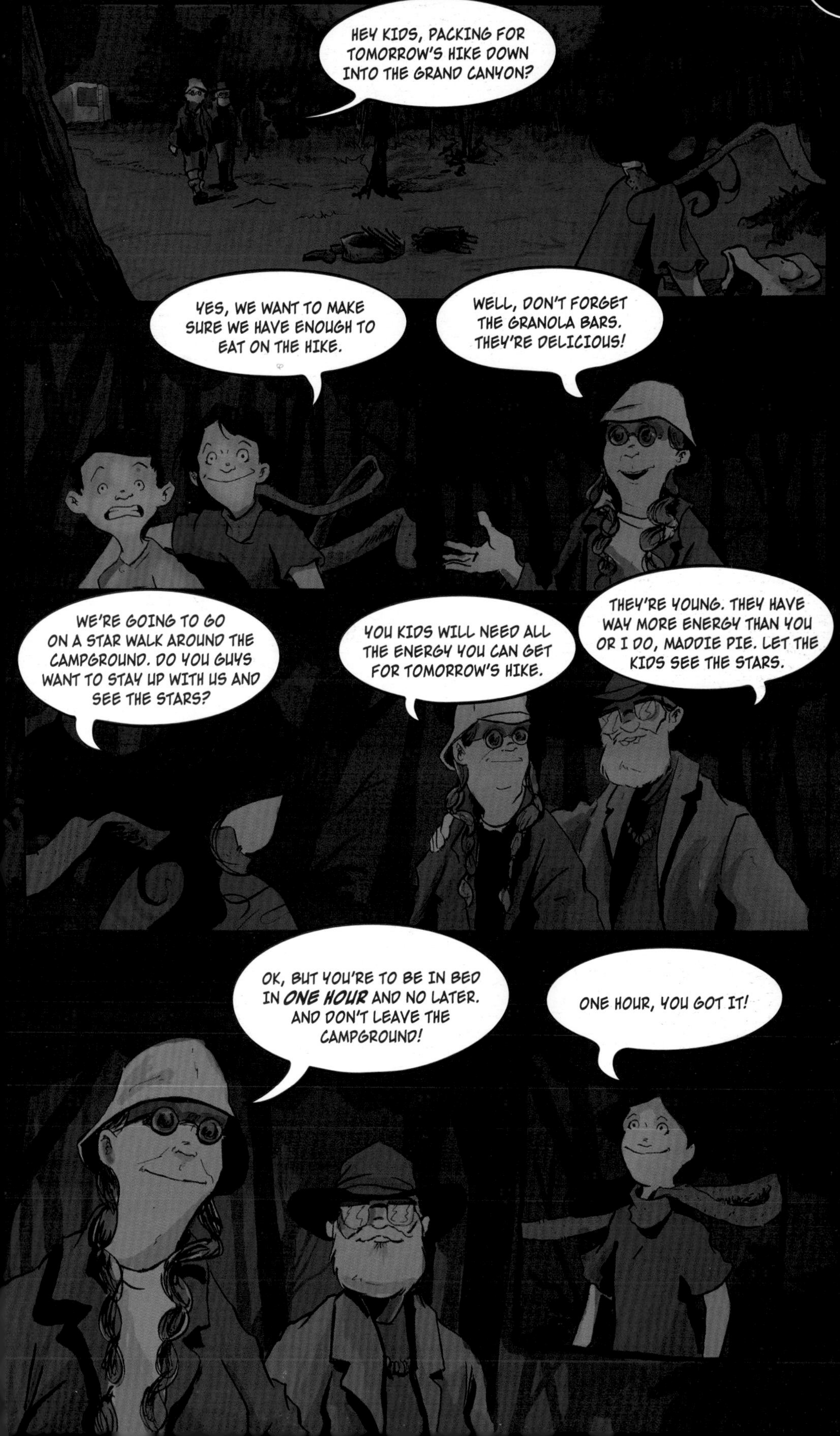
HEY KIDS, PACKING FOR TOMORROW'S HIKE DOWN INTO THE GRAND CANYON?
YES, WE WANT TO MAKE SURE WE HAVE ENOUGH TO EAT ON THE HIKE.
WELL, DON'T FORGET THE GRANOLA BARS. THEY'RE DELICIOUS!
WE'RE GOING TO GO ON A STAR WALK AROUND THE CAMPGROUND. DO YOU GUYS WANT TO STAY UP WITH US AND SEE THE STARS?
YOU KIDS WILL NEED ALL THE ENERGY YOU CAN GET FOR TOMORROW'S HIKE.
THEY'RE YOUNG. THEY HAVE WAY MORE ENERGY THAN YOU OR I DO, MADDIE PIE. LET THE KIDS SEE THE STARS.
OK, BUT YOU'RE TO BE IN BED IN ***ONE HOUR*** AND NO LATER. AND DON'T LEAVE THE CAMPGROUND!
ONE HOUR, YOU GOT IT!

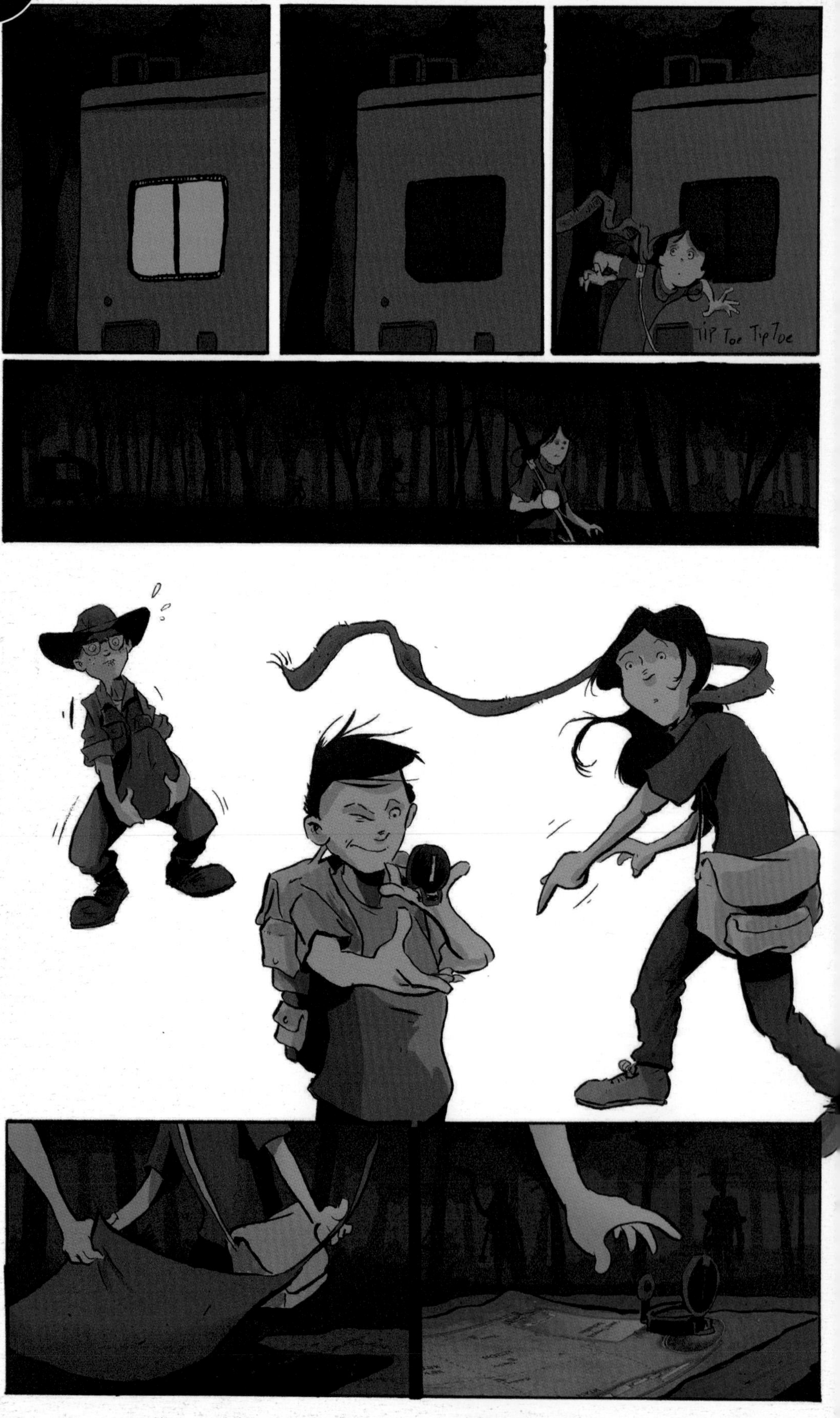
TIP Toe Tip Toe

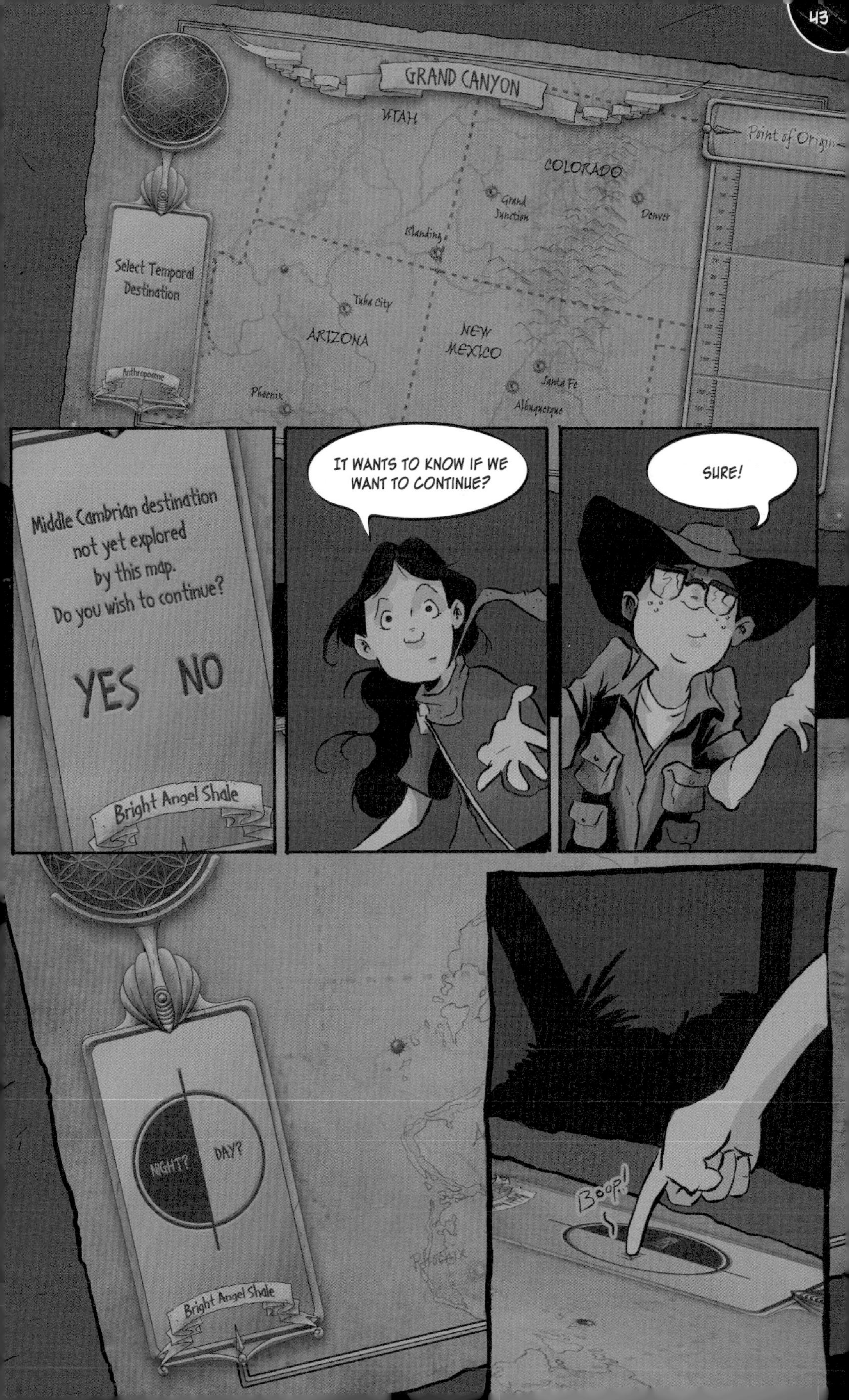
GRAND CANYON
UTAH
COLORADO
Point of Origin
Grand Junction
Denver
Blanding
Select Temporal Destination
Anthropocene
Tuba City
ARIZONA
NEW MEXICO
Santa Fe
Phoenix
Albuquerque
Middle Cambrian destination not yet explored by this map. Do you wish to continue?
YES
NO
Bright Angel Shale
IT WANTS TO KNOW IF WE WANT TO CONTINUE?
SURE!
NIGHT?
DAY?
Bright Angel Shale
BOOP!

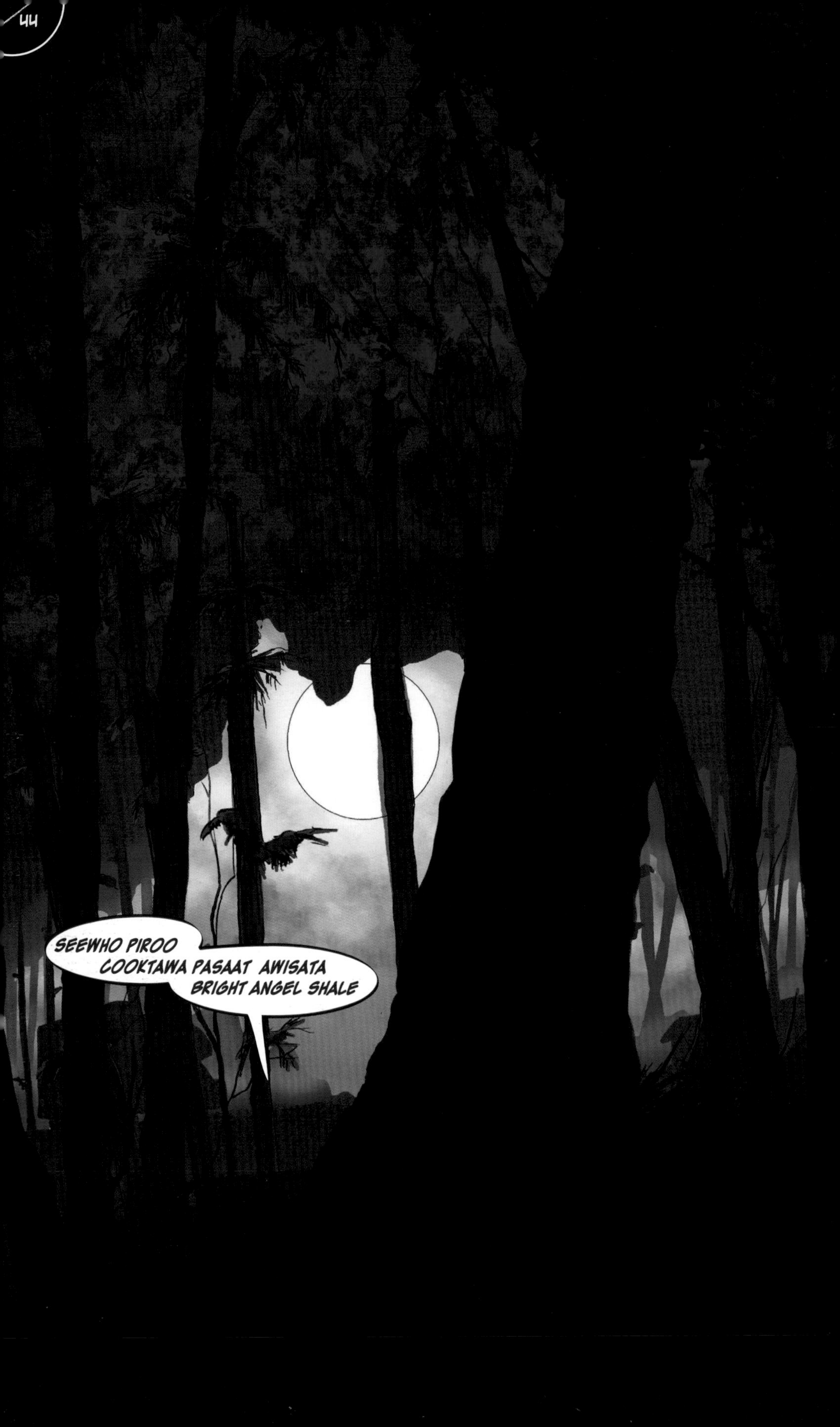
SEEWHO PIROO
COOKTAWA PASAAT AWISATA
BRIGHT ANGEL SHALE

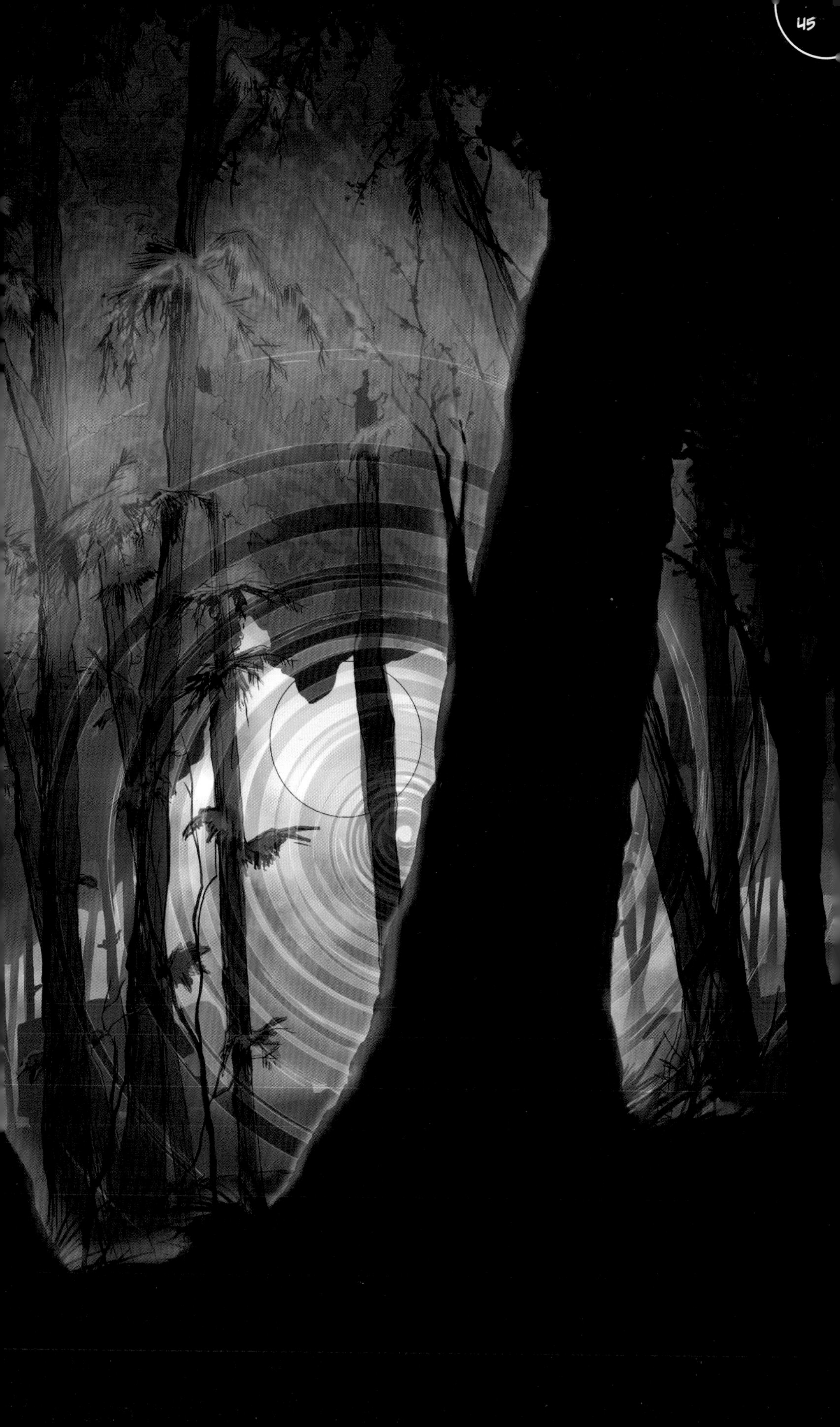

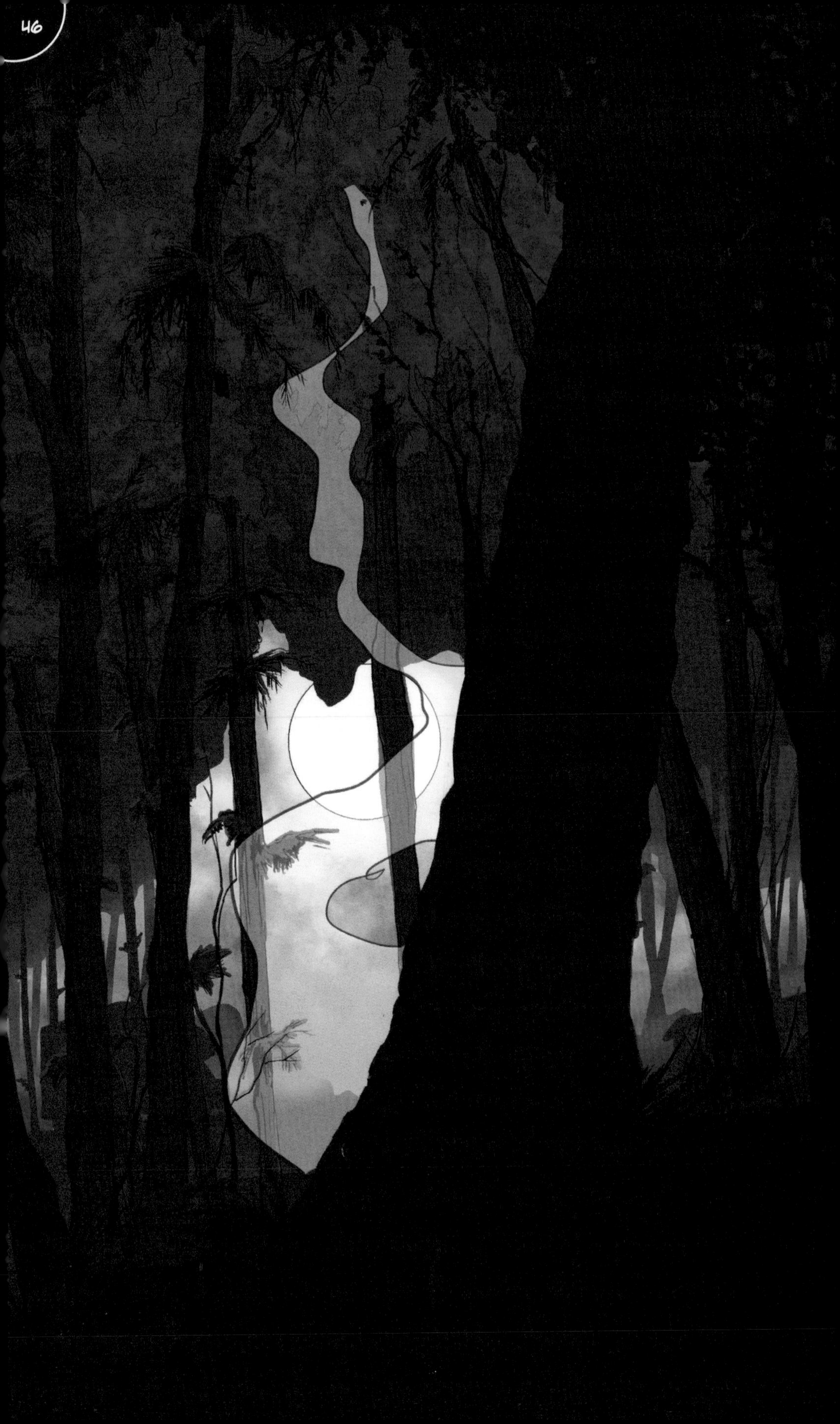

CHAPTER
THREE

BASEMENT ROCK!

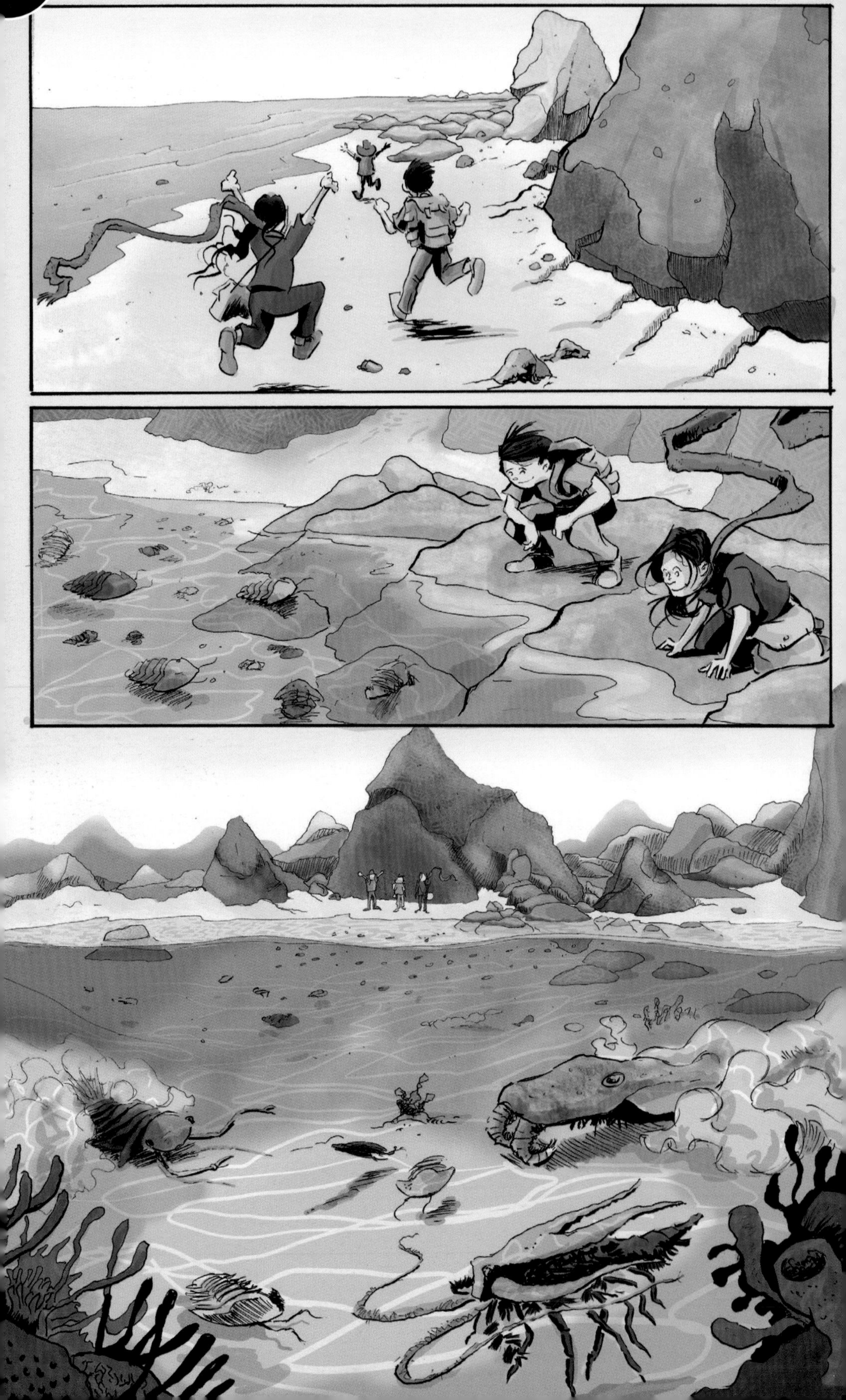

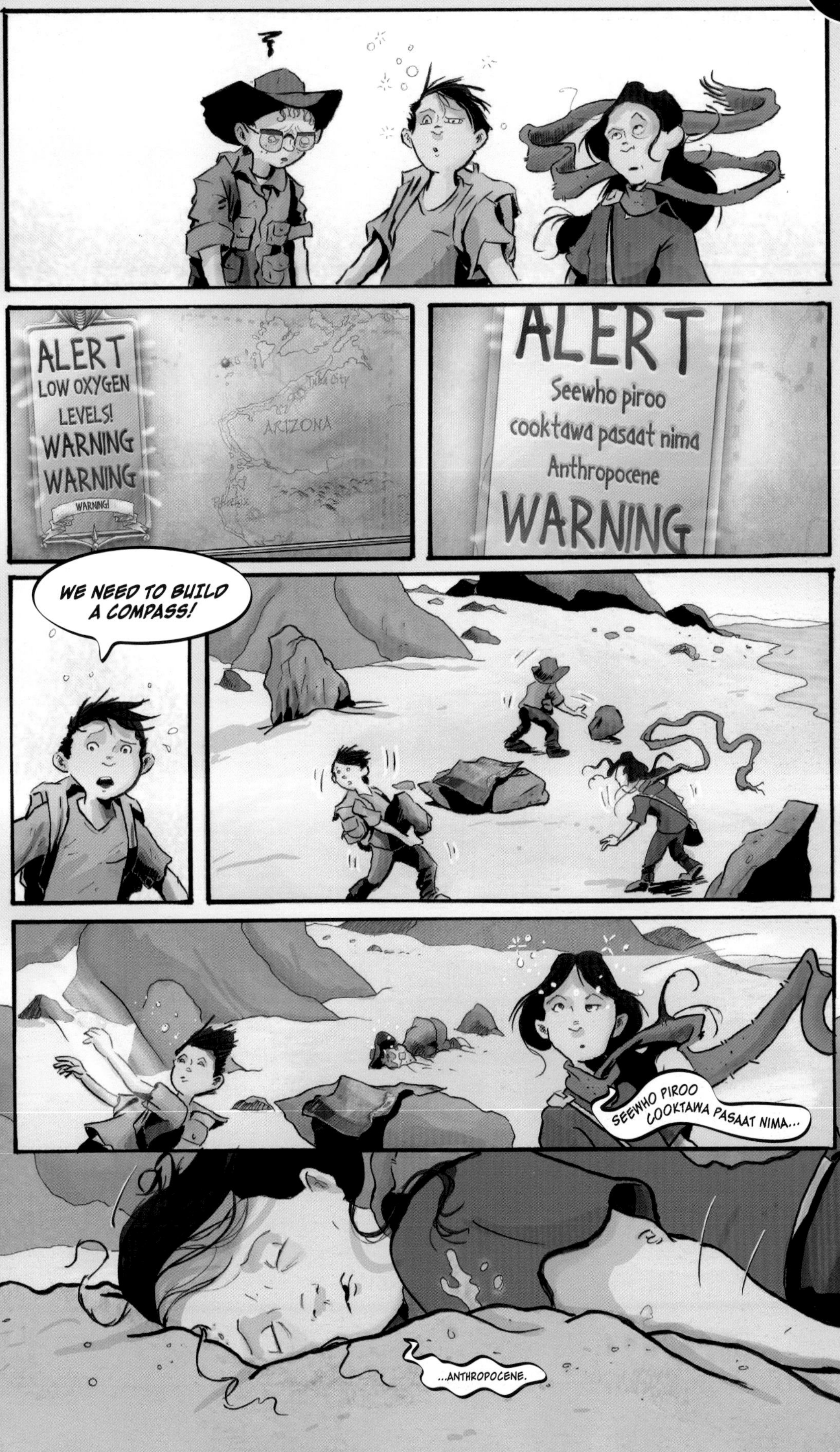
ALERT
LOW OXYGEN
LEVELS!
WARNING
WARNING
WARNING!
ARIZONA
Tuba City
ALERT
Seewho piroo
cooktawa pasaat nima
Anthropocene
WARNING
WE NEED TO BUILD A COMPASS!
SEEWHO PIROO COOKTAWA PASAAT NIMA...
...ANTHROPOCENE.

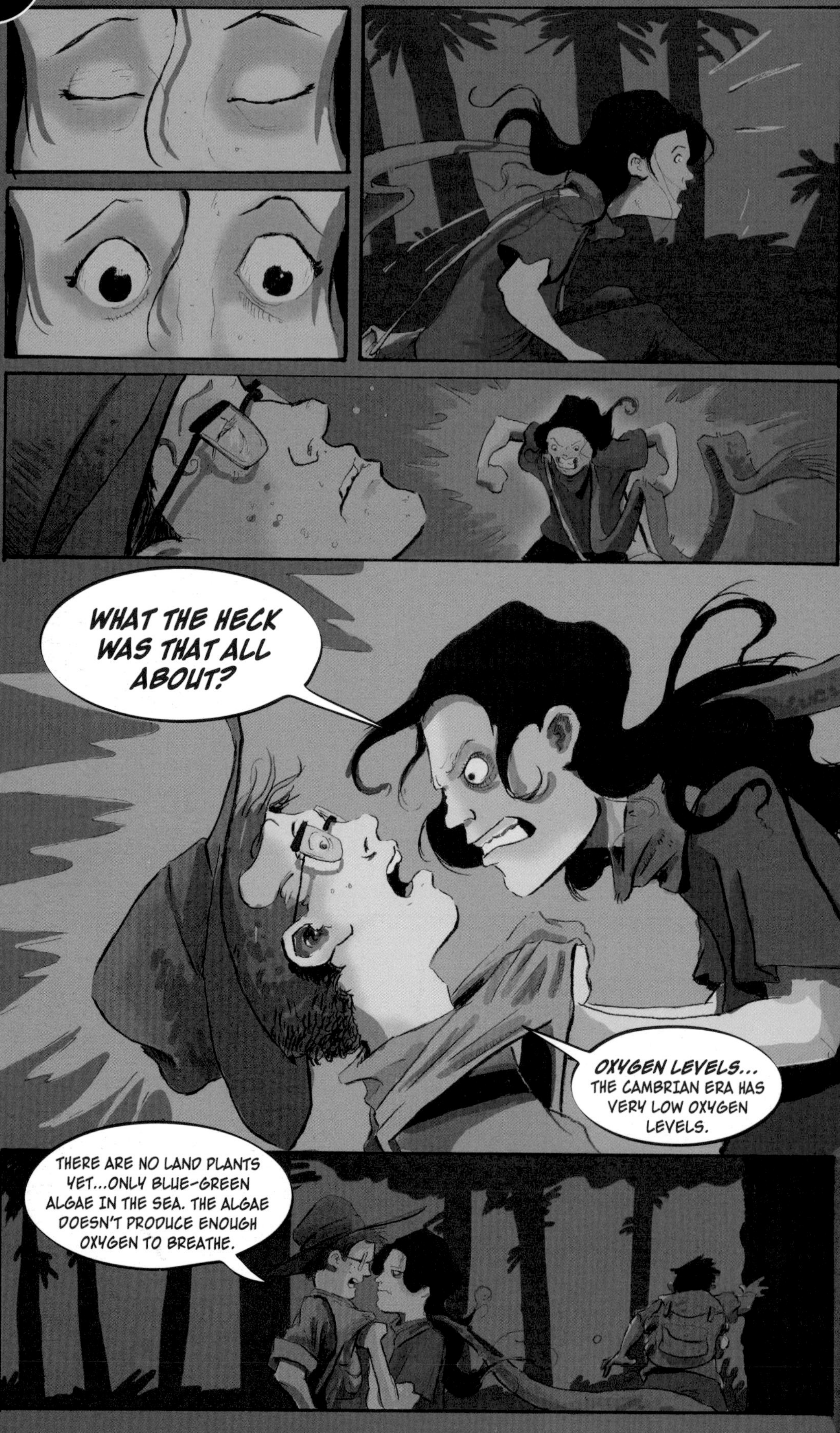
WHAT THE HECK WAS THAT ALL ABOUT?
OXYGEN LEVELS... THE CAMBRIAN ERA HAS VERY LOW OXYGEN LEVELS.
THERE ARE NO LAND PLANTS YET...ONLY BLUE-GREEN ALGAE IN THE SEA. THE ALGAE DOESN'T PRODUCE ENOUGH OXYGEN TO BREATHE.

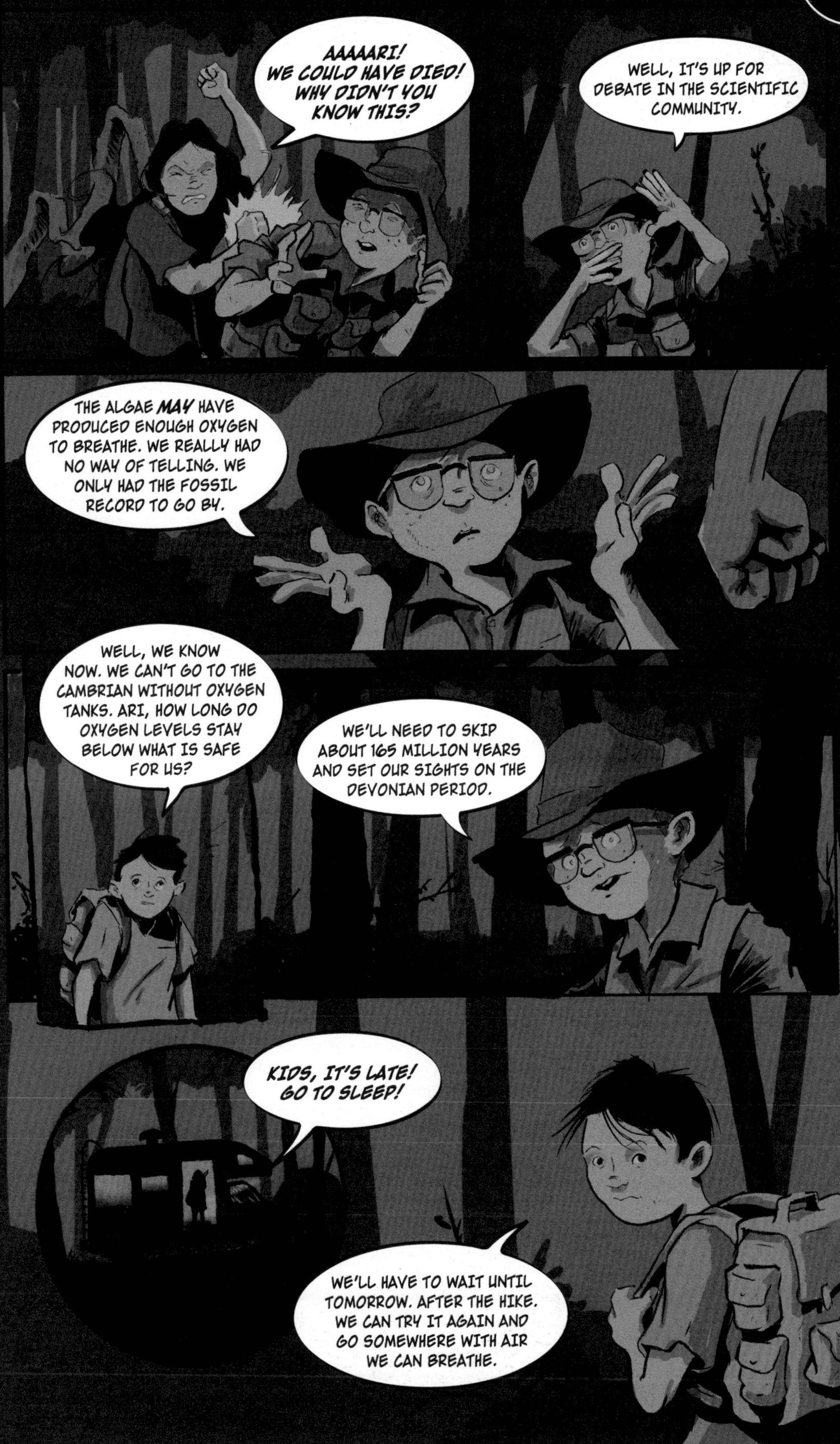
AAAAARI! WE COULD HAVE DIED! WHY DIDN'T YOU KNOW THIS?
WELL, IT'S UP FOR DEBATE IN THE SCIENTIFIC COMMUNITY.
THE ALGAE MAY HAVE PRODUCED ENOUGH OXYGEN TO BREATHE. WE REALLY HAD NO WAY OF TELLING. WE ONLY HAD THE FOSSIL RECORD TO GO BY.
WELL, WE KNOW NOW. WE CAN'T GO TO THE CAMBRIAN WITHOUT OXYGEN TANKS. ARI, HOW LONG DO OXYGEN LEVELS STAY BELOW WHAT IS SAFE FOR US?
WE'LL NEED TO SKIP ABOUT 165 MILLION YEARS AND SET OUR SIGHTS ON THE DEVONIAN PERIOD.
KIDS, IT'S LATE! GO TO SLEEP!
WE'LL HAVE TO WAIT UNTIL TOMORROW. AFTER THE HIKE. WE CAN TRY IT AGAIN AND GO SOMEWHERE WITH AIR WE CAN BREATHE.

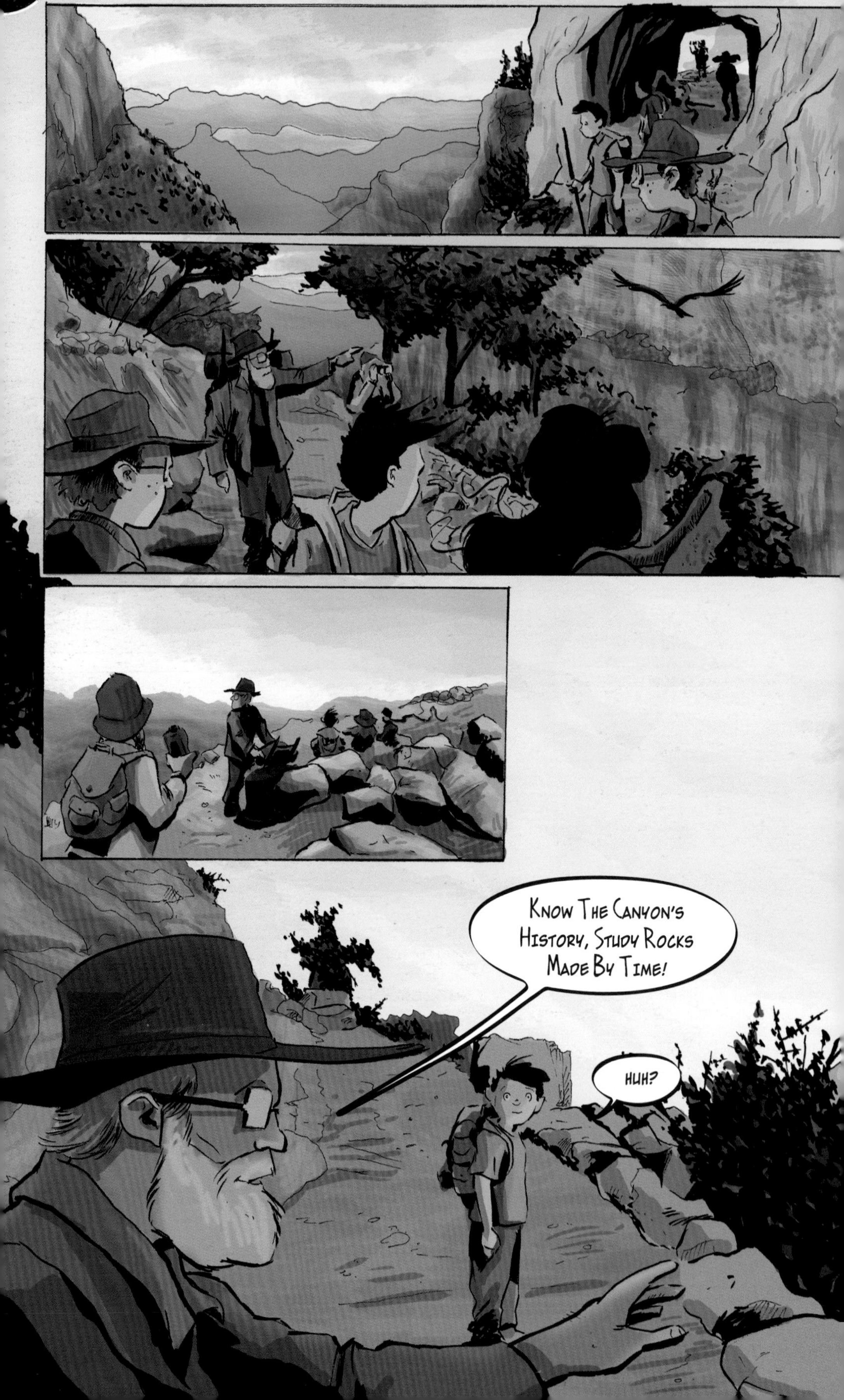
Know The Canyon's
History, Study Rocks
Made By Time!
HUH?

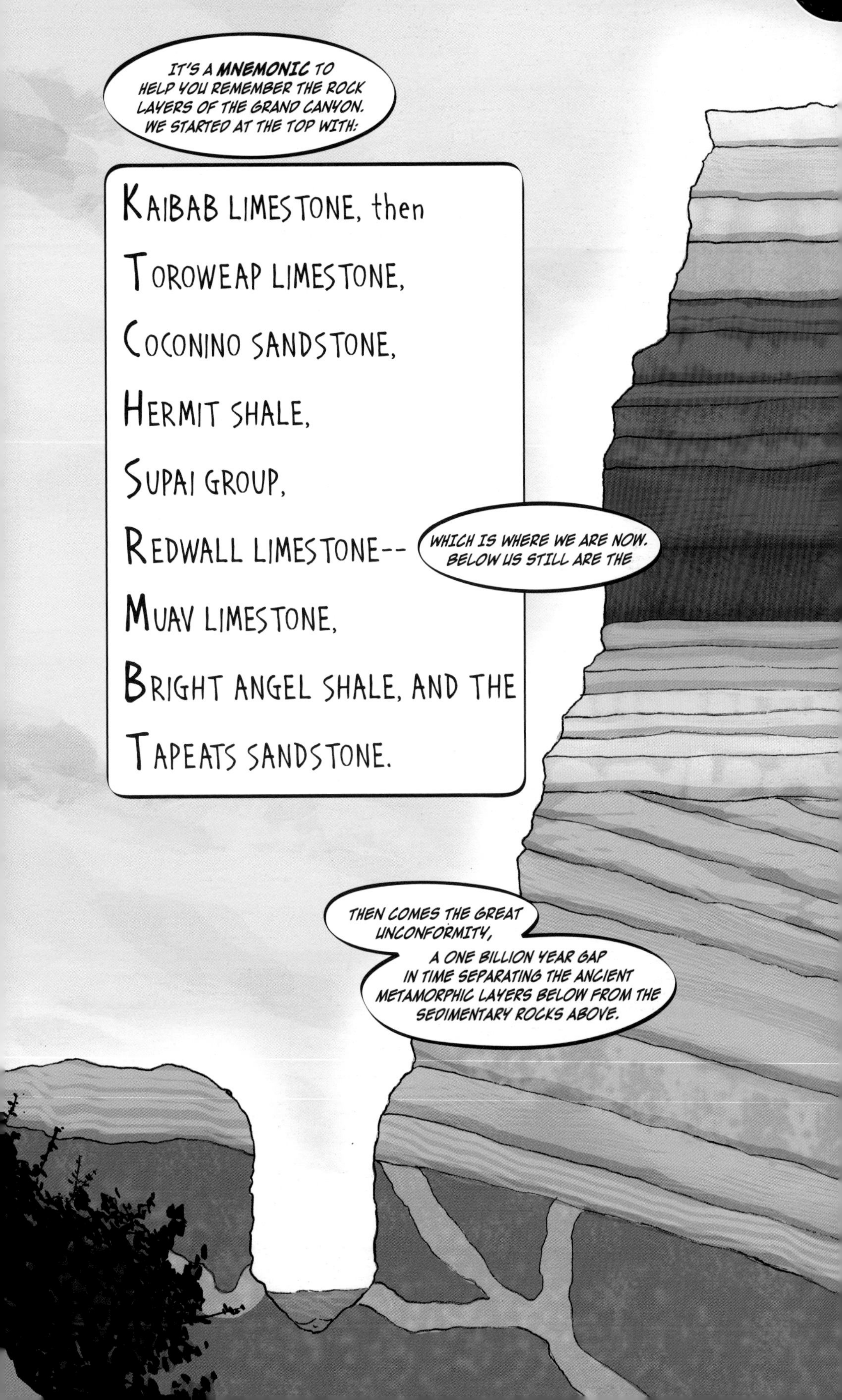
IT'S A MNEMONIC TO HELP YOU REMEMBER THE ROCK LAYERS OF THE GRAND CANYON. WE STARTED AT THE TOP WITH:
KAIBAB LIMESTONE, then
TOROWEAP LIMESTONE,
COCONINO SANDSTONE,
HERMIT SHALE,
SUPAI GROUP,
REDWALL LIMESTONE--
WHICH IS WHERE WE ARE NOW. BELOW US STILL ARE THE
MUAV LIMESTONE,
BRIGHT ANGEL SHALE, AND THE
TAPEATS SANDSTONE.
THEN COMES THE GREAT UNCONFORMITY,
A ONE BILLION YEAR GAP IN TIME SEPARATING THE ANCIENT METAMORPHIC LAYERS BELOW FROM THE SEDIMENTARY ROCKS ABOVE.

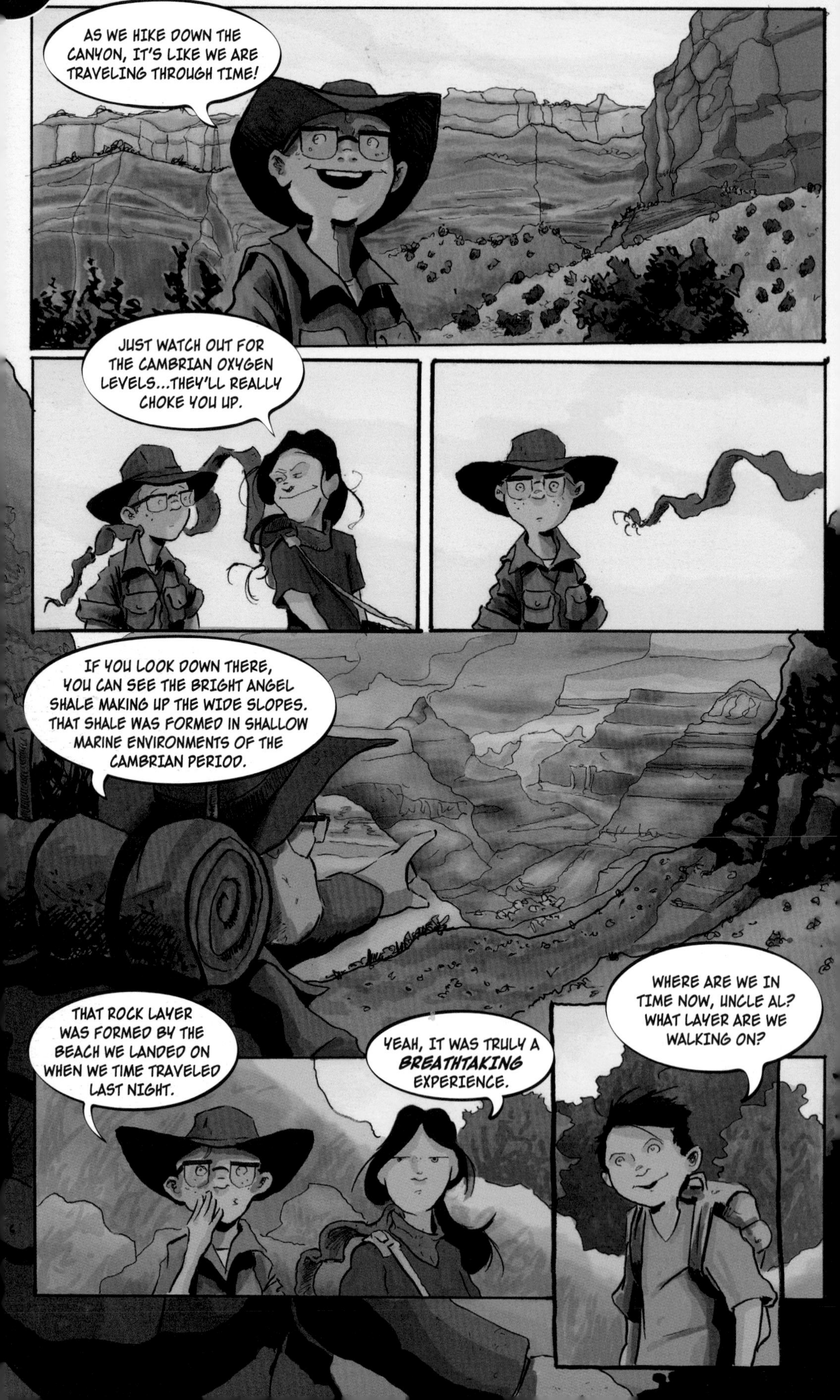
AS WE HIKE DOWN THE CANYON, IT'S LIKE WE ARE TRAVELING THROUGH TIME!
JUST WATCH OUT FOR THE CAMBRIAN OXYGEN LEVELS...THEY'LL REALLY CHOKE YOU UP.
IF YOU LOOK DOWN THERE, YOU CAN SEE THE BRIGHT ANGEL SHALE MAKING UP THE WIDE SLOPES. THAT SHALE WAS FORMED IN SHALLOW MARINE ENVIRONMENTS OF THE CAMBRIAN PERIOD.
THAT ROCK LAYER WAS FORMED BY THE BEACH WE LANDED ON WHEN WE TIME TRAVELED LAST NIGHT.
YEAH, IT WAS TRULY A ***BREATHTAKING*** EXPERIENCE.
WHERE ARE WE IN TIME NOW, UNCLE AL? WHAT LAYER ARE WE WALKING ON?

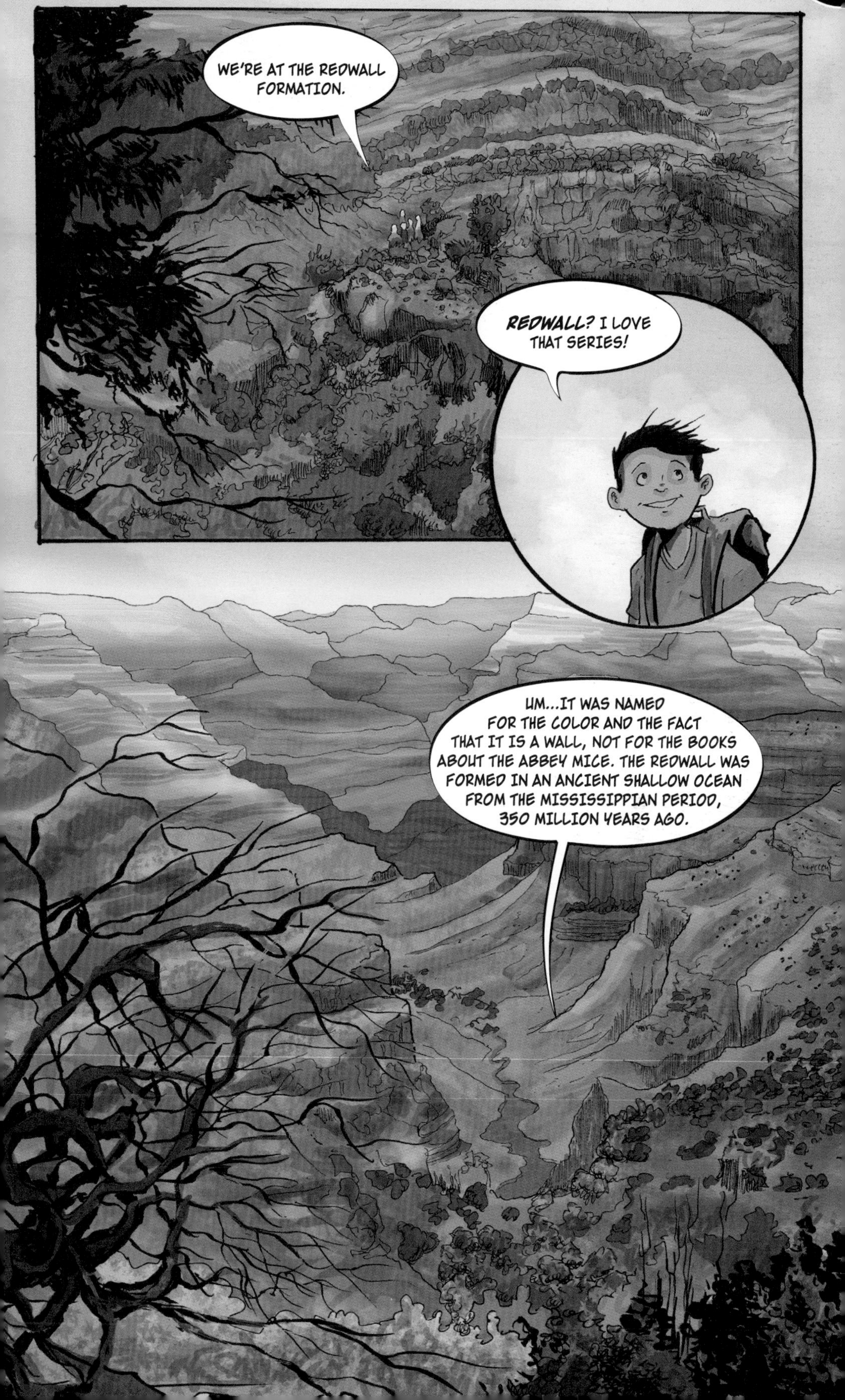
WE'RE AT THE REDWALL FORMATION.
REDWALL? I LOVE THAT SERIES!
UM...IT WAS NAMED FOR THE COLOR AND THE FACT THAT IT IS A WALL, NOT FOR THE BOOKS ABOUT THE ABBEY MICE. THE REDWALL WAS FORMED IN AN ANCIENT SHALLOW OCEAN FROM THE MISSISSIPPIAN PERIOD, 350 MILLION YEARS AGO.

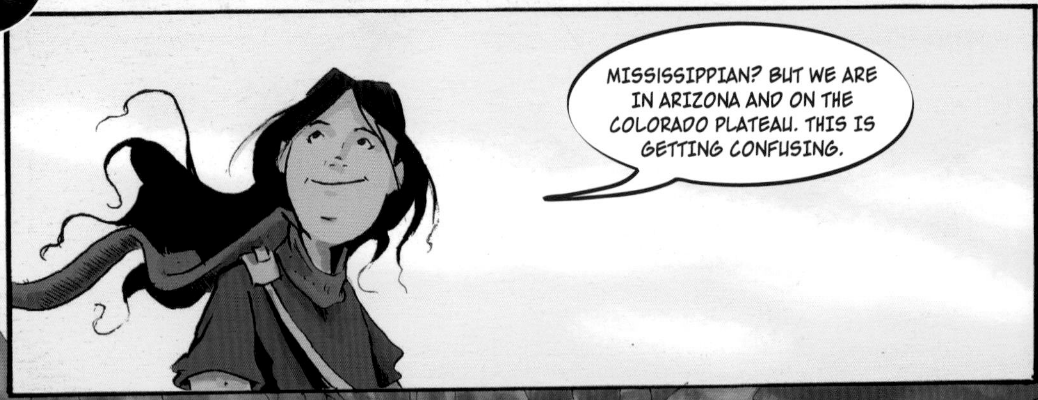
MISSISSIPPIAN? BUT WE ARE IN ARIZONA AND ON THE COLORADO PLATEAU. THIS IS GETTING CONFUSING.

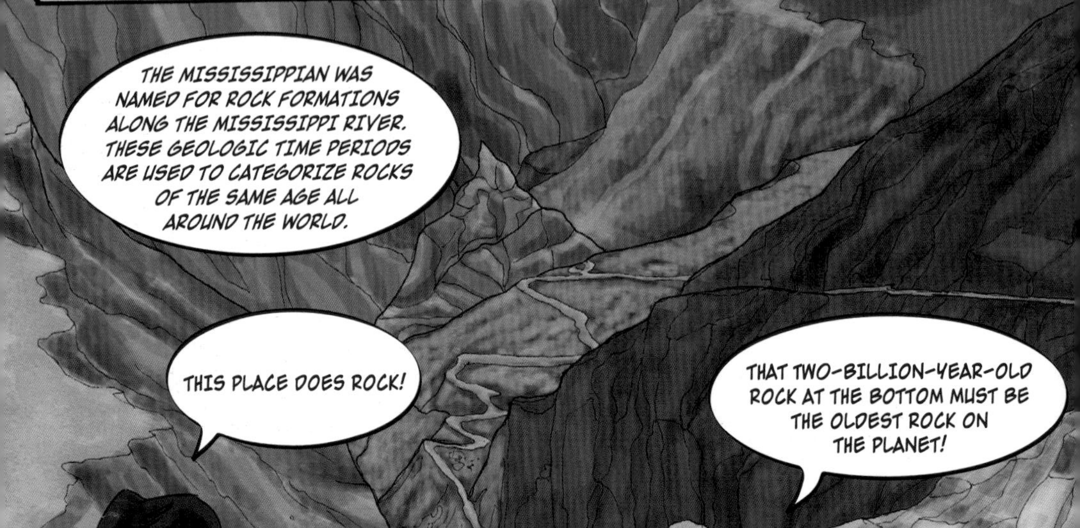
THE MISSISSIPPIAN WAS NAMED FOR ROCK FORMATIONS ALONG THE MISSISSIPPI RIVER. THESE GEOLOGIC TIME PERIODS ARE USED TO CATEGORIZE ROCKS OF THE SAME AGE ALL AROUND THE WORLD.
THIS PLACE DOES ROCK!
THAT TWO-BILLION-YEAR-OLD ROCK AT THE BOTTOM MUST BE THE OLDEST ROCK ON THE PLANET!

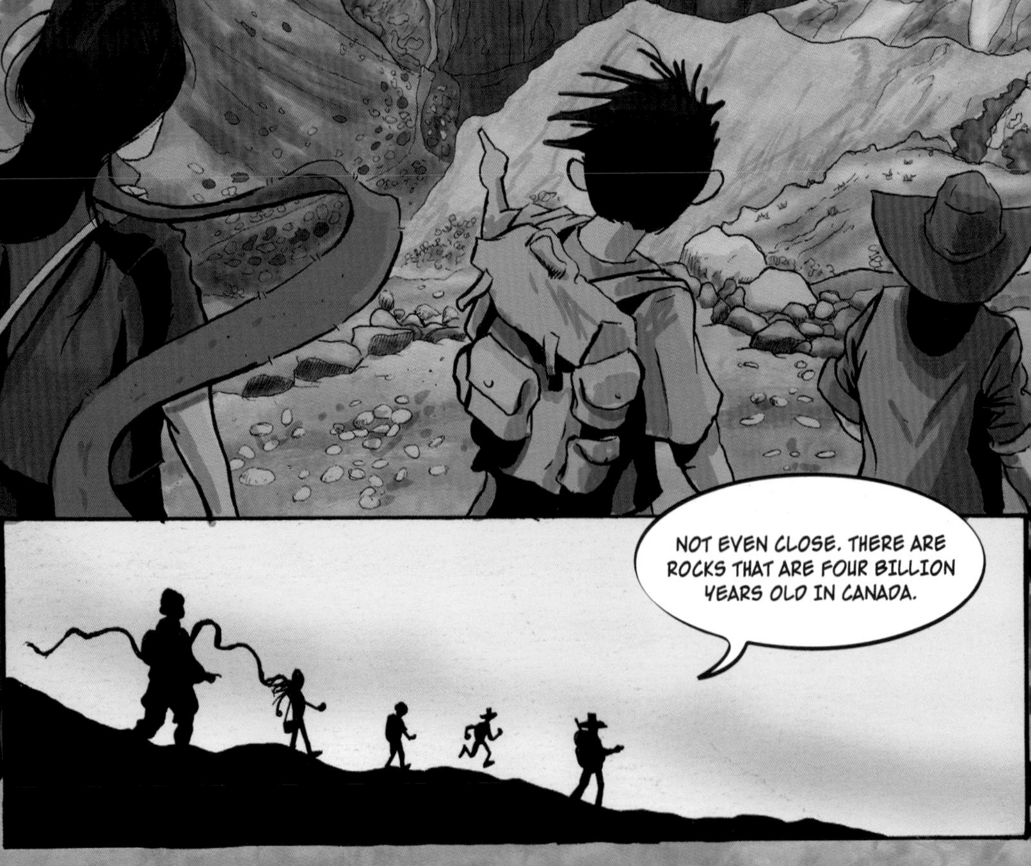
NOT EVEN CLOSE. THERE ARE ROCKS THAT ARE FOUR BILLION YEARS OLD IN CANADA.

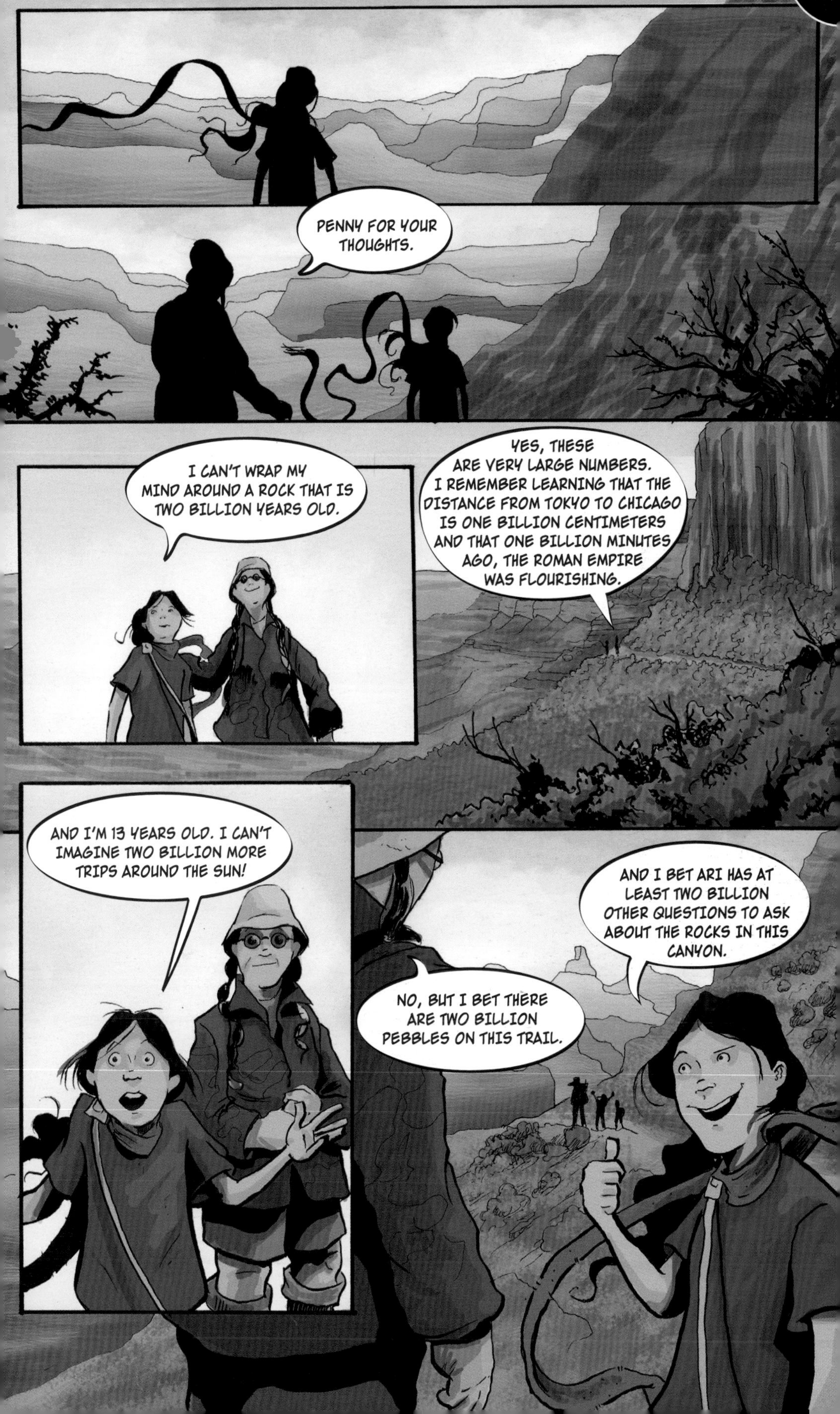
PENNY FOR YOUR THOUGHTS.
I CAN'T WRAP MY MIND AROUND A ROCK THAT IS TWO BILLION YEARS OLD.
YES, THESE ARE VERY LARGE NUMBERS. I REMEMBER LEARNING THAT THE DISTANCE FROM TOKYO TO CHICAGO IS ONE BILLION CENTIMETERS AND THAT ONE BILLION MINUTES AGO, THE ROMAN EMPIRE WAS FLOURISHING.
AND I'M 13 YEARS OLD. I CAN'T IMAGINE TWO BILLION MORE TRIPS AROUND THE SUN!
AND I BET ARI HAS AT LEAST TWO BILLION OTHER QUESTIONS TO ASK ABOUT THE ROCKS IN THIS CANYON.
NO, BUT I BET THERE ARE TWO BILLION PEBBLES ON THIS TRAIL.

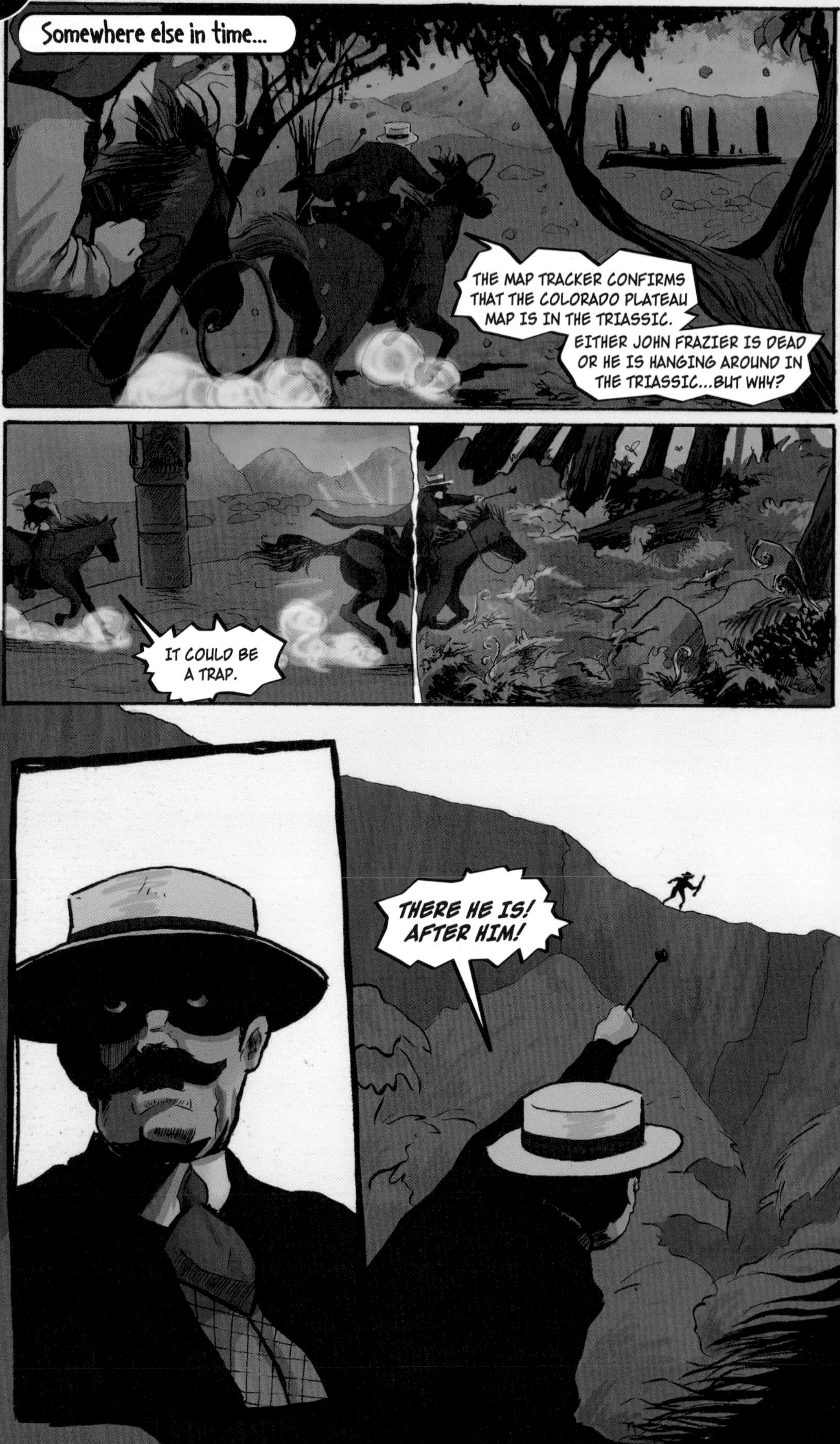
Somewhere else in time...
THE MAP TRACKER CONFIRMS THAT THE COLORADO PLATEAU MAP IS IN THE TRIASSIC.
EITHER JOHN FRAZIER IS DEAD OR HE IS HANGING AROUND IN THE TRIASSIC...BUT WHY?
IT COULD BE A TRAP.
THERE HE IS! AFTER HIM!

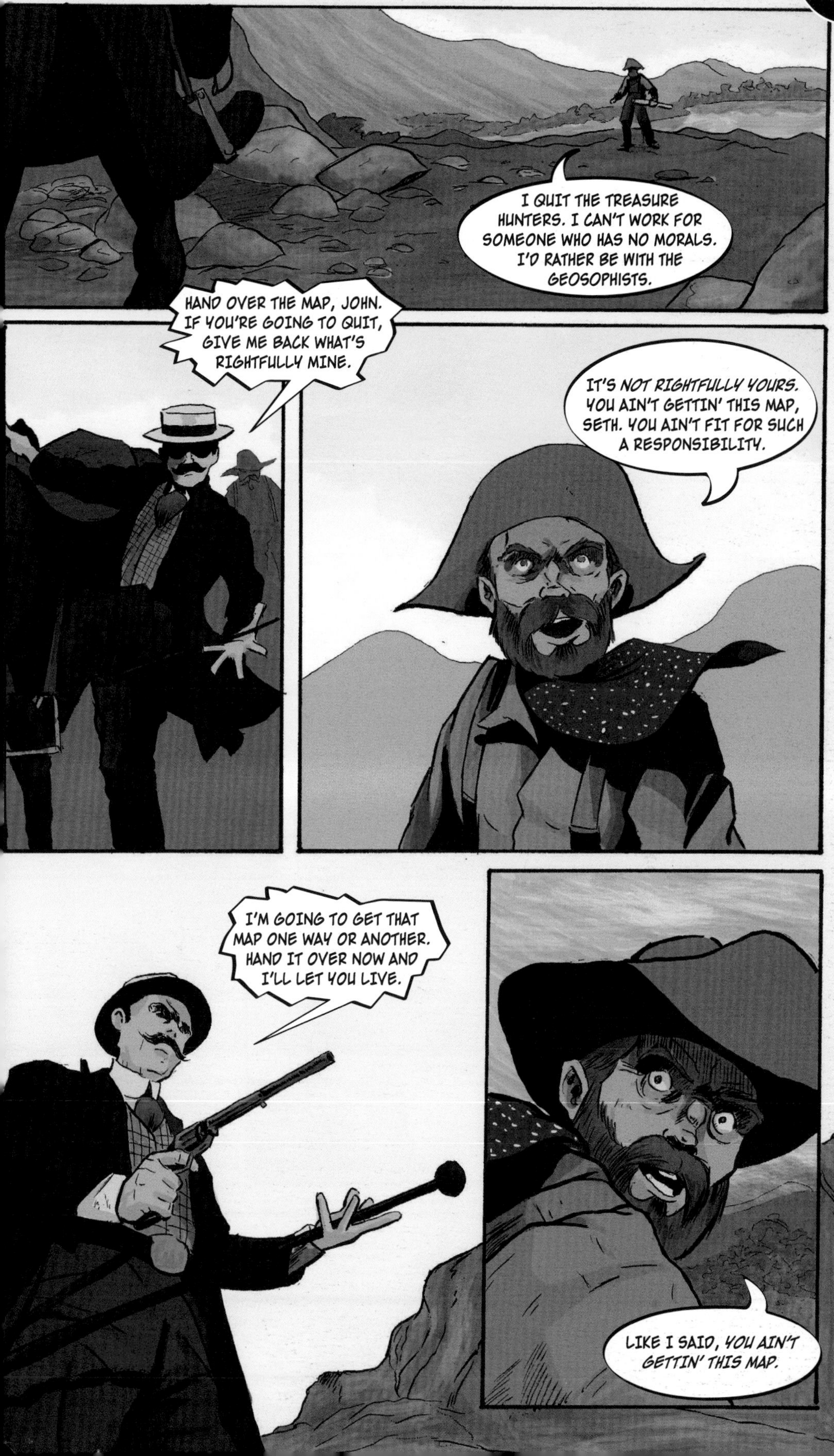
I QUIT THE TREASURE HUNTERS. I CAN'T WORK FOR SOMEONE WHO HAS NO MORALS. I'D RATHER BE WITH THE GEOSOPHISTS.
HAND OVER THE MAP, JOHN. IF YOU'RE GOING TO QUIT, GIVE ME BACK WHAT'S RIGHTFULLY MINE.
IT'S *NOT RIGHTFULLY YOURS*. YOU AIN'T GETTIN' THIS MAP, SETH. YOU AIN'T FIT FOR SUCH A RESPONSIBILITY.
I'M GOING TO GET THAT MAP ONE WAY OR ANOTHER. HAND IT OVER NOW AND I'LL LET YOU LIVE.
LIKE I SAID, *YOU AIN'T GETTIN' THIS MAP.*

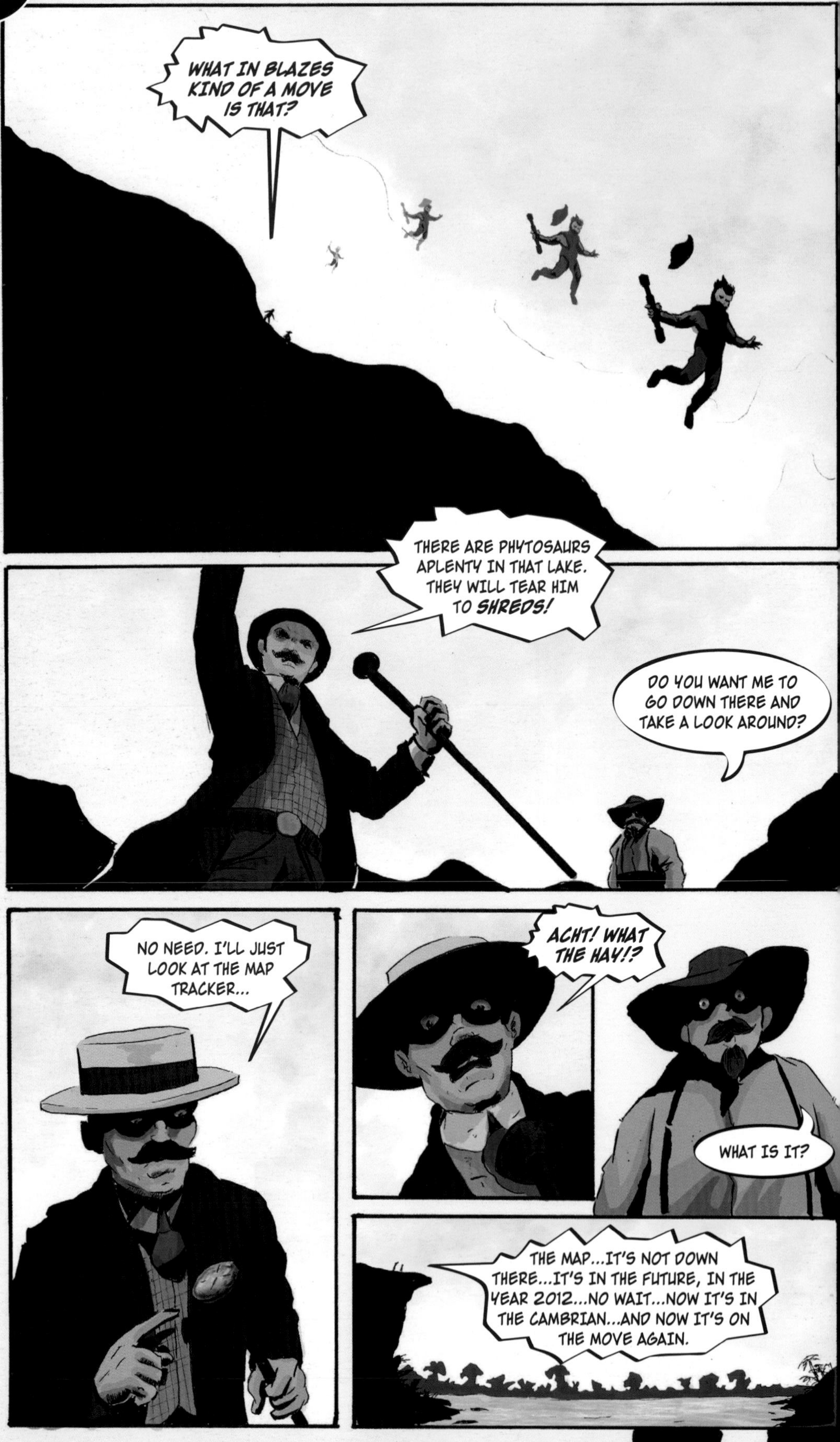
WHAT IN BLAZES KIND OF A MOVE IS THAT?
THERE ARE PHYTOSAURS APLENTY IN THAT LAKE. THEY WILL TEAR HIM TO SHREDS!
DO YOU WANT ME TO GO DOWN THERE AND TAKE A LOOK AROUND?
NO NEED. I'LL JUST LOOK AT THE MAP TRACKER...
ACHT! WHAT THE HAY!?
WHAT IS IT?
THE MAP...IT'S NOT DOWN THERE...IT'S IN THE FUTURE, IN THE YEAR 2012...NO WAIT...NOW IT'S IN THE CAMBRIAN...AND NOW IT'S ON THE MOVE AGAIN.

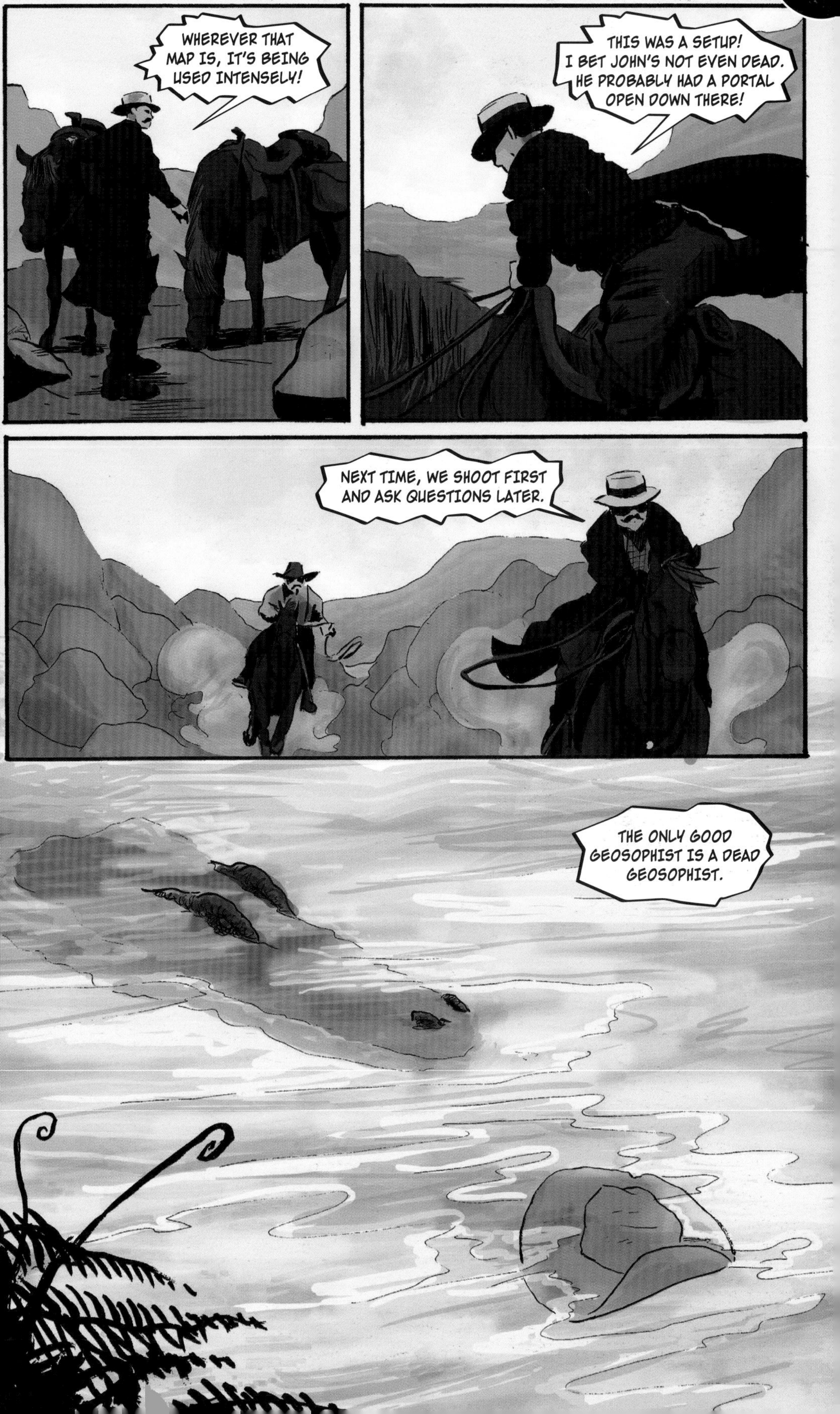
WHEREVER THAT MAP IS, IT'S BEING USED INTENSELY!
THIS WAS A SETUP! I BET JOHN'S NOT EVEN DEAD. HE PROBABLY HAD A PORTAL OPEN DOWN THERE!
NEXT TIME, WE SHOOT FIRST AND ASK QUESTIONS LATER.
THE ONLY GOOD GEOSOPHIST IS A DEAD GEOSOPHIST.

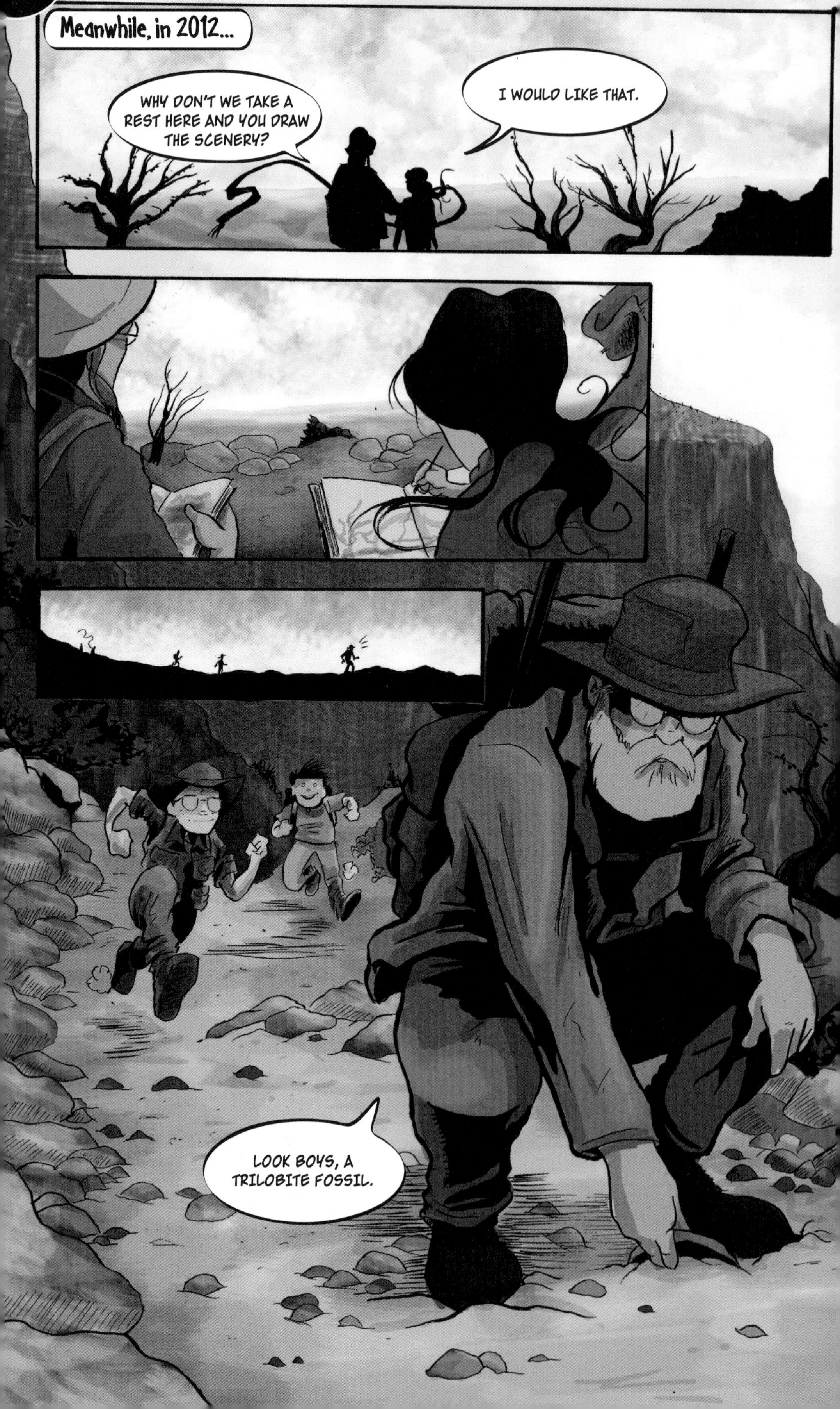
Meanwhile, in 2012...
WHY DON'T WE TAKE A REST HERE AND YOU DRAW THE SCENERY?
I WOULD LIKE THAT.
LOOK BOYS, A TRILOBITE FOSSIL.

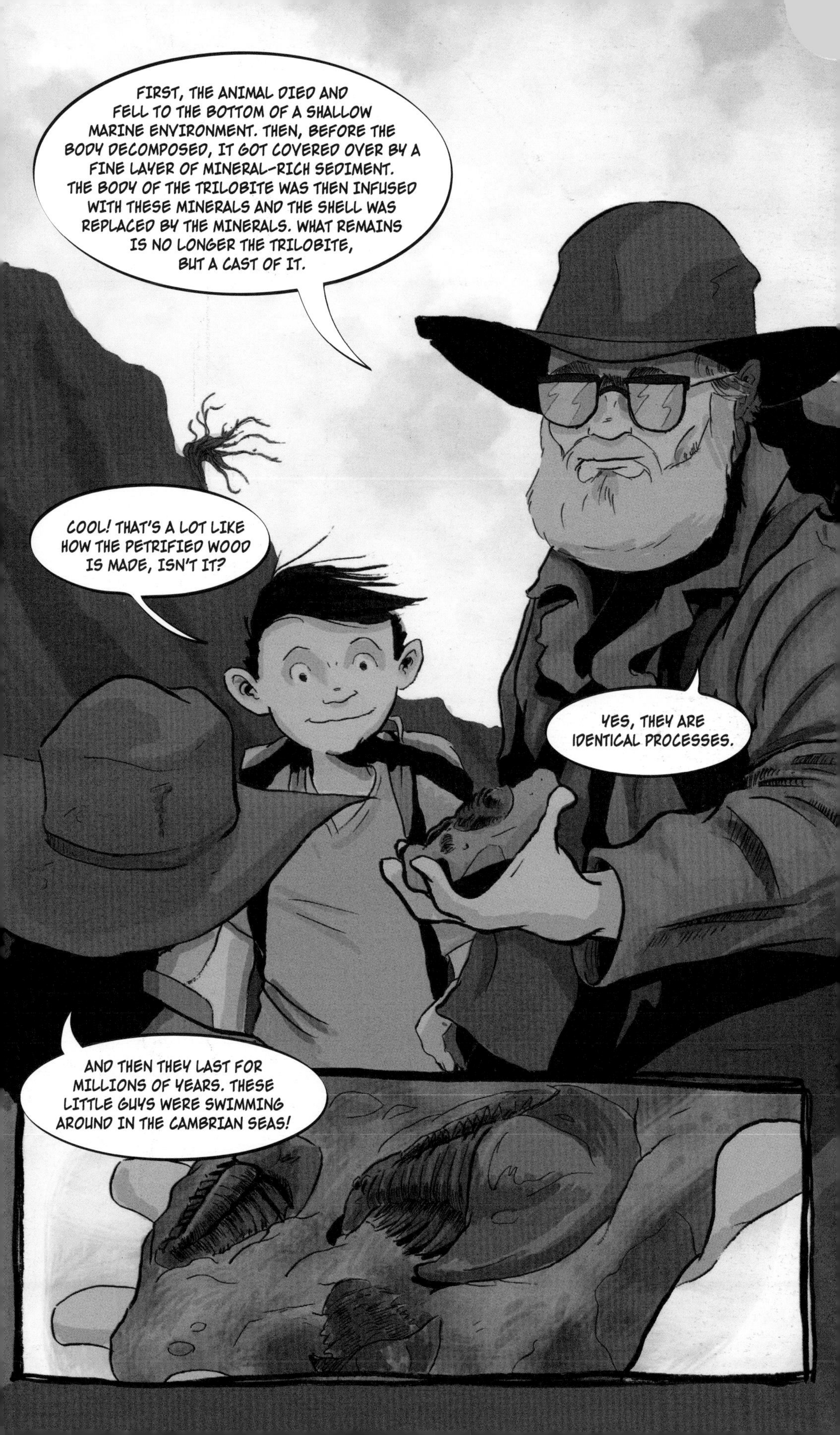
FIRST, THE ANIMAL DIED AND FELL TO THE BOTTOM OF A SHALLOW MARINE ENVIRONMENT. THEN, BEFORE THE BODY DECOMPOSED, IT GOT COVERED OVER BY A FINE LAYER OF MINERAL-RICH SEDIMENT. THE BODY OF THE TRILOBITE WAS THEN INFUSED WITH THESE MINERALS AND THE SHELL WAS REPLACED BY THE MINERALS. WHAT REMAINS IS NO LONGER THE TRILOBITE, BUT A CAST OF IT.
COOL! THAT'S A LOT LIKE HOW THE PETRIFIED WOOD IS MADE, ISN'T IT?
YES, THEY ARE IDENTICAL PROCESSES.
AND THEN THEY LAST FOR MILLIONS OF YEARS. THESE LITTLE GUYS WERE SWIMMING AROUND IN THE CAMBRIAN SEAS!

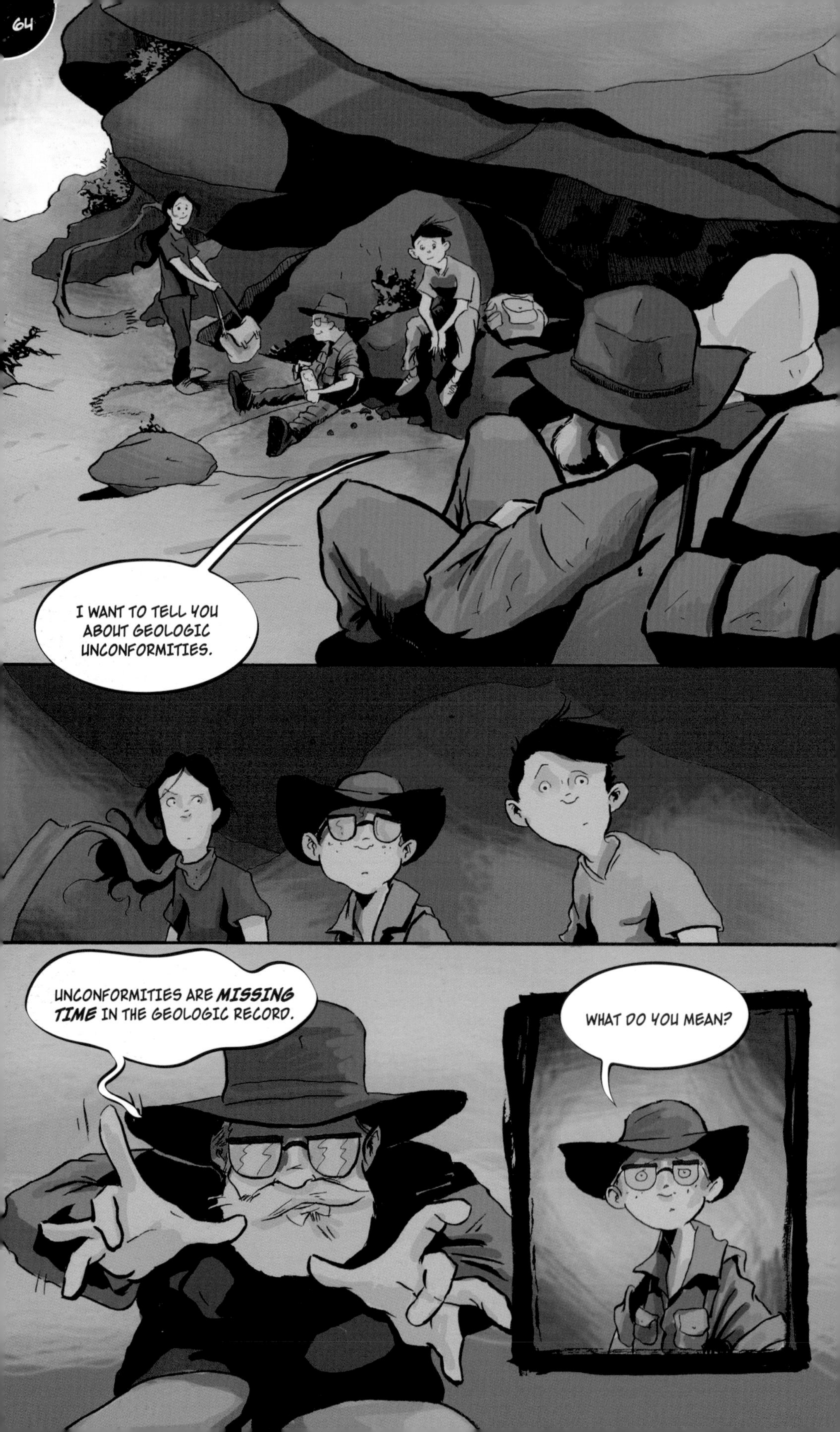
I WANT TO TELL YOU ABOUT GEOLOGIC UNCONFORMITIES.
UNCONFORMITIES ARE MISSING TIME IN THE GEOLOGIC RECORD.
WHAT DO YOU MEAN?

I HAVE ALREADY MENTIONED THE GREAT UNCONFORMITY, THE GRAND CANYON'S GAP IN GEOLOGIC TIME OF ONE BILLION YEARS. BUT THERE IS ANOTHER SIGNIFICANT MISSING PIECE OF THE GEOLOGIC PUZZLE.
THE ORDOVICIAN AND SILURIAN PERIODS, A TOTAL OF 114 MILLION YEARS AND A SIGNIFICANT PORTION OF THE STORY OF THE EVOLUTION OF LIFE ON EARTH, ARE ABSENT FROM THE GEOLOGIC RECORD HERE IN THE GRAND CANYON AND ACROSS THE ENTIRE COLORADO PLATEAU.
WELL, WHERE DID THEY *GO?*
NO ONE KNOWS. IT'S ONE OF THE BIGGER MYSTERIES OF THE CANYON. THE SEDIMENT MAY HAVE NEVER BEEN DEPOSITED, OR IT MIGHT HAVE ERODED AWAY ENTIRELY.
WHAT DO ***YOU*** THINK HAPPENED?
I'M NOT SURE. BUT I DO WANT TO POINT OUT THAT NOWHERE ON EARTH IS THE BOOK OF TIME *COMPLETE*.

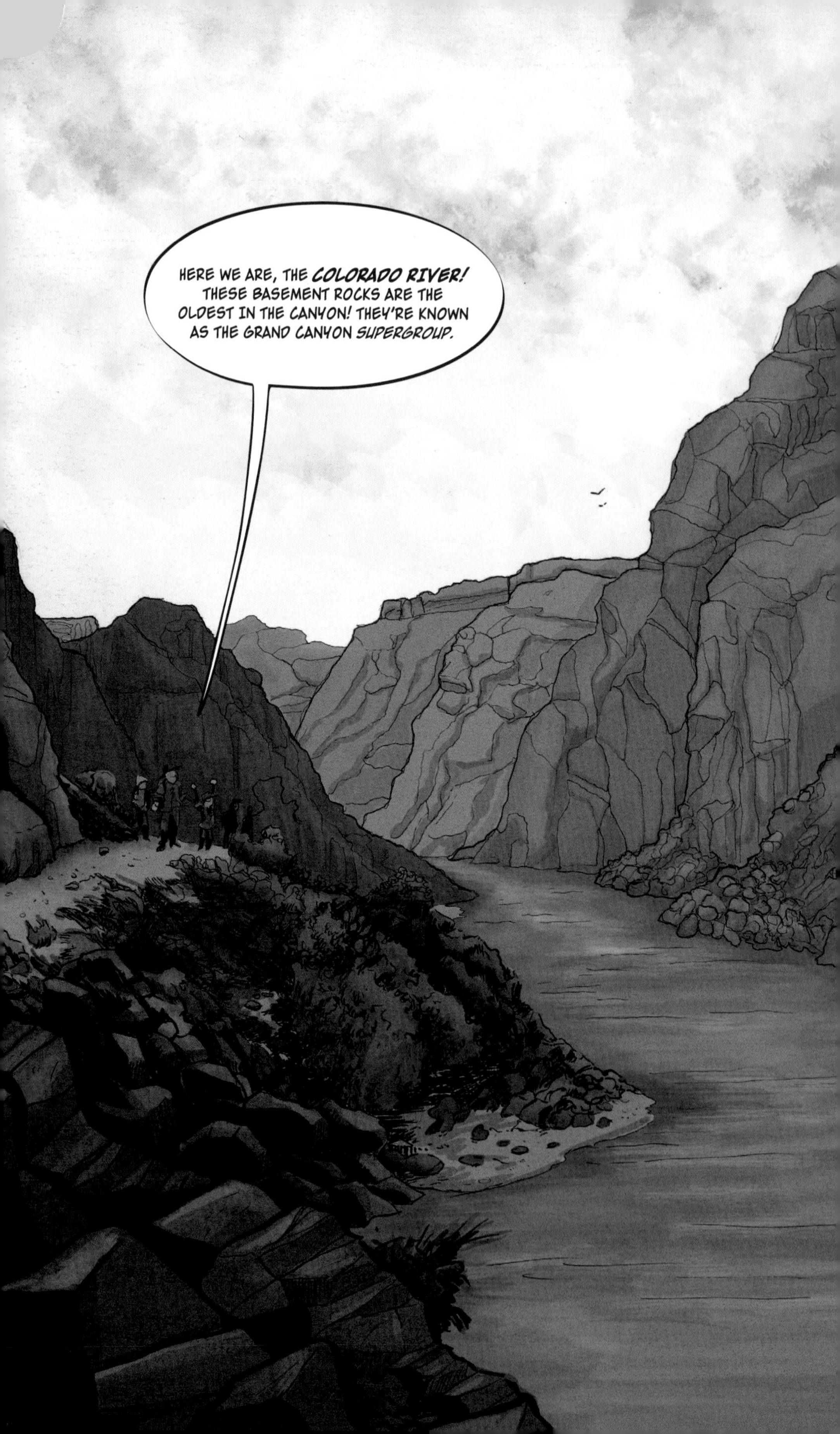
HERE WE ARE, THE COLORADO RIVER! THESE BASEMENT ROCKS ARE THE OLDEST IN THE CANYON! THEY'RE KNOWN AS THE GRAND CANYON SUPERGROUP.

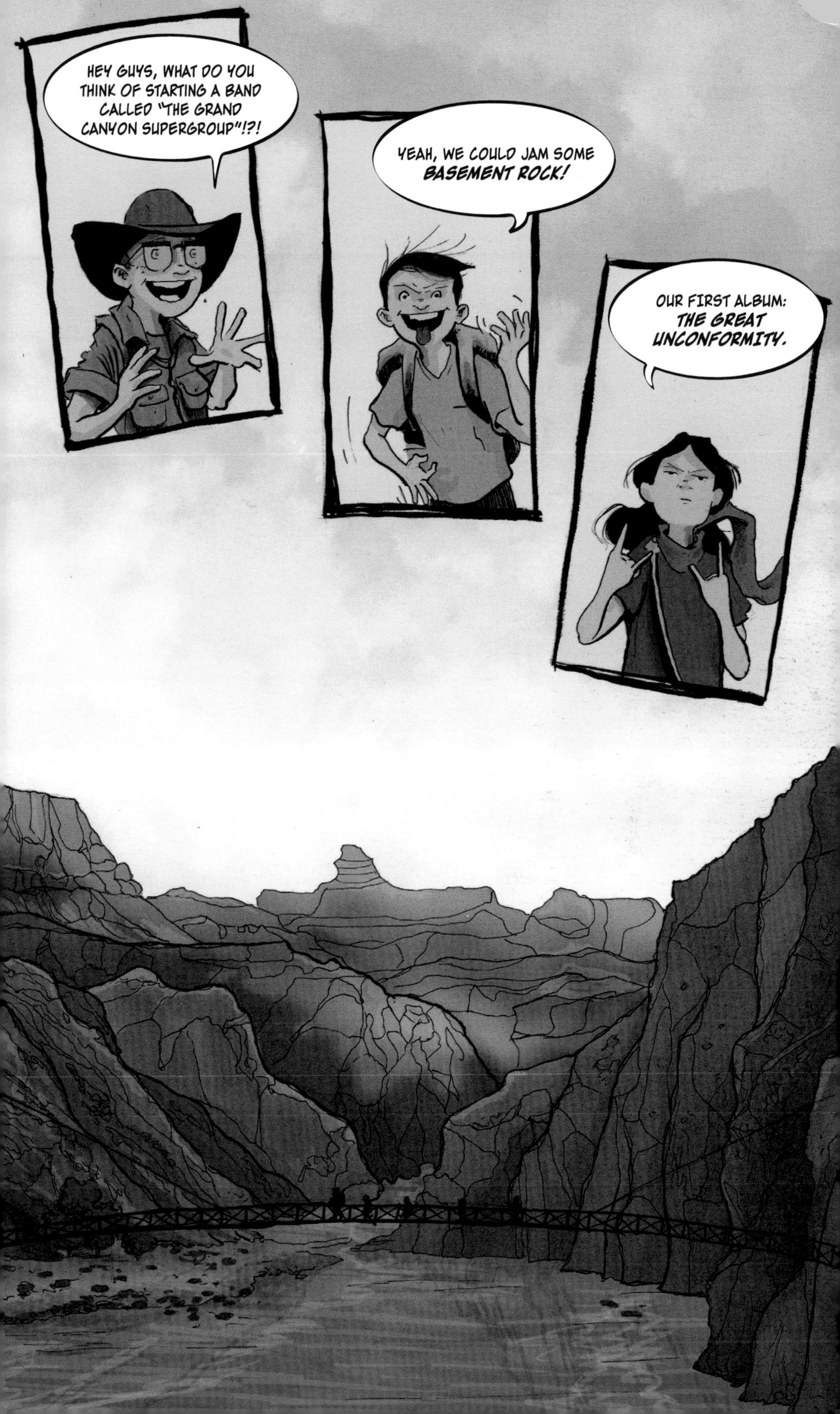
HEY GUYS, WHAT DO YOU THINK OF STARTING A BAND CALLED "THE GRAND CANYON SUPERGROUP"!?!
YEAH, WE COULD JAM SOME BASEMENT ROCK!
OUR FIRST ALBUM: THE GREAT UNCONFORMITY.

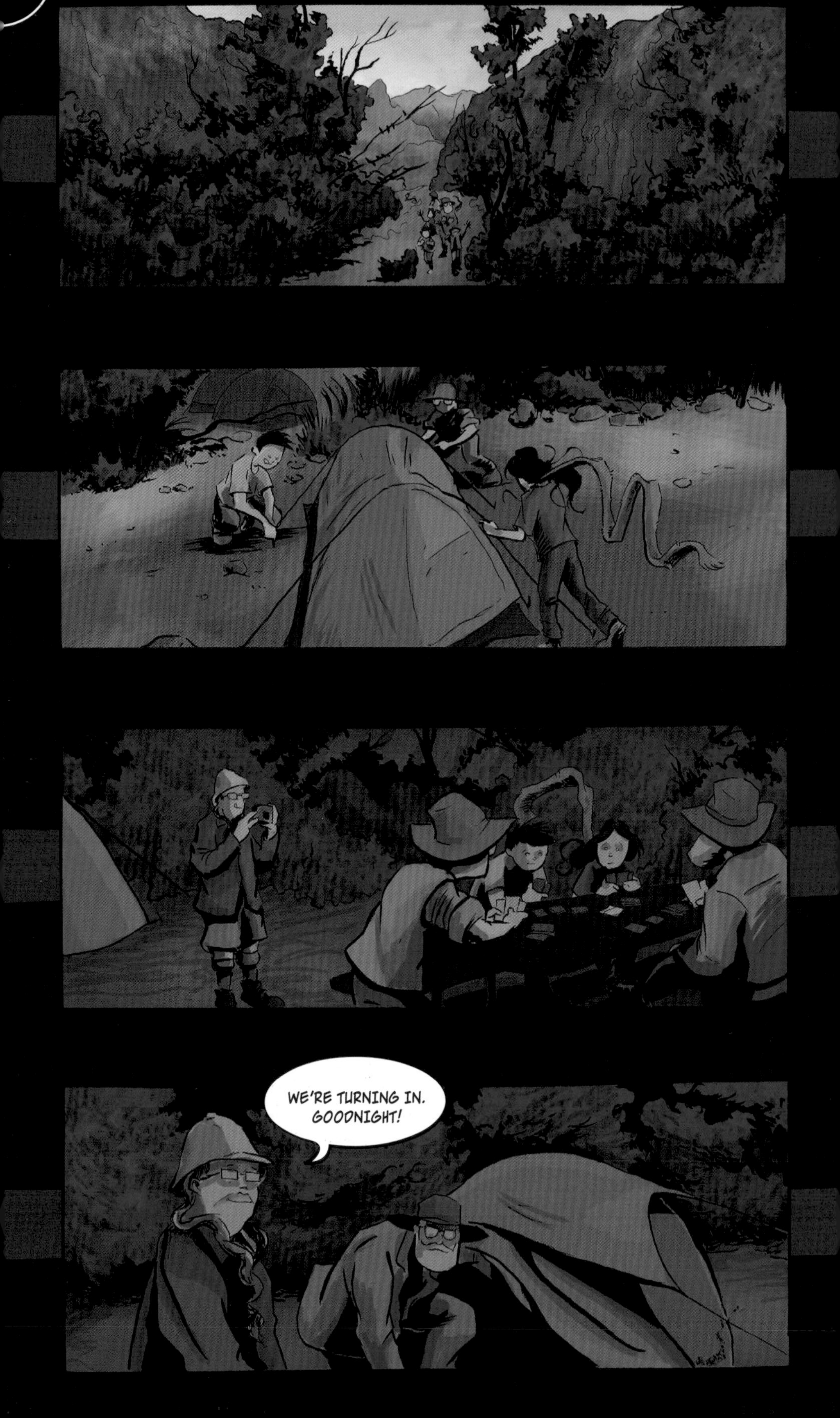
WE'RE TURNING IN. GOODNIGHT!

OH MAN, I'D LOVE TO GO TO THE DEVONIAN RIGHT NOW BUT MY LEGS FEEL LIKE JELL-O...
AND TOMORROW'S GOING TO BE EVEN TOUGHER GOING BACK UP.
YEAH, I'M READY FOR MY SLEEPING BAG.
LOOK OVER THERE!
A RINGTAIL CAT!
LOOKS LIKE HE'S READY FOR YOUR SLEEPING BAG TOO, JENNA!

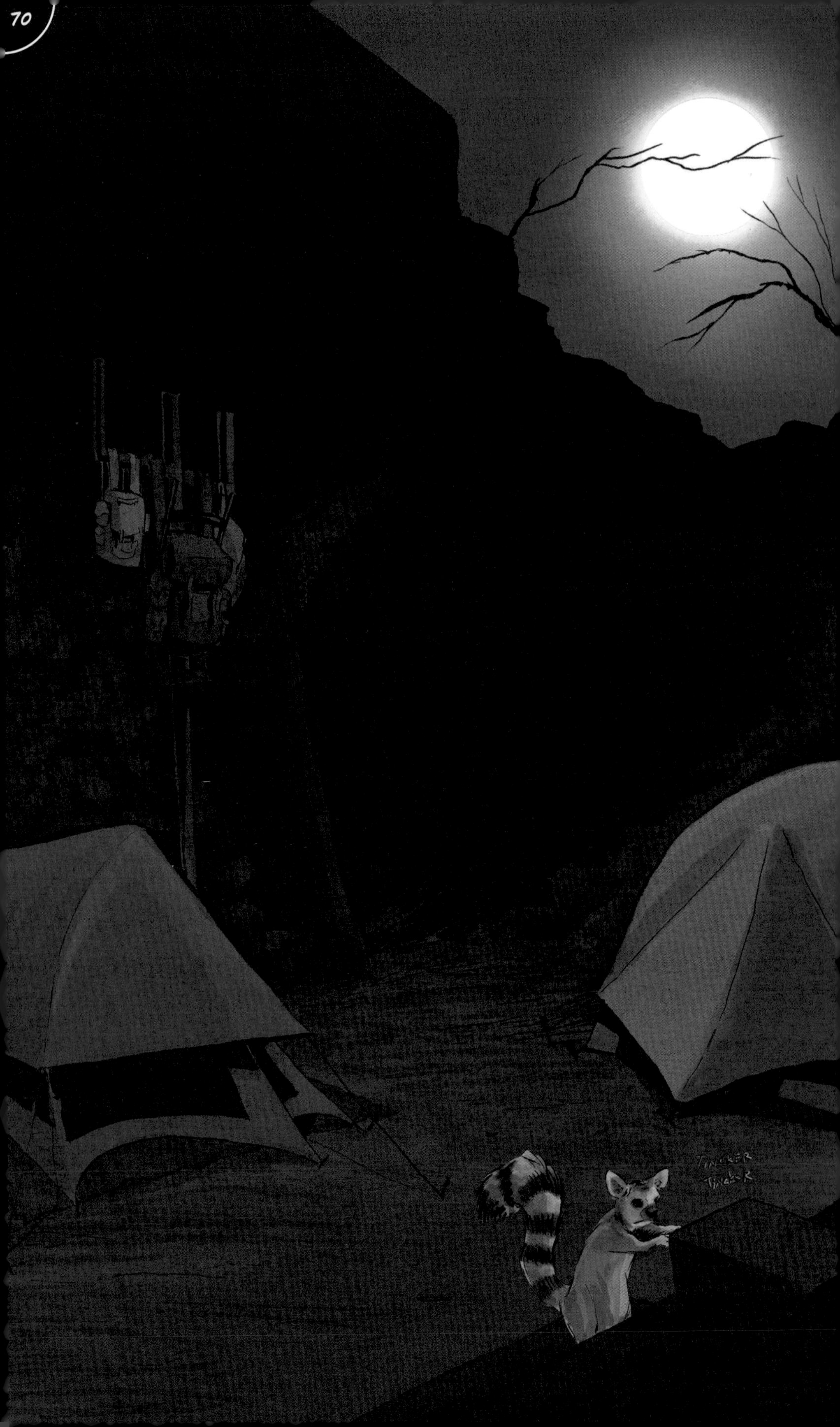

CHAPTER
FOUR

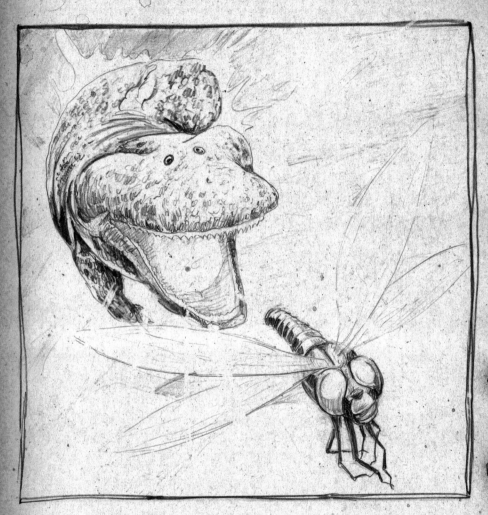

PALEOZOIC PURSUIT

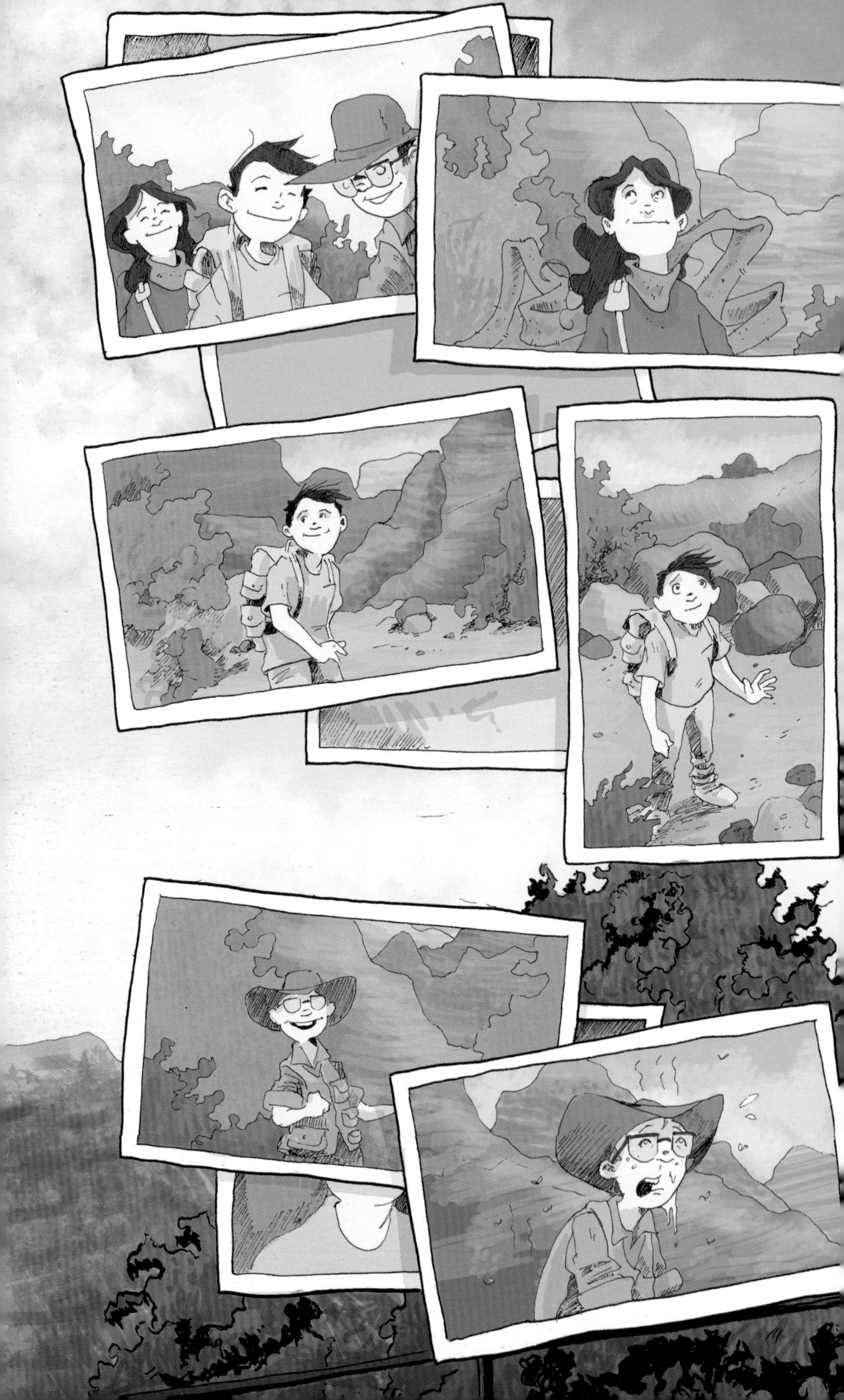

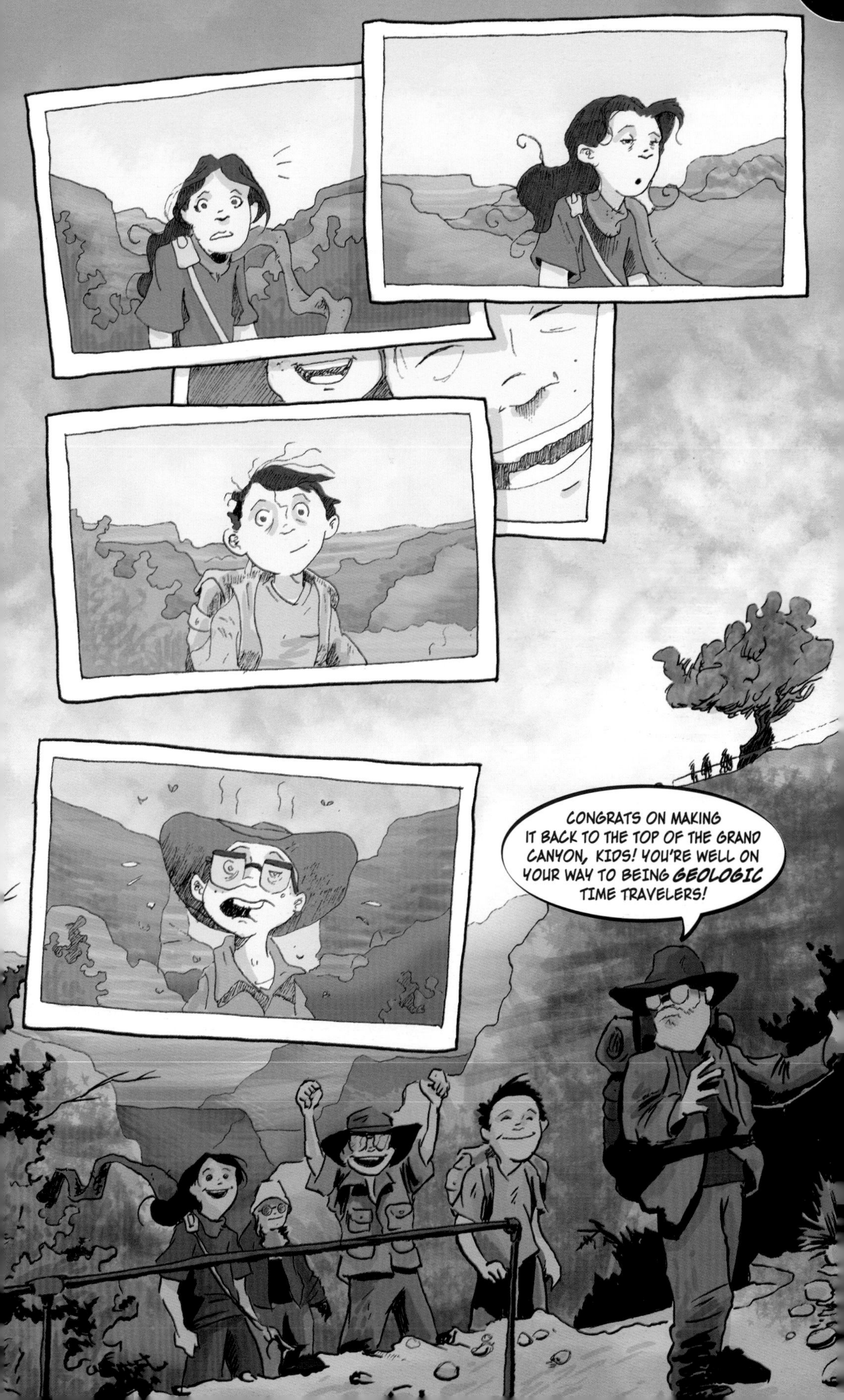
CONGRATS ON MAKING IT BACK TO THE TOP OF THE GRAND CANYON, KIDS! YOU'RE WELL ON YOUR WAY TO BEING GEOLOGIC TIME TRAVELERS!

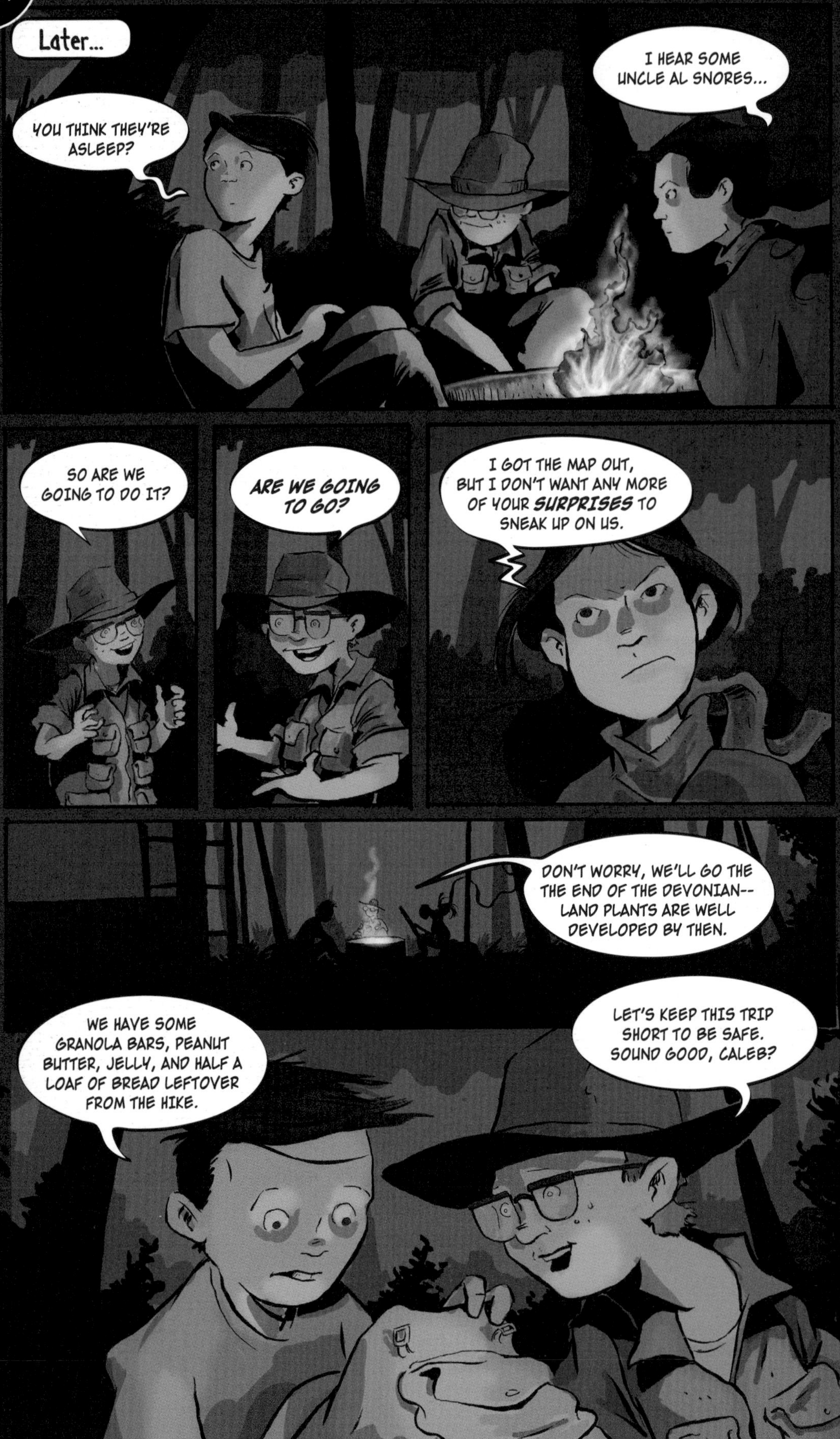
Later...
YOU THINK THEY'RE ASLEEP?
I HEAR SOME UNCLE AL SNORES...
SO ARE WE GOING TO DO IT?
ARE WE GOING TO GO?
I GOT THE MAP OUT, BUT I DON'T WANT ANY MORE OF YOUR SURPRISES TO SNEAK UP ON US.
DON'T WORRY, WE'LL GO THE THE END OF THE DEVONIAN-- LAND PLANTS ARE WELL DEVELOPED BY THEN.
WE HAVE SOME GRANOLA BARS, PEANUT BUTTER, JELLY, AND HALF A LOAF OF BREAD LEFTOVER FROM THE HIKE.
LET'S KEEP THIS TRIP SHORT TO BE SAFE. SOUND GOOD, CALEB?

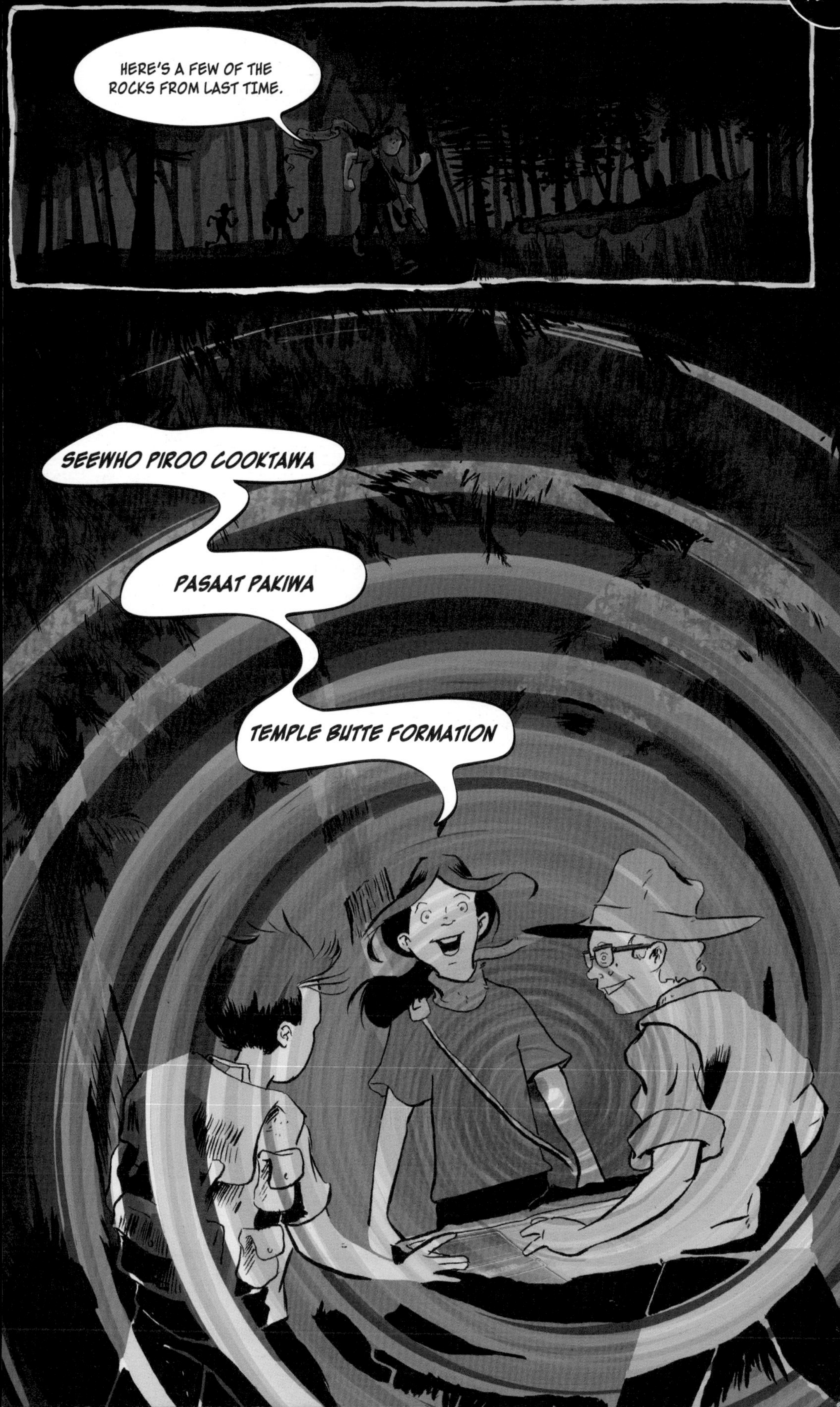
HERE'S A FEW OF THE ROCKS FROM LAST TIME.
SEEWHO PIROO COOKTAWA
PASAAT PAKIWA
TEMPLE BUTTE FORMATION

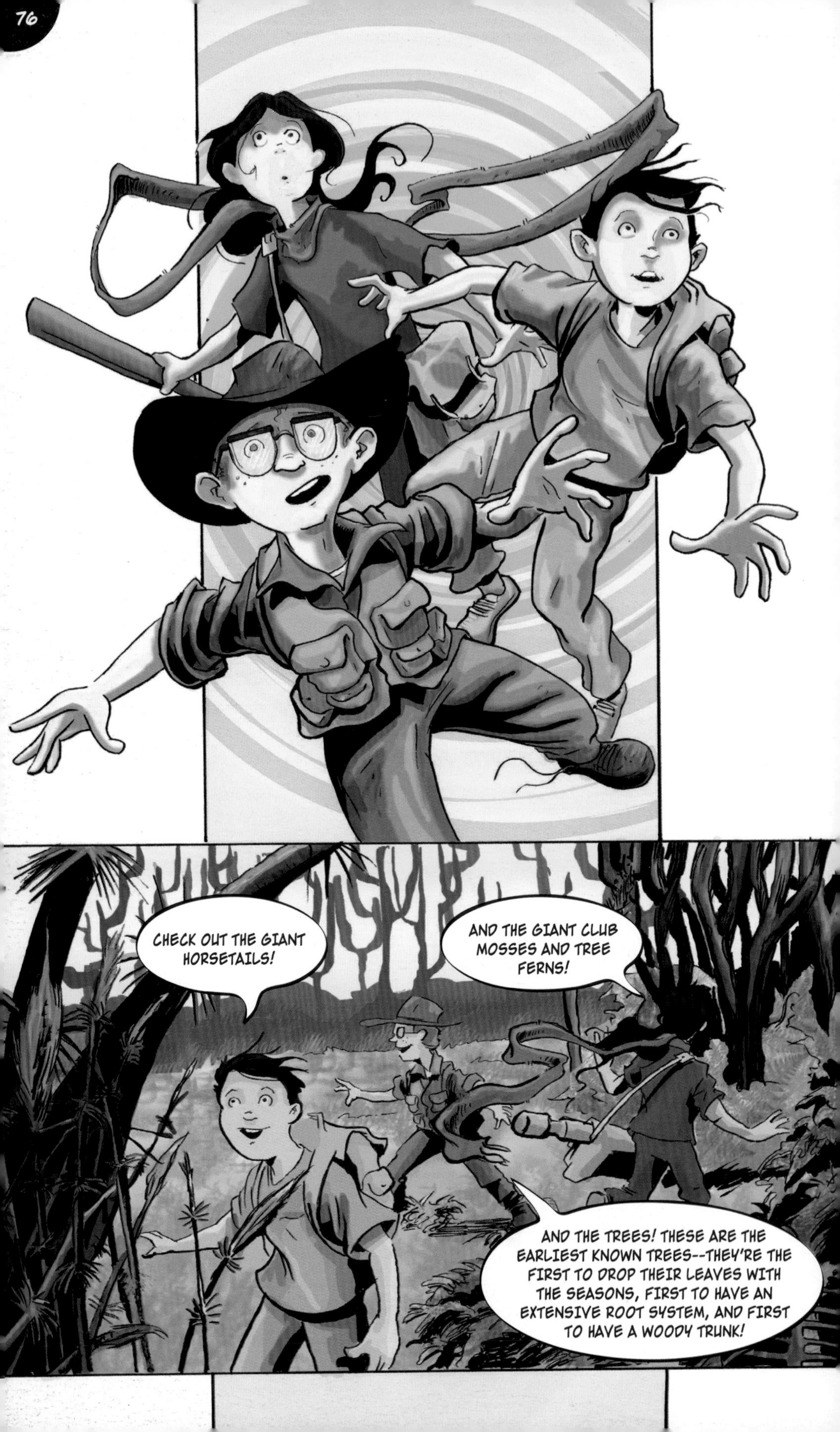
CHECK OUT THE GIANT HORSETAILS!
AND THE GIANT CLUB MOSSES AND TREE FERNS!
AND THE TREES! THESE ARE THE EARLIEST KNOWN TREES--THEY'RE THE FIRST TO DROP THEIR LEAVES WITH THE SEASONS, FIRST TO HAVE AN EXTENSIVE ROOT SYSTEM, AND FIRST TO HAVE A WOODY TRUNK!

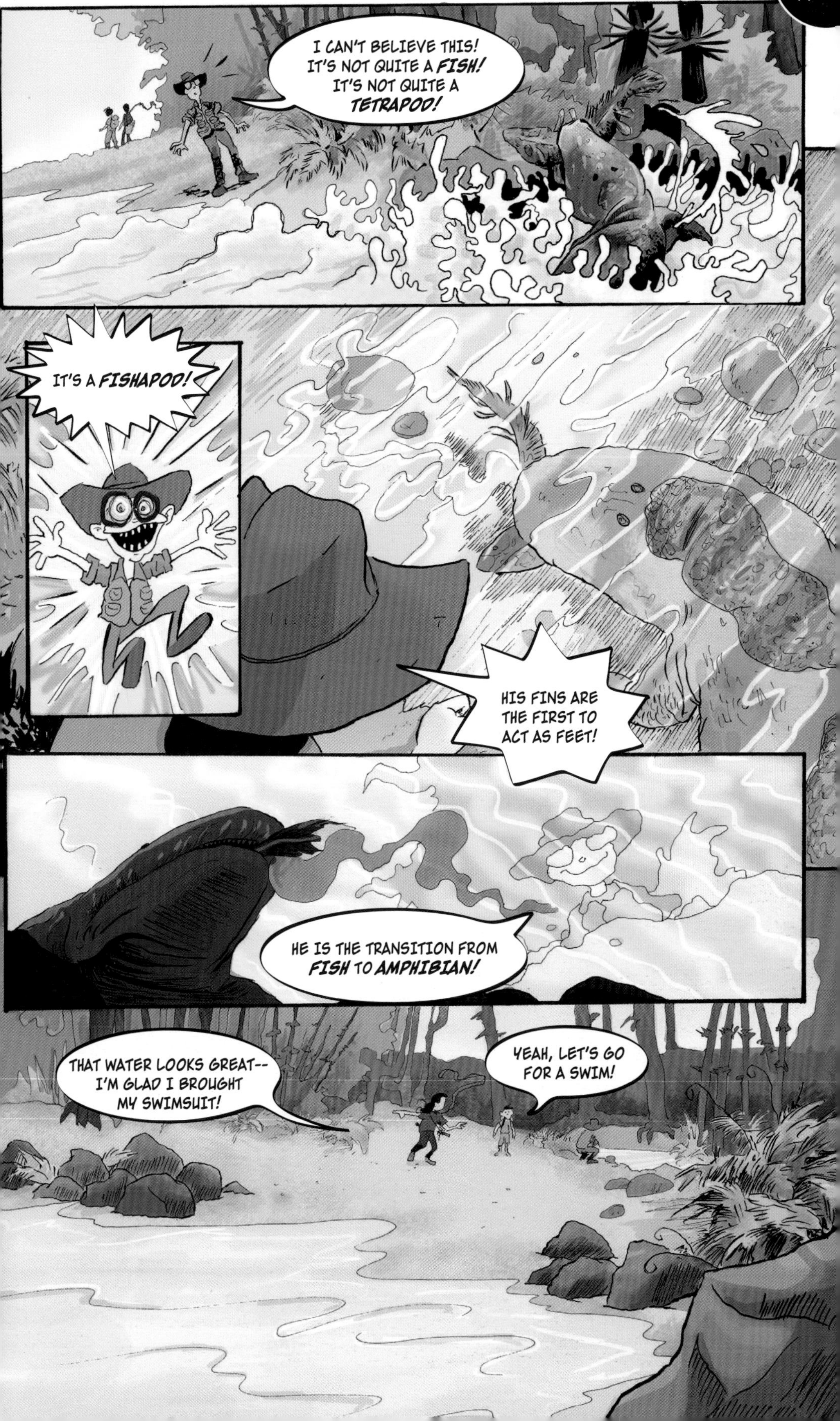
I CAN'T BELIEVE THIS! IT'S NOT QUITE A FISH! IT'S NOT QUITE A TETRAPOD!
IT'S A FISHAPOD!
HIS FINS ARE THE FIRST TO ACT AS FEET!
HE IS THE TRANSITION FROM FISH TO AMPHIBIAN!
THAT WATER LOOKS GREAT-- I'M GLAD I BROUGHT MY SWIMSUIT!
YEAH, LET'S GO FOR A SWIM!

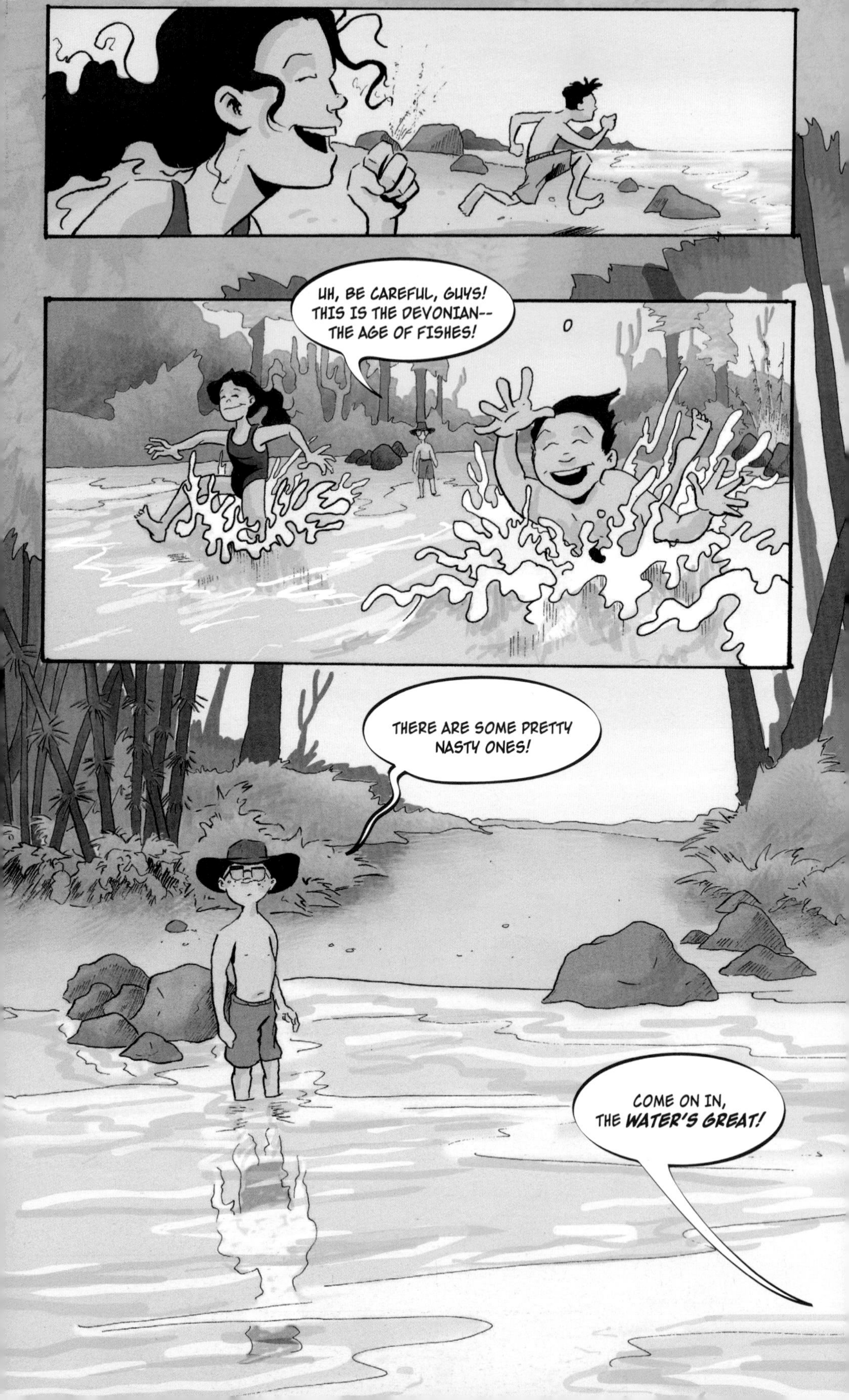
UH, BE CAREFUL, GUYS! THIS IS THE DEVONIAN-- THE AGE OF FISHES!
THERE ARE SOME PRETTY NASTY ONES!
COME ON IN, THE *WATER'S GREAT!*

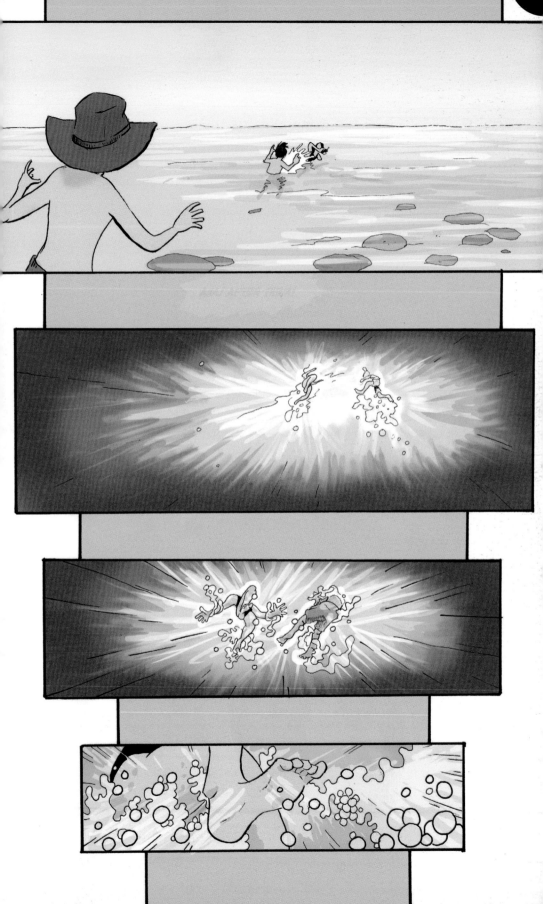

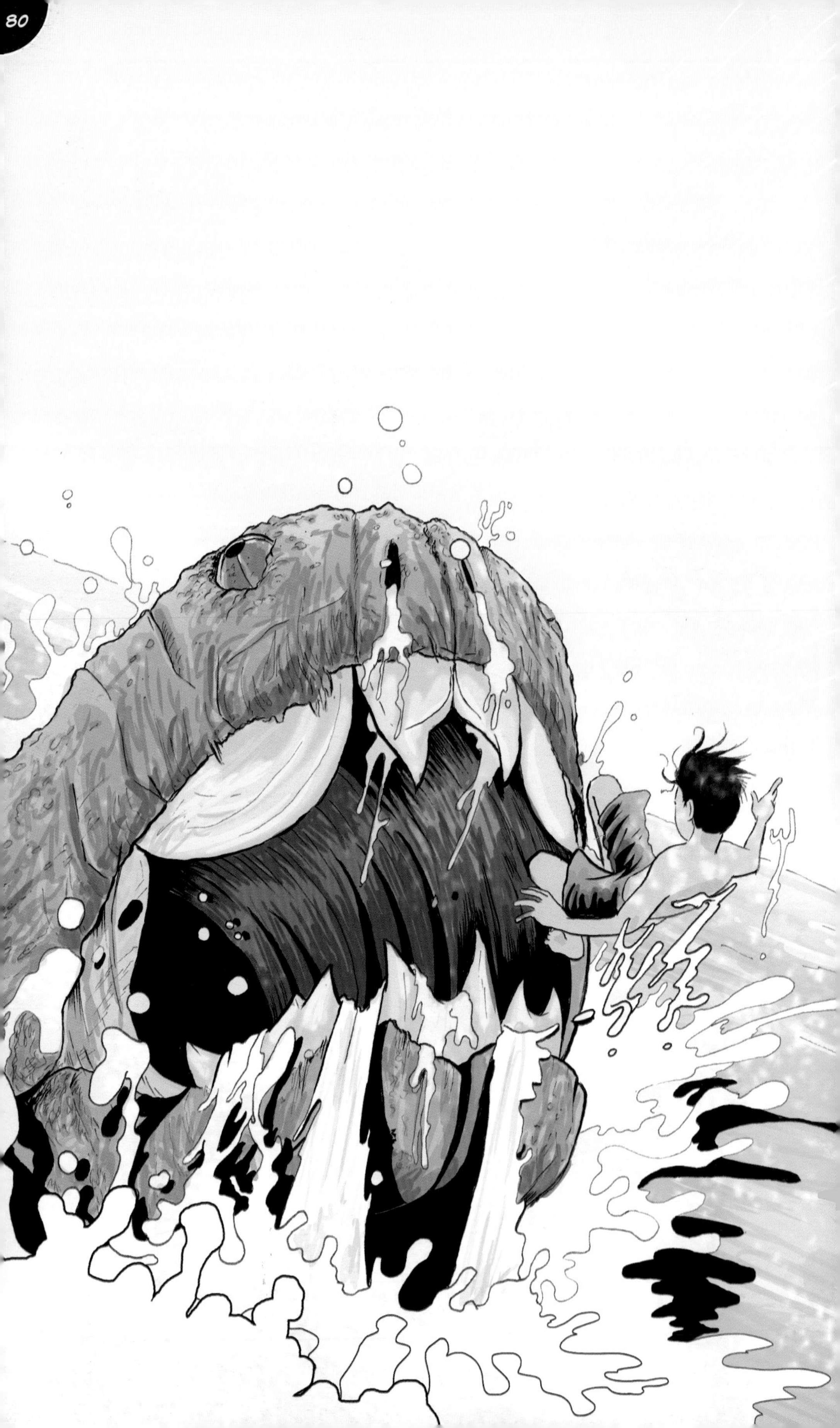

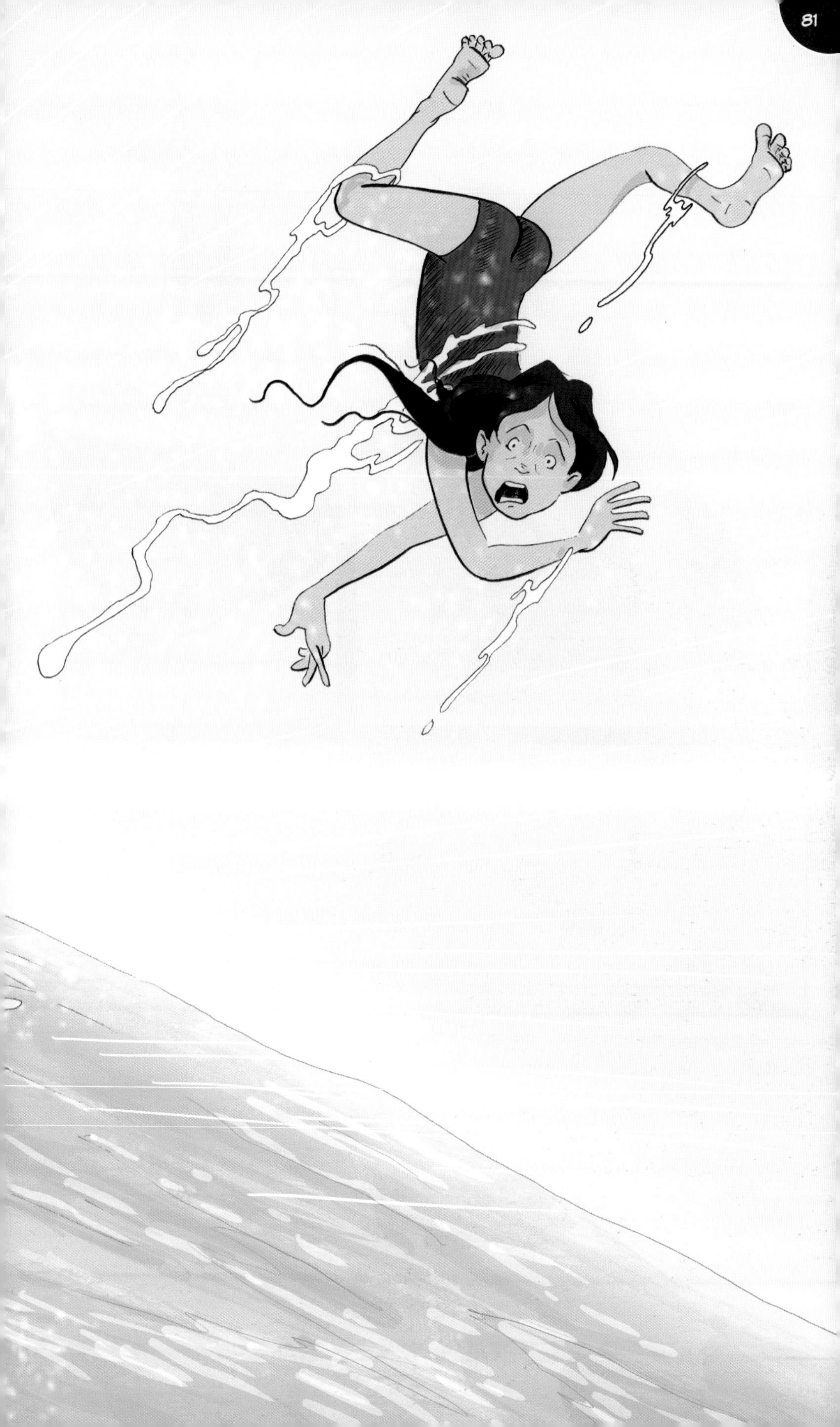

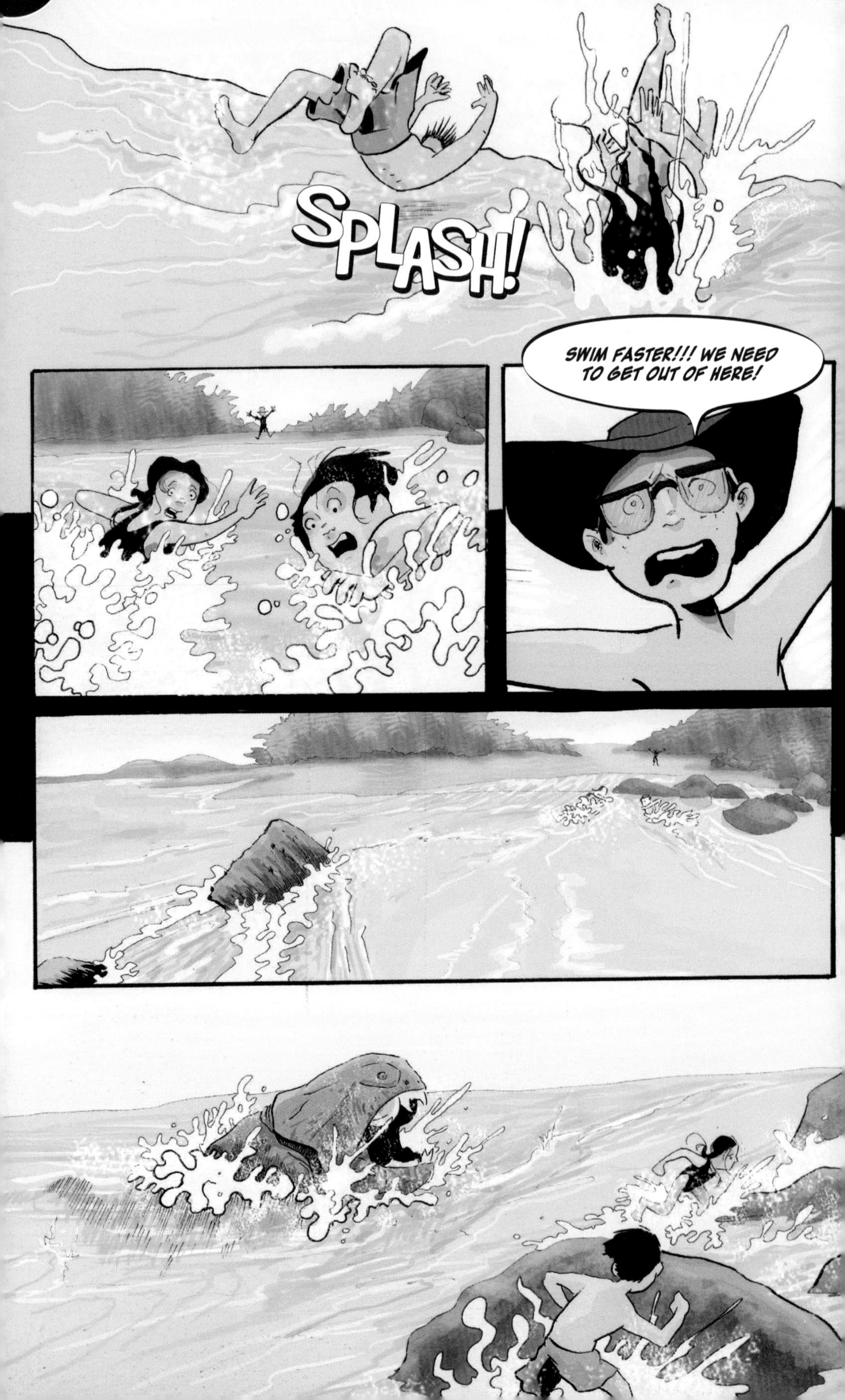
SPLASH!
SWIM FASTER!!! WE NEED TO GET OUT OF HERE!

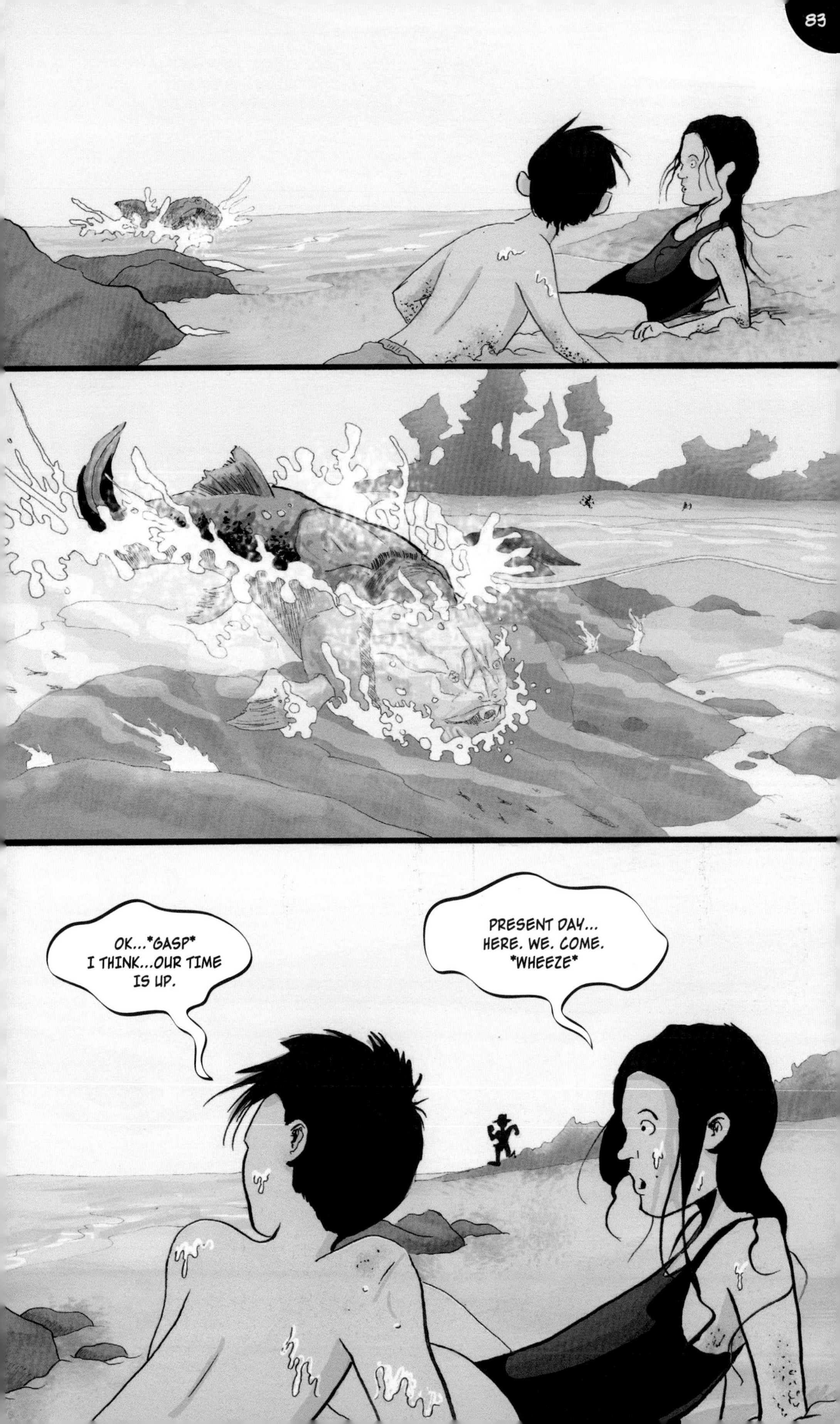
OK...*GASP*
I THINK...OUR TIME
IS UP.
PRESENT DAY...
HERE. WE. COME.
WHEEZE

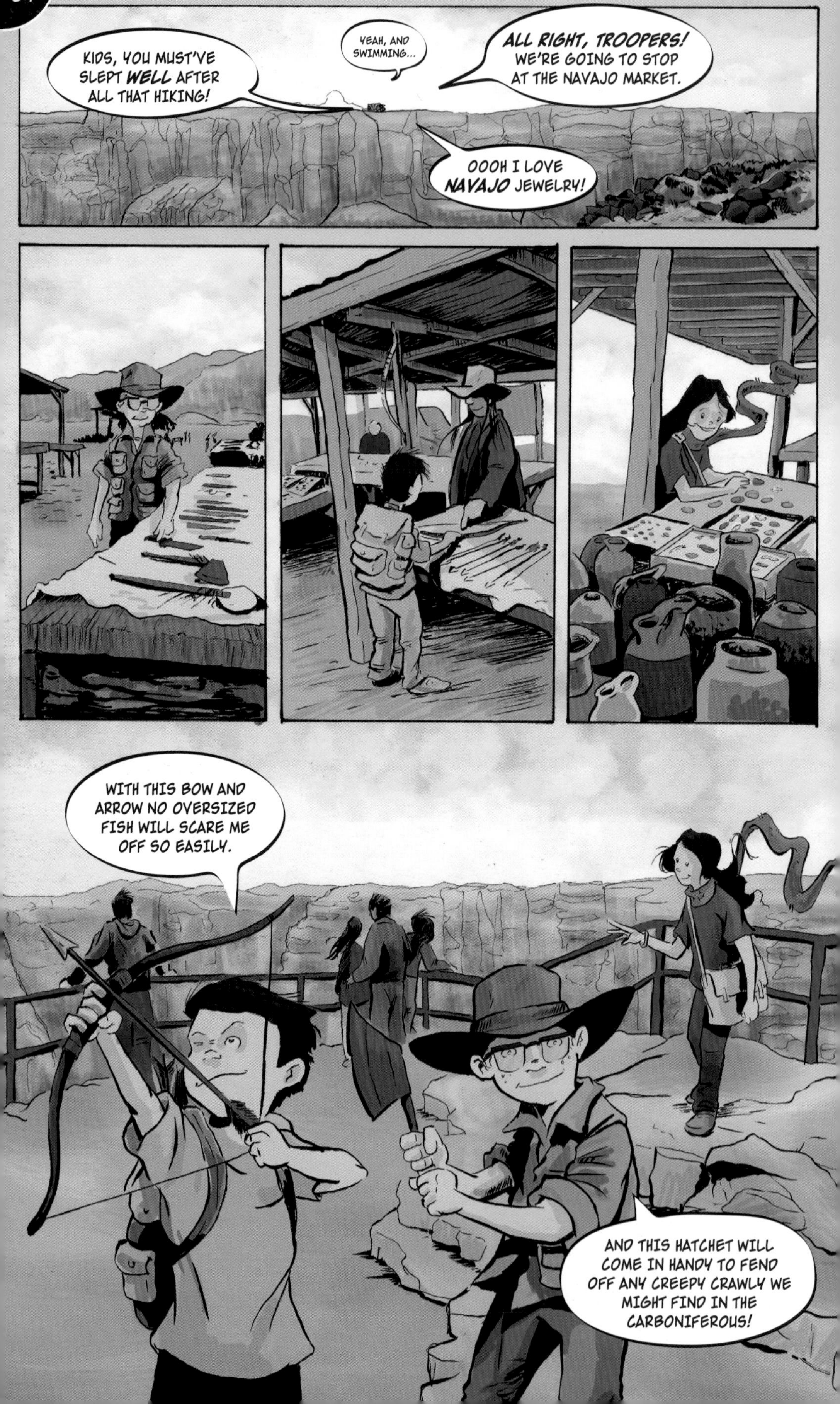
KIDS, YOU MUST'VE SLEPT WELL AFTER ALL THAT HIKING!
YEAH, AND SWIMMING...
ALL RIGHT, TROOPERS! WE'RE GOING TO STOP AT THE NAVAJO MARKET.
OOOH I LOVE NAVAJO JEWELRY!
WITH THIS BOW AND ARROW NO OVERSIZED FISH WILL SCARE ME OFF SO EASILY.
AND THIS HATCHET WILL COME IN HANDY TO FEND OFF ANY CREEPY CRAWLY WE MIGHT FIND IN THE CARBONIFEROUS!

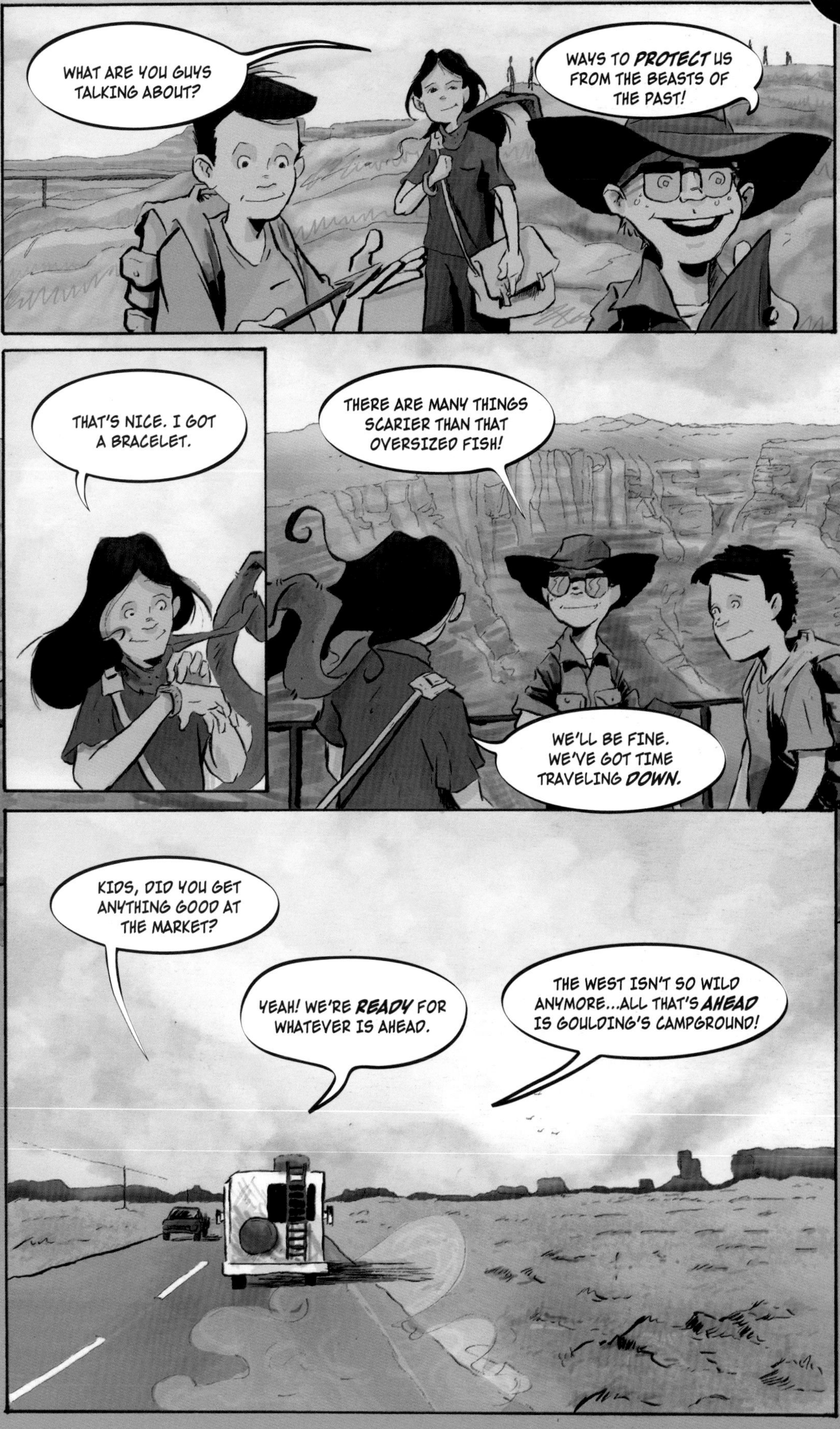
WHAT ARE YOU GUYS TALKING ABOUT?
WAYS TO PROTECT US FROM THE BEASTS OF THE PAST!
THAT'S NICE. I GOT A BRACELET.
THERE ARE MANY THINGS SCARIER THAN THAT OVERSIZED FISH!
WE'LL BE FINE. WE'VE GOT TIME TRAVELING DOWN.
KIDS, DID YOU GET ANYTHING GOOD AT THE MARKET?
YEAH! WE'RE READY FOR WHATEVER IS AHEAD.
THE WEST ISN'T SO WILD ANYMORE...ALL THAT'S AHEAD IS GOULDING'S CAMPGROUND!

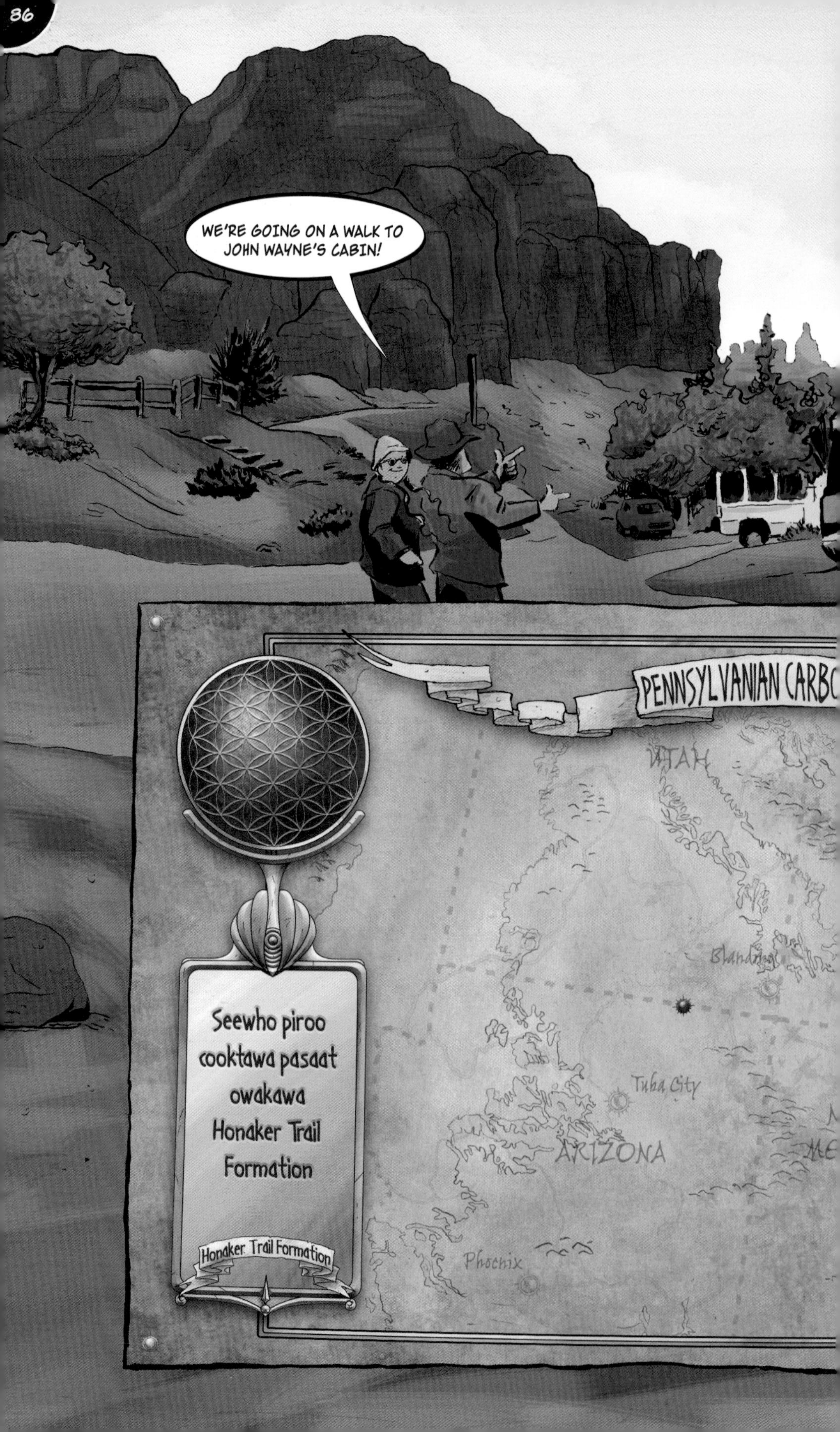
WE'RE GOING ON A WALK TO JOHN WAYNE'S CABIN!
PENNSYLVANIAN CARBO
UTAH
Blanding
Tuba City
ARIZONA
Phoenix
Seewho piroo cooktawa pasaat owakawa Honaker Trail Formation
Honaker Trail Formation

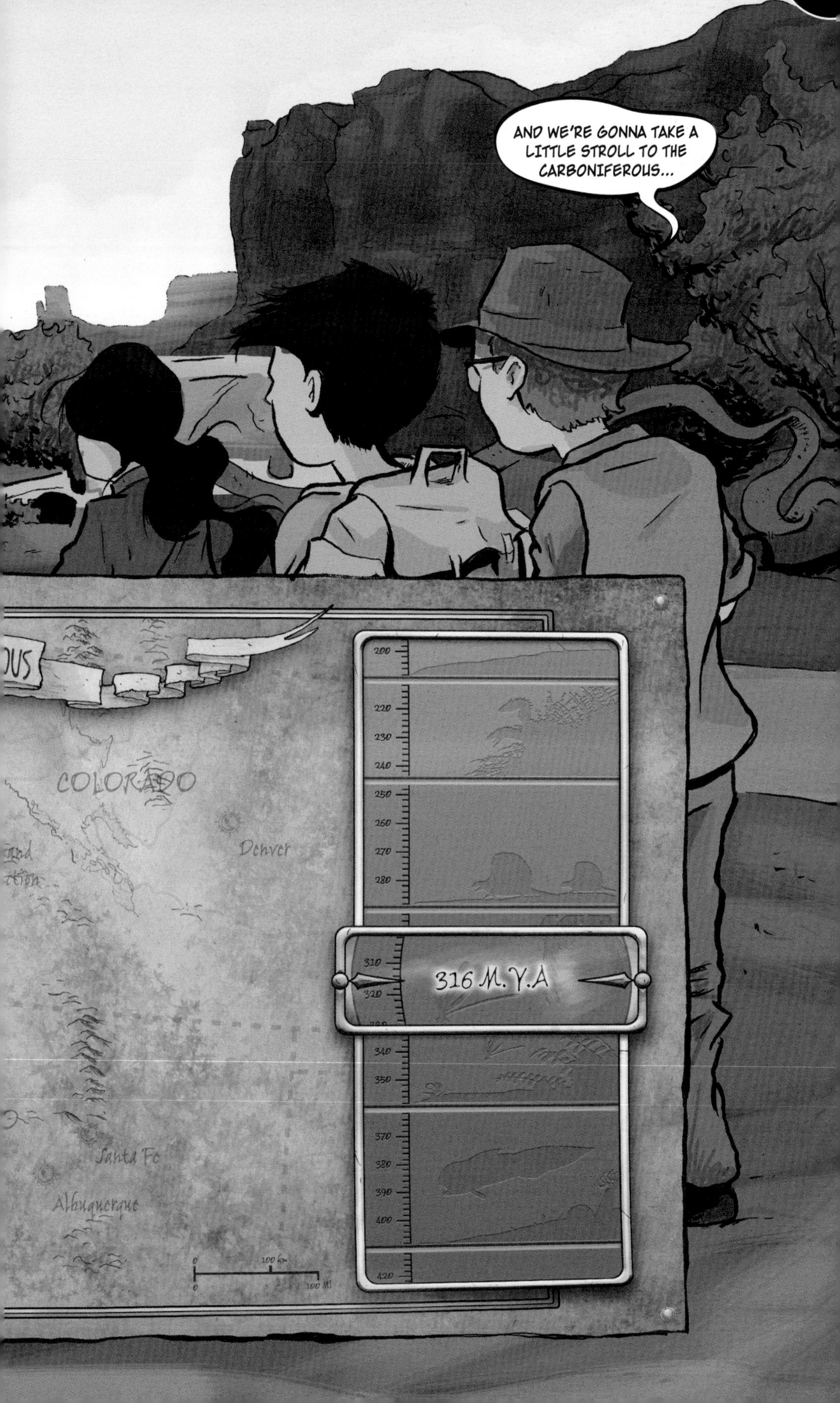
AND WE'RE GONNA TAKE A LITTLE STROLL TO THE CARBONIFEROUS...
OUS
COLORADO
Denver
Santa Fe
Albuquerque
200
220
230
240
250
260
270
280
310
320
340
350
370
380
390
400
420
316 M.Y.A

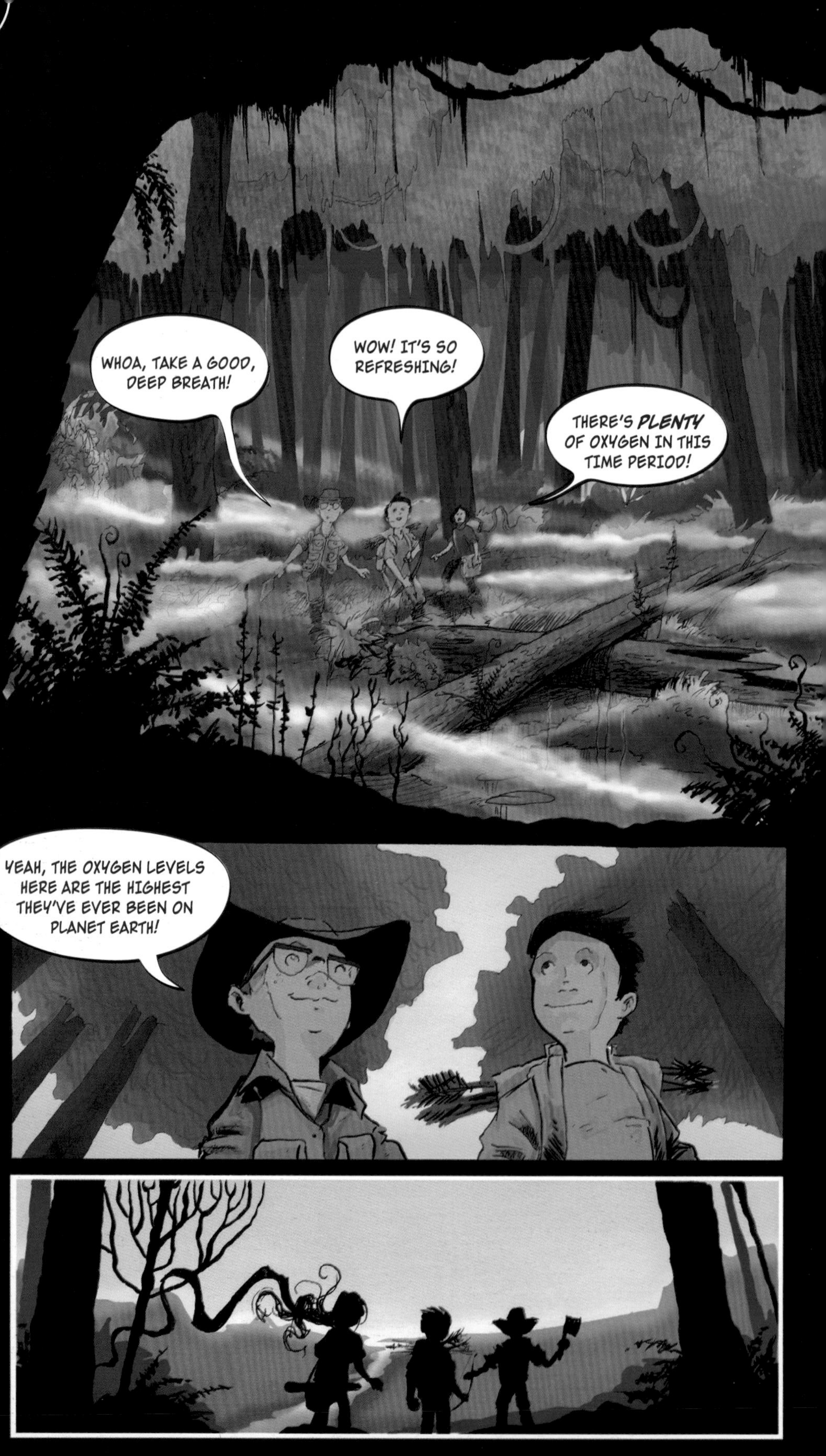
WHOA, TAKE A GOOD, DEEP BREATH!
WOW! IT'S SO REFRESHING!
THERE'S *PLENTY* OF OXYGEN IN THIS TIME PERIOD!
YEAH, THE OXYGEN LEVELS HERE ARE THE HIGHEST THEY'VE EVER BEEN ON PLANET EARTH!

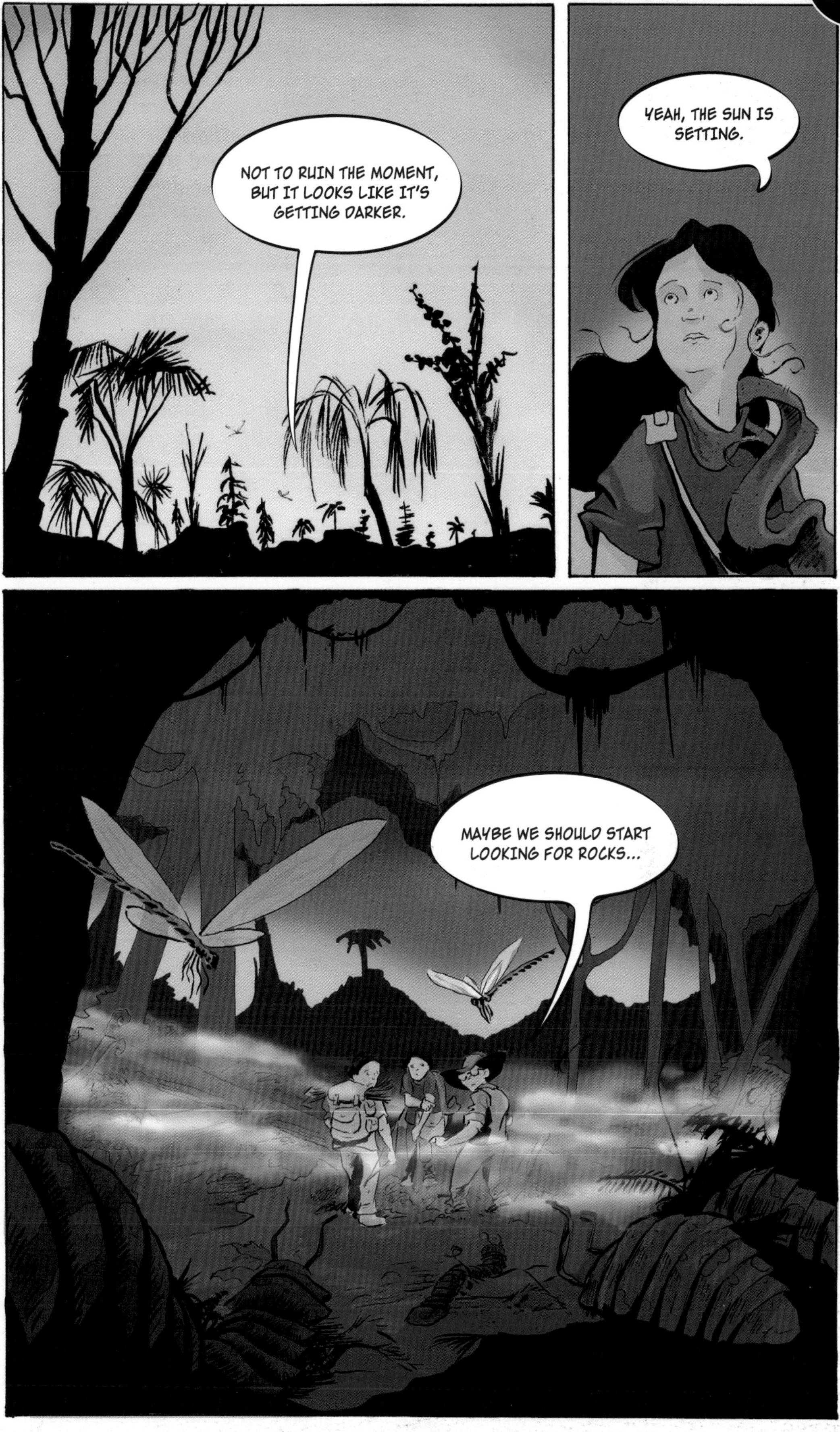
NOT TO RUIN THE MOMENT, BUT IT LOOKS LIKE IT'S GETTING DARKER.
YEAH, THE SUN IS SETTING.
MAYBE WE SHOULD START LOOKING FOR ROCKS...

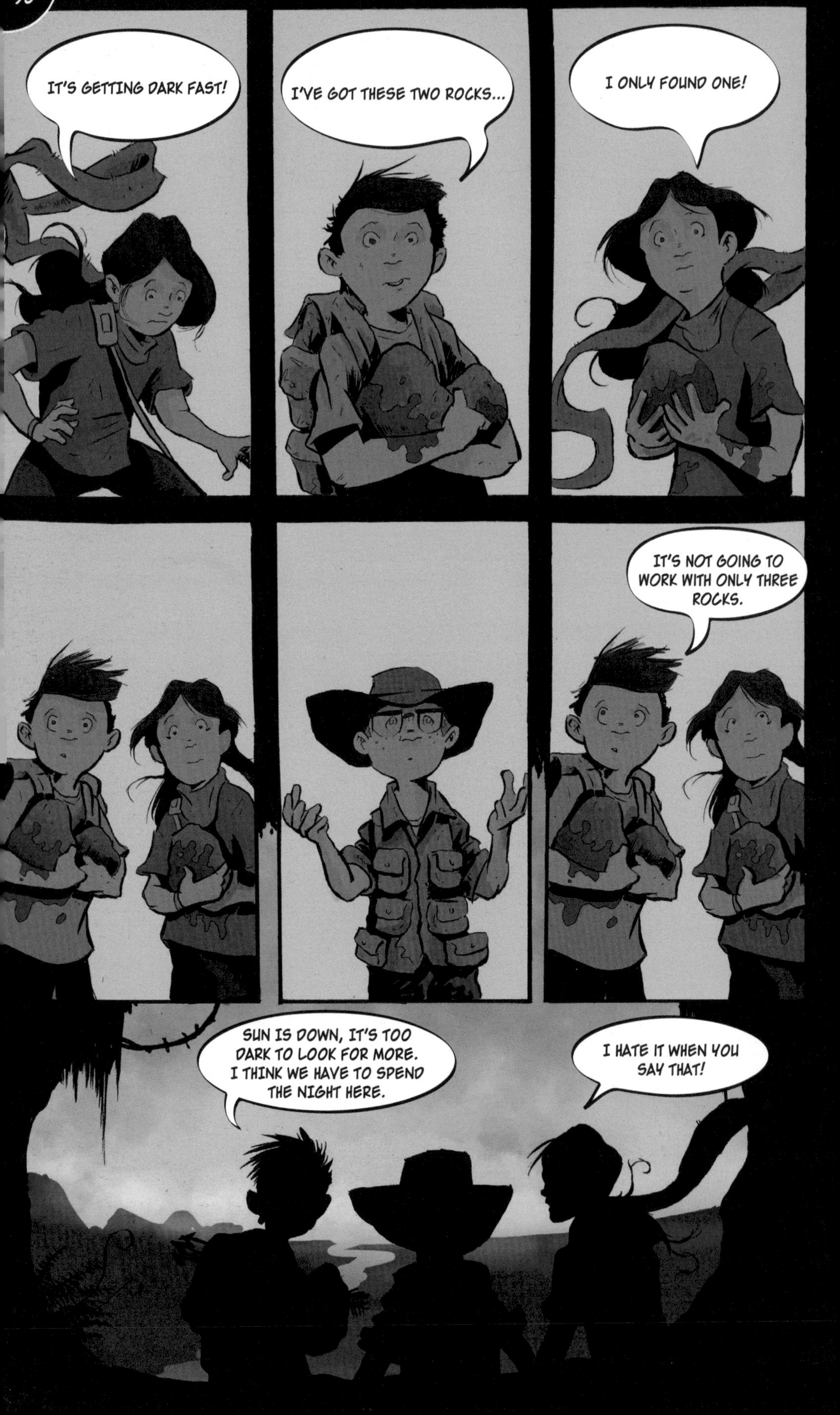

IT'S GETTING DARK FAST!
I'VE GOT THESE TWO ROCKS...
I ONLY FOUND ONE!
IT'S NOT GOING TO WORK WITH ONLY THREE ROCKS.
SUN IS DOWN, IT'S TOO DARK TO LOOK FOR MORE. I THINK WE HAVE TO SPEND THE NIGHT HERE.
I HATE IT WHEN YOU SAY THAT!

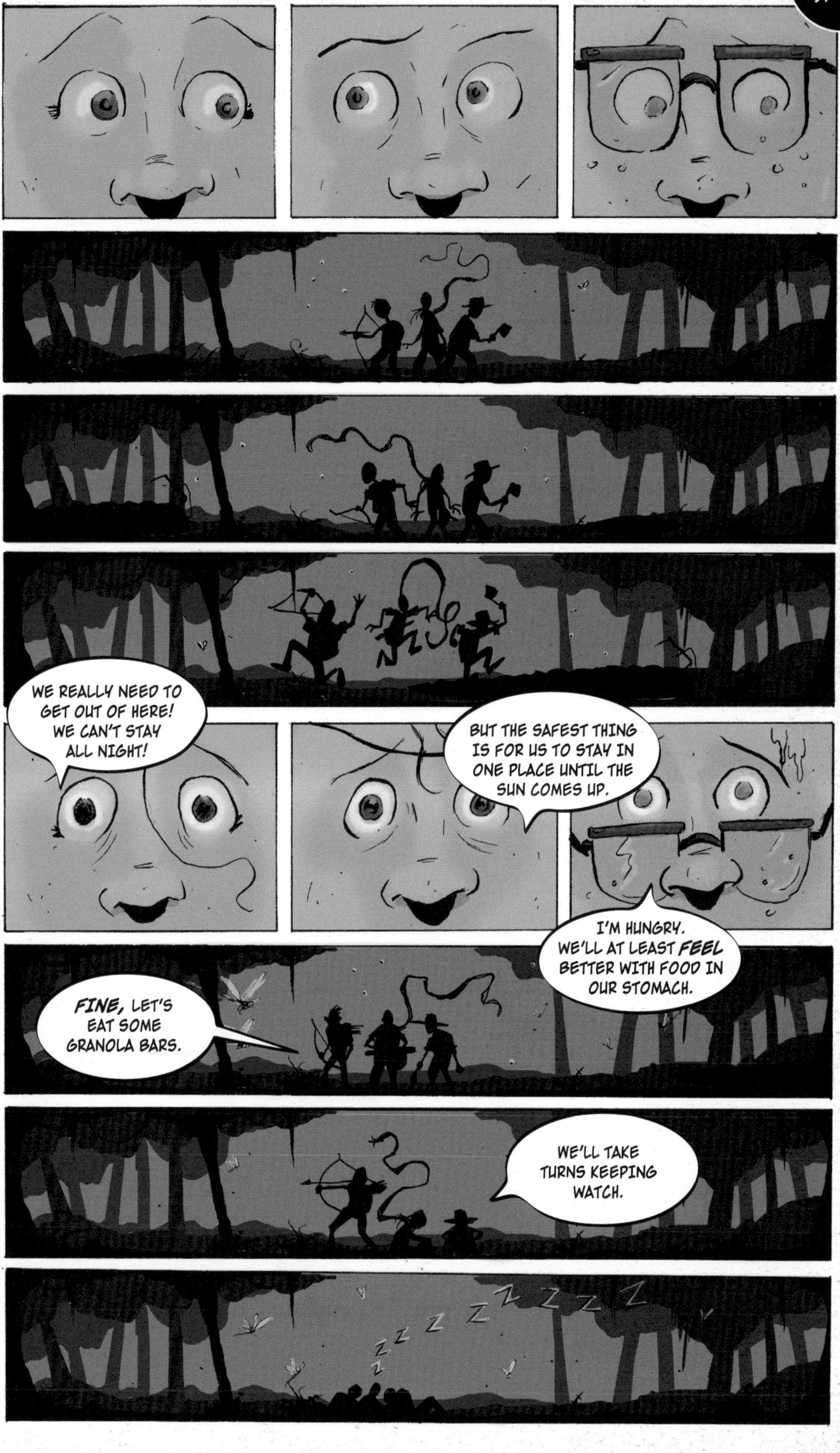
WE REALLY NEED TO GET OUT OF HERE! WE CAN'T STAY ALL NIGHT!
BUT THE SAFEST THING IS FOR US TO STAY IN ONE PLACE UNTIL THE SUN COMES UP.
I'M HUNGRY. WE'LL AT LEAST FEEL BETTER WITH FOOD IN OUR STOMACH.
FINE, LET'S EAT SOME GRANOLA BARS.
WE'LL TAKE TURNS KEEPING WATCH.
Z Z Z Z Z Z Z Z Z Z Z

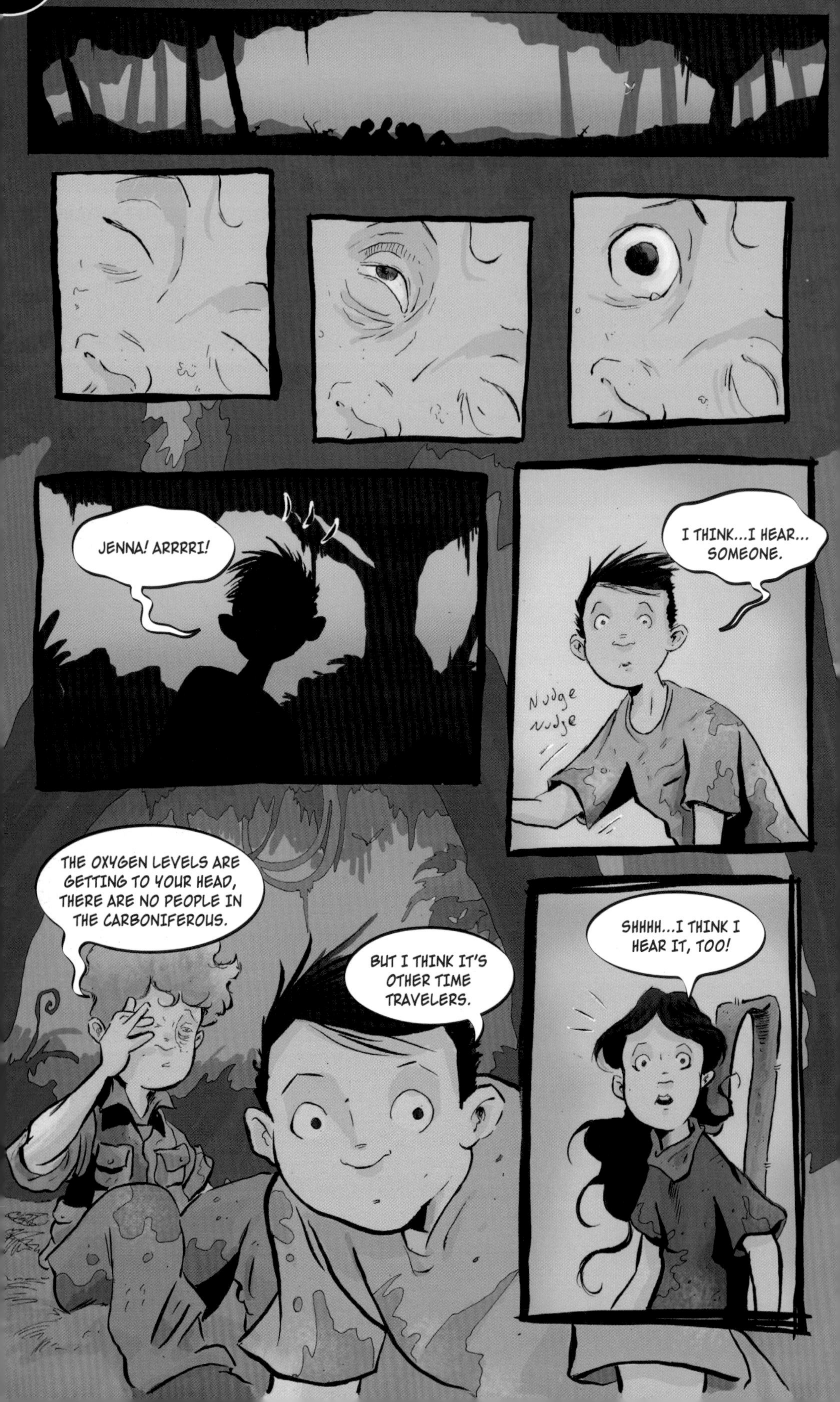
JENNA! ARRRRI!
I THINK...I HEAR... SOMEONE.
Nudge nudge
THE OXYGEN LEVELS ARE GETTING TO YOUR HEAD, THERE ARE NO PEOPLE IN THE CARBONIFEROUS.
BUT I THINK IT'S OTHER TIME TRAVELERS.
SHHHH...I THINK I HEAR IT, TOO!

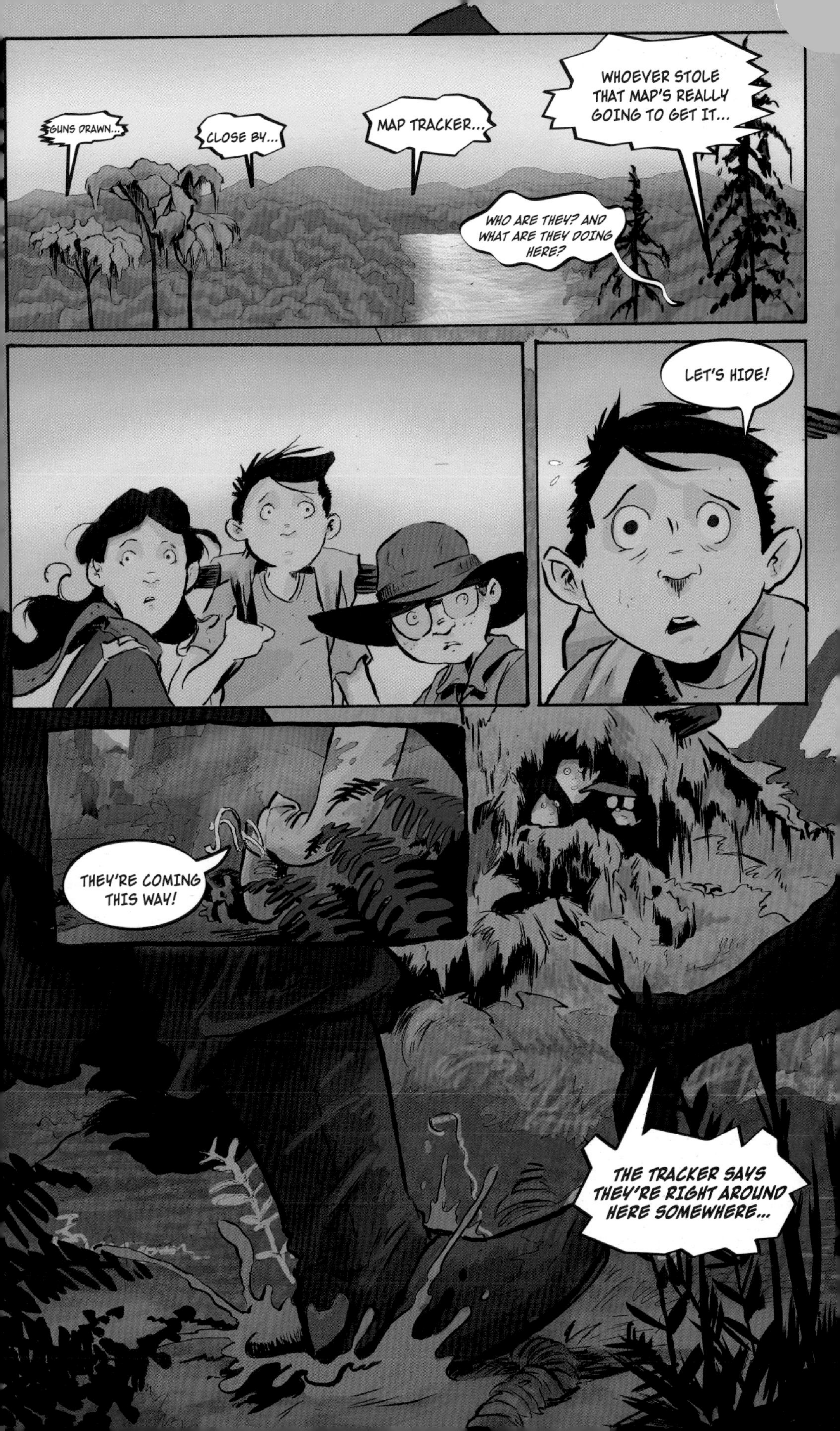
GUNS DRAWN...
CLOSE BY...
MAP TRACKER...
WHOEVER STOLE THAT MAP'S REALLY GOING TO GET IT...
WHO ARE THEY? AND WHAT ARE THEY DOING HERE?
LET'S HIDE!
THEY'RE COMING THIS WAY!
THE TRACKER SAYS THEY'RE RIGHT AROUND HERE SOMEWHERE...

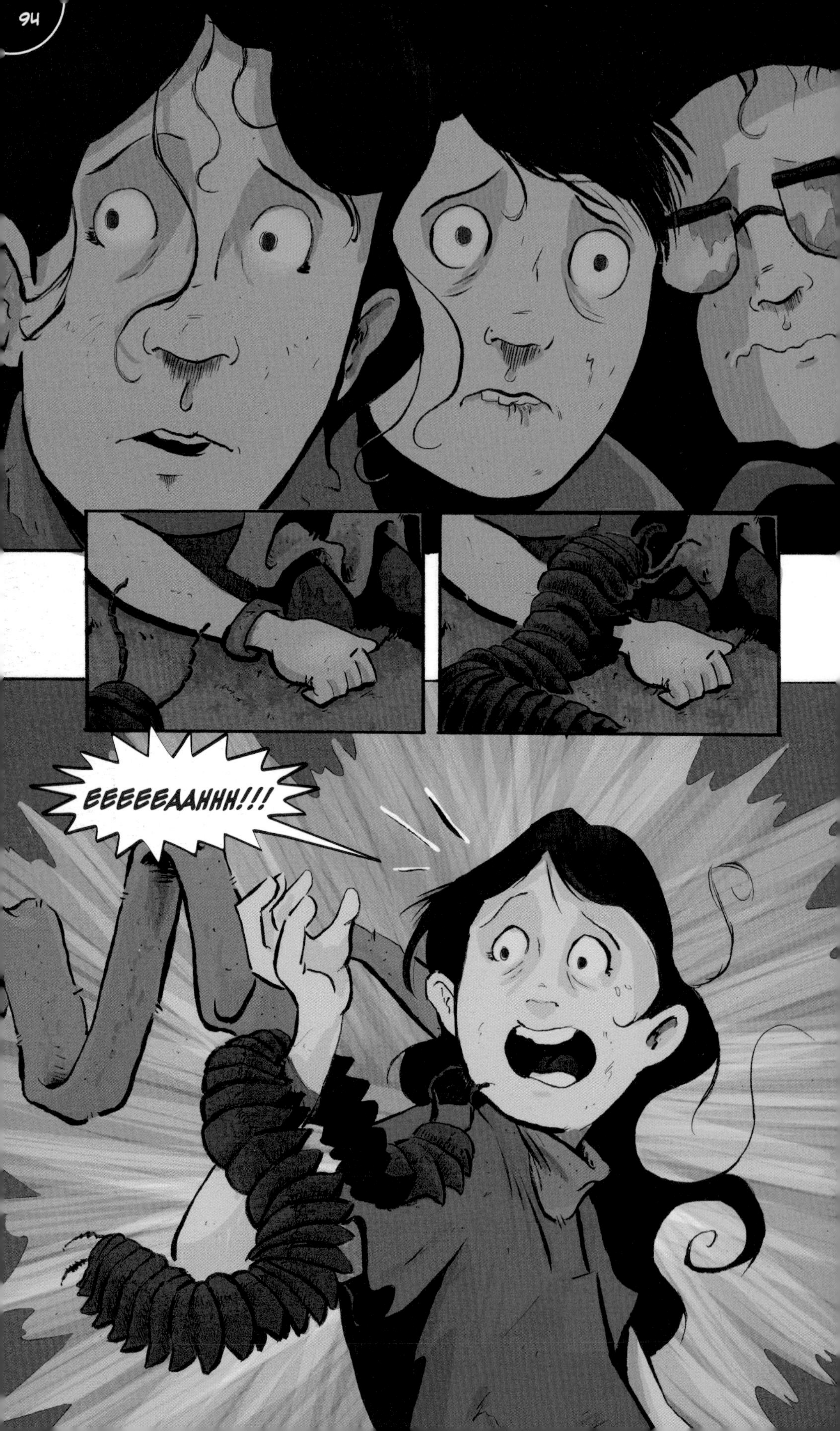
EEEEEEAAHHH!!!

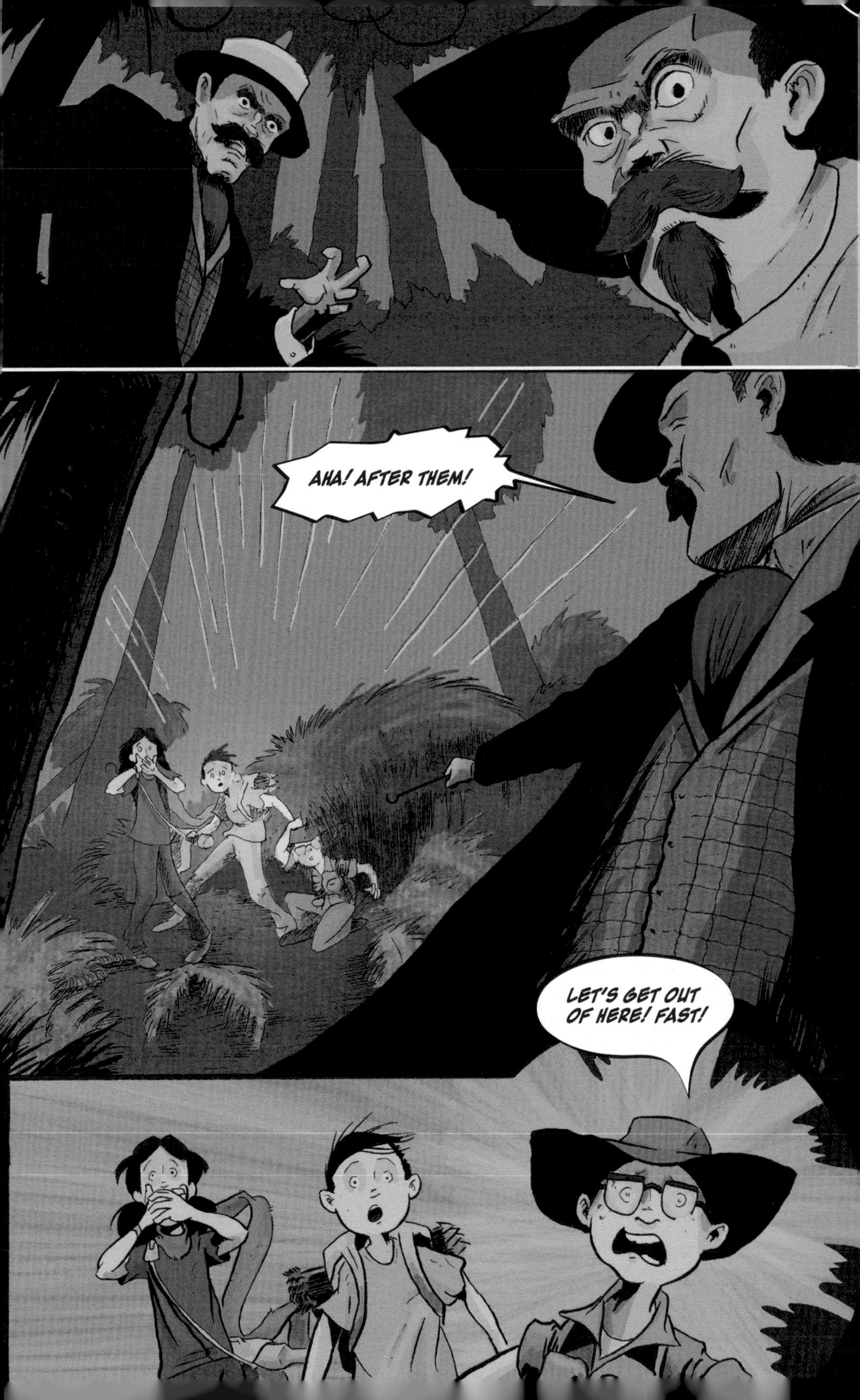
AHA! AFTER THEM!
LET'S GET OUT OF HERE! FAST!

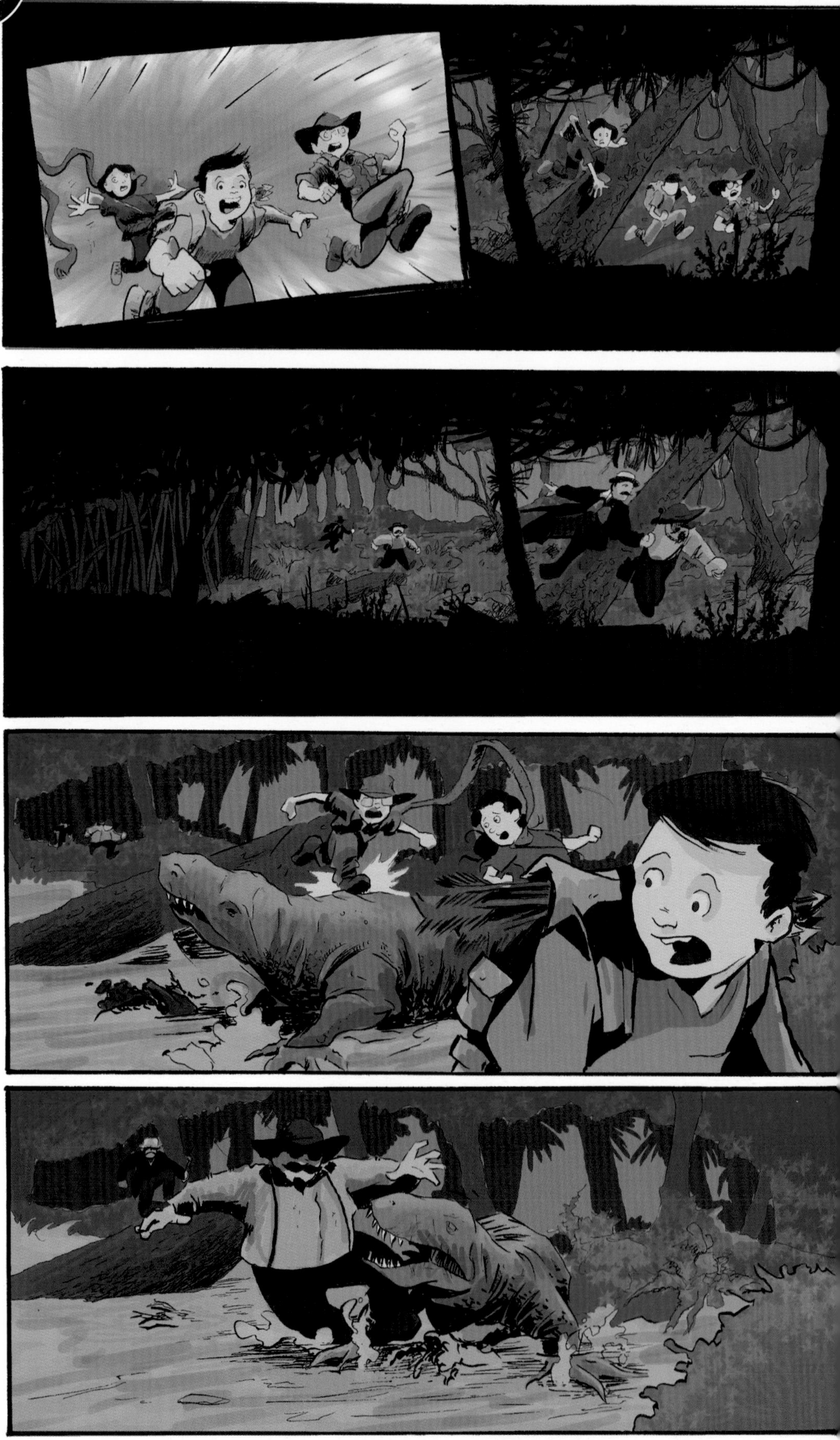

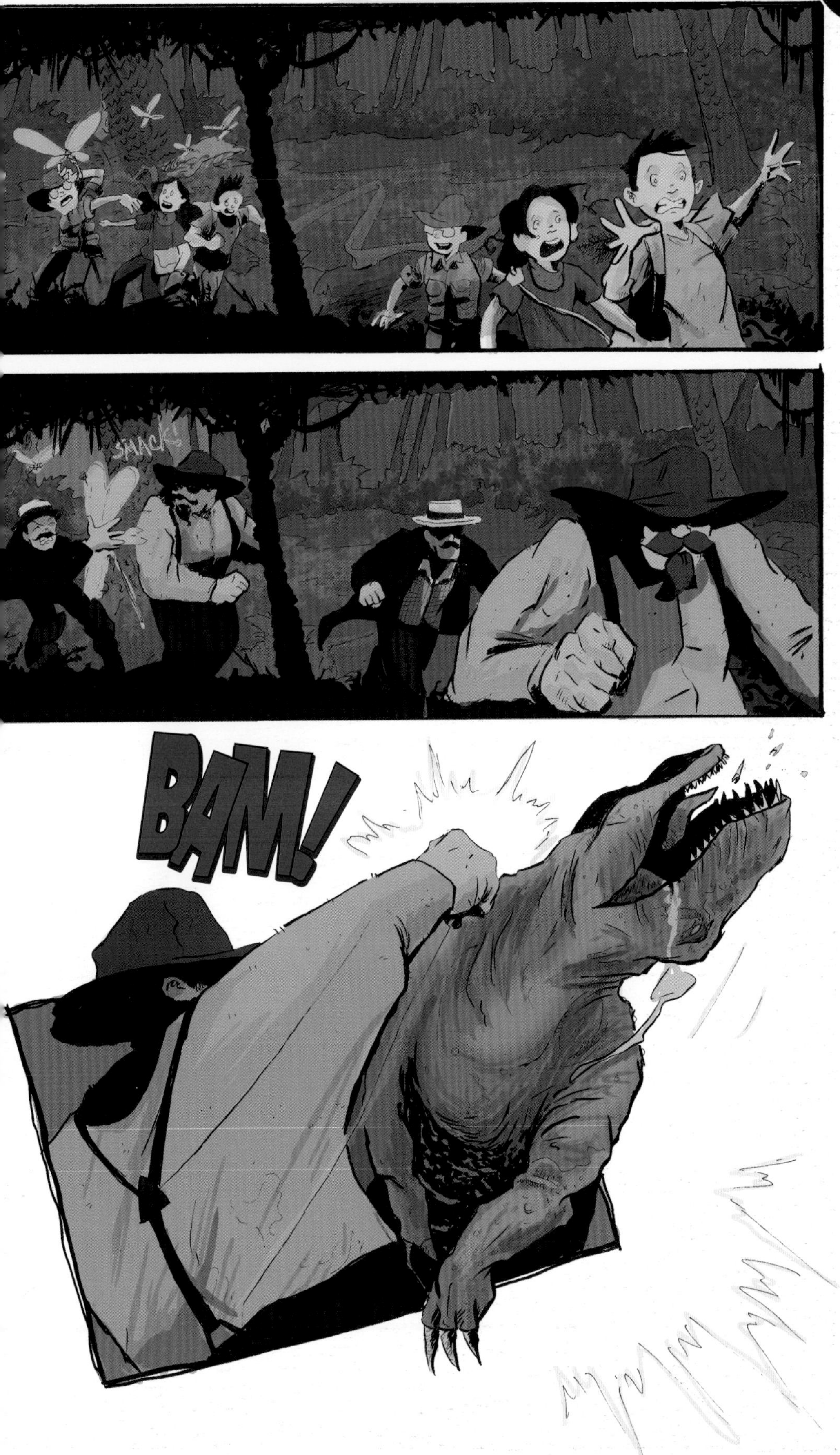
SMACK!
BAM!

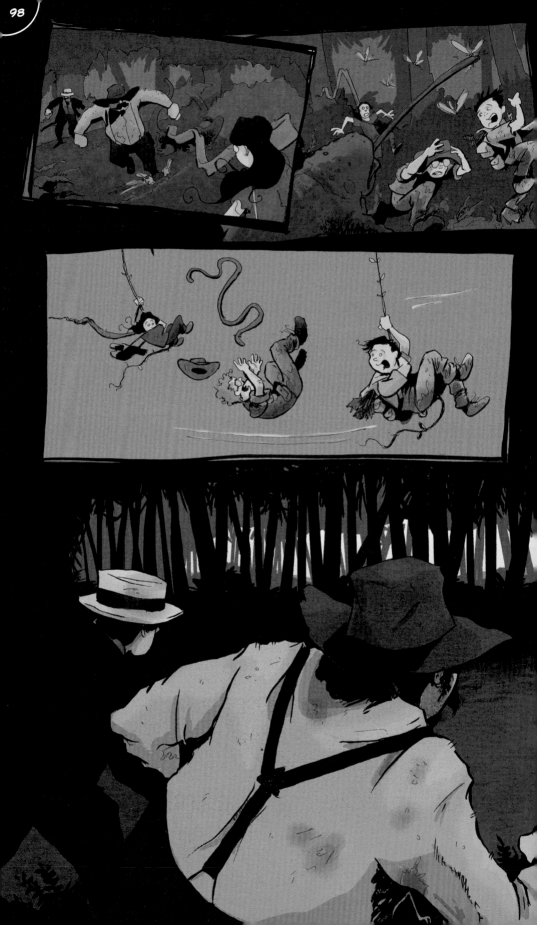

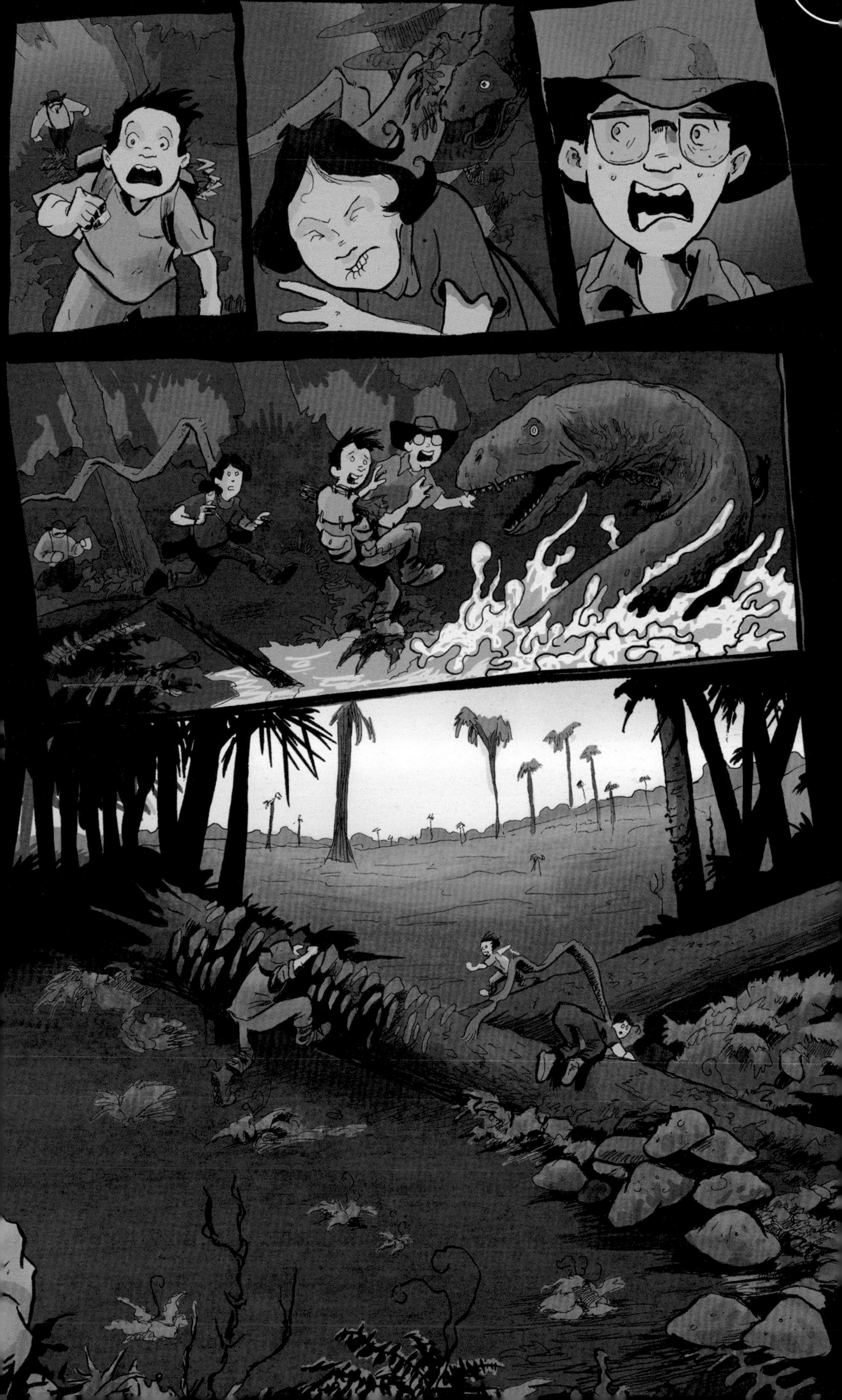

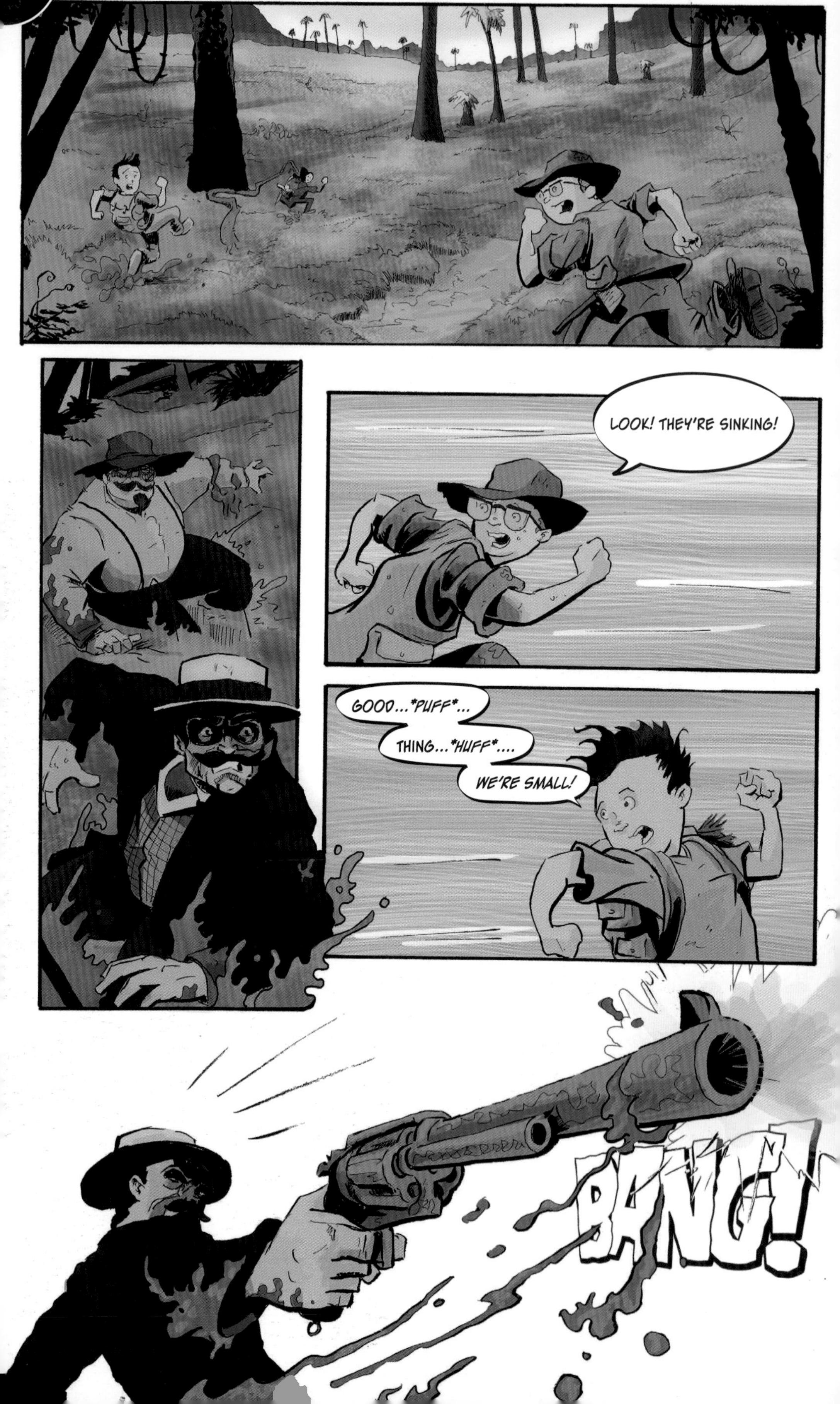
LOOK! THEY'RE SINKING!
GOOD...*PUFF*...
THING...*HUFF*....
WE'RE SMALL!
BANG!

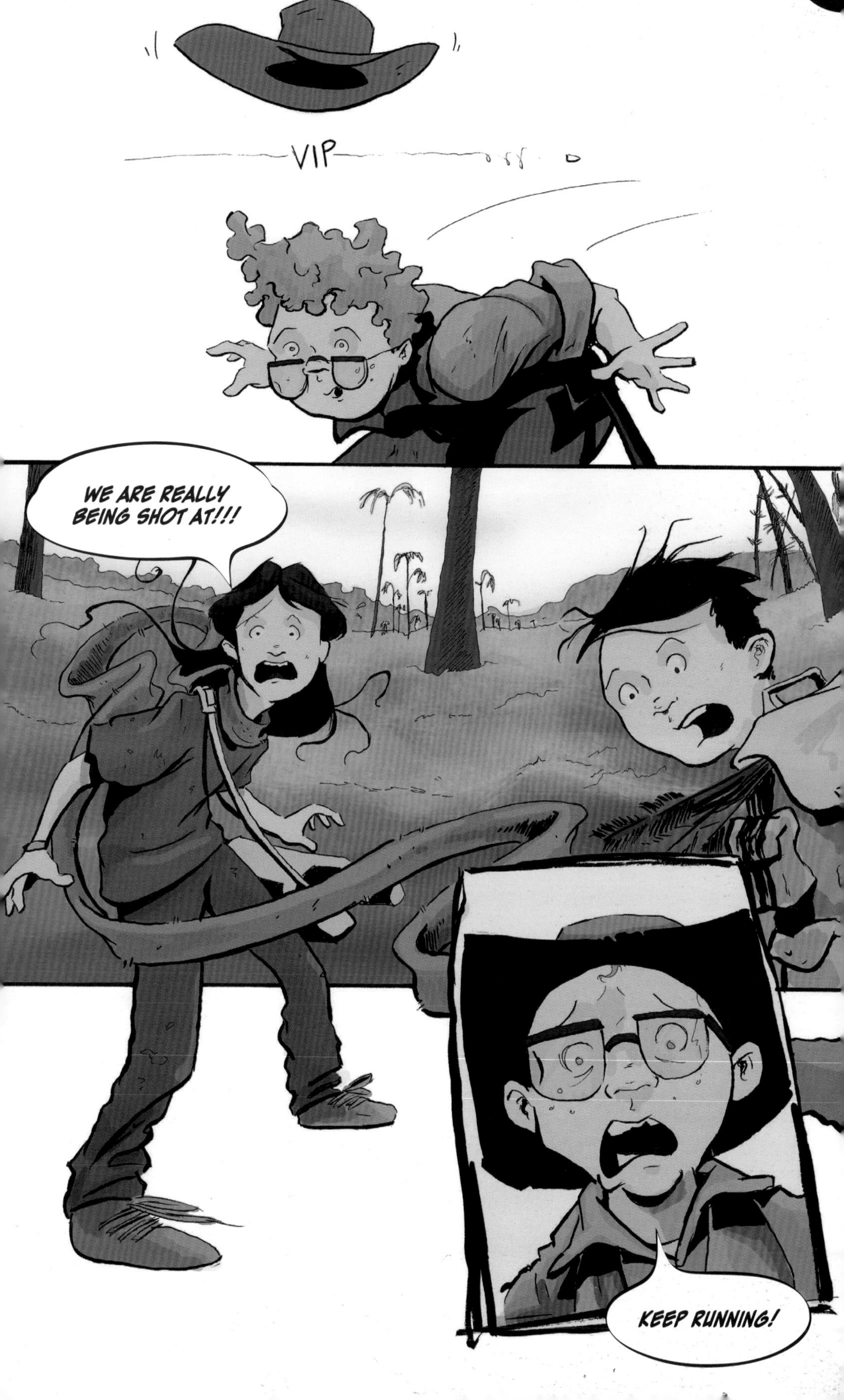
VIP
WE ARE REALLY BEING SHOT AT!!!
KEEP RUNNING!

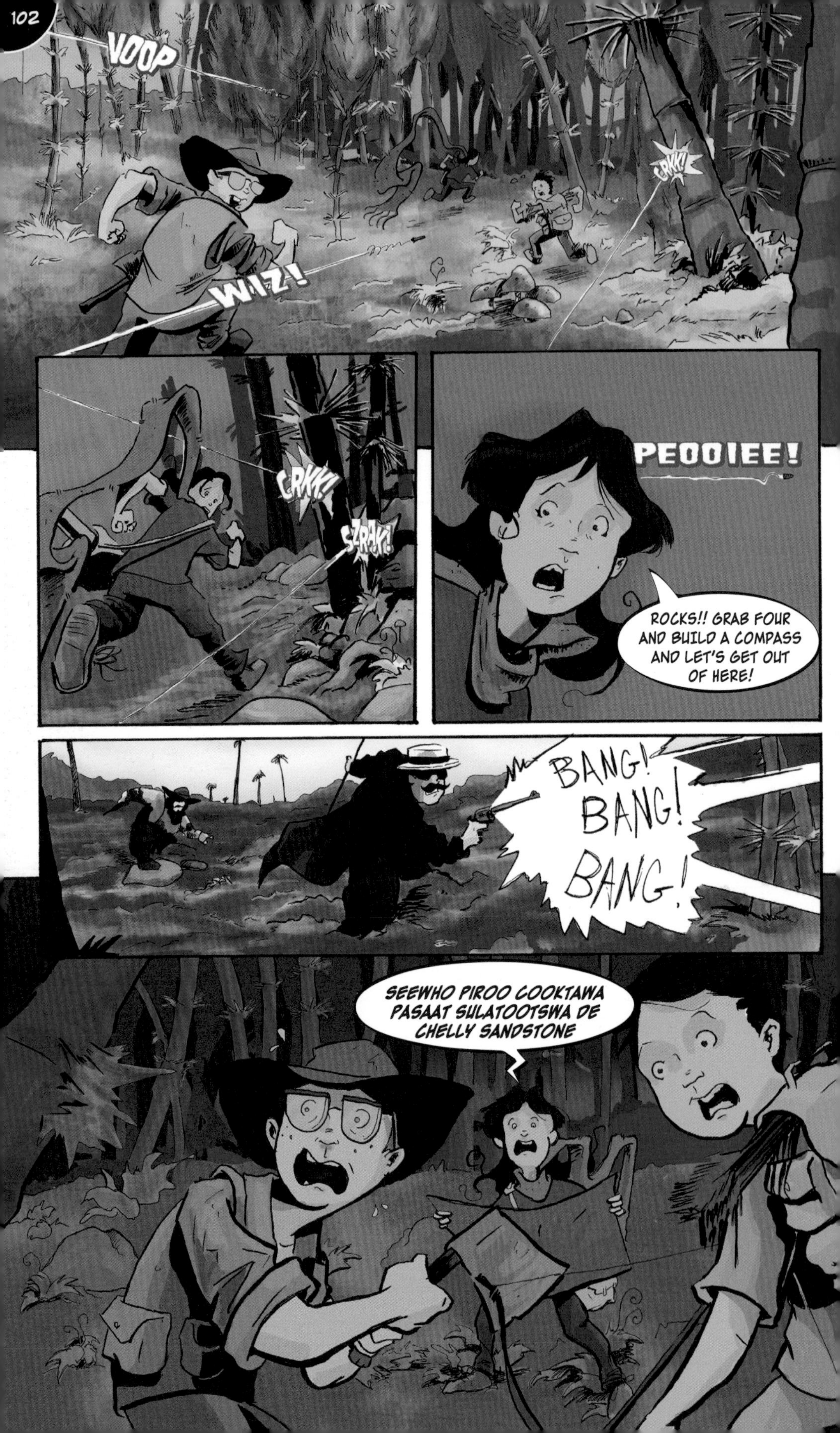
VOOP
CRKK!
WIZ!
CRKK!
SZRAK!
PEOOIEE!
ROCKS!! GRAB FOUR AND BUILD A COMPASS AND LET'S GET OUT OF HERE!
BANG! BANG! BANG!
SEEWHO PIROO COOKTAWA PASAAT SULATOOTSWA DE CHELLY SANDSTONE

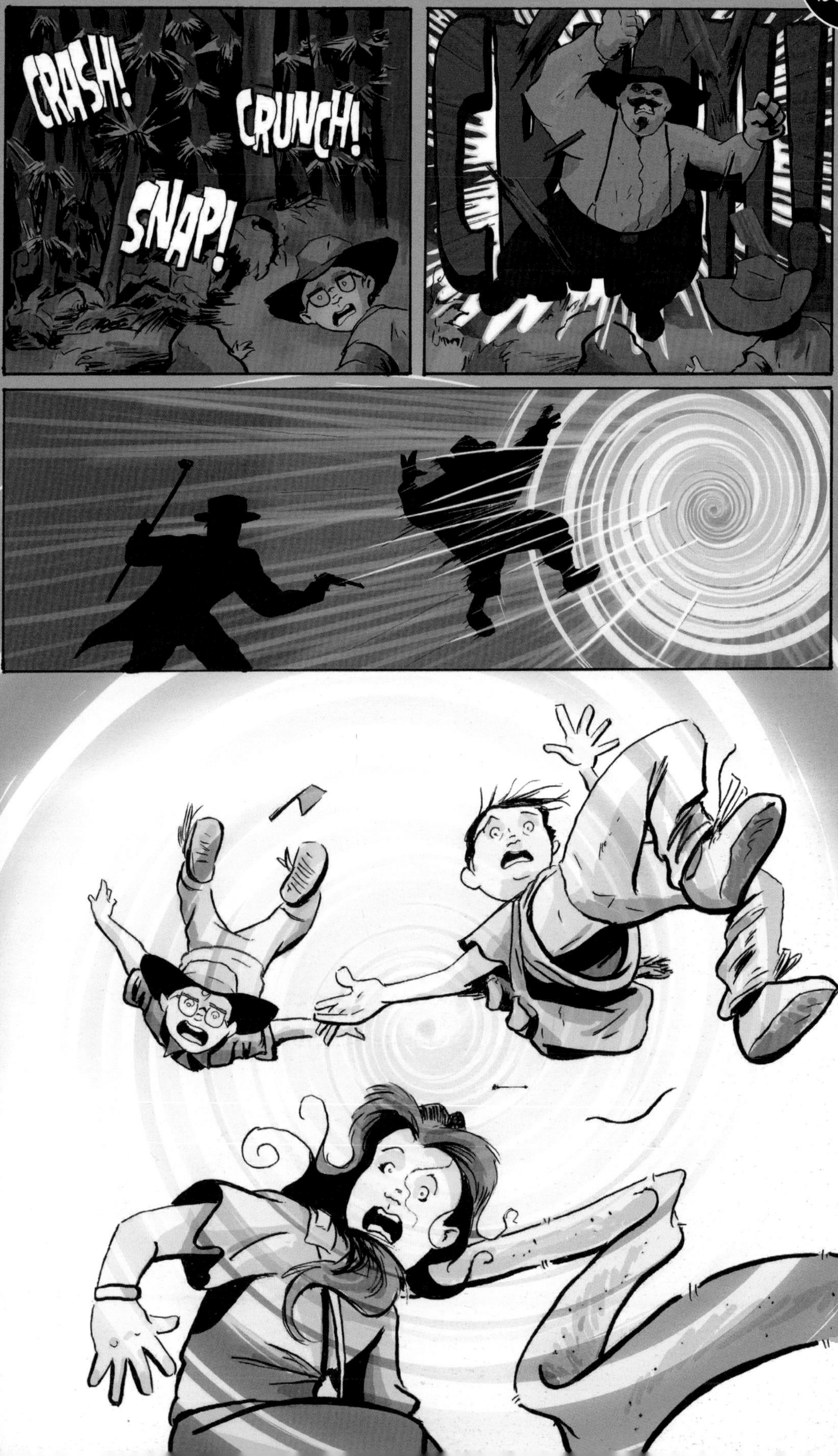
CRASH!
CRUNCH!
SNAP!

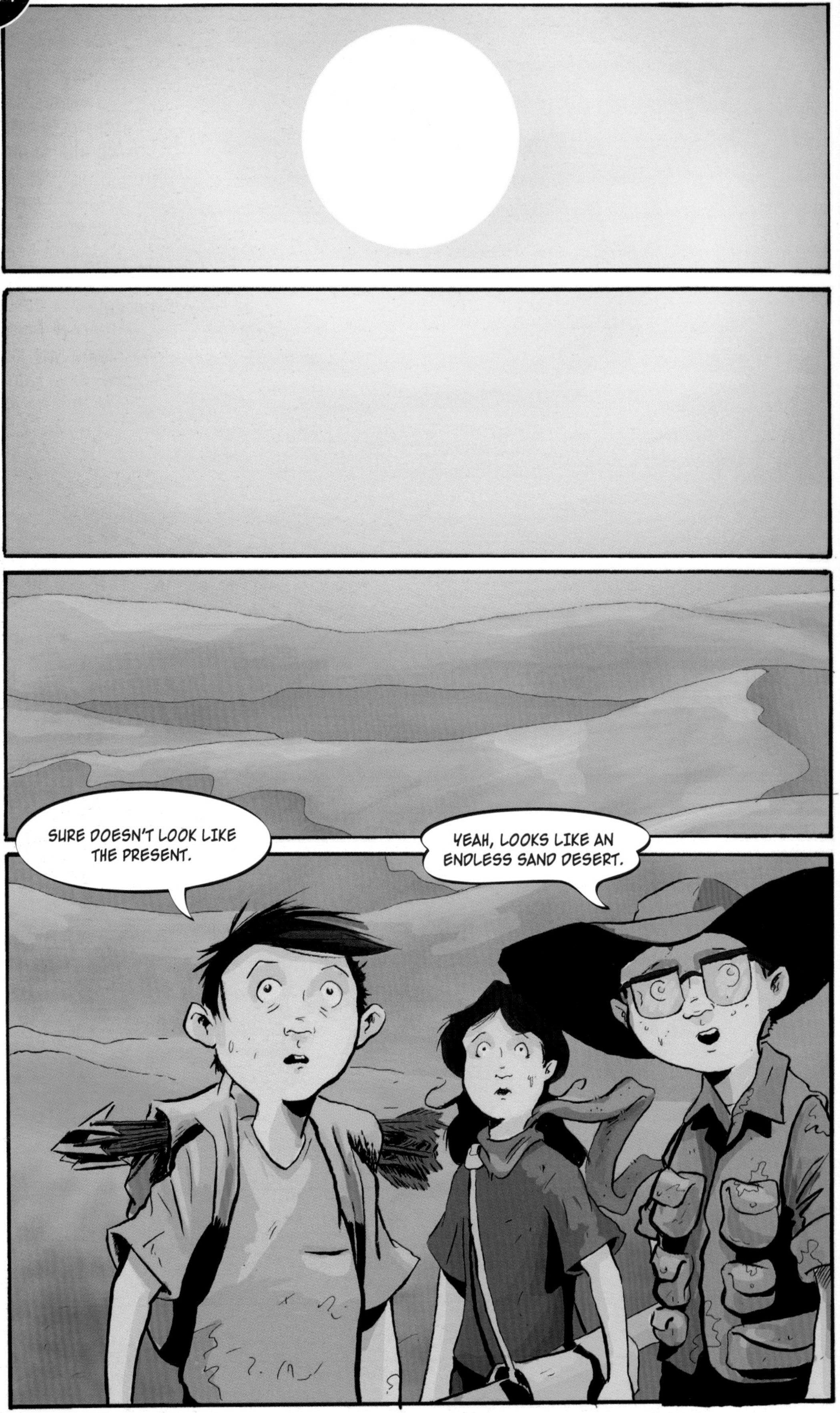
SURE DOESN'T LOOK LIKE THE PRESENT.
YEAH, LOOKS LIKE AN ENDLESS SAND DESERT.

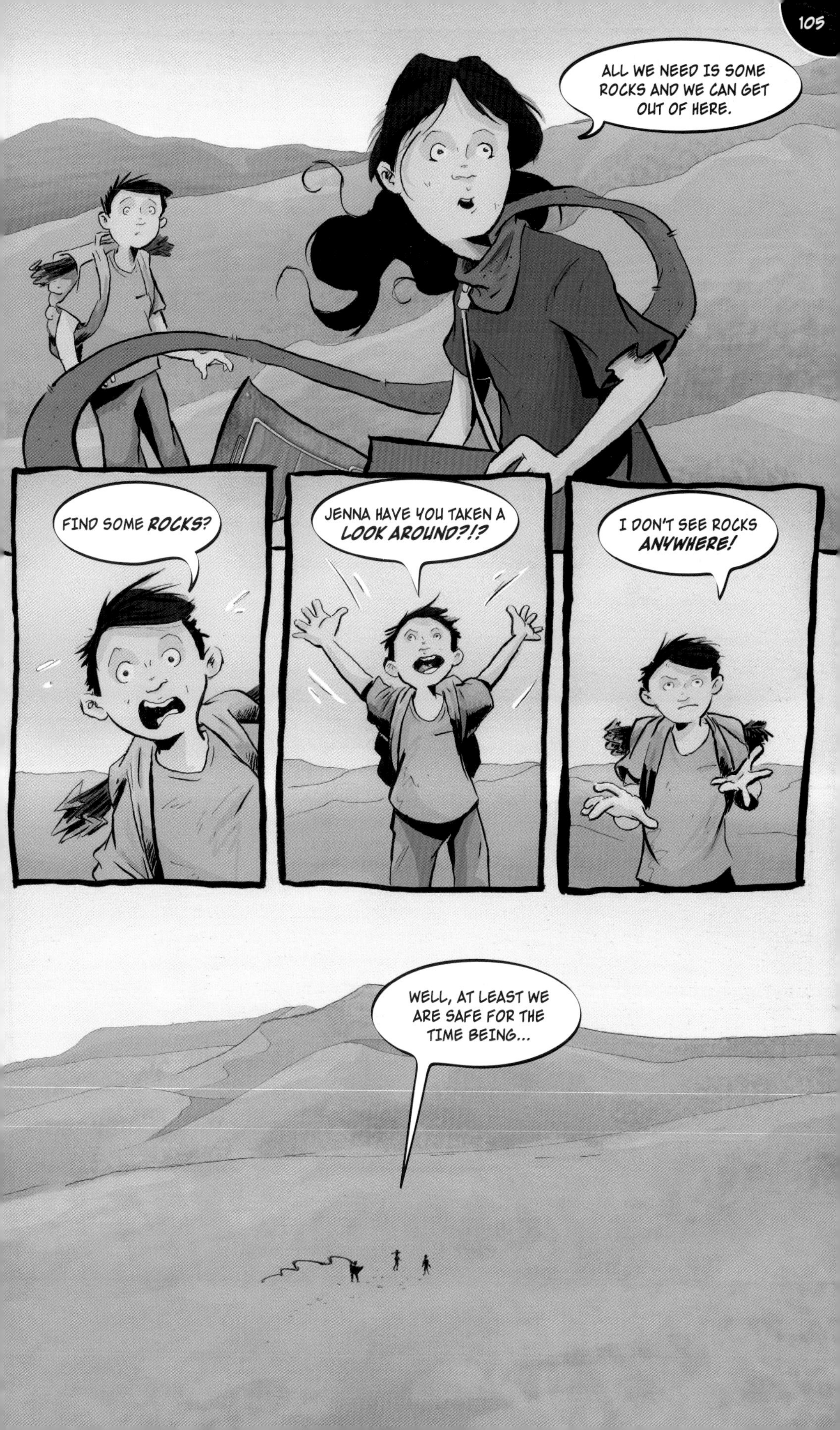
ALL WE NEED IS SOME ROCKS AND WE CAN GET OUT OF HERE.
FIND SOME ROCKS?
JENNA HAVE YOU TAKEN A LOOK AROUND?!?
I DON'T SEE ROCKS ANYWHERE!
WELL, AT LEAST WE ARE SAFE FOR THE TIME BEING...

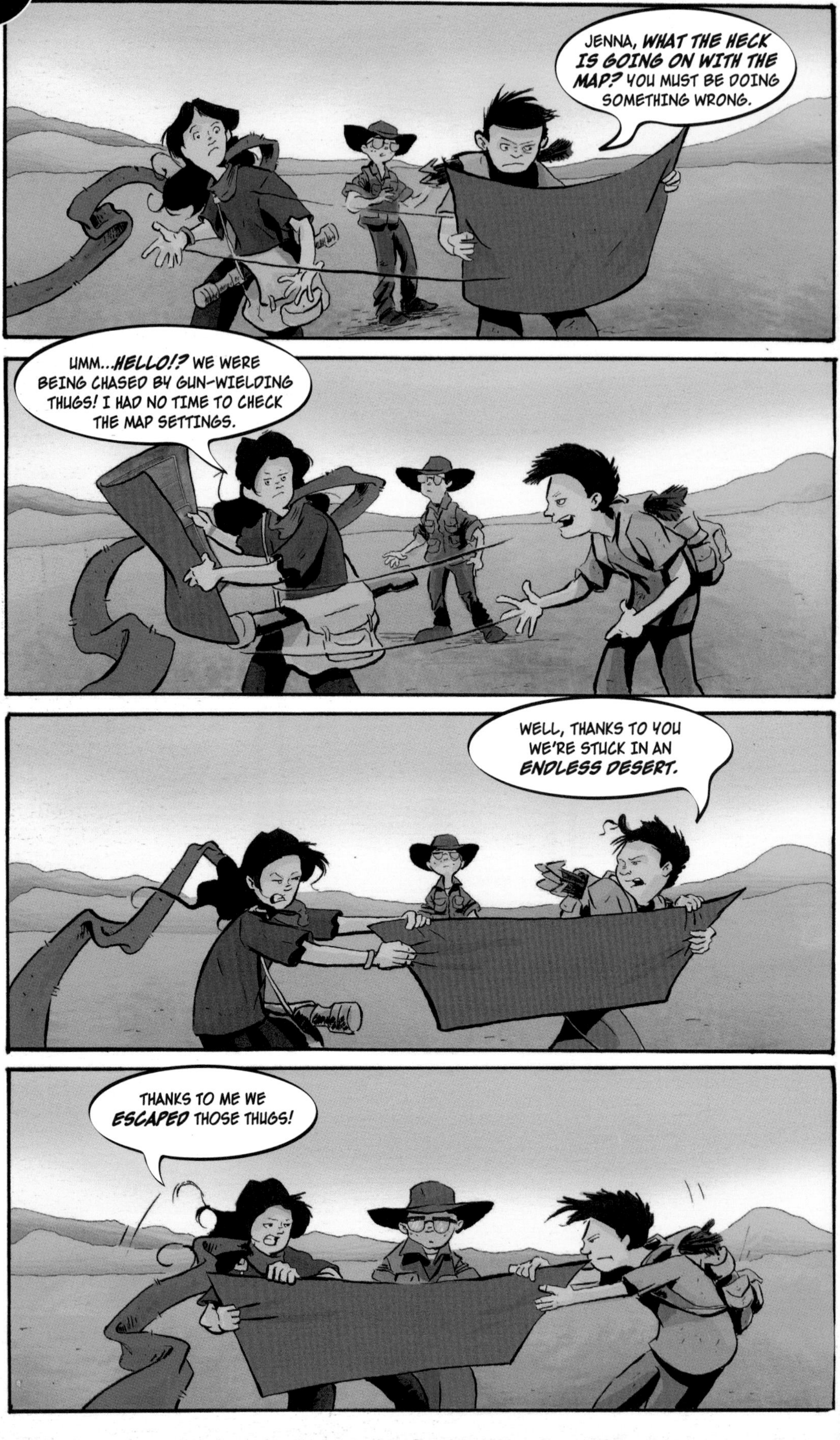
JENNA, WHAT THE HECK IS GOING ON WITH THE MAP? YOU MUST BE DOING SOMETHING WRONG.
UMM...HELLO!? WE WERE BEING CHASED BY GUN-WIELDING THUGS! I HAD NO TIME TO CHECK THE MAP SETTINGS.
WELL, THANKS TO YOU WE'RE STUCK IN AN ENDLESS DESERT.
THANKS TO ME WE ESCAPED THOSE THUGS!

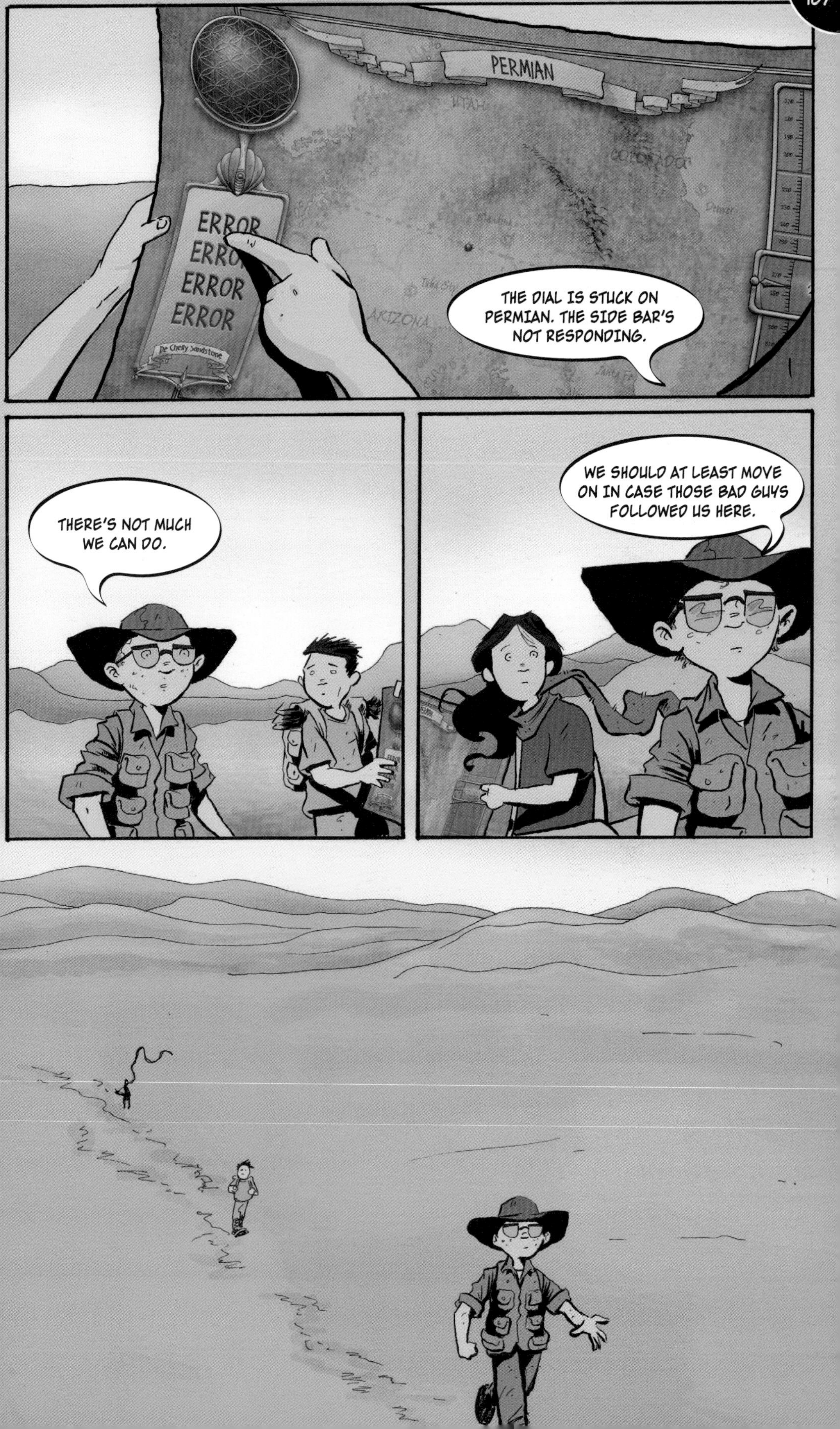
PERMIAN
UTAH
COLORADO
ERROR
ERROR
ERROR
ERROR
De Chelly Sandstone
ARIZONA
THE DIAL IS STUCK ON PERMIAN. THE SIDE BAR'S NOT RESPONDING.
THERE'S NOT MUCH WE CAN DO.
WE SHOULD AT LEAST MOVE ON IN CASE THOSE BAD GUYS FOLLOWED US HERE.

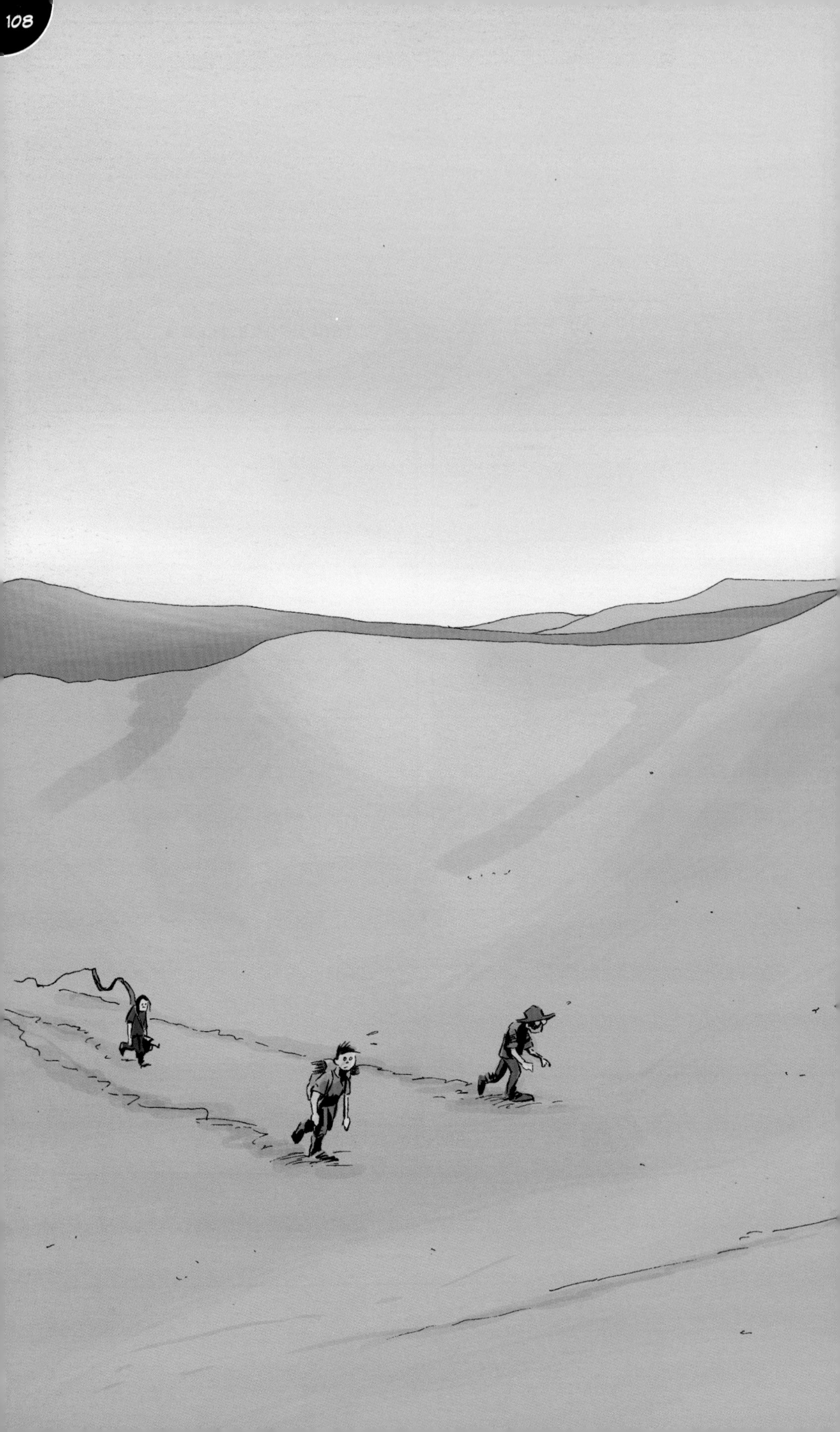

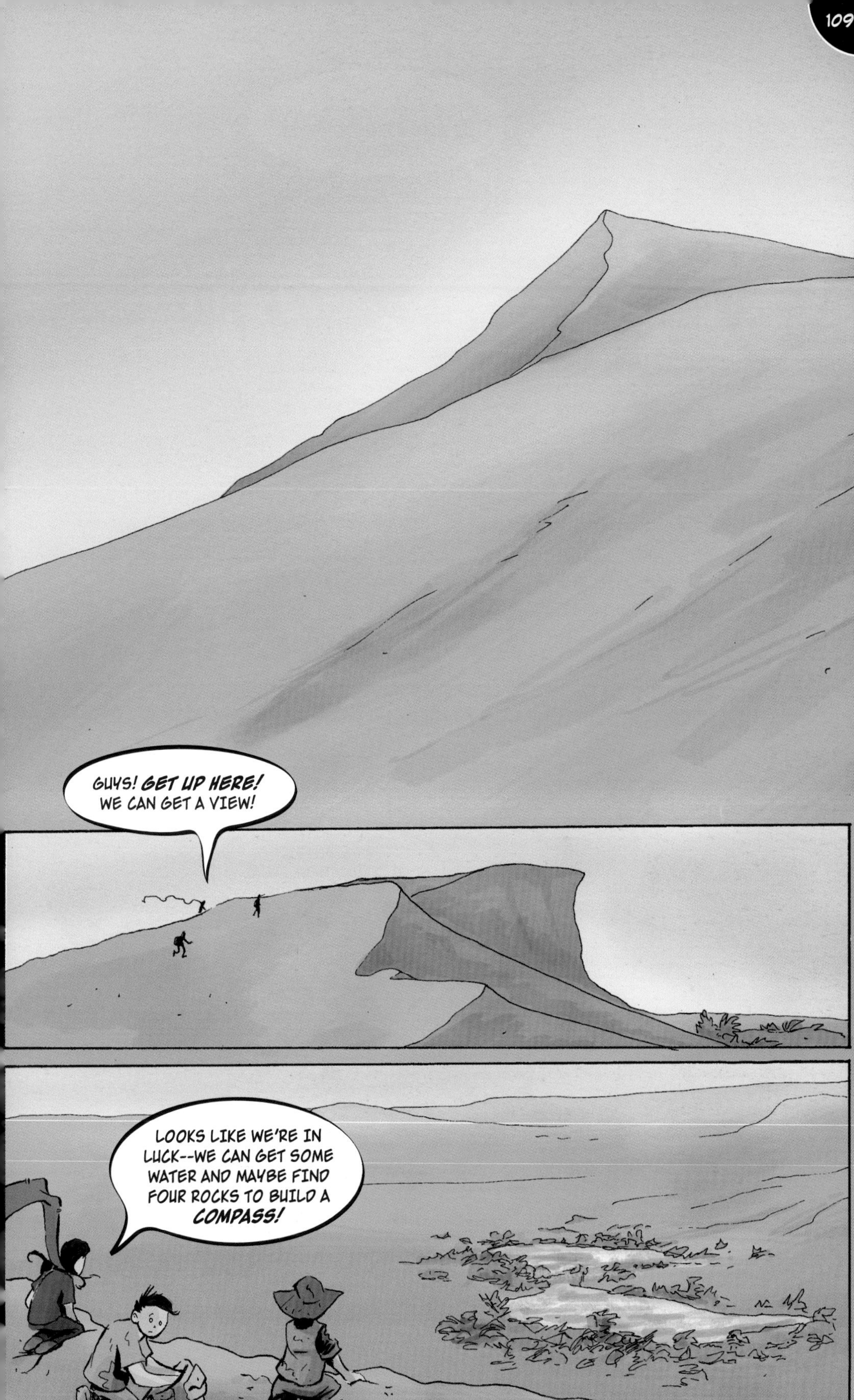
GUYS! GET UP HERE!
WE CAN GET A VIEW!
LOOKS LIKE WE'RE IN LUCK--WE CAN GET SOME WATER AND MAYBE FIND FOUR ROCKS TO BUILD A COMPASS!

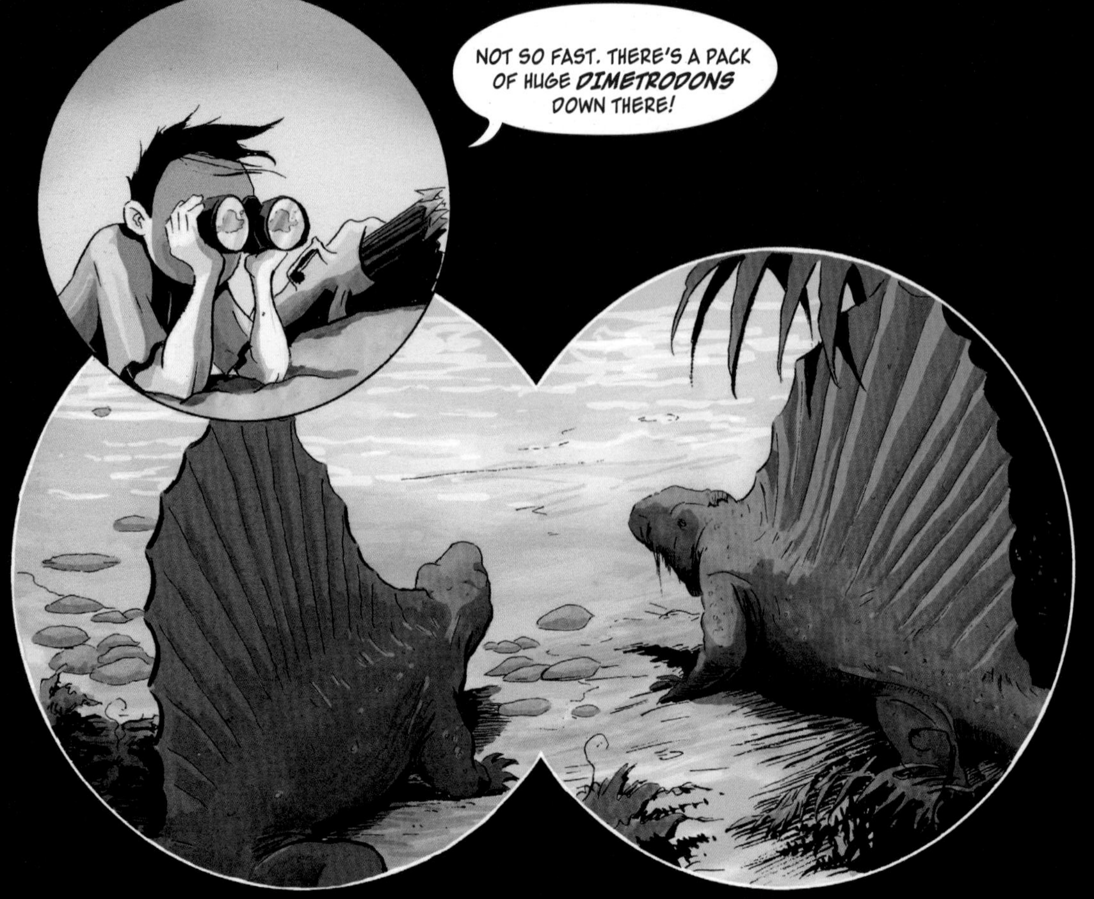
NOT SO FAST. THERE'S A PACK OF HUGE *DIMETRODONS* DOWN THERE!

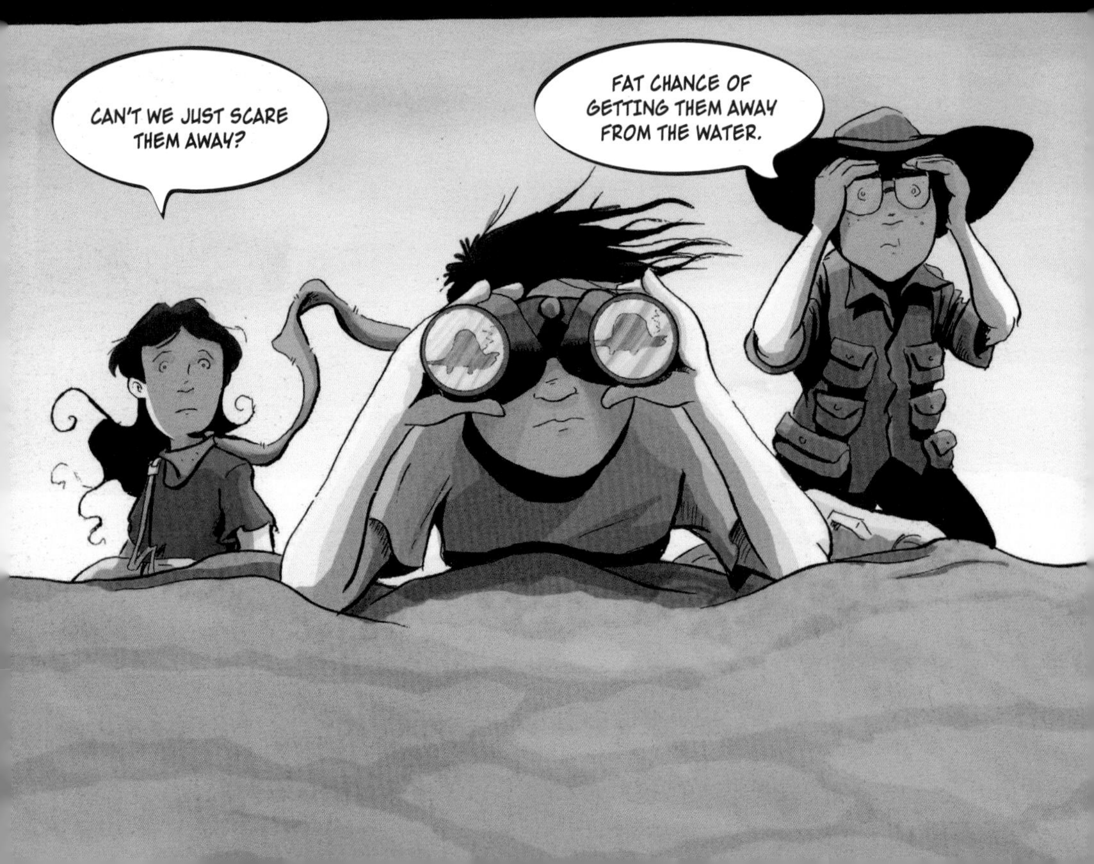
CAN'T WE JUST SCARE THEM AWAY?
FAT CHANCE OF GETTING THEM AWAY FROM THE WATER.

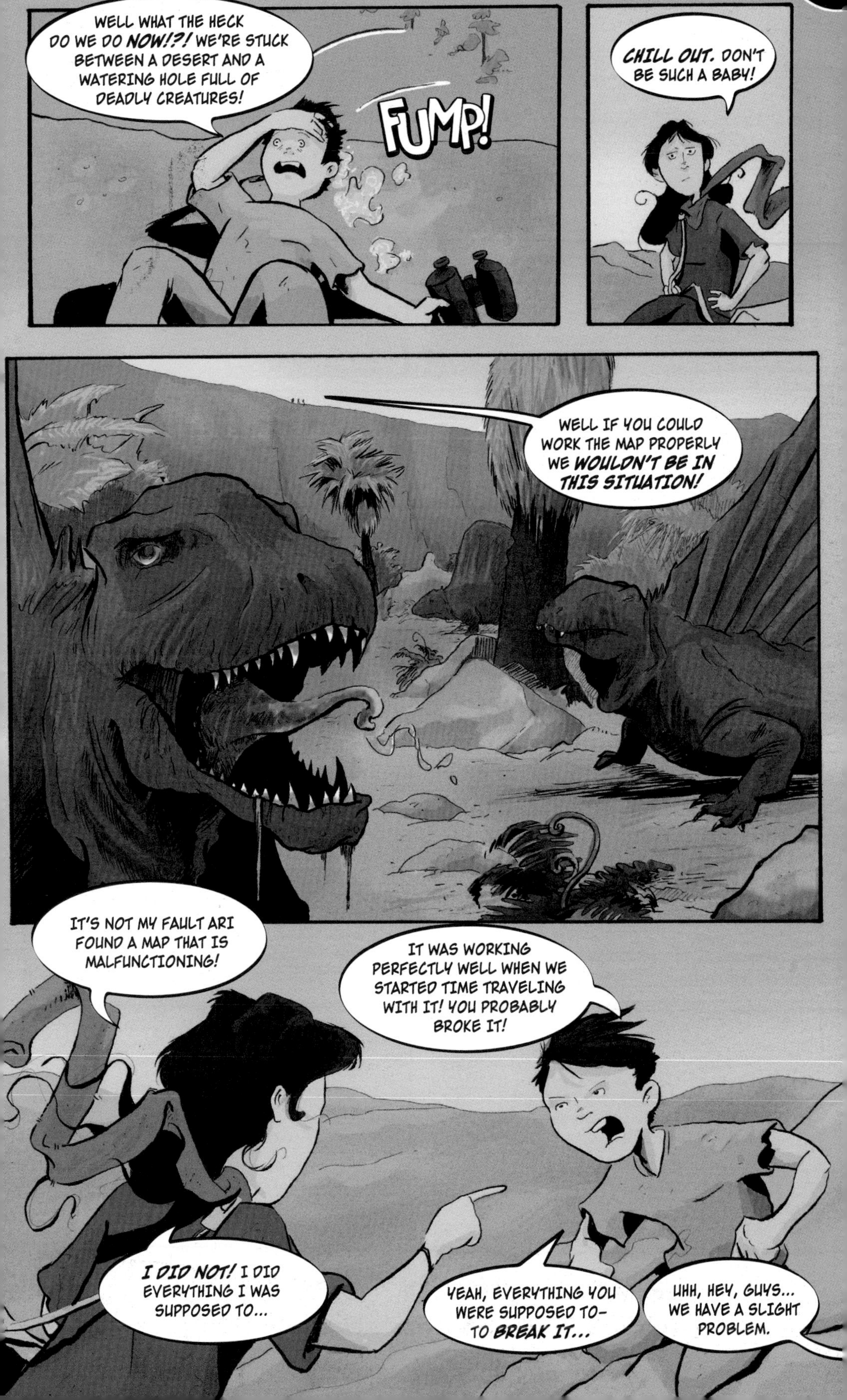
WELL WHAT THE HECK DO WE DO NOW!?! WE'RE STUCK BETWEEN A DESERT AND A WATERING HOLE FULL OF DEADLY CREATURES!
FUMP!
CHILL OUT. DON'T BE SUCH A BABY!
WELL IF YOU COULD WORK THE MAP PROPERLY WE WOULDN'T BE IN THIS SITUATION!
IT'S NOT MY FAULT ARI FOUND A MAP THAT IS MALFUNCTIONING!
IT WAS WORKING PERFECTLY WELL WHEN WE STARTED TIME TRAVELING WITH IT! YOU PROBABLY BROKE IT!
I DID NOT! I DID EVERYTHING I WAS SUPPOSED TO...
YEAH, EVERYTHING YOU WERE SUPPOSED TO-TO BREAK IT...
UHH, HEY, GUYS... WE HAVE A SLIGHT PROBLEM.

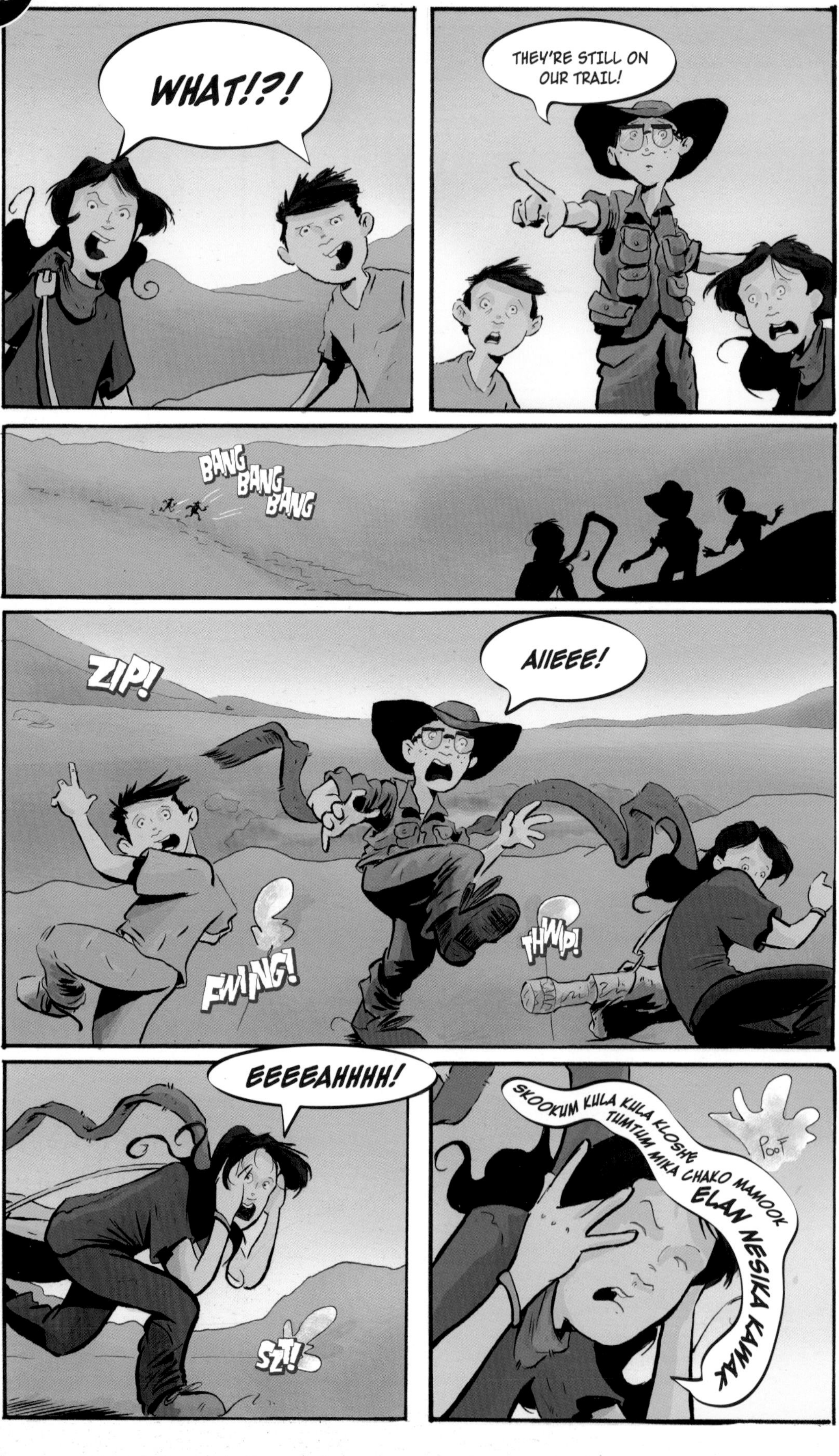
WHAT!?!
THEY'RE STILL ON OUR TRAIL!
BANG BANG BANG
ZIP!
AIIEEE!
FWING!
THWIP!
EEEEAHHHH!
SZT!
SKOOKUM KULA KULA KLOSHE TUMTUM MIKA CHAKO MAMOOK ELAN NESIKA KAWAK
POOF

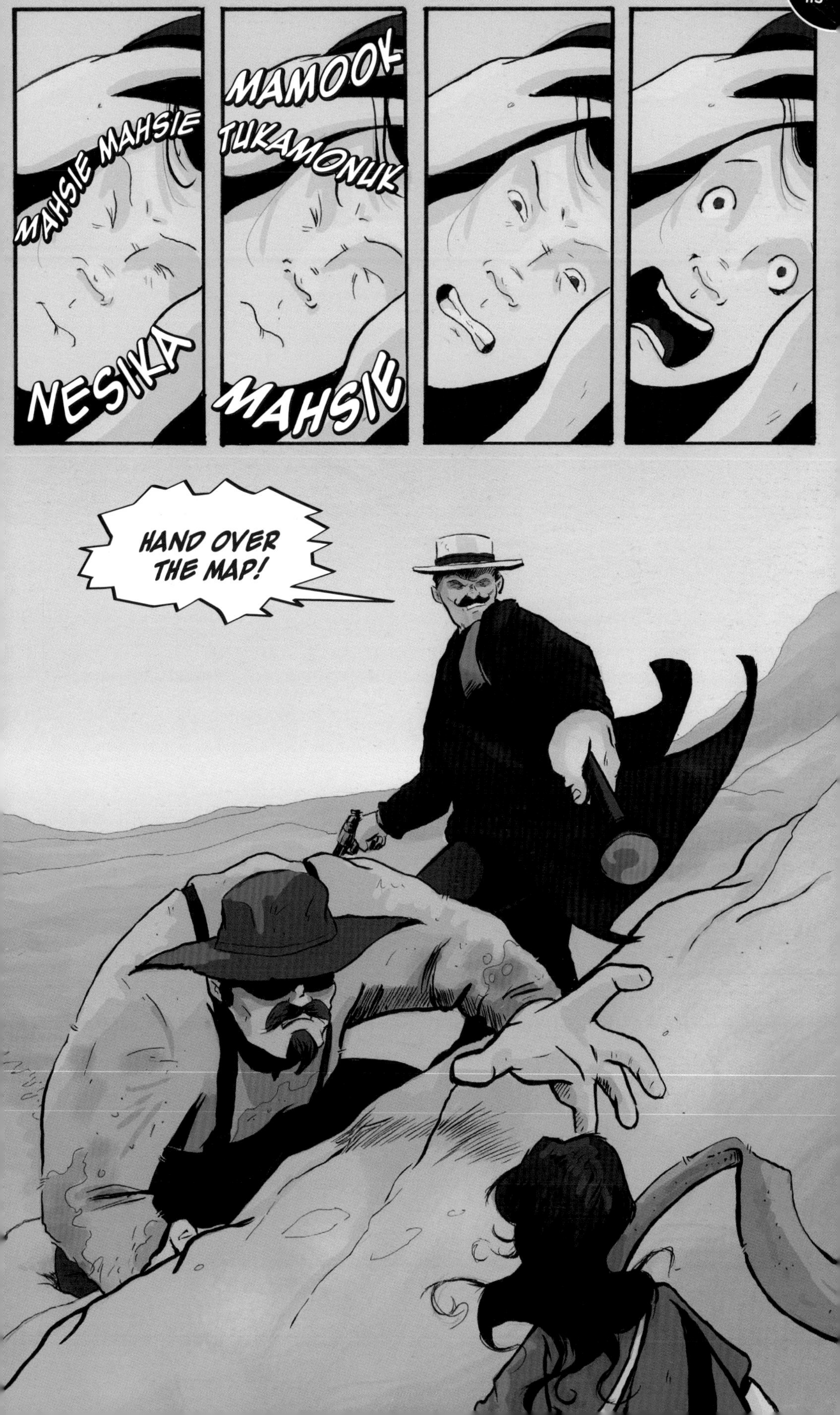
MAHSIE MAHSIE
NESIKA
MAMOOK
TUKAMONUK
MAHSIE
HAND OVER THE MAP!

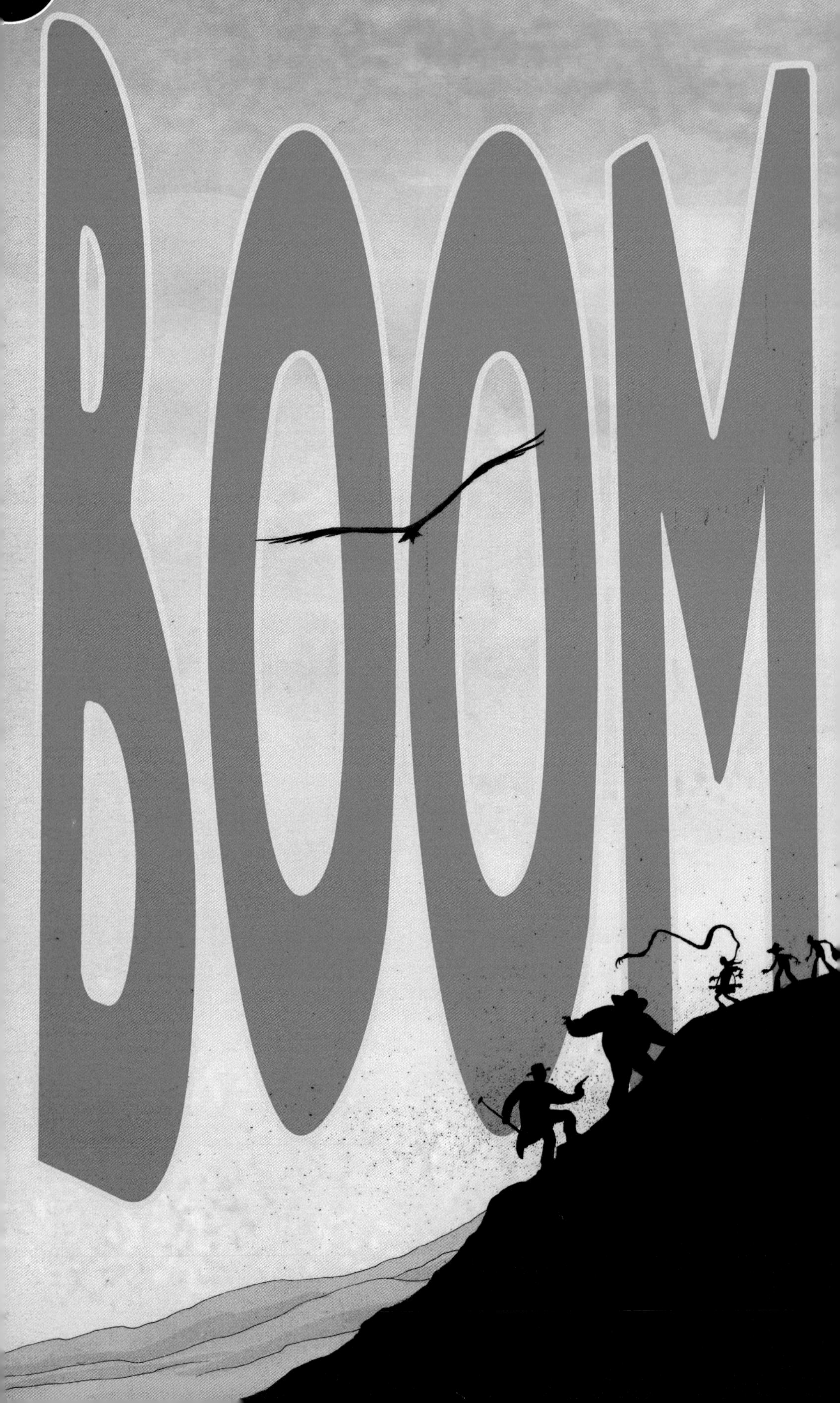
BOOM

CHAPTER FIVE

THE PERMIAN POST

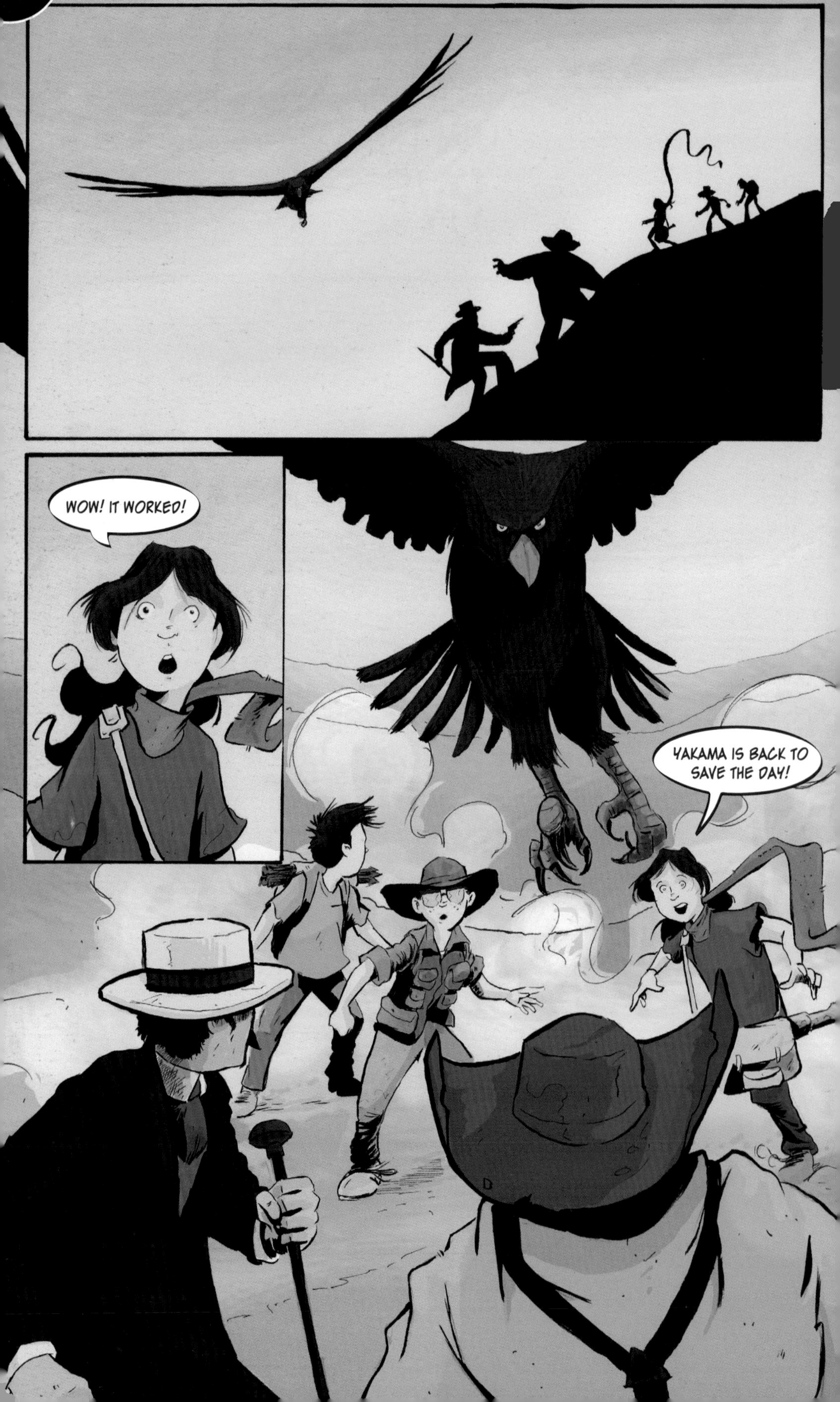
WOW! IT WORKED!
YAKAMA IS BACK TO SAVE THE DAY!

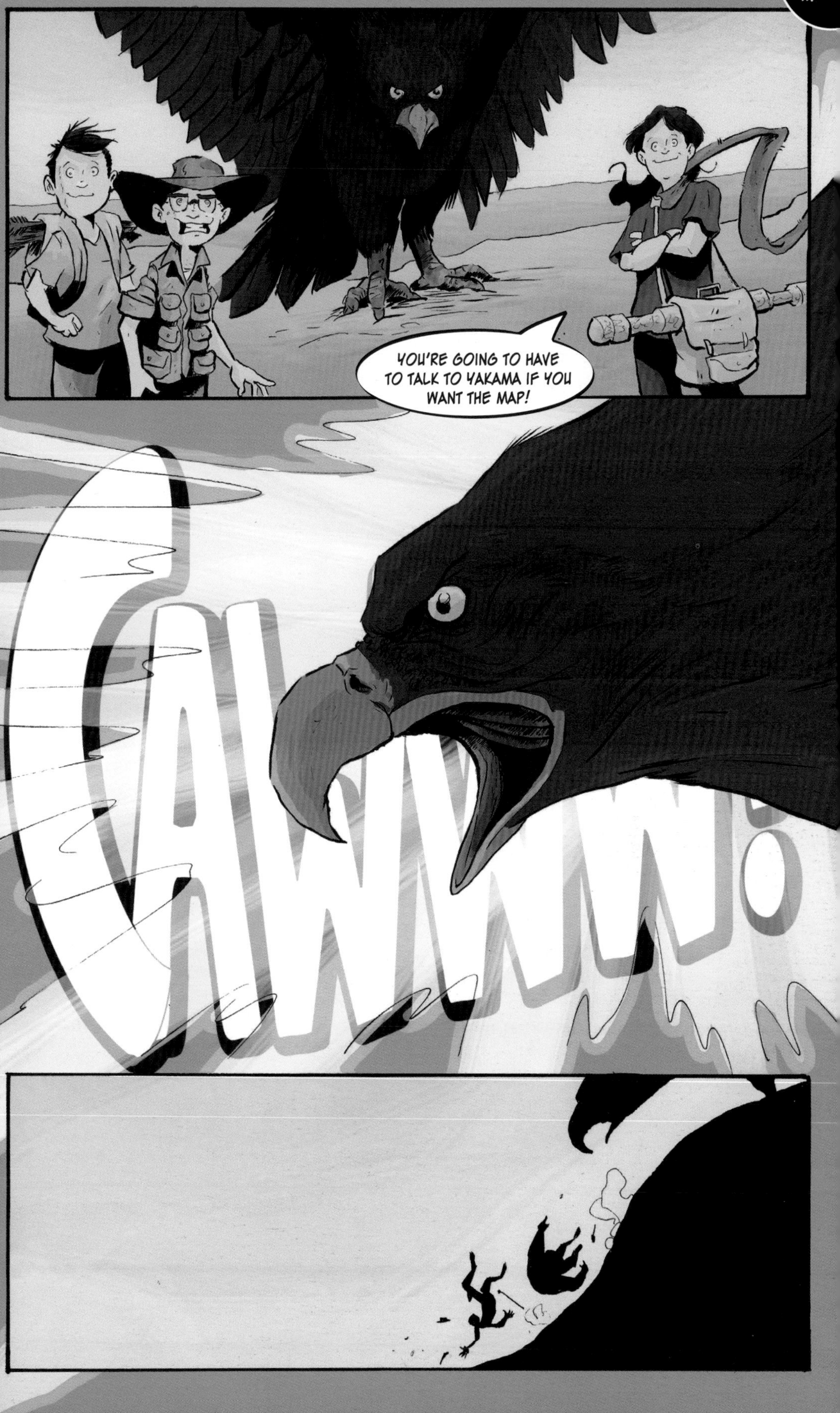
YOU'RE GOING TO HAVE TO TALK TO YAKAMA IF YOU WANT THE MAP!
CAWWW!

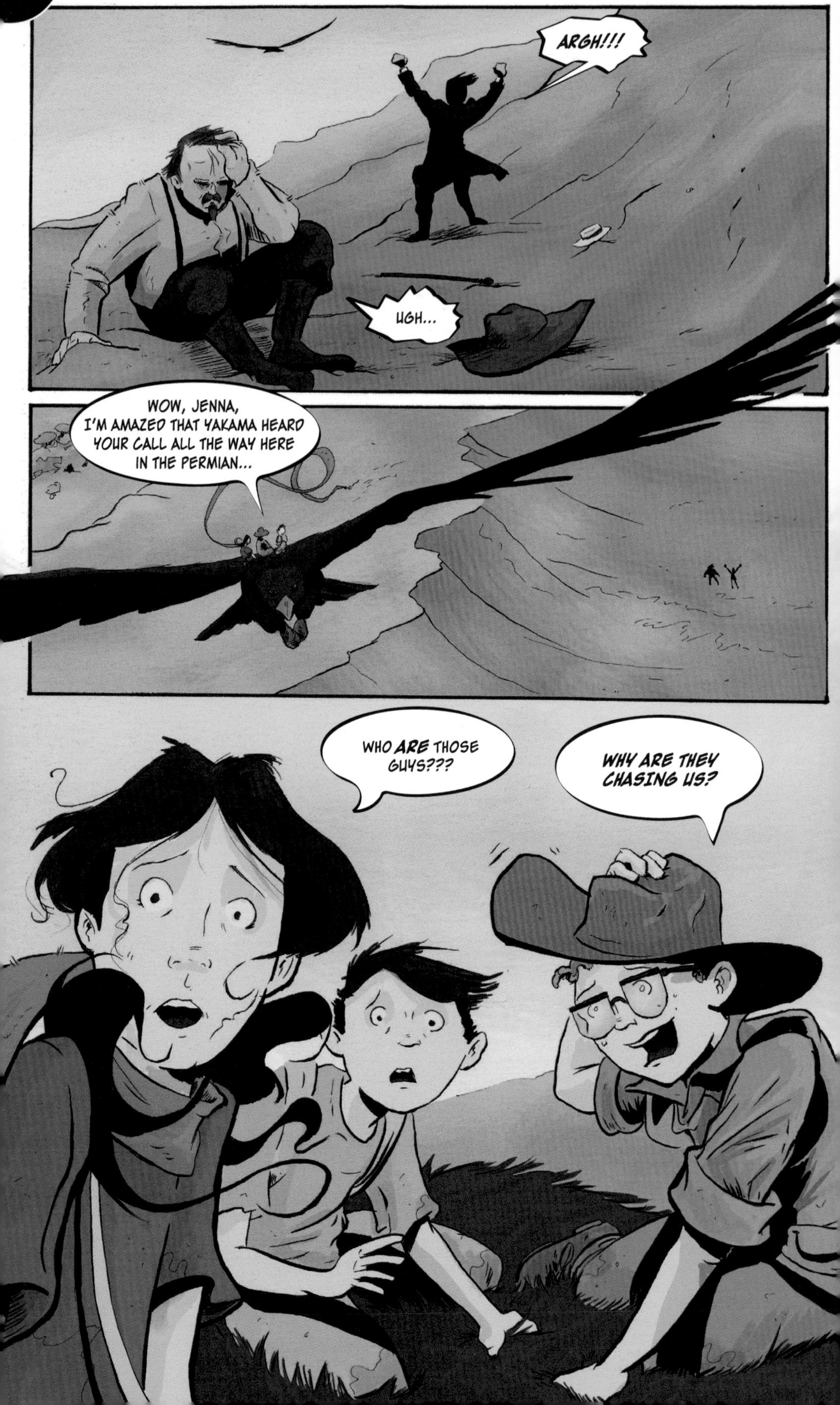
ARGH!!!
UGH...
WOW, JENNA, I'M AMAZED THAT YAKAMA HEARD YOUR CALL ALL THE WAY HERE IN THE PERMIAN...
WHO ARE THOSE GUYS???
WHY ARE THEY CHASING US?

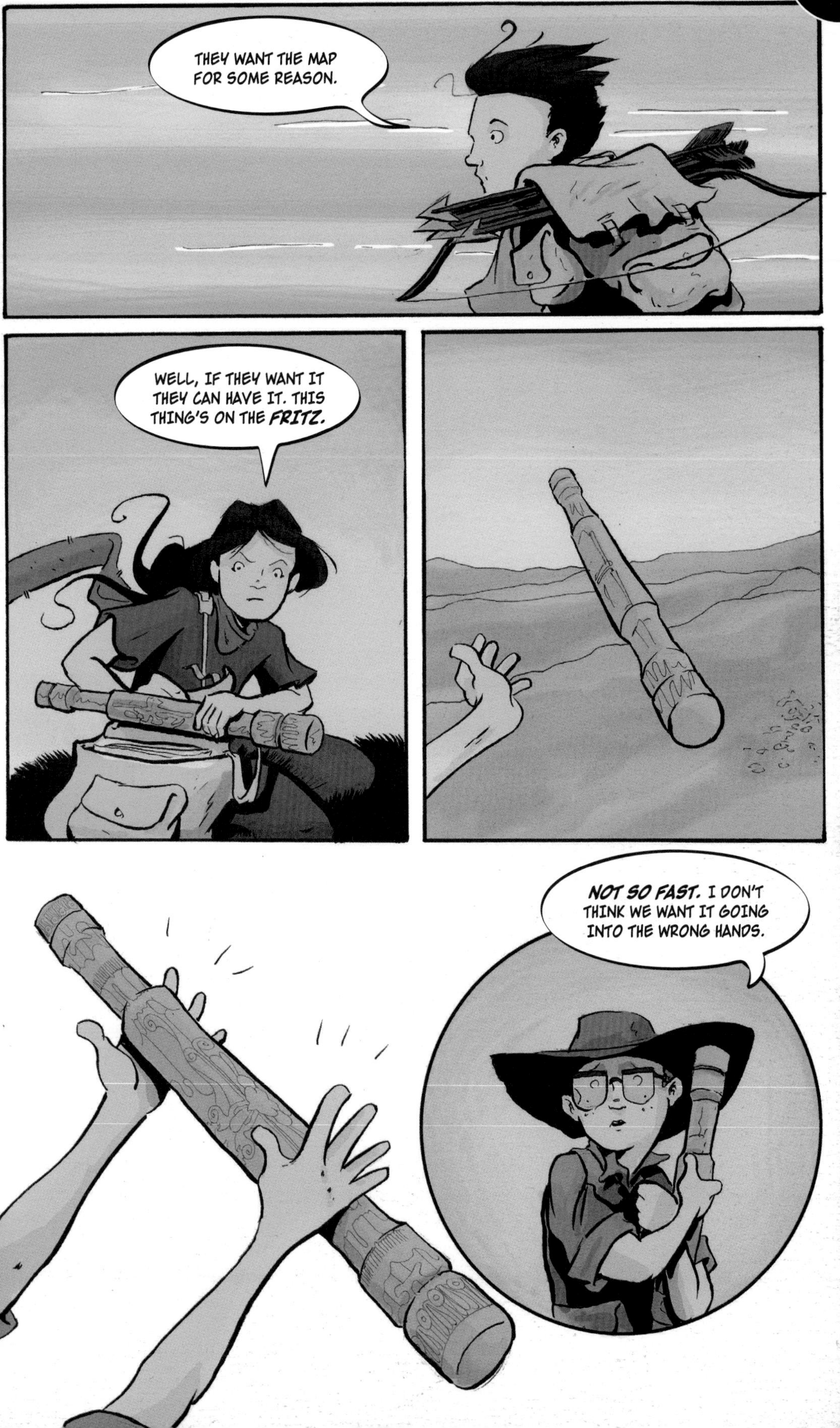
THEY WANT THE MAP FOR SOME REASON.
WELL, IF THEY WANT IT THEY CAN HAVE IT. THIS THING'S ON THE *FRITZ.*
NOT SO FAST. I DON'T THINK WE WANT IT GOING INTO THE WRONG HANDS.

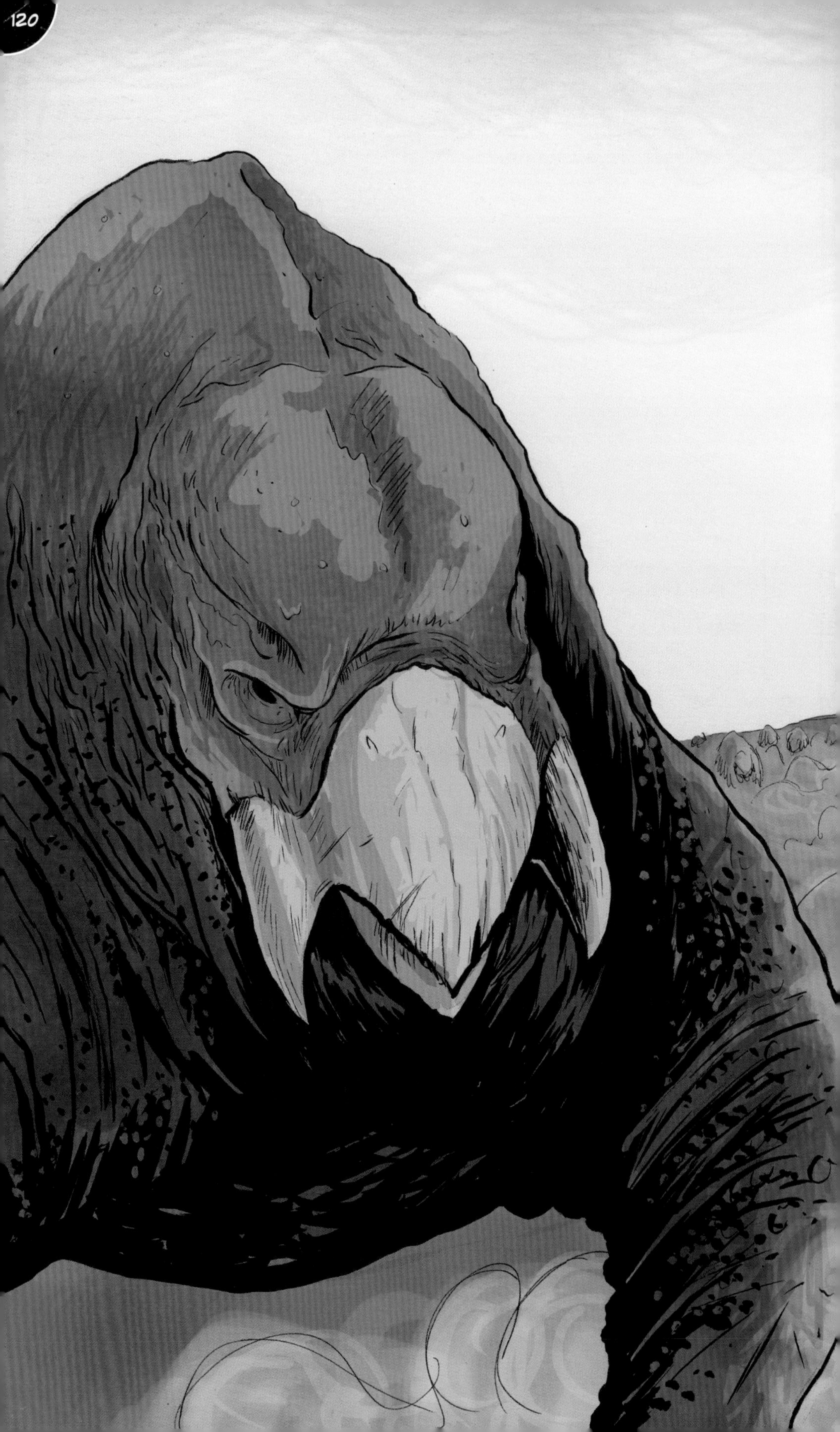

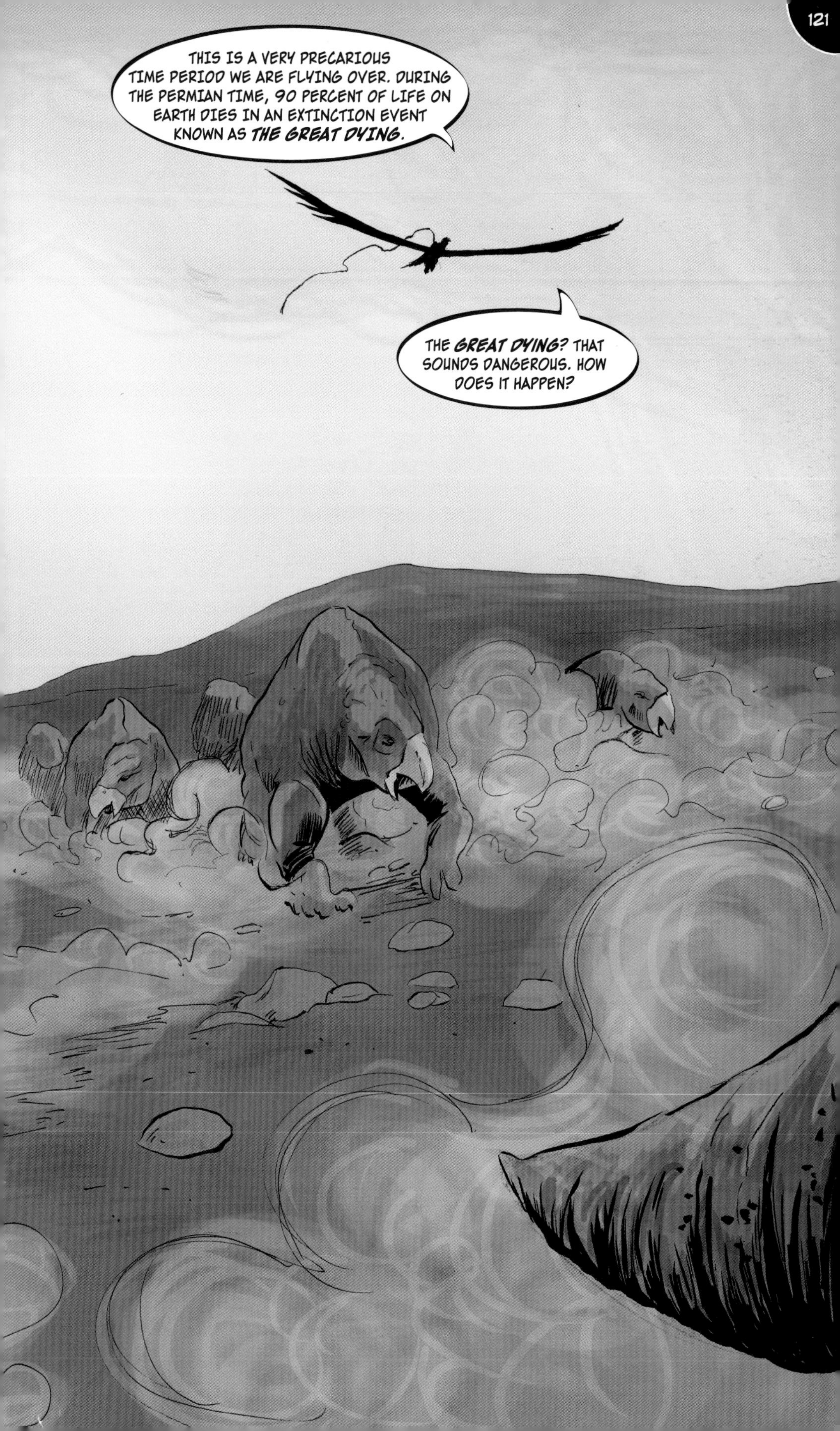
THIS IS A VERY PRECARIOUS TIME PERIOD WE ARE FLYING OVER. DURING THE PERMIAN TIME, 90 PERCENT OF LIFE ON EARTH DIES IN AN EXTINCTION EVENT KNOWN AS *THE GREAT DYING*.
THE *GREAT DYING*? THAT SOUNDS DANGEROUS. HOW DOES IT HAPPEN?

THE GREAT DYING BEGAN WITH THE BREAK-UP OF THE SUPERCONTINENT PANGEA.

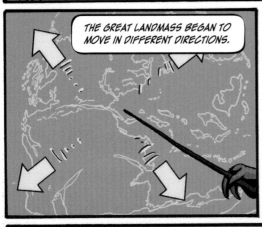

THE GREAT LANDMASS BEGAN TO MOVE IN DIFFERENT DIRECTIONS.

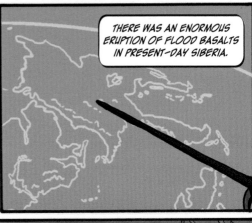

THERE WAS AN ENORMOUS ERUPTION OF FLOOD BASALTS IN PRESENT-DAY SIBERIA.

THESE LAVA FLOWS WOULD HAVE BEEN HUNDREDS OF MILES LONG AND WOULD HAVE ERUPTED FOR THOUSANDS OF YEARS.

TEMPERATURES WOULD HAVE DROPPED AT FIRST BECAUSE OF THE VOLCANIC ASH BLOCKING OUT DIRECT SUNLIGHT ACROSS THE GLOBE.

BUT THEN THE PLANET WOULD HAVE WARMED SIGNIFICANTLY BECAUSE OF THE GREENHOUSE GASES EMITTED FROM THE VOLCANIC ACTIVITY.

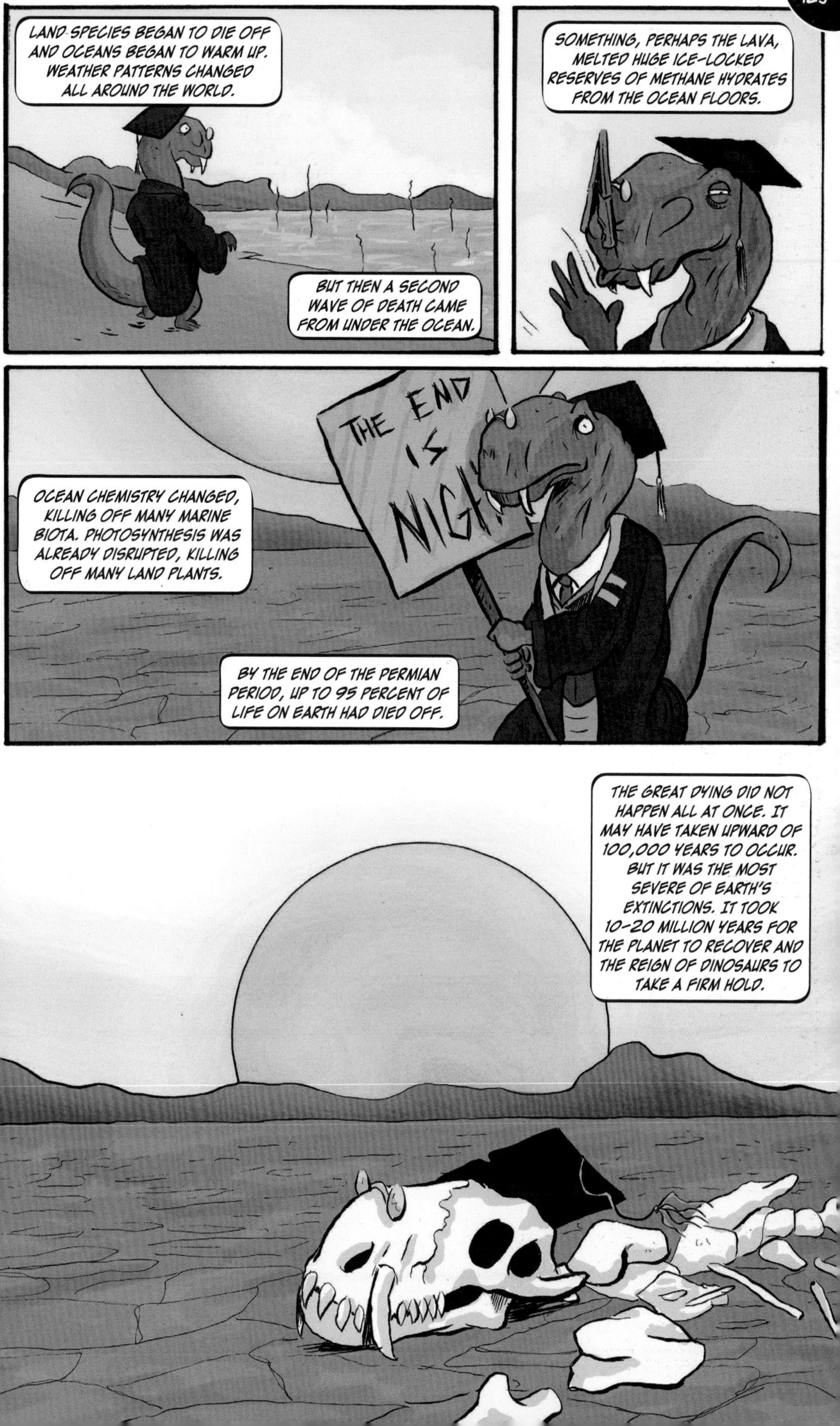
LAND SPECIES BEGAN TO DIE OFF AND OCEANS BEGAN TO WARM UP. WEATHER PATTERNS CHANGED ALL AROUND THE WORLD.
BUT THEN A SECOND WAVE OF DEATH CAME FROM UNDER THE OCEAN.
SOMETHING, PERHAPS THE LAVA, MELTED HUGE ICE-LOCKED RESERVES OF METHANE HYDRATES FROM THE OCEAN FLOORS.
THE END IS NIG
OCEAN CHEMISTRY CHANGED, KILLING OFF MANY MARINE BIOTA. PHOTOSYNTHESIS WAS ALREADY DISRUPTED, KILLING OFF MANY LAND PLANTS.
BY THE END OF THE PERMIAN PERIOD, UP TO 95 PERCENT OF LIFE ON EARTH HAD DIED OFF.
THE GREAT DYING DID NOT HAPPEN ALL AT ONCE. IT MAY HAVE TAKEN UPWARD OF 100,000 YEARS TO OCCUR. BUT IT WAS THE MOST SEVERE OF EARTH'S EXTINCTIONS. IT TOOK 10-20 MILLION YEARS FOR THE PLANET TO RECOVER AND THE REIGN OF DINOSAURS TO TAKE A FIRM HOLD.

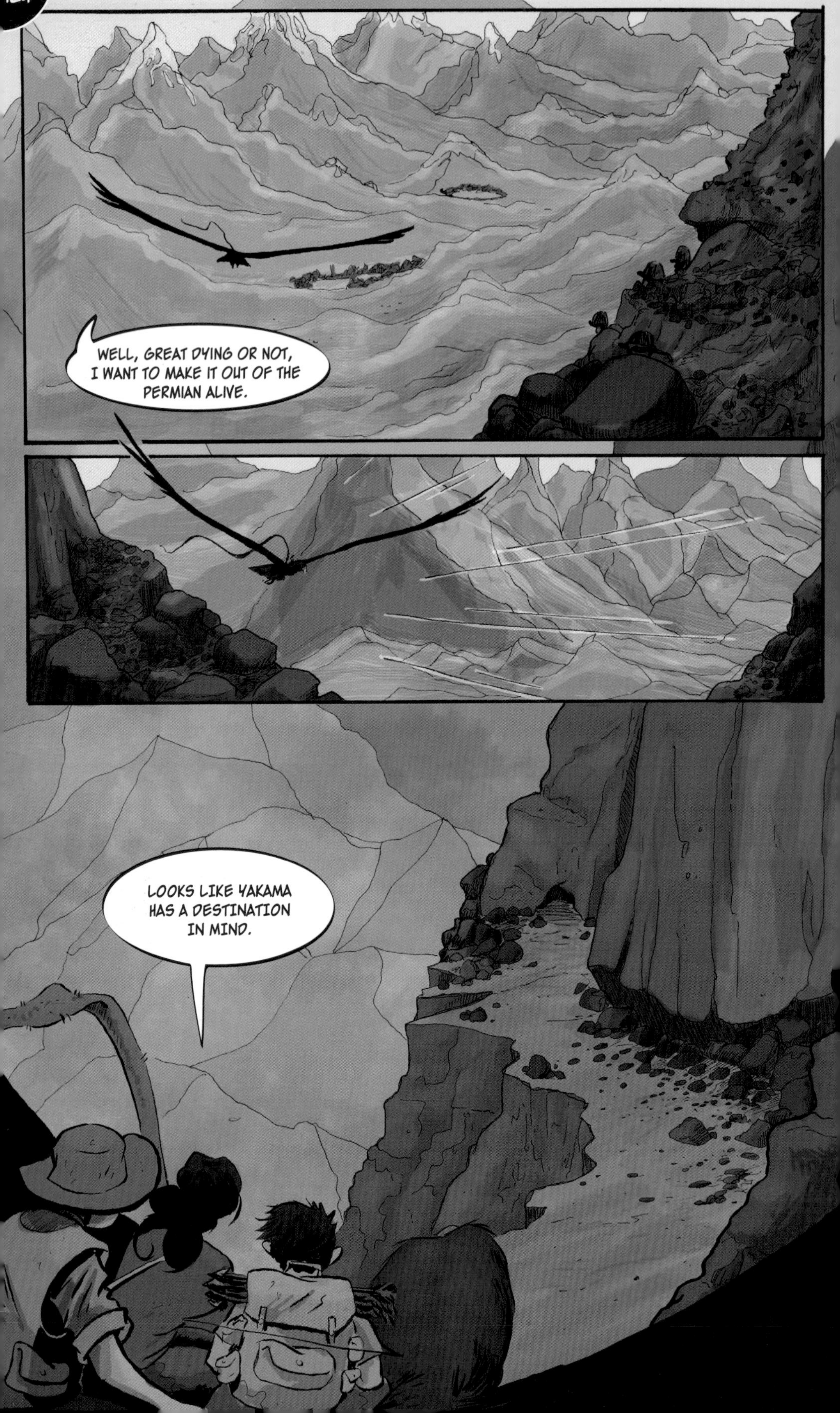
WELL, GREAT DYING OR NOT, I WANT TO MAKE IT OUT OF THE PERMIAN ALIVE.
LOOKS LIKE YAKAMA HAS A DESTINATION IN MIND.

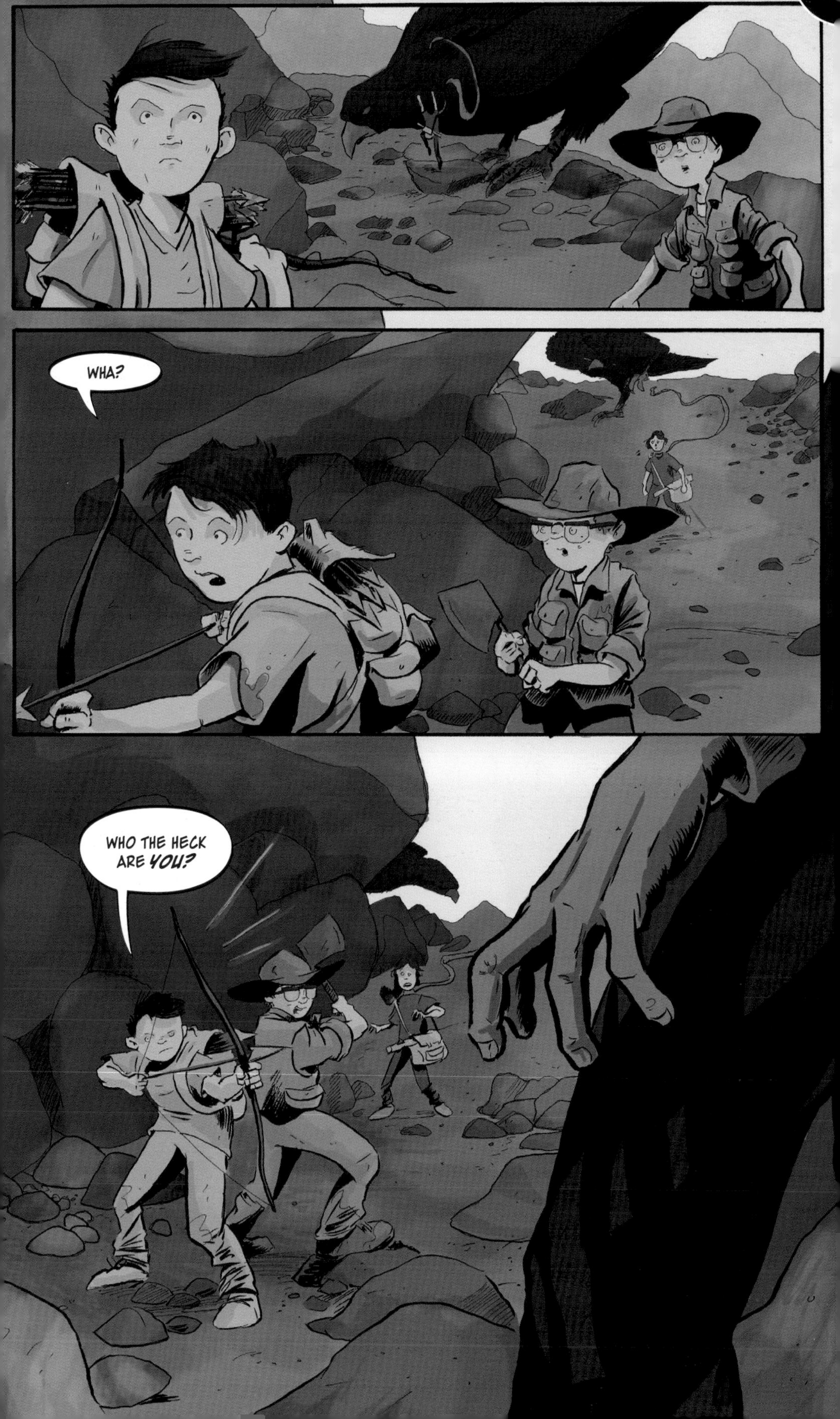
WHA?
WHO THE HECK ARE YOU?

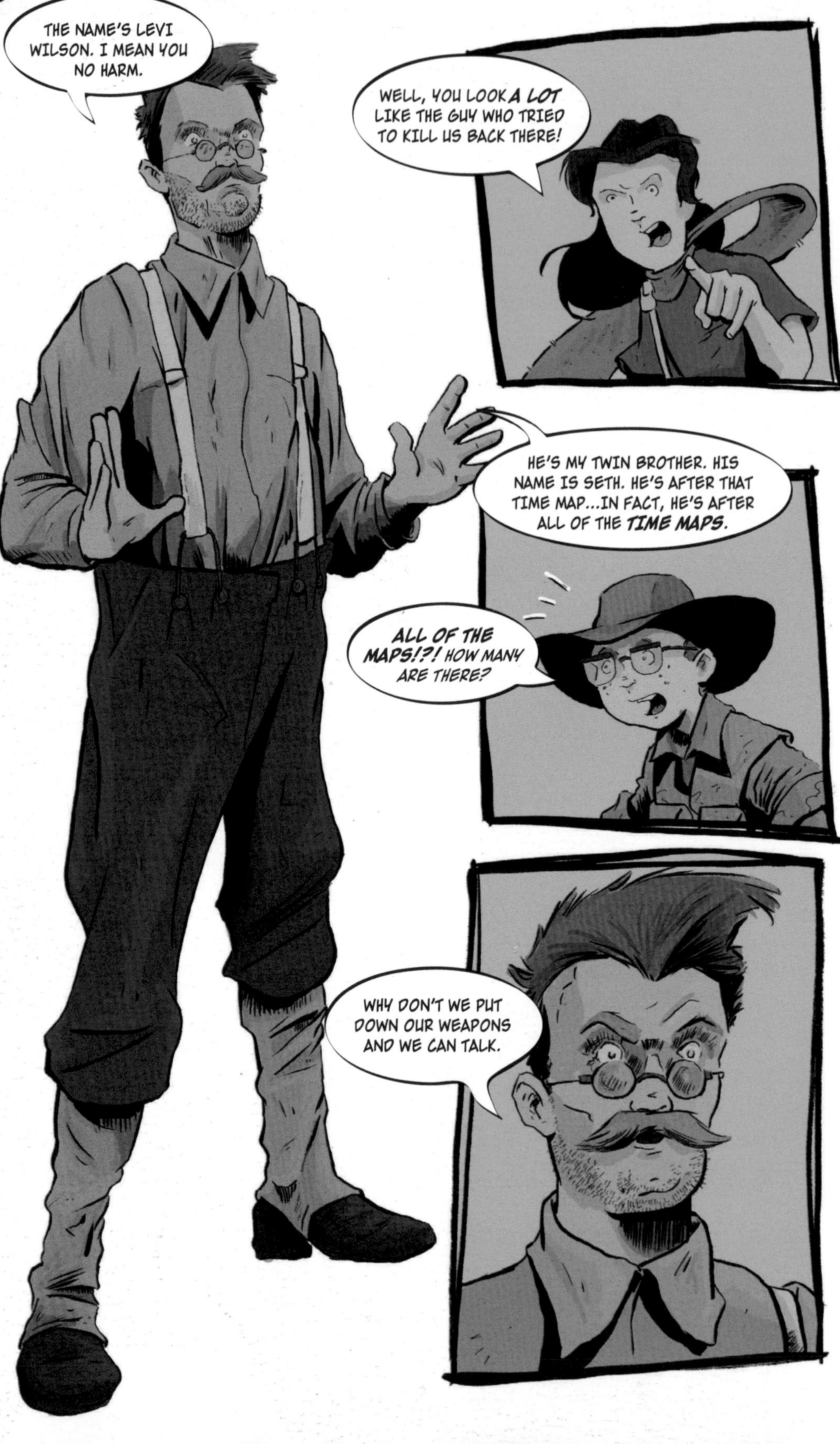
THE NAME'S LEVI WILSON. I MEAN YOU NO HARM.
WELL, YOU LOOK A LOT LIKE THE GUY WHO TRIED TO KILL US BACK THERE!
HE'S MY TWIN BROTHER. HIS NAME IS SETH. HE'S AFTER THAT TIME MAP...IN FACT, HE'S AFTER ALL OF THE TIME MAPS.
ALL OF THE MAPS!?! HOW MANY ARE THERE?
WHY DON'T WE PUT DOWN OUR WEAPONS AND WE CAN TALK.

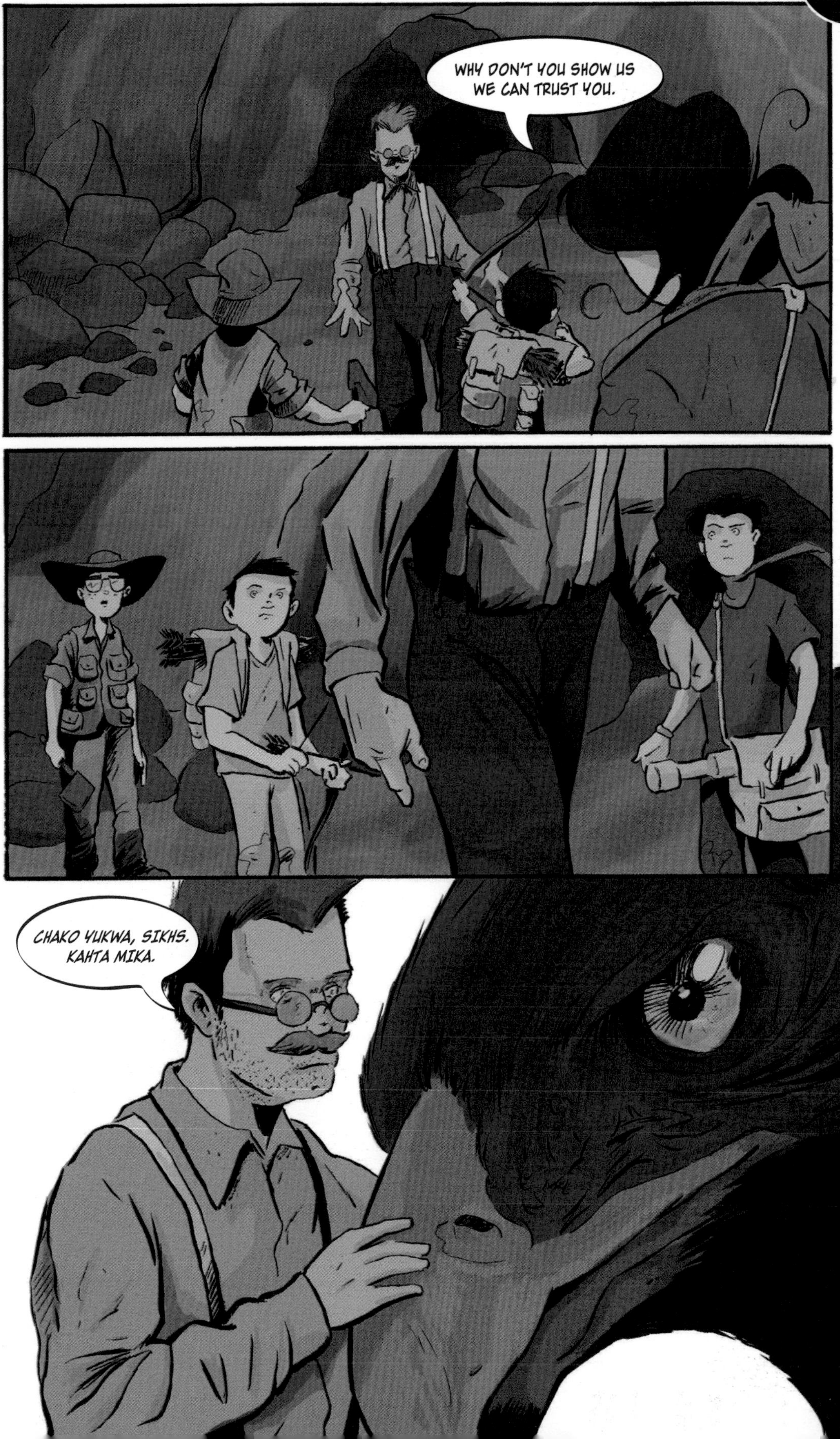
WHY DON'T YOU SHOW US WE CAN TRUST YOU.
CHAKO YUKWA, SIKHS. KAHTA MIKA.

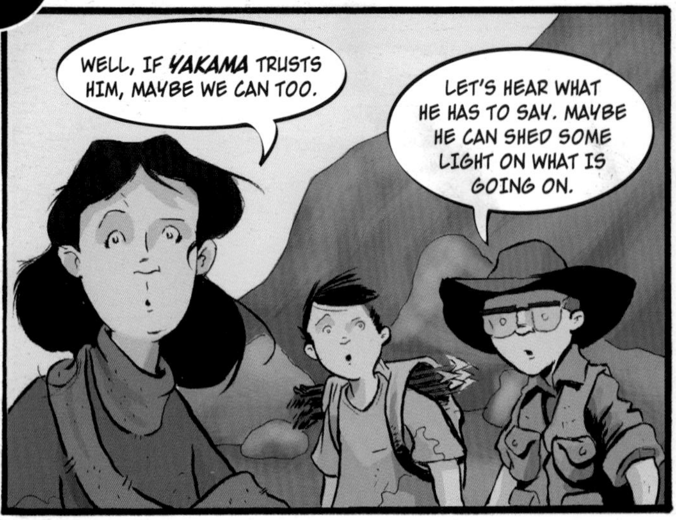
WELL, IF YAKAMA TRUSTS HIM, MAYBE WE CAN TOO.
LET'S HEAR WHAT HE HAS TO SAY. MAYBE HE CAN SHED SOME LIGHT ON WHAT IS GOING ON.

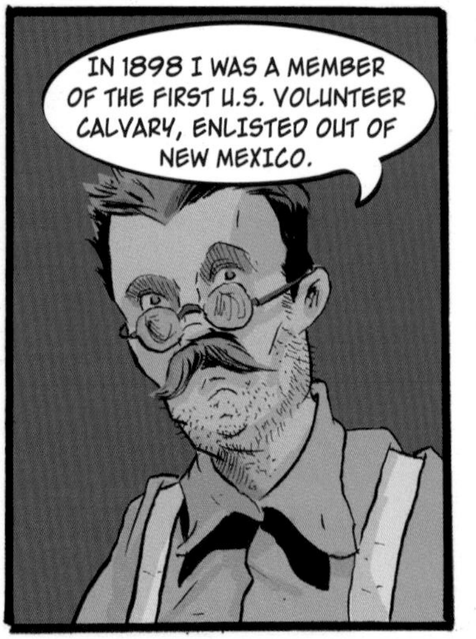
IN 1898 I WAS A MEMBER OF THE FIRST U.S. VOLUNTEER CALVARY, ENLISTED OUT OF NEW MEXICO.

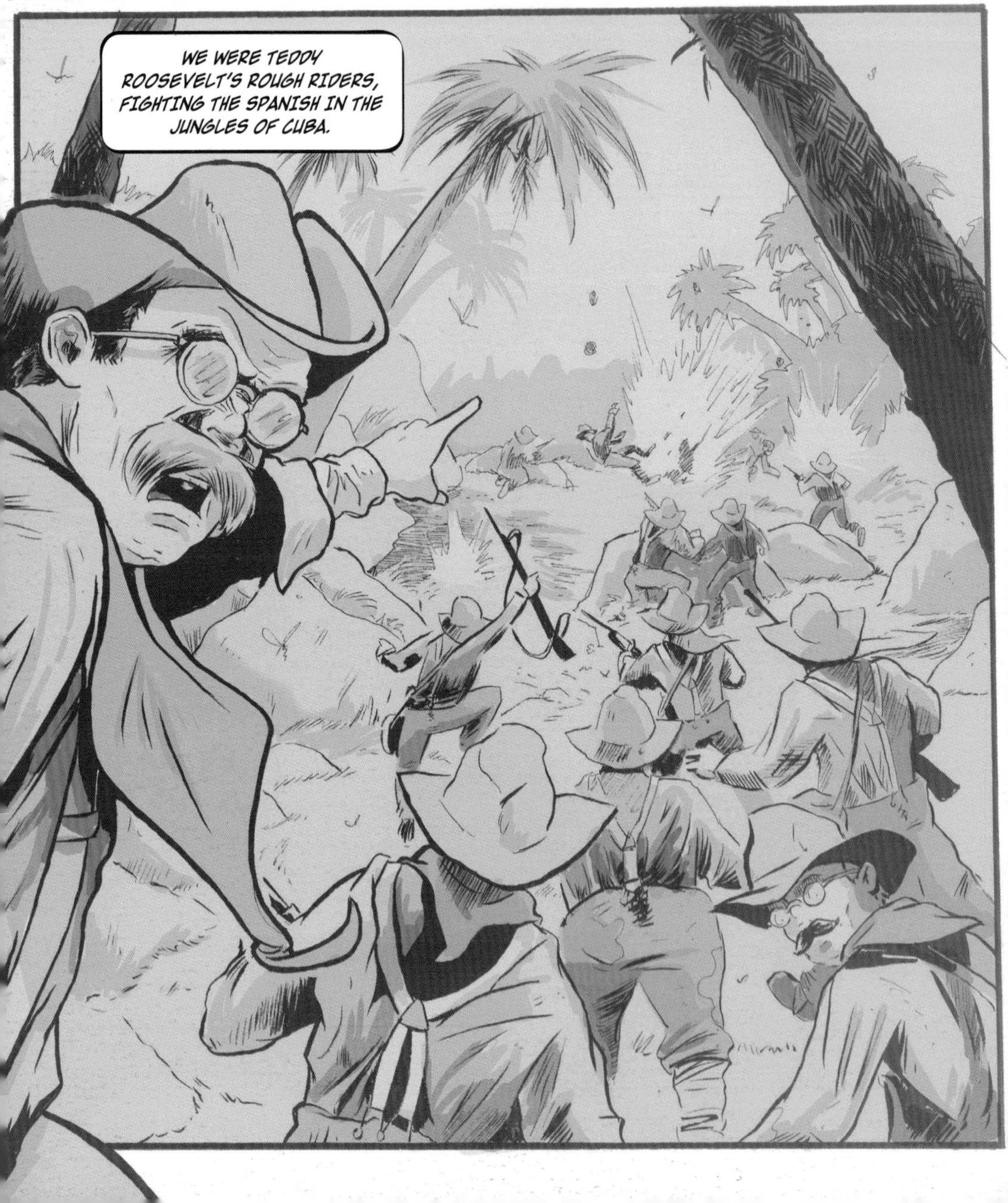
WE WERE TEDDY ROOSEVELT'S ROUGH RIDERS, FIGHTING THE SPANISH IN THE JUNGLES OF CUBA.

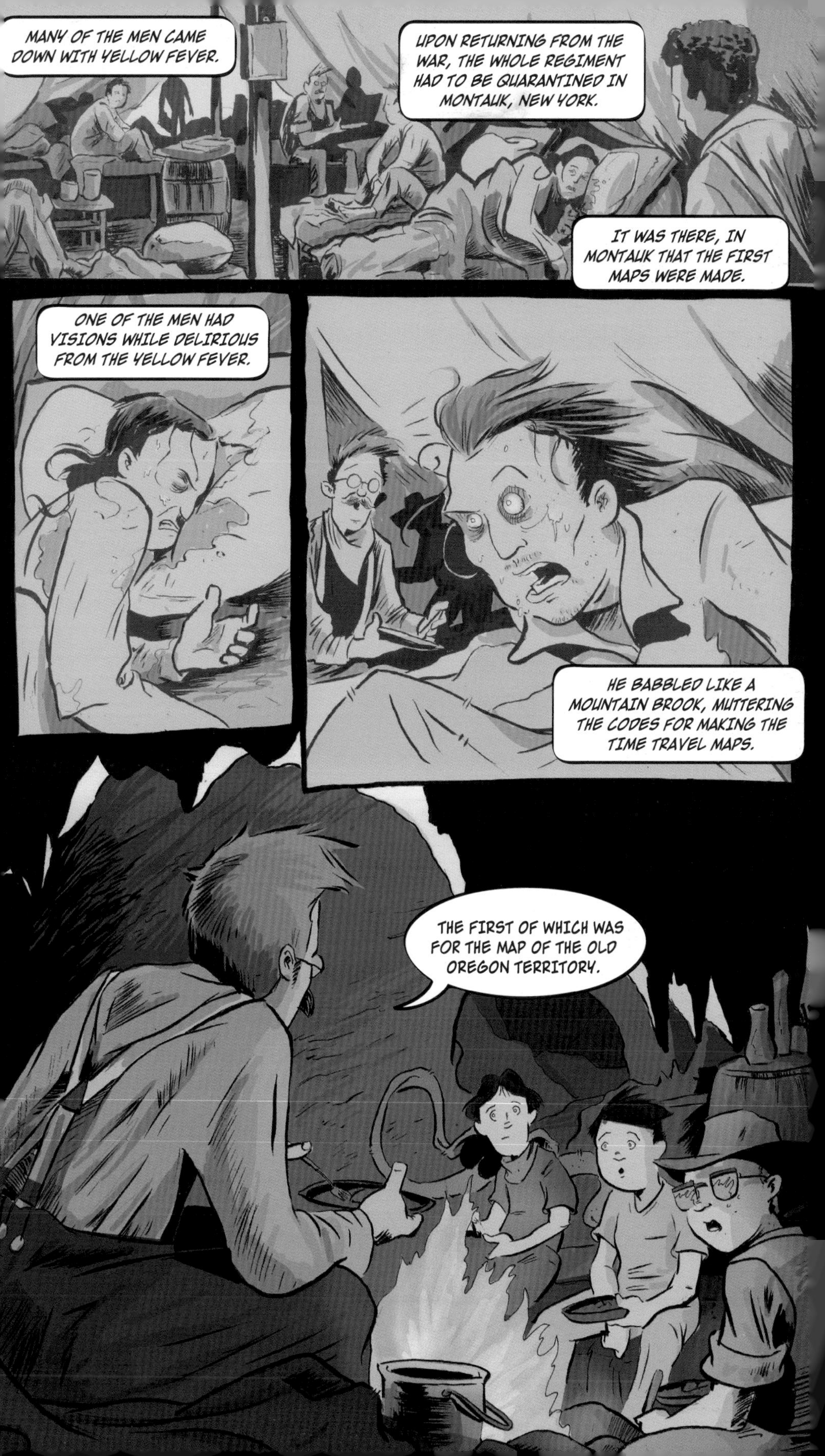
MANY OF THE MEN CAME DOWN WITH YELLOW FEVER.
UPON RETURNING FROM THE WAR, THE WHOLE REGIMENT HAD TO BE QUARANTINED IN MONTAUK, NEW YORK.
IT WAS THERE, IN MONTAUK THAT THE FIRST MAPS WERE MADE.
ONE OF THE MEN HAD VISIONS WHILE DELIRIOUS FROM THE YELLOW FEVER.
HE BABBLED LIKE A MOUNTAIN BROOK, MUTTERING THE CODES FOR MAKING THE TIME TRAVEL MAPS.
THE FIRST OF WHICH WAS FOR THE MAP OF THE OLD OREGON TERRITORY.

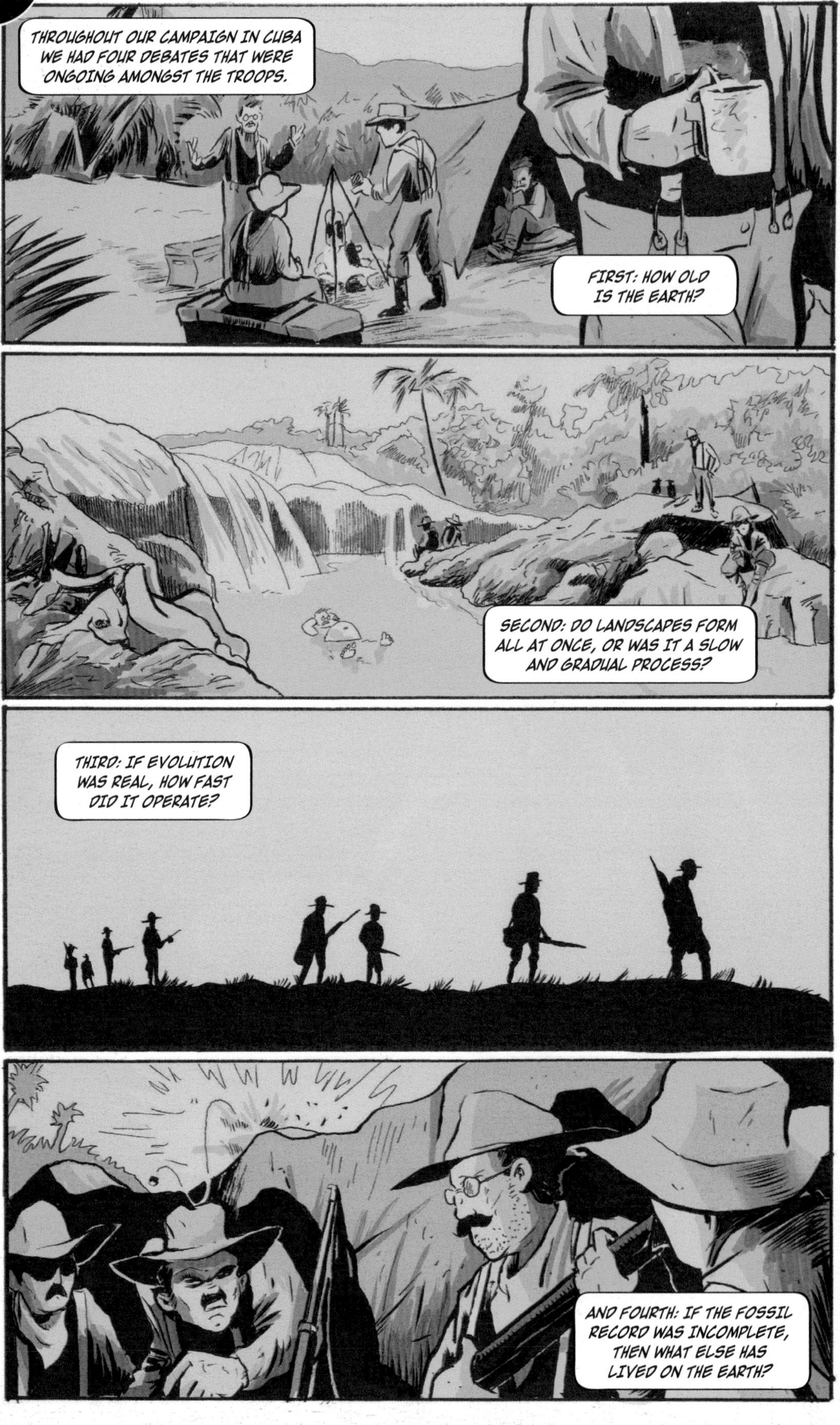
THROUGHOUT OUR CAMPAIGN IN CUBA WE HAD FOUR DEBATES THAT WERE ONGOING AMONGST THE TROOPS.
FIRST: HOW OLD IS THE EARTH?
SECOND: DO LANDSCAPES FORM ALL AT ONCE, OR WAS IT A SLOW AND GRADUAL PROCESS?
THIRD: IF EVOLUTION WAS REAL, HOW FAST DID IT OPERATE?
AND FOURTH: IF THE FOSSIL RECORD WAS INCOMPLETE, THEN WHAT ELSE HAS LIVED ON THE EARTH?

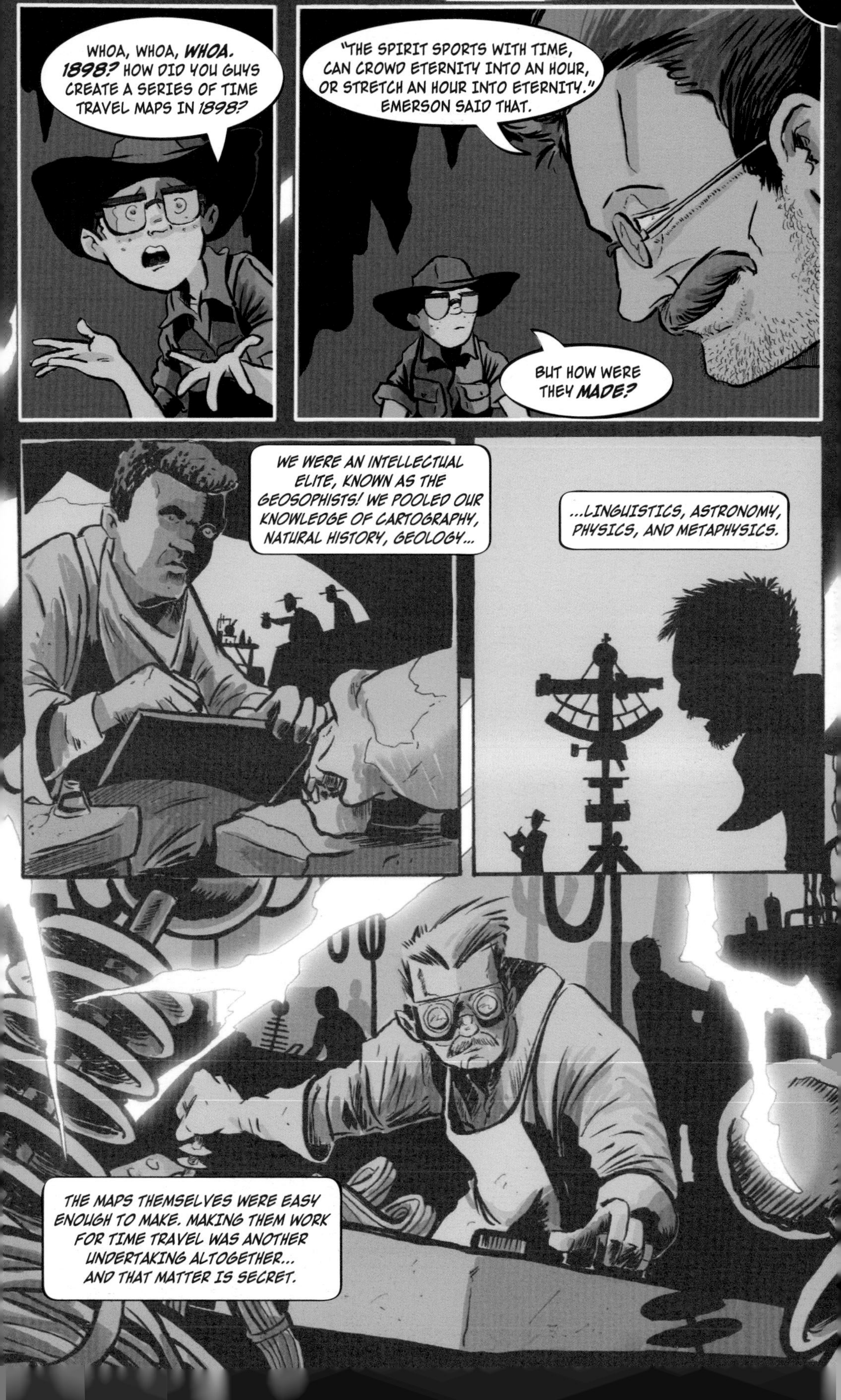
WHOA, WHOA, **WHOA.** *1898?* HOW DID YOU GUYS CREATE A SERIES OF TIME TRAVEL MAPS IN *1898?*
"THE SPIRIT SPORTS WITH TIME, CAN CROWD ETERNITY INTO AN HOUR, OR STRETCH AN HOUR INTO ETERNITY." EMERSON SAID THAT.
BUT HOW WERE THEY **MADE?**
WE WERE AN INTELLECTUAL ELITE, KNOWN AS THE GEOSOPHISTS! WE POOLED OUR KNOWLEDGE OF CARTOGRAPHY, NATURAL HISTORY, GEOLOGY...
...LINGUISTICS, ASTRONOMY, PHYSICS, AND METAPHYSICS.
THE MAPS THEMSELVES WERE EASY ENOUGH TO MAKE. MAKING THEM WORK FOR TIME TRAVEL WAS ANOTHER UNDERTAKING ALTOGETHER... AND THAT MATTER IS SECRET.

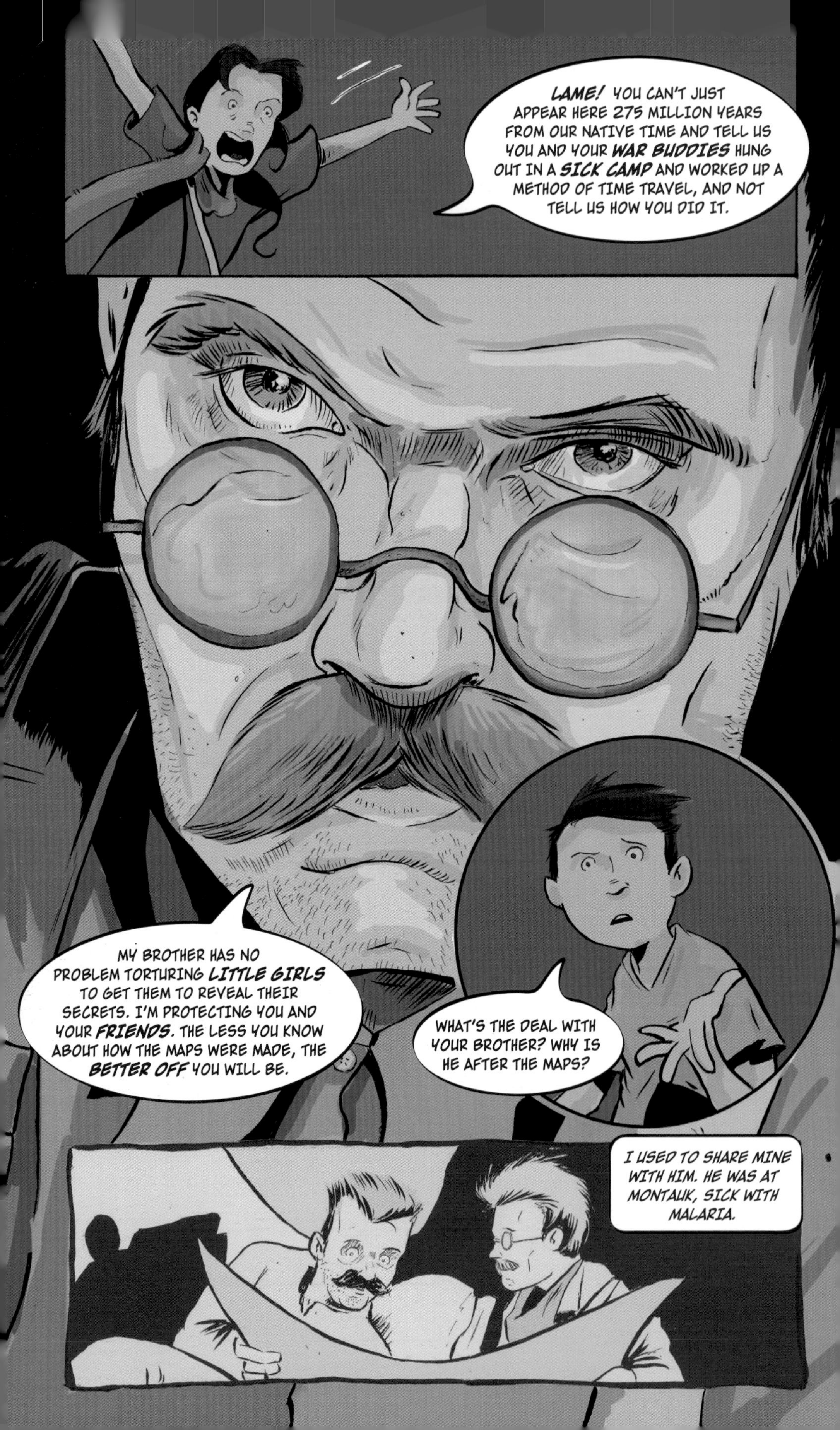
LAME! YOU CAN'T JUST APPEAR HERE 275 MILLION YEARS FROM OUR NATIVE TIME AND TELL US YOU AND YOUR WAR BUDDIES HUNG OUT IN A SICK CAMP AND WORKED UP A METHOD OF TIME TRAVEL, AND NOT TELL US HOW YOU DID IT.
WHAT'S THE DEAL WITH YOUR BROTHER? WHY IS HE AFTER THE MAPS?
MY BROTHER HAS NO PROBLEM TORTURING LITTLE GIRLS TO GET THEM TO REVEAL THEIR SECRETS. I'M PROTECTING YOU AND YOUR FRIENDS. THE LESS YOU KNOW ABOUT HOW THE MAPS WERE MADE, THE BETTER OFF YOU WILL BE.
I USED TO SHARE MINE WITH HIM. HE WAS AT MONTAUK, SICK WITH MALARIA.

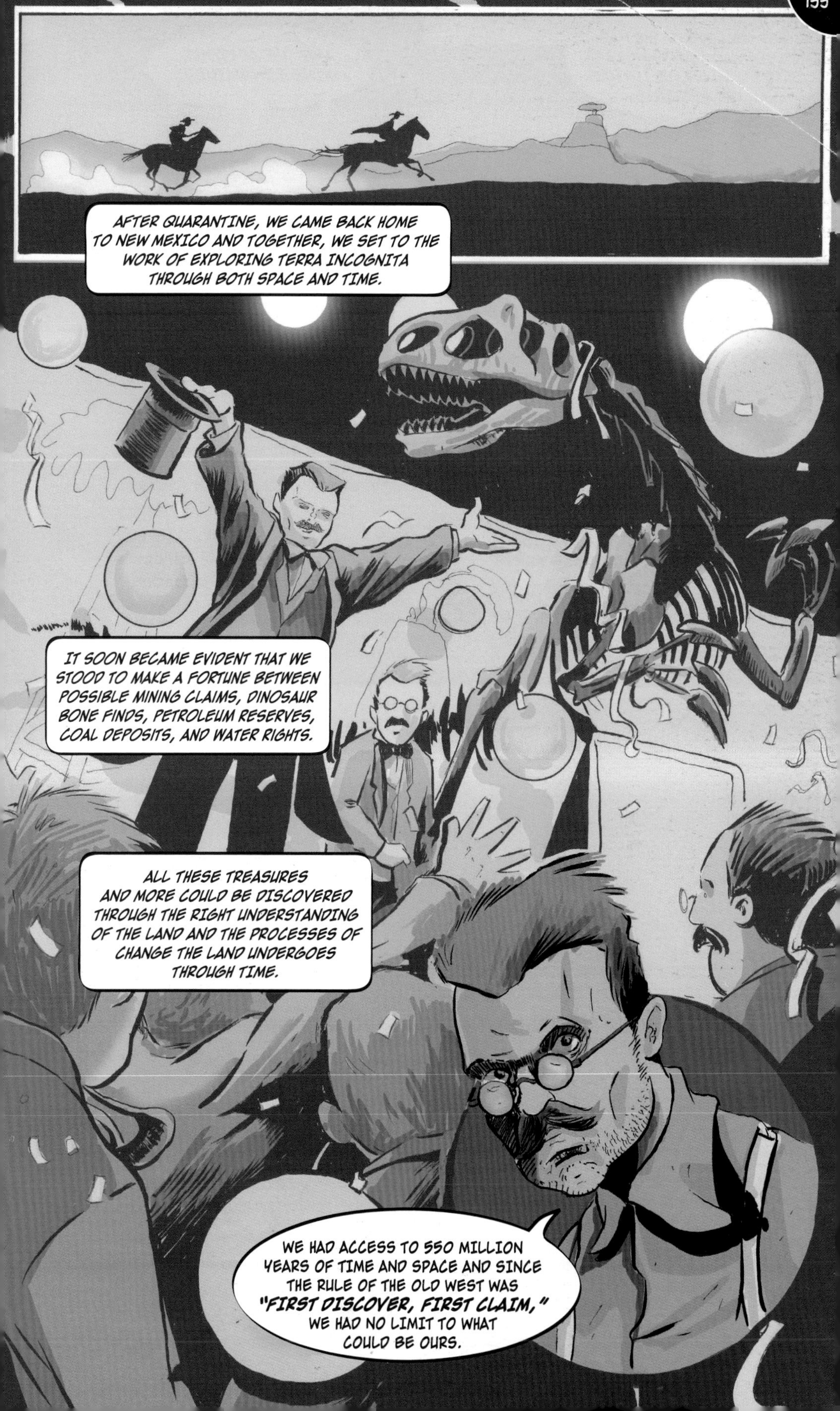
AFTER QUARANTINE, WE CAME BACK HOME TO NEW MEXICO AND TOGETHER, WE SET TO THE WORK OF EXPLORING TERRA INCOGNITA THROUGH BOTH SPACE AND TIME.
IT SOON BECAME EVIDENT THAT WE STOOD TO MAKE A FORTUNE BETWEEN POSSIBLE MINING CLAIMS, DINOSAUR BONE FINDS, PETROLEUM RESERVES, COAL DEPOSITS, AND WATER RIGHTS.
ALL THESE TREASURES AND MORE COULD BE DISCOVERED THROUGH THE RIGHT UNDERSTANDING OF THE LAND AND THE PROCESSES OF CHANGE THE LAND UNDERGOES THROUGH TIME.
WE HAD ACCESS TO 550 MILLION YEARS OF TIME AND SPACE AND SINCE THE RULE OF THE OLD WEST WAS ***"FIRST DISCOVER, FIRST CLAIM,"*** WE HAD NO LIMIT TO WHAT COULD BE OURS.

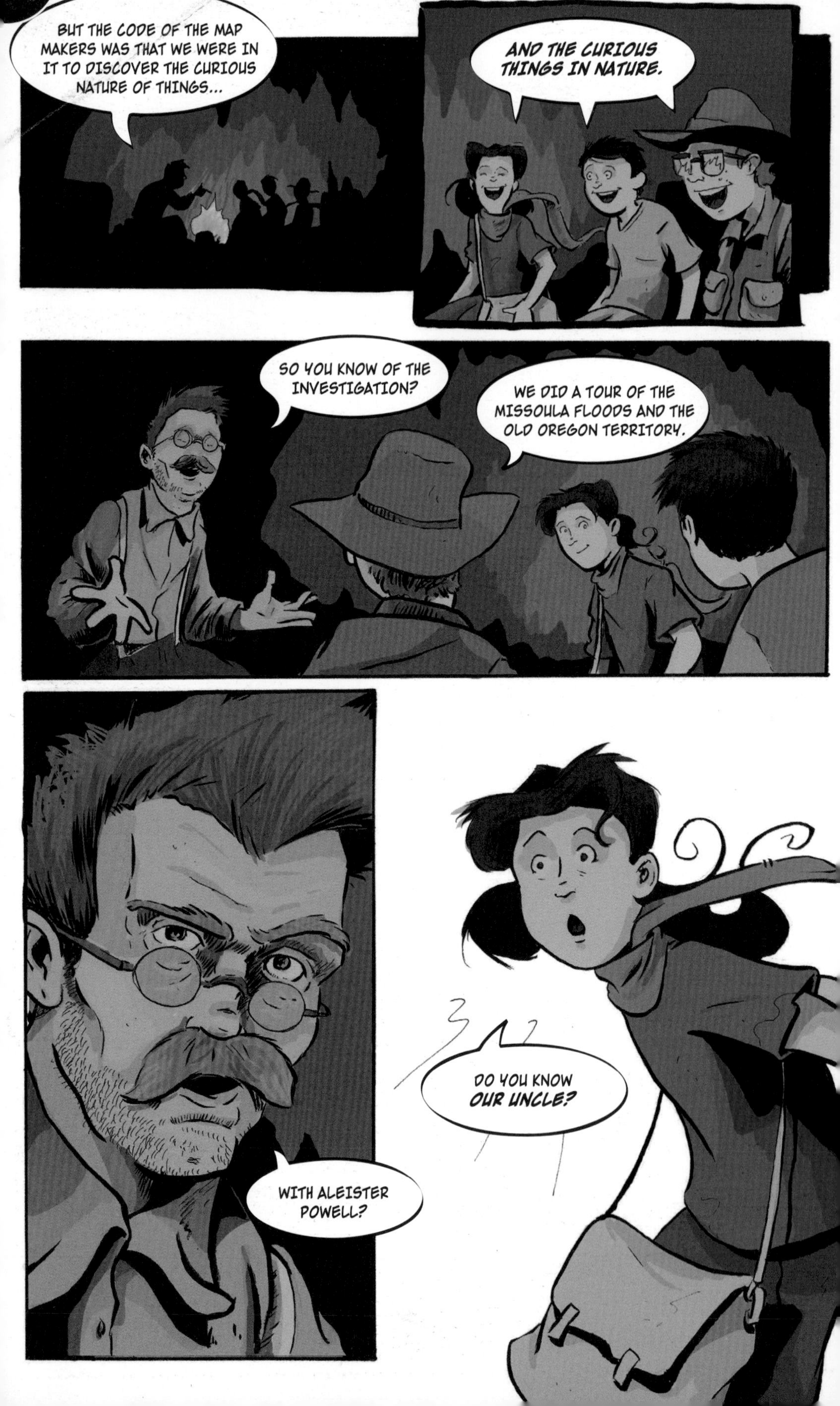
BUT THE CODE OF THE MAP MAKERS WAS THAT WE WERE IN IT TO DISCOVER THE CURIOUS NATURE OF THINGS...
AND THE CURIOUS THINGS IN NATURE.
SO YOU KNOW OF THE INVESTIGATION?
WE DID A TOUR OF THE MISSOULA FLOODS AND THE OLD OREGON TERRITORY.
WITH ALEISTER POWELL?
DO YOU KNOW OUR UNCLE?

I KNOW OF HIM.
WELL, I'D LIKE TO GET BACK TO HIM. HE'S IN ARIZONA IN 2012 WAITING FOR US.
WE'RE HAVING SOME TROUBLE WITH OUR MAP--MAYBE IT HAS SOME GLITCHES?
THE COLORADO PLATEAU CAN BE TRICKY AT TIMES. THIS MAP HAS BEEN MISSING SINCE THE GREAT DIVIDE OF THE GEOSOPHISTS.
PERMIAN
275 M.Y.A
ERROR
ERROR
ERROR
ERROR
ARIZONA
NEW MEXICO
I THOUGHT THE MAP WAS LOST. WHERE DID YOU FIND IT?
I FOUND IT IN THE CHINLE FORMATION IN 2012. IT WAS SEALED IN A CYLINDER AND BURIED IN THE DIRT.

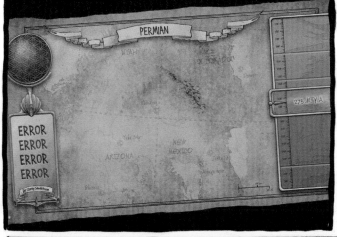

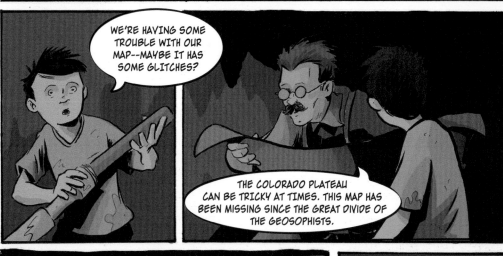

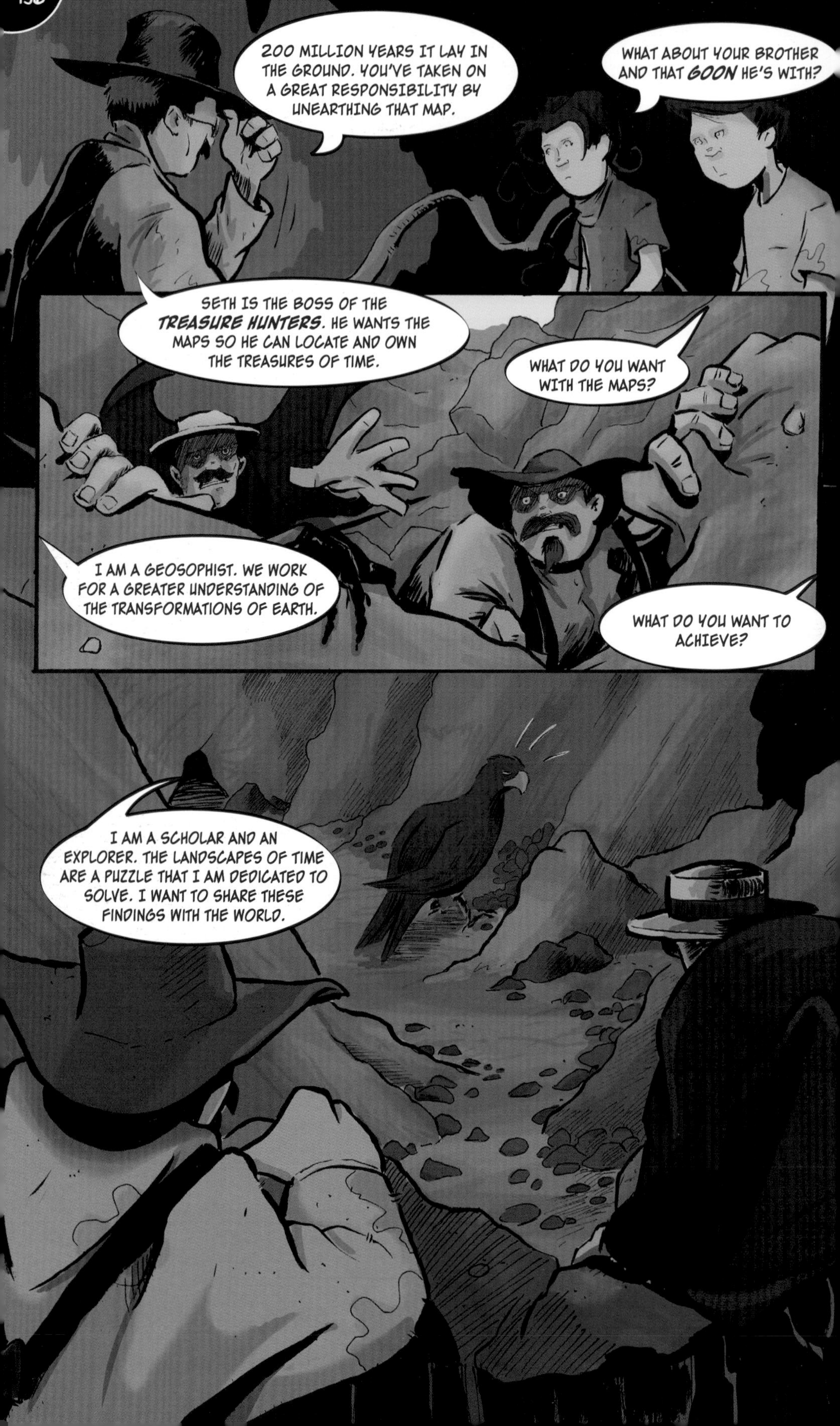
200 MILLION YEARS IT LAY IN THE GROUND. YOU'VE TAKEN ON A GREAT RESPONSIBILITY BY UNEARTHING THAT MAP.
WHAT ABOUT YOUR BROTHER AND THAT GOON HE'S WITH?
SETH IS THE BOSS OF THE TREASURE HUNTERS. HE WANTS THE MAPS SO HE CAN LOCATE AND OWN THE TREASURES OF TIME.
WHAT DO YOU WANT WITH THE MAPS?
I AM A GEOSOPHIST. WE WORK FOR A GREATER UNDERSTANDING OF THE TRANSFORMATIONS OF EARTH.
WHAT DO YOU WANT TO ACHIEVE?
I AM A SCHOLAR AND AN EXPLORER. THE LANDSCAPES OF TIME ARE A PUZZLE THAT I AM DEDICATED TO SOLVE. I WANT TO SHARE THESE FINDINGS WITH THE WORLD.

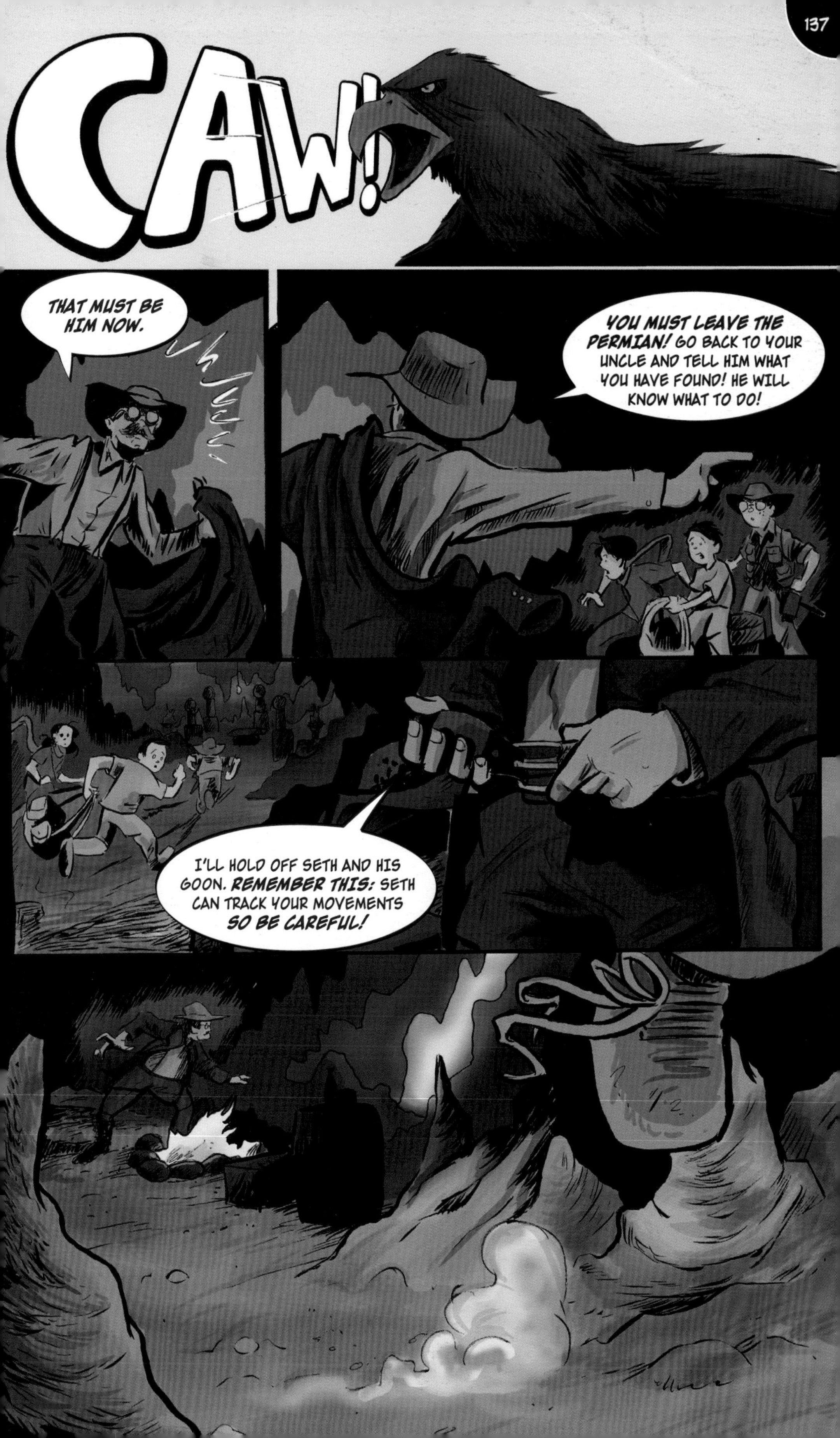
CAW!
THAT MUST BE HIM NOW.
YOU MUST LEAVE THE PERMIAN! GO BACK TO YOUR UNCLE AND TELL HIM WHAT YOU HAVE FOUND! HE WILL KNOW WHAT TO DO!
I'LL HOLD OFF SETH AND HIS GOON. REMEMBER THIS: SETH CAN TRACK YOUR MOVEMENTS SO BE CAREFUL!

LEVI! WE KNOW YOU'RE IN THERE!

click

KPCHK!

PUKCH!

PUKCH!

CPKKK!

PCKKK!

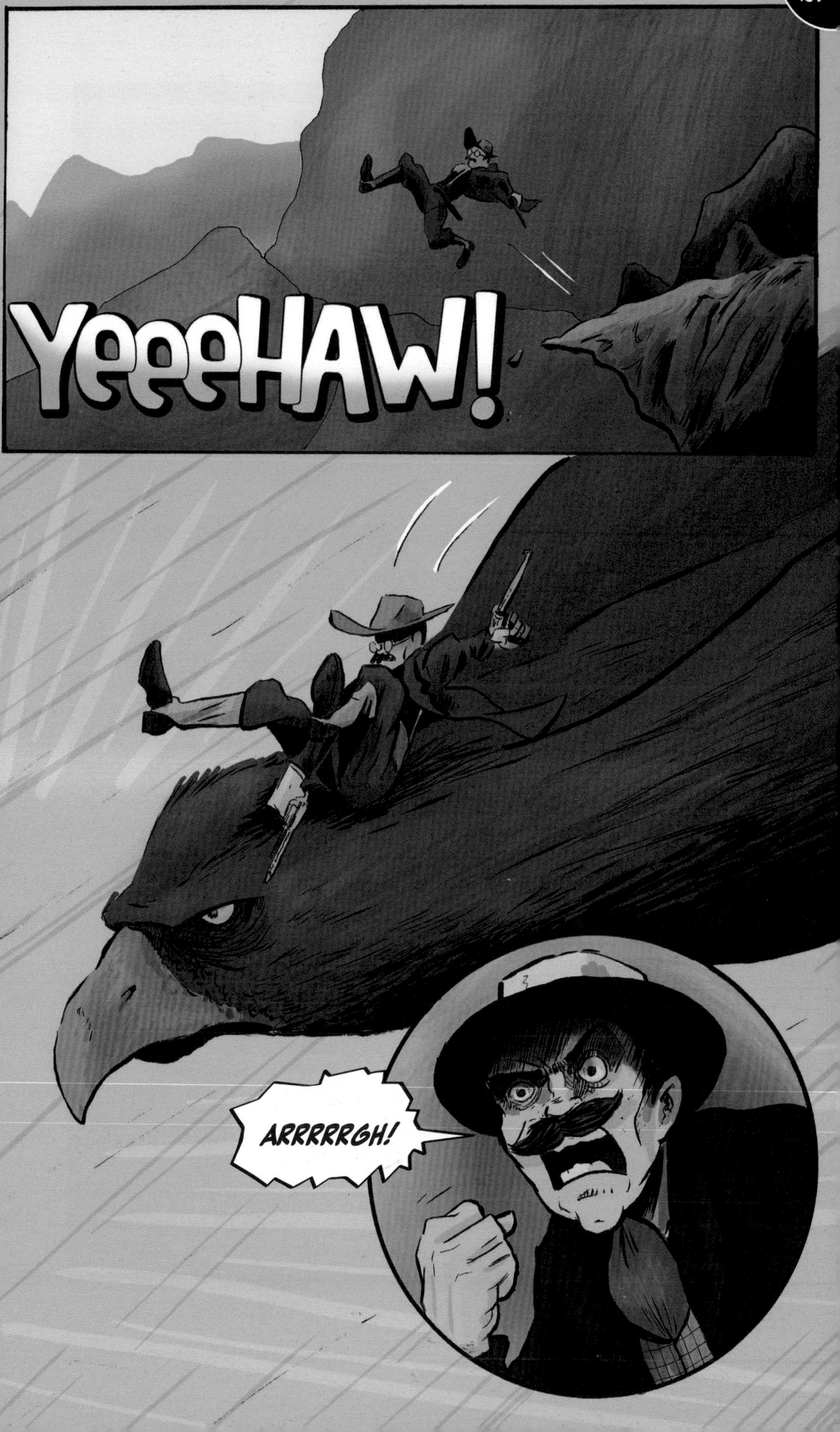
YEEEHAW!
ARRRRRGH!

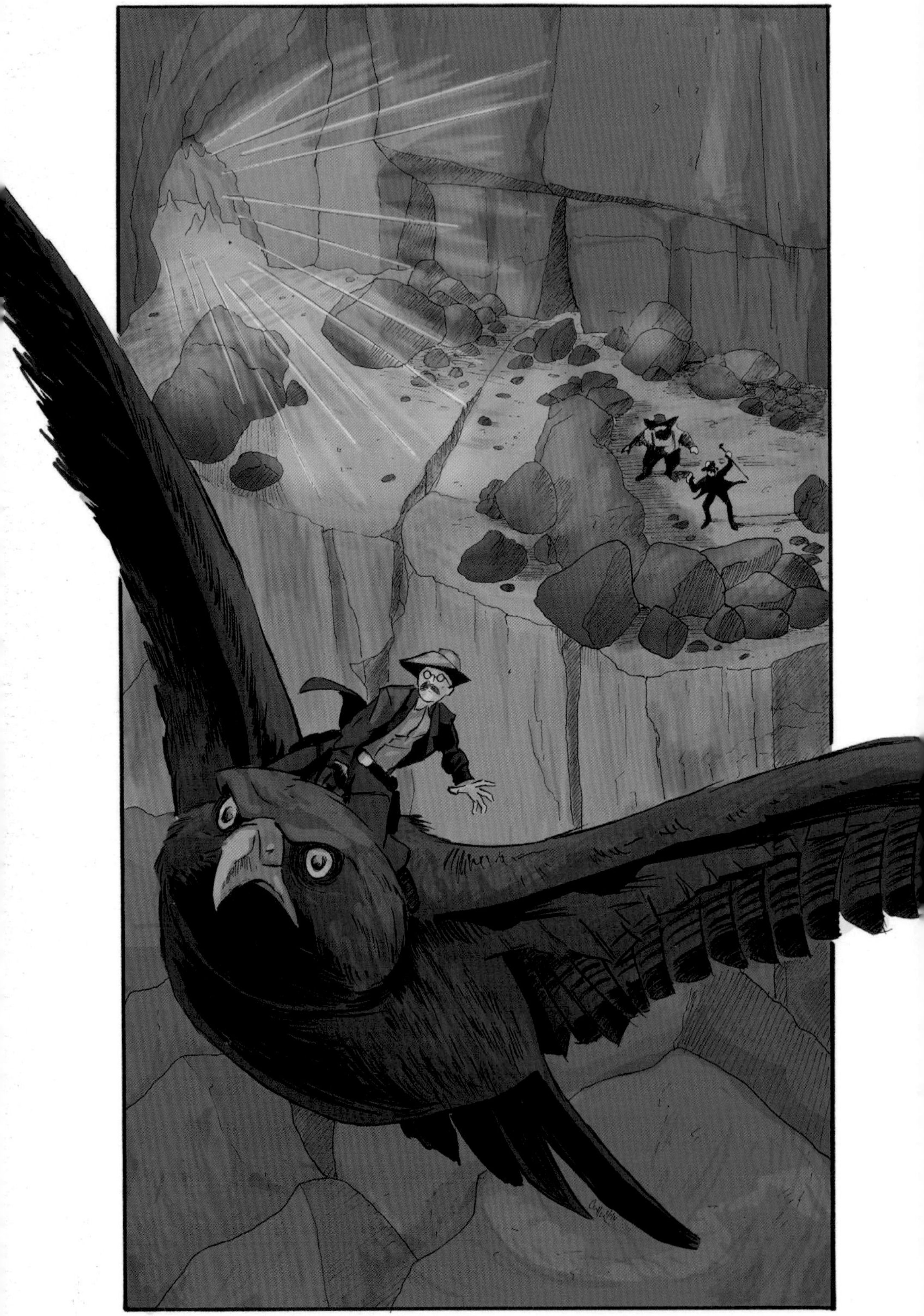

CHAPTER SIX

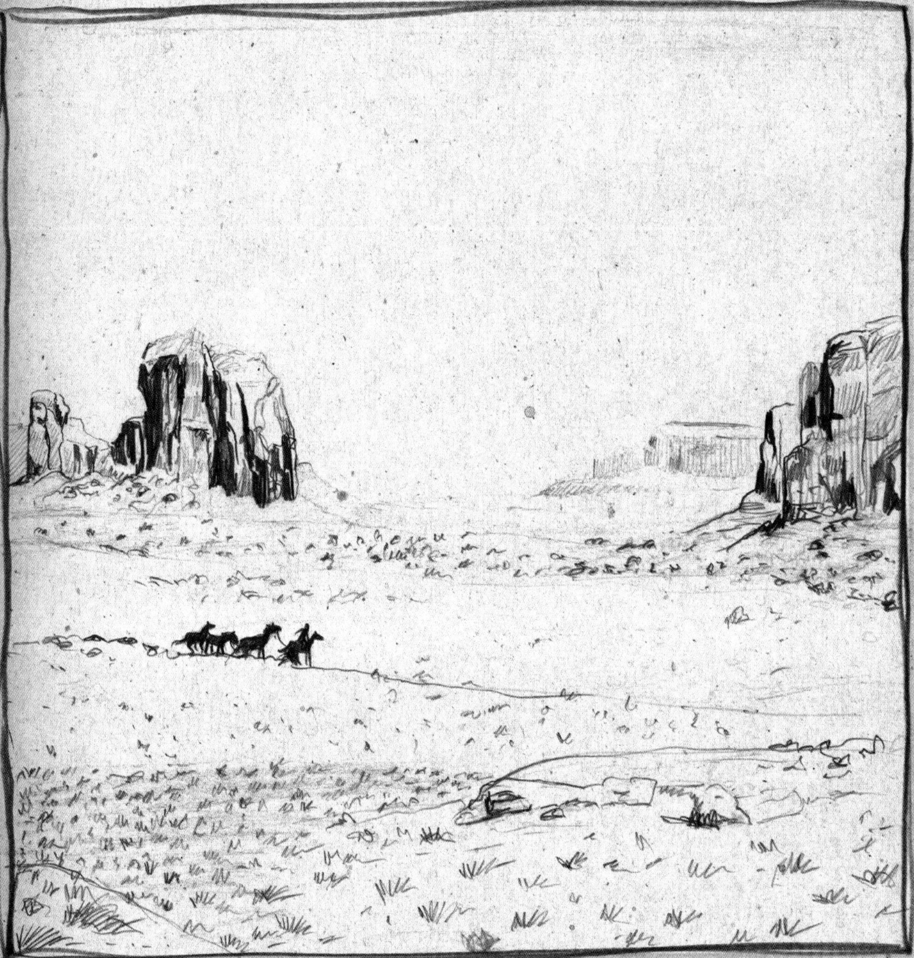

TSÉ BII' NDZISGAII

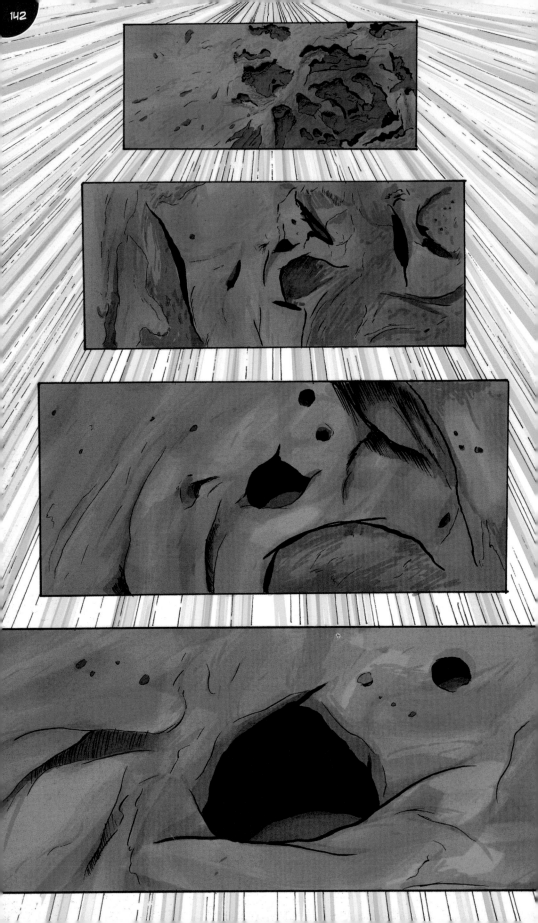

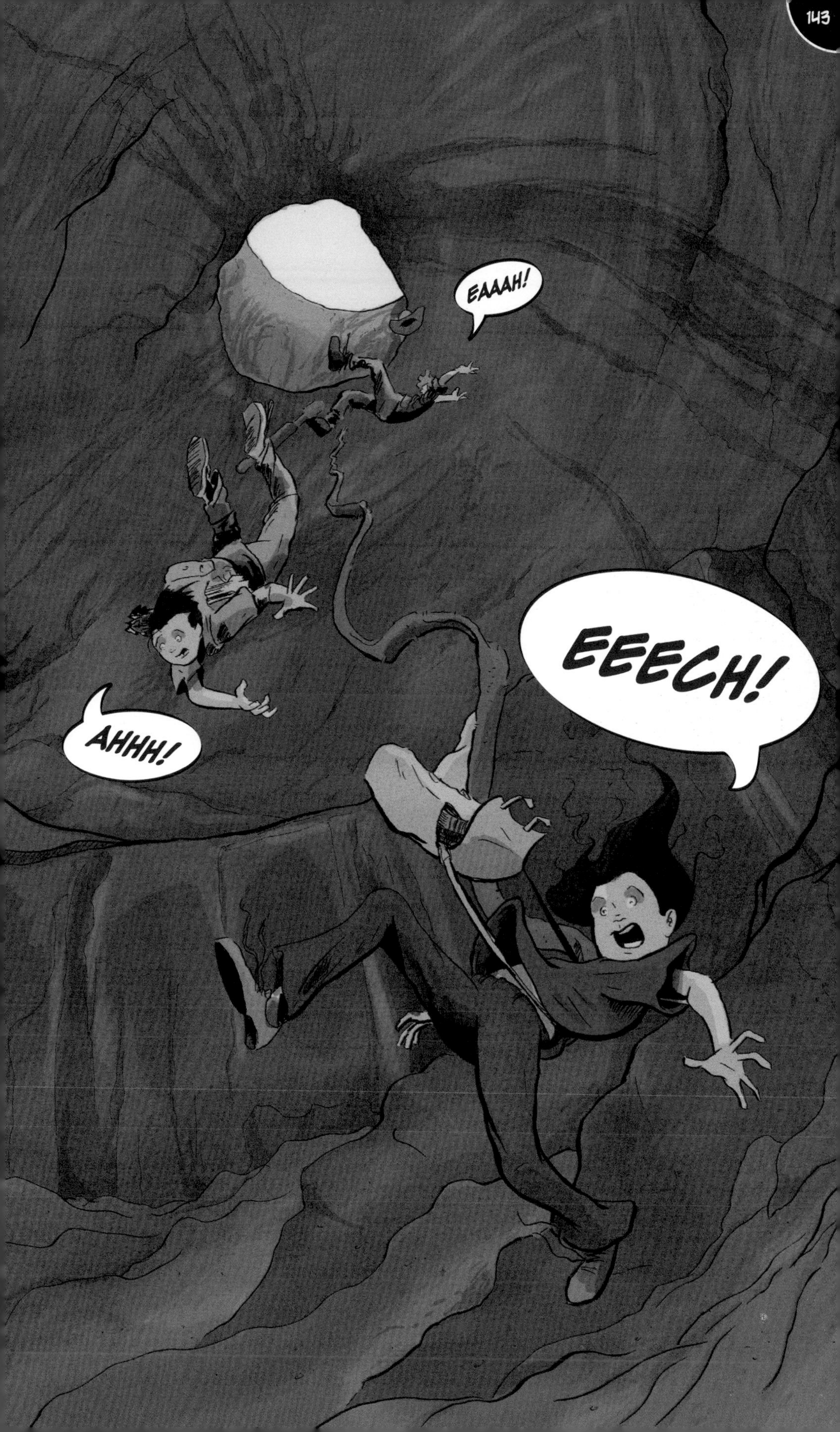
EAAAH!
AHHH!
EEECH!

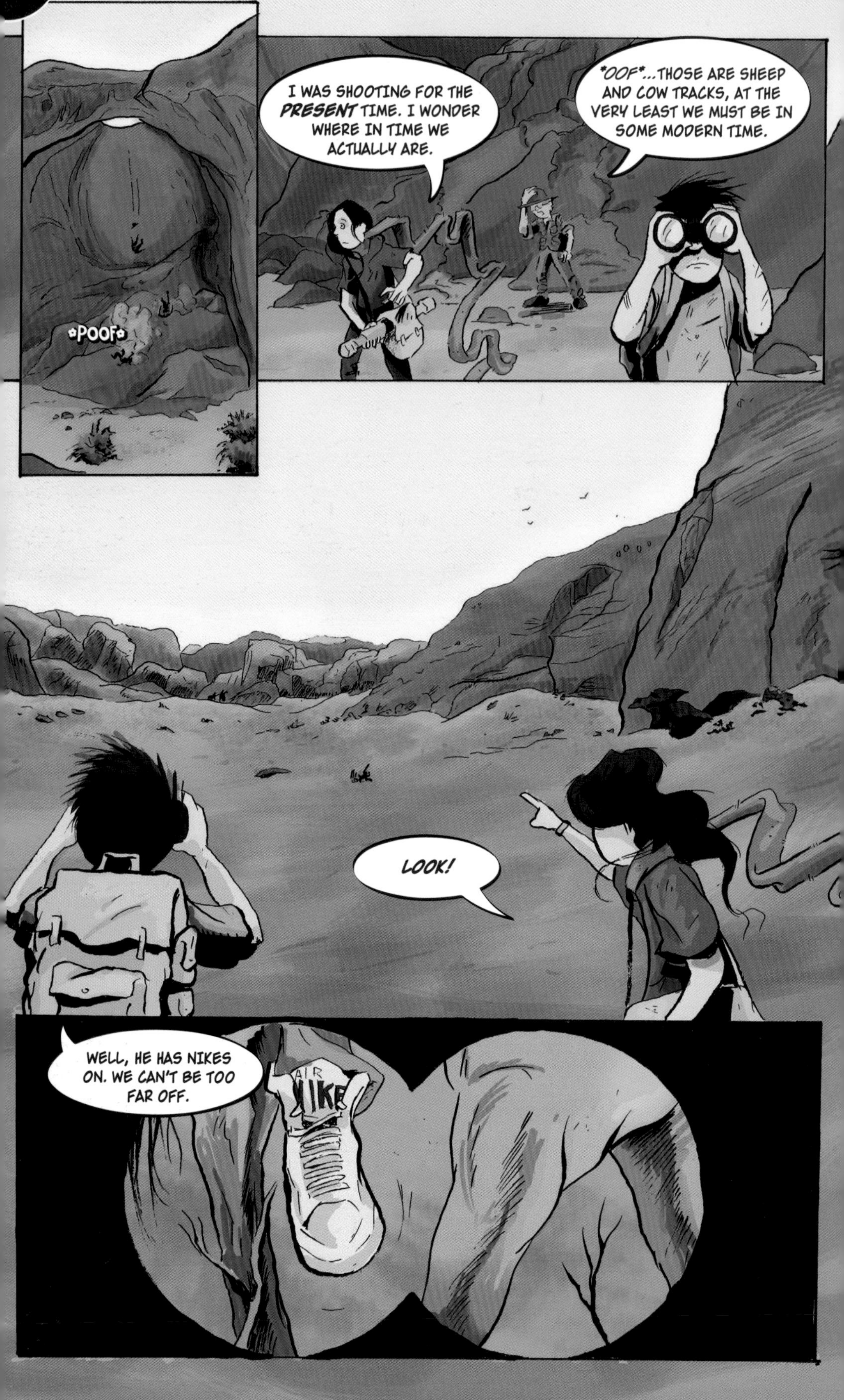
POOF
I WAS SHOOTING FOR THE PRESENT TIME. I WONDER WHERE IN TIME WE ACTUALLY ARE.
OOF...THOSE ARE SHEEP AND COW TRACKS, AT THE VERY LEAST WE MUST BE IN SOME MODERN TIME.
LOOK!
WELL, HE HAS NIKES ON. WE CAN'T BE TOO FAR OFF.
AIR
NIKE

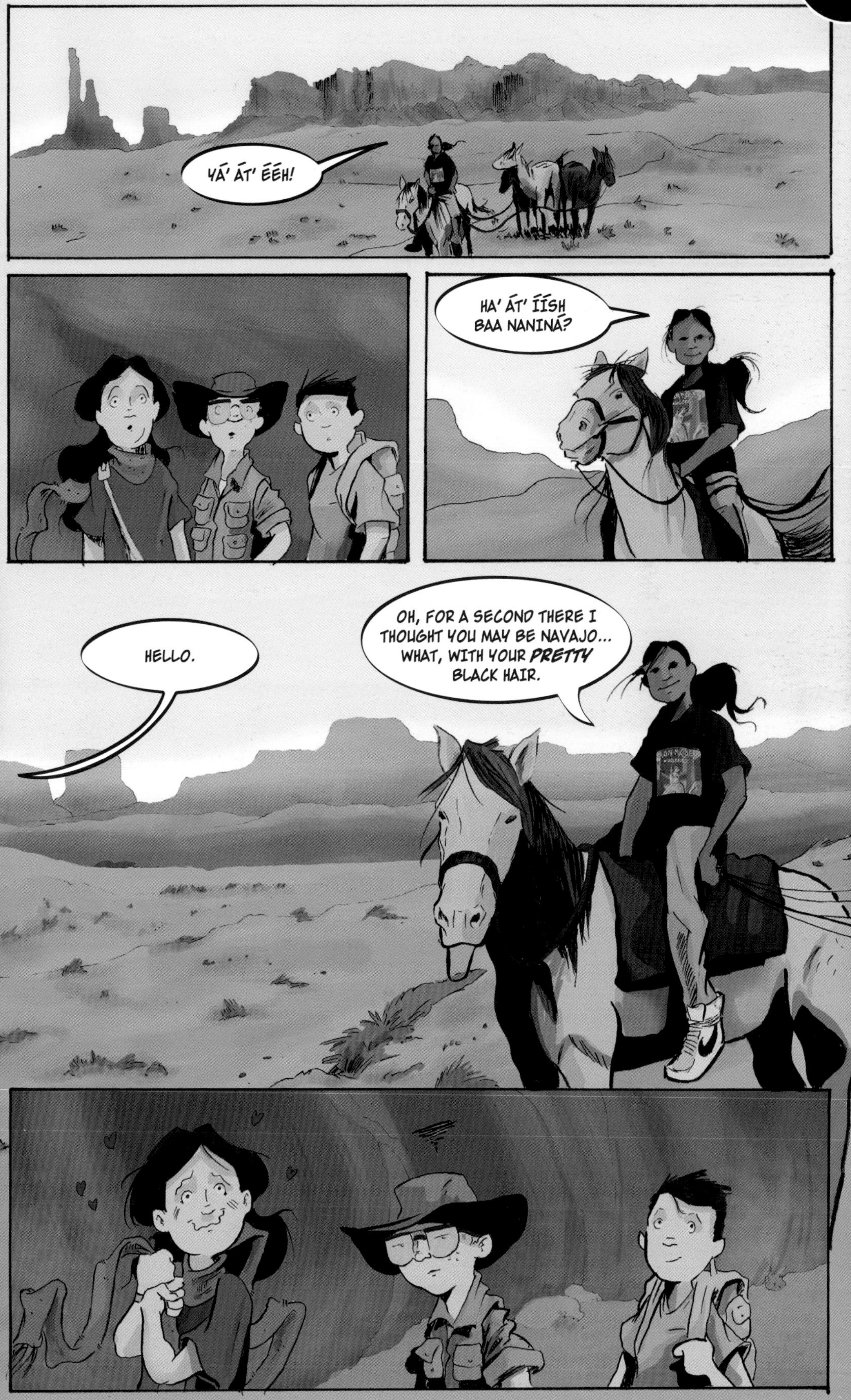
YÁ' ÁT' ÉÉH!
HA' ÁT' ÍÍSH BAA NANINÁ?
HELLO.
OH, FOR A SECOND THERE I THOUGHT YOU MAY BE NAVAJO... WHAT, WITH YOUR PRETTY BLACK HAIR.

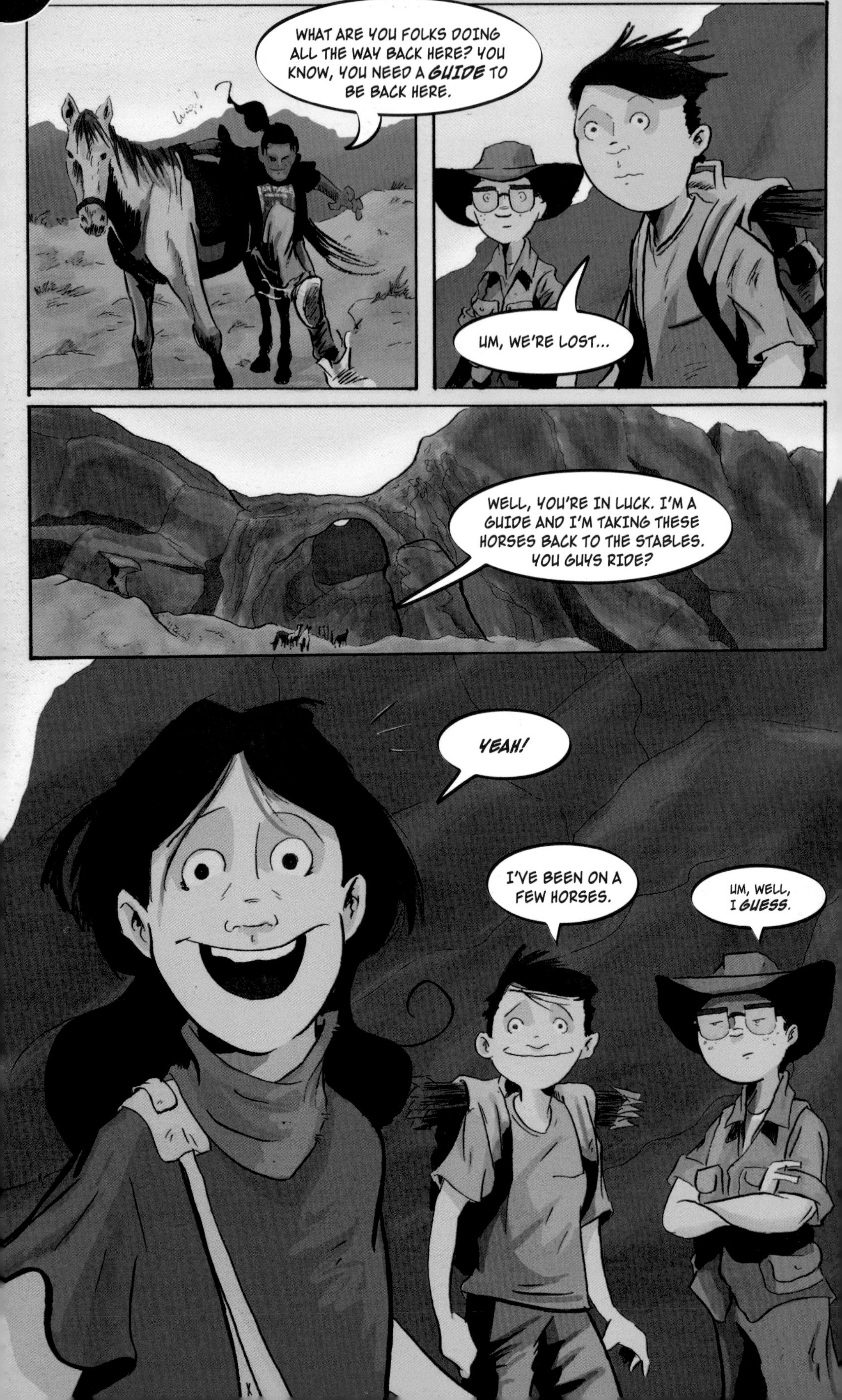
WHAT ARE YOU FOLKS DOING ALL THE WAY BACK HERE? YOU KNOW, YOU NEED A *GUIDE* TO BE BACK HERE.
UM, WE'RE LOST...
WELL, YOU'RE IN LUCK. I'M A GUIDE AND I'M TAKING THESE HORSES BACK TO THE STABLES. YOU GUYS RIDE?
YEAH!
I'VE BEEN ON A FEW HORSES.
UM, WELL, I *GUESS*.

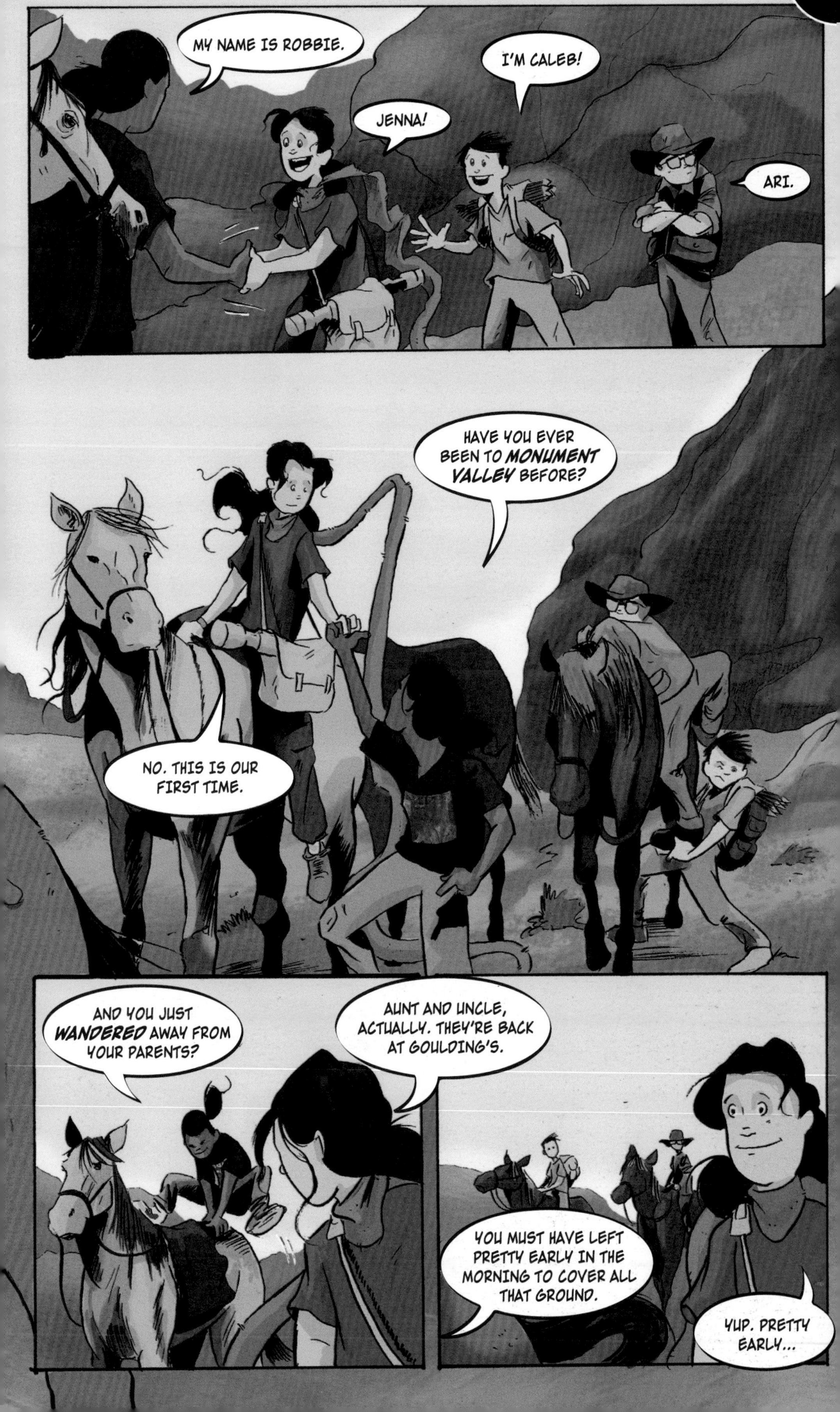
MY NAME IS ROBBIE.
JENNA!
I'M CALEB!
ARI.
HAVE YOU EVER BEEN TO MONUMENT VALLEY BEFORE?
NO. THIS IS OUR FIRST TIME.
AND YOU JUST WANDERED AWAY FROM YOUR PARENTS?
AUNT AND UNCLE, ACTUALLY. THEY'RE BACK AT GOULDING'S.
YOU MUST HAVE LEFT PRETTY EARLY IN THE MORNING TO COVER ALL THAT GROUND.
YUP. PRETTY EARLY...

WHAT KIND OF MUSIC DO YOU LIKE?
I'VE BEEN REALLY INTO BLIND PILOT LATELY...
I HAVEN'T HEARD OF THEM.
MUST BE A NORTHWEST THING. I'M FROM PORTLAND, OREGON. WHAT BANDS DO YOU LIKE?
METALLICA, ANTHRAX, AND OF COURSE, IRON MAIDEN. ONE OF MY CLIENTS JUST GAVE ME THIS NEW 1986 TOUR TEE.
THEY JUST SAW 'EM A FEW WEEKS AGO IN ALBUQUERQUE. I WAS SO PSYCHED. WE DON'T GET ANY MAJOR ACTS COMING THROUGH THE RESERVATION, SO I DON'T GET TO SEE THE MUSIC I LOVE LIVE...

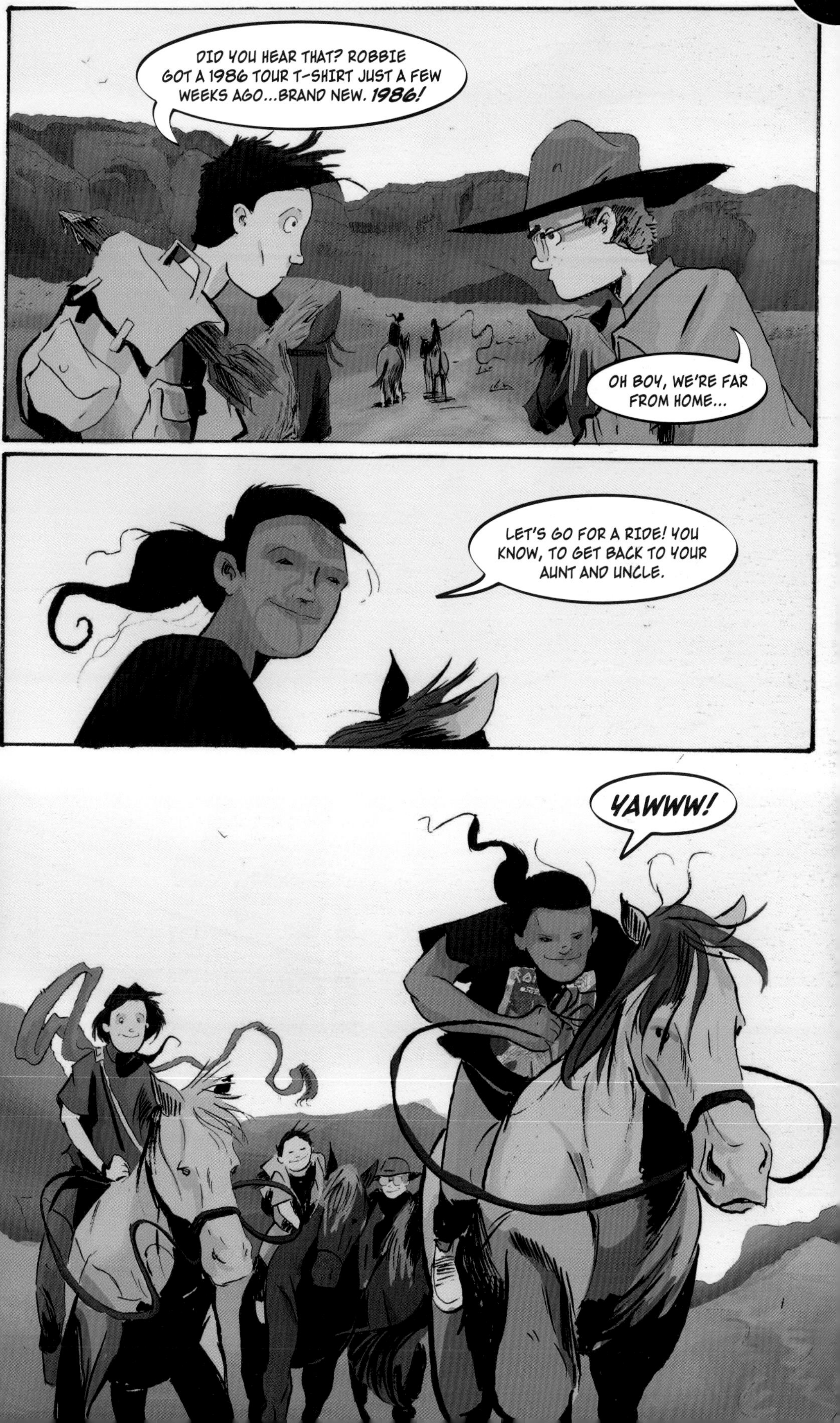
DID YOU HEAR THAT? ROBBIE GOT A 1986 TOUR T-SHIRT JUST A FEW WEEKS AGO...BRAND NEW. *1986!*
OH BOY, WE'RE FAR FROM HOME...
LET'S GO FOR A RIDE! YOU KNOW, TO GET BACK TO YOUR AUNT AND UNCLE.
YAWWW!

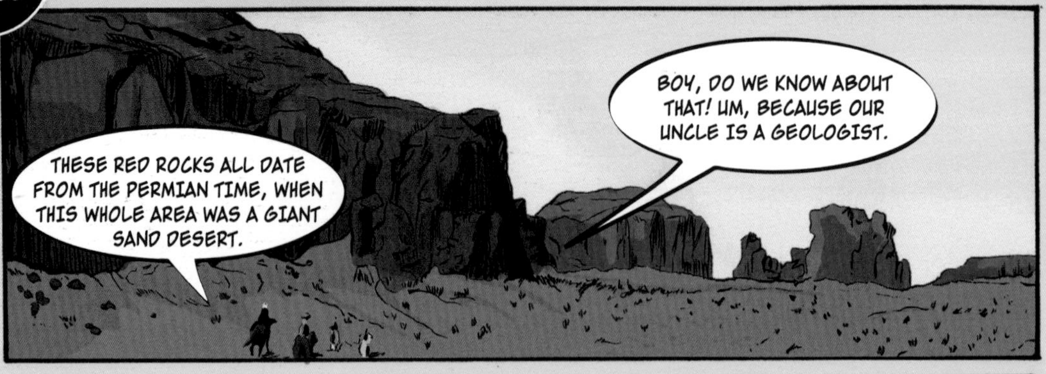
THESE RED ROCKS ALL DATE FROM THE PERMIAN TIME, WHEN THIS WHOLE AREA WAS A GIANT SAND DESERT.
BOY, DO WE KNOW ABOUT THAT! UM, BECAUSE OUR UNCLE IS A GEOLOGIST.

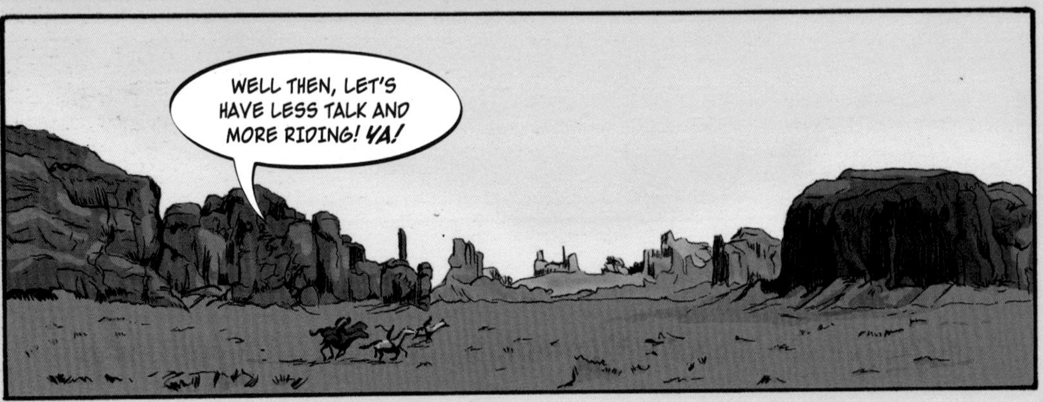
WELL THEN, LET'S HAVE LESS TALK AND MORE RIDING! YA!

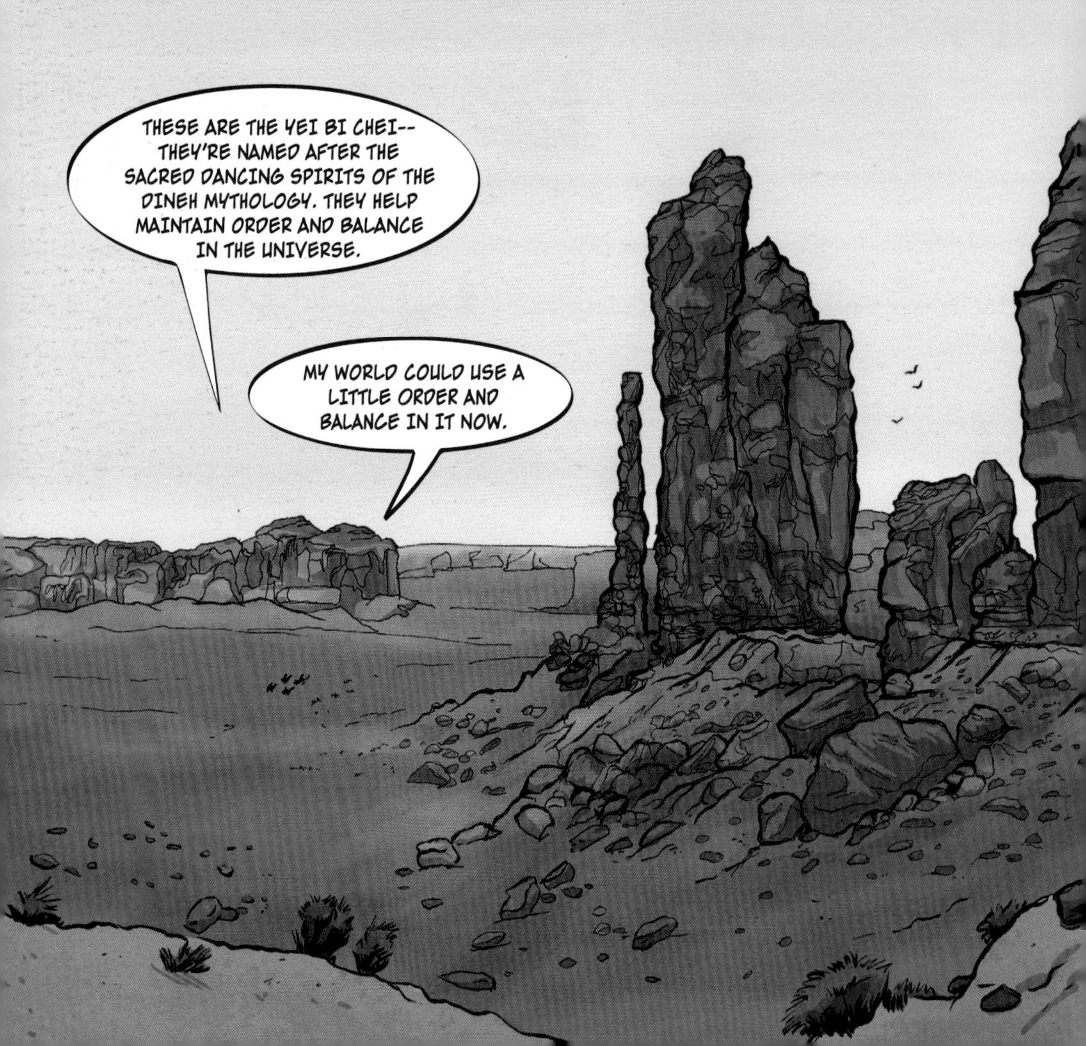
THESE ARE THE YEI BI CHEI-- THEY'RE NAMED AFTER THE SACRED DANCING SPIRITS OF THE DINEH MYTHOLOGY. THEY HELP MAINTAIN ORDER AND BALANCE IN THE UNIVERSE.
MY WORLD COULD USE A LITTLE ORDER AND BALANCE IN IT NOW.

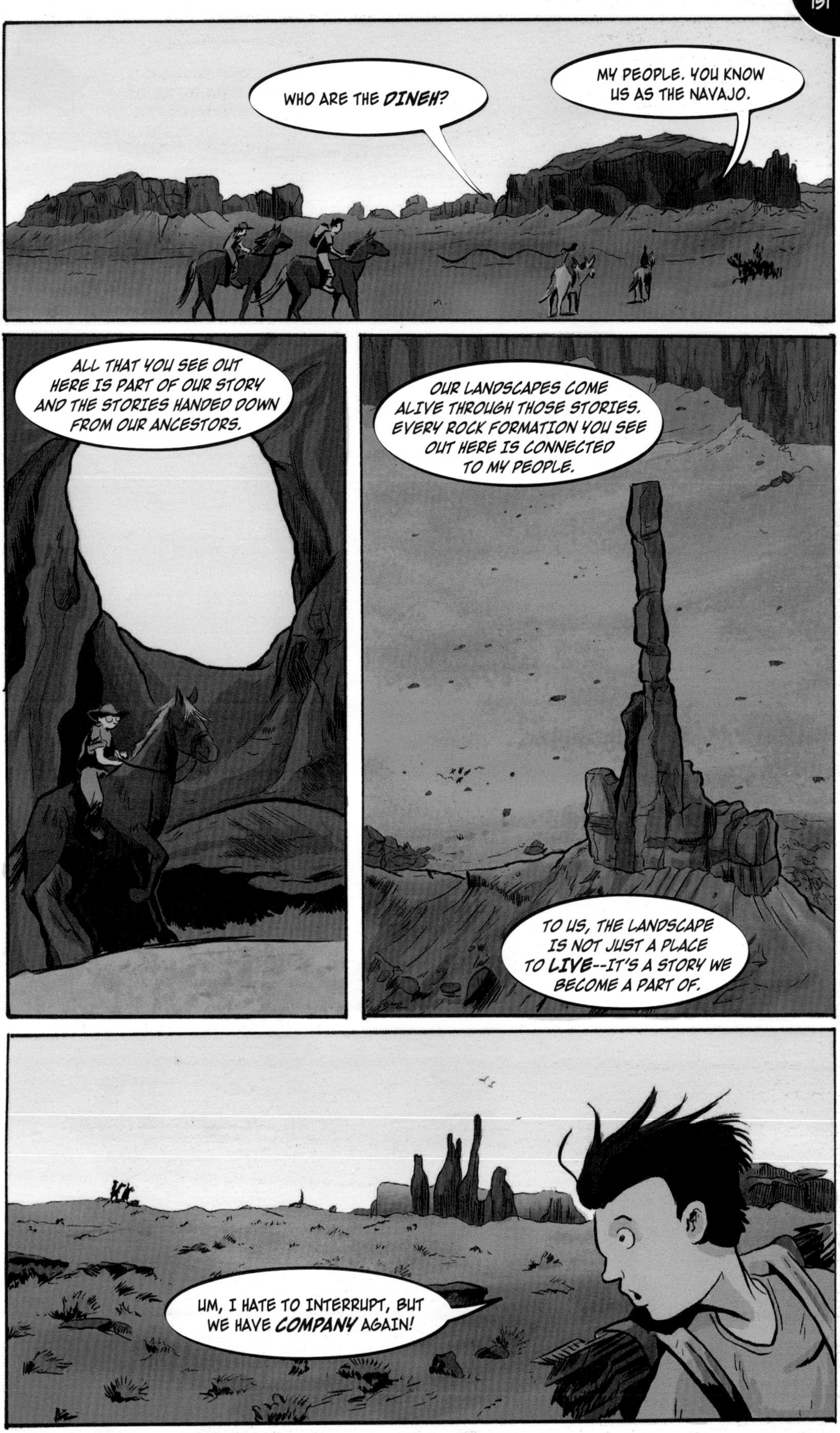
WHO ARE THE DINEH?
MY PEOPLE. YOU KNOW US AS THE NAVAJO.
ALL THAT YOU SEE OUT HERE IS PART OF OUR STORY AND THE STORIES HANDED DOWN FROM OUR ANCESTORS.
OUR LANDSCAPES COME ALIVE THROUGH THOSE STORIES. EVERY ROCK FORMATION YOU SEE OUT HERE IS CONNECTED TO MY PEOPLE.
TO US, THE LANDSCAPE IS NOT JUST A PLACE TO LIVE--IT'S A STORY WE BECOME A PART OF.
UM, I HATE TO INTERRUPT, BUT WE HAVE COMPANY AGAIN!

UM, ROBBIE, THOSE GUYS ARE REAL BAD NEWS AND THEY HAVE GUNS AND THEY REALLY WANT TO STEAL SOMETHING OF OURS!
WE'VE BEEN ON THE RUN FROM THEM FOR A WHILE NOW. THERE'S A LOT WE HAVEN'T TOLD YOU. IT'S KIND OF ***UNBELIEVABLE***... BUT WE'RE ALL IN REAL DANGER RIGHT NOW!
THEN LET'S RIDE. WE'LL MAKE FAT BOY AND HIS FRIEND WORK FOR IT!
THIS WAY, FOLLOW ME!

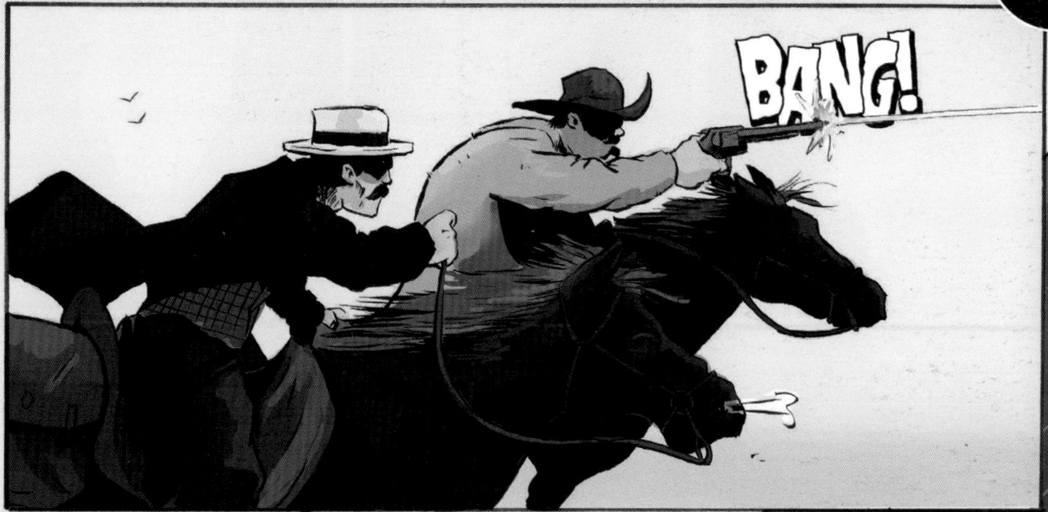
BANG!

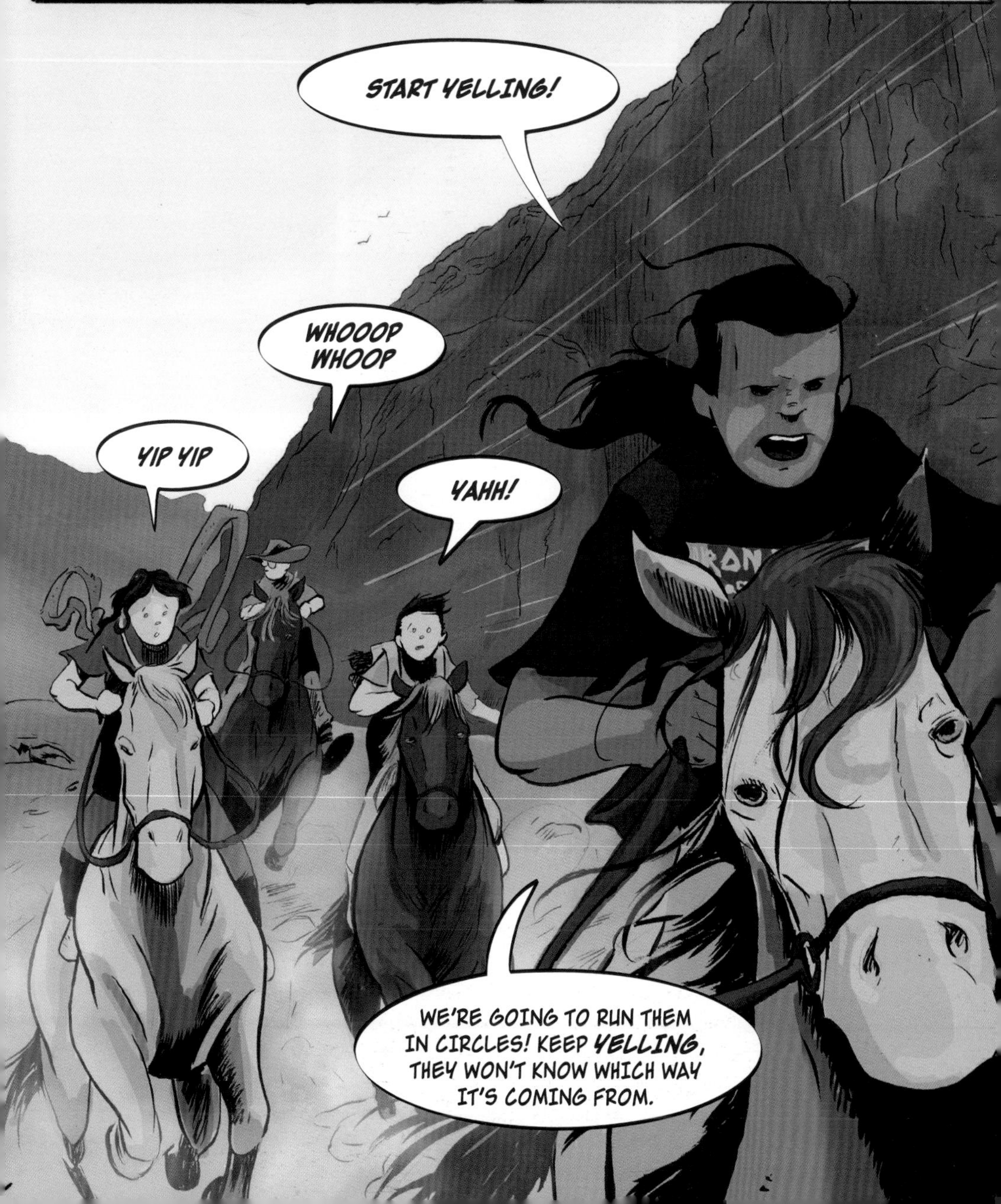
START YELLING!
WHOOOP WHOOP
YIP YIP
YAHH!
WE'RE GOING TO RUN THEM IN CIRCLES! KEEP YELLING, THEY WON'T KNOW WHICH WAY IT'S COMING FROM.

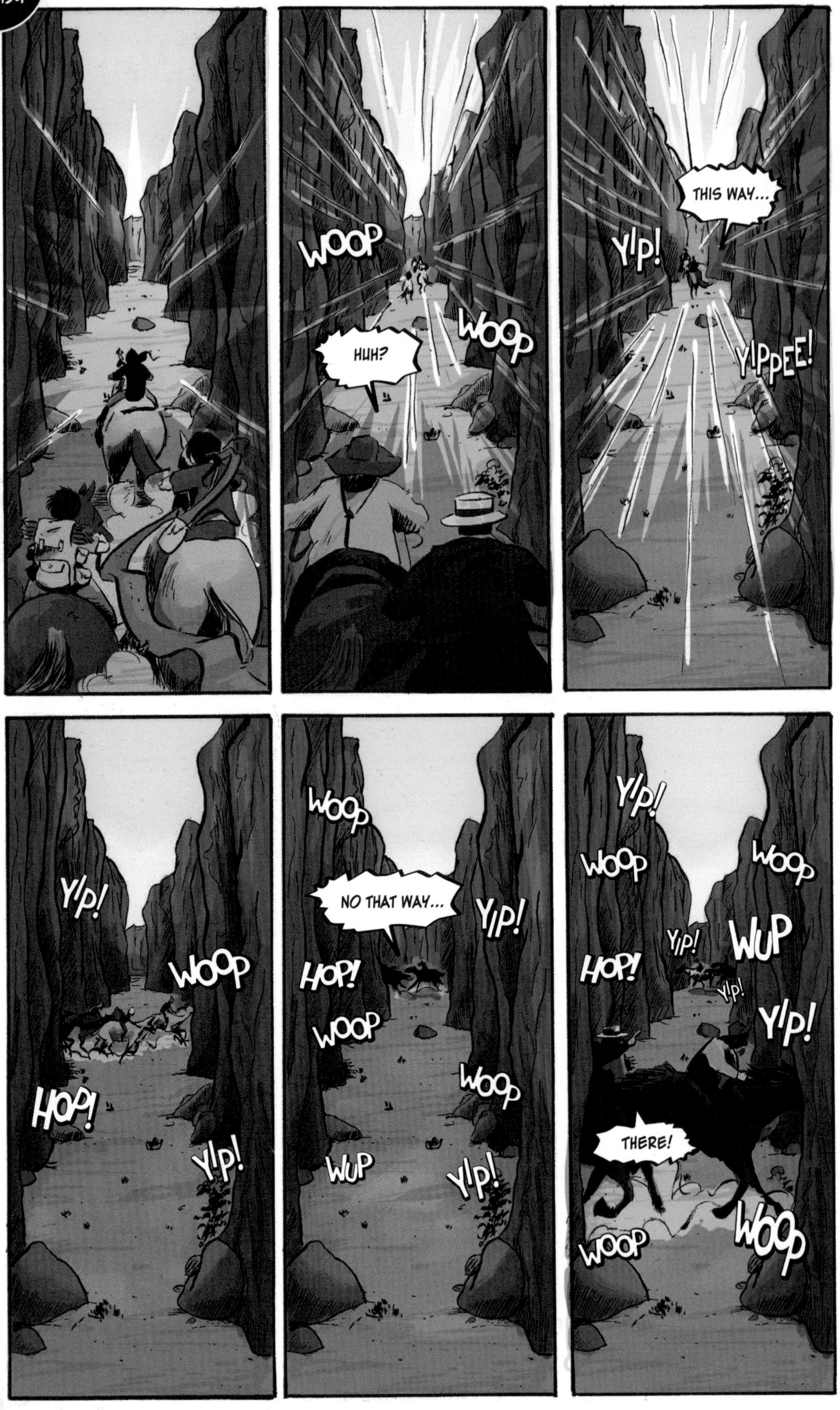
WOOP
HUH?
WOOP
YIP!
THIS WAY...
YIPPEE!
YIP!
WOOP
HOP!
YIP!
WOOP
NO THAT WAY...
YIP!
HOP!
WOOP
WOOP
WUP
YIP!
YIP!
WOOP
WOOP
YIP!
WUP
HOP!
YIP!
YIP!
THERE!
WOOP
WOOP

YIP!
WOOP
WOOP
YIP!
WUP
YIP!
YIP!
HOP!
YIPPEE!
WUP
YIP!
WHOOPEE!
WOOP
WOOP
WOOP
WUP
YIP!
HOP!
WHOOPEE!
HOP!
YIPPEE!
YIP!
WOOP
YIP!
WOOP
WHERE ARE THEY?
YIP YIP

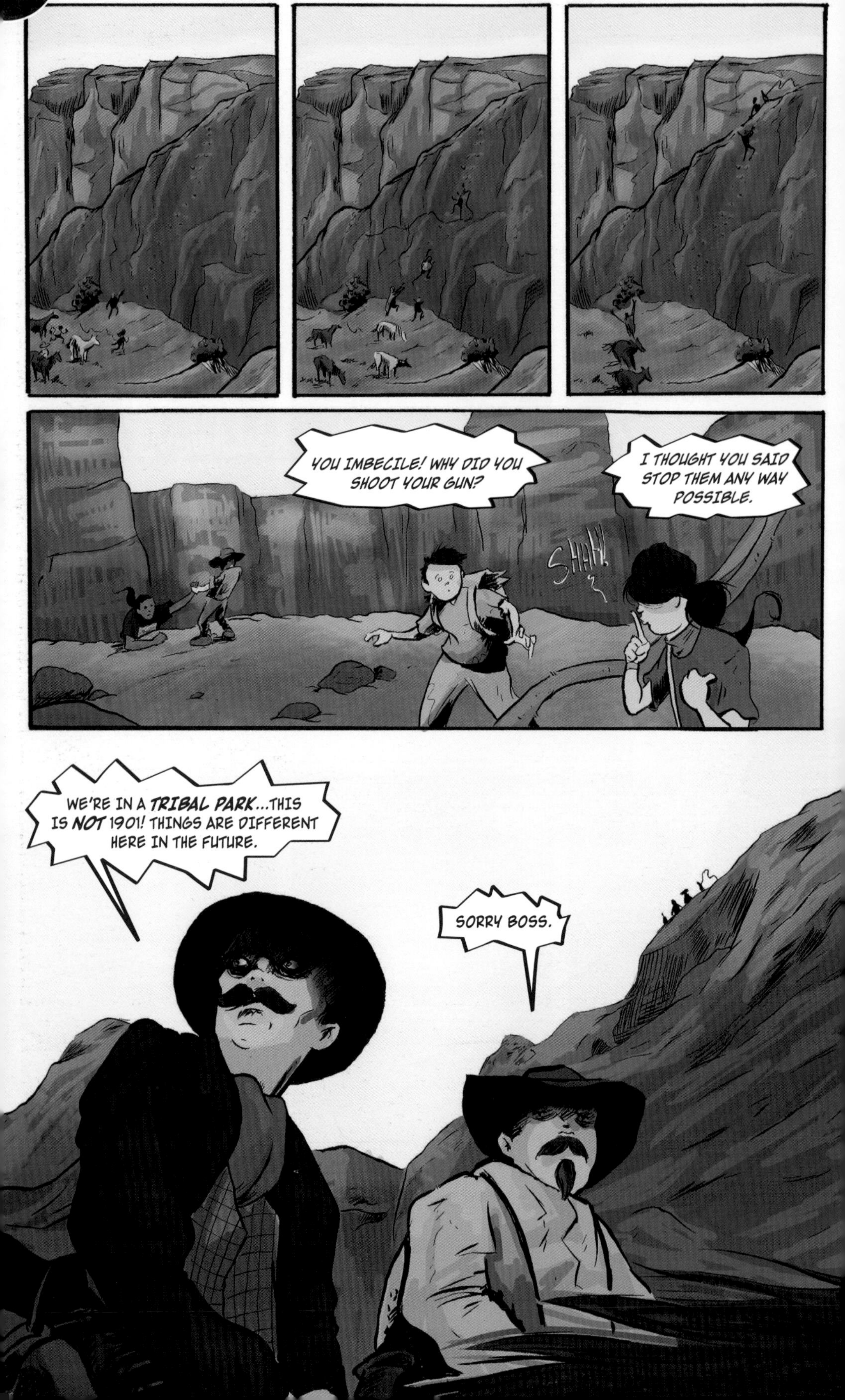
YOU IMBECILE! WHY DID YOU SHOOT YOUR GUN?
I THOUGHT YOU SAID STOP THEM ANY WAY POSSIBLE.
SHH!
WE'RE IN A **TRIBAL PARK**...THIS IS **NOT** 1901! THINGS ARE DIFFERENT HERE IN THE FUTURE.
SORRY BOSS.

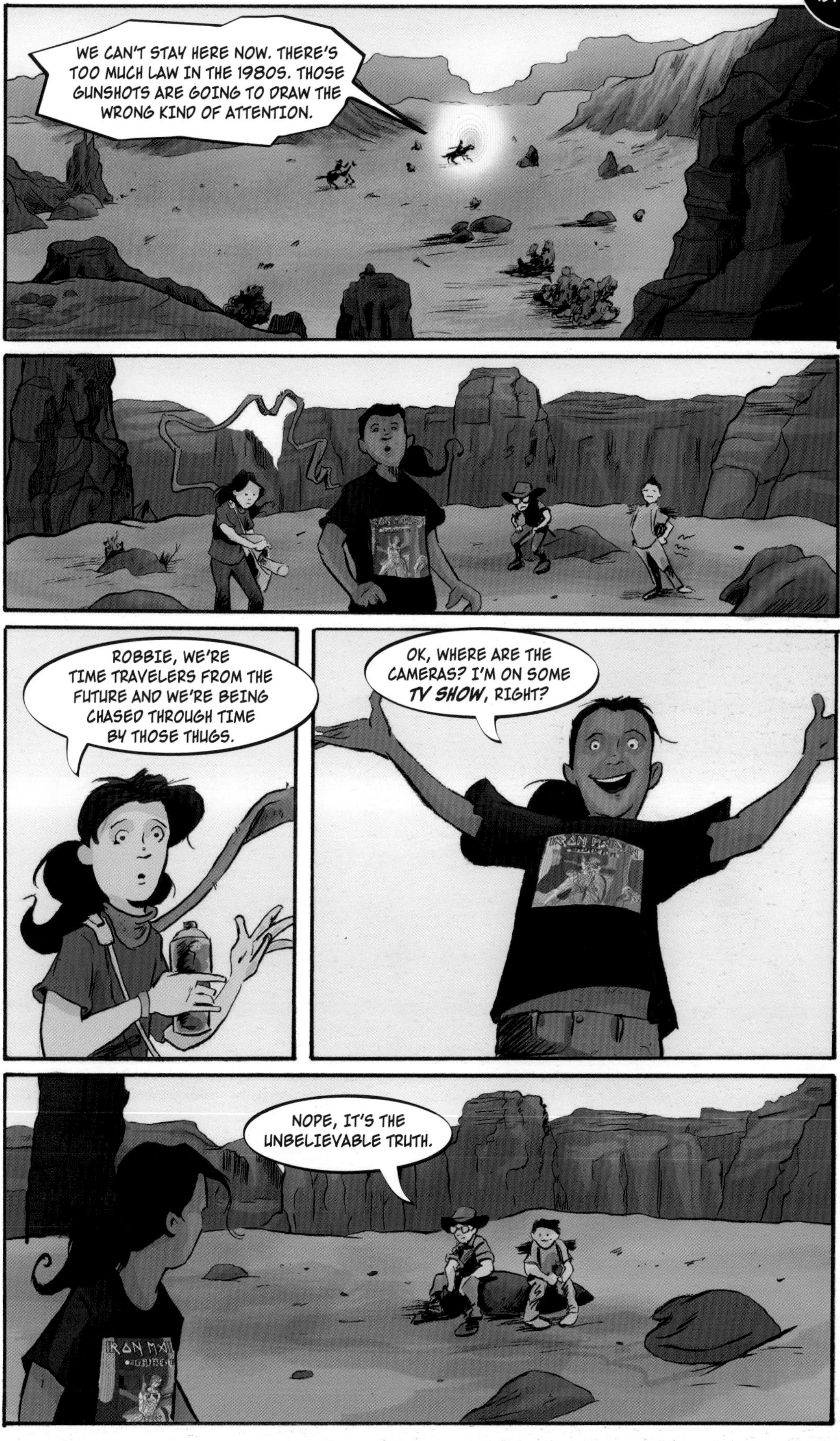
WE CAN'T STAY HERE NOW. THERE'S TOO MUCH LAW IN THE 1980S. THOSE GUNSHOTS ARE GOING TO DRAW THE WRONG KIND OF ATTENTION.
ROBBIE, WE'RE TIME TRAVELERS FROM THE FUTURE AND WE'RE BEING CHASED THROUGH TIME BY THOSE THUGS.
OK, WHERE ARE THE CAMERAS? I'M ON SOME *TV SHOW*, RIGHT?
NOPE, IT'S THE UNBELIEVABLE TRUTH.

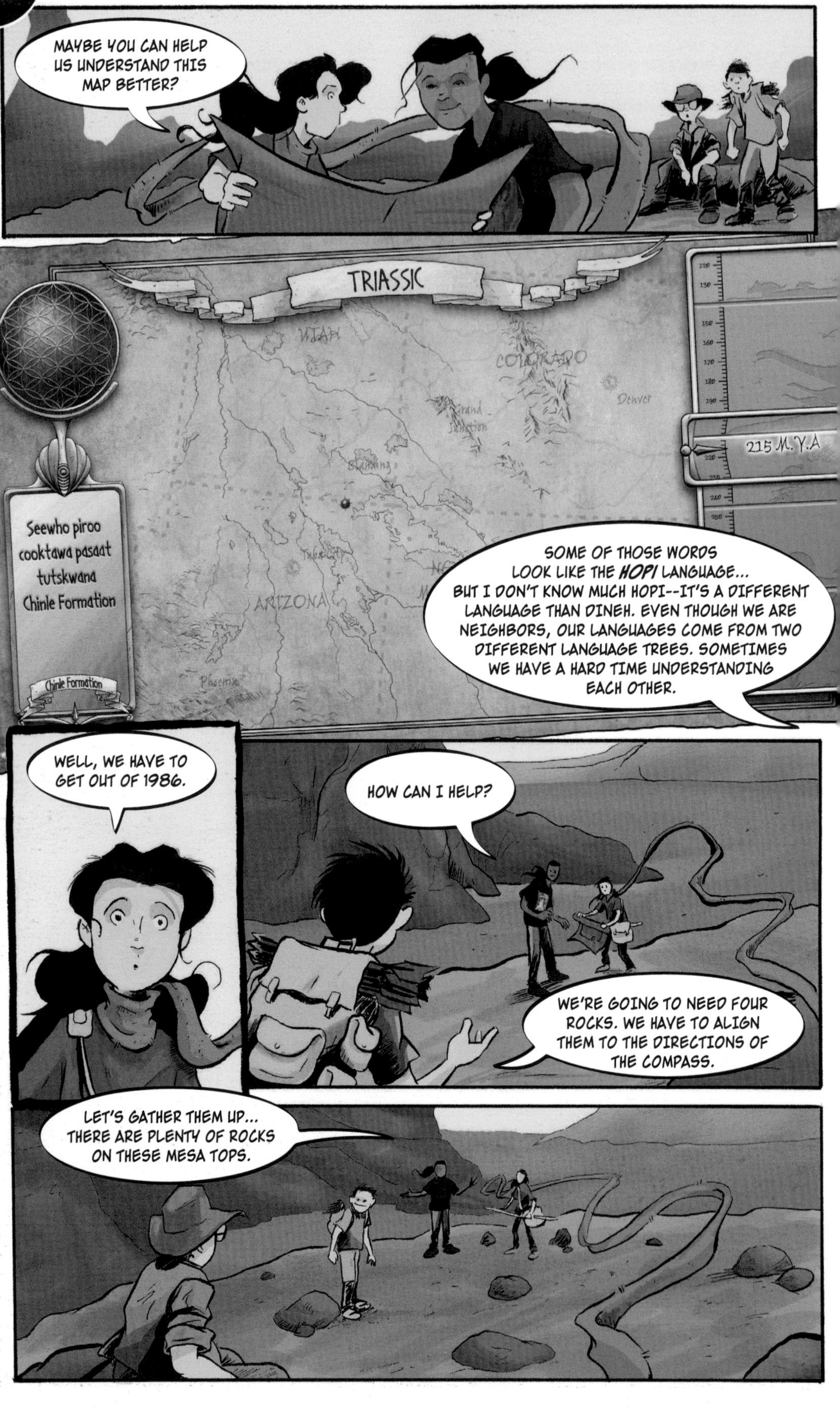
MAYBE YOU CAN HELP US UNDERSTAND THIS MAP BETTER?
TRIASSIC
UTAH
COLORADO
Denver
Grand Junction
Blanding
ARIZONA
Phoenix
215 M.Y.A
Seewho piroo cooktawa pasaat tutskwana Chinle Formation
Chinle Formation
SOME OF THOSE WORDS LOOK LIKE THE *HOPI* LANGUAGE... BUT I DON'T KNOW MUCH HOPI--IT'S A DIFFERENT LANGUAGE THAN DINEH. EVEN THOUGH WE ARE NEIGHBORS, OUR LANGUAGES COME FROM TWO DIFFERENT LANGUAGE TREES. SOMETIMES WE HAVE A HARD TIME UNDERSTANDING EACH OTHER.
WELL, WE HAVE TO GET OUT OF 1986.
HOW CAN I HELP?
WE'RE GOING TO NEED FOUR ROCKS. WE HAVE TO ALIGN THEM TO THE DIRECTIONS OF THE COMPASS.
LET'S GATHER THEM UP... THERE ARE PLENTY OF ROCKS ON THESE MESA TOPS.

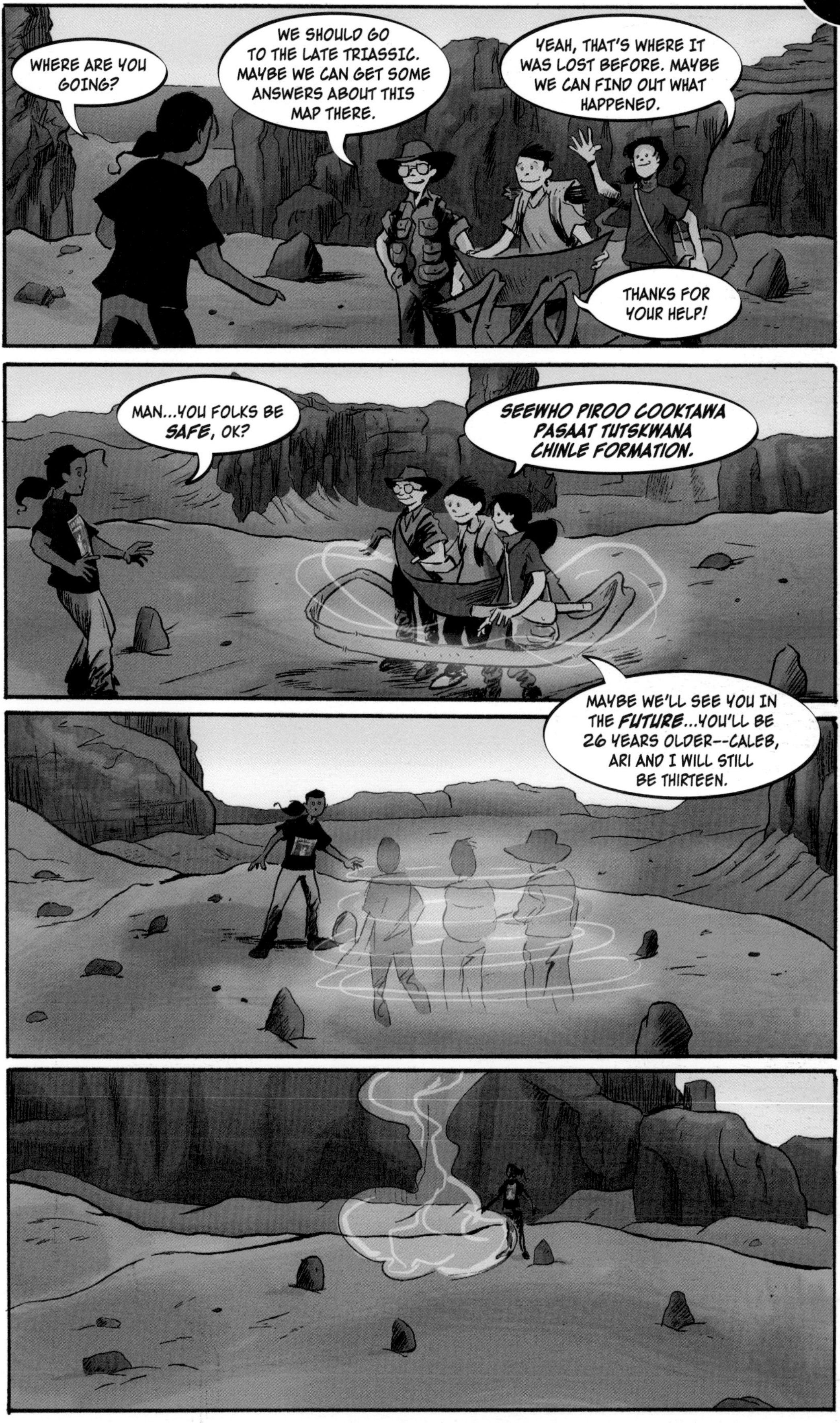
WHERE ARE YOU GOING?
WE SHOULD GO TO THE LATE TRIASSIC. MAYBE WE CAN GET SOME ANSWERS ABOUT THIS MAP THERE.
YEAH, THAT'S WHERE IT WAS LOST BEFORE. MAYBE WE CAN FIND OUT WHAT HAPPENED.
THANKS FOR YOUR HELP!
MAN...YOU FOLKS BE SAFE, OK?
SEEWHO PIROO COOKTAWA PASAAT TUTSKWANA CHINLE FORMATION.
MAYBE WE'LL SEE YOU IN THE FUTURE...YOU'LL BE 26 YEARS OLDER--CALEB, ARI AND I WILL STILL BE THIRTEEN.

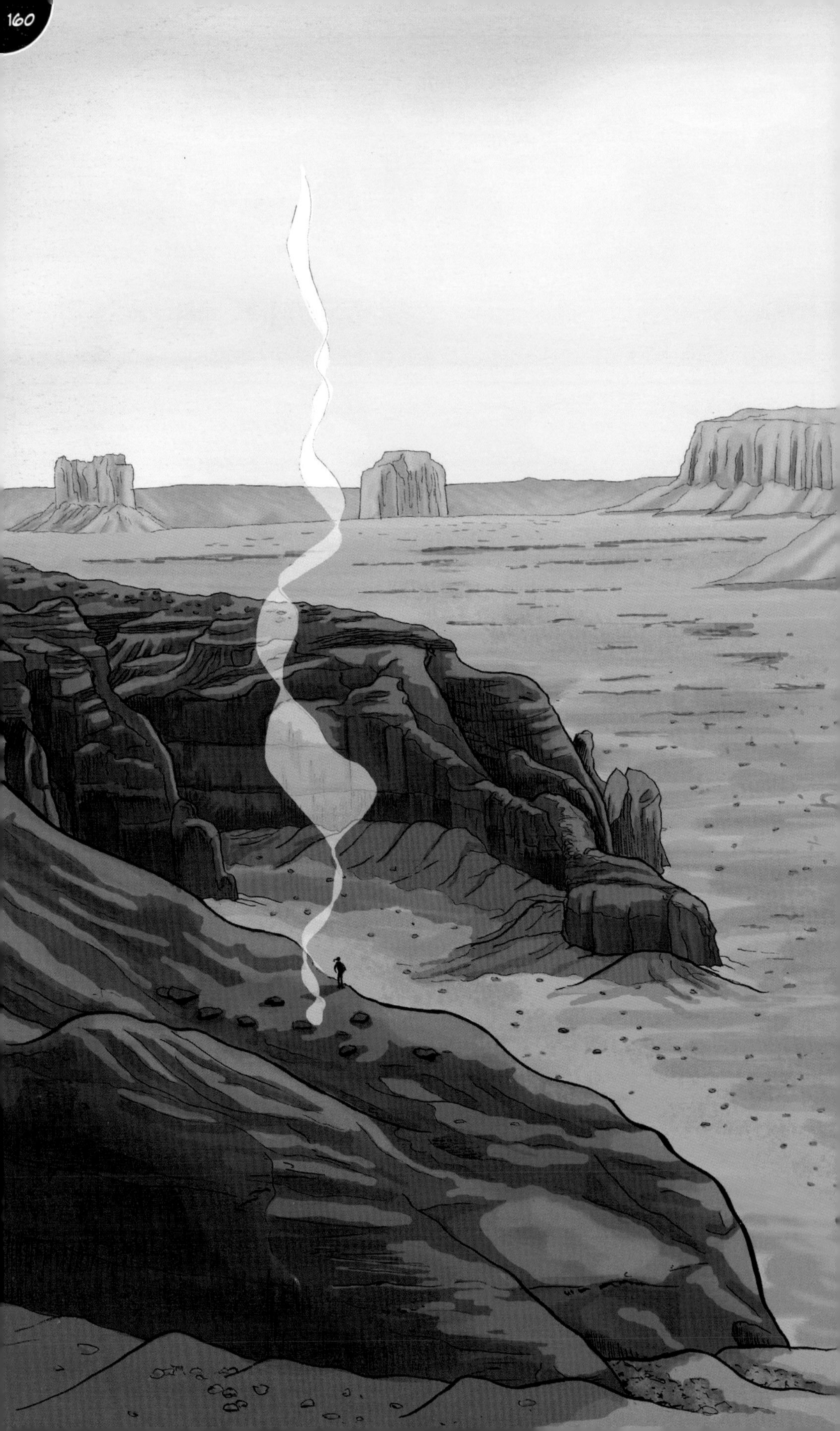

CHAPTER
SEVEN

TRIASSIC TIMES

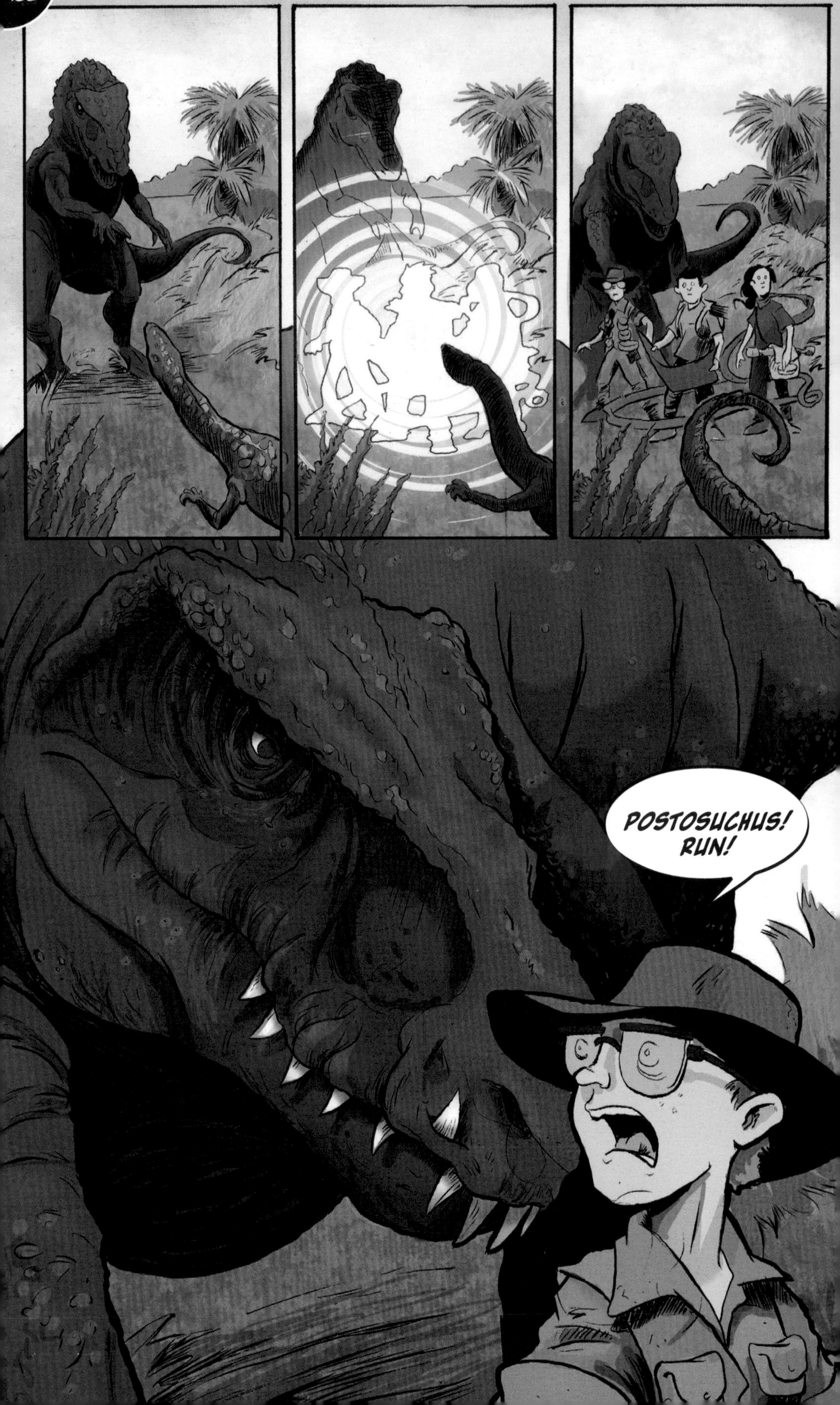
POSTOSUCHUS!
RUN!

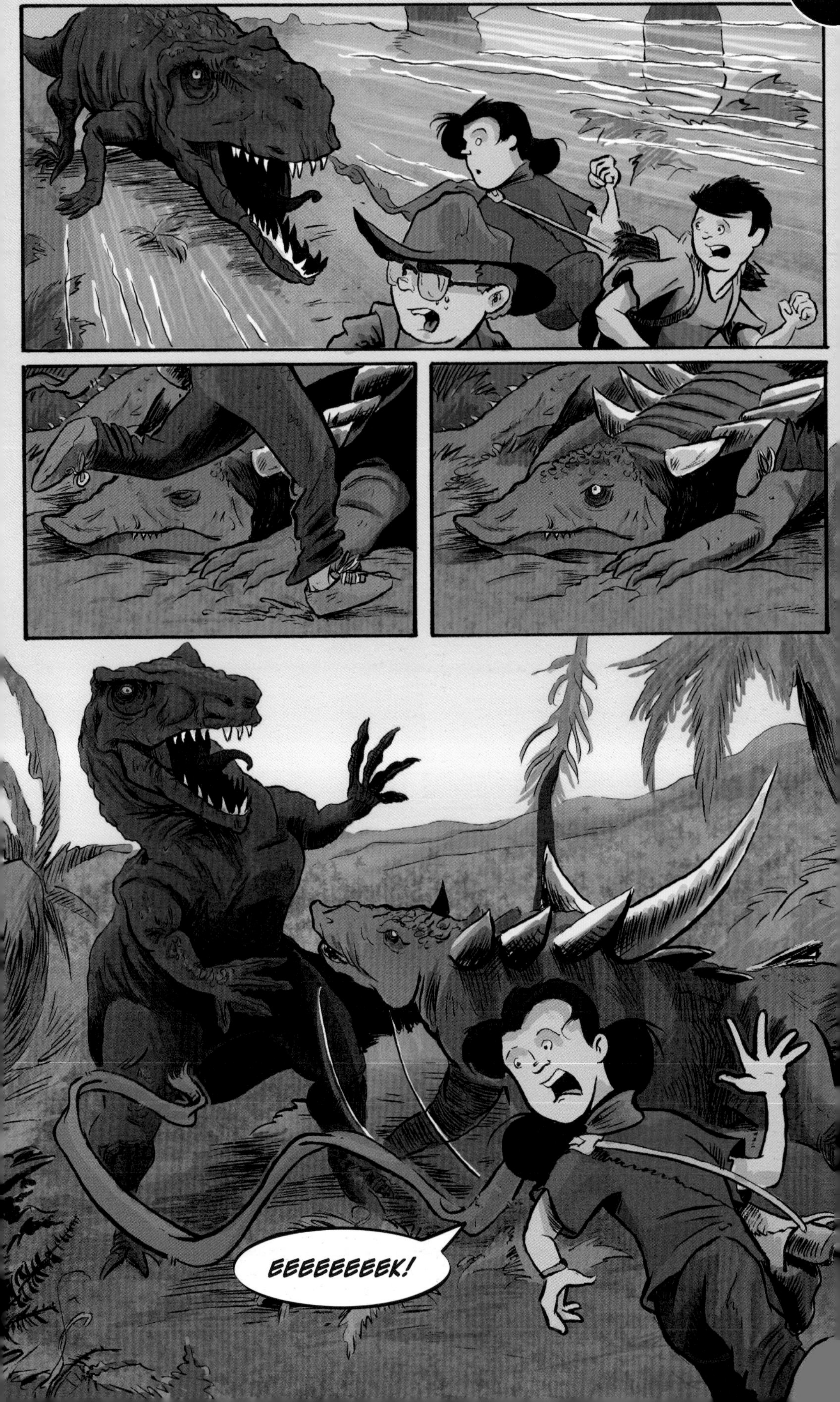
EEEEEEEEEK!

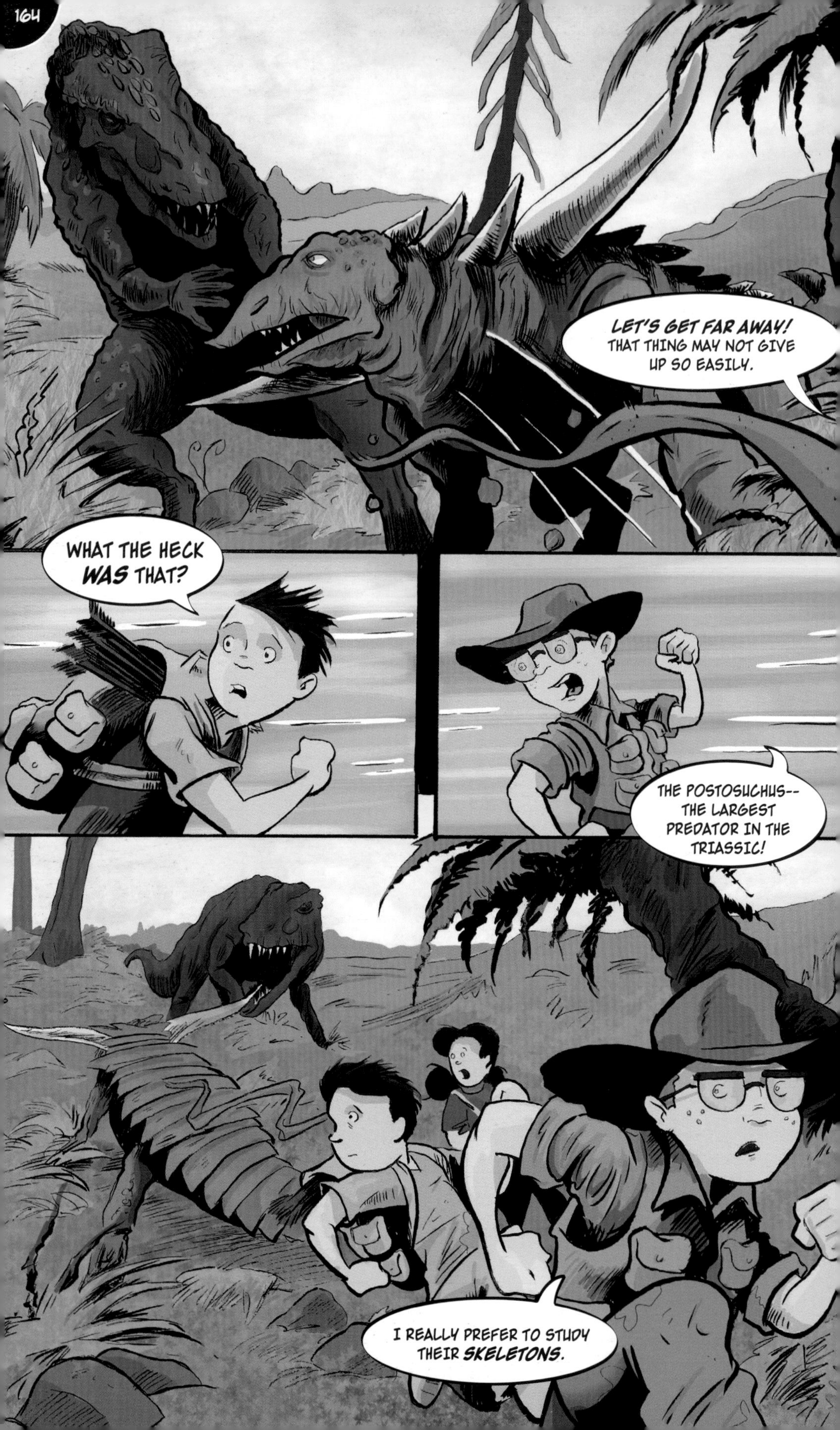
LET'S GET FAR AWAY! THAT THING MAY NOT GIVE UP SO EASILY.
WHAT THE HECK WAS THAT?
THE POSTOSUCHUS-- THE LARGEST PREDATOR IN THE TRIASSIC!
I REALLY PREFER TO STUDY THEIR SKELETONS.

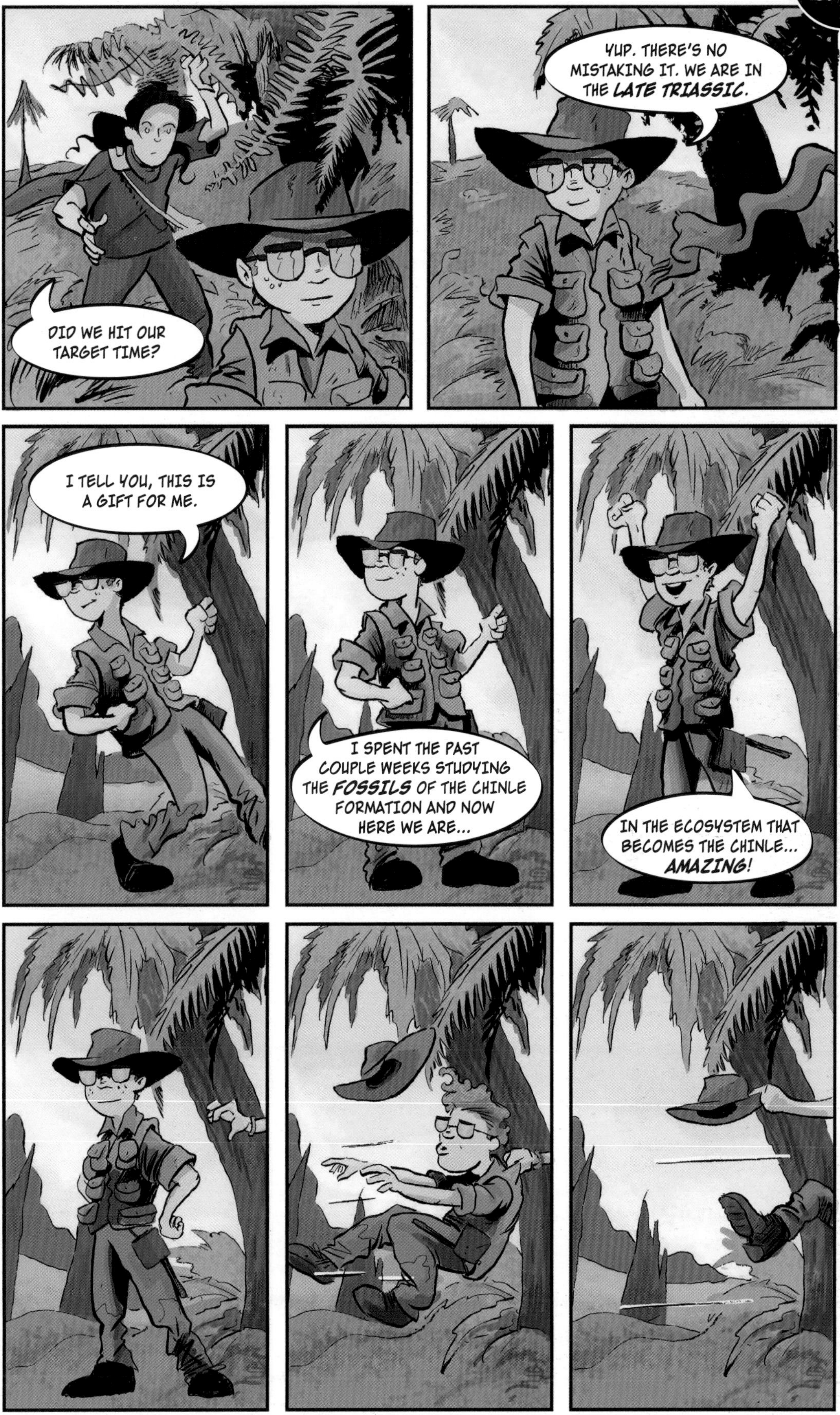
DID WE HIT OUR TARGET TIME?
YUP. THERE'S NO MISTAKING IT. WE ARE IN THE LATE TRIASSIC.
I TELL YOU, THIS IS A GIFT FOR ME.
I SPENT THE PAST COUPLE WEEKS STUDYING THE FOSSILS OF THE CHINLE FORMATION AND NOW HERE WE ARE...
IN THE ECOSYSTEM THAT BECOMES THE CHINLE... AMAZING!

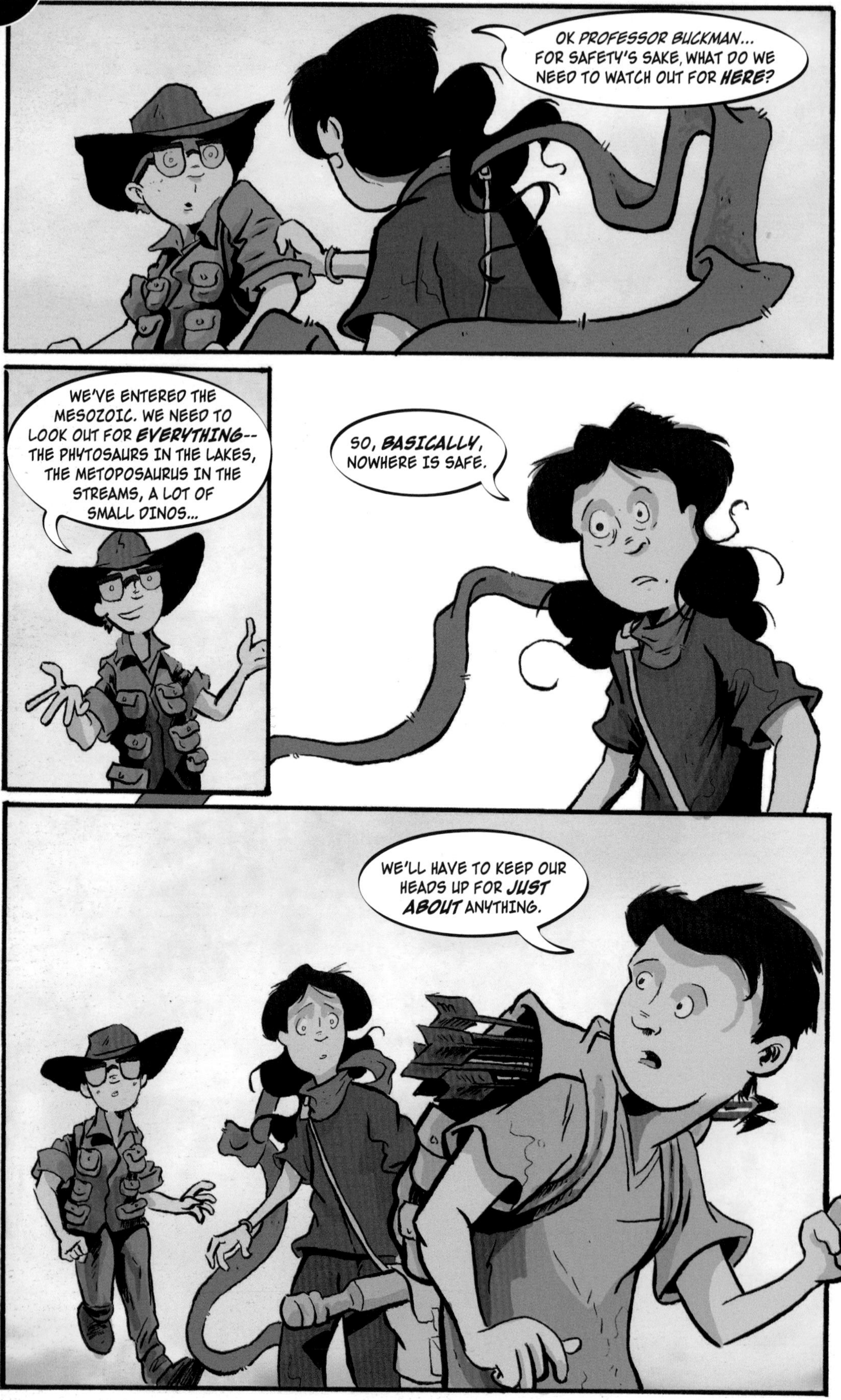
OK PROFESSOR BUCKMAN... FOR SAFETY'S SAKE, WHAT DO WE NEED TO WATCH OUT FOR *HERE*?
WE'VE ENTERED THE MESOZOIC. WE NEED TO LOOK OUT FOR *EVERYTHING*-- THE PHYTOSAURS IN THE LAKES, THE METOPOSAURUS IN THE STREAMS, A LOT OF SMALL DINOS...
SO, *BASICALLY*, NOWHERE IS SAFE.
WE'LL HAVE TO KEEP OUR HEADS UP FOR *JUST ABOUT* ANYTHING.

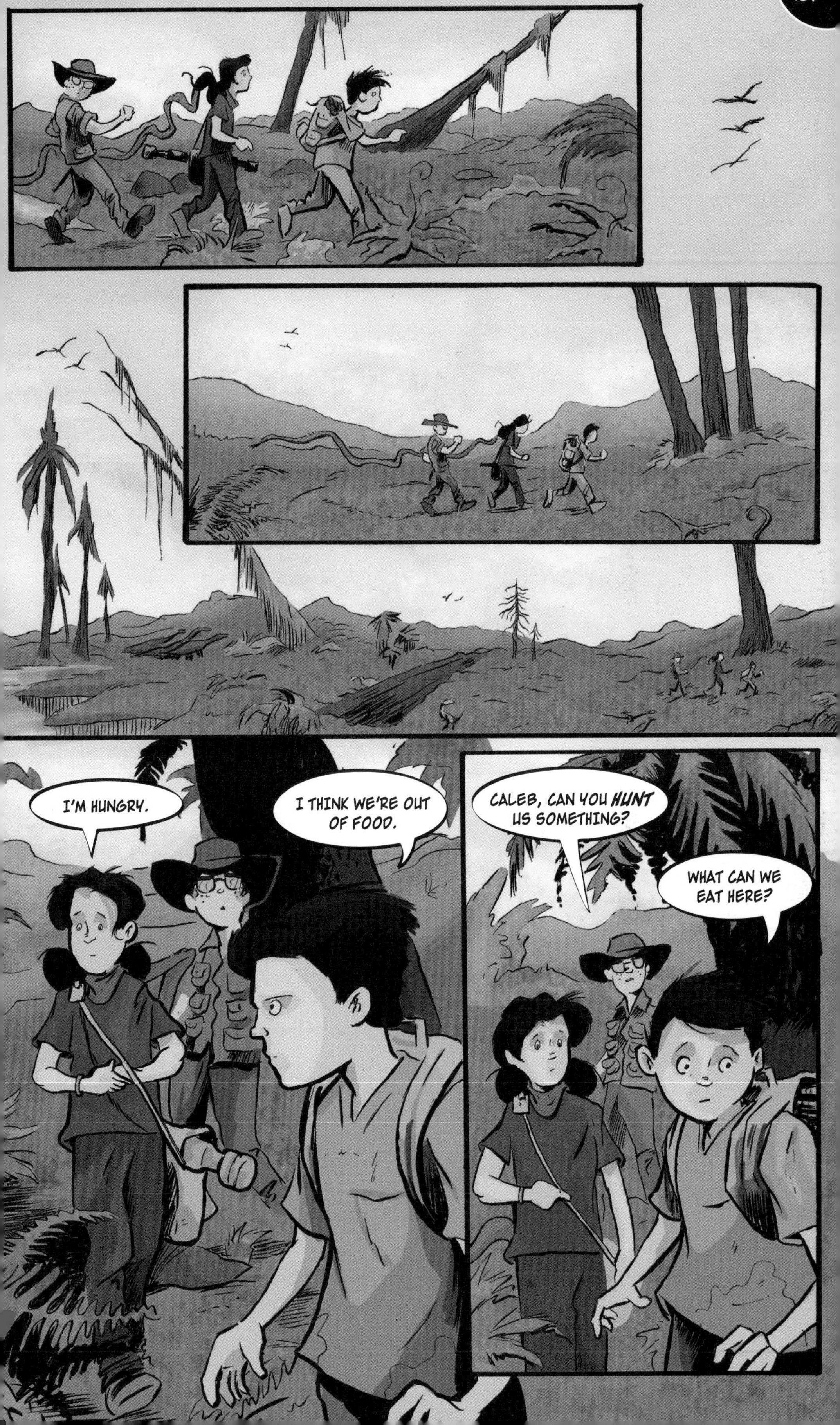
I'M HUNGRY.
I THINK WE'RE OUT OF FOOD.
CALEB, CAN YOU HUNT US SOMETHING?
WHAT CAN WE EAT HERE?

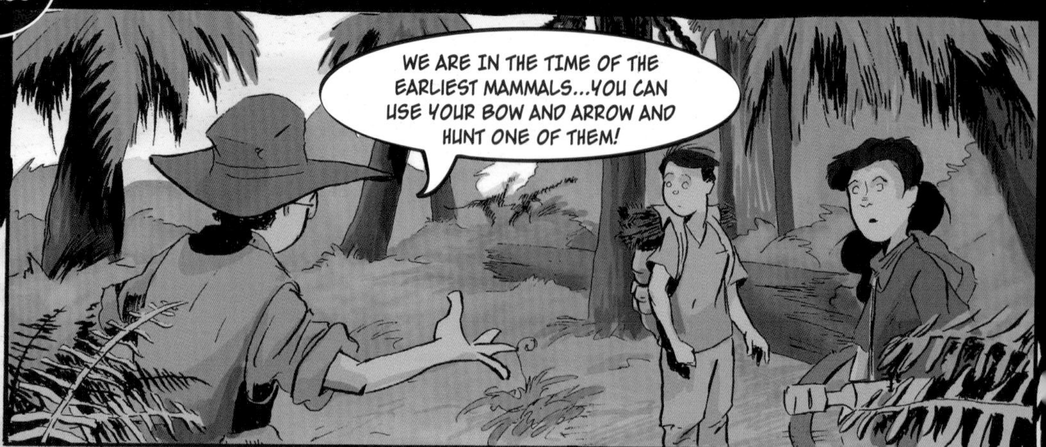
WE ARE IN THE TIME OF THE EARLIEST MAMMALS...YOU CAN USE YOUR BOW AND ARROW AND HUNT ONE OF THEM!

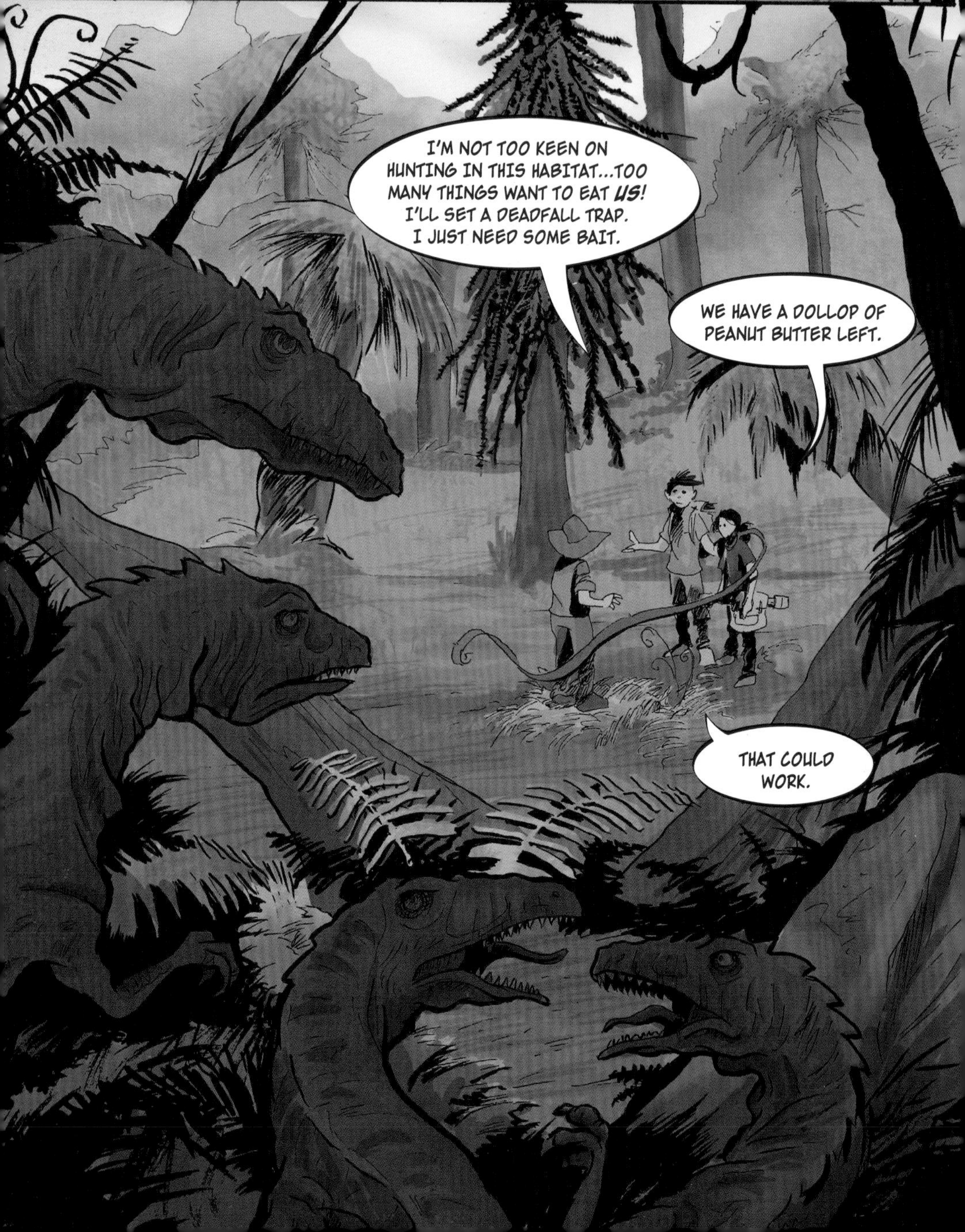
I'M NOT TOO KEEN ON HUNTING IN THIS HABITAT...TOO MANY THINGS WANT TO EAT *US*! I'LL SET A DEADFALL TRAP. I JUST NEED SOME BAIT.
WE HAVE A DOLLOP OF PEANUT BUTTER LEFT.
THAT COULD WORK.

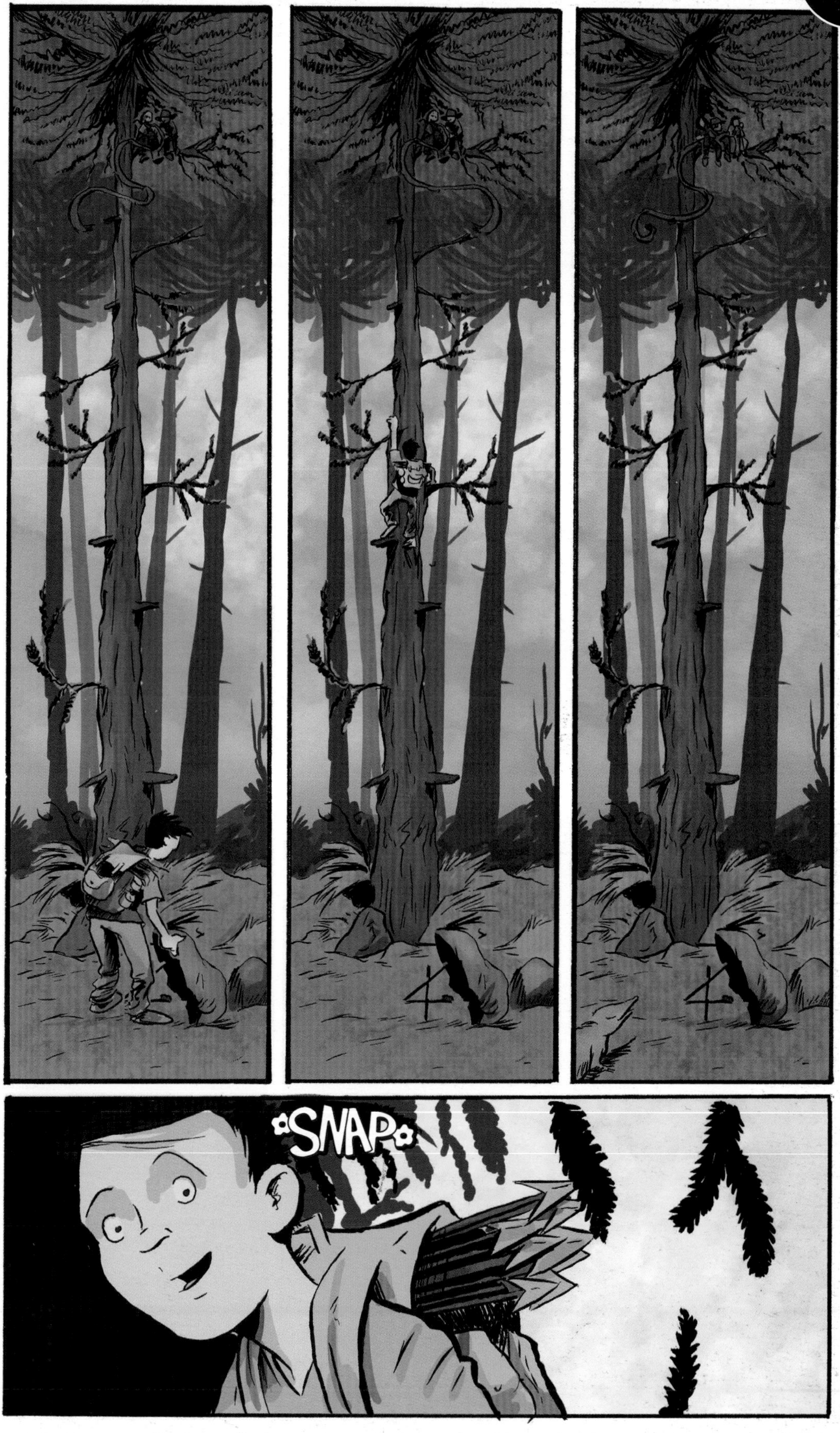
SNAP

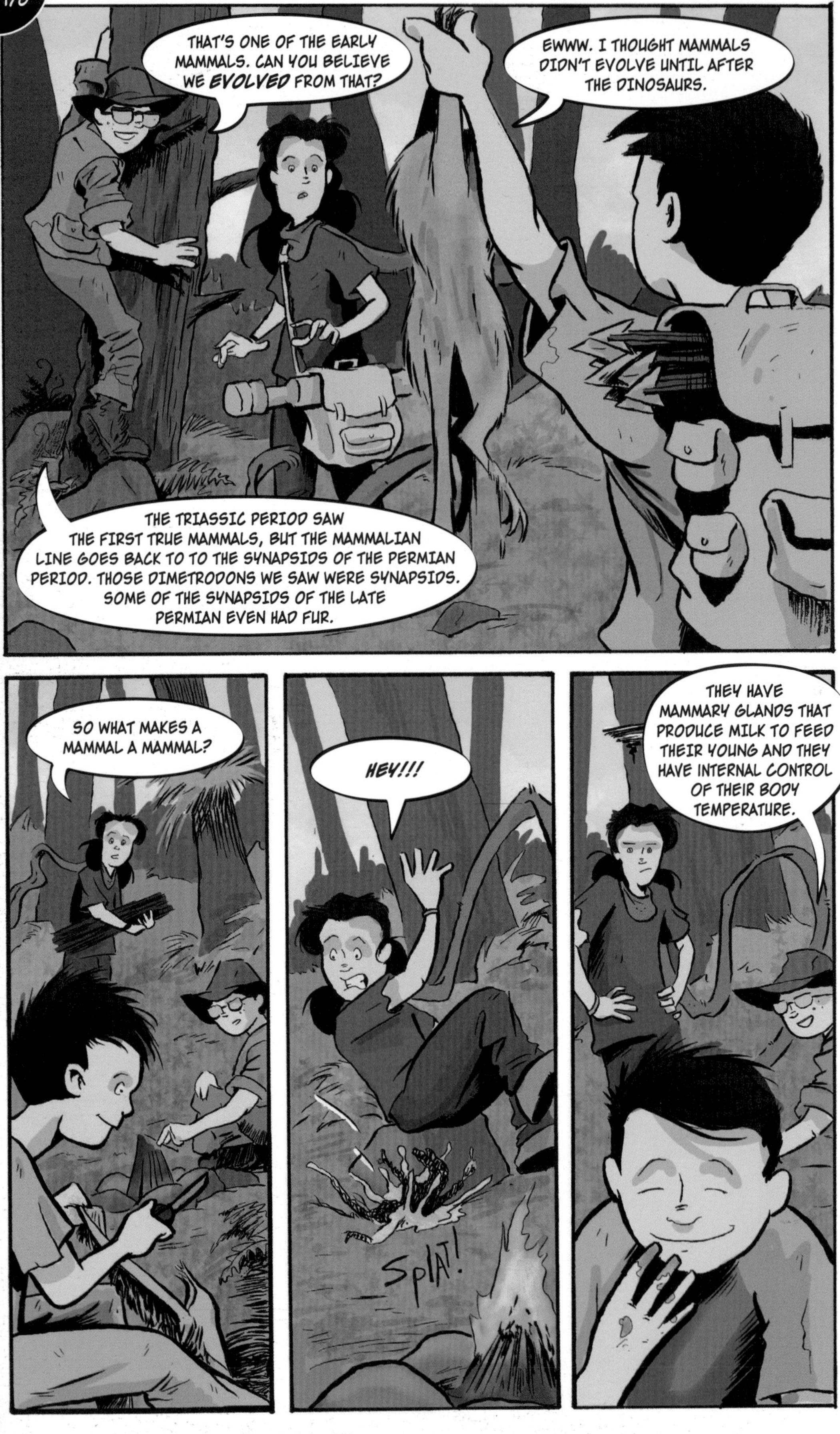
THAT'S ONE OF THE EARLY MAMMALS. CAN YOU BELIEVE WE EVOLVED FROM THAT?
EWWW. I THOUGHT MAMMALS DIDN'T EVOLVE UNTIL AFTER THE DINOSAURS.
THE TRIASSIC PERIOD SAW THE FIRST TRUE MAMMALS, BUT THE MAMMALIAN LINE GOES BACK TO TO THE SYNAPSIDS OF THE PERMIAN PERIOD. THOSE DIMETRODONS WE SAW WERE SYNAPSIDS. SOME OF THE SYNAPSIDS OF THE LATE PERMIAN EVEN HAD FUR.
SO WHAT MAKES A MAMMAL A MAMMAL?
HEY!!!
SPLAT!
THEY HAVE MAMMARY GLANDS THAT PRODUCE MILK TO FEED THEIR YOUNG AND THEY HAVE INTERNAL CONTROL OF THEIR BODY TEMPERATURE.

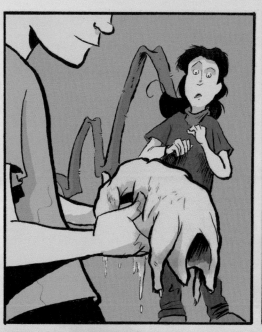

I THINK I LOST MY *APPETITE* FOR MEAT...

I JUST DON'T FEEL GOOD ABOUT EATING AN ANCESTOR OF MINE. AREN'T THERE FRUITS OR NUTS AROUND HERE?

SORRY, JENNA, THE FLOWERS THOSE THINGS COME FROM DO NOT EVOLVE UNTIL THE CRETACEOUS, ABOUT 100 MILLION YEARS IN THE FUTURE.

I AM *SO* BECOMING A VEGETARIAN WHEN I GET HOME.

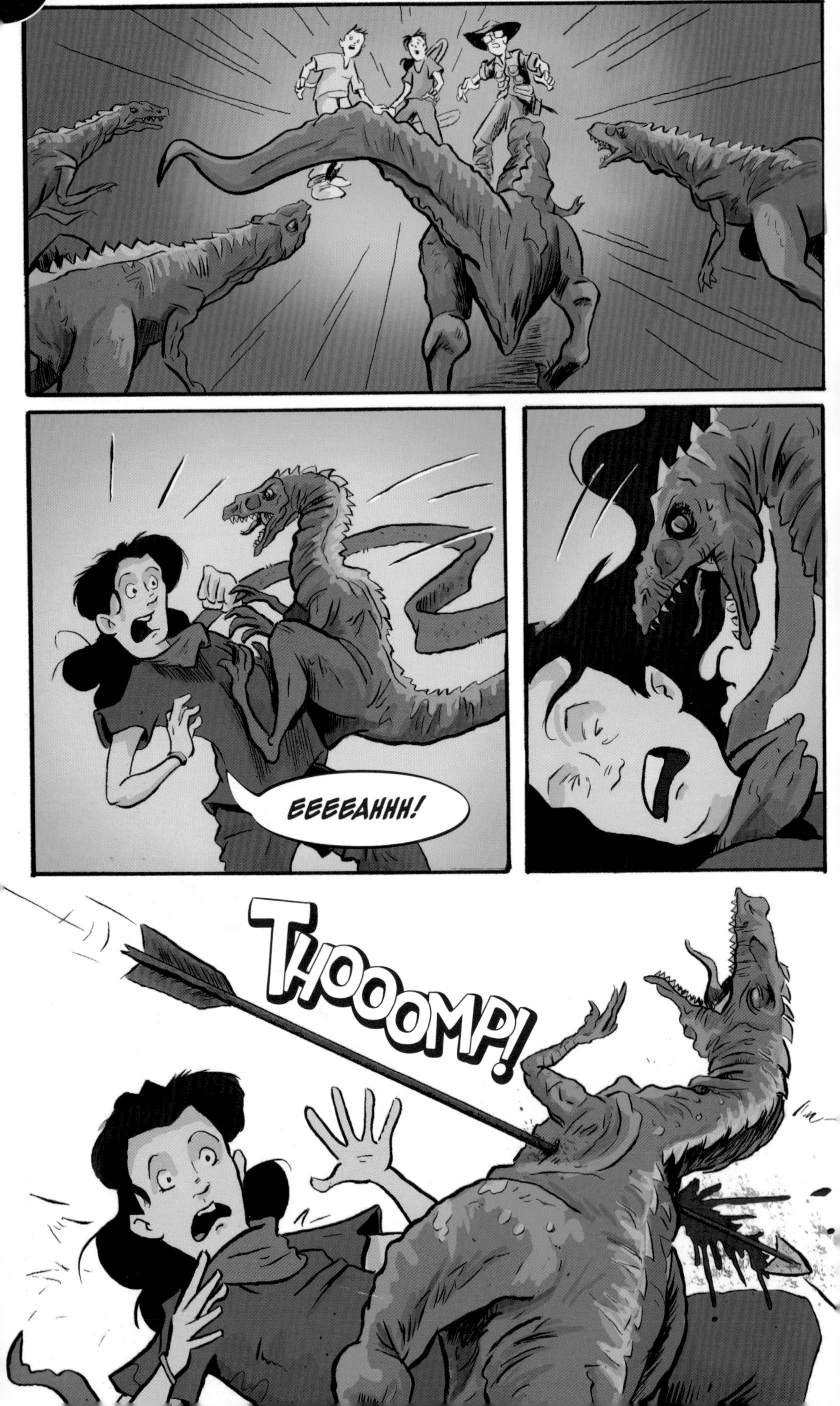
EEEEAHHH!
THOOOMP!

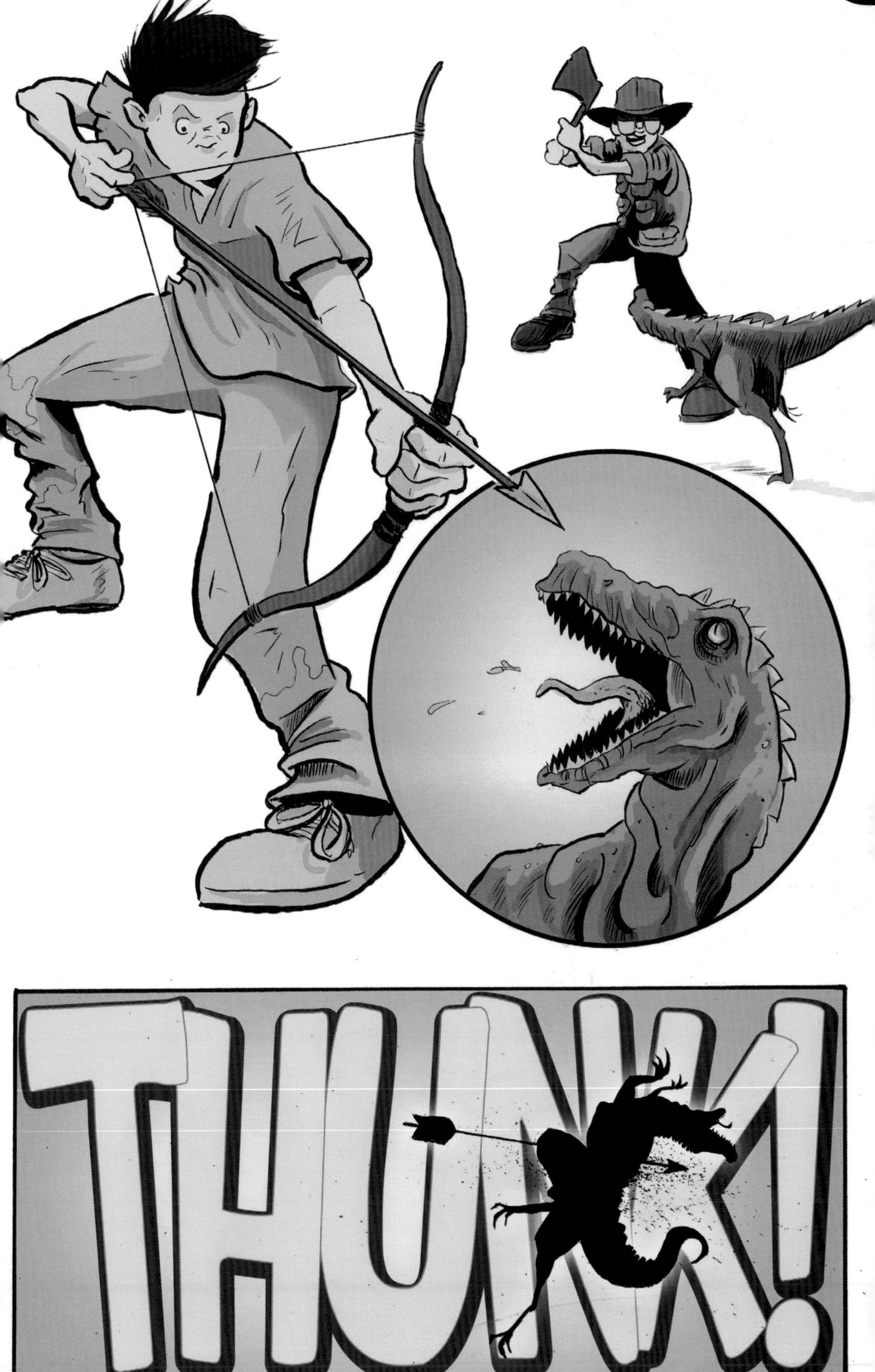
THUNK!

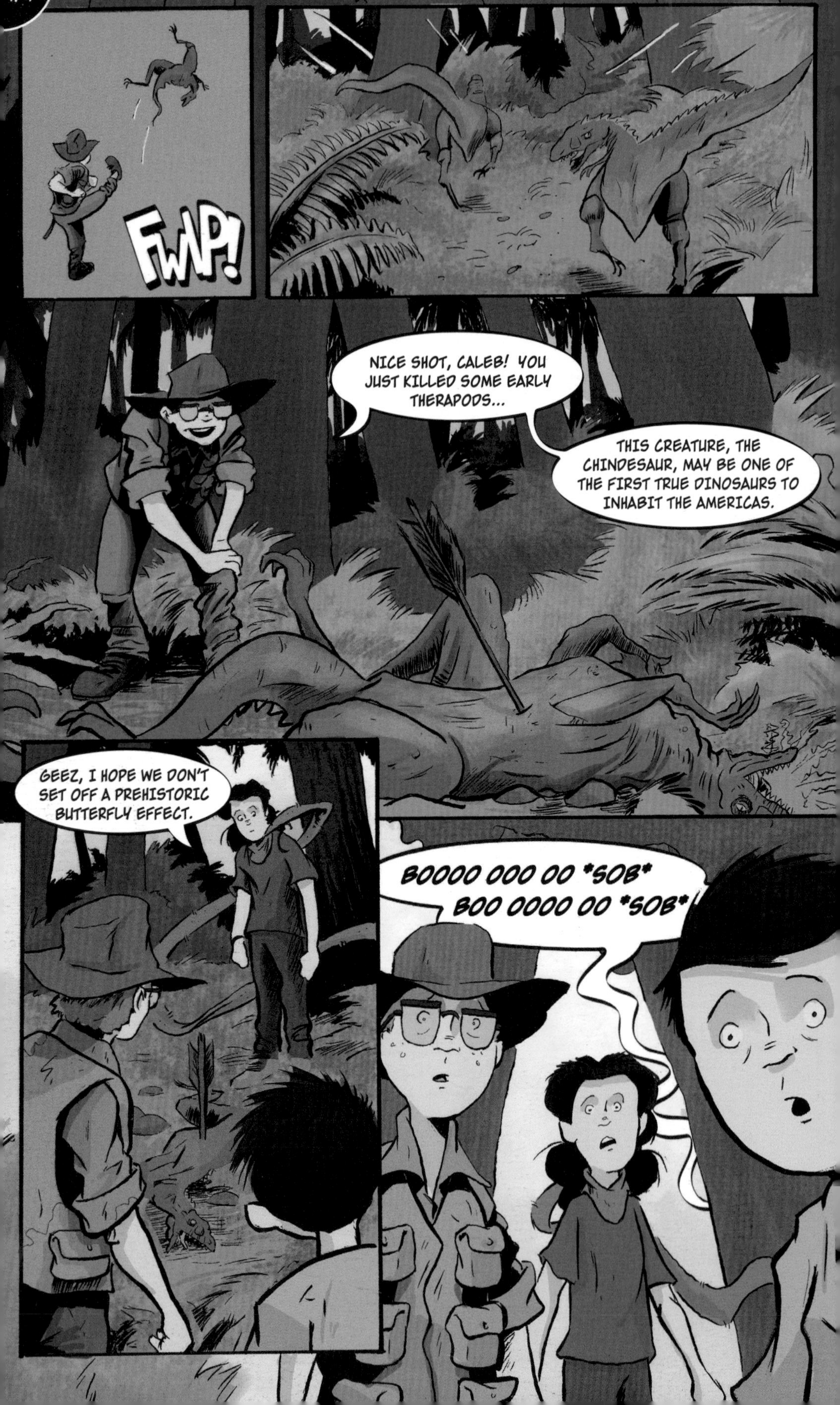
FWIP!
NICE SHOT, CALEB! YOU JUST KILLED SOME EARLY THERAPODS...
THIS CREATURE, THE CHINDESAUR, MAY BE ONE OF THE FIRST TRUE DINOSAURS TO INHABIT THE AMERICAS.
GEEZ, I HOPE WE DON'T SET OFF A PREHISTORIC BUTTERFLY EFFECT.
BOOOO OOO OO *SOB* BOO OOOO OO *SOB*

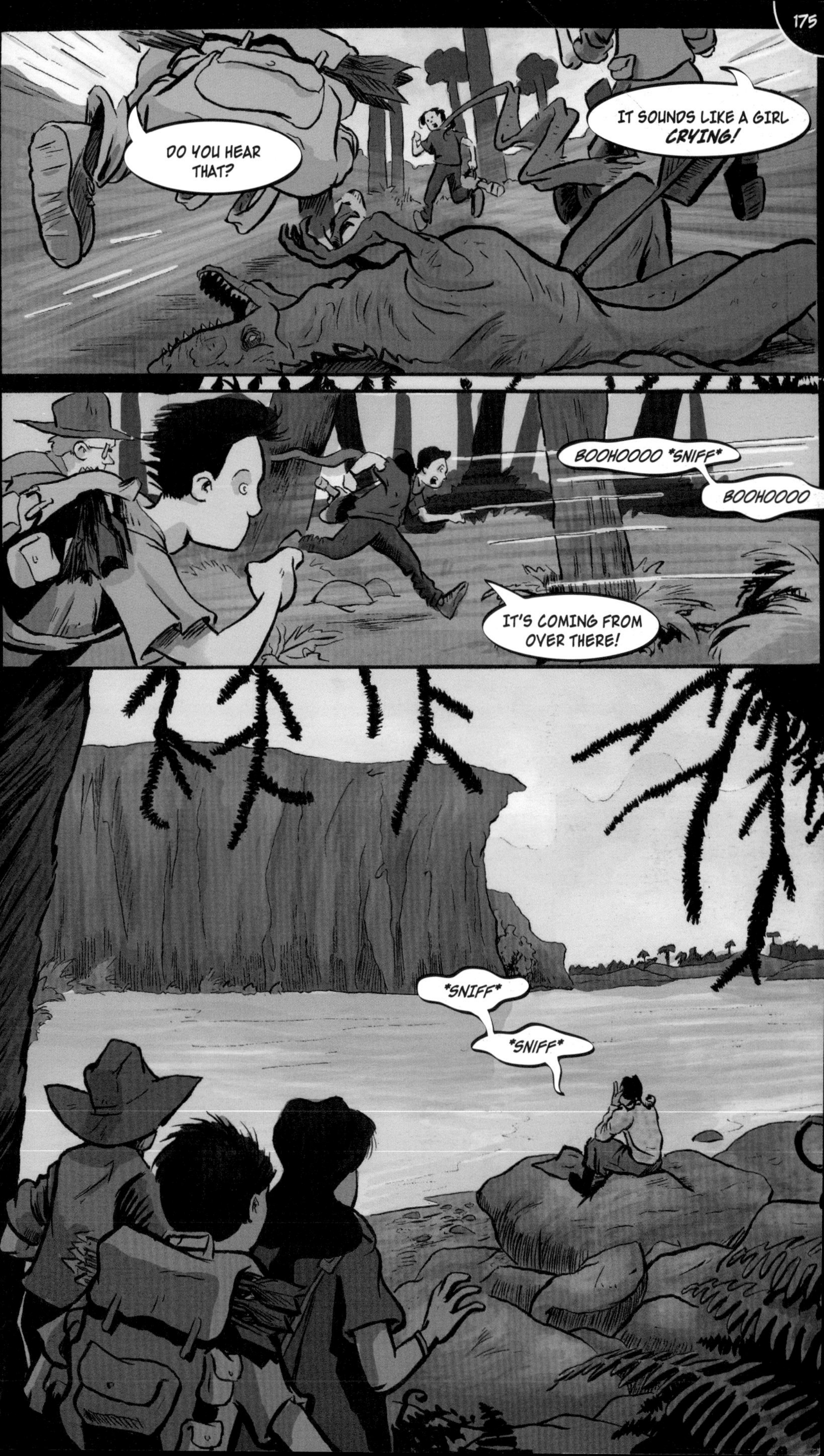
DO YOU HEAR THAT?
IT SOUNDS LIKE A GIRL CRYING!
BOOHOOOO *SNIFF*
BOOHOOOO
IT'S COMING FROM OVER THERE!
SNIFF
SNIFF

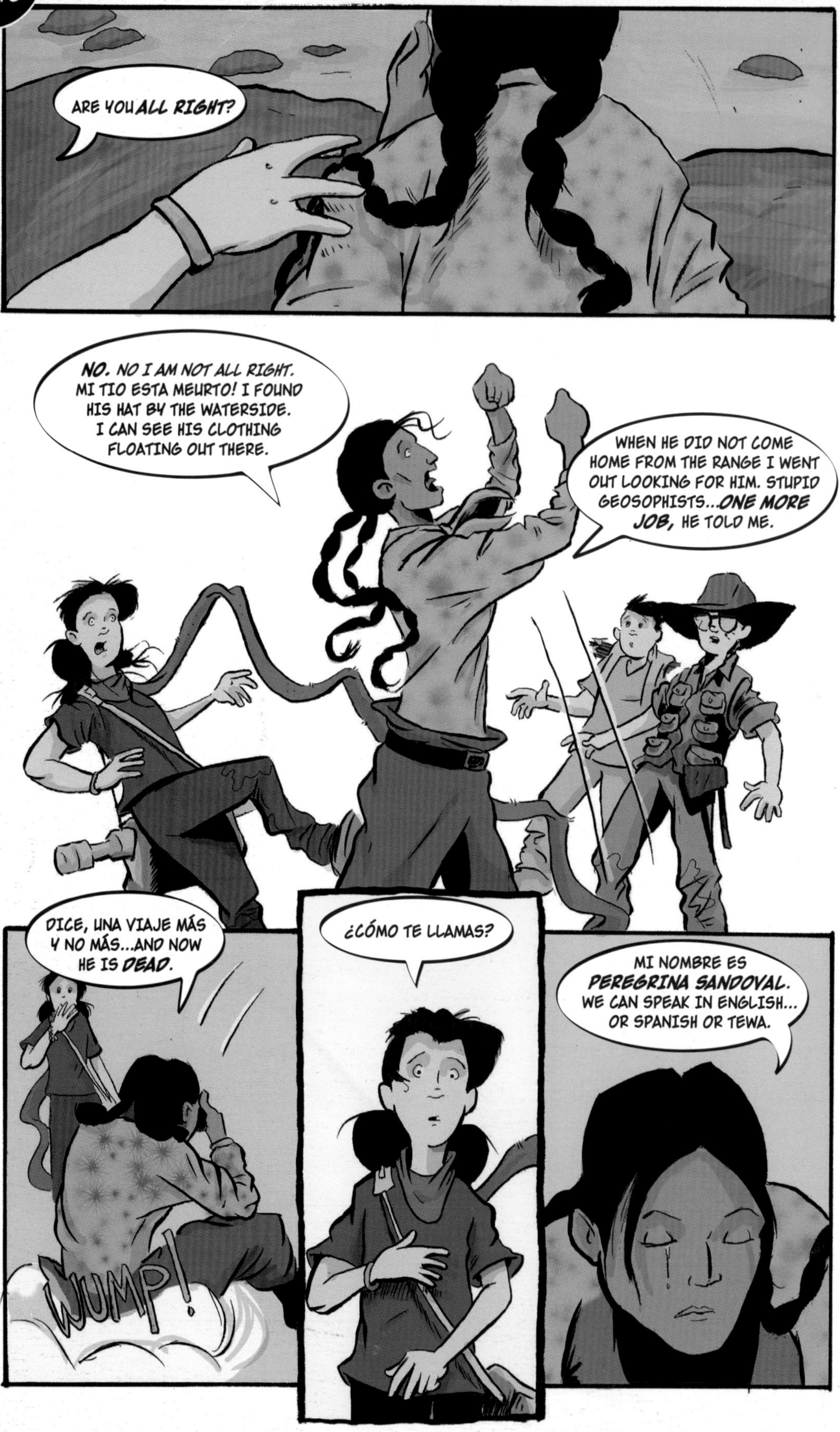
ARE YOU ALL RIGHT?
NO. NO I AM NOT ALL RIGHT. MI TIO ESTA MEURTO! I FOUND HIS HAT BY THE WATERSIDE. I CAN SEE HIS CLOTHING FLOATING OUT THERE.
WHEN HE DID NOT COME HOME FROM THE RANGE I WENT OUT LOOKING FOR HIM. STUPID GEOSOPHISTS...ONE MORE JOB, HE TOLD ME.
DICE, UNA VIAJE MÁS Y NO MÁS...AND NOW HE IS DEAD.
WUMP!
¿CÓMO TE LLAMAS?
MI NOMBRE ES PEREGRINA SANDOVAL. WE CAN SPEAK IN ENGLISH... OR SPANISH OR TEWA.

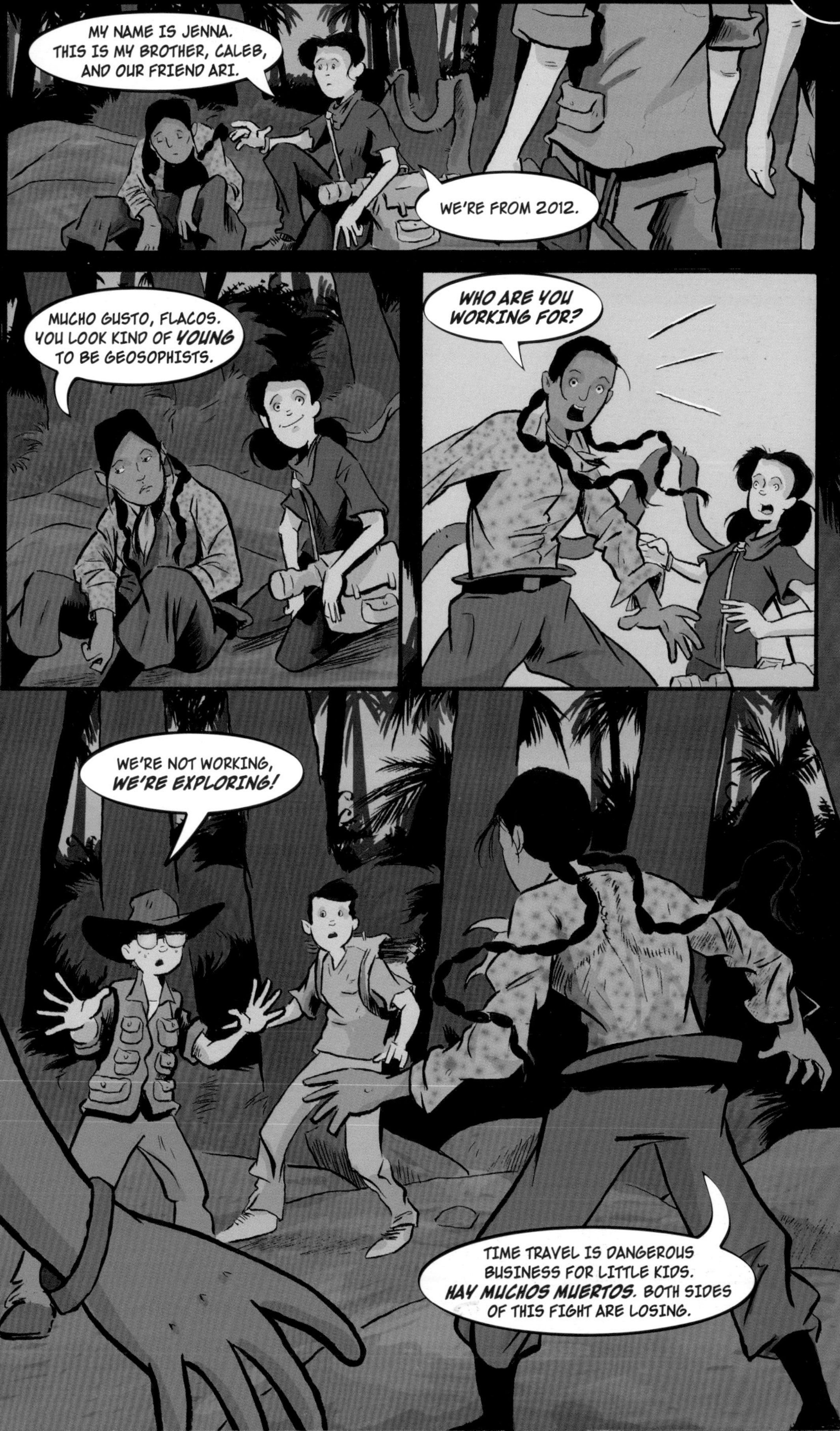
MY NAME IS JENNA.
THIS IS MY BROTHER, CALEB,
AND OUR FRIEND ARI.
WE'RE FROM 2012.
MUCHO GUSTO, FLACOS.
YOU LOOK KIND OF ***YOUNG***
TO BE GEOSOPHISTS.
WHO ARE YOU WORKING FOR?
WE'RE NOT WORKING,
WE'RE EXPLORING!
TIME TRAVEL IS DANGEROUS
BUSINESS FOR LITTLE KIDS.
HAY MUCHOS MUERTOS. BOTH SIDES
OF THIS FIGHT ARE LOSING.

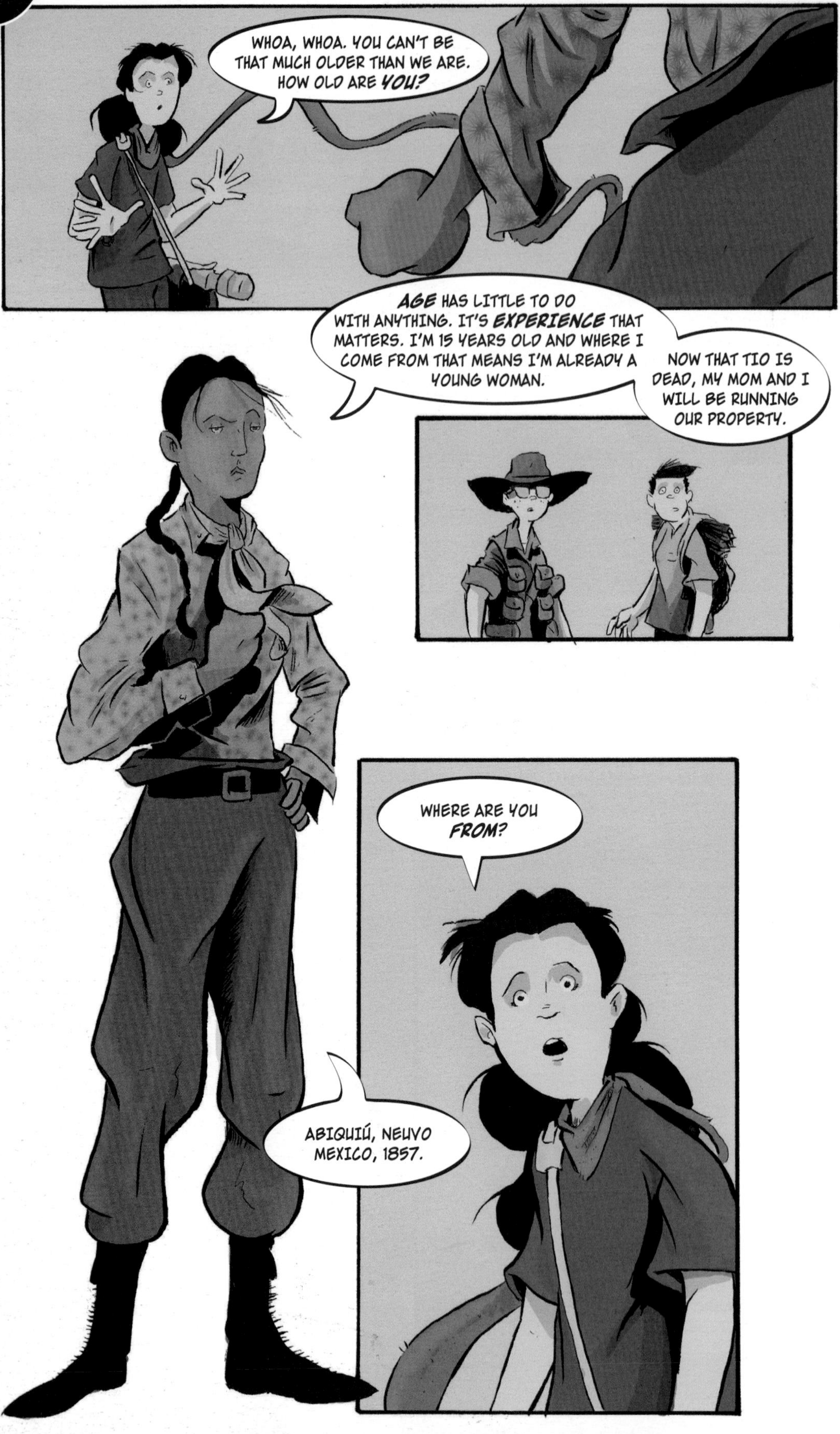
WHOA, WHOA. YOU CAN'T BE THAT MUCH OLDER THAN WE ARE. HOW OLD ARE YOU?
AGE HAS LITTLE TO DO WITH ANYTHING. IT'S EXPERIENCE THAT MATTERS. I'M 15 YEARS OLD AND WHERE I COME FROM THAT MEANS I'M ALREADY A YOUNG WOMAN.
NOW THAT TIO IS DEAD, MY MOM AND I WILL BE RUNNING OUR PROPERTY.
WHERE ARE YOU FROM?
ABIQUIÚ, NEUVO MEXICO, 1857.

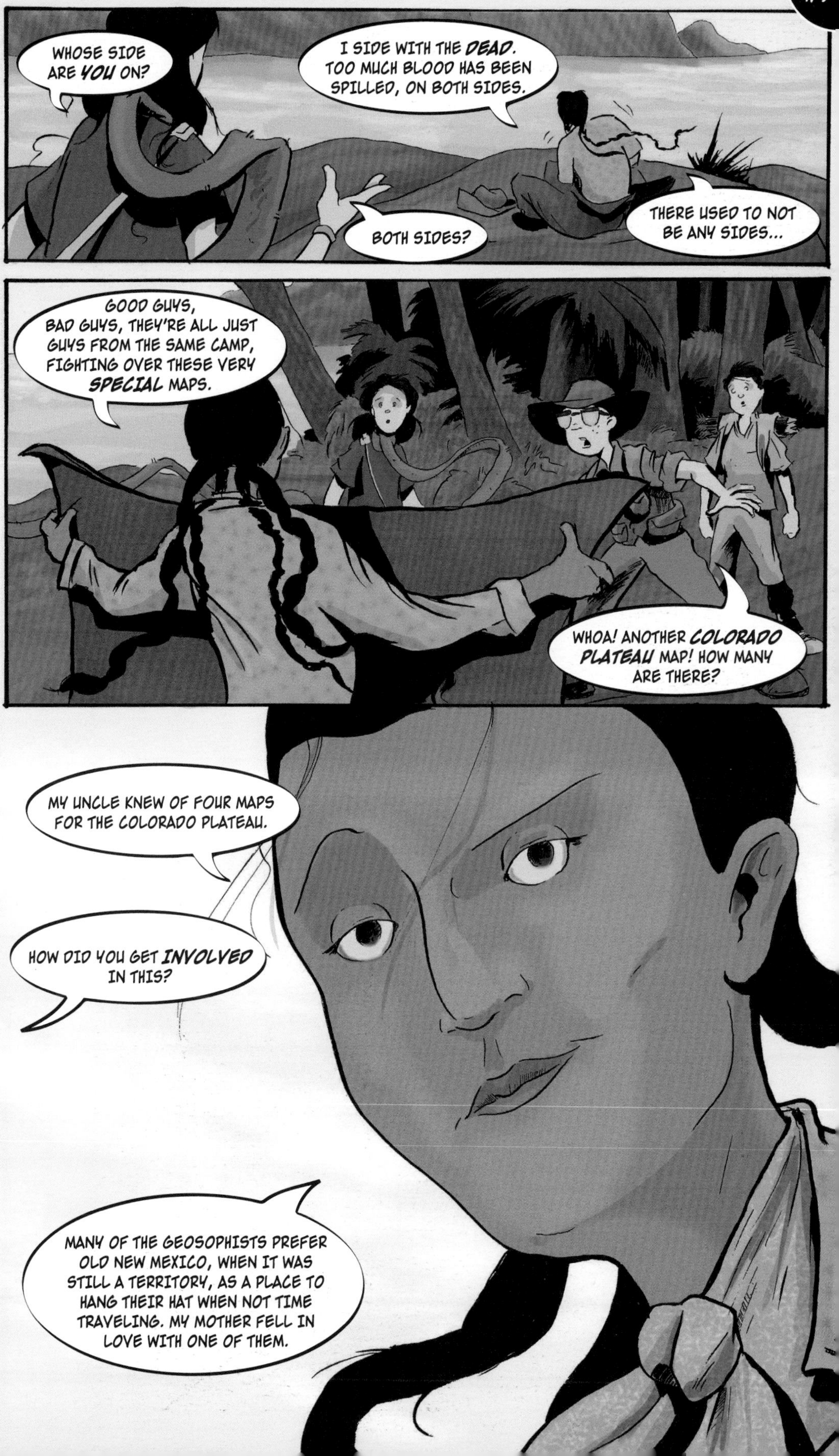
WHOSE SIDE ARE YOU ON?
I SIDE WITH THE DEAD. TOO MUCH BLOOD HAS BEEN SPILLED, ON BOTH SIDES.
BOTH SIDES?
THERE USED TO NOT BE ANY SIDES...
GOOD GUYS, BAD GUYS, THEY'RE ALL JUST GUYS FROM THE SAME CAMP, FIGHTING OVER THESE VERY SPECIAL MAPS.
WHOA! ANOTHER COLORADO PLATEAU MAP! HOW MANY ARE THERE?
MY UNCLE KNEW OF FOUR MAPS FOR THE COLORADO PLATEAU.
HOW DID YOU GET INVOLVED IN THIS?
MANY OF THE GEOSOPHISTS PREFER OLD NEW MEXICO, WHEN IT WAS STILL A TERRITORY, AS A PLACE TO HANG THEIR HAT WHEN NOT TIME TRAVELING. MY MOTHER FELL IN LOVE WITH ONE OF THEM.

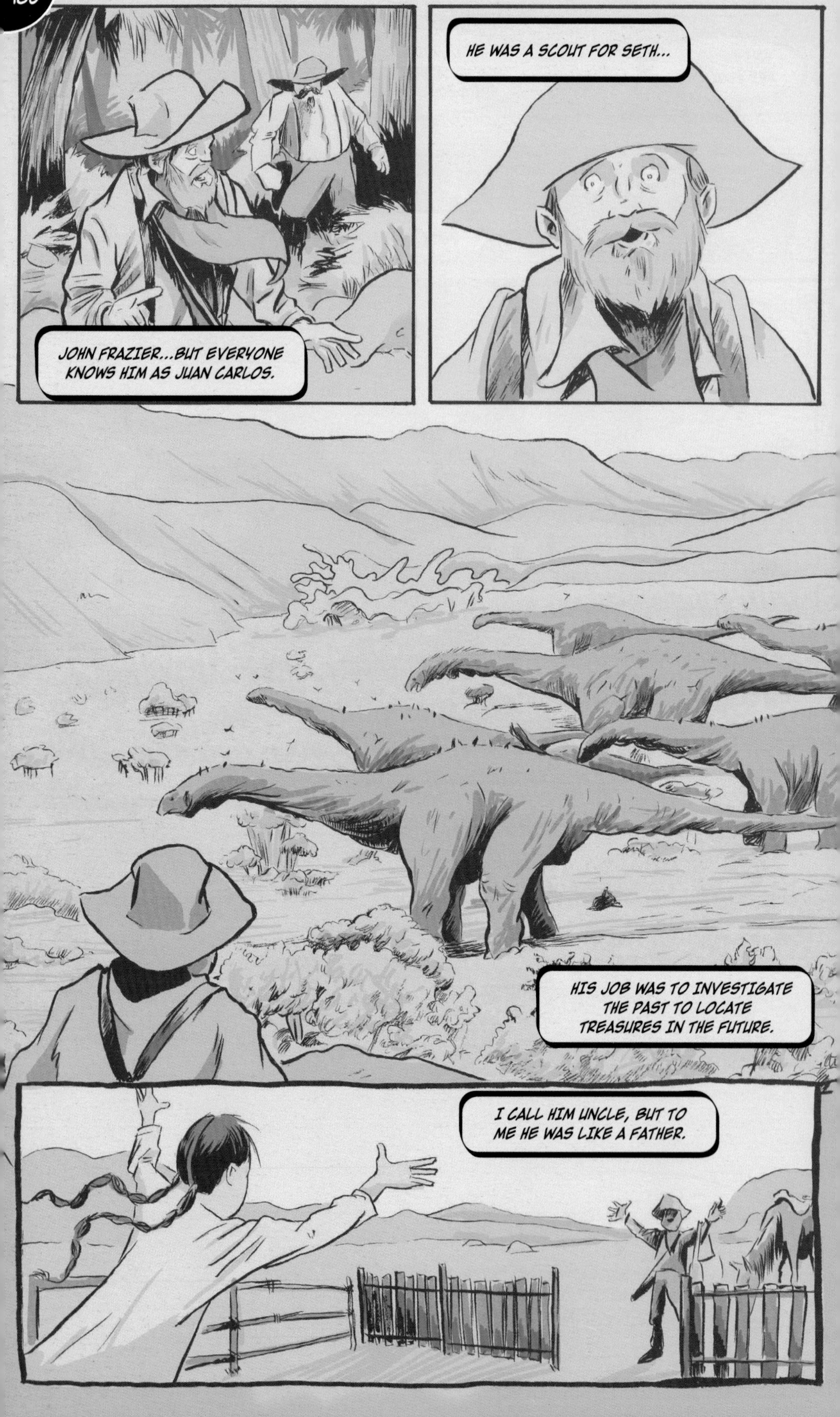
JOHN FRAZIER...BUT EVERYONE KNOWS HIM AS JUAN CARLOS.
HE WAS A SCOUT FOR SETH...
HIS JOB WAS TO INVESTIGATE THE PAST TO LOCATE TREASURES IN THE FUTURE.
I CALL HIM UNCLE, BUT TO ME HE WAS LIKE A FATHER.

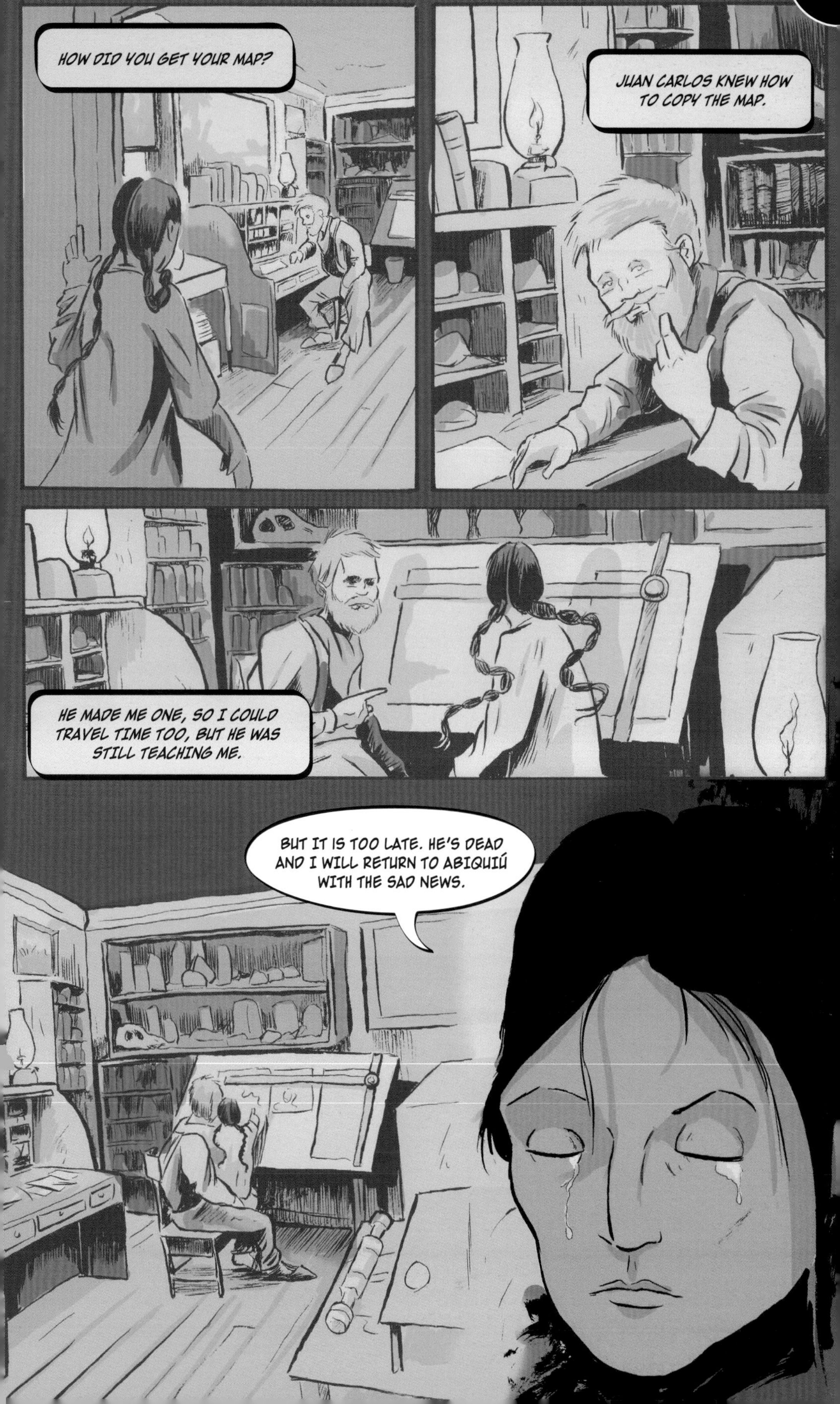
HOW DID YOU GET YOUR MAP?
JUAN CARLOS KNEW HOW TO COPY THE MAP.
HE MADE ME ONE, SO I COULD TRAVEL TIME TOO, BUT HE WAS STILL TEACHING ME.
BUT IT IS TOO LATE. HE'S DEAD AND I WILL RETURN TO ABIQUIÚ WITH THE SAD NEWS.

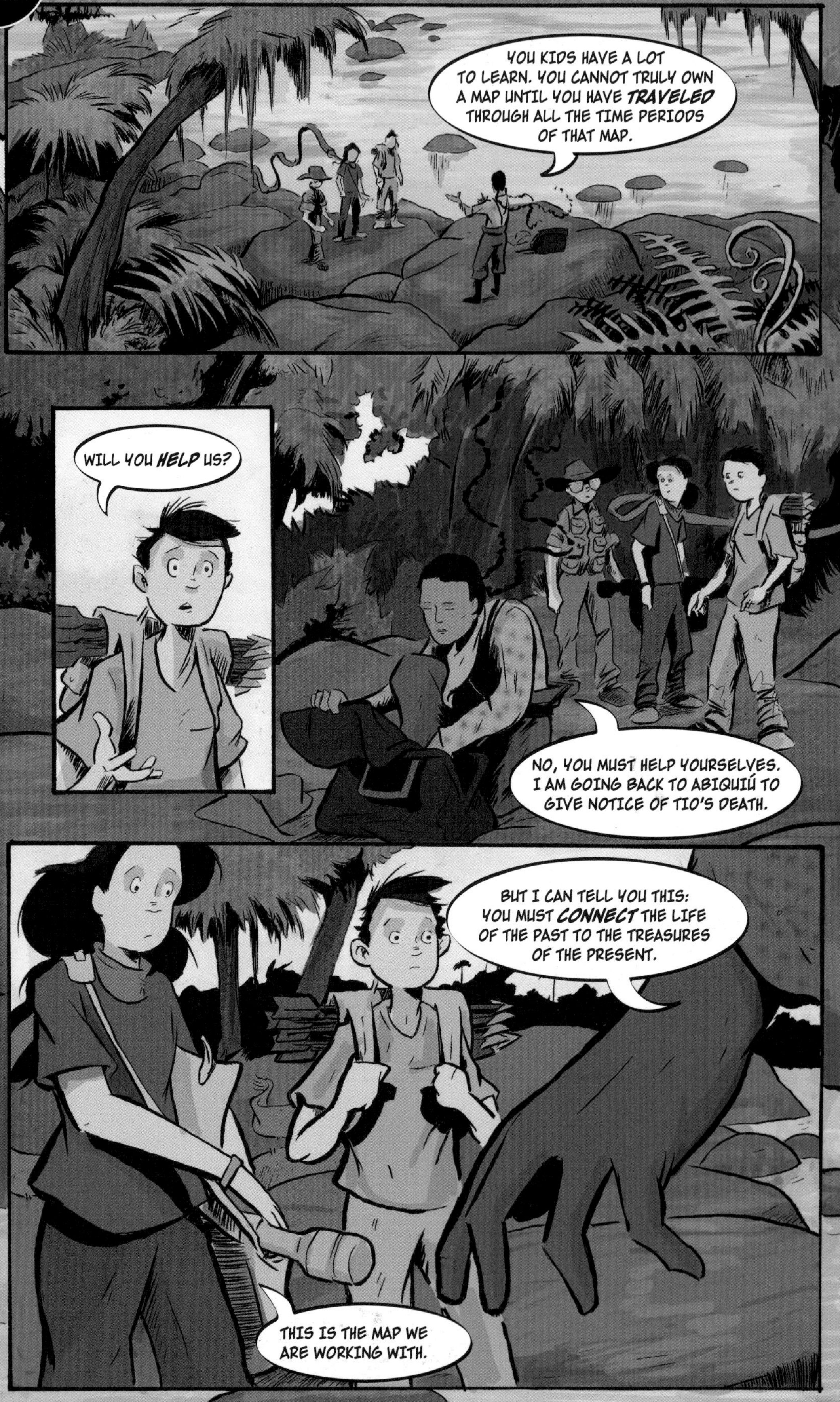
YOU KIDS HAVE A LOT TO LEARN. YOU CANNOT TRULY OWN A MAP UNTIL YOU HAVE TRAVELED THROUGH ALL THE TIME PERIODS OF THAT MAP.
WILL YOU HELP US?
NO, YOU MUST HELP YOURSELVES. I AM GOING BACK TO ABIQUIÚ TO GIVE NOTICE OF TIO'S DEATH.
BUT I CAN TELL YOU THIS: YOU MUST CONNECT THE LIFE OF THE PAST TO THE TREASURES OF THE PRESENT.
THIS IS THE MAP WE ARE WORKING WITH.

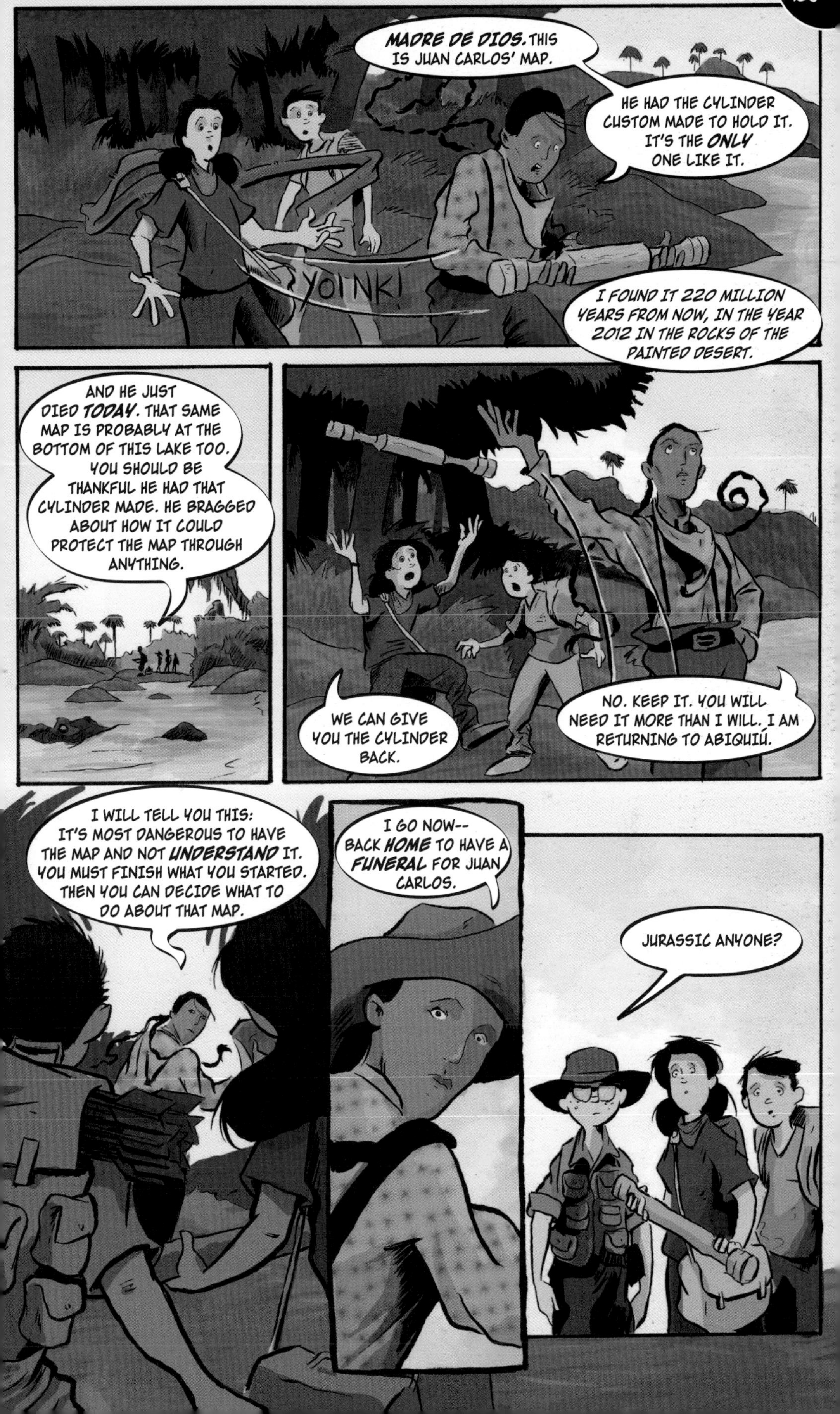
MADRE DE DIOS. THIS IS JUAN CARLOS' MAP.
HE HAD THE CYLINDER CUSTOM MADE TO HOLD IT. IT'S THE ONLY ONE LIKE IT.
YOINK!
I FOUND IT 220 MILLION YEARS FROM NOW, IN THE YEAR 2012 IN THE ROCKS OF THE PAINTED DESERT.
AND HE JUST DIED TODAY. THAT SAME MAP IS PROBABLY AT THE BOTTOM OF THIS LAKE TOO. YOU SHOULD BE THANKFUL HE HAD THAT CYLINDER MADE. HE BRAGGED ABOUT HOW IT COULD PROTECT THE MAP THROUGH ANYTHING.
WE CAN GIVE YOU THE CYLINDER BACK.
NO. KEEP IT. YOU WILL NEED IT MORE THAN I WILL. I AM RETURNING TO ABIQUIÚ.
I WILL TELL YOU THIS: IT'S MOST DANGEROUS TO HAVE THE MAP AND NOT UNDERSTAND IT. YOU MUST FINISH WHAT YOU STARTED. THEN YOU CAN DECIDE WHAT TO DO ABOUT THAT MAP.
I GO NOW-- BACK HOME TO HAVE A FUNERAL FOR JUAN CARLOS.
JURASSIC ANYONE?

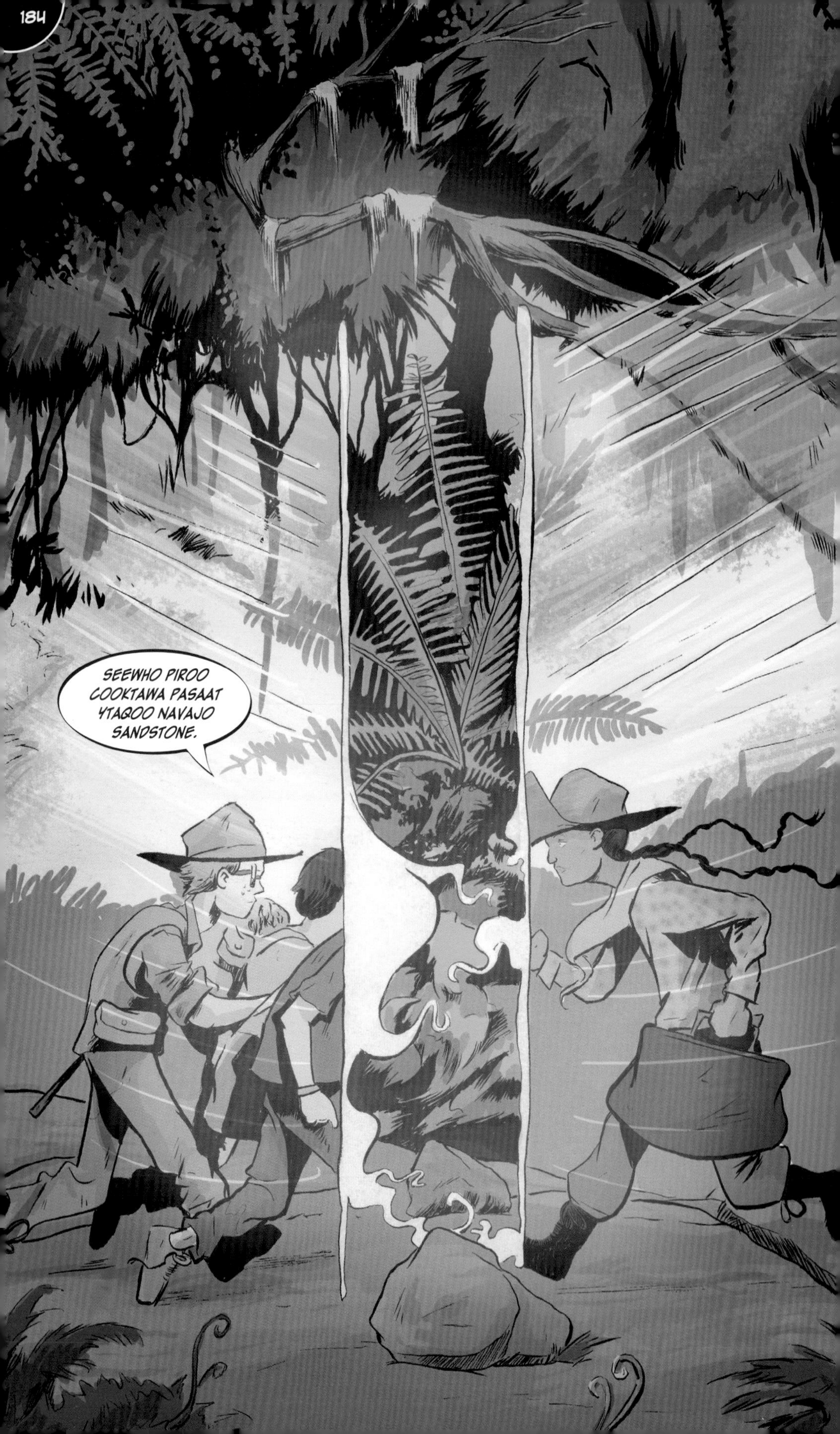
SEEWHO PIROO COOKTAWA PASAAT YTAQOO NAVAJO SANDSTONE.

CHAPTER
EIGHT

MOBILIS IN MOBILI

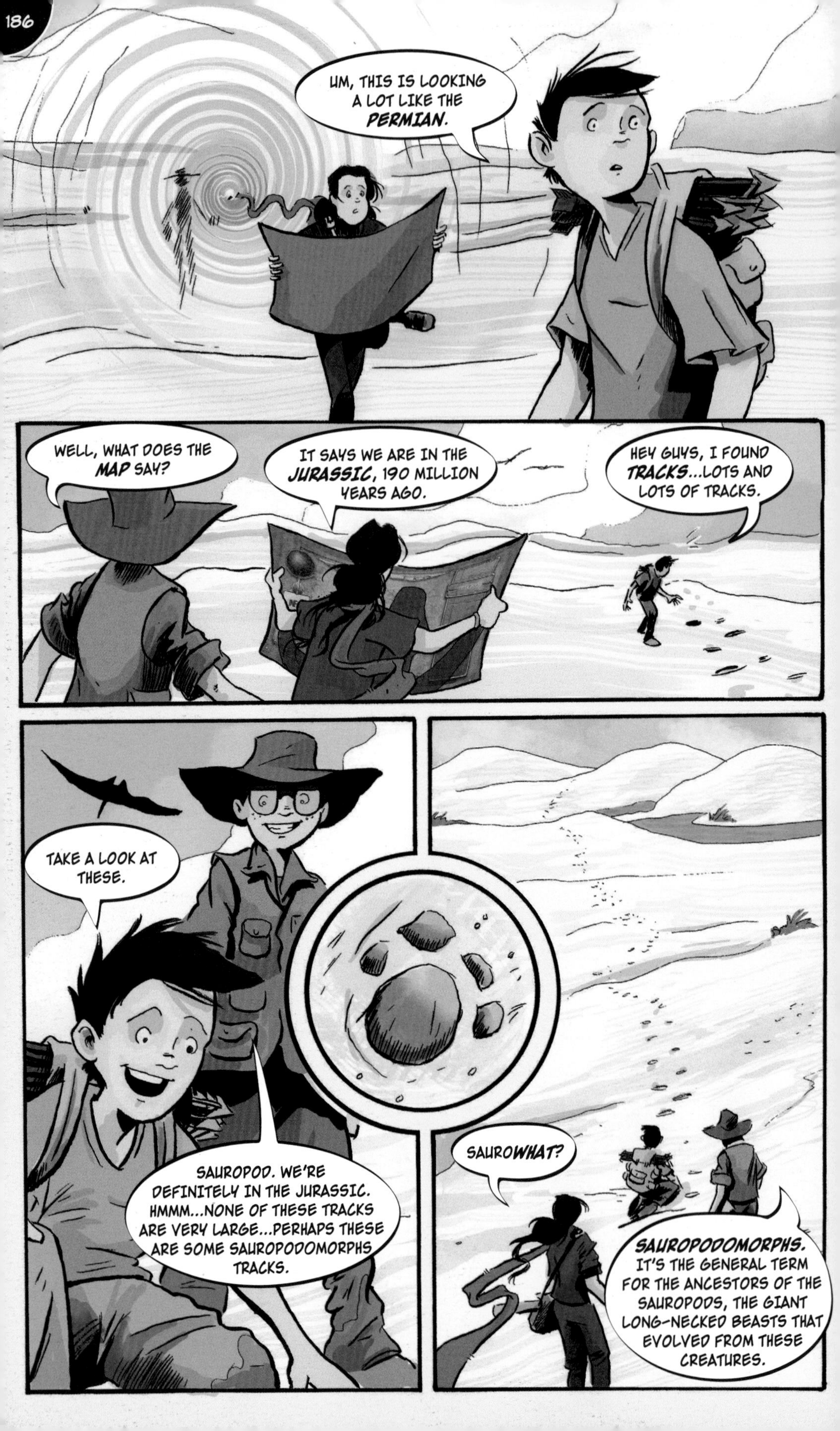
UM, THIS IS LOOKING A LOT LIKE THE PERMIAN.
WELL, WHAT DOES THE MAP SAY?
IT SAYS WE ARE IN THE JURASSIC, 190 MILLION YEARS AGO.
HEY GUYS, I FOUND TRACKS...LOTS AND LOTS OF TRACKS.
TAKE A LOOK AT THESE.
SAUROPOD. WE'RE DEFINITELY IN THE JURASSIC. HMMM...NONE OF THESE TRACKS ARE VERY LARGE...PERHAPS THESE ARE SOME SAUROPODOMORPHS TRACKS.
SAUROWHAT?
SAUROPODOMORPHS. IT'S THE GENERAL TERM FOR THE ANCESTORS OF THE SAUROPODS, THE GIANT LONG-NECKED BEASTS THAT EVOLVED FROM THESE CREATURES.

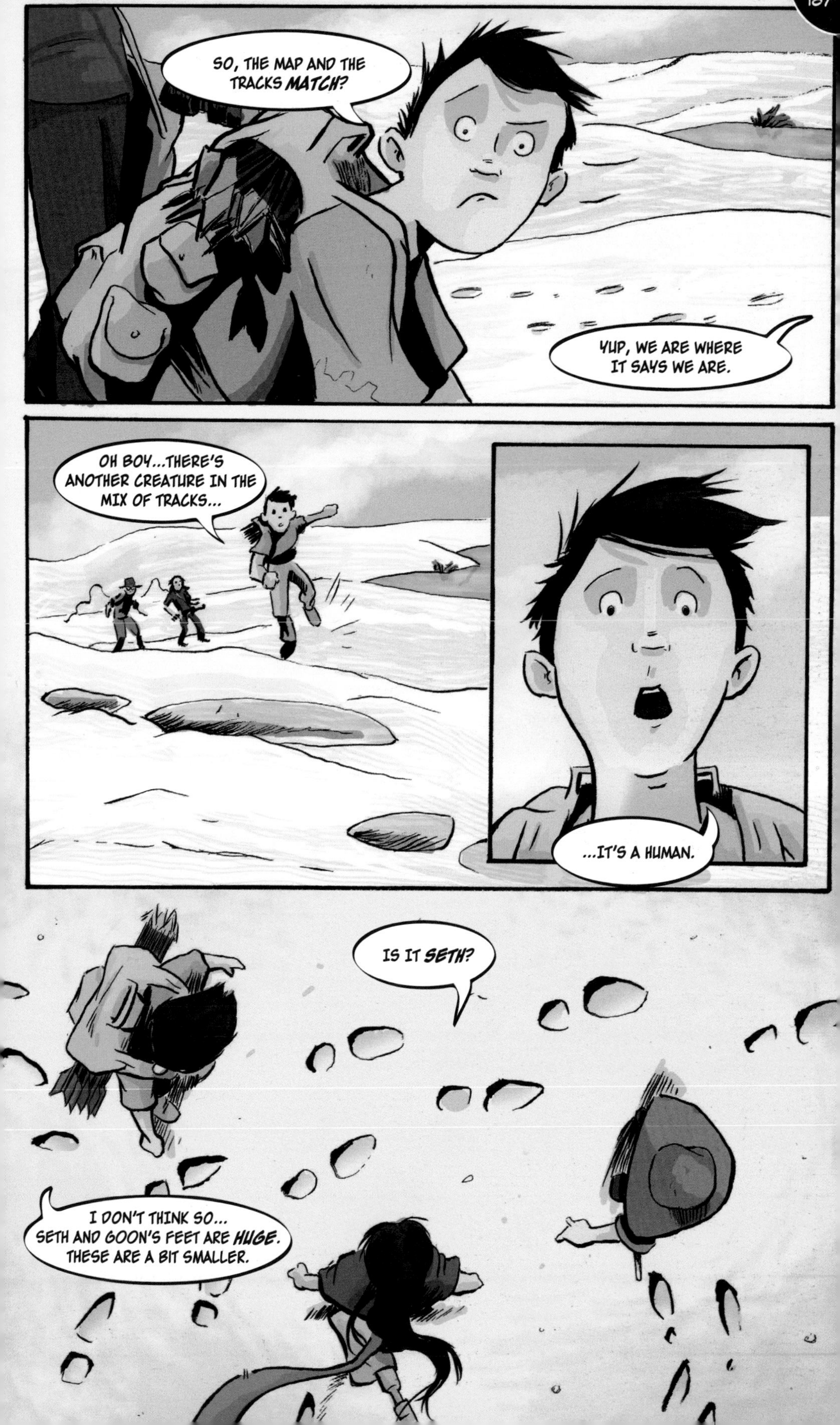
SO, THE MAP AND THE TRACKS MATCH?
YUP, WE ARE WHERE IT SAYS WE ARE.
OH BOY...THERE'S ANOTHER CREATURE IN THE MIX OF TRACKS...
...IT'S A HUMAN.
IS IT SETH?
I DON'T THINK SO... SETH AND GOON'S FEET ARE HUGE. THESE ARE A BIT SMALLER.

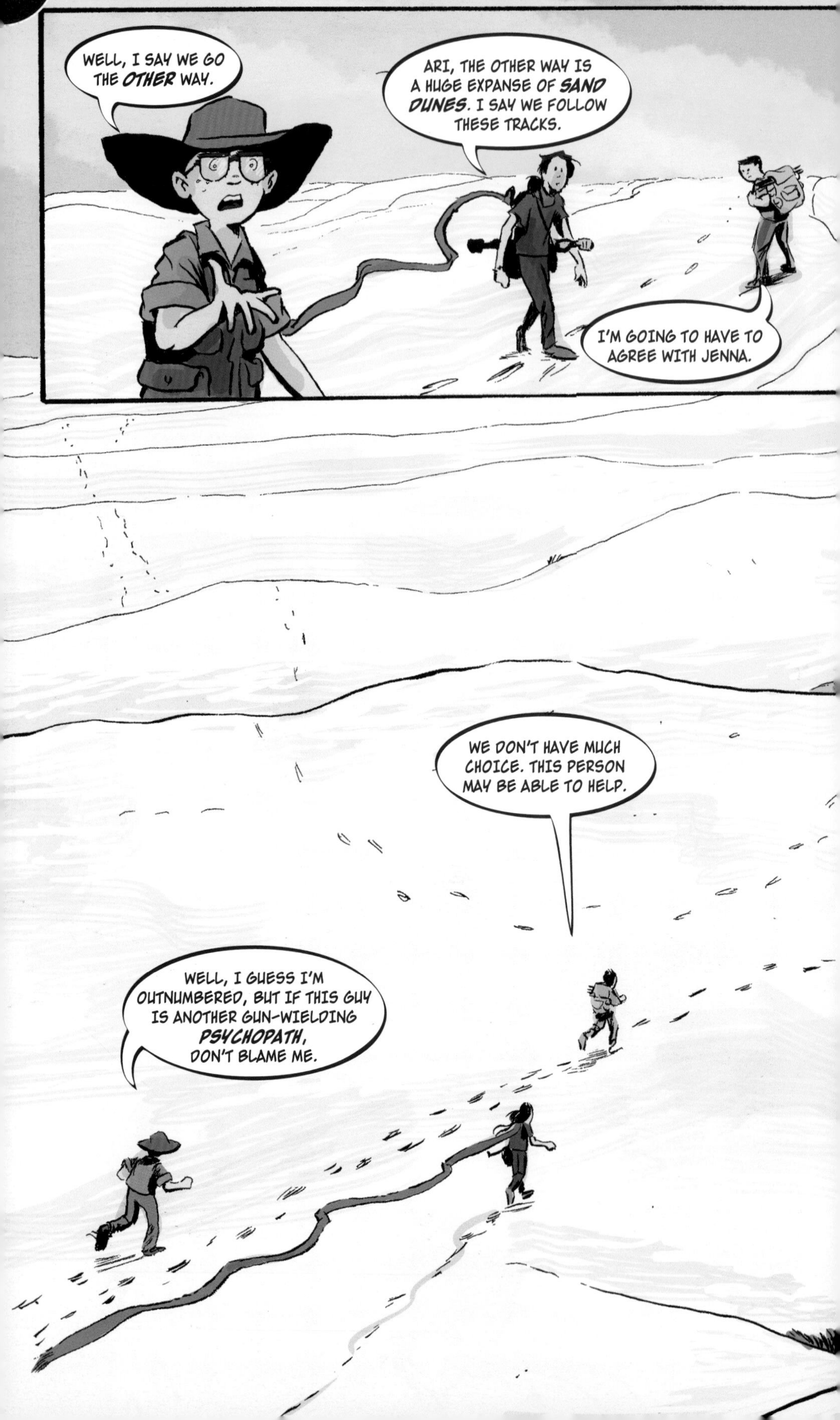
WELL, I SAY WE GO THE OTHER WAY.
ARI, THE OTHER WAY IS A HUGE EXPANSE OF SAND DUNES. I SAY WE FOLLOW THESE TRACKS.
I'M GOING TO HAVE TO AGREE WITH JENNA.
WE DON'T HAVE MUCH CHOICE. THIS PERSON MAY BE ABLE TO HELP.
WELL, I GUESS I'M OUTNUMBERED, BUT IF THIS GUY IS ANOTHER GUN-WIELDING PSYCHOPATH, DON'T BLAME ME.

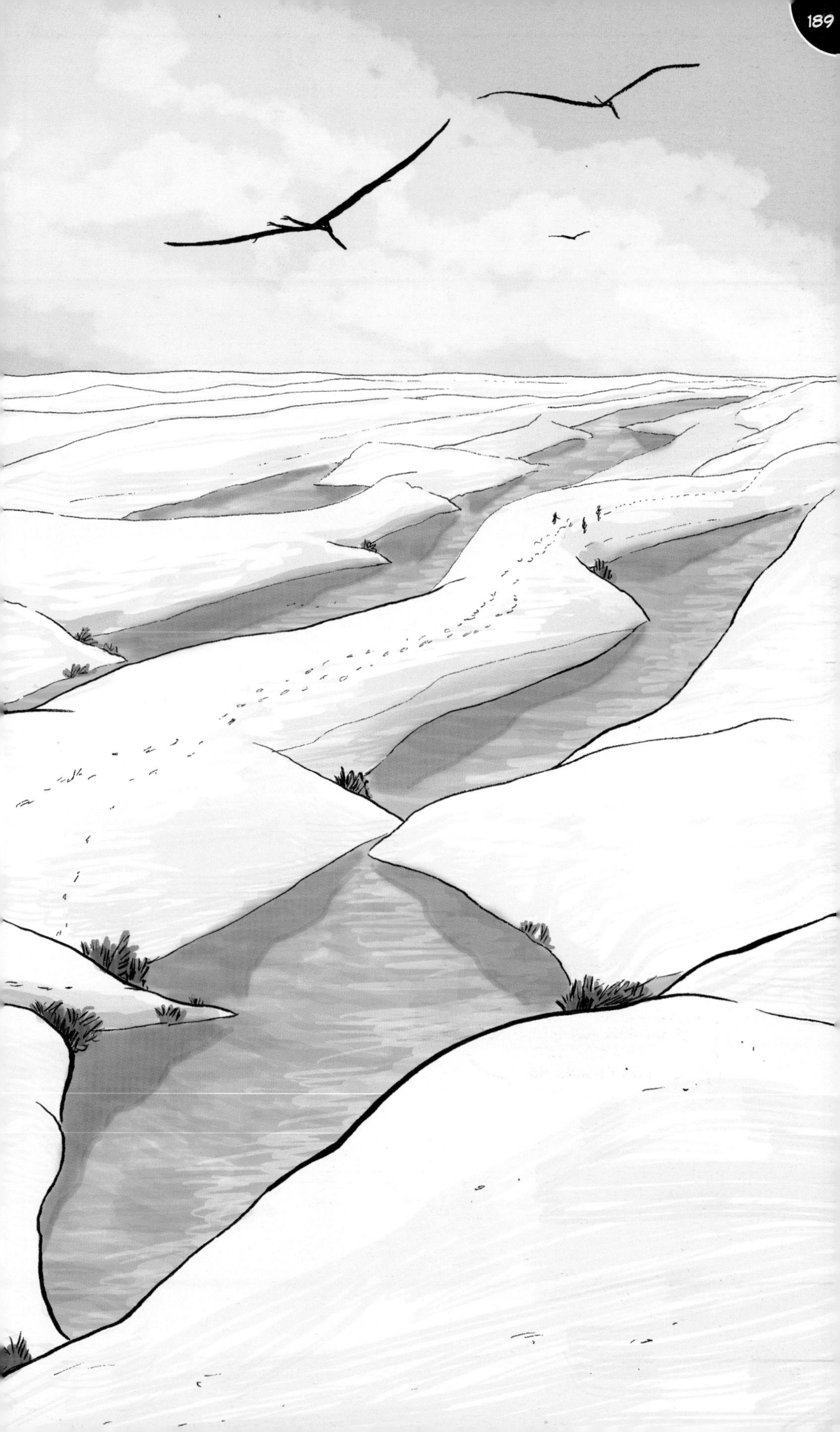

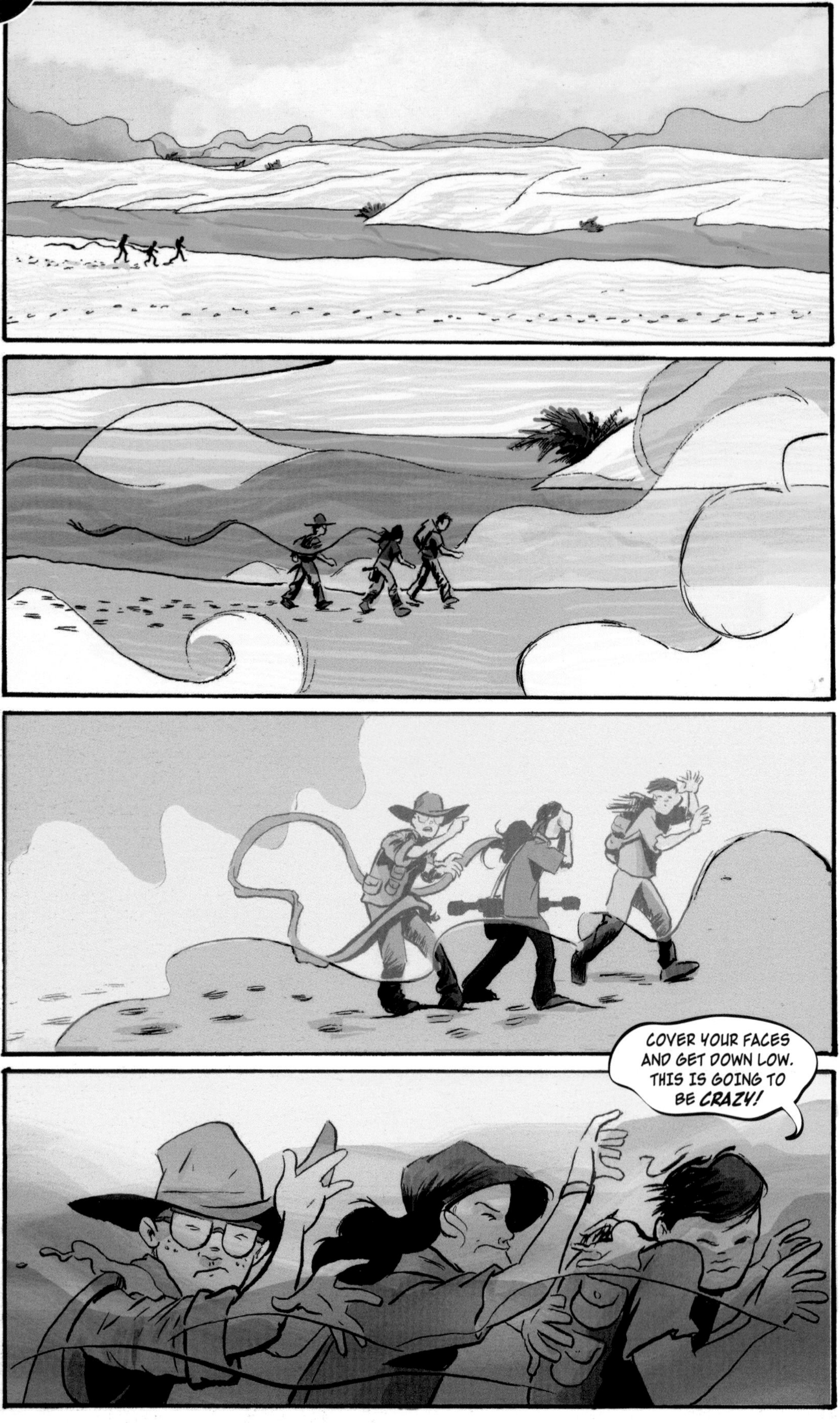
COVER YOUR FACES AND GET DOWN LOW. THIS IS GOING TO BE *CRAZY!*

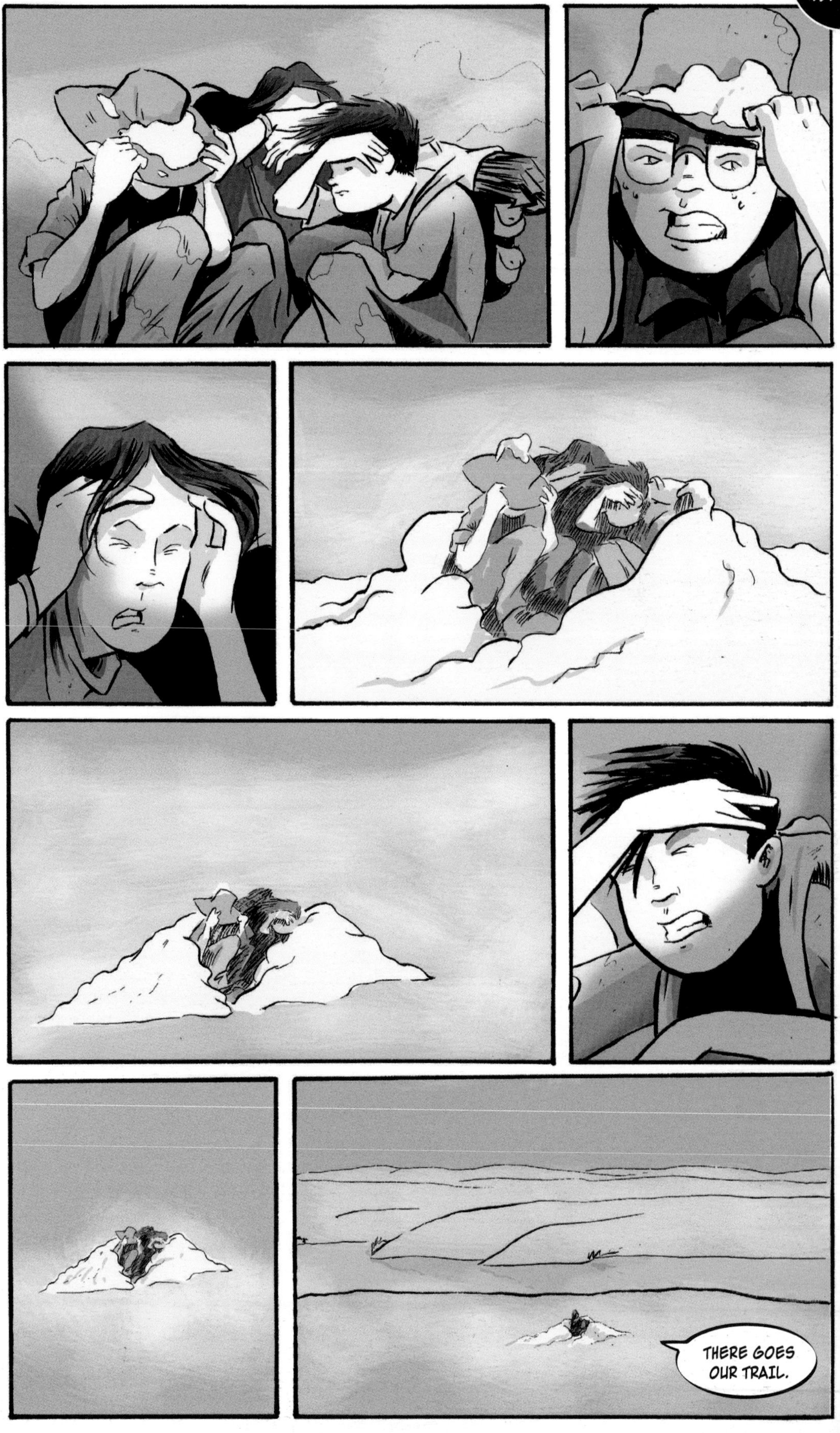
THERE GOES OUR TRAIL.

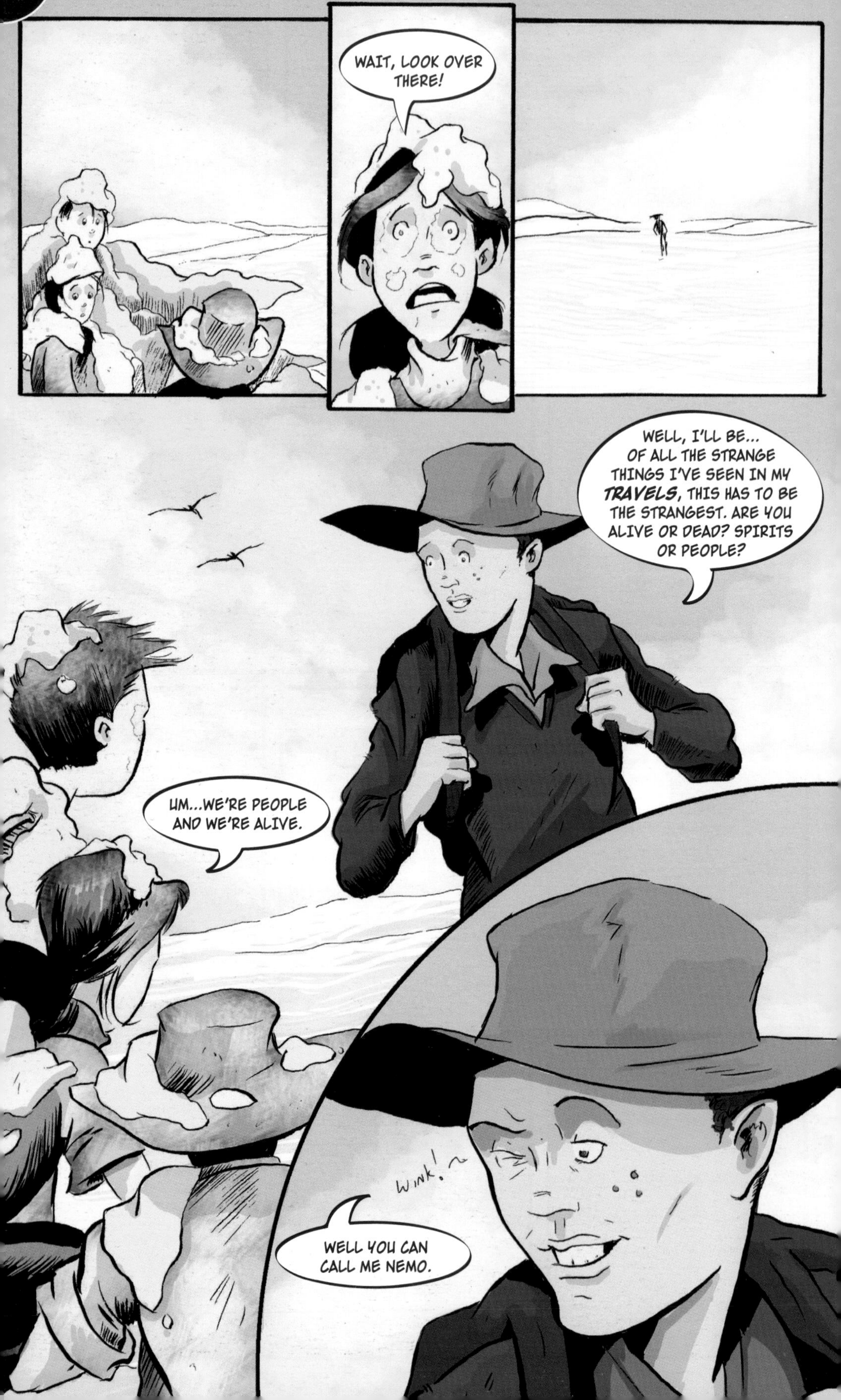
WAIT, LOOK OVER THERE!
WELL, I'LL BE... OF ALL THE STRANGE THINGS I'VE SEEN IN MY TRAVELS, THIS HAS TO BE THE STRANGEST. ARE YOU ALIVE OR DEAD? SPIRITS OR PEOPLE?
UM...WE'RE PEOPLE AND WE'RE ALIVE.
Wink!
WELL YOU CAN CALL ME NEMO.

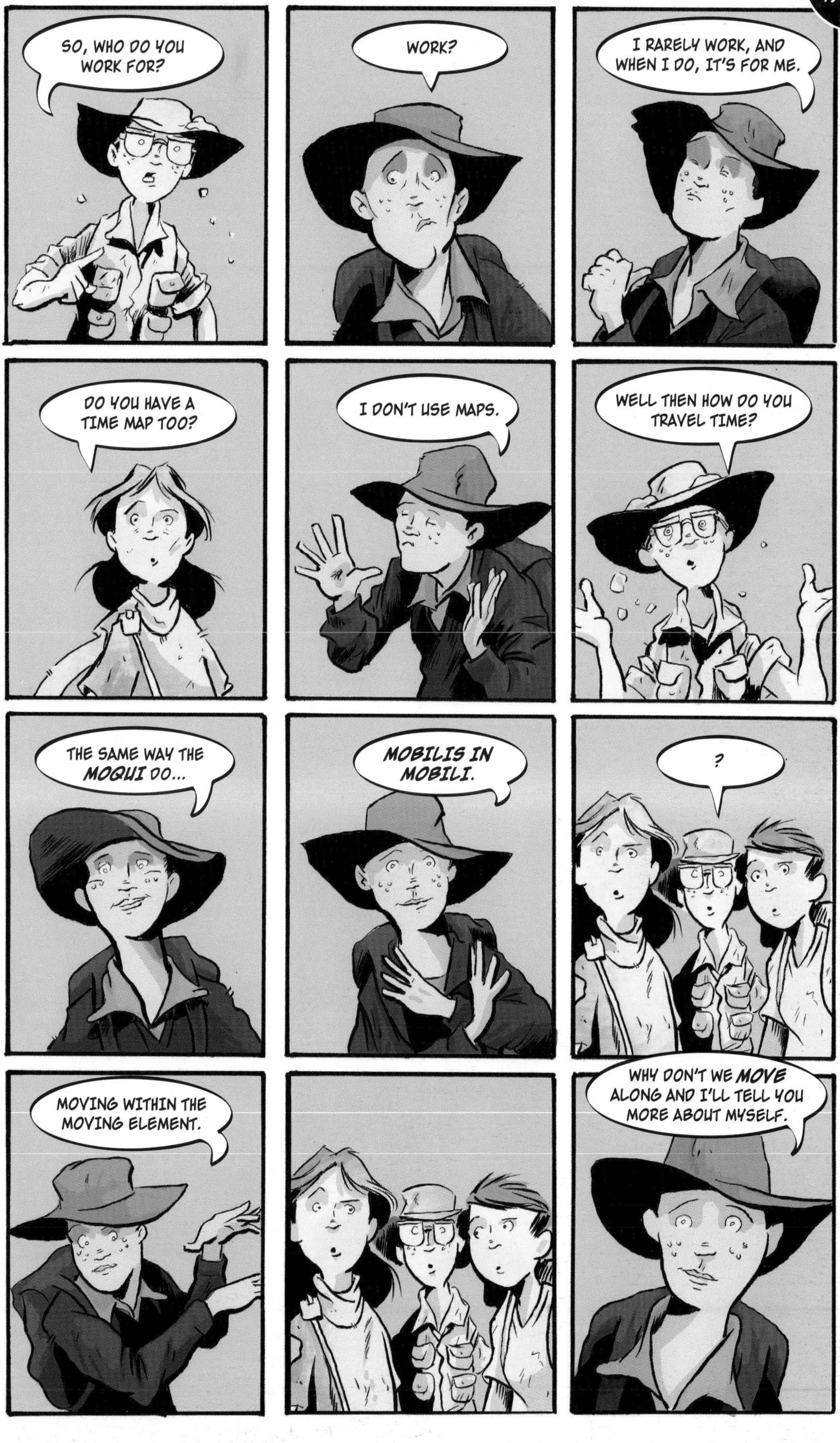
SO, WHO DO YOU WORK FOR?
WORK?
I RARELY WORK, AND WHEN I DO, IT'S FOR ME.
DO YOU HAVE A TIME MAP TOO?
I DON'T USE MAPS.
WELL THEN HOW DO YOU TRAVEL TIME?
THE SAME WAY THE *MOQUI* DO...
MOBILIS IN MOBILI.
?
MOVING WITHIN THE MOVING ELEMENT.
WHY DON'T WE *MOVE* ALONG AND I'LL TELL YOU MORE ABOUT MYSELF.

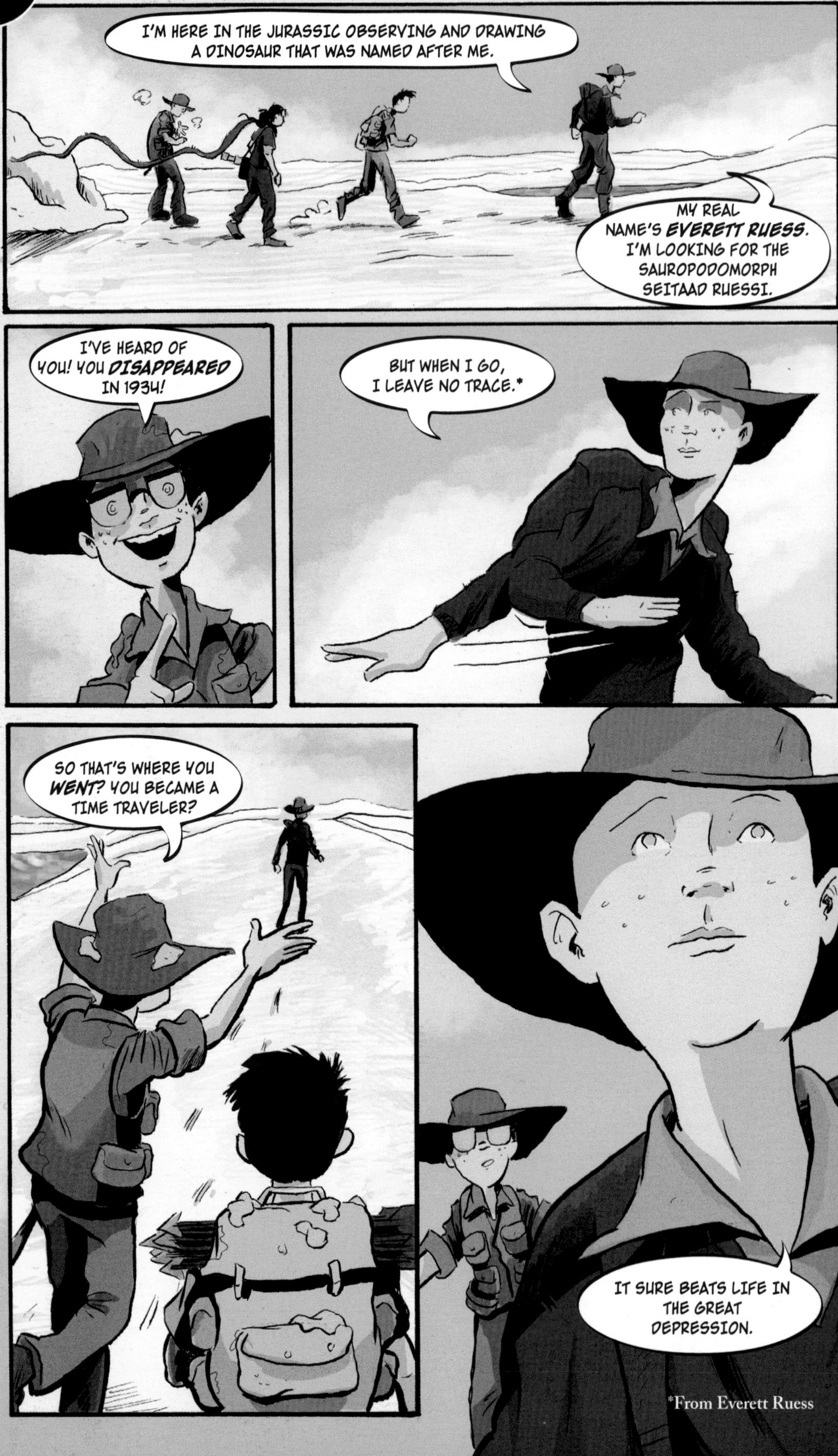
I'M HERE IN THE JURASSIC OBSERVING AND DRAWING A DINOSAUR THAT WAS NAMED AFTER ME.
MY REAL NAME'S **EVERETT RUESS**. I'M LOOKING FOR THE SAUROPODOMORPH SEITAAD RUESSI.
I'VE HEARD OF YOU! YOU ***DISAPPEARED*** IN 1934!
BUT WHEN I GO, I LEAVE NO TRACE.*
SO THAT'S WHERE YOU ***WENT***? YOU BECAME A TIME TRAVELER?
IT SURE BEATS LIFE IN THE GREAT DEPRESSION.

*From Everett Ruess

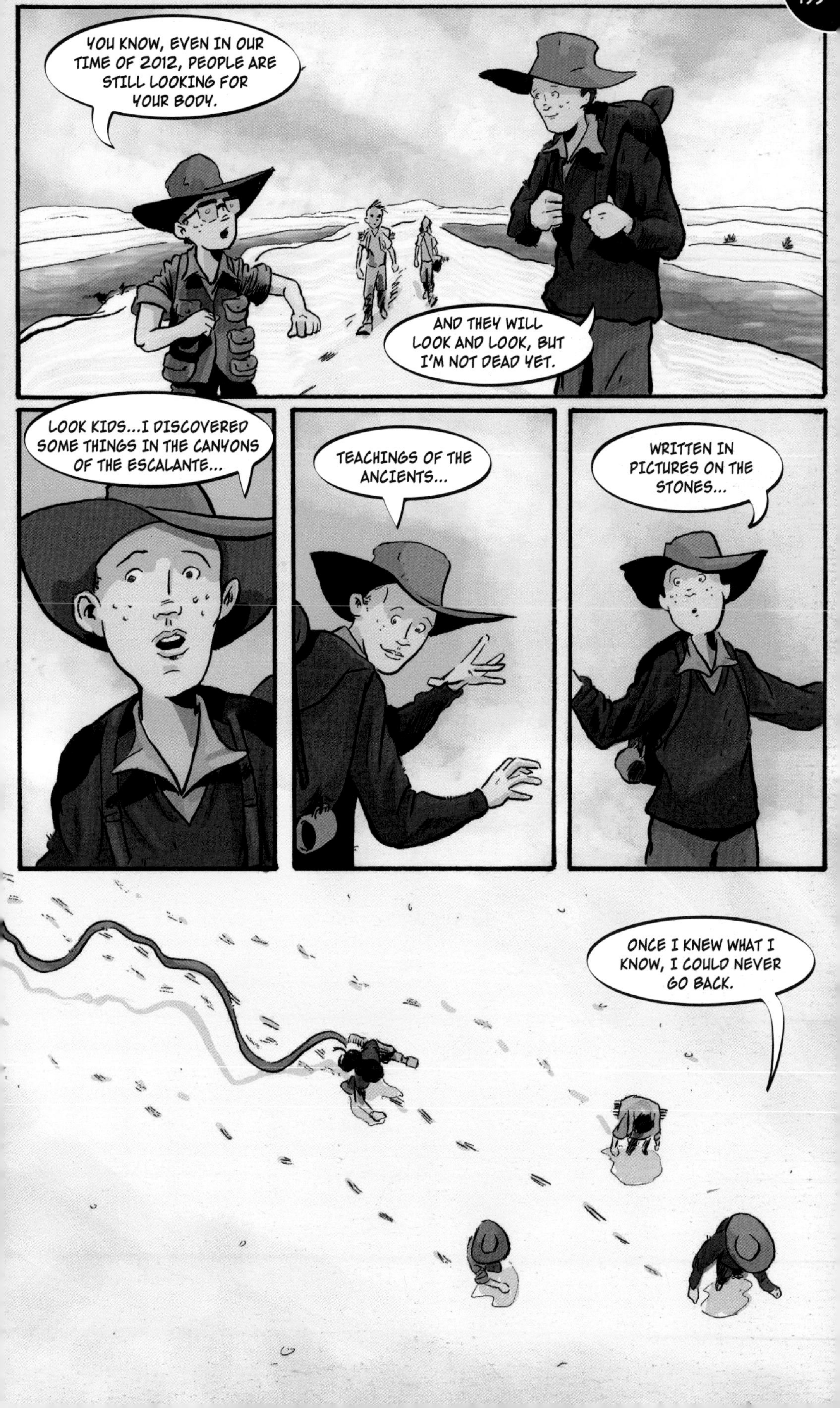
YOU KNOW, EVEN IN OUR TIME OF 2012, PEOPLE ARE STILL LOOKING FOR YOUR BODY.
AND THEY WILL LOOK AND LOOK, BUT I'M NOT DEAD YET.
LOOK KIDS...I DISCOVERED SOME THINGS IN THE CANYONS OF THE ESCALANTE...
TEACHINGS OF THE ANCIENTS...
WRITTEN IN PICTURES ON THE STONES...
ONCE I KNEW WHAT I KNOW, I COULD NEVER GO BACK.

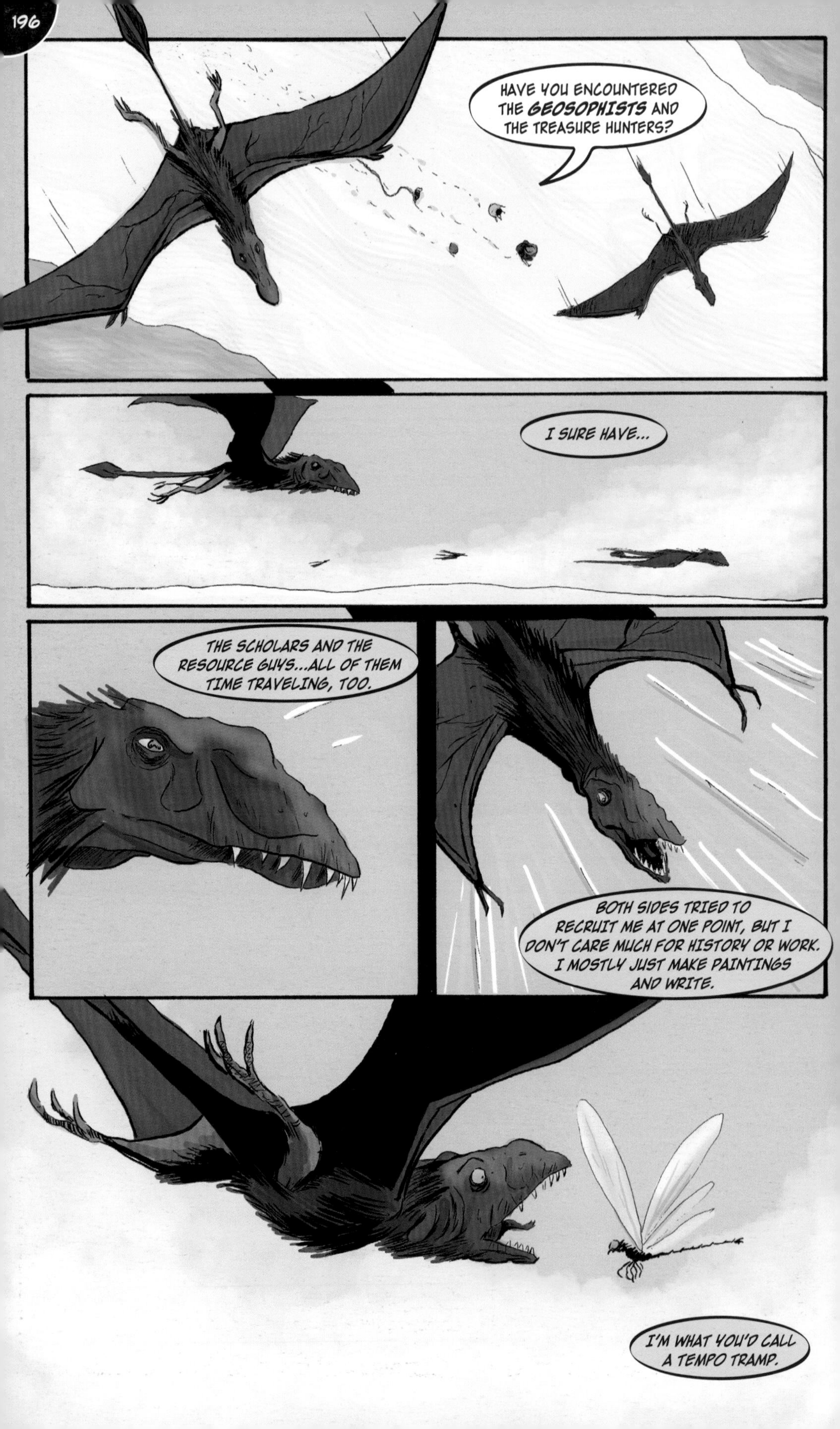
HAVE YOU ENCOUNTERED THE GEOSOPHISTS AND THE TREASURE HUNTERS?
I SURE HAVE...
THE SCHOLARS AND THE RESOURCE GUYS...ALL OF THEM TIME TRAVELING, TOO.
BOTH SIDES TRIED TO RECRUIT ME AT ONE POINT, BUT I DON'T CARE MUCH FOR HISTORY OR WORK. I MOSTLY JUST MAKE PAINTINGS AND WRITE.
I'M WHAT YOU'D CALL A TEMPO TRAMP.

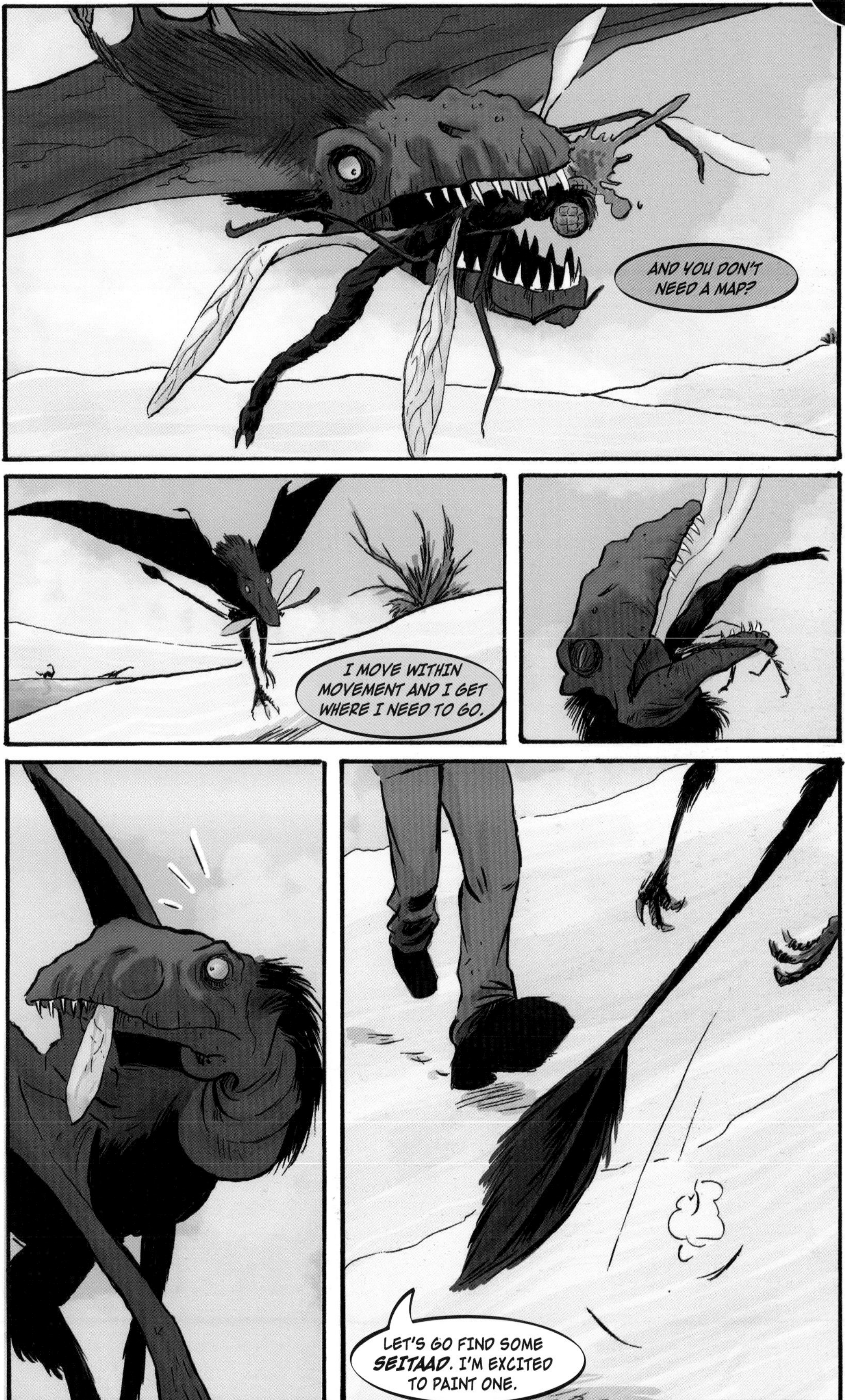
AND YOU DON'T NEED A MAP?
I MOVE WITHIN MOVEMENT AND I GET WHERE I NEED TO GO.
LET'S GO FIND SOME SEITAAD. I'M EXCITED TO PAINT ONE.

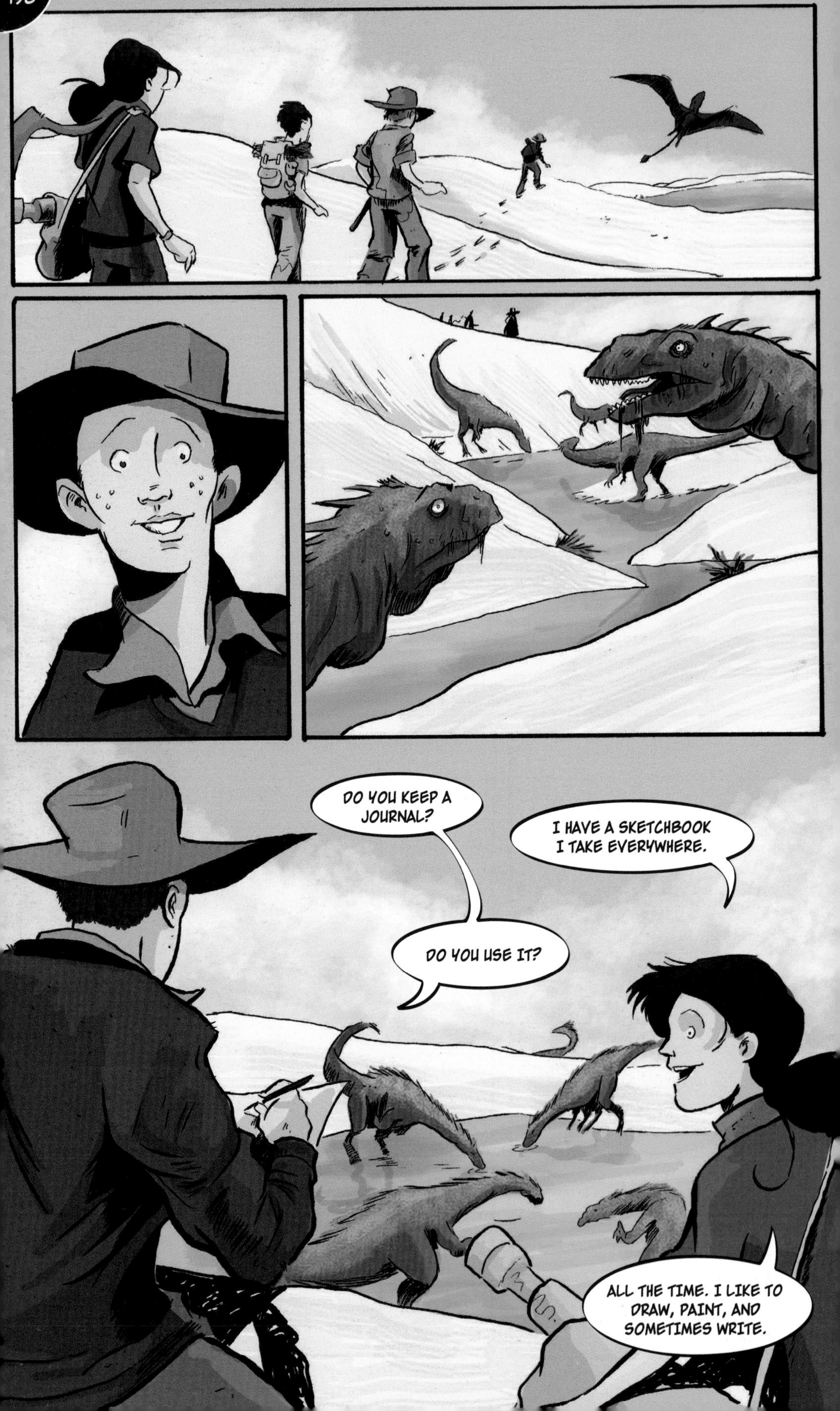
DO YOU KEEP A JOURNAL?
I HAVE A SKETCHBOOK I TAKE EVERYWHERE.
DO YOU USE IT?
ALL THE TIME. I LIKE TO DRAW, PAINT, AND SOMETIMES WRITE.

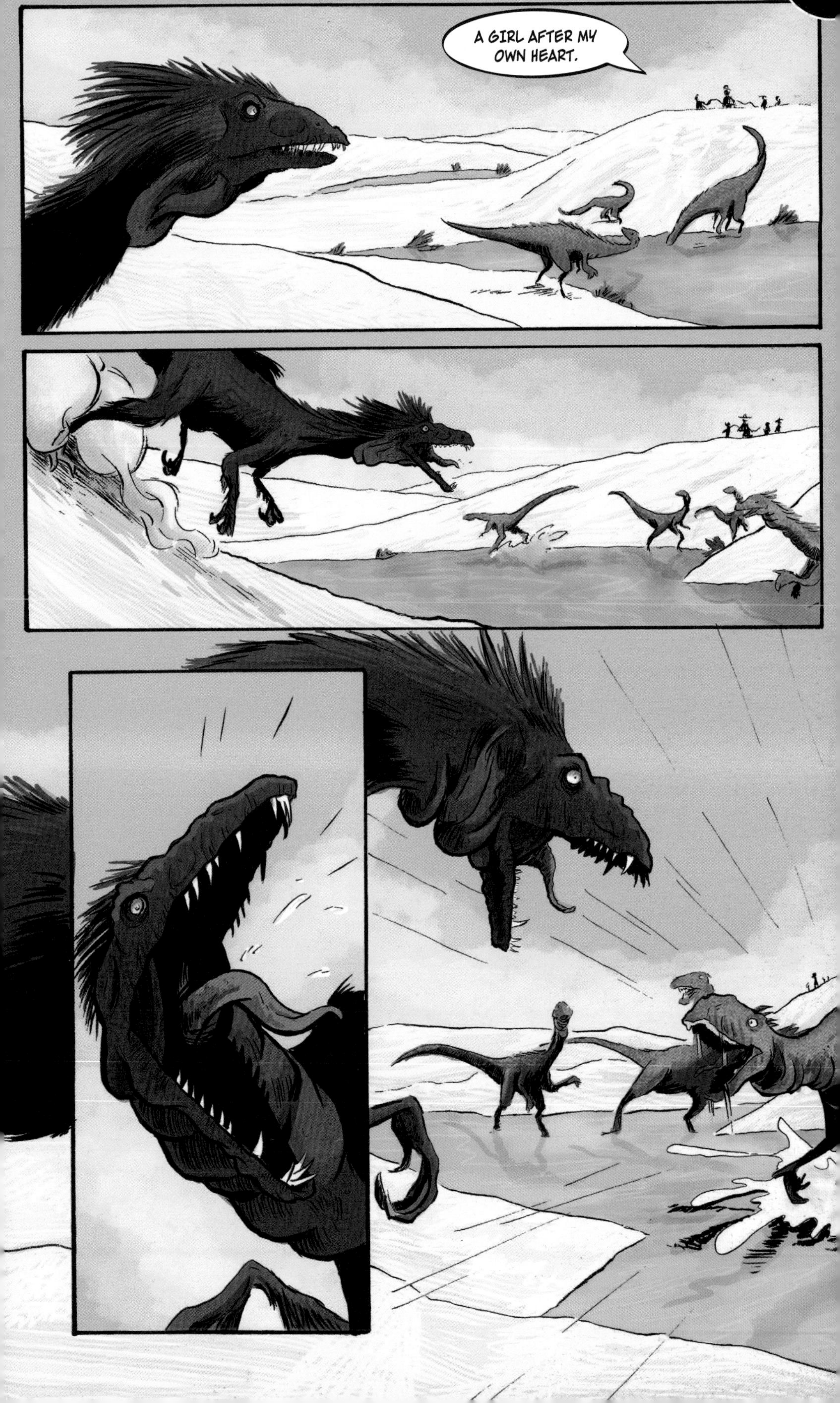
A GIRL AFTER MY
OWN HEART.

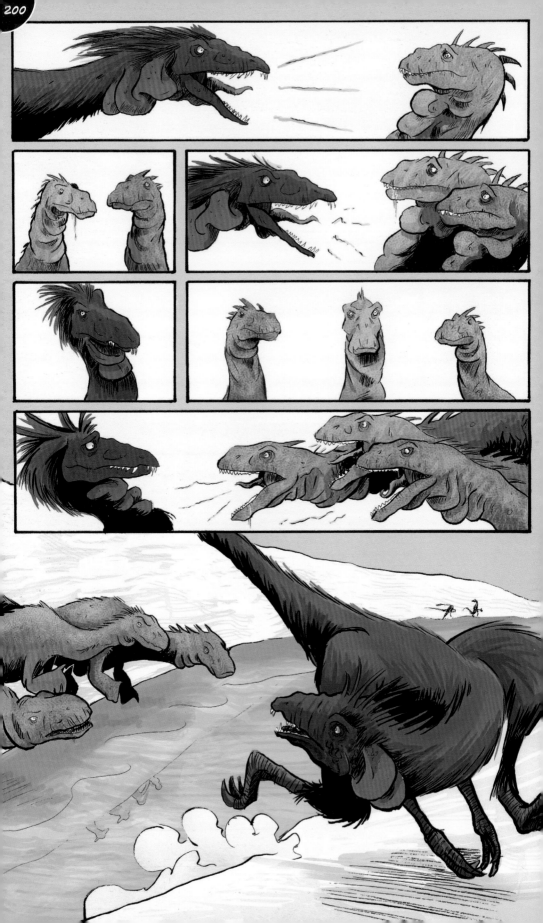

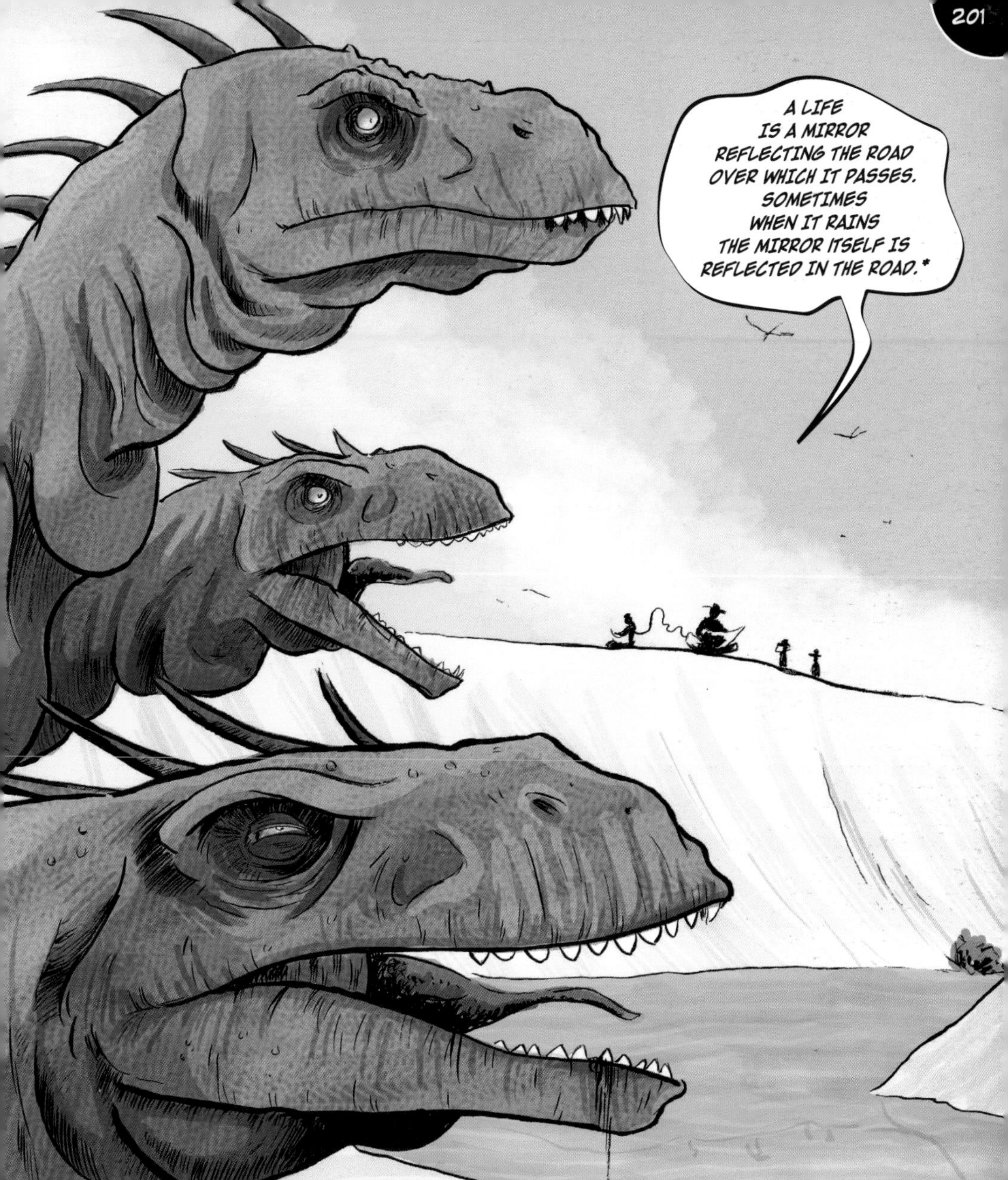
A LIFE IS A MIRROR REFLECTING THE ROAD OVER WHICH IT PASSES. SOMETIMES WHEN IT RAINS THE MIRROR ITSELF IS REFLECTED IN THE ROAD.*

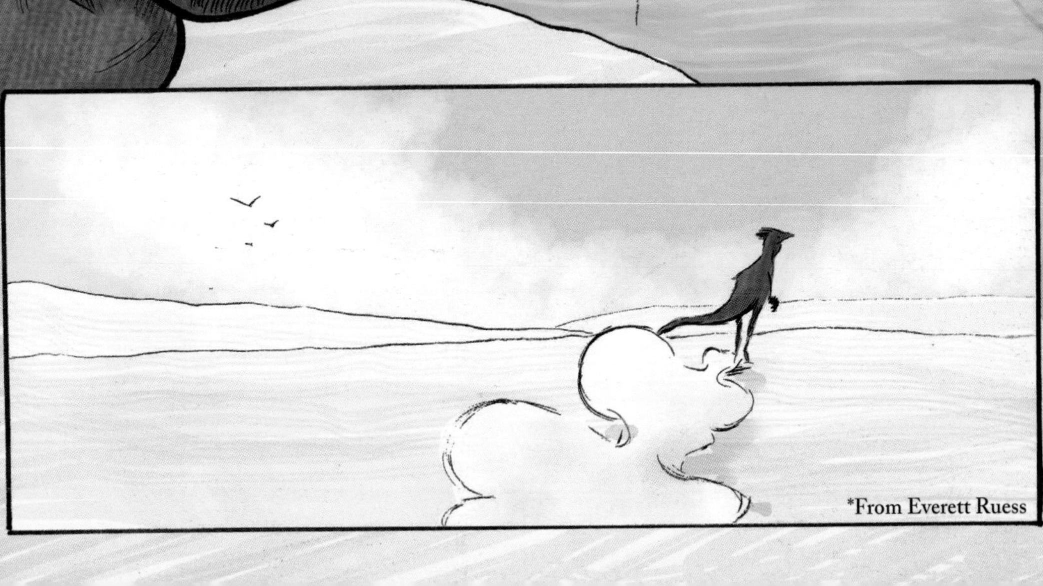

*From Everett Ruess

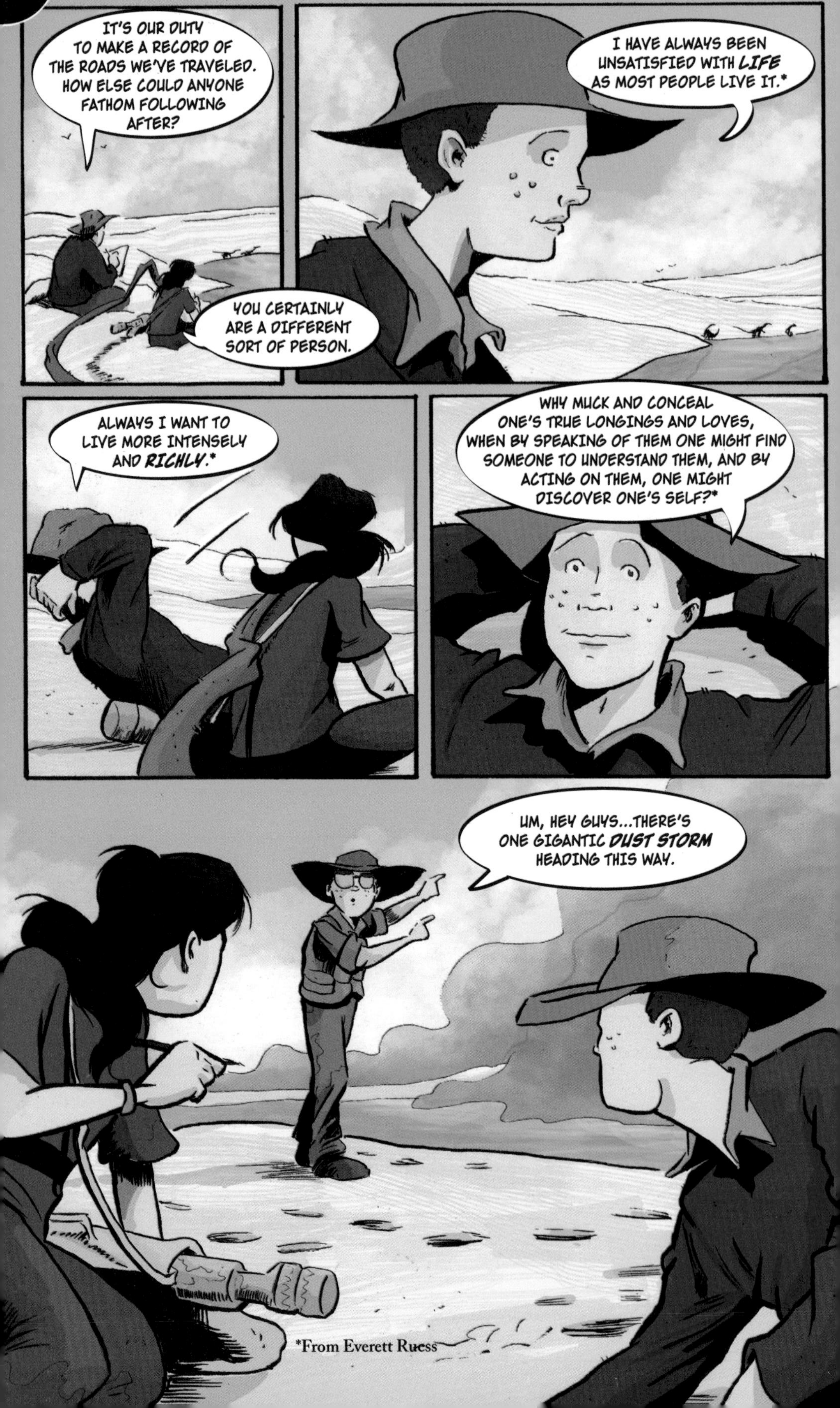
IT'S OUR DUTY TO MAKE A RECORD OF THE ROADS WE'VE TRAVELED. HOW ELSE COULD ANYONE FATHOM FOLLOWING AFTER?
YOU CERTAINLY ARE A DIFFERENT SORT OF PERSON.
I HAVE ALWAYS BEEN UNSATISFIED WITH LIFE AS MOST PEOPLE LIVE IT.*
ALWAYS I WANT TO LIVE MORE INTENSELY AND RICHLY.*
WHY MUCK AND CONCEAL ONE'S TRUE LONGINGS AND LOVES, WHEN BY SPEAKING OF THEM ONE MIGHT FIND SOMEONE TO UNDERSTAND THEM, AND BY ACTING ON THEM, ONE MIGHT DISCOVER ONE'S SELF?*
UM, HEY GUYS...THERE'S ONE GIGANTIC DUST STORM HEADING THIS WAY.

*From Everett Ruess

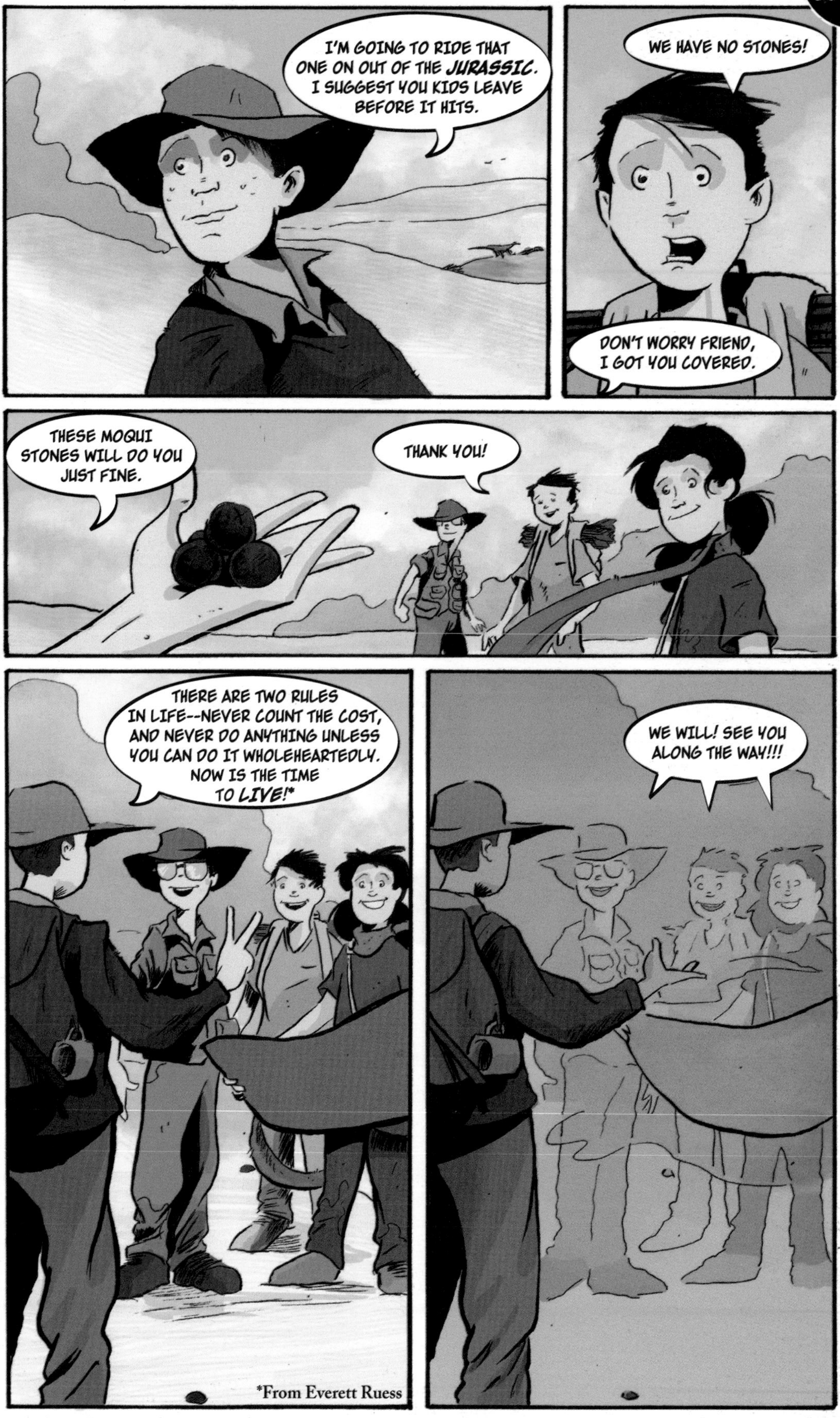
I'M GOING TO RIDE THAT ONE ON OUT OF THE *JURASSIC*. I SUGGEST YOU KIDS LEAVE BEFORE IT HITS.
WE HAVE NO STONES!
DON'T WORRY FRIEND, I GOT YOU COVERED.
THESE MOQUI STONES WILL DO YOU JUST FINE.
THANK YOU!
THERE ARE TWO RULES IN LIFE--NEVER COUNT THE COST, AND NEVER DO ANYTHING UNLESS YOU CAN DO IT WHOLEHEARTEDLY. NOW IS THE TIME TO *LIVE*!*
WE WILL! SEE YOU ALONG THE WAY!!!
*From Everett Ruess

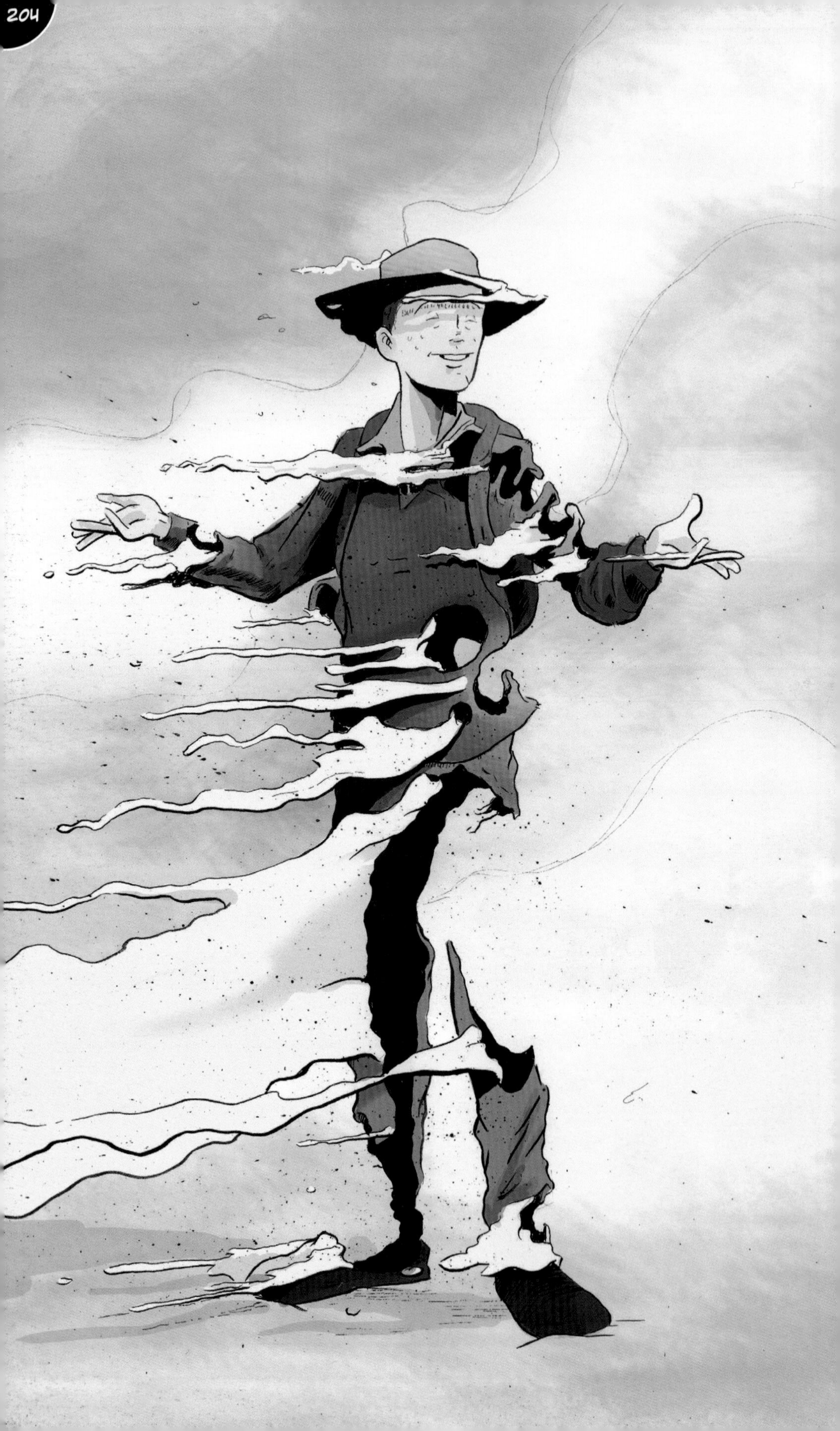

CHAPTER NINE

CREEPY CRETACEOUS

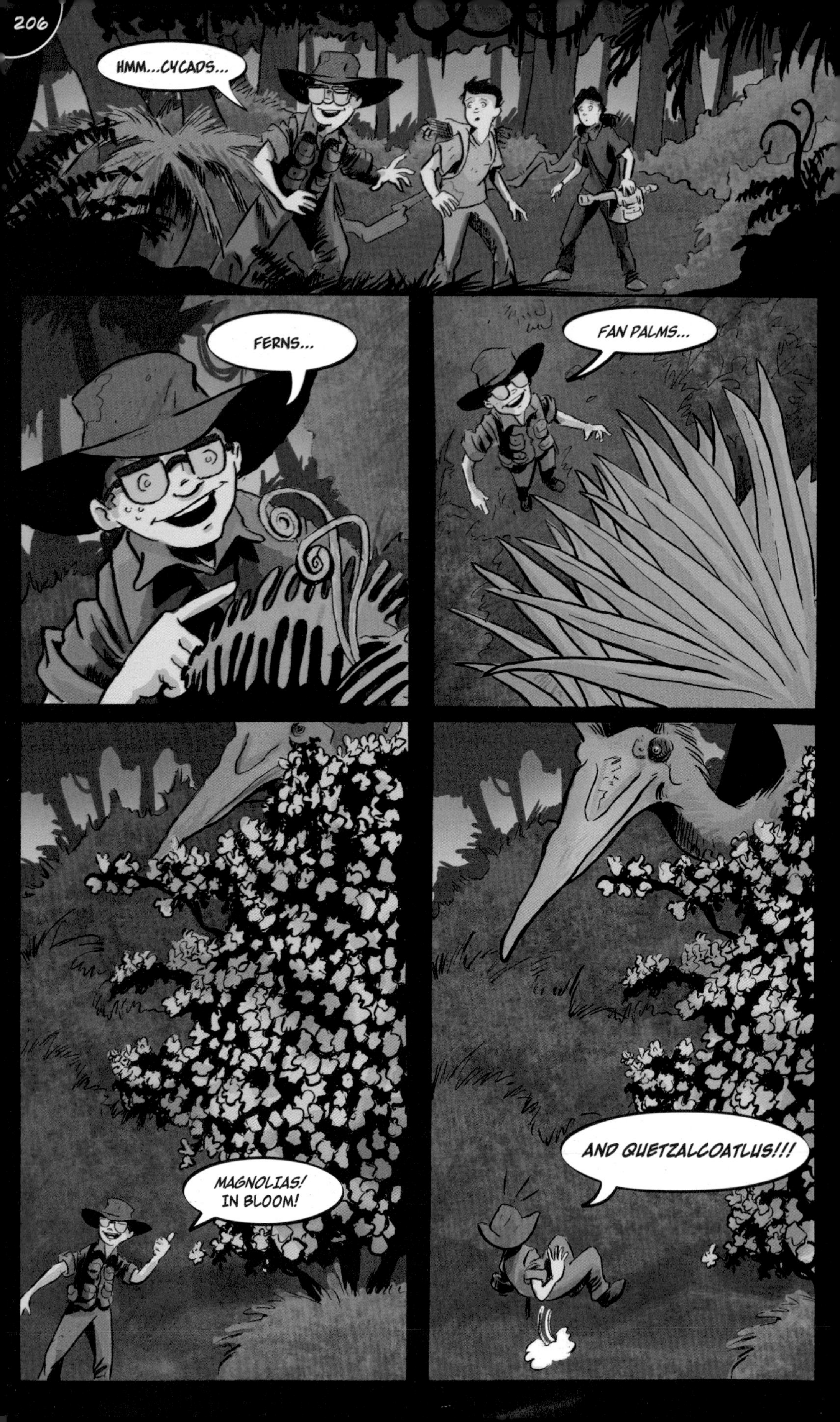
HMM...CYCADS...
FERNS...
FAN PALMS...
MAGNOLIAS! IN BLOOM!
AND QUETZALCOATLUS!!!

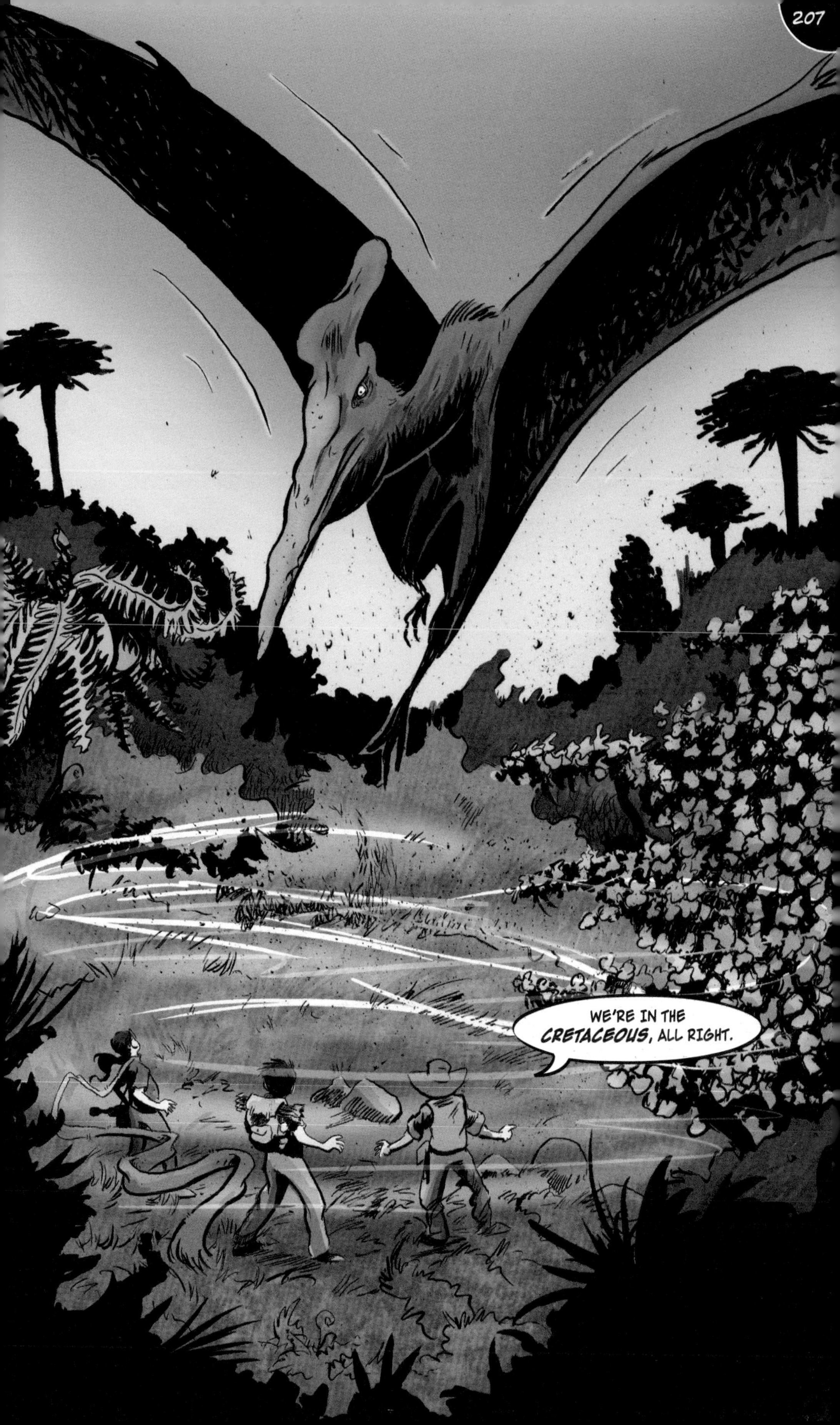
WE'RE IN THE *CRETACEOUS*, ALL RIGHT.

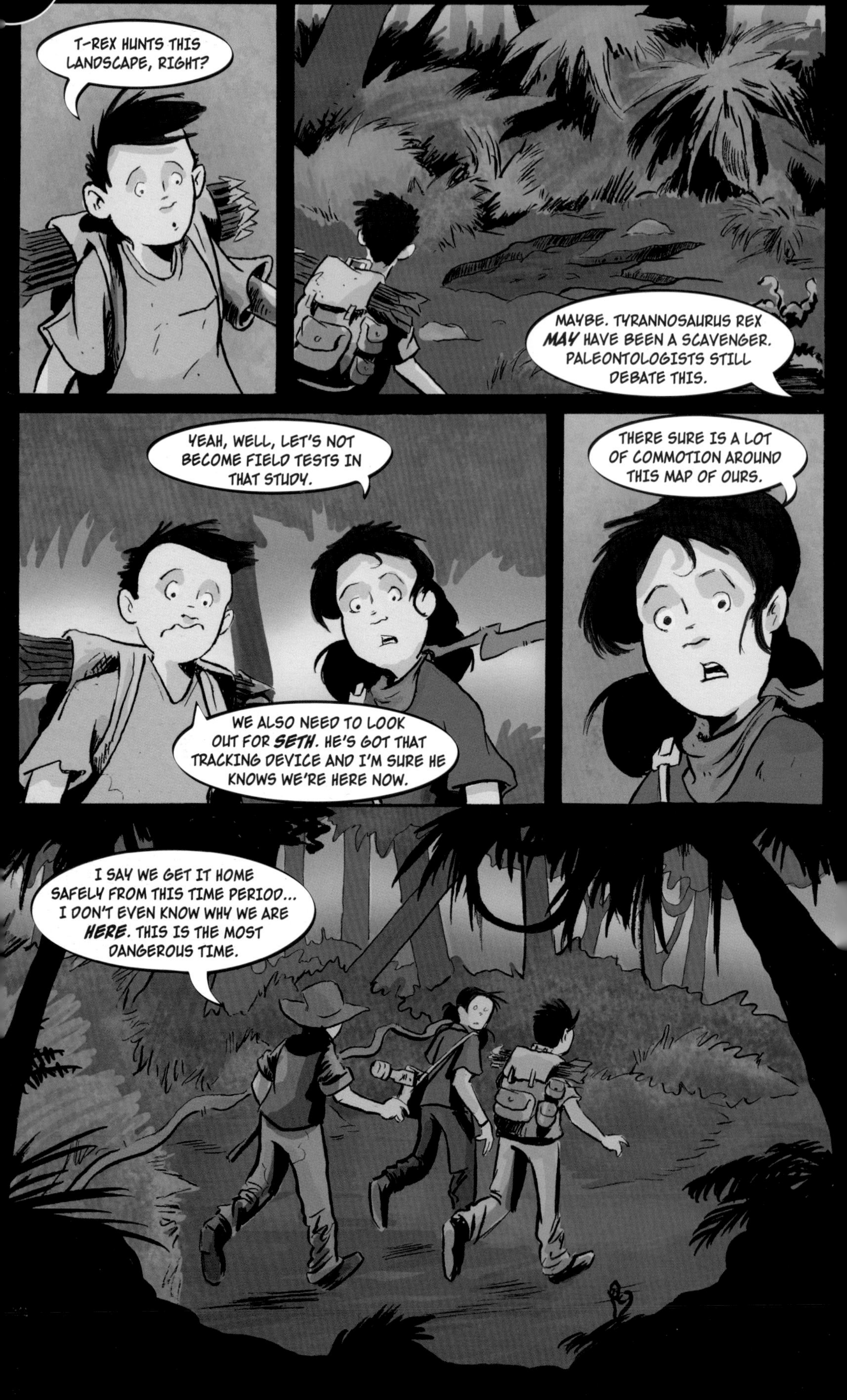

T-REX HUNTS THIS LANDSCAPE, RIGHT?
MAYBE. TYRANNOSAURUS REX MAY HAVE BEEN A SCAVENGER. PALEONTOLOGISTS STILL DEBATE THIS.
YEAH, WELL, LET'S NOT BECOME FIELD TESTS IN THAT STUDY.
WE ALSO NEED TO LOOK OUT FOR SETH. HE'S GOT THAT TRACKING DEVICE AND I'M SURE HE KNOWS WE'RE HERE NOW.
THERE SURE IS A LOT OF COMMOTION AROUND THIS MAP OF OURS.
I SAY WE GET IT HOME SAFELY FROM THIS TIME PERIOD... I DON'T EVEN KNOW WHY WE ARE HERE. THIS IS THE MOST DANGEROUS TIME.

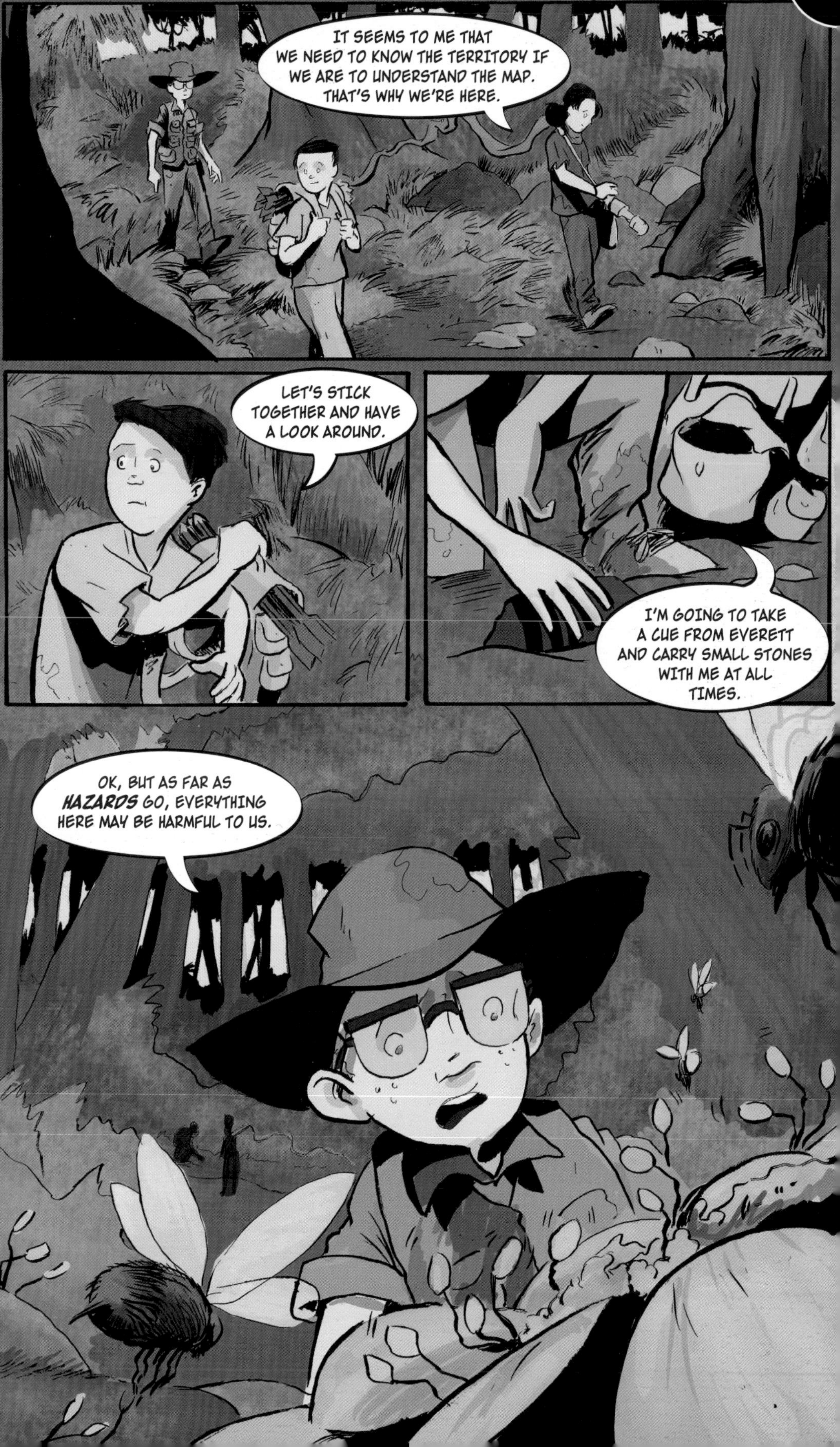
IT SEEMS TO ME THAT WE NEED TO KNOW THE TERRITORY IF WE ARE TO UNDERSTAND THE MAP. THAT'S WHY WE'RE HERE.
LET'S STICK TOGETHER AND HAVE A LOOK AROUND.
I'M GOING TO TAKE A CUE FROM EVERETT AND CARRY SMALL STONES WITH ME AT ALL TIMES.
OK, BUT AS FAR AS **HAZARDS** GO, EVERYTHING HERE MAY BE HARMFUL TO US.

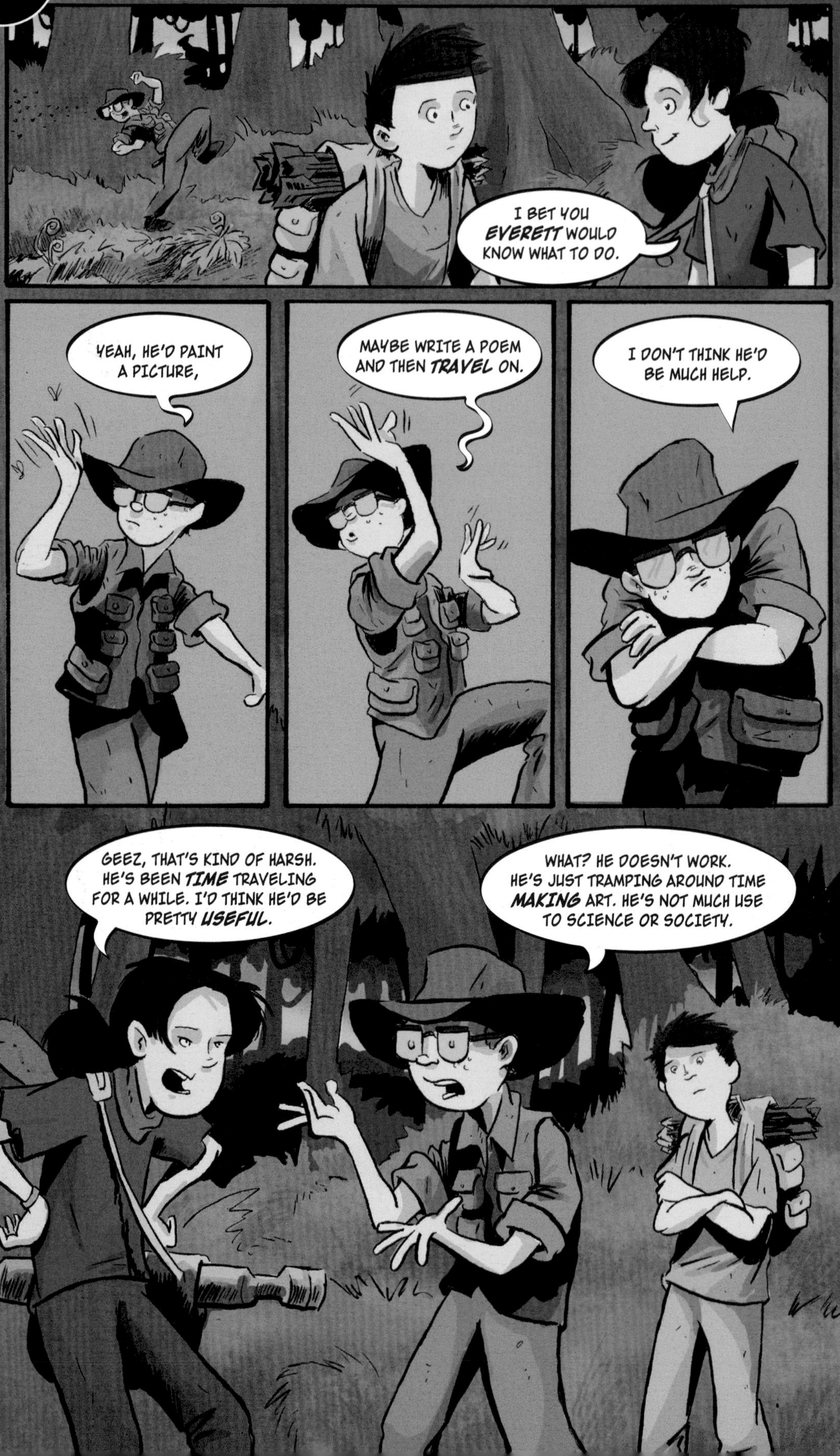
I BET YOU EVERETT WOULD KNOW WHAT TO DO.
YEAH, HE'D PAINT A PICTURE,
MAYBE WRITE A POEM AND THEN TRAVEL ON.
I DON'T THINK HE'D BE MUCH HELP.
GEEZ, THAT'S KIND OF HARSH. HE'S BEEN TIME TRAVELING FOR A WHILE. I'D THINK HE'D BE PRETTY USEFUL.
WHAT? HE DOESN'T WORK. HE'S JUST TRAMPING AROUND TIME MAKING ART. HE'S NOT MUCH USE TO SCIENCE OR SOCIETY.

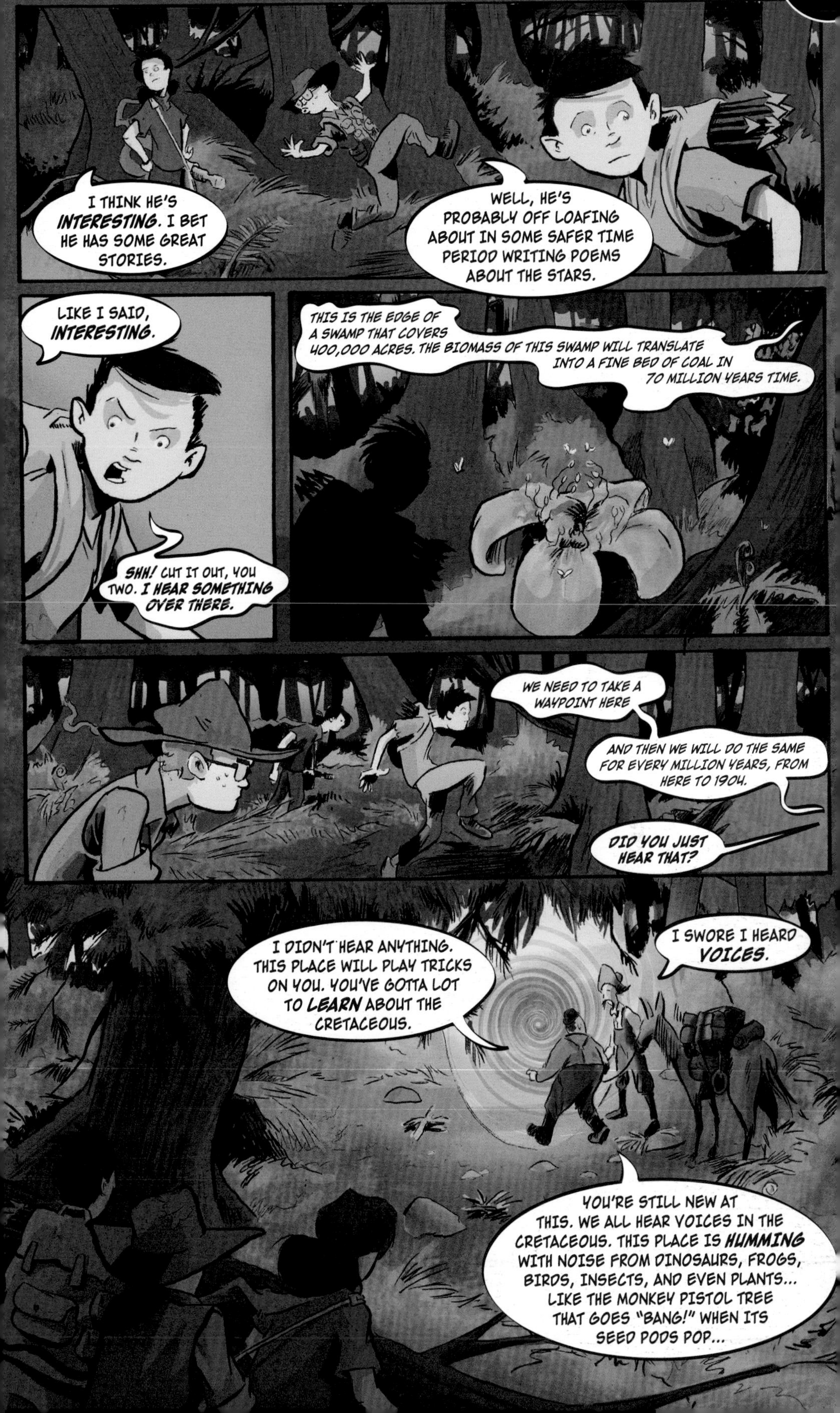
I THINK HE'S INTERESTING. I BET HE HAS SOME GREAT STORIES.
WELL, HE'S PROBABLY OFF LOAFING ABOUT IN SOME SAFER TIME PERIOD WRITING POEMS ABOUT THE STARS.
LIKE I SAID, INTERESTING.
SHH! CUT IT OUT, YOU TWO. I HEAR SOMETHING OVER THERE.
THIS IS THE EDGE OF A SWAMP THAT COVERS 400,000 ACRES. THE BIOMASS OF THIS SWAMP WILL TRANSLATE INTO A FINE BED OF COAL IN 70 MILLION YEARS TIME.
WE NEED TO TAKE A WAYPOINT HERE
AND THEN WE WILL DO THE SAME FOR EVERY MILLION YEARS, FROM HERE TO 1904.
DID YOU JUST HEAR THAT?
I DIDN'T HEAR ANYTHING. THIS PLACE WILL PLAY TRICKS ON YOU. YOU'VE GOTTA LOT TO LEARN ABOUT THE CRETACEOUS.
I SWORE I HEARD VOICES.
YOU'RE STILL NEW AT THIS. WE ALL HEAR VOICES IN THE CRETACEOUS. THIS PLACE IS HUMMING WITH NOISE FROM DINOSAURS, FROGS, BIRDS, INSECTS, AND EVEN PLANTS... LIKE THE MONKEY PISTOL TREE THAT GOES "BANG!" WHEN ITS SEED PODS POP...

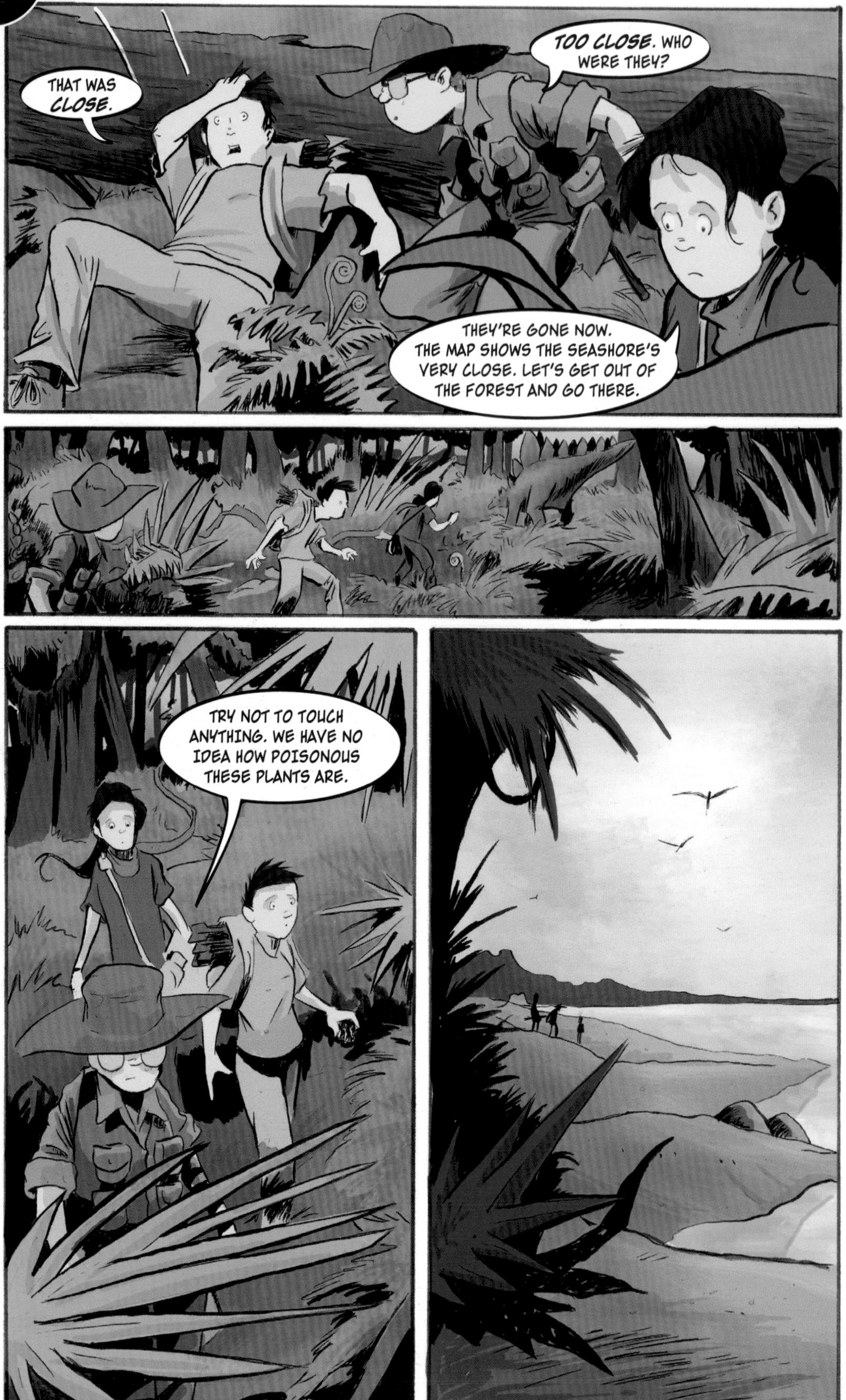
THAT WAS CLOSE.
TOO CLOSE. WHO WERE THEY?
THEY'RE GONE NOW. THE MAP SHOWS THE SEASHORE'S VERY CLOSE. LET'S GET OUT OF THE FOREST AND GO THERE.
TRY NOT TO TOUCH ANYTHING. WE HAVE NO IDEA HOW POISONOUS THESE PLANTS ARE.

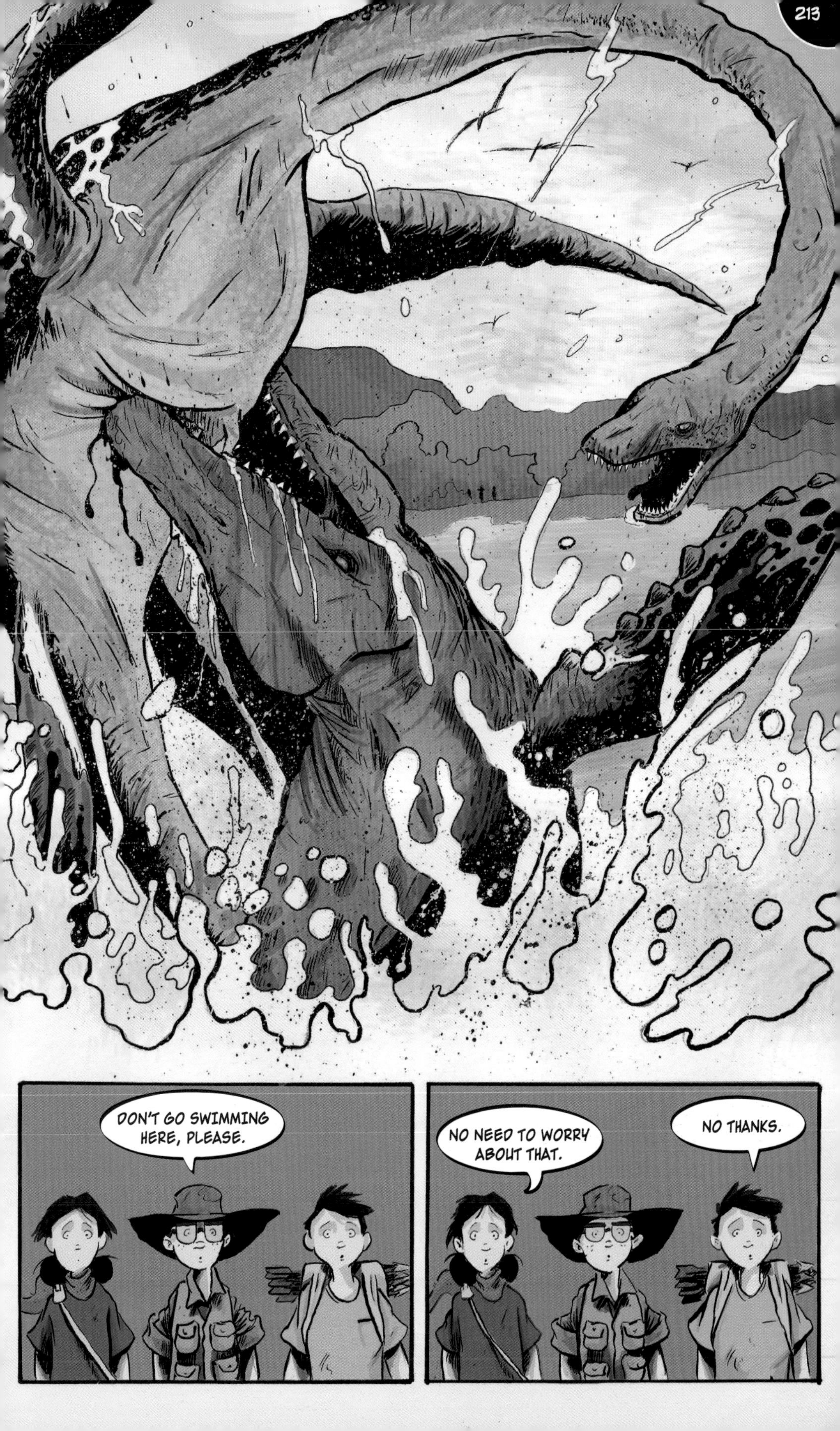
DON'T GO SWIMMING HERE, PLEASE.
NO NEED TO WORRY ABOUT THAT.
NO THANKS.

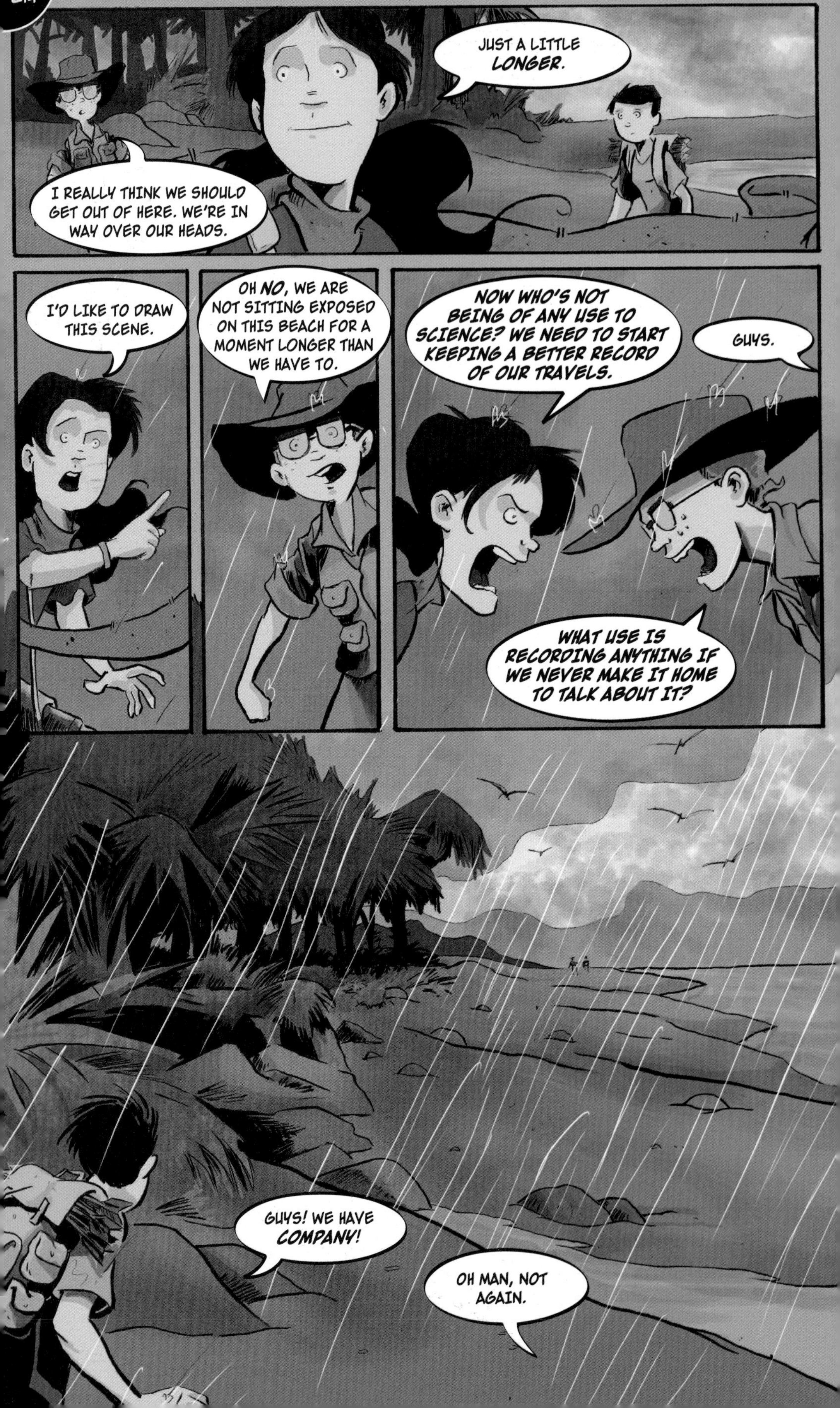
JUST A LITTLE LONGER.
I REALLY THINK WE SHOULD GET OUT OF HERE. WE'RE IN WAY OVER OUR HEADS.
I'D LIKE TO DRAW THIS SCENE.
OH NO, WE ARE NOT SITTING EXPOSED ON THIS BEACH FOR A MOMENT LONGER THAN WE HAVE TO.
NOW WHO'S NOT BEING OF ANY USE TO SCIENCE? WE NEED TO START KEEPING A BETTER RECORD OF OUR TRAVELS.
GUYS.
WHAT USE IS RECORDING ANYTHING IF WE NEVER MAKE IT HOME TO TALK ABOUT IT?
GUYS! WE HAVE COMPANY!
OH MAN, NOT AGAIN.

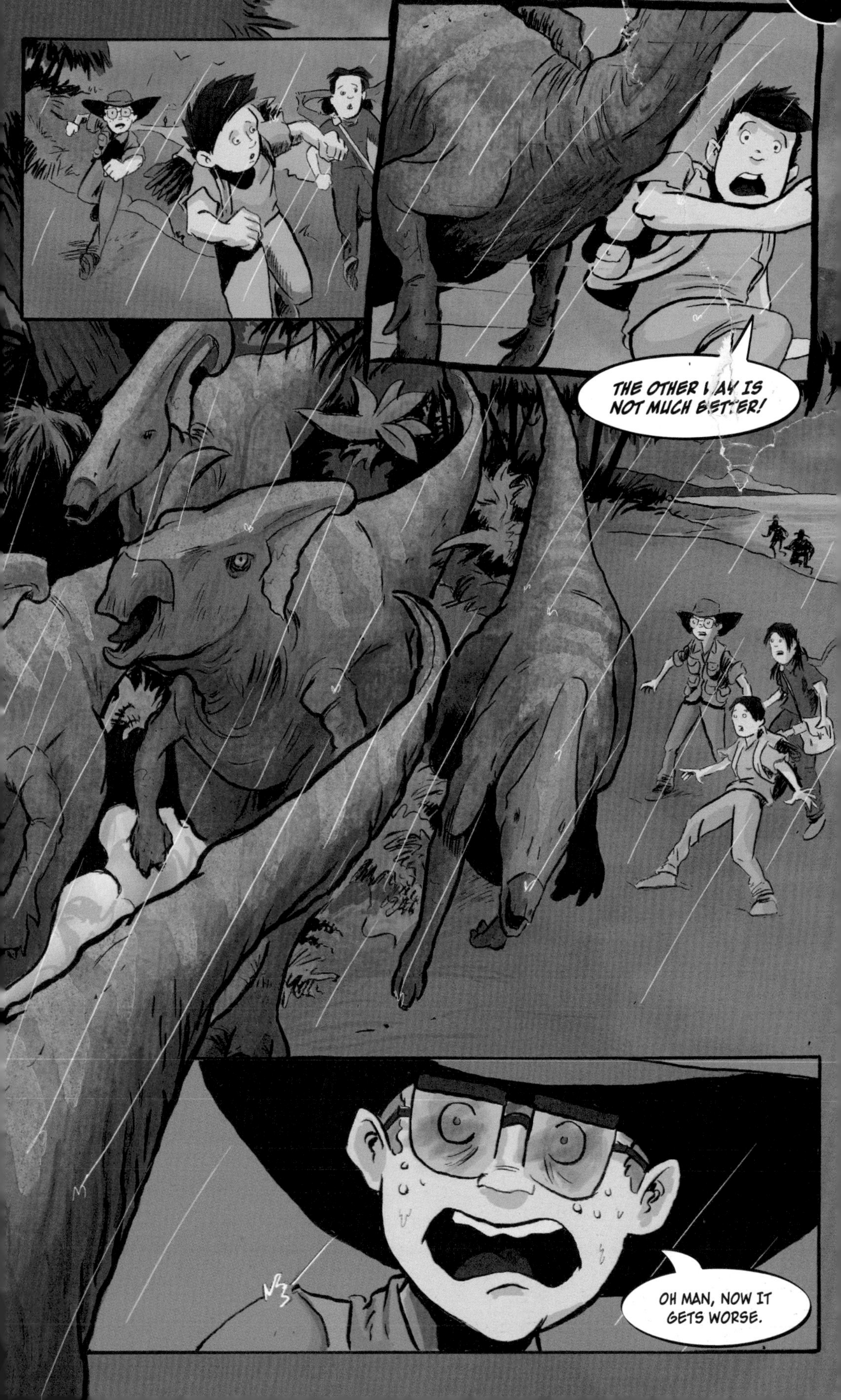
THE OTHER WAY IS NOT MUCH BETTER!
OH MAN, NOW IT GETS WORSE.

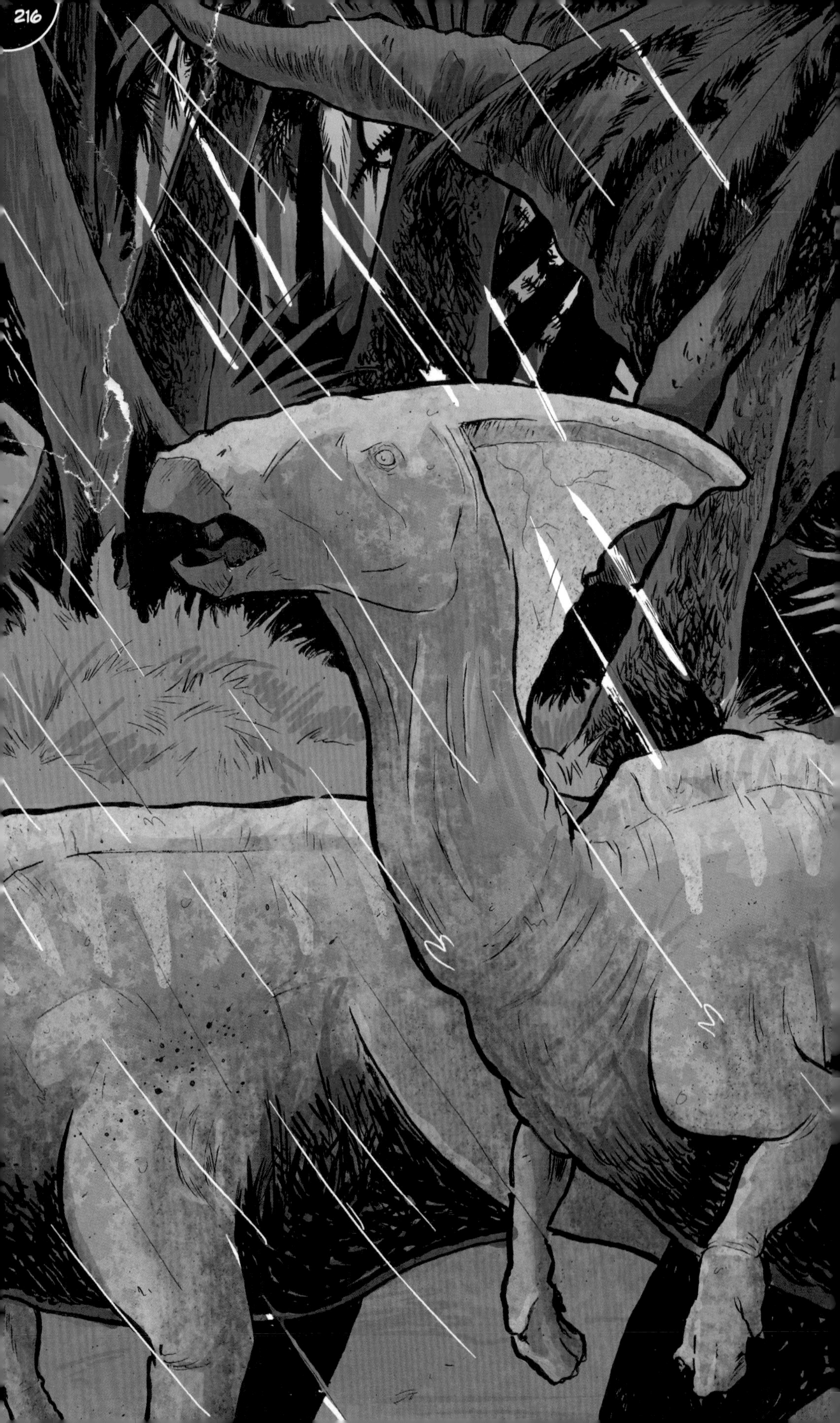

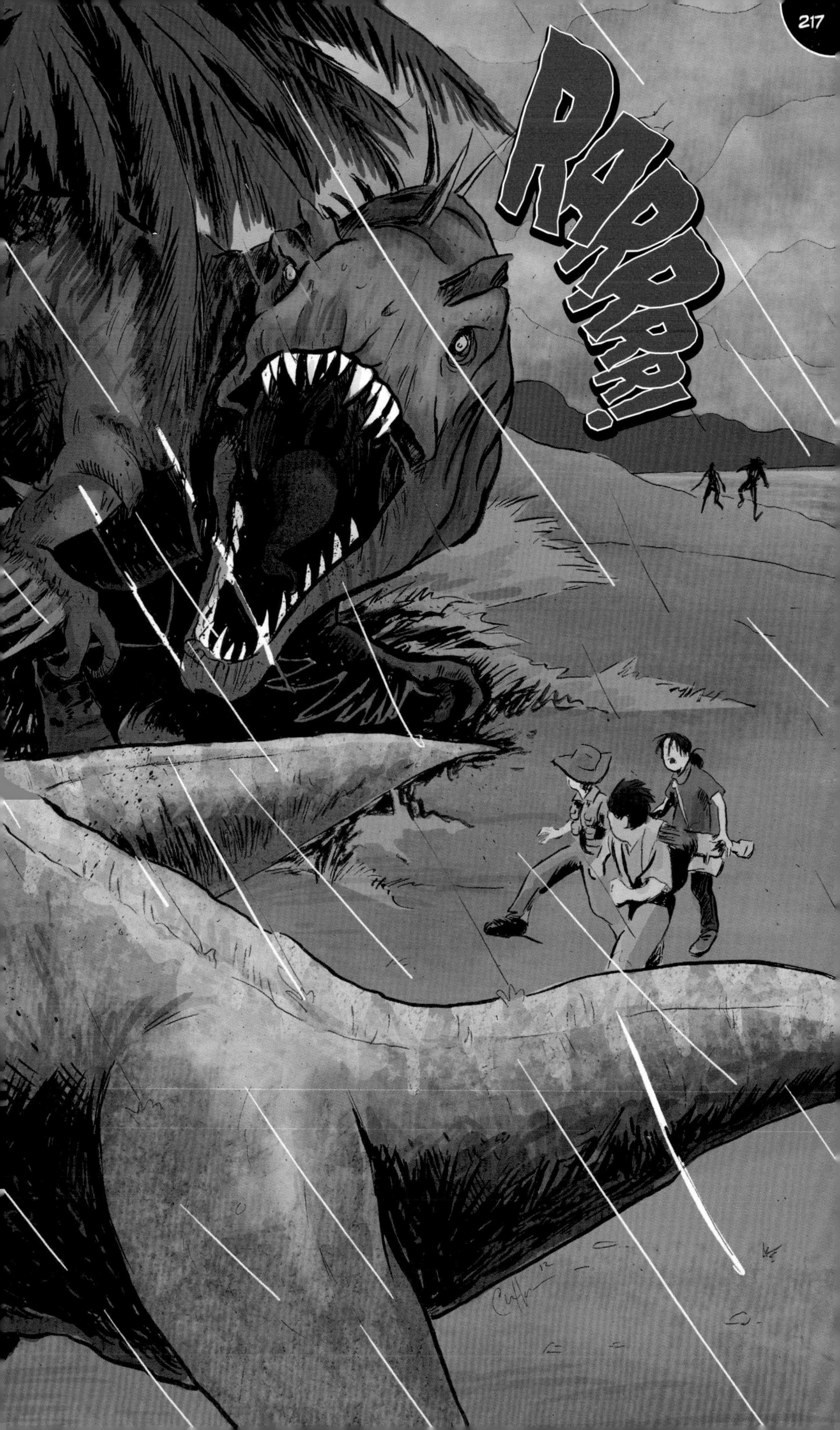
RARRRR!!

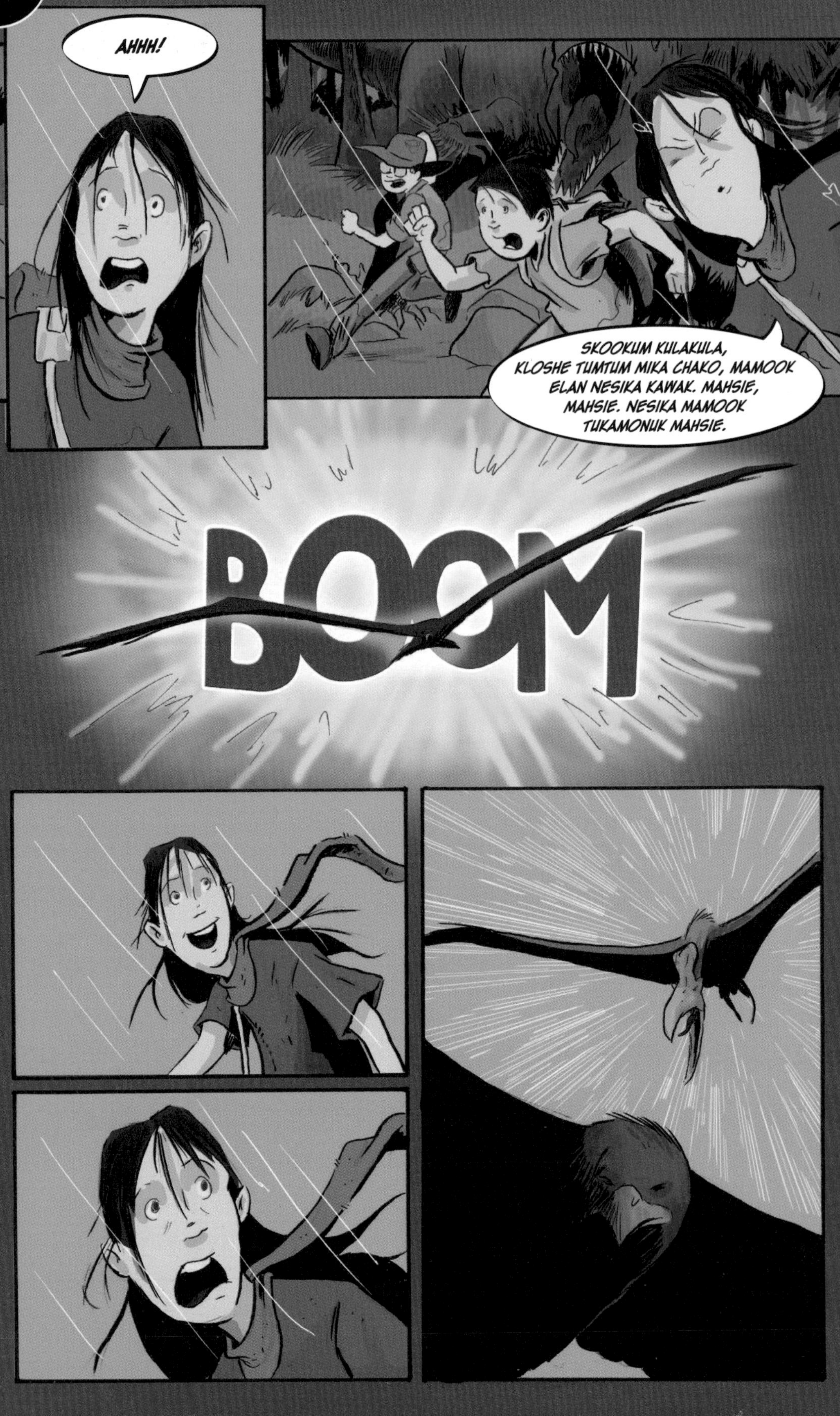
AHHH!
SKOOKUM KULAKULA, KLOSHE TUMTUM MIKA CHAKO, MAMOOK ELAN NESIKA KAWAK. MAHSIE, MAHSIE. NESIKA MAMOOK TUKAMONUK MAHSIE.
BOOM

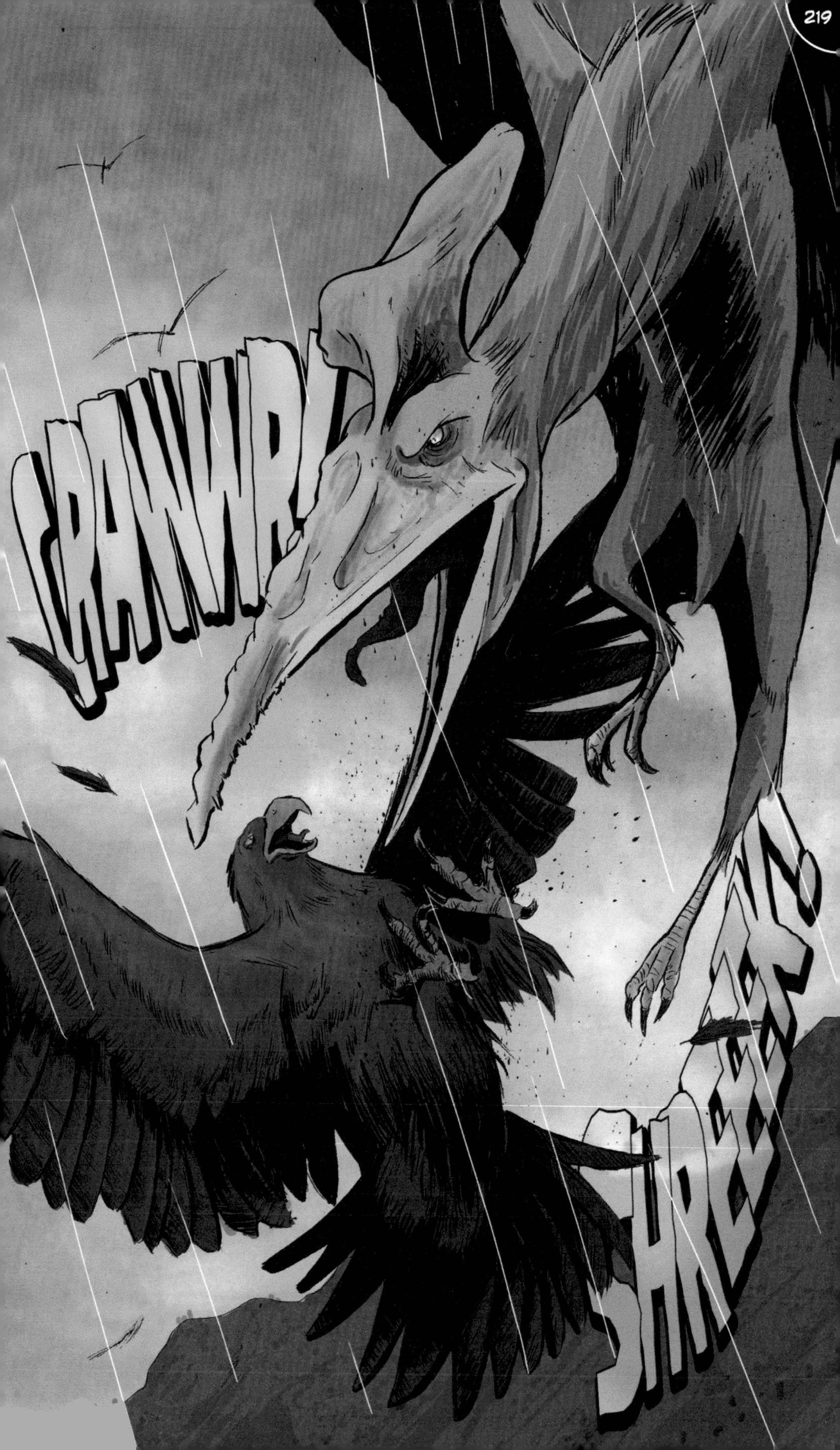
CRAWWR!
SHREEEEK!

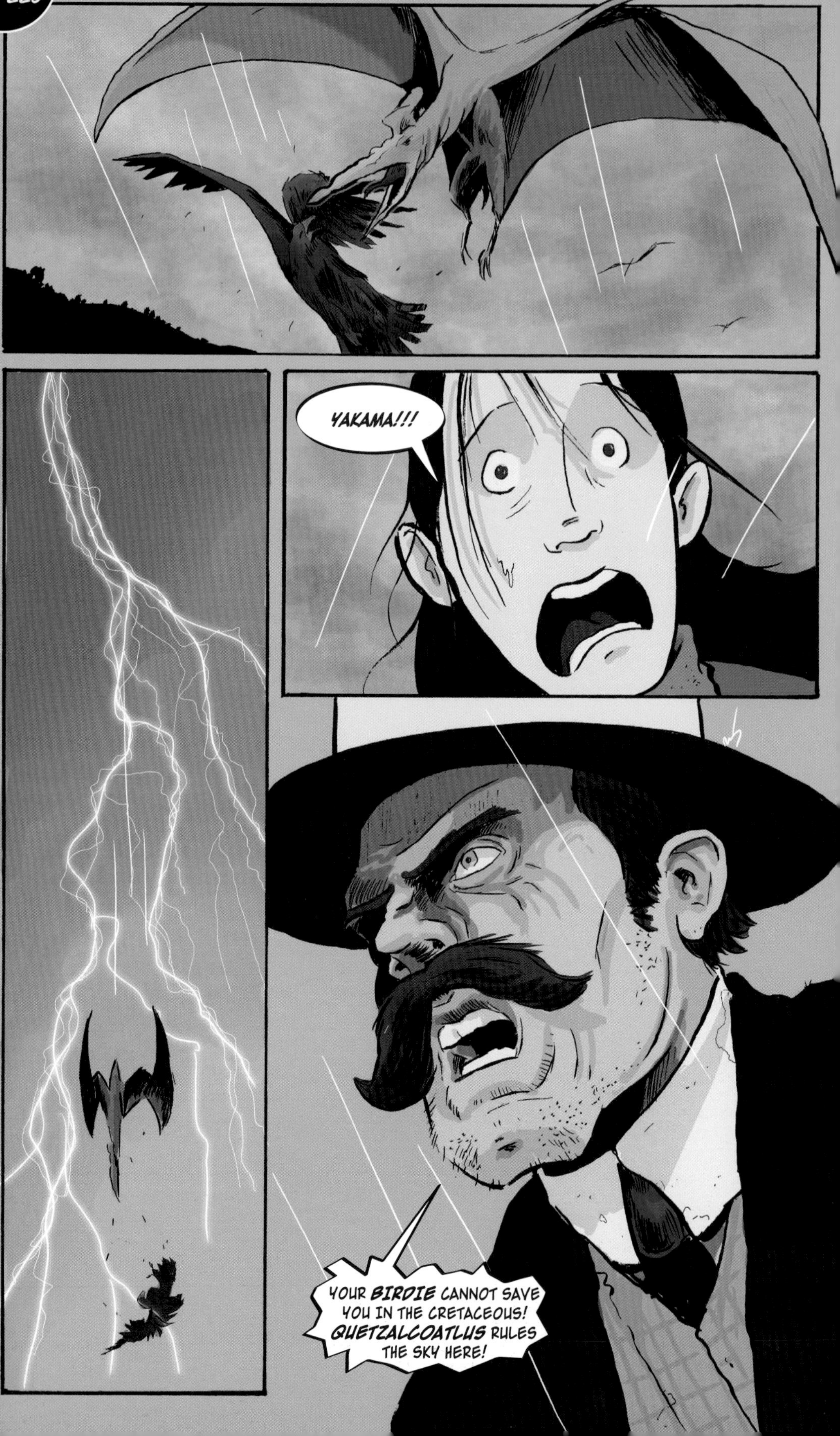
YAKAMA!!!
YOUR BIRDIE CANNOT SAVE YOU IN THE CRETACEOUS! QUETZALCOATLUS RULES THE SKY HERE!

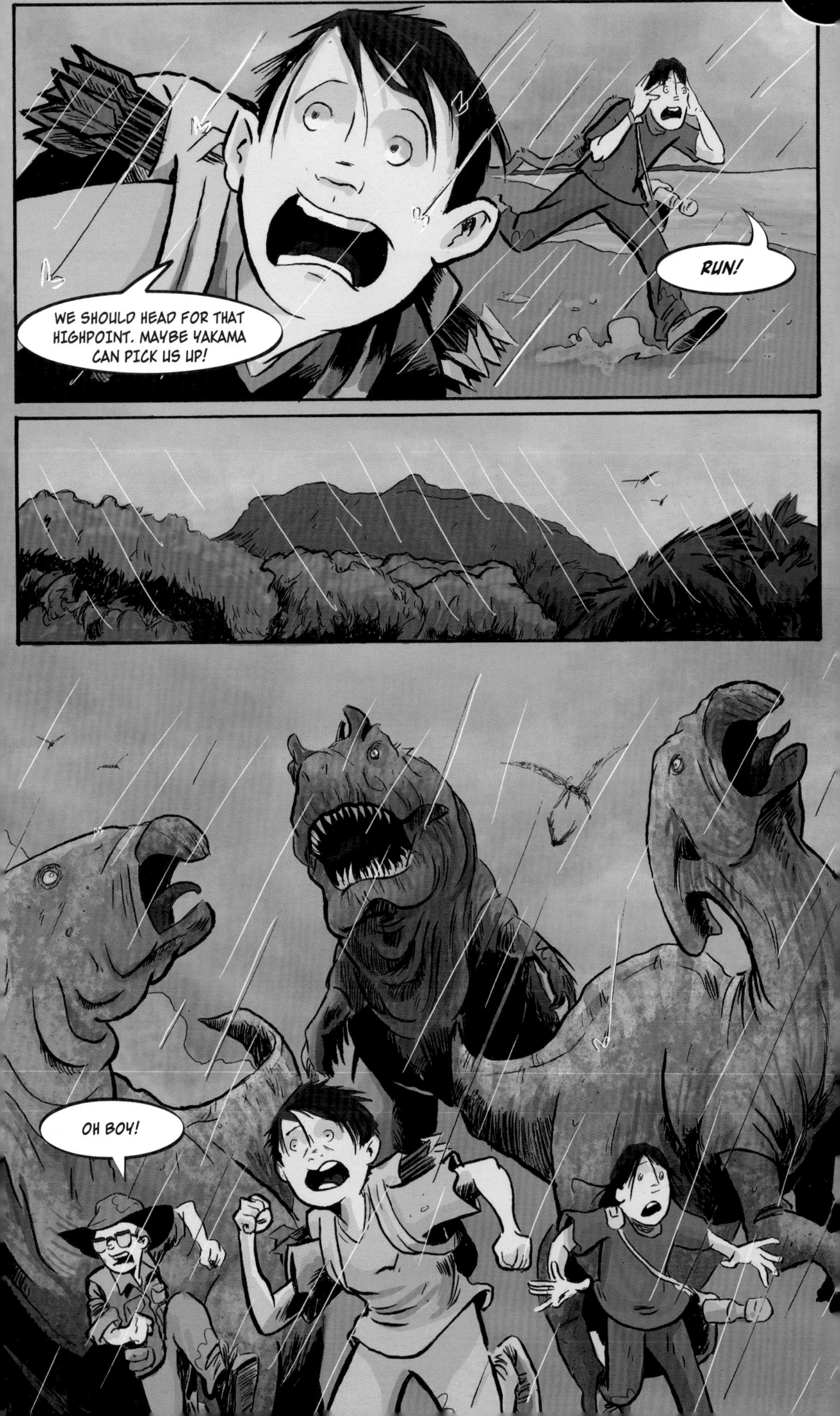
WE SHOULD HEAD FOR THAT HIGHPOINT. MAYBE YAKAMA CAN PICK US UP!
RUN!
OH BOY!

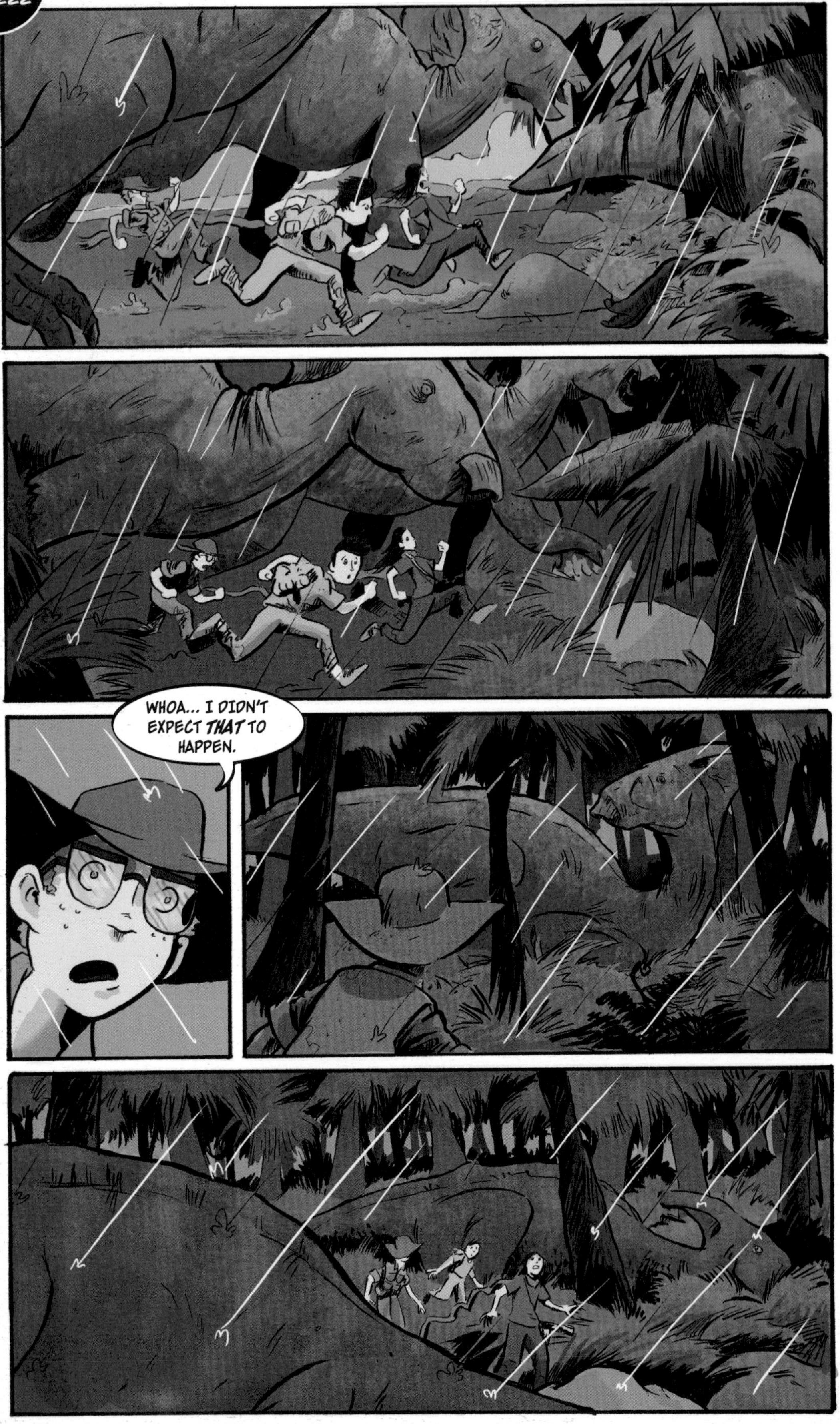
WHOA... I DIDN'T EXPECT *THAT* TO HAPPEN.

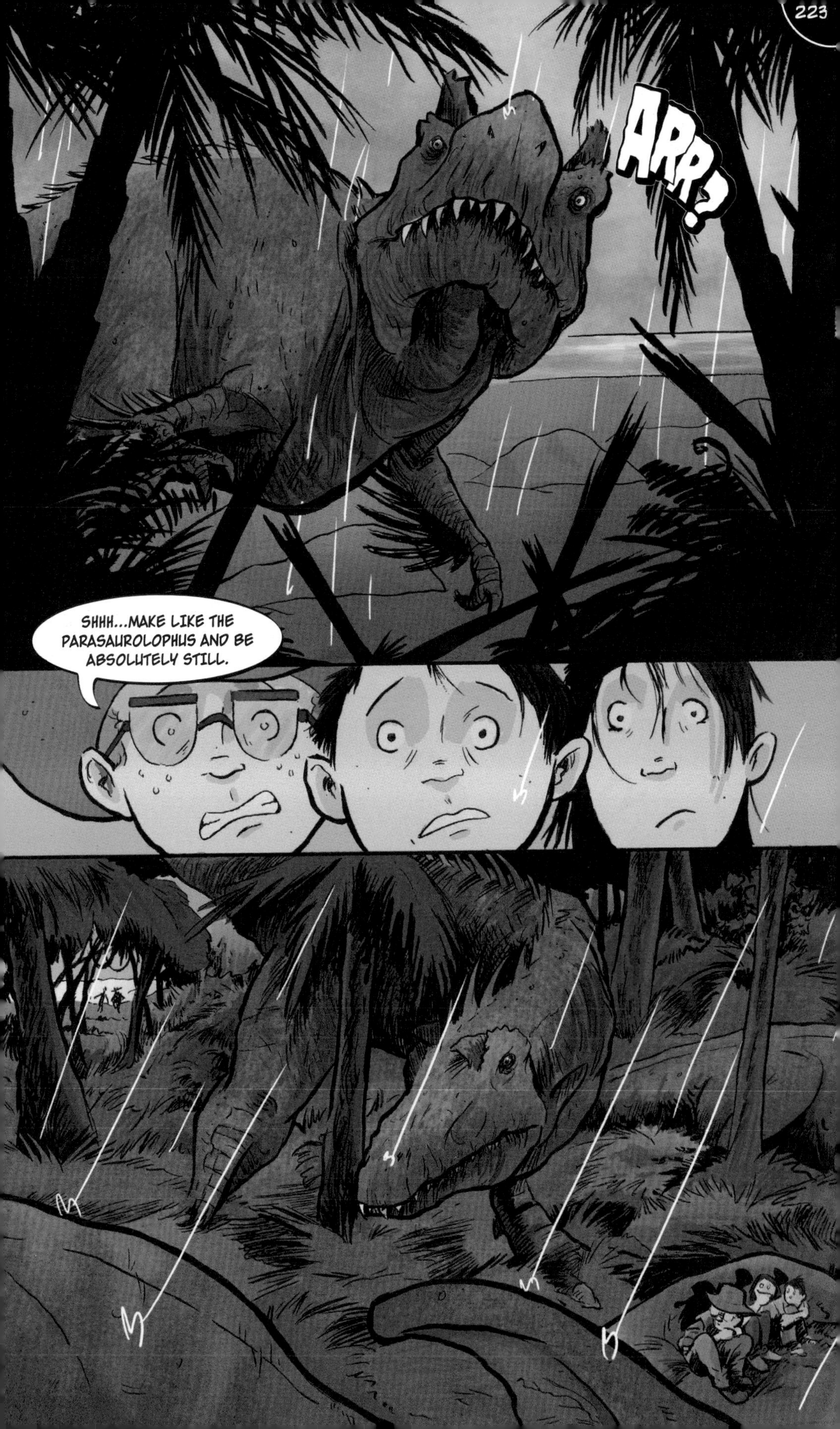
ARR?
SHHH...MAKE LIKE THE PARASAUROLOPHUS AND BE ABSOLUTELY STILL.

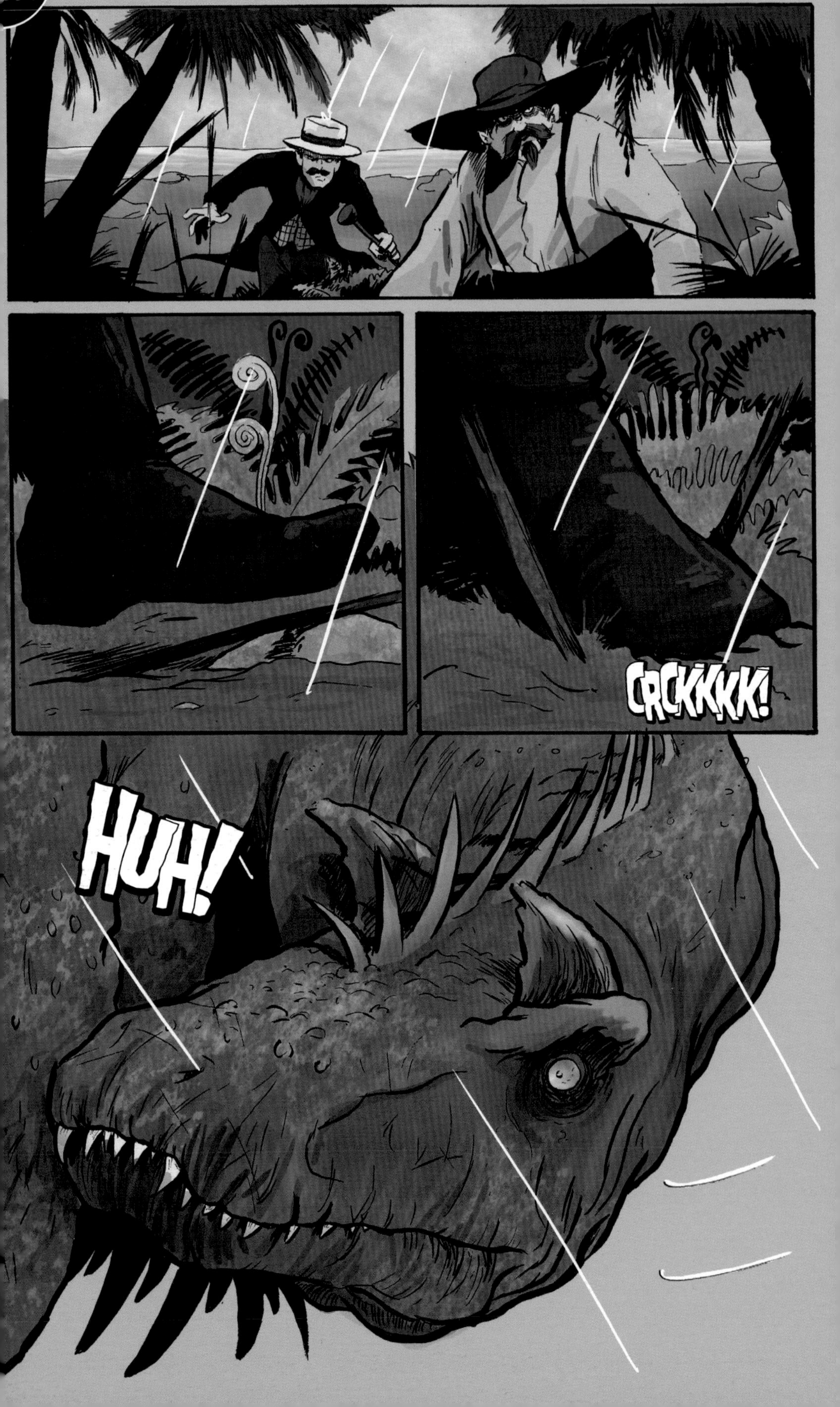
CRCKKKK!
HUH!

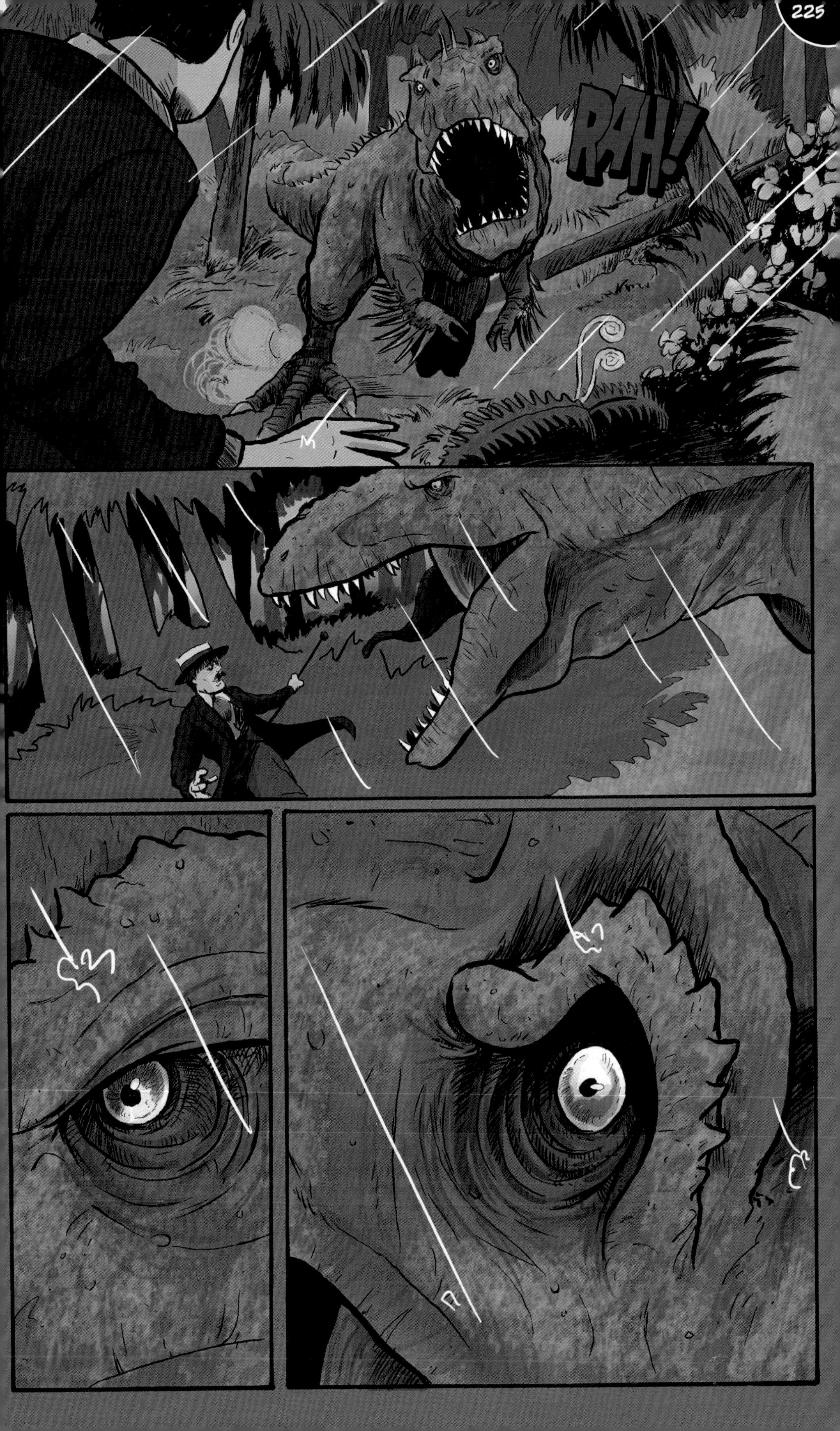
RAH!

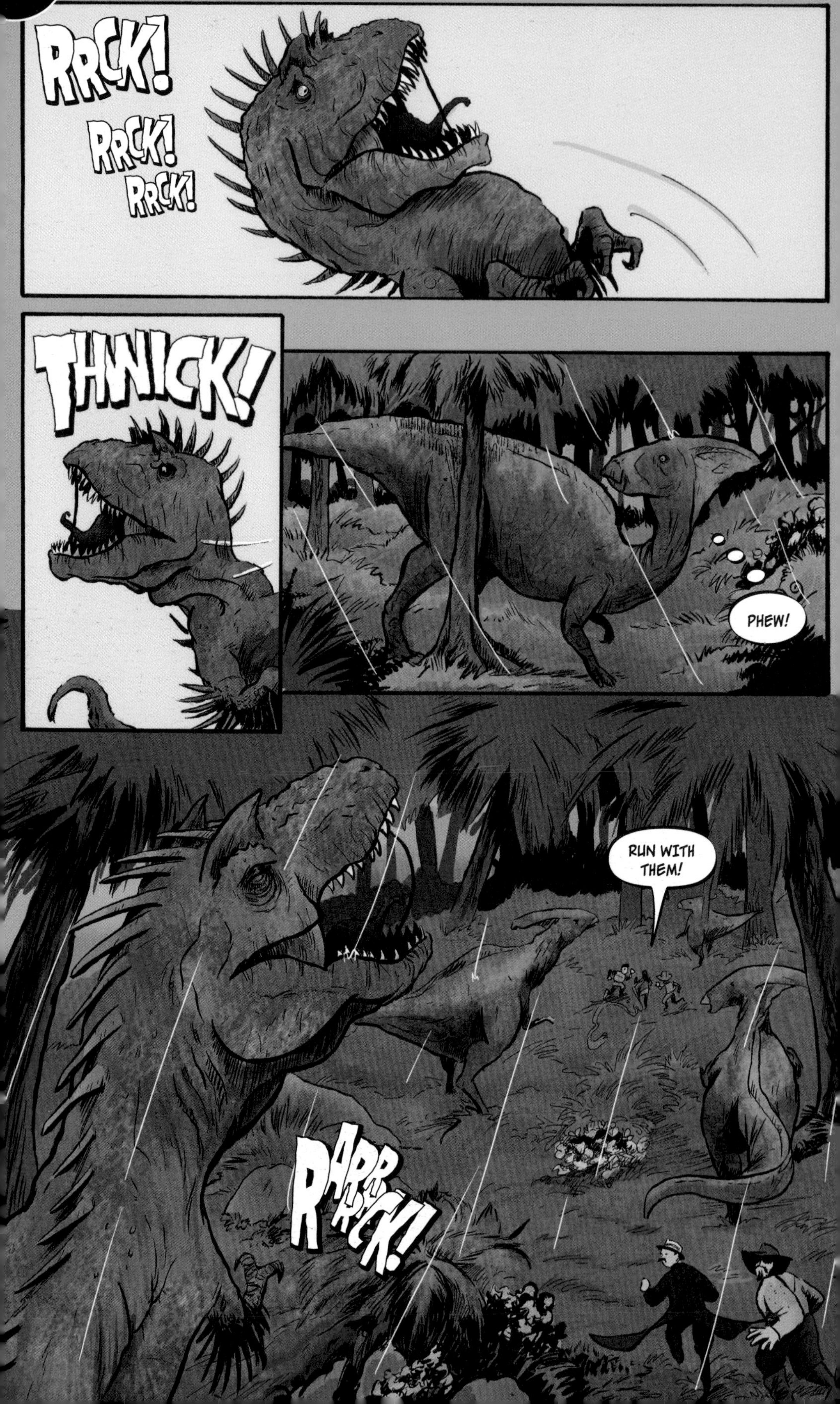
RRCK!
RRCK!
RRCK!
THWICK!
PHEW!
RUN WITH THEM!
RARRRRCK!

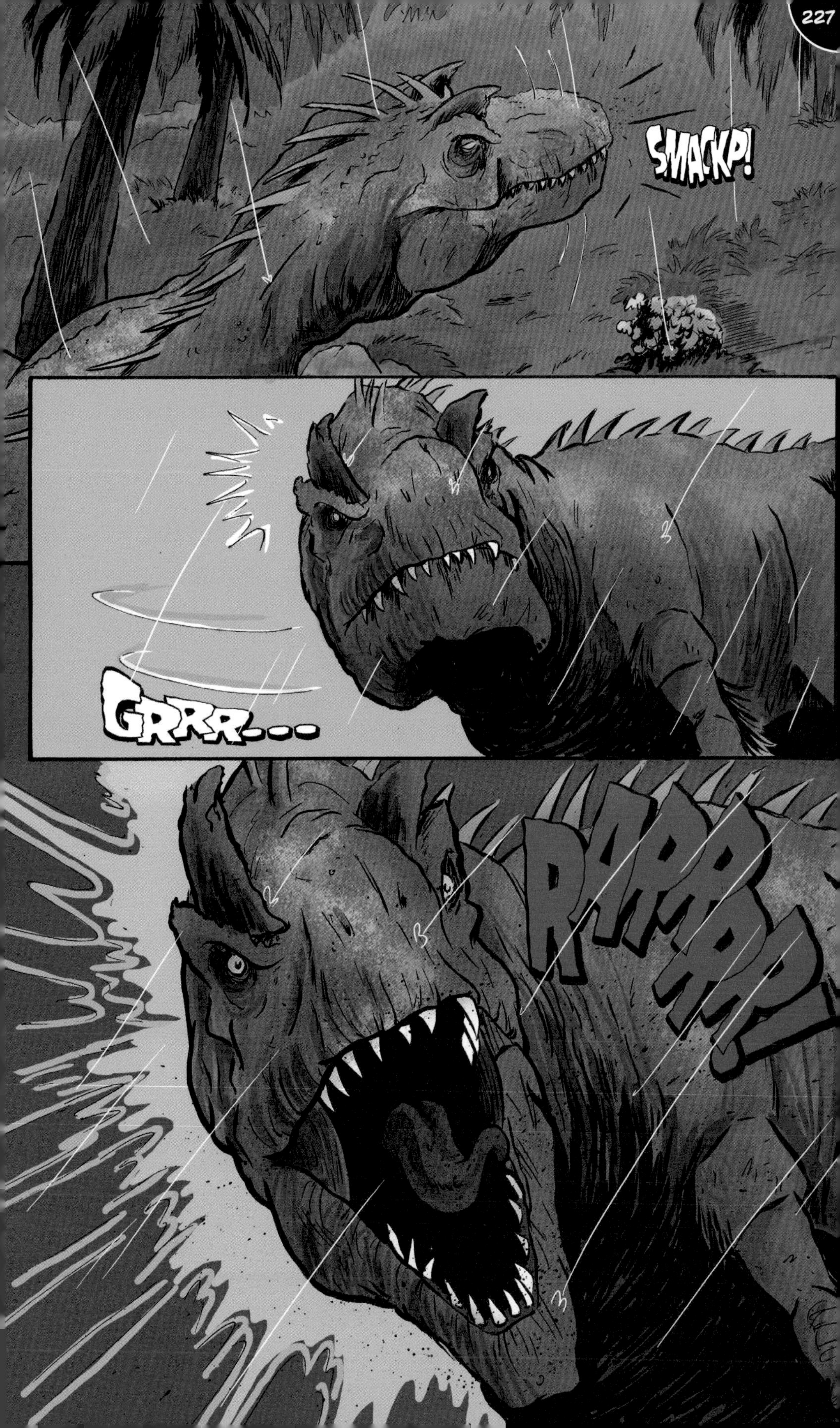
SMACKP!
GRRR...
RAAARR!

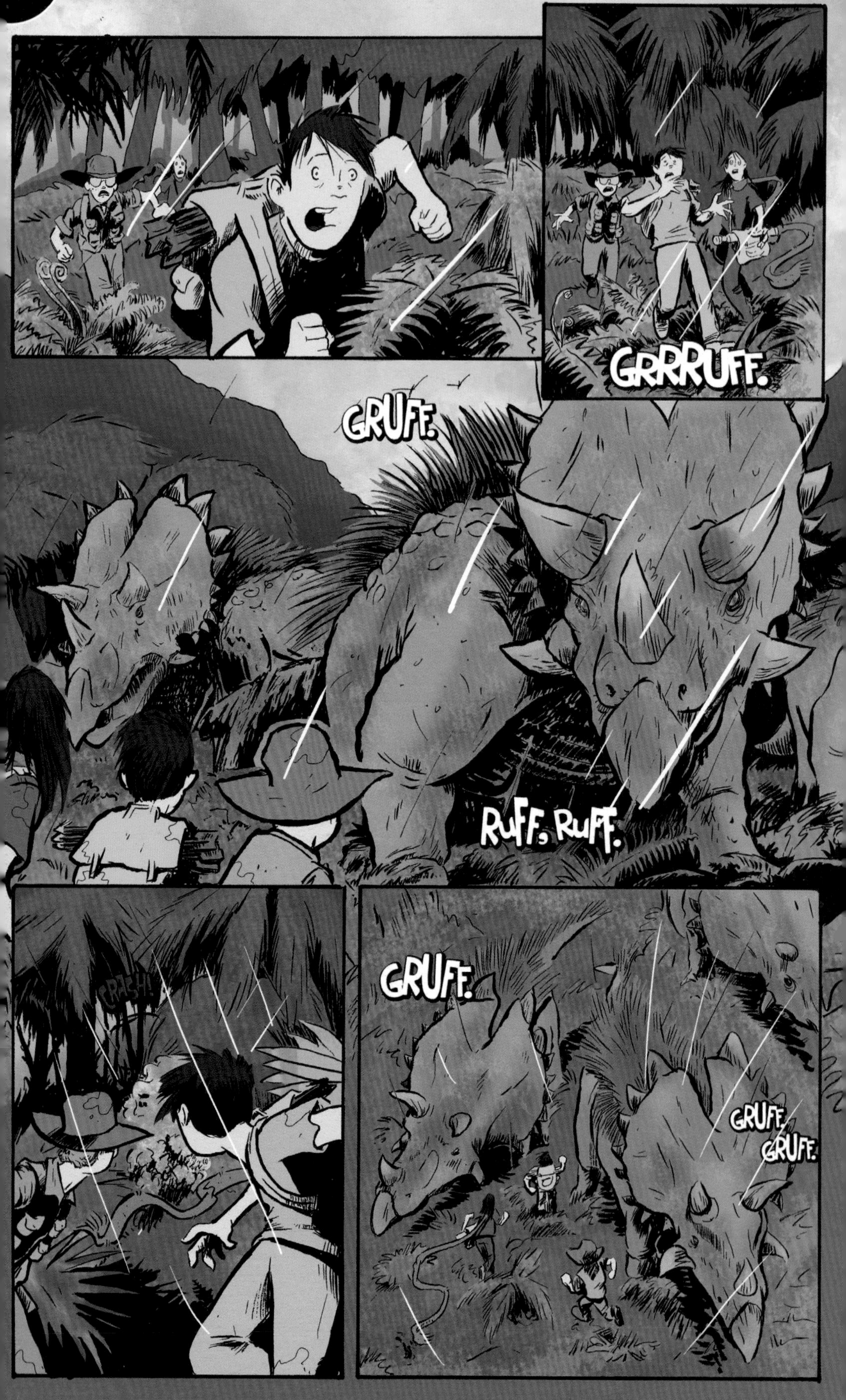
GRRRUFF.
GRUFF.
RUFF, RUFF.
CRASH!
GRUFF.
GRUFF,
GRUFF.

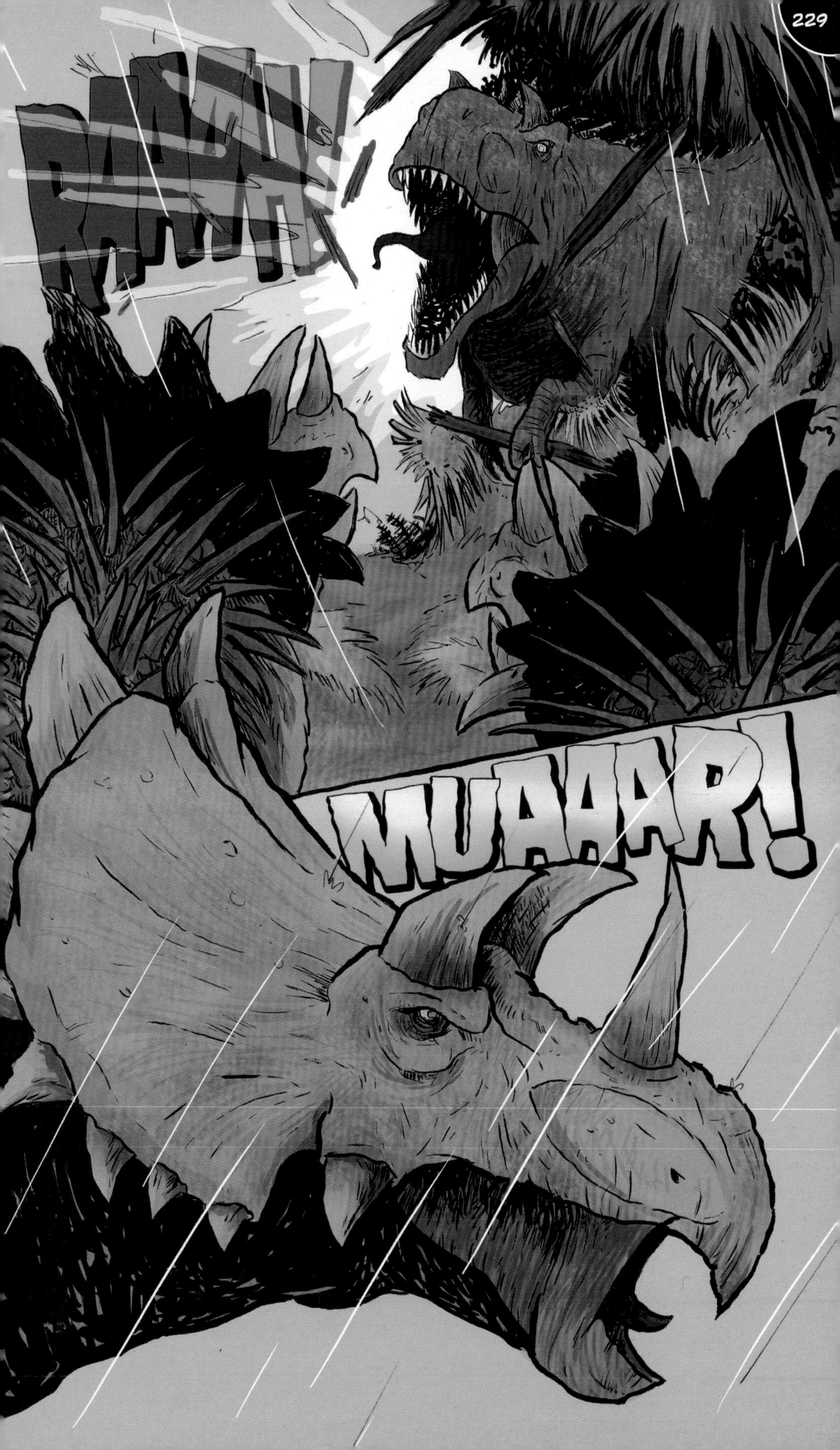
MUAAAR!

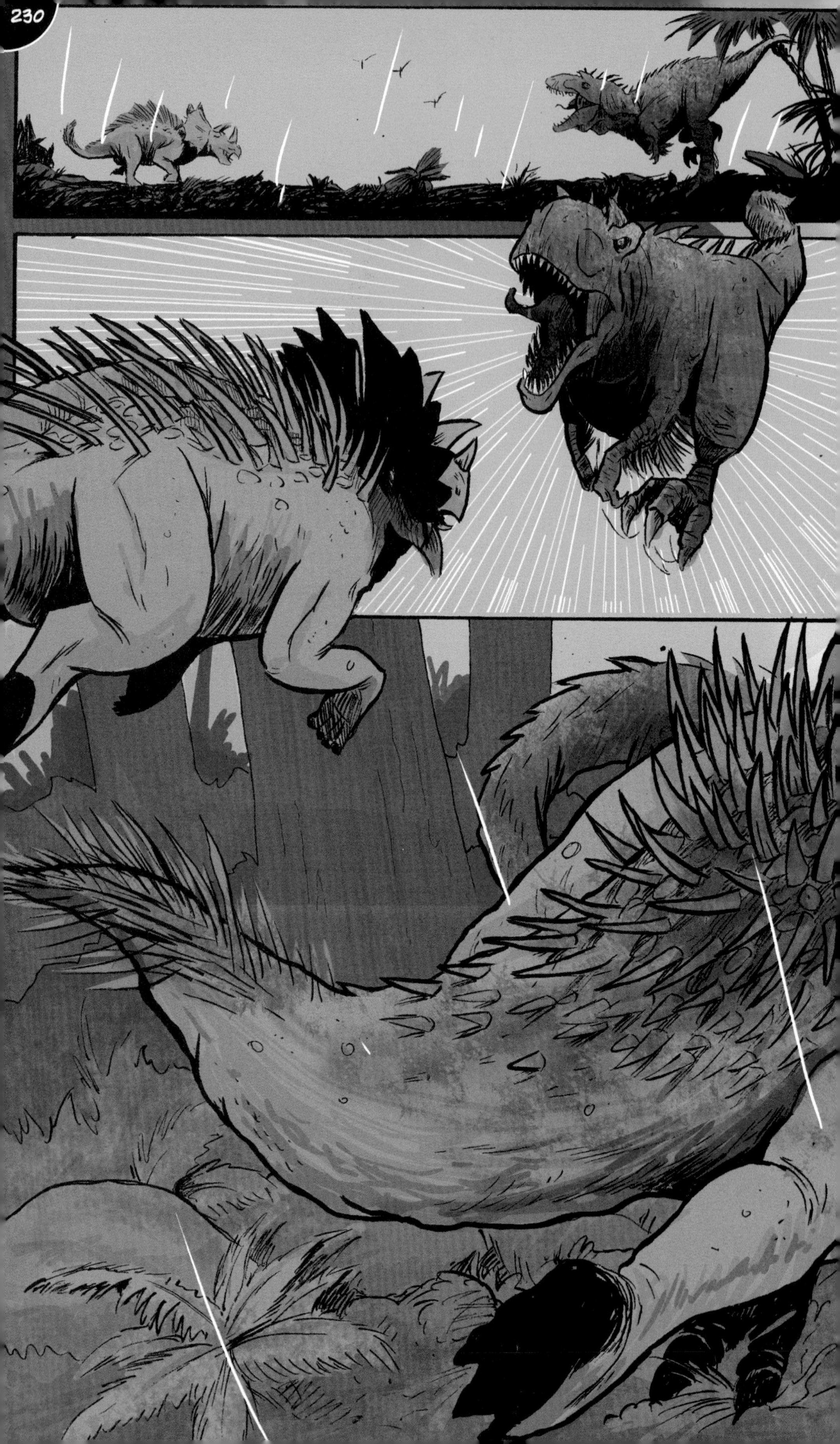

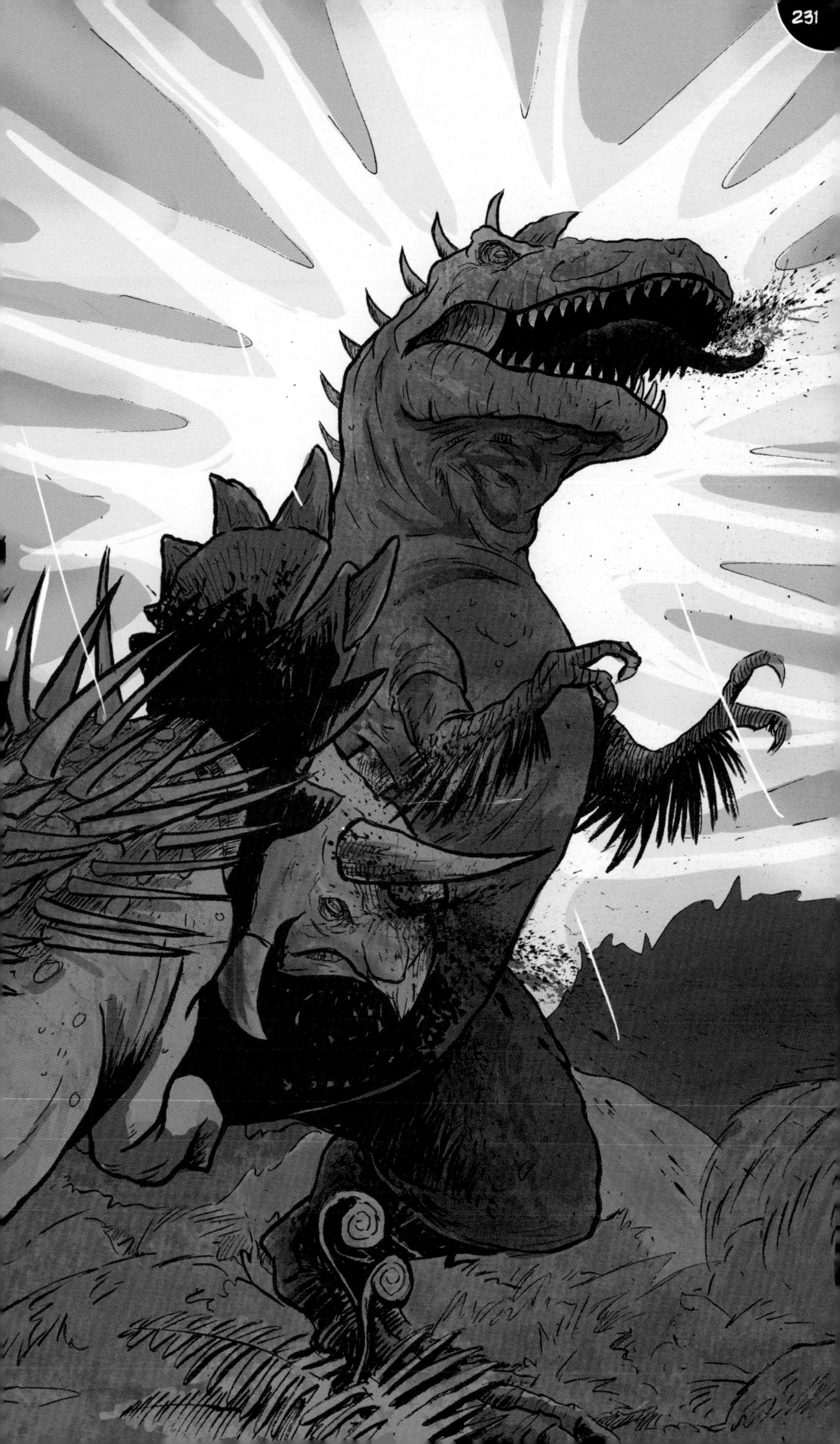

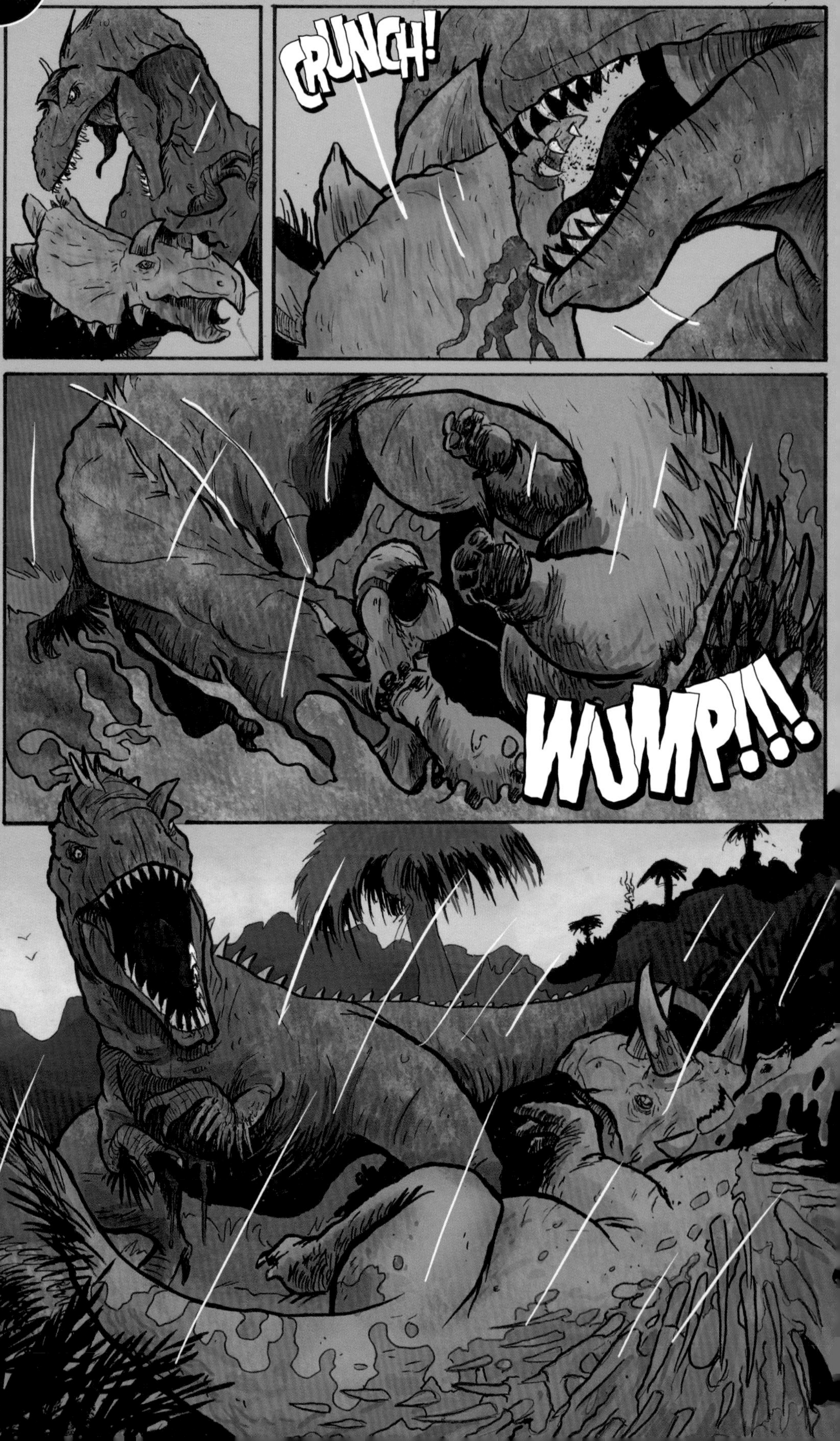
CRUNCH!
WUMP!!!

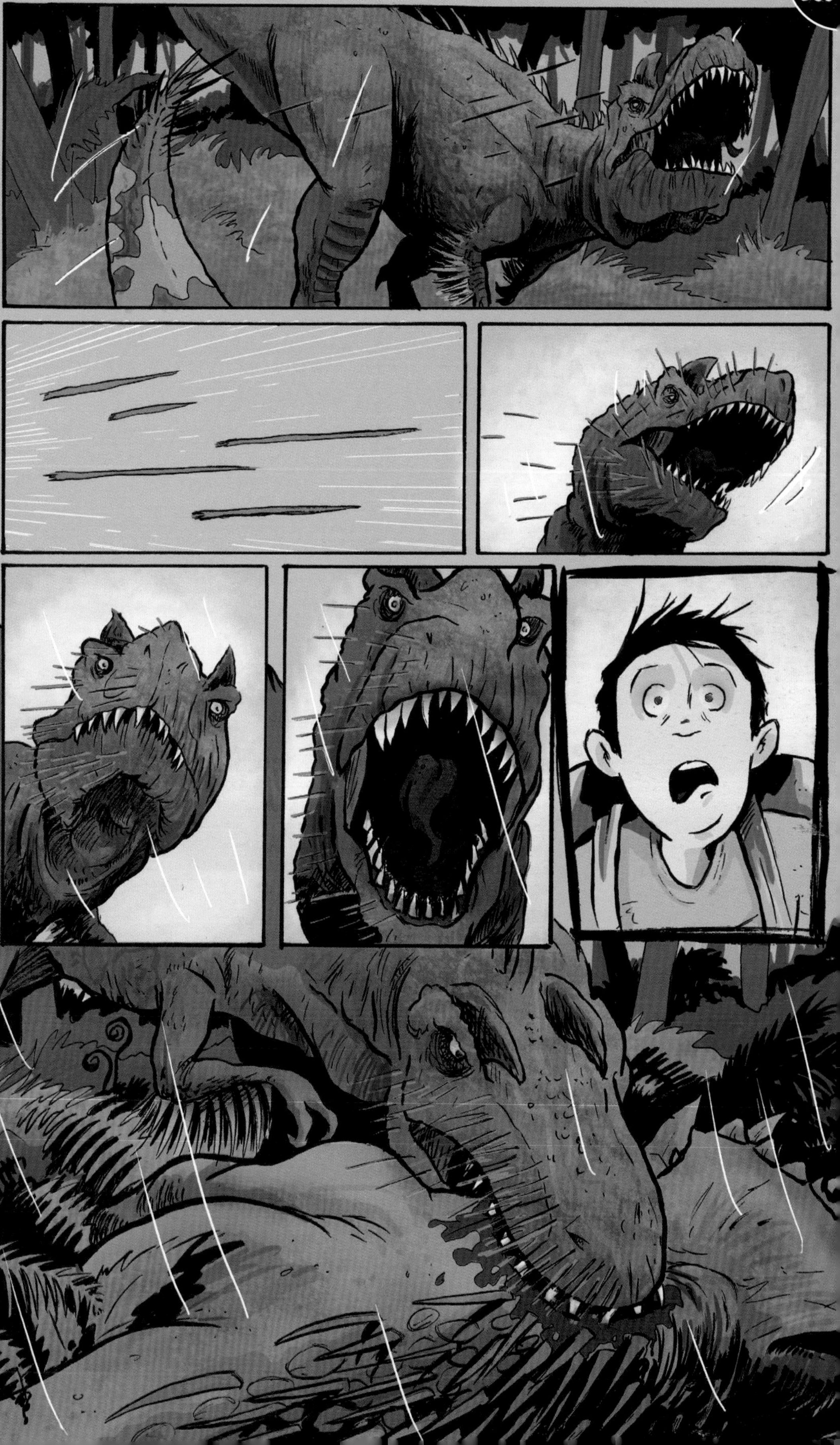

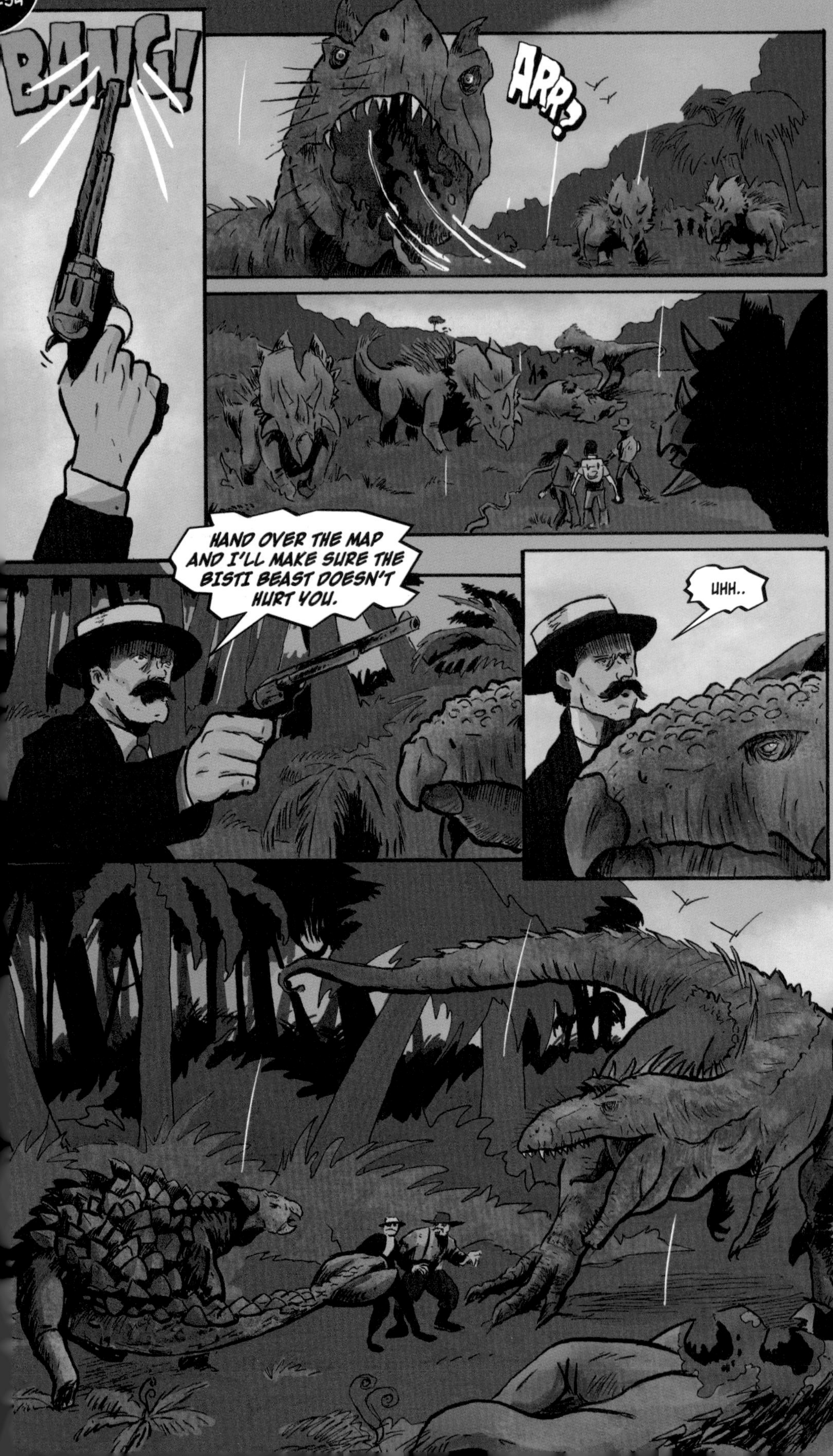
BANG!
ARR?
HAND OVER THE MAP AND I'LL MAKE SURE THE BISTI BEAST DOESN'T HURT YOU.
UHH..

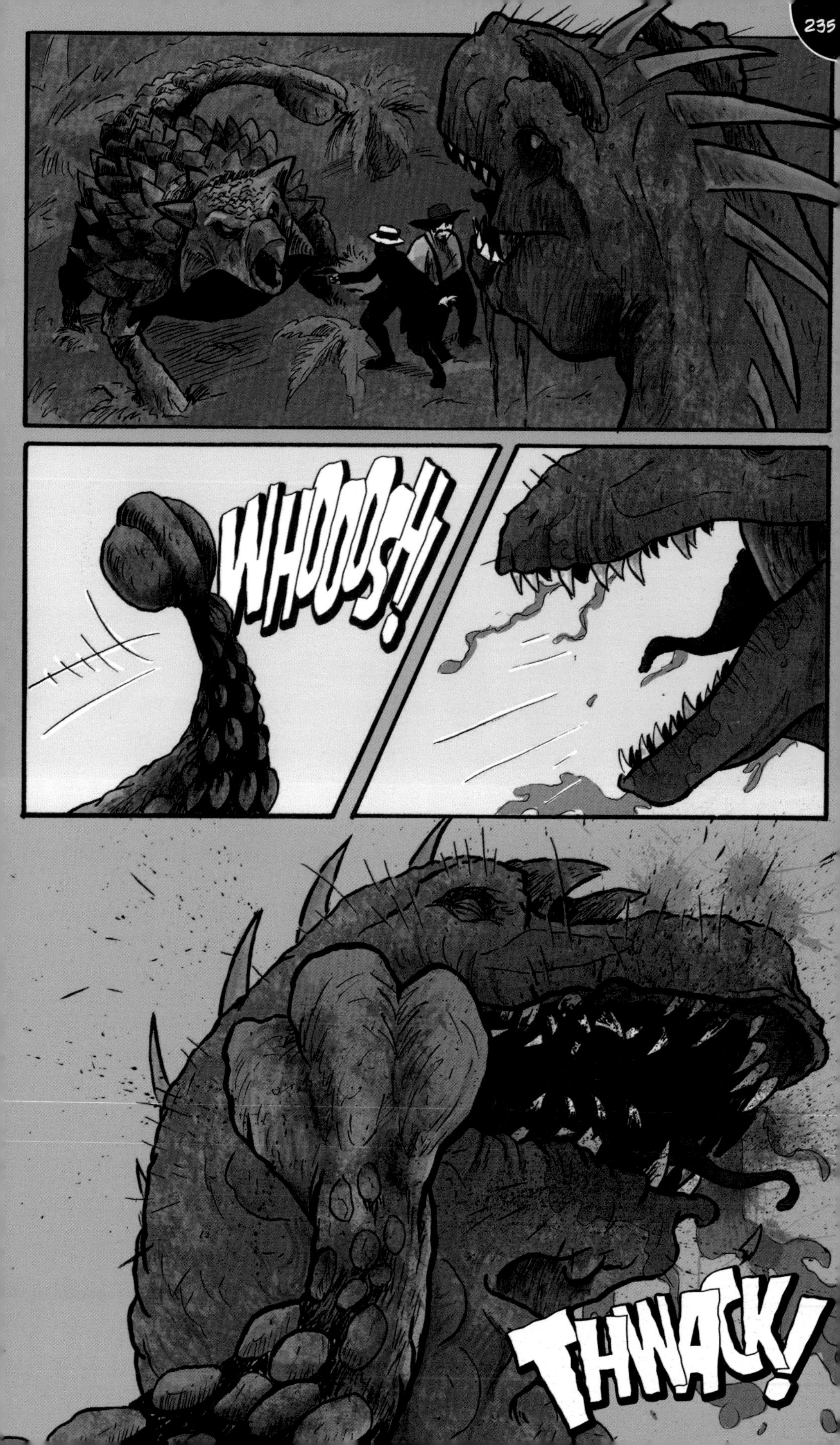
WHOOOSH!!
THWACK!

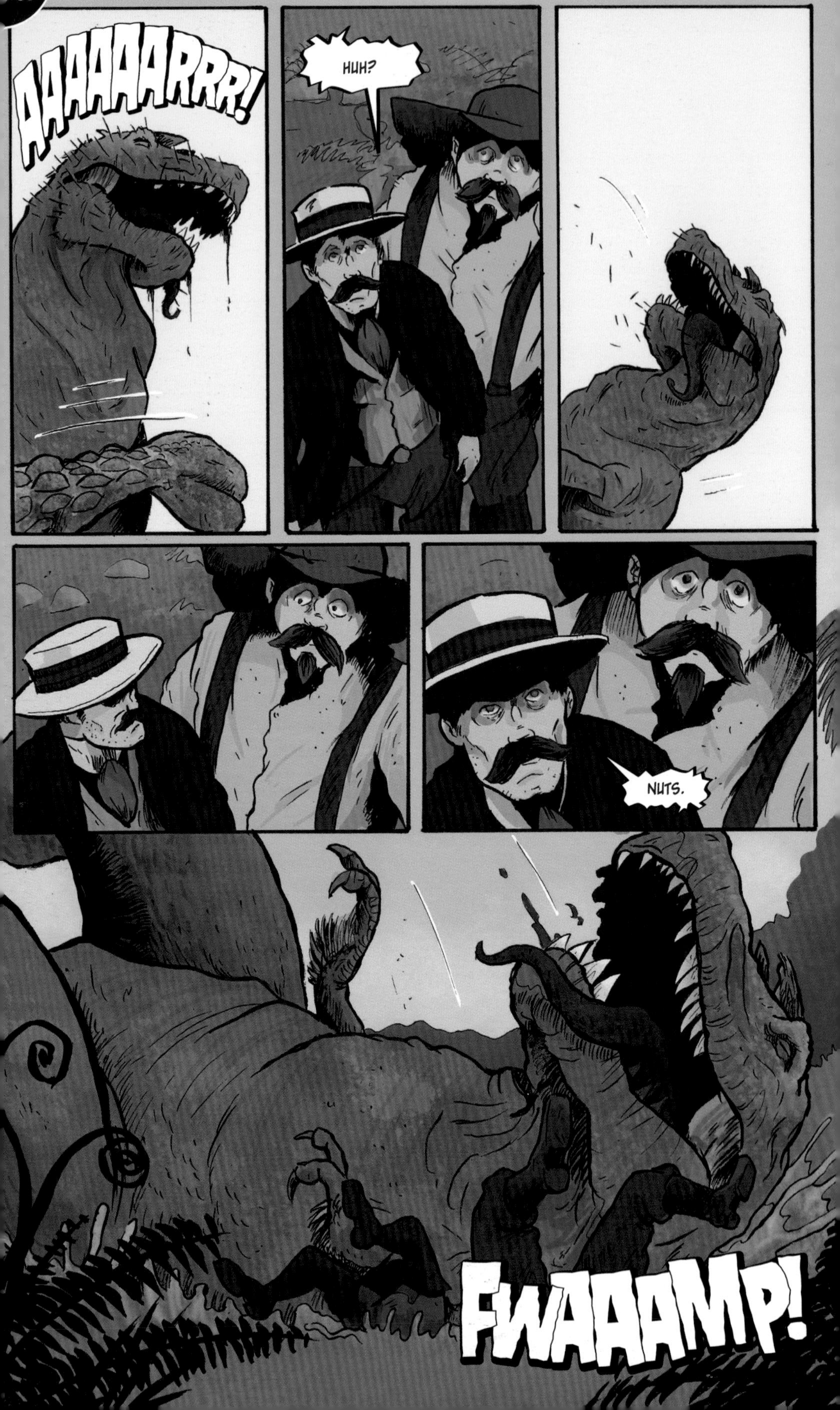
AAAAAARRRR!
HUH?
NUTS.
FWAAAMP!

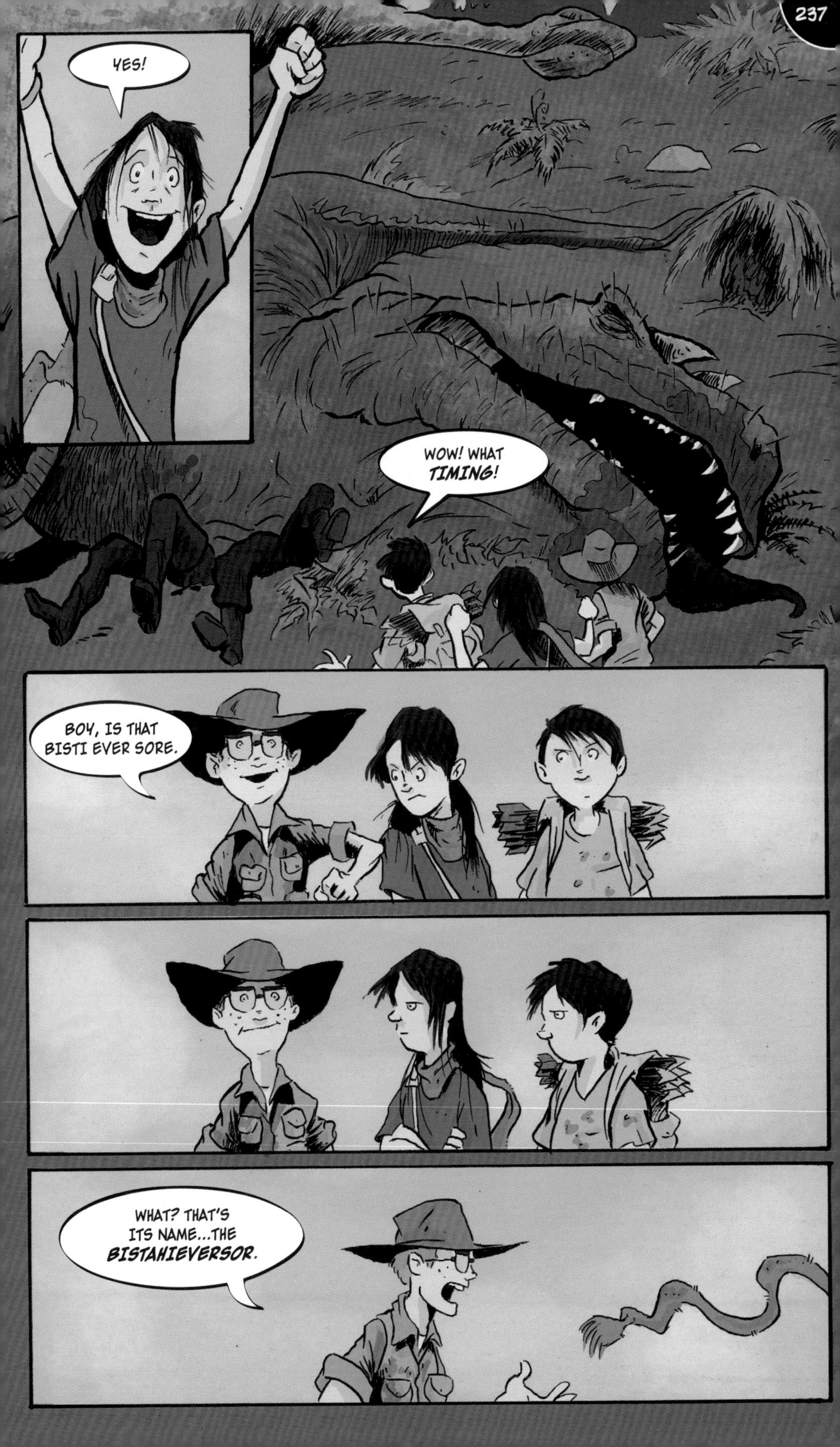
YES!
WOW! WHAT TIMING!
BOY, IS THAT BISTI EVER SORE.
WHAT? THAT'S ITS NAME...THE BISTAHIEVERSOR.

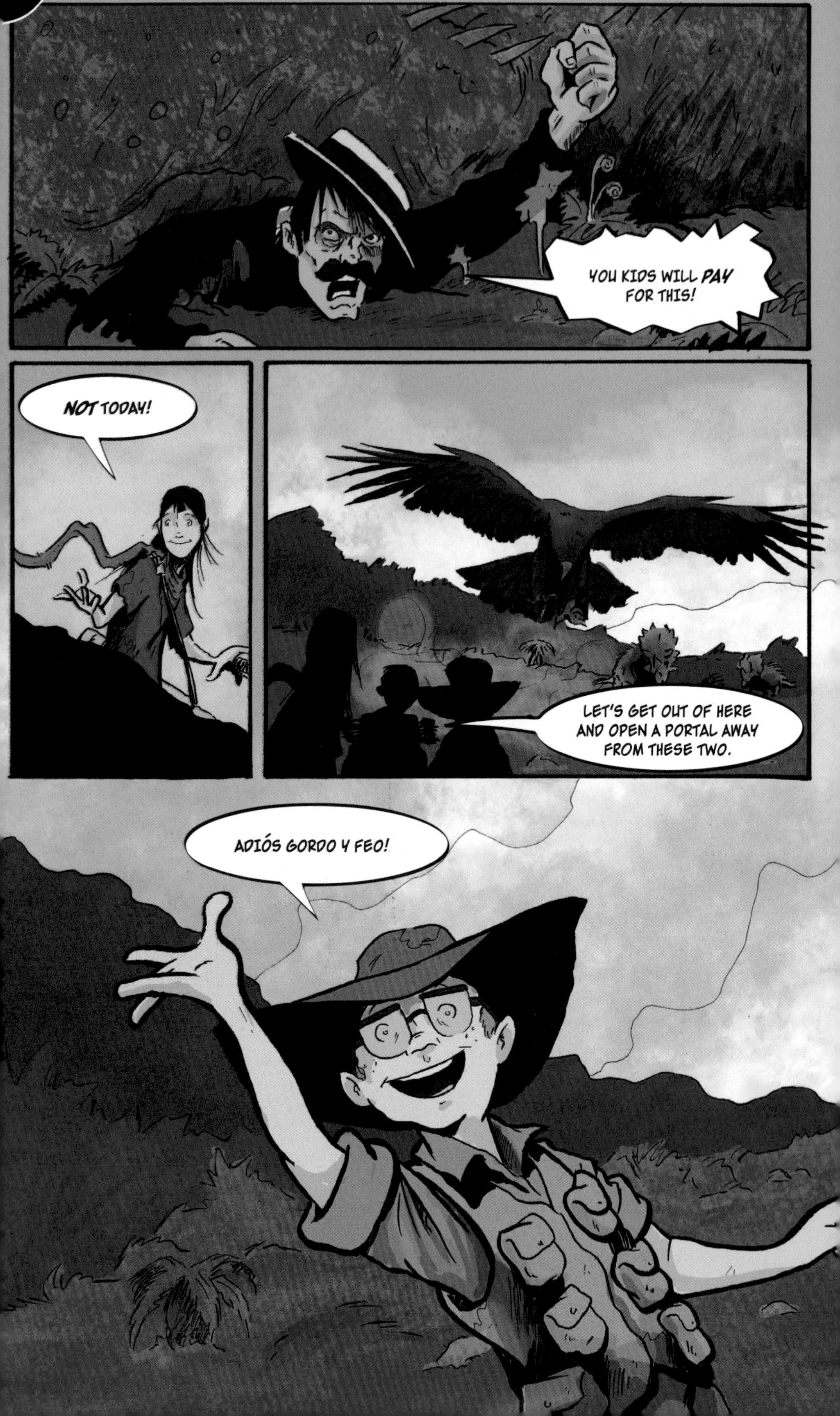
YOU KIDS WILL **PAY** FOR THIS!
NOT TODAY!
LET'S GET OUT OF HERE AND OPEN A PORTAL AWAY FROM THESE TWO.
ADIÓS GORDO Y FEO!

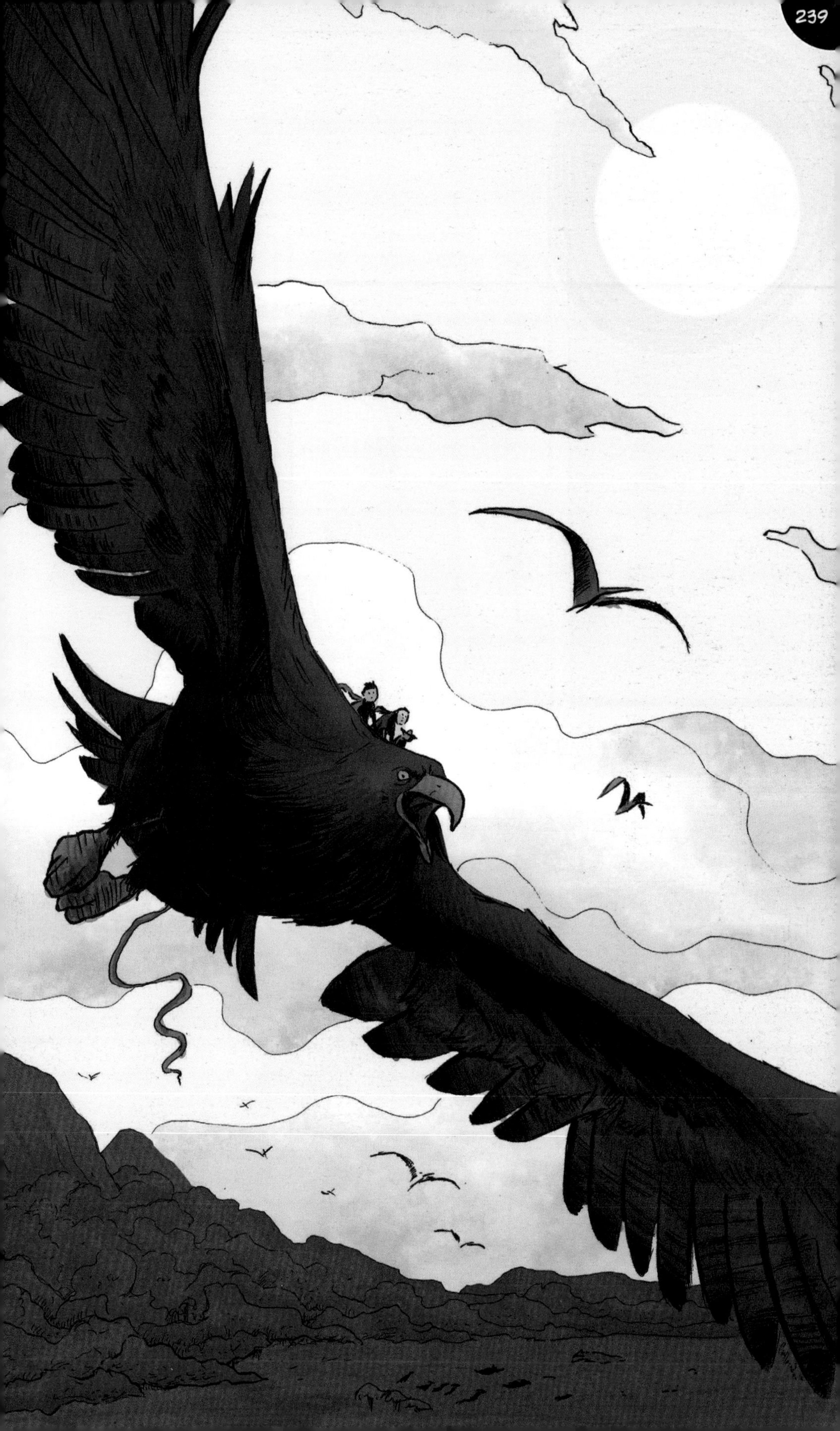

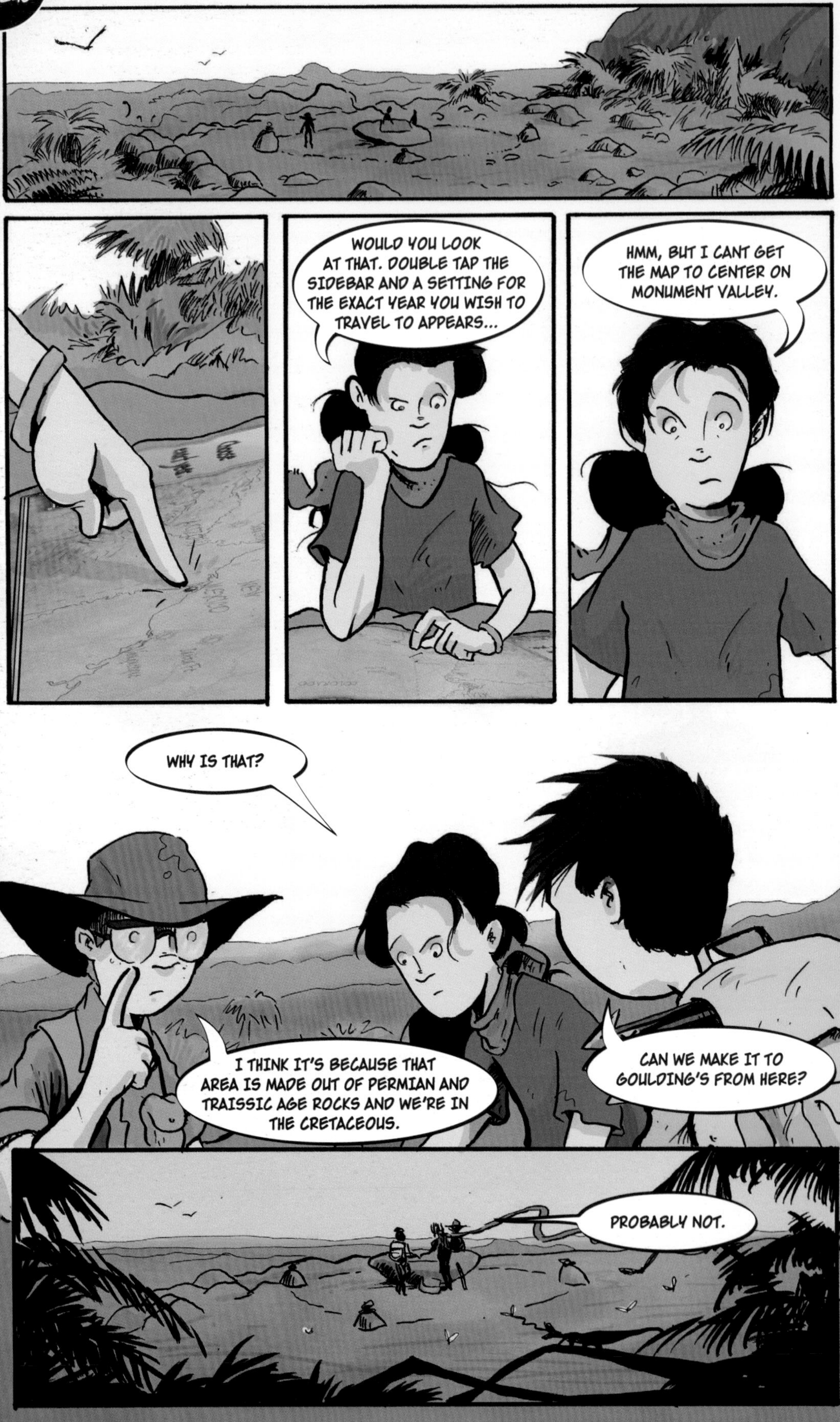
WOULD YOU LOOK AT THAT. DOUBLE TAP THE SIDEBAR AND A SETTING FOR THE EXACT YEAR YOU WISH TO TRAVEL TO APPEARS...
HMM, BUT I CANT GET THE MAP TO CENTER ON MONUMENT VALLEY.
WHY IS THAT?
I THINK IT'S BECAUSE THAT AREA IS MADE OUT OF PERMIAN AND TRAISSIC AGE ROCKS AND WE'RE IN THE CRETACEOUS.
CAN WE MAKE IT TO GOULDING'S FROM HERE?
PROBABLY NOT.

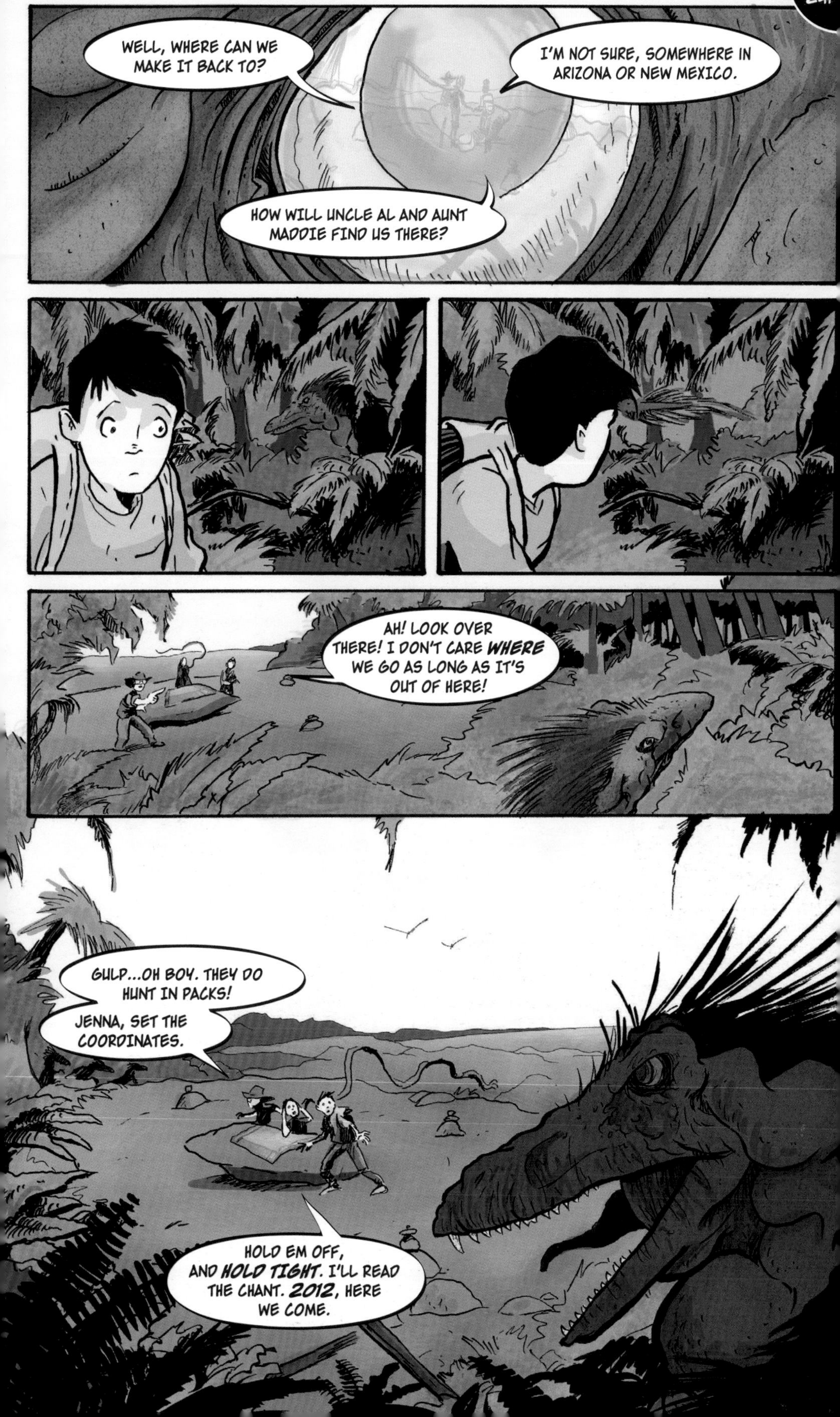
WELL, WHERE CAN WE MAKE IT BACK TO?
I'M NOT SURE, SOMEWHERE IN ARIZONA OR NEW MEXICO.
HOW WILL UNCLE AL AND AUNT MADDIE FIND US THERE?
AH! LOOK OVER THERE! I DON'T CARE WHERE WE GO AS LONG AS IT'S OUT OF HERE!
GULP...OH BOY. THEY DO HUNT IN PACKS!
JENNA, SET THE COORDINATES.
HOLD EM OFF, AND HOLD TIGHT. I'LL READ THE CHANT. 2012, HERE WE COME.

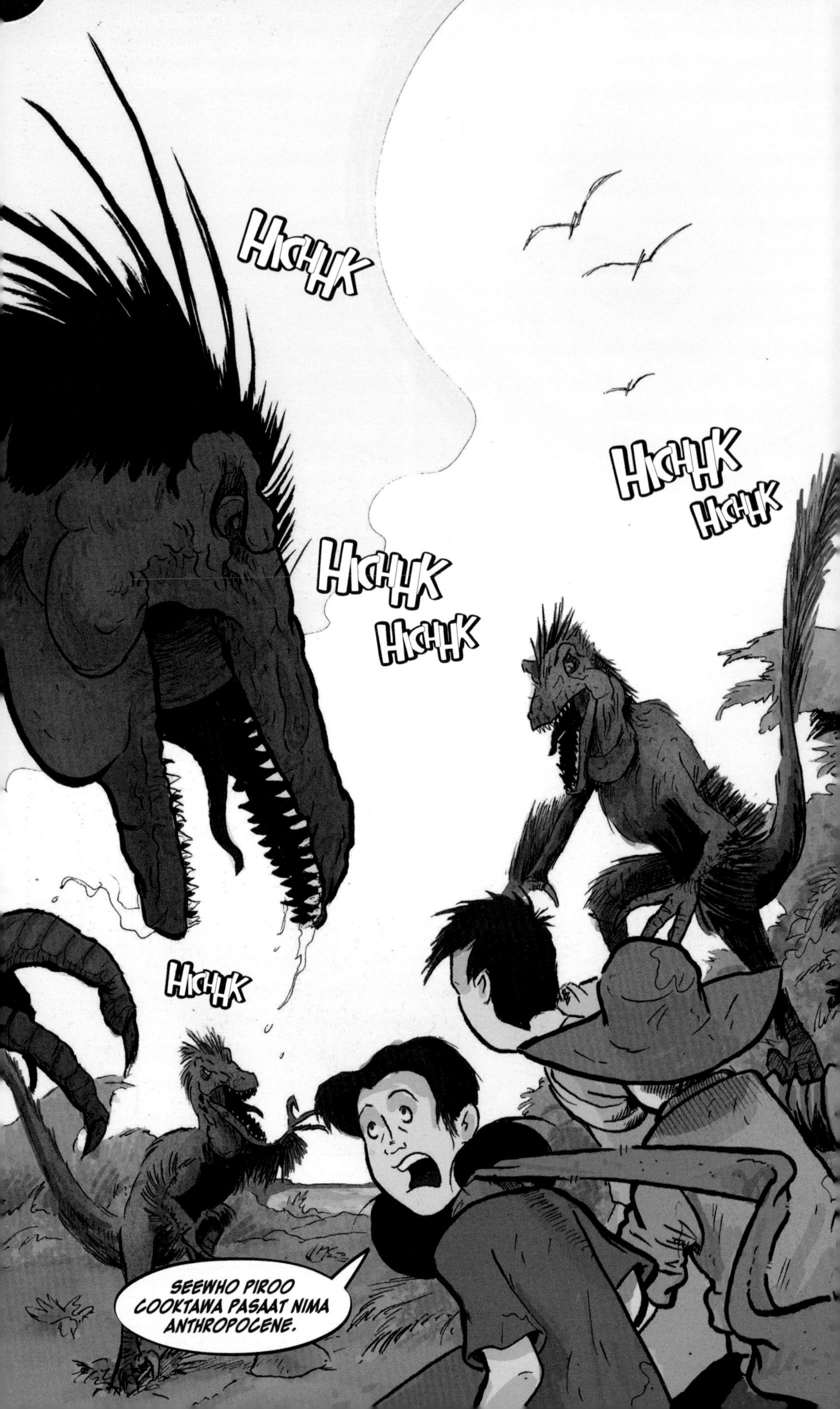
HICHHK
HICHHK
HICHHK
HICHHK
HICHHK
HICHHK
SEEWHO PIROO COOKTAWA PASAAT NIMA ANTHROPOCENE.

CHAPTER
TEN

HOME FROM THE RANGE

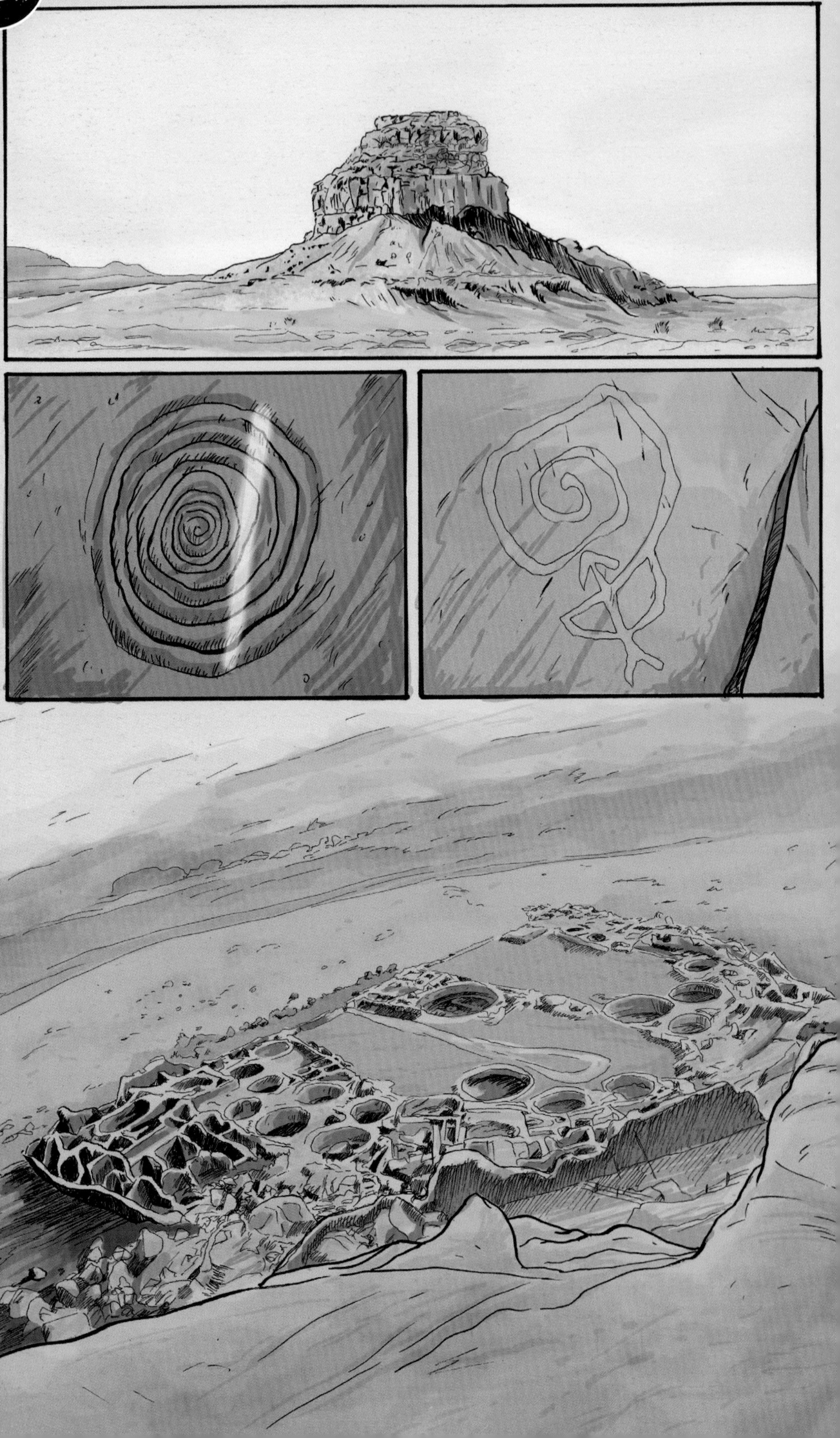

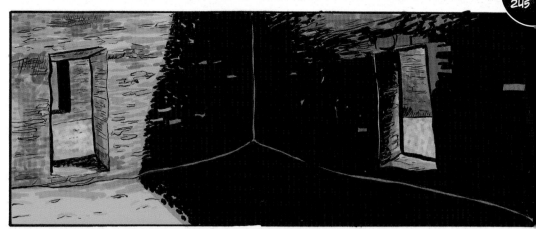

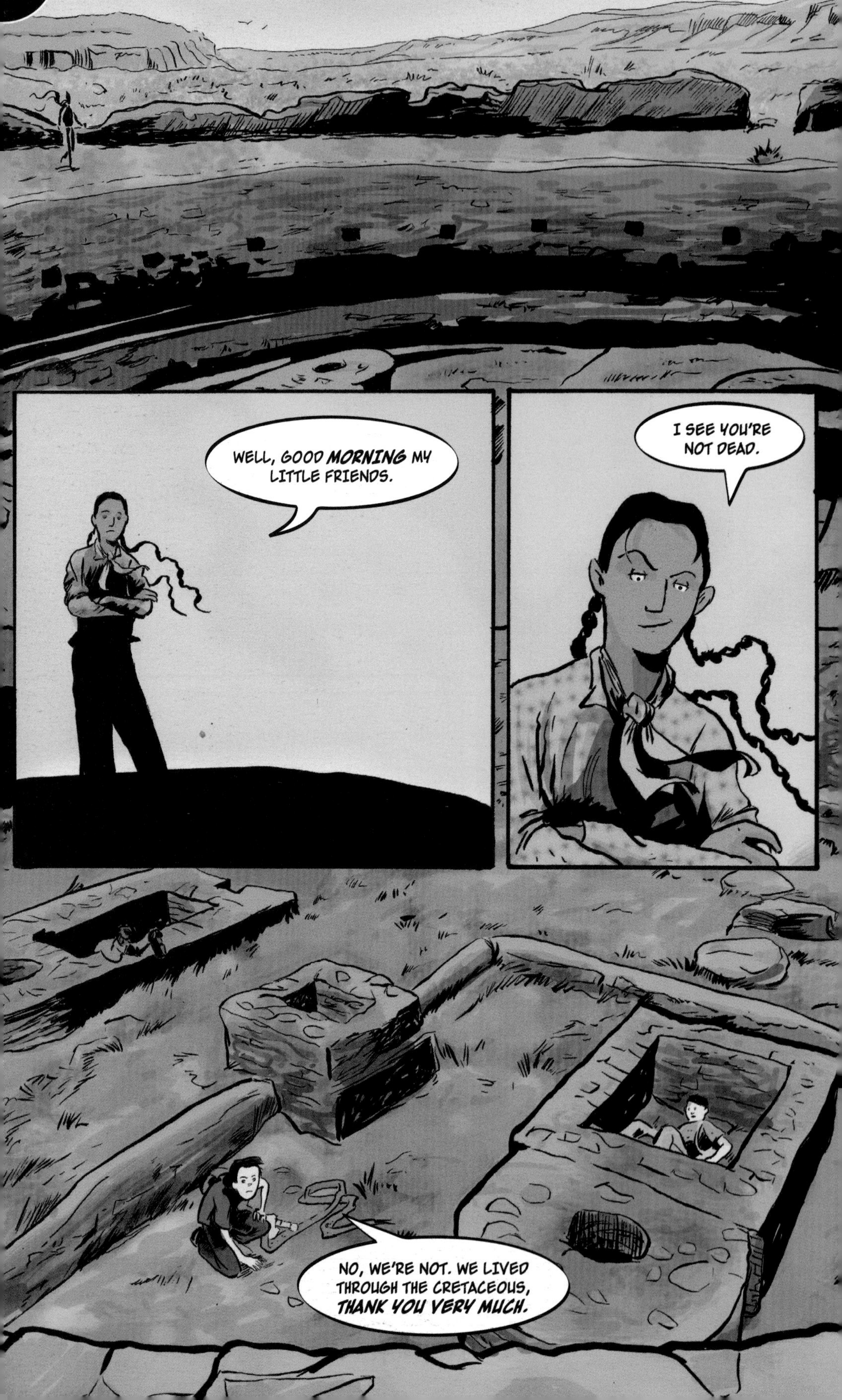
WELL, GOOD MORNING MY LITTLE FRIENDS.
I SEE YOU'RE NOT DEAD.
NO, WE'RE NOT. WE LIVED THROUGH THE CRETACEOUS, THANK YOU VERY MUCH.

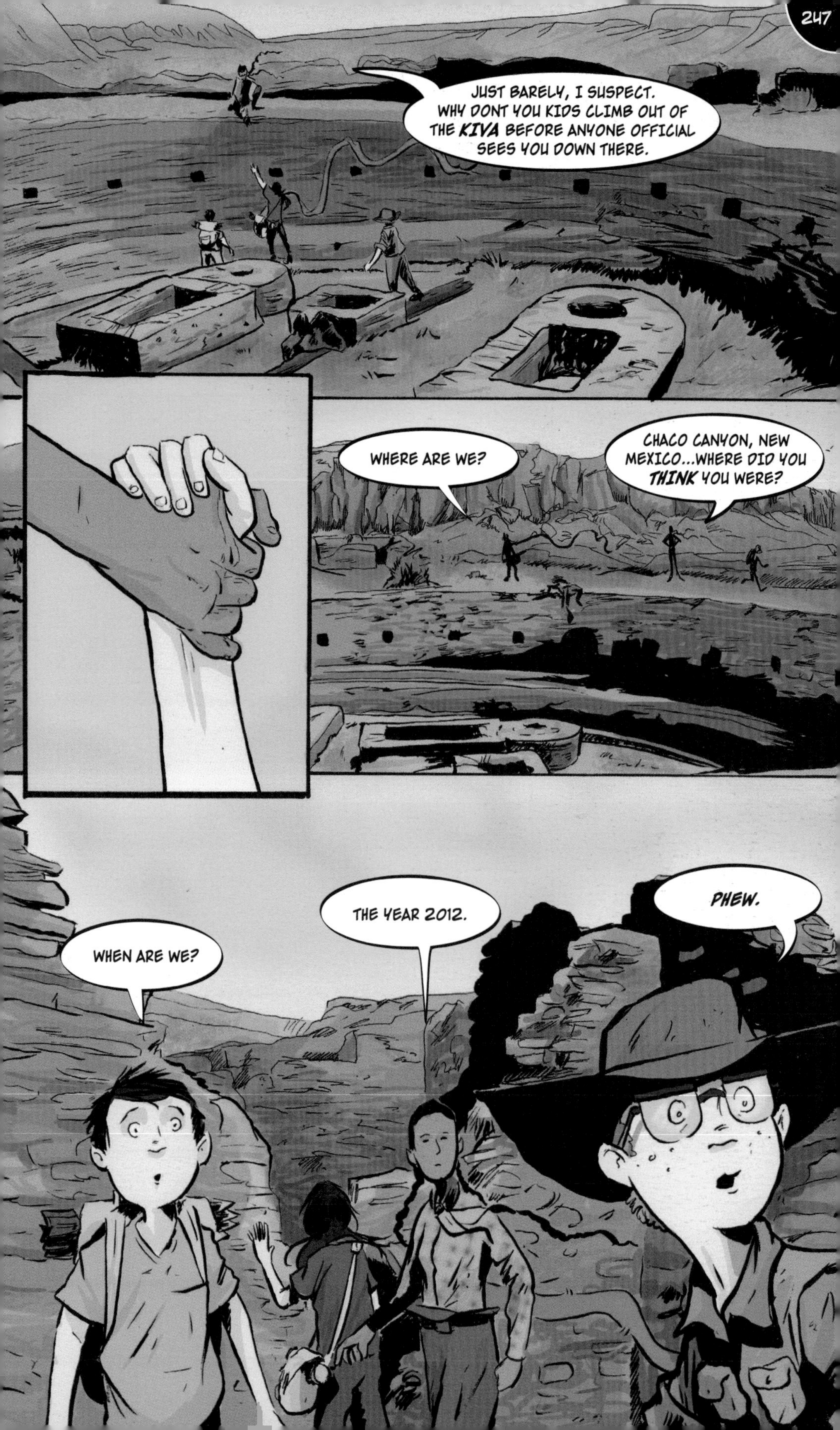
JUST BARELY, I SUSPECT. WHY DONT YOU KIDS CLIMB OUT OF THE *KIVA* BEFORE ANYONE OFFICIAL SEES YOU DOWN THERE.
WHERE ARE WE?
CHACO CANYON, NEW MEXICO...WHERE DID YOU *THINK* YOU WERE?
WHEN ARE WE?
THE YEAR 2012.
PHEW.

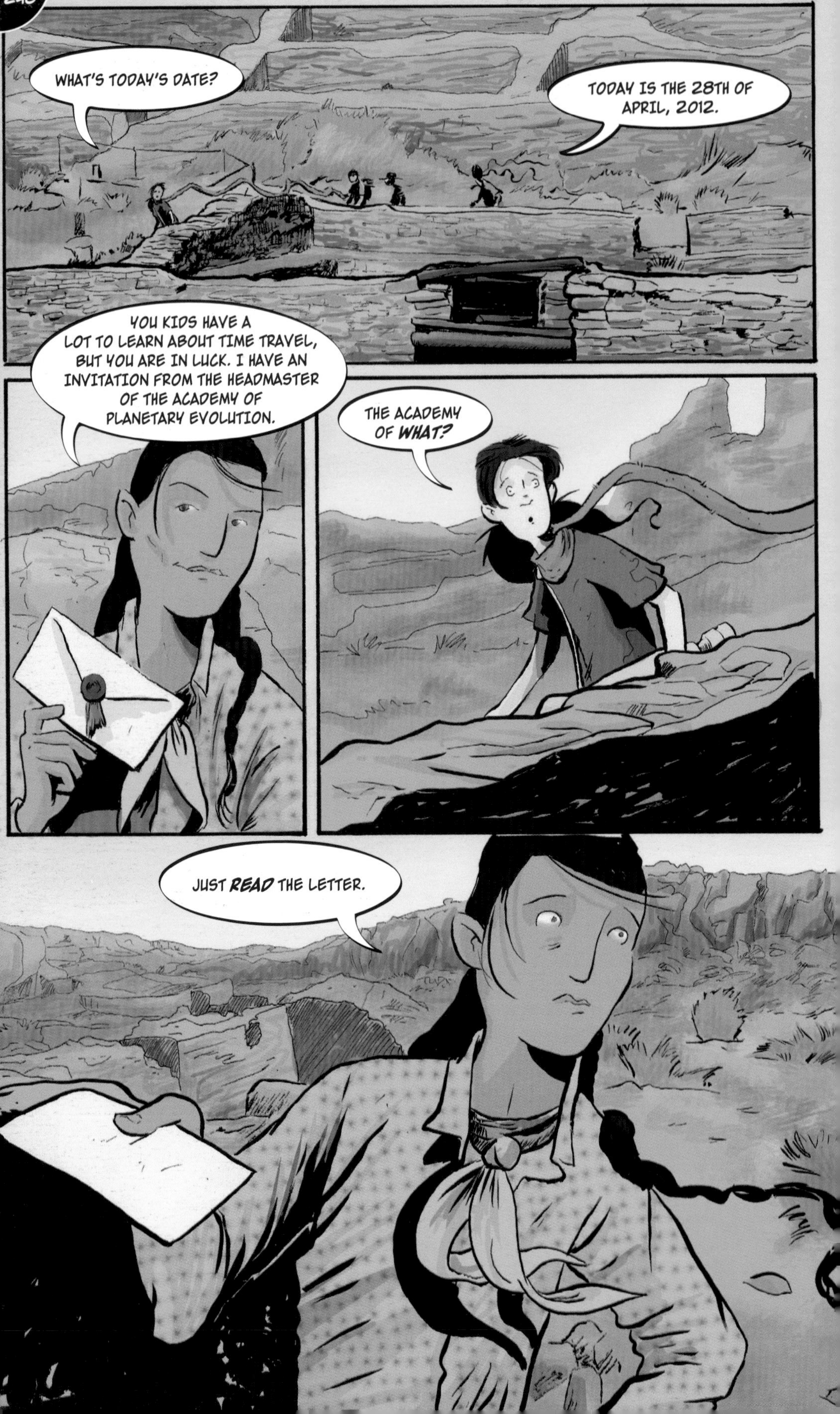
WHAT'S TODAY'S DATE?
TODAY IS THE 28TH OF APRIL, 2012.
YOU KIDS HAVE A LOT TO LEARN ABOUT TIME TRAVEL, BUT YOU ARE IN LUCK. I HAVE AN INVITATION FROM THE HEADMASTER OF THE ACADEMY OF PLANETARY EVOLUTION.
THE ACADEMY OF ***WHAT?***
JUST ***READ*** THE LETTER.

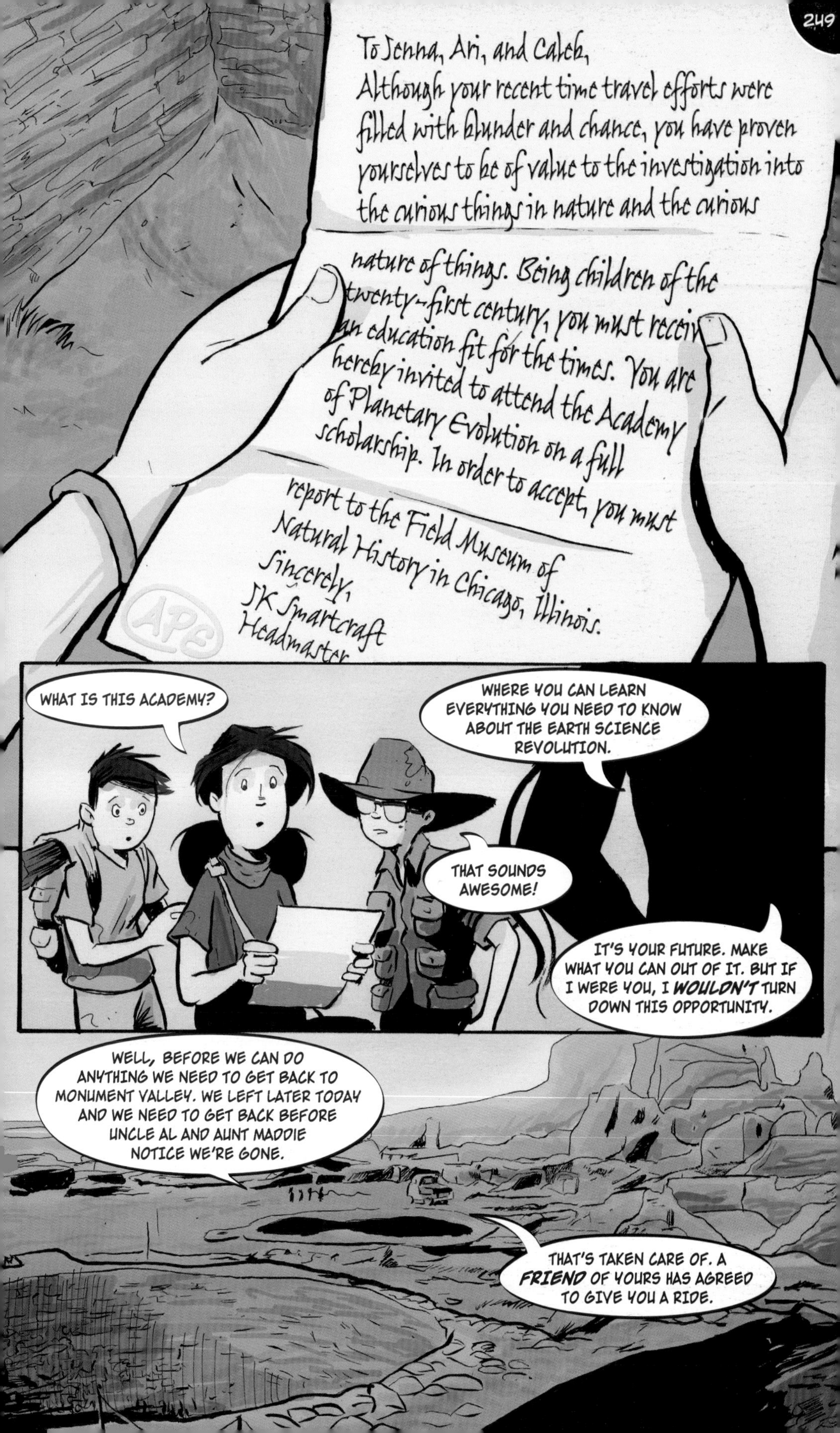

To Jenna, Ari, and Caleb,
Although your recent time travel efforts were filled with blunder and chance, you have proven yourselves to be of value to the investigation into the curious things in nature and the curious
nature of things. Being children of the twenty-first century, you must receiv
an education fit for the times. You are hereby invited to attend the Academy of Planetary Evolution on a full scholarship. In order to accept, you must
report to the Field Museum of Natural History in Chicago, Illinois.
Sincerely,
JK Smartcraft
WHAT IS THIS ACADEMY?
WHERE YOU CAN LEARN EVERYTHING YOU NEED TO KNOW ABOUT THE EARTH SCIENCE REVOLUTION.
THAT SOUNDS AWESOME!
IT'S YOUR FUTURE. MAKE WHAT YOU CAN OUT OF IT. BUT IF I WERE YOU, I ***WOULDN'T*** TURN DOWN THIS OPPORTUNITY.
WELL, BEFORE WE CAN DO ANYTHING WE NEED TO GET BACK TO MONUMENT VALLEY. WE LEFT LATER TODAY AND WE NEED TO GET BACK BEFORE UNCLE AL AND AUNT MADDIE NOTICE WE'RE GONE.
THAT'S TAKEN CARE OF. A ***FRIEND*** OF YOURS HAS AGREED TO GIVE YOU A RIDE.

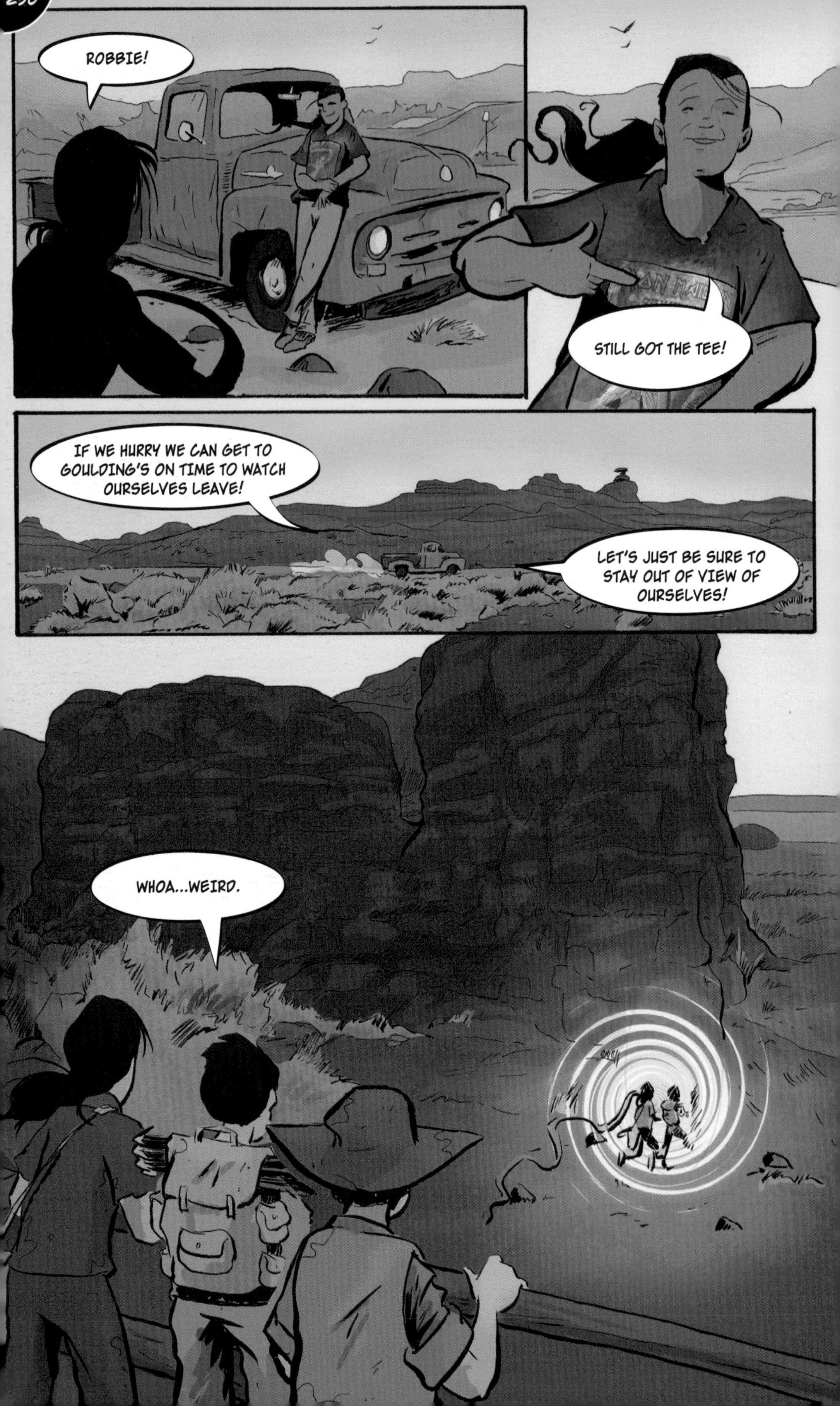
ROBBIE!
STILL GOT THE TEE!
IF WE HURRY WE CAN GET TO GOULDING'S ON TIME TO WATCH OURSELVES LEAVE!
LET'S JUST BE SURE TO STAY OUT OF VIEW OF OURSELVES!
WHOA...WEIRD.

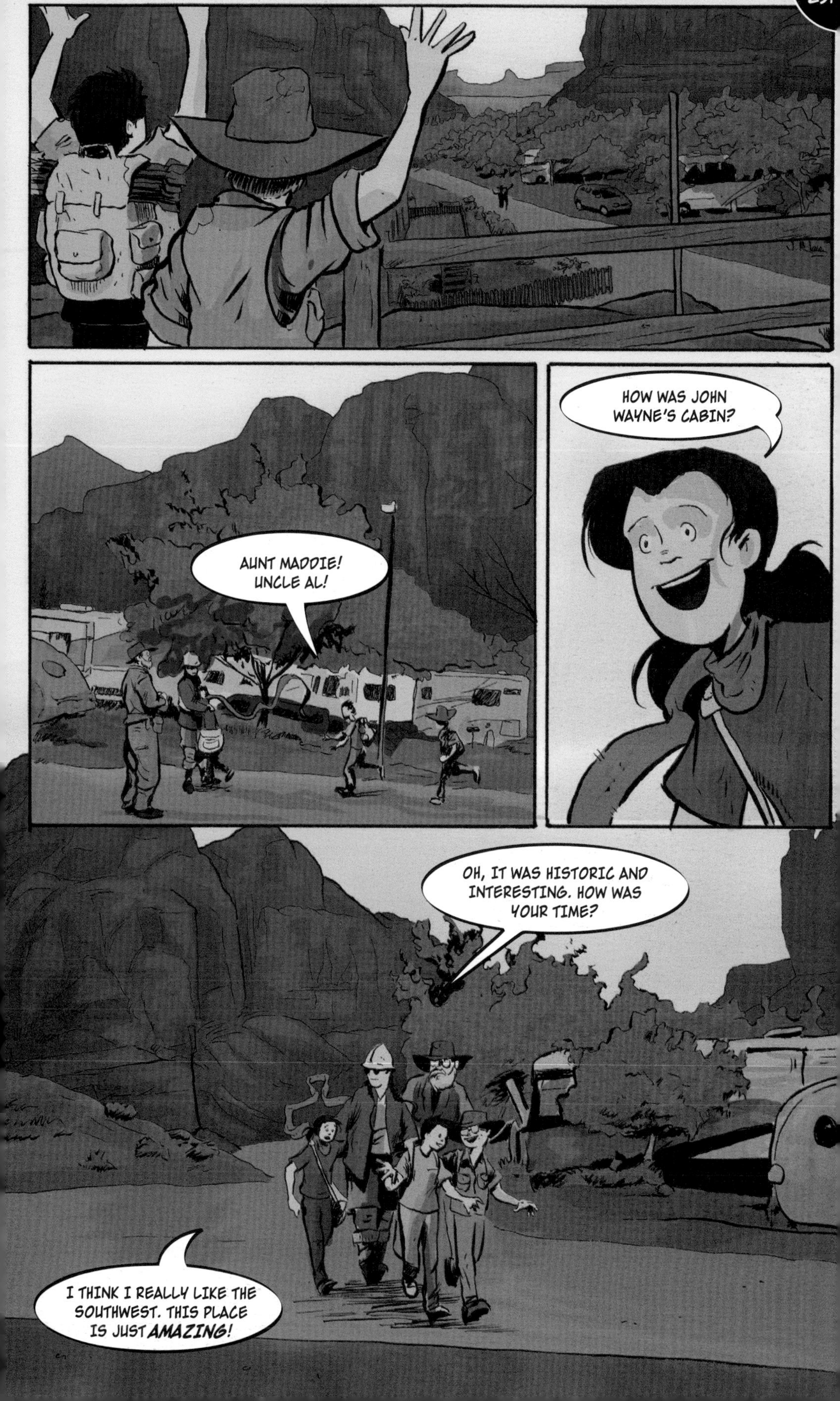
AUNT MADDIE!
UNCLE AL!
HOW WAS JOHN WAYNE'S CABIN?
OH, IT WAS HISTORIC AND INTERESTING. HOW WAS YOUR TIME?
I THINK I REALLY LIKE THE SOUTHWEST. THIS PLACE IS JUST AMAZING!

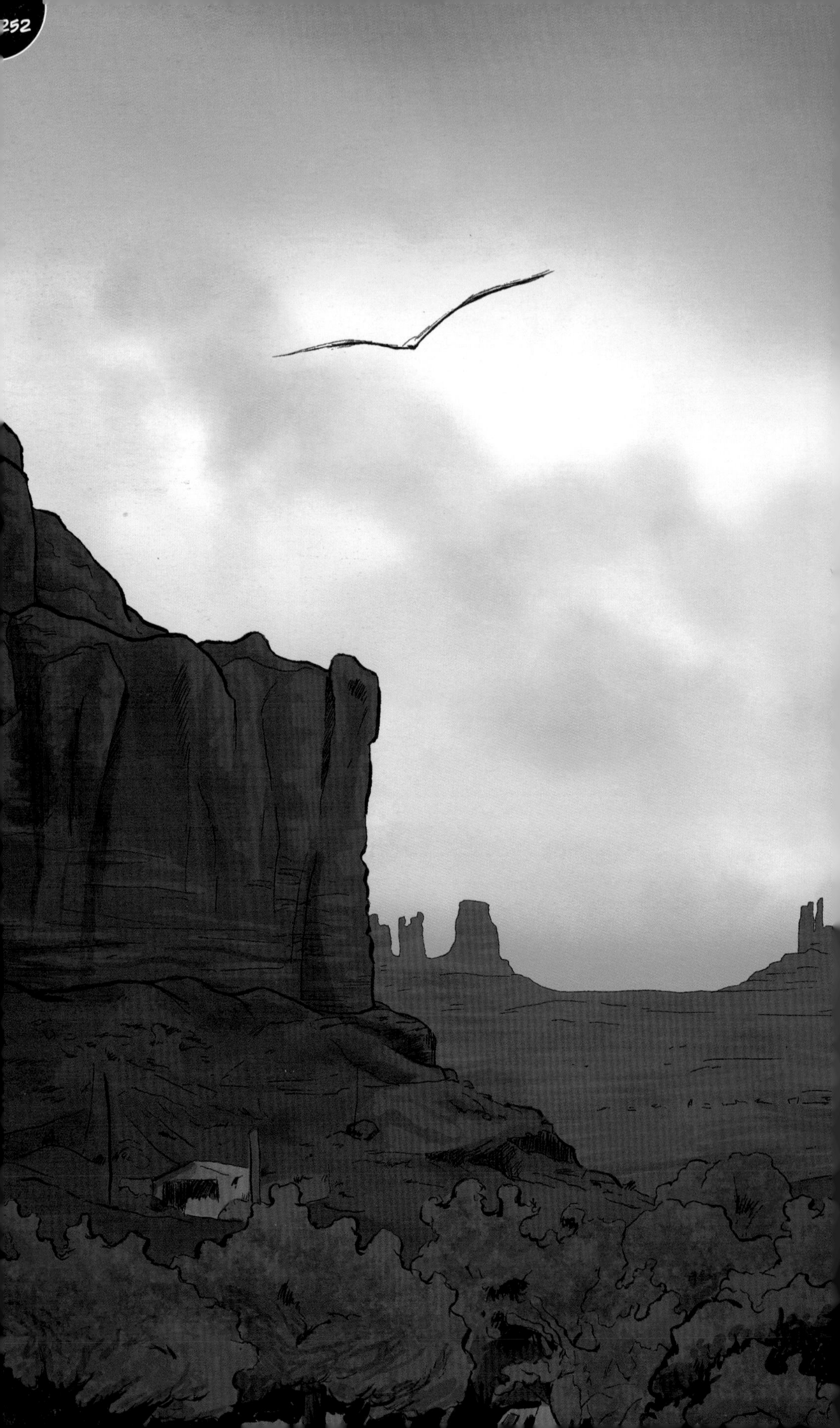

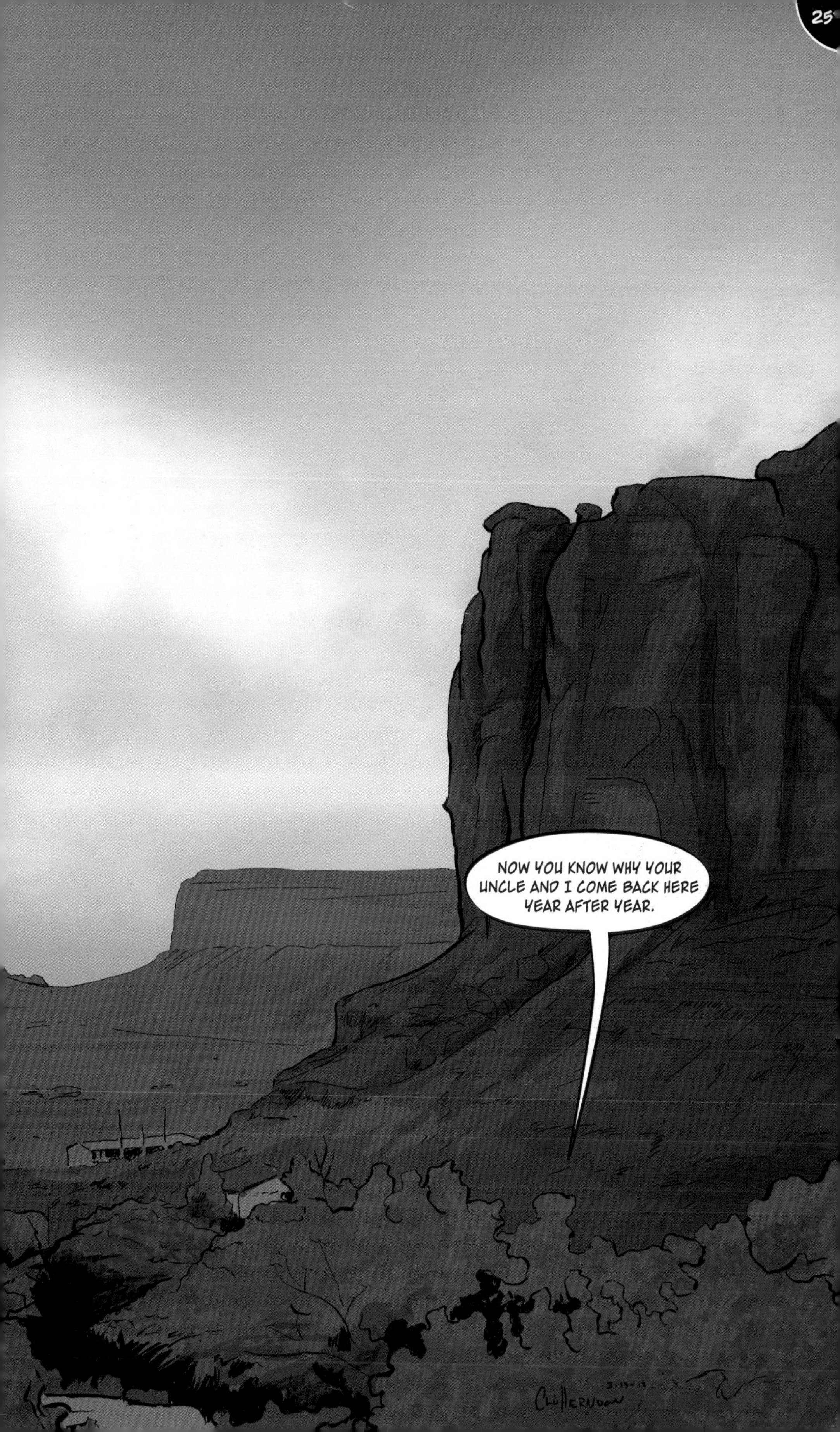
NOW YOU KNOW WHY YOUR UNCLE AND I COME BACK HERE YEAR AFTER YEAR.

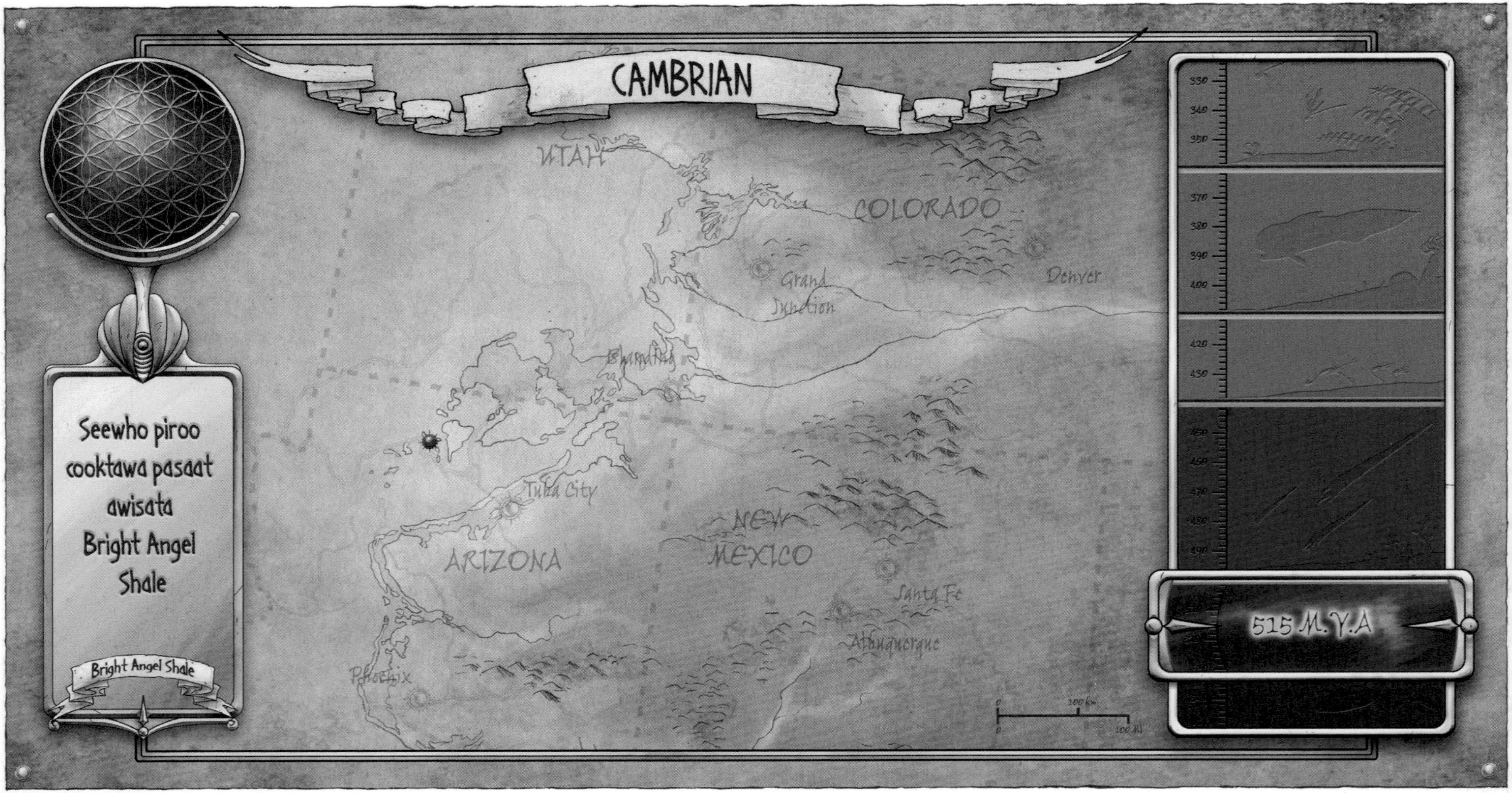
CAMBRIAN
Seewho piroo
cooktawa pasaat
awisata
Bright Angel
Shale
Bright Angel Shale
UTAH
COLORADO
Grand Junction
Denver
Tuba City
ARIZONA
NEW MEXICO
Santa Fe
Albuquerque
Phoenix
515 M.Y.A
330
340
350
370
380
390
400
420
430
450
460
470
480
490
0
100 km

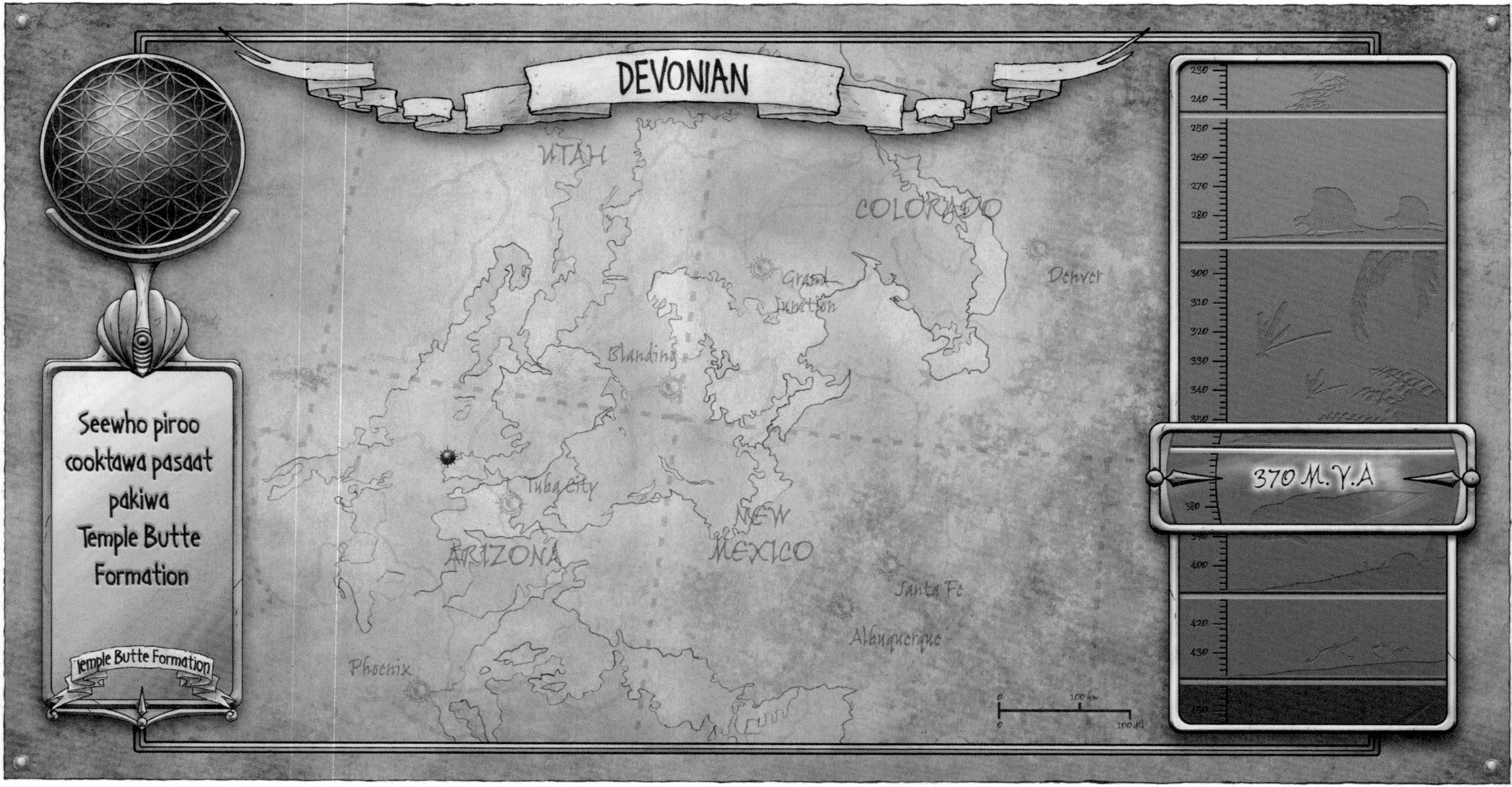
DEVONIAN
UTAH
COLORADO
Denver
Grand Junction
Blanding
Tuba City
ARIZONA
NEW MEXICO
Santa Fe
Albuquerque
Phoenix
Seewho piroo cooktawa pasaat pakiwa Temple Butte Formation
Temple Butte Formation
370 M.Y.A
230
240
250
260
270
280
300
310
320
330
340
350
380
400
420
430
450
100 km
100 mi

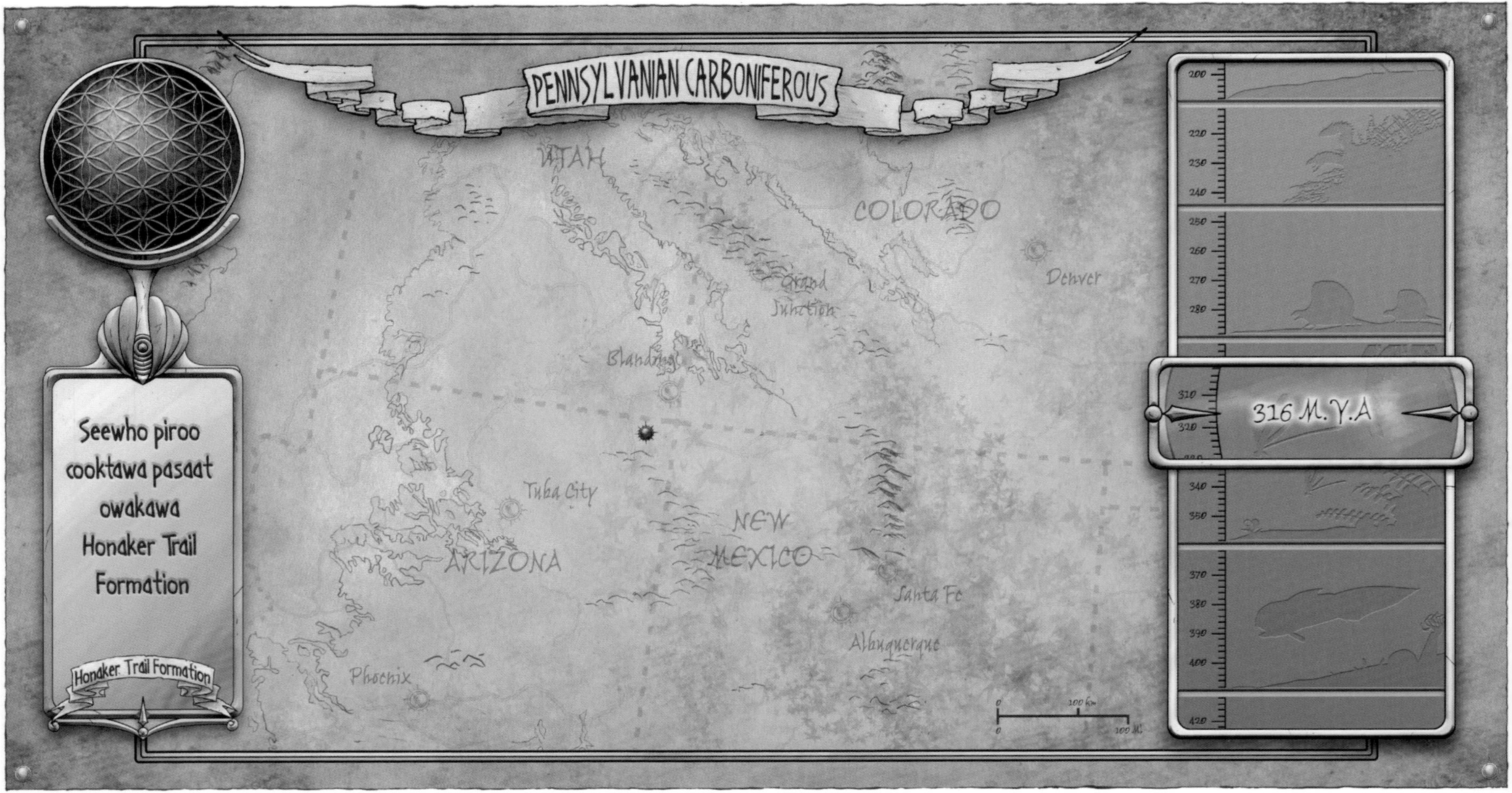
PENNSYLVANIAN CARBONIFEROUS
Seewho piroo
cooktawa pasaat
owakawa
Honaker Trail
Formation
Honaker Trail Formation
UTAH
COLORADO
Denver
Grand Junction
Blanding
Tuba City
NEW MEXICO
ARIZONA
Santa Fe
Albuquerque
Phoenix
0
100 km
100 Mi
316 M.Y.A
200
220
230
240
250
260
270
280
310
320
340
350
370
380
390
400
420

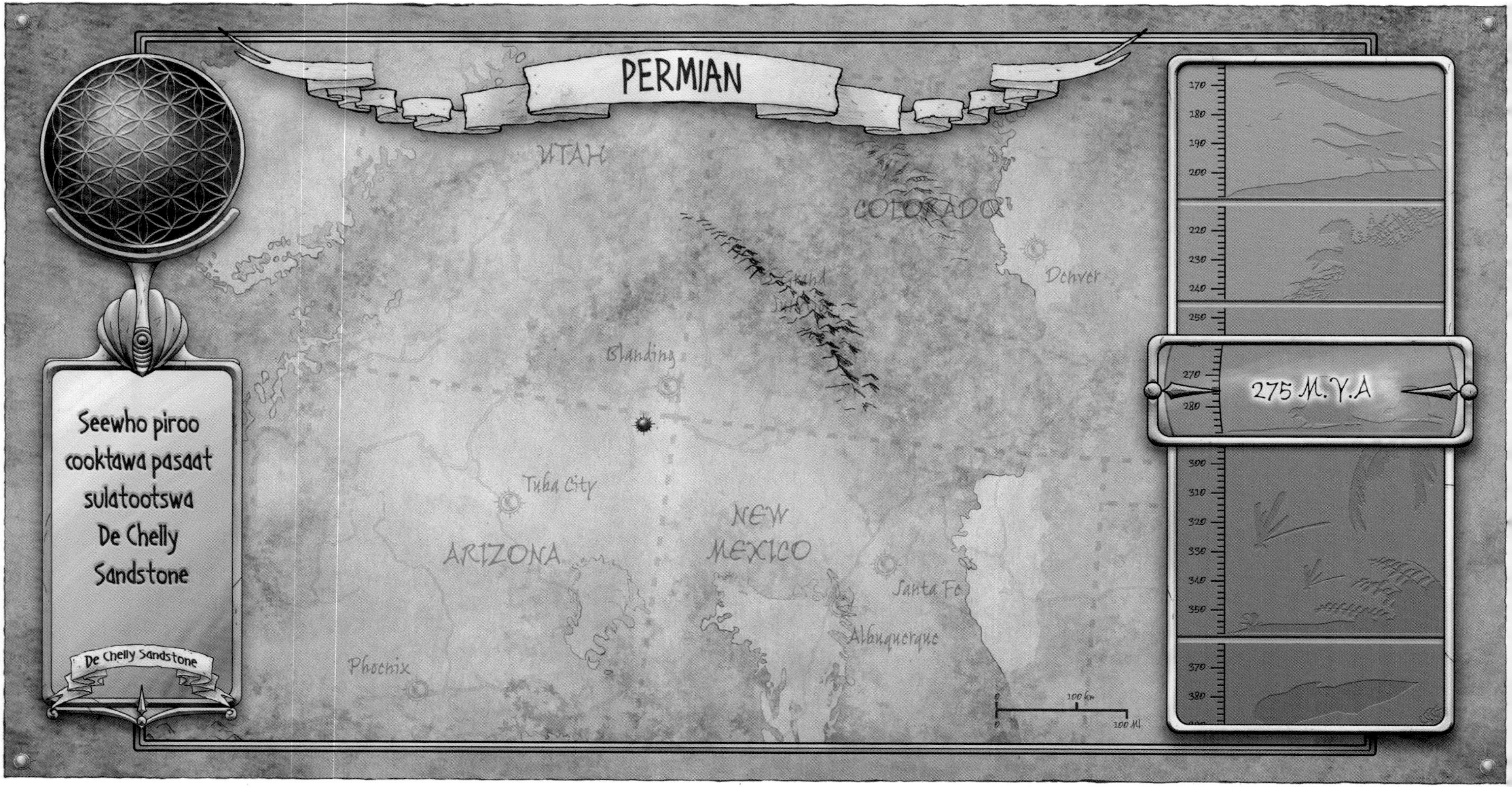
PERMIAN
UTAH
COLORADO
Grand Junction
Denver
Blanding
Tuba City
ARIZONA
NEW MEXICO
Santa Fe
Albuquerque
Phoenix
100 km
100 Mi
275 M.Y.A
Seewho piroo cooktawa pasaat sulatootswa De Chelly Sandstone
De Chelly Sandstone

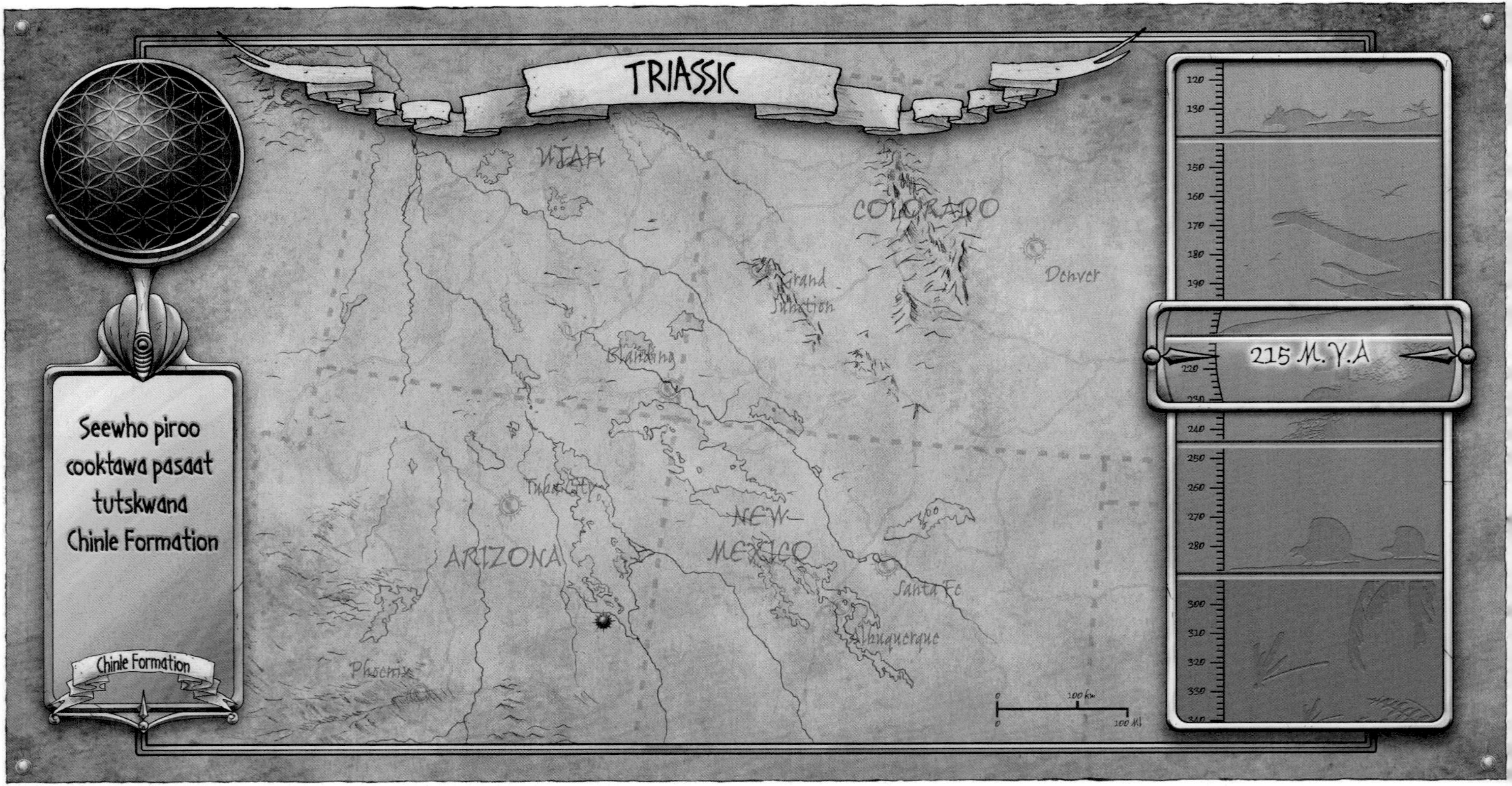
TRIASSIC
Seewho piroo
cooktawa pasaat
tutskwana
Chinle Formation
Chinle Formation
UTAH
COLORADO
Denver
Grand Junction
Blanding
Tuba City
ARIZONA
NEW MEXICO
Santa Fe
Albuquerque
Phoenix
0
100 km
100 Mi
215 M.Y.A
120
130
150
160
170
180
190
220
230
240
250
260
270
280
300
310
320
330
340

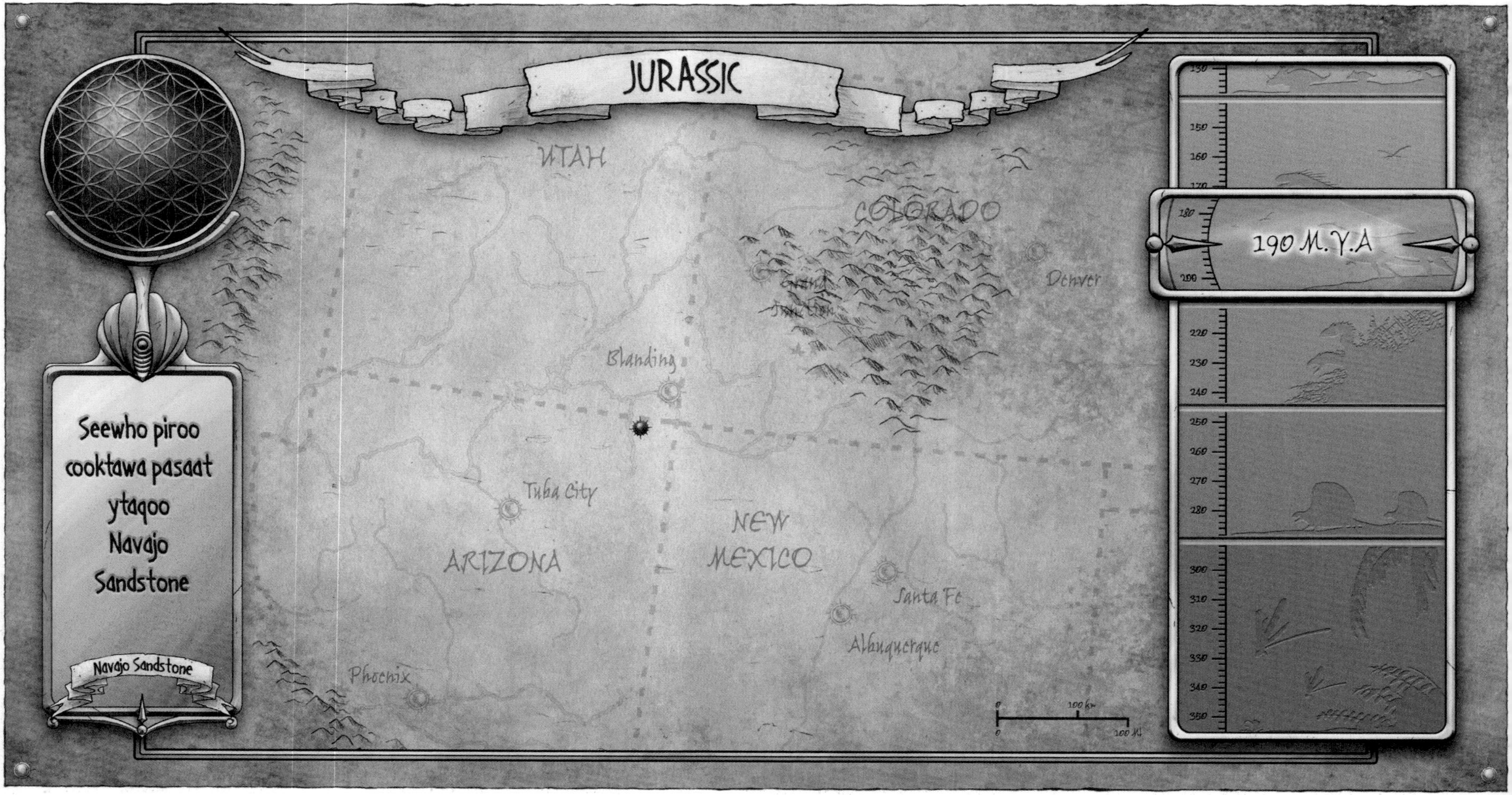
JURASSIC
UTAH
COLORADO
Denver
Grand Junction
Blanding
Tuba City
ARIZONA
NEW MEXICO
Santa Fe
Albuquerque
Phoenix
190 M.Y.A
Seewho piroo cooktawa pasaat ytaqoo Navajo Sandstone
Navajo Sandstone

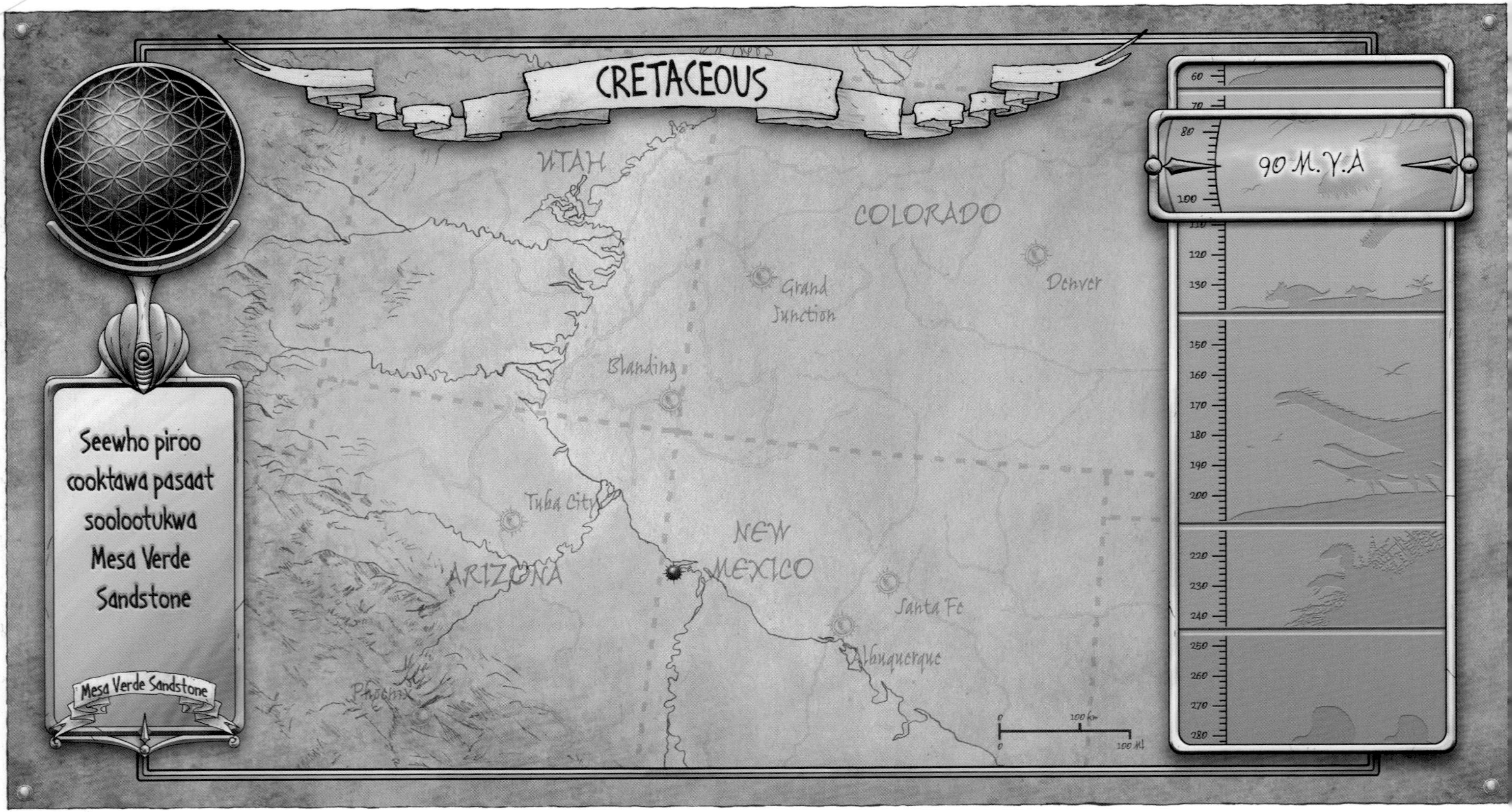
CRETACEOUS
90 M.Y.A
60
70
80
100
110
120
130
150
160
170
180
190
200
220
230
240
250
260
270
280
UTAH
COLORADO
Grand Junction
Denver
Blanding
Tuba City
NEW MEXICO
ARIZONA
Santa Fe
Albuquerque
Phoenix
0
100 km
100 mi
Seewho piroo cooktawa pasaat soolootukwa Mesa Verde Sandstone
Mesa Verde Sandstone

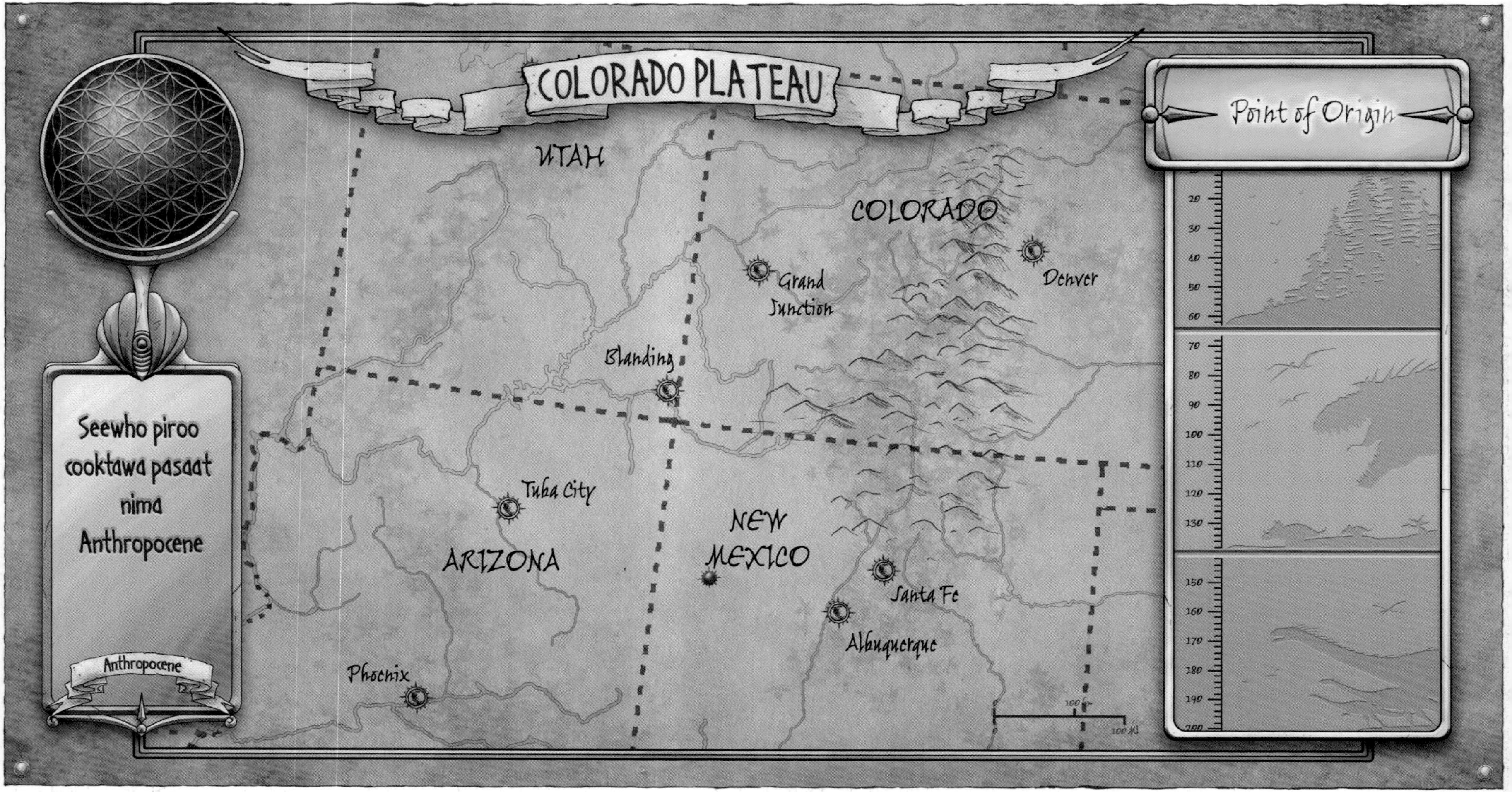

COLORADO PLATEAU
Point of Origin
UTAH
COLORADO
ARIZONA
NEW MEXICO
Grand Junction
Denver
Blanding
Tuba City
Santa Fe
Albuquerque
Phoenix
Seewho piroo cooktawa pasaat nima Anthropocene
Anthropocene
20
30
40
50
60
70
80
90
100
110
120
130
150
160
170
180
190
200
100 Ml

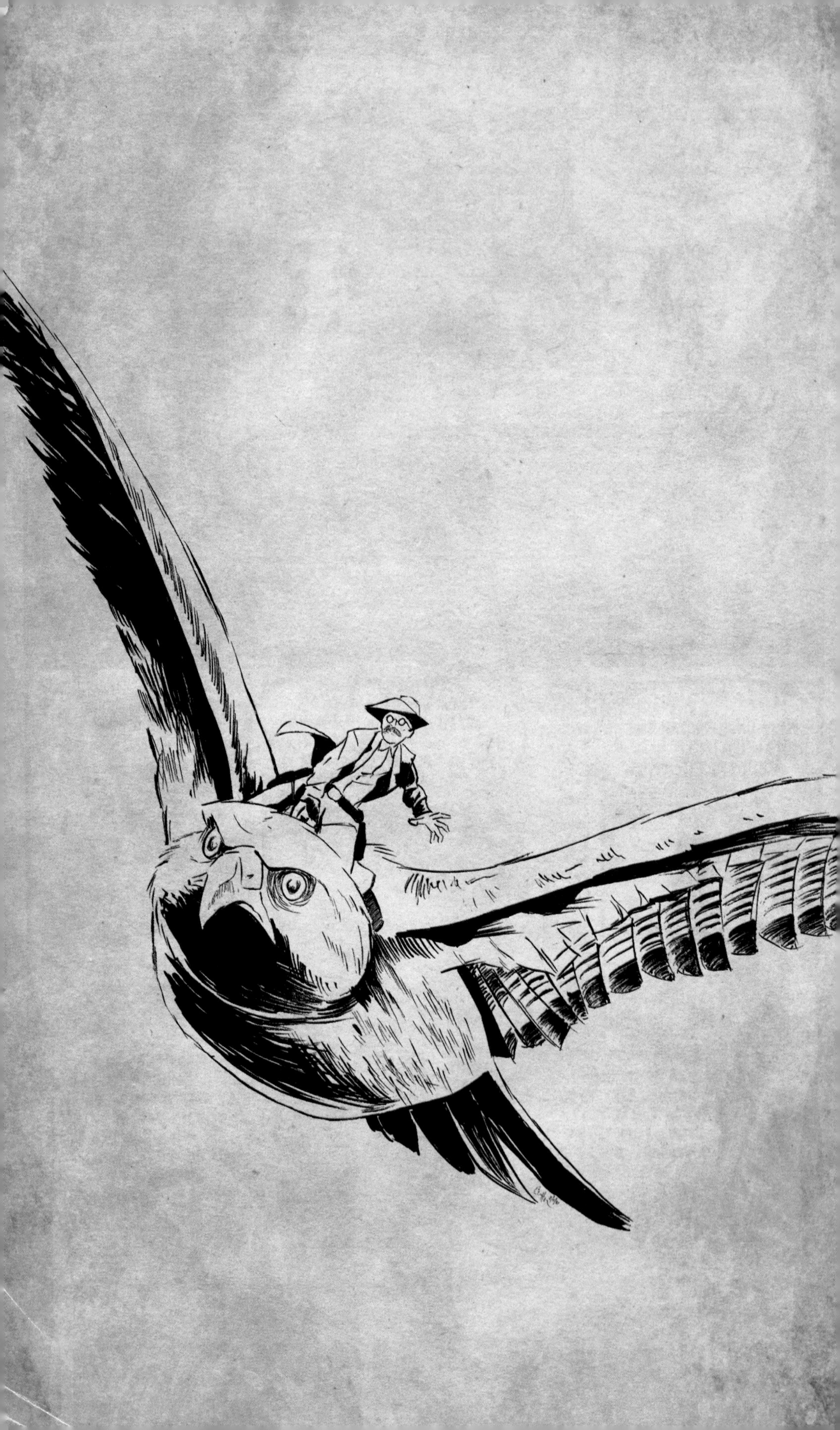

Acknowledgements

Excerpts from *Everett Ruess, a Vagabond for Beauty* by W. L. Rusho. Everett Ruess copyright © 2013. Reproduced with permission of Gibbs Smith.

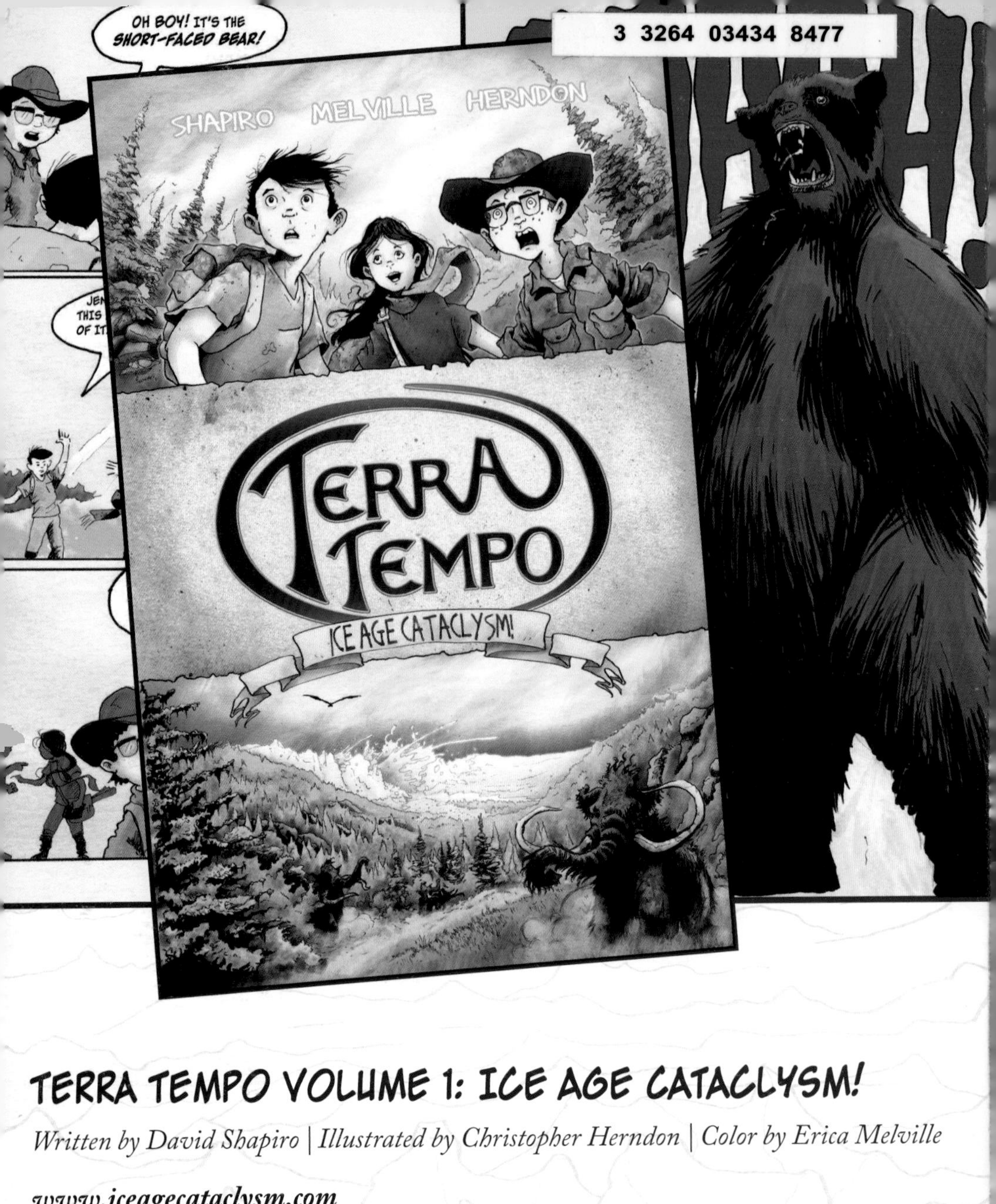
OH BOY! IT'S THE SHORT-FACED BEAR!
SHAPIRO
MELVILLE
HERNDON
TERRA TEMPO
ICE AGE CATACLYSM!

TERRA TEMPO VOLUME 1: ICE AGE CATACLYSM!

Written by David Shapiro | Illustrated by Christopher Herndon | Color by Erica Melville

www.iceagecataclysm.com

ISBN: 978-0-98444-221-8

"Naturalist David Shapiro has crafted an unforgettable story, brought to life with vivid portrayals of the landscape and its creatures by Christopher Herndon. *Terra Tempo: Ice Age Cataclysm!* is an excellent gift for young people and a worthy addition to public library children's graphic novel collections."

—*Midwest Book Review*

"Fans of action and fans of science, especially budding naturalists, paleontologists, and archeologists, will find a lot to enjoy here." —*School Library Journal*

"Time travel, adventure and the graphic novel format of this book make it an easy and fun read." —Alice Berger, *Bergers Book Review*